Praise for
HARRY TURTLEDOVE

"Harry Turtledove has established himself as a grand master of the alternative history form."
—POUL ANDERSON

"Turtledove has proved he can divert his readers to astonishing places. He's developed a cult following over the years; and if you've already been there, done that with real-history novelists Patrick O'Brian, Dorothy Dunnett, or George MacDonald Fraser, for your Next Big Enthusiasm you might want to try Turtledove. I know I'd follow his imagination almost anywhere."
—*San Jose Mercury News*

"Harry Turtledove [is] probably the best-known practitioner of alternate history working today."
—*American Heritage*

"The definitive alternate history saga of its time."
—*Booklist* (starred review)
on *The Great War: American Front*

The Great War:
BREAKTHROUGHS

Harry Turtledove

THE BALLANTINE PUBLISHING GROUP • NEW YORK

A Del Rey® Book
Published by The Ballantine Publishing Group

www.randomhouse.com/delrey/

Library of Congress Catalog Card Number: 2001116538

ISBN 0-345-40564-1

Manufactured in the United States of America

First Hardcover Edition: August 2000
First Mass Market Edition: July 2001

10   9   8   7   6   5   4   3   2   1

To my readers

I

Klaxons hooted the call to battle stations. George Enos sprinted along the deck of the USS *Ericsson* toward the one-pounder gun near the stern. The destroyer was rolling and pitching in the heavy swells of an Atlantic winter storm. Freezing rain made the metal deck slick as a Boston Common ice-skating rink.

Enos ran as confidently as a mountain goat bounding from crag to crag. Ice and heavy seas were second nature to him. Before the war sucked him into the Navy, he'd put to sea in fishing boats from Boston's T Wharf at every season of the year, and gone through worse weather in craft a lot smaller than this one. The thick peacoat was warmer than a civilian slicker, too.

Petty Officer Carl Sturtevant and most of his crew were already at the depth-charge launcher near the one-pounder. The other sailors came rushing up only moments after Enos took his place at the antiaircraft gun.

He stared every which way, though with the weather so bad he would have been hard pressed to spot an aeroplane before it crashed on the *Ericsson*'s deck. A frigid gust of wind tried to yank off his cap. He grabbed it and jammed it back in place. Navy barbers kept his brown hair trimmed too close for it to hold in any heat on its own.

"What's up?" he shouted to Sturtevant through the wind. "Somebody spot a periscope, or think he did?" British, French, and Confederate submersibles all prowled the Atlantic. For that matter, so did U.S. and German boats. If a friendly skipper made a mistake and launched a spread of fish at the *Ericsson*, her crew would be in just as much trouble as if the Rebs or limeys had attacked.

"Don't know." The petty officer scratched at his dark Kaiser Bill mustache. "Shit, you expect 'em to go and tell us stuff? All I know is, I heard the hooter and I ran like hell." He scratched his mustache again. "Long as we're standing next to each other, George, happy New Year."

"Same to you," Enos answered in surprised tones. "It is today, isn't it? I hadn't even thought about it, but you're right. Back when this damn war started, who would have thought it'd last into 1917?"

"Not me, I'll tell you that," Sturtevant said.

"Me, neither," George Enos said. "I sailed into Boston harbor with a hold full of haddock the day the Austrian grand duke got himself blown up in Sarajevo. I figured the fight would be short and sweet, same as everybody else."

"Yeah, so did I," Sturtevant said. "Didn't quite work out that way, though. The Kaiser's boys didn't make it into Paris, we didn't make it into Toronto, and the goddamn Rebs did make it into Washington, and almost into Philadelphia. Nothin' comes easy, not in this fight."

"Ain't it the truth?" Enos agreed fervently. "I was in river monitors on the Mississippi and the Cumberland. I know how tough it's been."

"The snapping-turtle fleet," Sturtevant said with the good-natured scorn sailors of the oceanic Navy reserved for their inland counterparts. Having served in both branches, George knew the scorn was unjustified. He also knew he had no chance of convincing anyone who hadn't served in a river monitor that that was so.

Lieutenant Armstrong Crowder came toward the stern, a pocket watch in one hand, a clipboard with some increasingly soggy papers in the other. Seeing him thus made Enos relax inside, though he did not ease his vigilant posture. Lieutenant Crowder took notes or checked boxes or did whatever he was supposed to do with those papers.

After he was done writing, he said, "Men, you may stand easy. This was only an exercise. Had the forces of the Entente been foolish enough to try our mettle, I have no doubt we would have sunk them or driven them off."

He set an affectionate hand on the depth-charge launcher. It was a new gadget; until a few months before, ashcans had been "launched" by rolling them off the stern. Crowder loved new gadgets, and depth charges from this one actually had crippled a Confederate submarine. With a fisherman's ingrained pessimism, George Enos thought that going from one crippled boat to a sure sinking was a long leap of faith.

Eventually, Lieutenant Crowder shut up and went away. Carl Sturtevant rolled his eyes. He had even less faith in gadgets than Enos did. "If that first torpedo nails us," he said, "odds are we're nothing but a whole raft of 'The Navy Department regrets' telegrams waiting to happen."

"Oh, yeah." George nodded. The all-clear sounded. He didn't leave the one-pounder right away even so. As long as he had reason to be here by the rail, he aimed to take a good long look at as much of the Atlantic as he could. Just because the call to battle stations had been a drill did not mean no enemy submarines lurked out there looking for a target.

Quite a few sailors lingered by the rail, despite the rain and sleet riding the wind. "Don't know why I'm bothering," Carl Sturtevant said. "Half the Royal Navy could sail by within a quarter-mile of us and we'd never be the wiser."

"Yeah," Enos said again. "Well, this makes it harder for the submersibles to spot us, too."

"I keep telling myself that," the petty officer answered. "Sometimes it makes me feel better, sometimes it doesn't. What it puts me in mind of is playing blindman's buff where everybody's got a blindfold on and everybody's carrying a six-shooter. A game like that gets scary in a hurry."

"Can't say you're wrong," Enos replied, riding the deck shifting under his feet with automatic ease. He was a good sailor with a strong stomach, which got him respect from his shipmates even though, unlike so many of them, he wasn't a career Navy man. "Could be worse, though—we could be running guns into Ireland again, or playing hide-and-seek with the limeys around the icebergs way up north."

"You're right—both of those would be worse," Sturtevant agreed. "Sooner or later, we *will* cut that sea bridge between England and Canada, and then the Canucks *will* be in the soup."

"Sooner or later," George echoed mournfully. Before the war, the plan had been for the German High Seas Fleet to break out of the North Sea and rendezvous with the U.S. Atlantic Fleet, smashing the Royal Navy between them. But the Royal Navy had had plans of its own, and only the couple of squadrons of the High Seas Fleet actually on the high seas when war broke out were fighting alongside their American allies. "Sooner or later,"

Enos went on, "I'll get some leave and see my wife and kids again, too, but I'm not holding my breath there, either. Christ, George, Jr., turns seven this year."

"It's hard," Sturtevant said with a sigh that made a young fog-bank grow in front of his face. He peered out at the ocean again, then shook his head. "Hellfire, I'm only wasting my time and trying to fool myself into thinking I'll be able to spot anything anyhow."

That was probably true. George shook his head. No, that was almost certainly true. It didn't keep him from staring at the sea till his eyelashes started icing up. If he saw a periscope—

At last, he concluded he wasn't going to see a periscope, not even if a dozen of them were out there. Reluctantly, he headed back toward the bulkhead from which he'd been chipping paint. One big difference he'd discovered between the Navy and a fishing boat was that you had to look busy all the time in the Navy, regardless of whether you were.

Smoke poured from the *Ericsson*'s four stacks. No one had ever claimed beauty for the destroyer's design. There were good and cogent reasons why no one had ever claimed beauty for it. Some people did claim she looked like a French warship, a claim that would have been vicious enough to start barroom brawls during shore leave if it hadn't held such a large measure of truth.

Enos picked up the chisel he'd set down when the exercise began. He went back to work—chip, chip, chip. He spotted no rust under the paint he was removing, only bright metal. That meant his work was essentially wasted effort, but he'd had no way of knowing as much in advance. He went right on chipping. He couldn't get in trouble for doing as he was told.

A chief petty officer swaggered by. He had less rank than any officer but more authority than most. For a moment, he beamed around his cigar at George's diligence. Then, as if angry at letting himself be seen in a good mood, he growled, "You *will* police up those paint scraps from the deck, sailor." His gravelly voice said he'd been smoking cigars for a lot of years.

"Oh, yes, Chief, of course," Enos answered, his own voice dripping virtue. Since he really had intended to sweep up the paint chips, he wasn't even acting. Propitiated, the petty officer went on his way. George thought about making a face behind his back, then thought better of it. Long tours aboard fishing boats even more cramped than the *Ericsson* had taught him he was always likely to be under somebody's eyes, whether he thought so or not.

Another strip of gray paint curled against the blade of his chisel and fell to the deck. It crunched under his shoes as he took half a step down the corridor. His hands did their job with automatic competence, letting his mind wander where it would.

It wandered, inevitably, back to his family. He smiled at imagining his son seven years old. That was halfway to man-sized, by God. And Mary Jane would be turning four. He wondered what sort of fits she was giving Sylvia these days. She'd hardly been more than a toddler when he went into the Navy.

And, of course, he thought about Sylvia. Some of his thoughts about his wife were much more interesting than chipping paint. He'd been at sea a long time. But he didn't just imagine her naked in the dark with him, making the mattress in their upstairs flat creak. She'd been different, distant, the last time he'd got leave in Boston. He knew he never should have got drunk enough to tell her about being on the point of going with that colored whore when his monitor got blown out of the water. But it wasn't just that; Sylvia had been different ever since she'd got a job in the fish-packing plant: more on her own, less *his wife*.

He frowned as he tapped the chisel yet again. He wished she hadn't had to go to work, but the allotment she took from his salary wasn't enough to keep body and soul together, especially not with the Coal Board and the Ration Board and all the other government bureaus tightening the screws on civilians harder every day to support the war.

Then he frowned again, in a different way. The throb of the engines changed. He not only heard it, he felt it through his shoes. The *Ericsson* picked up speed and swung through a long, smooth turn.

A few minutes later, the chief petty officer came back down the corridor. "Why'd we change course?" Enos asked him. "Which way are we heading now?"

"Why? Damned if I know." The chief sounded as if the admission pained him. "But I know which way we're heading, by Jesus. We're heading south."

Private First Class Jefferson Pinkard sat in the muddy bottom of a trench east of Lubbock, Texas, staring longingly at the tin coffeepot above the little fire burning there. The wood that made the fire had been part of somebody's fence or somebody's house not so long before. Pinkard didn't give a damn about that. He just wanted the coffee to boil so he could drink it.

A few hundred yards to the south, a couple of Yankee three-inch field guns opened up and started hitting the Confederate lines opposite them. "God damn those sons of bitches to hell and gone," Pinkard said to anybody who would listen. "What the hell good do they think they're going to do? They'll just kill a few of us and maim a few more, and that'll be that. They're not going to break through. Shitfire, they're not even *trying* to break through. Nothin' but throwin' a little death around for the fun of it, is all."

The nearest soldier happened to be Hipolito Rodriguez. The stocky little farmer from the state of Sonora was darning socks, a useful soldierly skill not taught in basic training. He looked up from his work and said, "This whole war, it don't make no sense to me. Why you think any one part of it is supposed to make sense when the whole thing don't?"

"Damn good question, Hip," Pinkard said. "Wish I had me a damn good answer." He overtopped Rodriguez by nearly a head and could have broken him in half; he'd been a steelworker in Birmingham till conscription pulled him into the Army, and had the frame to prove it. Not only that, he was a white man, while Hip Rodriguez, like other Sonorans and Chihuahuans and Cubans, didn't fit neatly into the Confederate States' scheme of things. Rodriguez wasn't quite black, but he wasn't quite white, either—his skin was just about the color of his butternut uniform. What he was, Pinkard had discovered, was a fine soldier.

The coffee did boil then, and Jeff poured some into his tin cup. He drank. It was hotter than the devil's front porch in July and strong enough to grow hair on a little old lady's chest, but that suited him fine. Winter in Texas was worse than anything he'd known in Alabama, and he'd never tried passing an Alabama winter in a soggy trench, either.

Rodriguez came over and filled his cup, too. Sergeant Albert Cross paused on his way down the trench line. He squatted down by the fire and rolled himself a cigarette. "Don't know where the dickens this war is getting to," he remarked as he held the cigarette to the flames.

Pinkard and Rodriguez looked at each other. Sergeant Cross was a veteran, one of the trained cadre around whom the regiment had been formed. He wore the ribbon for the Purple Heart to show he'd been wounded in action. That was about all that kept the other two men from braining him with the coffeepot. Pinkard couldn't begin to remember how many times over the past few weeks Cross had made the same weary joke.

Wearily, Pinkard pointed north and east. "Town of Dickens is over that way, Sarge," he said. "Christ, I wish we'd run the damnyankees back toward Lubbock a ways, just to get us the hell out of Dickens County and make you come up with somethin' new to say."

"Godalmightydamn," Cross said. "Put a stripe on somebody's sleeve and listen to how big his mouth gets." But he was chuckling as he sipped his coffee. He knew how often he said the same thing. He just couldn't stop himself from doing it.

And then, with flat, harsh, unemphatic bangs, U.S. artillery began shelling the stretch of trench where Pinkard and his comrades sheltered. His coffee went flying as he dove for the nearest dugout. The shells screamed in. They burst all around. Blast tried to tear the air out of Pinkard's lungs and hammered his ears. Shrapnel balls and fragments of shell casing scythed by.

Lying next to him in the hole scraped under the forward wall of the trench, Sergeant Cross shouted, "Leastways it ain't gas."

"Yeah," Pinkard said. He hadn't heard any of the characteristic duller explosions of gas shells, and no one was screaming out warnings or pounding on a shell casing with a rifle butt to get men to put on their masks. "Ain't seen gas but once or twice here."

Even as they were being shelled, Cross managed a chuckle with real amusement in it. "Sonny boy, this front ain't important enough to waste a lot of gas on it. And you know what else? I ain't a bit sorry, neither."

Before Pinkard could answer, rifles and machine guns opened up all along the line. Captain Connolly, the company commander, shouted, "Up! Get up and fight, damn it! Everybody to the firing steps, or the damnyankees'll roll right over us."

Shells were still falling. Fear held Pinkard in what seemed a safer position for a moment. But he knew Connolly was right. If U.S. troops got into the Confederate trenches, they'd do worse than field guns could.

He grabbed his rifle and scrambled out of the dugout. Yankee bullets whined overhead. If he thought about exposing himself to them, his bowels would turn to water. Doing was better than thinking. Up to the firing step he went.

Sure enough, here came the U.S. soldiers across no-man's-land, all of them in the world seemingly headed straight toward him. Their green-gray uniforms were splotched with mud, the same as his butternut tunic and trousers. They wore what looked like round pots on their heads, not the British-style iron derbies the Confederates called tin hats. Pinkard reached up to adjust his own helmet, not that the damned thing would stop a direct hit from a rifle bullet.

He rested his Tredegar on the dirt of the parapet and started firing. Enemy soldiers dropped, one after another. He couldn't tell for certain whether he was scoring any of the hits. A lot of bullets were in the air. Not all the Yankees were falling because they'd been shot, either. A lot of them went down so they could advance at a crawl, taking advantage of the cover shell holes and bushes offered.

Sometimes a few U.S. soldiers would send a fusillade of rifle fire at the nearest stretch of trench line. That would make the Confederates put their heads down and let the Yankees' pals move forward. Then the pals would bob up out of whatever hiding places they'd found and start blazing away in turn. Firing and moving, the U.S. troops worked their way forward.

Pinkard's rifle clicked harmlessly when he pulled the trigger. He slammed in a new ten-round clip, worked the bolt to bring a cartridge up into the chamber, and aimed at a Yankee trotting his way. He pulled the trigger. The man in green-gray crumpled.

Pinkard felt the same surge of satisfaction he did when controlling a stream of molten steel back at the Sloss Works: he'd done something difficult and dangerous and done it well. He worked the bolt. The spent cartridge casing leaped out of the Tredegar and fell at his feet. He swung the rifle toward the next target.

In the fighting that made the headlines, in southern Kentucky or northern Tennessee, on the Roanoke front, or up in Pennsylvania and Maryland, attackers had to work their way through enormous belts of barbed wire to close with their foes. It wasn't like that in west Texas, however much Jefferson Pinkard might have wished it were. Hereabouts, not enough men tried to cover too many miles of trenches with not enough wire. A few sad, rusty strands ran from pole to pole. They would have been fine for keeping cattle from straying into the trenches. Against a determined enemy, they did little good.

A roar in the air, a long hammering noise, screams running up and down the Confederate line. The U.S. aeroplane zoomed away after strafing the trenches from what would have been treetop height had any trees grown within miles. Pinkard sent a bullet after it, sure the round would be wasted—and it was.

"That ain't fair!" he shouted to Sergeant Cross, who had also fired at the aeroplane. "Not many flying machines out here, any more'n there's a lot of gas. Why the hell did this one have to shoot up our stretch of trench?"

"Damned if I know," Cross answered. "Must be our lucky day."

Stretcher bearers carried groaning wounded men back toward aid stations behind the line. Another soldier was walking back under his own power. "What the devil are you doing, Stinky?" Pinkard demanded.

"Christ, I hate that nickname," Christopher Salley said with dignity. He was a skinny, precise little pissweed who'd been a clerk before the Conscription Bureau sent him his induction letter. He was, at the moment, a skinny, precise, wounded little pissweed: he held up his left hand to display a neat bullet hole in the flesh between thumb and forefinger. Blood dripped from the wound. "I really ought to get this seen to, don't you think?"

"Go ahead, go ahead." Pinkard turned most of his attention back to the Yankees. A minute or so later, though, he spoke to Sergeant Cross in tones of barely disguised envy: "Lucky bastard."

"Ain't it the truth?" Cross said. "He's hurt bad enough to get out of the fight, but that'll heal clean as a whistle. Shit, they might even ship him home on convalescent leave."

That appalling prospect hadn't occurred to Jeff. He swore. The idea of Stinky Salley getting to go home while he was stuck out here God only knew how far from Emily . . .

Then he forgot about Salley, for the U.S. soldiers were making their big push toward the trench line. The last hundred yards of savage fire proved more than flesh and blood could bear. Instead of storming forward and leaping down in among the Confederates, the soldiers in green-gray broke and ran back toward their own line, dragging along as many of their wounded as they could.

The firefight couldn't have lasted longer than half an hour. Pinkard felt a year or two older, or maybe like a cat that had just used up one of its lives. He looked around for his tin cup. There it was, where he'd dropped it when the shelling started. Somebody had stomped on it. For good measure, it had a bullet hole in it, too, probably from the aeroplane. He let out a long sigh.

"Amen," Sergeant Cross said.

"Wonder when they're going to start bringin' nigger troops into line," Pinkard said. "Wouldn't mind seein' it, I tell you. Save some white men from getting killed, that's for damn sure."

"You really think so?" Cross shook his head to show he didn't. "Half o' those black bucks ain't nothin' but the Red rebels who were trying to shoot our asses off when they rose up. I think I'd sooner trust a damnyankee than a nigger with a rifle in his hands. Damnyankees, you *know* they're the enemy."

Pinkard shrugged. "I was one of the last white men conscripted out of the Sloss Works, so I spent a deal of time alongside niggers who were doin' the work of whites who'd already gone into the Army. Treat 'em decent and they were all right. Besides, we got any hope of winning this war without 'em?"

Albert Cross didn't answer that at all.

Iron wheels screaming against steel rails, the train slowed to a halt. The conductor worked his way through the cars, calling out the destination: "Philadelphia! All out for Philadelphia!"

Flora Hamburger's heart thudded in her chest. Until this train ride, she had never been out of New York State—never, come to that, been out of New York City. But here she was, arriving in the de facto national capital as the newly elected Socialist member of the House of Representatives for her Lower East Side district.

She wished the train had not come into the Broad Street station at night. Blackout curtains on the windows kept light from leaking out of the cars—and kept her from seeing her new home. The Confederates' night bombers were not hitting Philadelphia so hard as the aeroplanes of the United States were punishing Richmond—they had to fly a long way from Virginia—but no one wanted to give them any targets at which they might aim.

Her lip curled. She had opposed the war from the beginning, and wished her party had been more steadfast in opposing it. After once supporting war loans, the Socialists had been unable to avoid doing it again and again.

No one sharing the car with her knew who she was. Several young officers—and a couple of older men in business suits—had tried to strike up a conversation on the way down from New York City. As was her way in such situations, she'd been polite but resolutely distant. Most of them were likely to be Democrats, and few if any were likely to be Jews. She wondered what living outside the crowded and solidly Jewish neighborhood in which she'd grown up would be like. So many changes . . .

She got up, put on the overcoat she'd removed as soon as she boarded the car, and filed off with everyone else. "Be watching your step, ma'am," a porter with a face like a freckled map of Ireland said as she descended to the platform.

Broad Street Station was an impressive pile of brick, terra cotta, and granite. It would have been more impressive without the cloth awnings that helped shield the electric lights inside from the air. It would also have been more impressive had more of those lights been shining. As things were, walls and doors and windows barely emerged from twilight. Shadows leaped and swooped wildly as people hurried by.

"How crowded it is!" someone behind her exclaimed. She had to smile. Whoever said that had never seen the Lower East Side.

A man walked slowly along the platform holding a square of cardboard with a couple of words printed on it in large letters. Peering through the gloom, she finally made them out: CONGRESSWOMAN HAMBURGER. She waved to catch the man's attention, then called, "Here I am!"

"You're Miss Hamburger?" he asked. At her nod, his eyes widened a little. With a shrug, he tossed the sign into the nearest rubbish barrel. His laugh was on the rueful side. "I knew you were young. I didn't expect you to be quite so young."

He was probably twice her age: an erect but portly fellow in his early fifties, with a gray mustache and gray hair peeping out from under a somber black homburg. "I don't know what you expected," she said, a little more sharply than she'd intended. "I *am* Flora Hamburger." She held out her hand, man-fashion.

That surprised him again. He hesitated a moment before shaking hands. If he'd paused any longer, she would have grown angry. His grip, though, proved pleasantly firm. "I am pleased to meet you," he said, and tipped his hat. "I'm Hosea Blackford."

"Oh!" she said, now surprised in her turn. "The congressman from Dakota!" She felt foolish. She'd expected the Socialists to have someone waiting to meet her at the station, but she'd thought the fellow would be a local ward captain or organizer. That a U.S. Representative—*another U.S. Representative,* she thought with more than a little pride—would come here had never crossed her mind.

"I do have that honor, yes," he said. "Shall we collect your baggage? I have a motorcar outside. I'll take you to the flat we've found for you. It happens to be in the building where I have my own flat, so there is some method to the madness. You've got your claim tickets, I trust?"

"Yes." Flora knew she sounded dazed. It wasn't just because Congressman Blackford was meeting her here. The idea of having a flat to herself was every bit as astonishing. Back in New York, she'd shared one with her father and mother, two sisters, a brother (her other brother having gone into the Army not long before), and a nephew. What would she do, with so much space to herself? What would she do with so much quiet?

A porter with a dolly wheeled Flora's trunks out to Blackford's automobile, a small, sedate Ford, and heaved them into it. The congressman tipped the fellow, who thanked him in Italian-accented English. Despite the chilly breeze, Flora's face went hot. She should have tipped the man herself, but she hadn't thought of it till too late. Till now, she hadn't been in a lot of situations where she was supposed to tip.

Blackford cranked the engine into life. It started readily, which meant it hadn't been sitting long. The headlamps had masking tape over most of their surface, so they cast only the faintest glow out ahead of the motorcar. Congressman Blackford drove slowly and carefully, so as not to run into anything before he knew it was there.

"Thank you for taking all this trouble over me," Flora said above the Ford's grunts and rattles and squeaks.

"Don't make it out to be something bigger than it is," Blackford answered. "I'm not just taking you home: I'm taking myself home, too. And believe me, the Socialist Party needs every representative and senator it can lay its hands on. If you have a strong voice, you will be able to make yourself heard, I promise you."

"Yes, but how much good will it do?" Flora could not hide her bitterness. "The Democrats have such a majority, they can do as they please."

Blackford shrugged. "We do what we can. Lincoln didn't quote the Scripture that says, 'As your Father in heaven is perfect, be ye also perfect,' because he wanted people to truly be perfect. He wanted them to do their best."

"Yes," Flora said, and no more. Blackford's comment went over less well than he'd no doubt intended. For one thing, the Scripture Lincoln had quoted was not Flora's. And, for another, while Lincoln had made the Socialist Party in the USA strong by bringing in his wing of the Republicans after the fiasco of the Second Mexican War, Socialism in New York City stayed closer to its Marxist roots than was true in most of the country.

Blackford said, "I met Lincoln once—more than thirty-five years ago, it was."

"Did you?" Now Flora put more interest in her voice. Whether or not she agreed with all of Lincoln's positions, without him the Socialists likely would have remained a splinter group instead of overtaking the Republicans as the chief opposition to the Democratic Party.

He nodded. "It changed my life. I'd been mining in Montana, with no better luck than most. I was taking the train back to Dakota to farm with my kin, and I happened to have the seat next to his. We talked for hours, till I came to my stop and got off. He opened my eyes, Miss Hamburger. Without him, I never would have thought to read law or go into politics. I'd still be trying to coax wheat out of the ground out West."

"He inspired a lot of people," Flora said. After losing the War of Secession and having to yield independence to the Confederate States, he'd inspired a lot of people to hate him, too.

The Ford stuttered to a stop in front of a four-story brick building. Hosea Blackford pointed west. "Liberty Hall is just a couple of blocks over that way. It's an easy walk, unless the weather is very bad. They'll swear you in day after tomorrow, and the new Congress will get down to business."

A doorman came over to the motorcar. He nodded to Blackford, then spoke to Flora: "You must be Congresswoman Hamburger. Very pleased to meet you, ma'am. I'm Hank. Whatever you need, you let me know. Right now, I expect you'll want your bags taken up to your flat. Don't you worry about a thing. I'll handle it."

And he did, with efficiency and dispatch. She remembered to tip him, and must have gauged the amount about right, for he touched a forefinger to the patent-leather brim of his cap in salute before he vanished. Flora was amazed she remembered anything. The flat was astonishing beyond her wildest flights of fancy. All for herself, she had twice the room her entire family enjoyed—or sometimes did not enjoy—on the Lower East Side.

Congressman Blackford stood in the doorway. Careful of convention, he did not go into her flat. He said, "I'm straight across the hall, in 3C. If Hank can't help you with something, maybe I can. Good night."

"Good night," Flora said vaguely. She kept staring at all the space she was somehow supposed to occupy by herself. She had thought the Congressional salary of $7,500 a year—far, far more than her entire family made—the most luxurious part of the position. Now she wasn't so sure.

Opening the trunk in which she'd packed her nightgowns, she put on a long wool flannel one and went to bed. Tomorrow, she told herself, she would explore Philadelphia. The day after tomorrow, she would go to work. For all her good intentions, she was a long time falling asleep. Not long after she did, she woke up to the distant pounding of antiaircraft guns and the roar of aeroplane engines right overhead. No bombs fell nearby, so those engines probably belonged to U.S. pursuit aeroplanes, not Confederate raiders.

When morning came, she discovered the kitchen was stocked with everything she might want. After coffee and eggs, she found a shirtwaist and black wool skirt that weren't impossibly wrinkled, put them on along with a floral hat, threw on the coat she'd worn the night before, and went downstairs. Hank was already on duty. "I'll see that everything is pressed for you, ma'am," he promised when she inquired. "Don't you worry about a thing. I'll take care of it. You look like you're going out. Enjoy yourself. I vote Socialist, too, you know. I hope you keep coming back to Philadelphia for years and years."

She nodded her thanks, more than a little dazed. She'd never had so much attention lavished on her. No one in her family had ever had time to lavish so much attention on her. Out she went, to see what Philadelphia was like.

It struck her as being a more serious, more disciplined place than New York City. Big, forthright, foursquare government buildings—some of them showing bomb damage, others being repaired—dominated downtown. They were all fairly new, having gone up since the Second Mexican War. Not only had the government grown greatly since then, but Philadelphia had taken on more and more of the role of capital. Washington, though remaining in law the center of government, was hideously vulnerable to Confederate guns—and had, in fact, been occupied by the CSA since the earliest days of the fighting.

Liberty Hall was another pile of brick and granite, rather less impressive than the Broad Street station. It looked more like the home of an insurance firm than that of a great democracy. Down in Washington, the Capitol was splendid . . . or had been, till Confederate cannon damaged it.

Liberty Hall stood near one of the many buildings through which the War Department sprawled. Men in uniform were everywhere on the street, far more common than in New York. New York at most accepted the war—reluctantly, sometimes angrily. Philadelphia embraced it. Seeing that sobered Flora. She wondered how parochial her opposition would seem.

She stayed out all day. When she got back, she found her clothes unpacked, pressed as promised, and set neatly in closets and drawers. Nothing was missing—she checked. Seven cents in change lay on the nightstand. It must have been in one of her trunks.

She dressed in her best tailored suit, a black and white plaid, for her first trip to the House. Despite her businesslike appearance, a functionary in semimilitary uniform tried to keep her out of the House chamber, saying, "The stairs to the visitors' gallery are on your right, ma'am."

"I am Congresswoman Flora Hamburger," she said in a wintry voice, and had the satisfaction of seeing him turn pale. Another uniformed aide took her down to her desk.

She looked around the immense chamber, which was filling rapidly. The only other woman in the House was a Democrat, an elderly widow from outside of Pittsburgh whose husband had held the district for decades till he died a few days before the war broke out. Flora didn't expect to have much in common with her. She didn't expect to have much in common with the plump, prosperous men who were the majority here, either, though she did wave back when Hosea Blackford waved to her.

Then she was on her feet with her right hand raised in a different fashion. "I, Flora Hamburger, do solemnly swear that I will faithfully execute the office of Representative of the United

States, and will to the best of my ability preserve, protect and defend the Constitution of the United States."

When she sat down again, her face bore an enormous smile. She belonged here. It was official. "Now to set this place to rights," she muttered under her breath.

Winter nights up in southern Manitoba were long. Arthur McGregor wished they were longer still. If he lay in bed asleep, he would not have to think of his son Alexander, executed by the U.S. occupiers for sabotage—sabotage he had not committed, sabotage McGregor was convinced he had not even planned.

He stirred in bed, wishing he could sleep: a big, strong, hard-faced Scots farmer in his early forties, his dark hair grayer than it had been before the war started, grayer than it would have been had the Yankees stayed on their own side of the border. *Damn them.* His mouth silently shaped the words.

Maude stirred beside him. "You can't bring him back, Arthur," she murmured, as if he'd shouted instead of soundlessly whispering. "All you can do is make yourself feel worse. Rest if you can."

"I want to," he answered. "The harder I chase after sleep, though, the faster it runs away. It didn't used to be like this."

Maude lay quiet. *It's because I'm right,* McGregor thought. Before the Americans came, he'd fallen asleep every night as if he were a blown-out lantern. Farm work did that to a man. It did that to a woman, too; Maude hadn't lain awake beside him. Now worry and anguish fought their exhaustion to a standstill.

"We have to go on," Maude said. "We have to go on for the sake of the girls."

"Julia's turning into a woman," he said in dull wonder. "Thirteen. God, where does the time go? And Mary . . ." He didn't go on. What he'd started to say was, *Mary would kill every American in Manitoba if she could.* That wasn't the sort of thing you should say about an eight-year-old girl, even if it was true— maybe especially if it was true.

"Arthur—" Maude began. She fell silent again, and then spoke once more: "Whatever you do, Arthur, be careful."

"I don't know what you're talking about," he answered stolidly. "Been a goodish while since I let the horse kick me."

"That's not what I meant." Maude rolled over, turning her

back on him. She was angry. She would have been angrier if she hadn't had to tell him that, though. He was sure of it.

Eventually, he slept. When he went downstairs the next morning, Julia had oatmeal ready and fried a couple of eggs while he ate it. The oatmeal and the eggs came straight from what the farm produced. The coffee Julia poured, however, he'd bought in Rosenfeld, the nearest town. He made a face when he drank it. "I'm sorry, Father. Didn't I make it right?" Julia asked anxiously.

"It's as good as it can be," he answered. "It's about one part coffee to ten parts burnt roots and grain, is all. I expect the Americans think they're good-hearted for letting us have any of the real bean at all."

"Are you sure it's all right?" Julia said. McGregor was a serious man in a practical way, as farmers have to be. Julia was serious, too, but more thoughtfully so; she'd been outraged at the lies the Yankees were having the schools teach, and even more outraged because some of her classmates accepted those lies for truth. Now she seemed to wonder if her father was trying to deceive her about the coffee.

"I'm sure," he told her. "Your mother couldn't have made it any better." That did reassure her. McGregor went on, "And no matter what else, it's hot. The Yanks can't take that from us—unless they rob us of fuel, too, that is."

"I wouldn't put it past them," Julia said darkly.

McGregor wouldn't have put it past them, either. As far as he was concerned, the Americans were nothing but locusts eating their way through everything he and the rest of the Canadians whose land they occupied had spent years—sometimes generations—building up. Whatever fragments they happened to leave behind, the Canadians could keep. His mouth twisted in what was not a smile. He hoped such generosity wouldn't bankrupt them.

After finishing breakfast, he put on his coat, mittens, earmuffs, and a stout felt hat. He was already wearing two undershirts under a wool shirt and two pairs of long johns under jeans. Thus fortified against the weather, he opened the door, slamming it behind him as fast as he could.

As always, the first breath of outside air made him feel as if he'd inhaled a lungful of knives and saws. His work boots crunched in the snow as he made his slow way toward the barn. The second breath wasn't so bad; by the third, the air was just cold. He'd felt it much colder; he doubted it was any more than ten below. This sort of winter weather came with living in Manitoba.

A north-south dirt road marked the eastern boundary of his farm. Most winters, it would have been all but empty of traffic. Not this one, nor the two previous. Big snorting White trucks painted green-gray growled over the frozen ground, hauling men and supplies toward the front south of Winnipeg.

"Not far enough south of Winnipeg," McGregor said under his steaming breath. Canadian and British troops still held the United States out of the link between the west and the more densely populated provinces to the east, but the sound of artillery from the front was no more than a low mutter on the horizon, not the thunder it had been the summer before, when for a while he'd hoped the Yanks would be driven from his land.

Horse-drawn wagons and columns of marching men supplemented the trucks. McGregor hoped the marching soldiers would all come down with frostbite. Some of them surely would; the United States did not have winters to match these.

Other trucks carried soldiers south, away from the fighting. Ambulances with red crosses painted on their green-gray side panels carried soldiers away from the fighting, too, probably for good. Any man hurt badly enough to need treatment so far away from the front was likely to be in bad shape. McGregor hoped so.

He went into the barn and tended to the livestock. He didn't have so much livestock to tend as he'd had before the war started; U.S. requisitions had made sure of that. He milked the cow and fed it and the horse and the pigs. He shoveled dung. When spring came, he'd manure his acres as best he could. He gathered eggs from under the chickens, who squawked and tried to peck. He put corn in a trough for them, glad he still had corn to give.

Before too long, the work with the animals was done. He could have gone back to the house and its warmth. But it wasn't so cold in here; the enclosed space and the body heat of the livestock brought the temperature up a good deal. He took off his mittens and stuffed them into a coat pocket.

Along with the animals, he kept all sort of tools and supplies in the barn. Most of those tools were openly displayed, hung on pegs above his workbench. Near the workbench lay an old wagon wheel, a couple of wooden spokes broken, the iron tire streaked with rust the color of old blood. It looked as if it had lain there for a long time. It was supposed to look as if it had lain there for a long time.

With a grunt, he picked it up and leaned it against the wall. A rake swept away the dirt under it, the dirt that concealed a board which he heaved up and leaned against the wagon wheel. Under the board was a hole in which sat a wooden crate about half full of sticks of dynamite, a couple of medium-sized wooden boxes, and a small cardboard box of blasting caps, a long coil of fuse, and, carefully greased against rust, a fuse cutter and crimper.

McGregor looked down into the hole with considerable satisfaction. "If Captain Hannebrink ever finds out I've got this stuff, he puts me against a wall, the same as he did Alexander," he said. He whistled a couple of bars of "God Save the King," to which the Americans had written their own asinine lyrics. "Well, one fine day Captain Hannebrink *will* find out—and won't he be surprised?"

He laughed then. Contemplating revenge on the U.S. officer who had arrested his son and later ordered the youth's execution was one of the few things that could take the scowl off his face these days.

He picked up a blasting cap, a couple of sticks of dynamite, and the crimper and carried them over to the workbench. A case waited for them there, one more box made from scrap lumber and carefully varnished and smeared with petroleum jelly to keep moisture from getting in. Before he got to work on loading the explosives into it, he blew on his hands till his fingers were as warm and supple as they could be.

When he was done working, he set the bomb in the hole along with the crimper. He put the board over the top of the hole, then raked and swept dirt and straw onto it till it looked no different from the surrounding ground. With another grunt, he put the old wagon wheel back where it had been. While it was there, no searcher would step on the board and hear the hollow sound a footfall made.

He put on his mittens again, then left the barn. The tracks in the snow he had made coming from the house were still unchanged. He grimaced as he started back. As long as snow lay quiet, he couldn't go out and use any of his toys, not without leaving a trail that would lead Captain Hannebrink and his chums straight back to the farmhouse.

"A blizzard," he whispered hoarsely. "Give me a blizzard, God." If the snow was falling fast and blowing hard, it would hide his tracks almost as soon as he made them. And, if he did come across a Yankee sentry then, he would have bet on himself in the snow against any Yankee ever born. He'd known Canadian winters all his life—and he'd served his hitch as a conscript soldier, too, half a lifetime before. He knew the tricks of the business.

Business . . . Instead of going straight back to the house, he made a detour to the outhouse. He did his business there as fast as he could. During winter, a man thanked God if he was constipated; the fewer trips you made, the better. The only advantage to winter was that it held down the stink.

He set his clothes to rights in jig time, then started back to the farmhouse. He was halfway there when he realized he'd forgotten the milk in the barn. Cursing under his breath, he went back and retrieved it. When he went into the farmhouse, the first breath of warm air inside was almost as shocking as going the other way had been. "What took you so long, Pa?" Mary asked.

"I was working," he told his youngest daughter. Mary's gingery eyebrows rose; she knew how long his chores should have taken. He didn't care, not at the moment. Turning to his wife, he asked, "What smells so good?"

"Blackberry pie—our own berries from down by the creek." Maude asked him no questions about why he'd worked so long in the barn. She never asked him any questions about things like that. He didn't think she wanted to know. But she never told him to stop, either.

Along with a good part of Greenville, South Carolina's, population—both white and black—Scipio spent a Sunday afternoon in City Park watching Negro recruits for the Confederate Army practice marching and countermarching over the broad expanse of grass.

"Ho there, Jeroboam!" called one of the colored men who worked at the same textile mill as did Scipio. "How you is?"

"I's middlin'," he answered. "How *you* is, Titus?" Jeroboam was a safer name than his own. As Scipio, he had a price on his head. The government of the Confederate States and the government of South Carolina would both hang him if they caught him. He'd been a leader in the revolutionary Congaree Socialist Republic, one of the many black Socialist republics that had flared to life in the great uprising at the end of 1915—and been crushed, one after another, the following year.

Bayonets glittered on the black recruits' Tredegars. Scipio wondered how many of those soldiers who now wore butternut had worn the red armband of revolution a year earlier. Without a doubt, some had. Why were they serving the government they had tried to overthrow? To learn what they had not known before, what they would need to know to make their next uprising succeed? Or—

Titus came up alongside Scipio. Like Scipio's, his hair had some gray in it. He said, "Wish I was young enough to jine up my own self. Them sojers, when they gets out, they be as good as white in the eyes of the law."

"De gummint say so," Scipio answered dubiously. "De gummint need we niggers now. De gummint don' need we no mo', what happen den?" His accent was thicker and richer than Titus': the accent of the swamp country down by the Congaree River, south and east of Greenville.

When he chose, he could also speak like an educated white. Before he unwillingly became a revolutionary, he'd been the butler at Anne Colleton's Marshlands plantation. If God was kind, he would never have to talk like a white man again. If God was very kind, he would never see Anne Colleton again.

Titus said, "They git to vote, don't they, once they's done bein' sojers? They git to sit on juries, don't they, once they's out o' the Army?"

"De gummint say so," Scipio repeated. "I hopes de gummint tell de truth. But it de gummint."

That got through to Titus. "Maybe so, Jeroboam. Maybe so. They make a law today say one thing, they make another one tomorrow, say somethin' else." He pointed. "But the law they make today, it give 'em niggers with guns. Niggers with guns, they ain't so easy to trifle with."

Scipio nodded. Titus couldn't read and signed his name with an X, but he wasn't stupid. Black men who'd carried rifles and shown they could fight would be harder to cheat after the war was over. Maybe it was only because the Negro had shown he could fight in the Red uprisings that the Confederate government had decided to put him into the line against the United States. If the USA crushed the CSA, the Confederate way of life was wrecked forever. If the Negro helped save the CSA, change would also come, but perhaps less of it.

A white drill sergeant put the black troops through their paces. "By the right flank . . . *harch!*" he barked, and they went as one man to the right. "To the rear . . . *harch!*" The recruits turned back on themselves. "By the left flank . . . *harch!*" They changed direction once more. "Eyes . . . right!" Their heads swung so that they looked into the crowd as they marched past Scipio and Titus. "Count cadence—count!"

"One! . . . Two! . . . Three! . . . Four!" the Negro soldiers shouted in unison, calling out a number at every other step. Then they doubled the pace of the count: "One two three four! One two three four!"

"Companeee—halt!" the drill sergeant shouted. His men might suddenly have turned to stone. He nodded, then looked angry at himself for betraying the slightest hint of approval. "Present—arms!" The Tredegars that had been on the Negroes' shoulders leaped in front of their faces, held by both hands. "Shoulder—arms!" The rifles returned to the men's shoulders. "For'ard . . . *harch!*" Like a well-oiled machine, the company went back into motion.

After a few minutes, Scipio said, "I's goin' on home. See you in de mornin'." Titus nodded absently. The soldiers seemed to entrance him.

The room Scipio rented was large and cheap. He kept it scrupulously clean. That was a leftover from his days at Marshlands, though he didn't think of it as such. All he knew was, dirt annoyed him. He bathed more often than most of his fellow boarders, too. He wished he had a bathtub in his own room. The one down at the end of the hall would have to do, though.

He read under the gaslight till six o'clock, then went downstairs to supper. It was a stew of rice and carrots and turnips and okra and a little chicken. A cook at Marshlands who turned out such a stingy supper would have been looking for a new situation the next morning. Scipio ate a big plateful and said not a word. Since the ill-fated black revolt broke out, he'd learned a full belly, however obtained, was nothing at which to sneer.

His cheap alarm clock jangled far too early the next morning. He shaved in cold water at the sink in his room, put on wool pants and a collarless cotton shirt, threw a cotton jacket over the shirt, and plopped a flat cap on his head. Coffee and rolls were waiting downstairs. The coffee was brewed from about as much chicory as the real bean, but it made his eyes come open, which counted for more. The only word he had for the rolls was *delicious*.

Thus fortified, he made his way to the mill where he worked. The morning was brisk, but not so chilly as to make walking unpleasant. He fell in with a couple of other Negro men who worked at the same mill. One of his friends told a lewd, improbable, and highly entertaining story about his exploits with several women—just how many kept changing from one minute to another.

Black faces streamed in at the entry gate. Only a few whites put salt among the pepper. Most of the white faces belonged to women, the rest to men either unfit for service or too badly injured to go back into the military.

"Befo' the war," one of Scipio's friends said, "niggers couldn't get these here jobs, 'cept maybe the dirtiest ones an' the hardest ones. They was all fo' the buckra, but nowadays the buckra all off fightin' the Yankees. If us niggers don't do the work, the work don't get did."

"That's a fac'," Scipio said. He never expressed an opinion of that sort on his own. To have done so might have drawn attention to him. The more nearly invisible he was, the better. Agreeing with what someone else said, though, seemed safe enough.

He punched the time clock and went to work: throwing heavy bolts of butternut cloth onto a low cart with tiny wheels and pushing the cart from the enormous room where the cloth was woven to the equally enormous one where it was cut into uniforms. He got three dollars a day, up from the $2.50 the mill had paid when he first hired on. Part of the increase was because wages were rising along with prices, though not so fast. The rest came simply from his staying on the job. A lot of men started, lasted a couple of days or a couple of weeks, and quit. Some got better work elsewhere, while others left the factory for the service.

At forty-four—give or take a year—Scipio was too old to join the service. He wasn't particularly interested in better work, either. The job he had was hard, but not too hard. He had better wind and a slimmer waistline than he'd owned back at Marshlands. He also had work that he did and did well, without anyone giving him orders every other minute.

He hadn't learned what a luxury that was till his first factory job in Columbia, after he'd managed to escape the collapsing Congaree Socialist Republic. Before then, all he'd ever known were Anne Colleton's endless commands, and those of her brothers, and, in earlier days, those of her father.

Now all he had to do was shove this cart across fifty feet of bumpy floor, unload the bolts of cloth, and then pull the cart back and fill it up again. He had plenty of time to think while he worked, and his natural pace was fast enough to keep the foreman happy. Had the foreman pushed him, he could easily have worked half again as hard; the fellow never would have lasted as an overseer in the Marshlands cotton fields.

At noon, the lunch whistle blew. Scipio clocked out, hurried to one of the many little greasy spoons across the street from the mill, and bought a ham sandwich on fresh-baked bread, with homemade mustard sharp enough to bring tears to his eyes. Then it was back to the mill, and an afternoon just like the morning.

His replacement on the evening shift, a fellow about half his age named Midas, got there a couple of minutes before the shift whistle blew. Scipio was pleasantly surprised; this was the first time in several days Midas had been early. They gossiped till the whistle screeched. Then Scipio said, "See you in de mornin'," and headed for the boardinghouse.

Supper that evening was another starchy, watery stew, this one eked out with bits of salt pork. Scipio wolfed it down as if he never expected to eat again, then took the stairs to his room two at a time. That got him into the bathtub ahead of any of the other four people on his floor. Feeling clean and contented, he went back to his room to read and relax for an hour or two before he had to go to bed.

About half past eight, someone knocked on the door. When he got up and opened it, he found two large white men outside. They did not look friendly. One of them pointed a large, heavy revolver at his chest, which seemed anything but friendly. In a flat voice, the other one said, "You are a nigger named Scipio."

Had Scipio been white, he would have turned pale. "No, suh." He shook his head violently. "I's Jeroboam. I's had de name all my born days."

"Passbook," the white man holding the revolver said.

Now, were Scipio white, he would have flushed. "Ain't got

none," he admitted. He put the best face on it he could: "Hell of a lot of niggers ain't got no passbook no mo'. De war, de nasty uprisin'—" Frantically, he wondered who had recognized him and turned him in. Titus? One of the soldiers who'd marched past him in the park? He doubted he would ever know.

"Liar," the white man with the pistol said. His comrade whispered something to him. Reluctantly, he nodded. When he spoke again, his tone was grudging: "We do want to make sure you really are Scipio the Red, so we know we're killin' the right nigger and not letting him run loose to make more mischief. So I ain't gonna get rid of you now, not unless you do somethin' stupid like try and run. So we'll take you to somebody who damn well knows who you are. Once we're certain sure, *then* we stretch your goddamn neck."

"Whoever say I ain't Jeroboam, he a liar," Scipio declared.

"Anne Colleton ain't no *he*," the white man without the gun said. Scipio had the presence of mind not to betray that he knew the name. That helped now. It wouldn't help for long. The tough guy with the gun gestured. "Come on," the other one growled. Numbly, Scipio came.

Sergeant Chester Martin wrinkled his long, rather beaky nose as he made his way up the muddy zigzag of the communications trench toward the front line. He'd lived with mud and the stink of rotting meat and shit and garbage from the U.S. invasion of the Roanoke valley when the war was new till he got wounded the autumn before. Convalescing in Toledo, he'd almost managed to forget the nature of the stench, but it came back in a hurry.

He rubbed his chin, which was as pointed as his nose. Now the United States were getting ready to invade Virginia again, this time from the north rather than the west. In the early days of the fighting, the CSA had overrun Maryland and southern Pennsylvania before being halted on the line of the Susquehanna. The grinding war since then had driven the Rebels back toward their own border. Now—

Now the United States had bridgeheads south of the Potomac, on Confederate soil. Martin trudged past a wrecked barrel—a Confederate model, with treads all around the hull—from which Army engineers were scavenging whatever they could.

A shell burst a couple of hundred yards to Martin's left. He didn't bother ducking; going home to heal hadn't made him lose the knack for knowing when an incoming round was dangerous and when it wasn't. Rifle and machine-gun fire told him he was getting very close to the front. The shooting was sporadic, almost desultory. Neither side was pushing hard here, not right this second.

A grimy, tired-looking fellow with several days' growth of beard was leaning against the wall of the trench while he smoked a cigarette. Martin paused. The soldier studied him. He could read the fellow's thoughts. Nearly clean uniform—a point against. New Purple Heart ribbon—a point for, maybe even a point and a half, because it explained the clean uniform. Sergeant's stripes—three points against, without a doubt.

But the stripes also meant the fellow couldn't safely ignore him. Sure enough, after another drag on the hand-rolled cigarette, the soldier asked, "You lookin' for somebody in particular, Sergeant?"

"B Company, 91st Regiment," Martin answered. "They told me back at division HQ it was up this way."

"They gave you the straight goods," the soldier said with a nod. "Matter of fact, I'm in B Company myself. Name's Tilden Russell."

"Chester Martin," Martin said.

Russell looked him over again, this time with more interest. "You don't mind me askin', Sarge, where'd you pick up your grape-jelly ribbon there?"

What kind of soldier are you? the question meant. *What kind of action have you seen?* "Roanoke front," Martin answered crisply. "Spent two years there, till I took one in the arm in the Rebs' big counterattack last fall."

"Two years on the Roanoke front?" Russell's eyebrows rose toward the brim of his helmet. "Come on. I'll take you up to the line myself. God damn, you can play on my team any day of the week."

"Thanks." Martin hid a smile. If he'd come from Arkansas or, say, Sequoyah, Tilden Russell wouldn't have wanted to give him the time of day, let alone escort him up to the forward trenches. Compared to this front, the fighting out west wasn't anything to speak of. The fighting in the Roanoke valley, though, didn't take a back seat to anything.

"Captain Cremony!" Russell called as he came into the front-line trenches, and then, to a soldier in a green-gray uniform,

"You seen the captain, Eddie? This here's our new sergeant—spent two years on the Roanoke front." He sounded as proud of that as if he'd done the fighting himself.

"Yeah?" Eddie looked impressed, too. He pointed to the nearest vertical jog in the horizontal trench. "He ducked into that traverse there, last I saw him."

"Thanks. Come on, Sergeant." Russell led Martin down the firebay toward the traverse. Some of the trench floor was corduroyed with wood. Some was just mud, into which Martin's boots sank with wet, squelching noises. He rounded the corner on Tilden Russell's heels. Russell let out a pleased grunt and said, "Hey, Captain, I found our new sergeant comin' up to the line. His name's Martin, sir—he was on the Roanoke front before he got wounded."

In spite of a fearsomely waxed, upthrusting Kaiser Bill mustache, Captain Cremony couldn't have seen his twenty-fifth birthday. He was skinny and swarthy and looked more like a clerk than a soldier, but clerks didn't commonly have two oak-leaf clusters under their Purple Heart ribbons. "Roanoke, eh?" he said. "You'll know what it's all about, then."

"I hope so, sir," Martin answered.

"You ought to fit in well," the company commander said. "You mark my words, Sergeant—when the weather clears up, this front will see movement like nothing since the early days."

"I hope so, sir," Martin said again. In the early days, the Confederates had been doing all the moving on this front. He was willing to assume that wasn't what Captain Cremony meant.

"About time, too," Cremony said. "We've owed these bastards for two wars and fifty years. Now we're going to get our own back."

"Yes, sir!" Martin's voice took on real warmth. "My grandfather lost a leg in the War of Secession. He died before we got to pay the Rebs back for that and for everything else. Next to what he got, this"—he waggled his arm—"isn't anything worth talking about."

He listened to himself in something close to amazement. After two and a half years of what surely came closer to hell than anything else man had managed to build on earth, he could still sound like a patriot. If that didn't mean he was crazy, it did mean the United States had owed a hell of a big debt for a hell of a long time: a debt of pain, a debt of humiliation. And if they won this time, they would pay it back in the same coin. Martin didn't look forward to the fighting that lay ahead. But the repayment . . . oh, yes, he looked forward to the repayment.

Captain Cremony said, "Russell, take him down the line to the section he'll be leading. The sooner he fits himself into the scheme of things, the better for everybody."

"Yes, sir," Tilden Russell said. "You come with me, Sergeant. It's not far." As soon as he and Martin were out of earshot of Captain Cremony, he added, "The one you're going to have to watch out for, Sarge, is Corporal Reinholdt. He's been running the section since Sergeant Kelly stopped a Tredegar round with his ear, and he was steamed when they didn't give him his third stripe."

"I'll take care of that," Martin said. He didn't blame Reinholdt for being steamed. If you were doing a three-striper's job, you deserved a third stripe. A file card with Martin's name on it must have popped up in the War Department at just the wrong moment for Reinholdt.

Either that, Martin thought, *or the guy doesn't deserve two stripes, let alone three.* He'd have to see about that, too.

Quietly, Russell said, "Here we are, Sarge." Then he raised his voice: "Heads up, you lugs. This here is Sergeant Martin. He's off convalescent leave—spent the whole damn war till now on the Roanoke front."

One of the men Martin would be leading was stirring a kettle of stew. A couple were on the firing step, though they weren't shooting at the Rebels. One was dealing from a battered deck of cards for himself and three friends. A couple were cleaning their rifles. One was repairing a tunic, using a needle and thread with what Martin could see at a glance was extraordinary skill. A few were asleep, rolled in blankets.

Everybody who was awake gave Martin a once-over. He was a stranger here, and so an object of suspicion, and in a clean uniform, and so doubly an object of suspicion. He looked the men over, too. The tailor, or whatever he was in civilian life, was a kid. So were one of the fellows on the firing step, a cardplayer, and one of the men working with gun oil and cleaning rod. The rest, Martin guessed, had been in the fight longer.

He looked around for Corporal Reinholdt, and found him glowering at the cards he was holding. Reinholdt looked like somebody who spent a lot of time glowering. Martin decided to try it the smooth way first: "Corporal, I hope you'll give me a hand getting to know people."

By way of answer, Reinholdt only grunted. His eyes went back to his hand, but kept flicking toward Martin's face. Martin sighed. The smooth way wasn't going to work. Sooner or later, he'd have trouble with the disgruntled corporal. He resolved to make it sooner, and to pick the time himself.

Holding in his temper, Martin spoke to the men of the section: "Tell me who you are. I'll get it wrong for a while, but not for long."

Names washed over him: Willie and Parker and Zeb and Cal and two guys named Joe and one, the fellow with needle and thread, who seemed to be called Hamburger. "That a first name or a last name?" Martin asked, and got a laugh from everybody except Corporal Reinholdt.

"Hey, don't get him mad at you," one of the Joes said. "His sister's a congressman—congresslady—whatever the hell they call her."

"Yeah, and I'm Queen of the May," Martin said.

That got more laughter, but the soldiers said things like, "We're not shitting you, Sarge." "She really is." "We ain't lyin'."

Martin still didn't believe it. Pointing at the kid named Hamburger—David, his first name turned out to be—he asked, "Listen, if your sister's in Congress, what the hell are you doin' *here*? She don't like you or somethin'?"

"She likes me fine," Hamburger said through more laughter. His swarthy face flushed. "She just doesn't think it's right to use her job to make things soft for her family. That's not why the working people elected her."

Socialist, Martin thought from the way the kid said *working people.* It didn't faze him; about one soldier in three voted that way. "New York City?" he asked.

"Yeah." Hamburger nodded. "You can tell from the way I talk, I bet."

"Right the first time," Martin said. He would have tagged the kid for a dago from his looks, but with that last name he was likelier to be a Jew. "Your old man a peddler?"

"No—he sews for a living, same as me, same as my other two sisters." That explained the deft hand with a needle. "How about you, Sarge?"

"I was a steelworker in Toledo before the war, like my pa still is," Martin answered. "He makes the stuff, and we throw it at the Rebs. That works out pretty good, hey?" David Hamburger nodded again. Martin thought he'd get on here well enough—except he didn't like Corporal Reinholdt's eyes.

II

Anne Colleton paced back and forth like a caged lioness in the little room she'd rented in St. Matthews, South Carolina. "I will not go any farther from Marshlands," she snapped, as if someone had insisted that she should.

A wisp of dark blond hair escaped from its pin and tickled her cheek. She forced it back into place without breaking her furious stride. The Red uprising of 1915 had sent the Marshlands mansion up in flames; her brother Jacob, an invalid after the damnyankees gassed him, died then, too. She'd been in Charleston when the Negroes rebelled, and, unlike so many white landowners, returned to her plantation after the revolt was quelled. She'd even managed to bring in a cotton crop of sorts. And then—

"God damn you, Cassius," she said softly. In the days before the war, he'd been the chief hunter at Marshlands—and a secret Red, when she'd thought the Negroes there had no secrets from her. In the rebellion, he'd headed the murderous outfit that styled itself the Congaree Socialist Republic. He still led a ragtag band of black brigands who skulked through the swamps, eluding the authorities and calling murder and thievery acts of revolution.

They had friends among the Negroes who'd gone back to work at Marshlands. They had more friends among them than Anne had imagined. A month or so earlier, on Christmas night, 1916, they'd come horrifyingly close to killing her.

"I will have my revenge," she said, as she'd said a hundred times since managing to escape. "I will have—" A knock on the door interrupted her. She stormed over to it and threw it open. "What is it?" she demanded.

Even though the delivery boy for the Confederate Wire Service wore a uniform close in color and cut to that of the Army, he couldn't have been a day above fifteen years old. The sight of a

31

tall, fierce, beautiful blond woman twice his age glaring at him unstrung him altogether. He tried to stammer out why he had come, but words failed him. After a couple of clucks a hen would have been ashamed to claim, he dropped the envelope he carried and incontinently fled.

Feeling triumph over so lowly a male would have demeaned Anne. She bent, scooped up the envelope, tore it open, and unfolded the telegram inside. REGRET NO CONFEDERATE TROOPS AVAILABLE TO AID SOUTH CAROLINA FORCES IN HUNTING DOWN BANDITS. HOPE ALL OTHERWISE WELL. GABRIEL SEMMES, PRESIDENT OF THE CONFEDERATE STATES.

She crumpled up the telegram and flung it into the wickerwork wastebasket that had come with the room. "You stingy son of a bitch!" she snarled. "I poured money into your campaign. The niggers burned down Marshlands, and I still twisted arms to help get your bill for Negro troops through Congress. And now you won't—"

She broke off. Some of her rage evaporated. The only reason Semmes had wanted to arm Negroes was that the war, as it was presently being fought, was going so badly. It hadn't gone any better lately. Maybe the president of the CSA really couldn't spare any decent soldiers to help the lame, the halt, and the elderly of South Carolina's militia go after Cassius and his guerrillas.

"If they can't handle the job, I'll damn well have to take care of it myself," she said. Somehow, that didn't surprise her. Cassius had made the fight personal when he burned the mansion where her family had lived for most of a century. He'd made it even more personal when he tried to give her a bullet for Christmas. "If that's how he wants it, that's how he'll have it."

She walked over to the closet, slid the door on its squeaking track, and scowled at the few sorry dresses and skirts and shirtwaists that hung there. She was used to ordering gowns from Paris and London and (in peacetime) New York. What she'd been able to buy in St. Matthews was to her eye one short step up from the burlap feed sacks poor Negroes and shiftless whites used to cover their nakedness.

But, after she'd pushed aside the clothes, she smiled. Against the back wall of the closet leaned a Tredegar her surviving brother, Tom, had sent on learning of her escape. It was a sniper's rifle, with a telescopic sight. She'd been a tomboy as a girl—

good training for competing against men as an adult. She knew how to handle guns.

During the Red rebellion, the authorities hadn't let her fight against the Negroes of the Congaree Socialist Republic. Now—

Now she picked up her handbag (which held, among other things, a revolver to replace the one she'd lost when Cassius burned her cabin) and went downstairs. It was cool, not cold; whatever winter might do up in the USA, it rested lightly on Low Country South Carolina. She headed for the haberdasher's.

St. Matthews had been a cotton town before the war. It was still a cotton town—of sorts. Most of the nearby plantations were either corpses or crippled remnants of their former selves. Most of the white men in town were gone for soldiers or gone to the grave. Most of the black men were gone, too: drafted into labor battalions, fled into revolt, or now wearing butternut themselves. Only a little of the damage done when Confederate forces recaptured the town from the Congaree Socialist Republic had been repaired. No labor for that, and no money, either.

By what sort of luck Anne could scarcely imagine, Rosenblum's Clothes had escaped everything. One of the bricks near the plate-glass window bore a bright bullet scar; other than that, the place was untouched. Inside, Aaron Rosenblum clacked away on a treadle-powered sewing machine, as he'd been doing for as long as Anne could remember.

When the bell above the door jangled, he looked up over the tops of his gold-framed half-glasses. Seeing Anne, he jumped to his feet and gave her a nod that was almost a bow. "Good day to you, Miss Colleton," he said.

"Good day, Mr. Rosenblum." As always, Anne hid the smile that wanted to leap out onto her face whenever she heard him talk. His accent, half Low Country drawl, half guttural Yiddish, was among the strangest she'd ever encountered.

"And what can I do for you today?" Rosenblum asked, running a hand over his bald head. He would never go into the Army; he had to be nearer seventy than fifty.

"I want half a dozen pairs of stout trousers of the sort men use to go hunting in the swamps of the Congaree," she answered.

He nodded. "These would be for your brother, after—God willing—he comes home safe from the war? Shall I alter them thinking he will be the same size he was when he went into the Army?"

"I'm sorry," Anne said. "You misunderstand, Mr. Rosenblum. These trousers are for me."

"For—you?" His eyes went wide. The lenses of his spectacles magnified his stare even more. "You are joking with me." Instead of staring, he really looked at her. "No, you are not joking. But—what would a woman want with trousers?"

"To go hunting in the swamps of the Congaree," she repeated patiently. "I can't very well do that in gingham or lace, can I?"

"What would you hunt?" he asked, still not believing.

"Reds." Anne Colleton's voice was flat and determined. "I will want these trousers as soon as you can have them ready. They shouldn't be hard to alter to fit me; I'm as tall as a good many men."

"Well, yes, but—" He blushed to the crown of his head, then blurted, "My wife is visiting our daughter in Columbia. Who will measure you?"

Again, Anne didn't laugh out loud. "Go ahead, Mr. Rosenblum. Being so careful, you won't take any undue liberties. I'm sure of it." *And if you try, I'll give you such a licking, you won't know yesterday from next week.*

He coughed and muttered, then blushed once more. "If you do this thing, Miss Colleton, will you wear a corset while you are doing it?"

Anne felt like giving herself a licking. She'd defied a lot of conventions, but some she didn't even notice till someone reminded her they were there. She dashed into the dressing room, yanked the curtain shut, and divested herself of boning and elastic. When she came out, she was so comfortable, she wondered why she wore the damn thing. Fashion made a harsh mistress.

Aaron Rosenblum still hawed instead of hemming. In the end, though, he did as she wanted. In the end, almost everyone did as she wanted. He looked a little happier when she set two butternut-colored twenty-dollar bills on his sewing machine, but only a little. "I still do not know if this is decent," he muttered.

"I'll worry about that," she answered, by which she meant she would not worry in the slightest.

The telephone rang a few minutes after she got back to her room. "Hello?" she said into the mouthpiece. "What? . . . Really? . . . Yes, bring him here. We'll see. Greenville, you say? . . . You should have him here by evening. . . . Of course I'll pay for train fare. I want to get to the bottom of this, too." She hung the mouthpiece on its hook, then let out a long sigh that was also a name: "Scipio."

After he'd fled Columbia, he'd gone up into the northwestern part of the state, had he? Now he was found out there, too. He knew how to get things done, did Scipio. A butler who didn't know how to get things done wasn't worth having. From things she'd heard, Scipio had been Cassius' right-hand man in the Congaree Socialist Republic, and a big reason it held together as long as it did.

What did she owe him for that? After what the Reds' revolutionary tribunals had done to so many white landowners, how many times did any official of the Congaree Socialist Republic deserve to die?

Waiting was hard, even though she knew Scipio was coming from more than a hundred miles away. She'd lighted the gas lamps before a knock sounded on her door. She opened it. The two whites who stood in the hall had the look of city policemen: middle-aged, rugged, wary, wearing suits that would have been fashionable about 1910 but were dowdy now. "Miss Colleton?" one of them asked in an Up Country accent. When she nodded, the policeman pointed to the Negro who stood, hands manacled behind his back, between him and his partner. "This boy the Scipio you know, ma'am?"

She carefully studied the black man, then slowly and regretfully shook her head. "I'm sorry, but I'm afraid not. There must be some mistake. I've never set eyes on this man before in my life."

Both white policemen stared at her in astonished dismay. Scipio stared, too, in equal astonishment—though not dismay—but only for an instant. Then, very smoothly, he went back to playing the innocent wronged. "You see?" he shouted to the policemen. "I ain't dat bad nigger. I tol' you I ain't dat bad nigger!"

"Shut up, God damn you," one of them growled. Perfunctorily, he added, "Sorry, ma'am." Then he and his partner put their heads together.

Anne looked at Scipio. He was looking at her. She'd known he would be. *You are mine,* she mouthed silently. *Do you understand me?* His head moved up and down—only a little, but enough. *You are mine,* she repeated, and watched him nod again.

* * *

Major Abner Dowling slogged through freezing Tennessee mud from his tent toward the farmhouse where the general commanding the U.S. First Army made his headquarters. Dowling supposed the mud couldn't have been quite freezing. In that case, it would have been hard. It wasn't.

When the general's adjutant lifted one booted foot out of the muck, pounds of it came up, stuck to the sole and sides. For one of the few times in his life, Dowling wished he were seventy-five pounds lighter. Far more often than not, he'd found, being fat mattered little, and he dearly loved to eat. But his bulk made him sink deeper into the ooze than he would have had he been thin.

Puffing his way up onto the porch, he paused to knock as much mud off his boots as he could. Cornelia, the colored housekeeper the general had hired after First Army's attack on Nashville stalled the winter before, would not be happy if he left filthy tracks in the hall and parlor. Even if she was a mulatto, she was such a good-looking young woman, he didn't want her glaring at him.

Delicious frying odors filled the air when he went inside. He sighed. Not only was Cornelia a fine-looking wench, she could cook with the best of them, too.

Neat in a white shirtwaist and long black skirt, she came sweeping out of the kitchen. "Mornin', Major," she said. "The general and his missus, they still finishin' breakfast. You want to sit yourself down in the parlor, I bring you some coffee while you wait."

He knew he could have gone straight into the kitchen, had he had anything more urgent than the usual morning briefing. But he also knew the general would not appreciate being disturbed at his ham and eggs and hotcakes, or whatever other delicacies Cornelia had devised. "Coffee will be fine," he said. She made good coffee, too.

The parlor window gave him a good view of a couple of anti-aircraft guns sitting out there in the mud, and of the wet, cold, miserable soldiers who served them. The Rebs had stepped up bombing attacks against First Army lately. More pursuit aeroplanes were supposed to be coming, but every Army commander screamed for more aeroplanes at the top of his lungs.

Cornelia brought him his coffee, pale with cream and—he sipped—very sweet, just the way he liked it. "Thank you, my dear," he said. She smiled at him, but he was wise enough—which wasn't too far removed from saying *old enough*—to recognize it as a smile of service, not one of invitation.

Dowling had taken only a couple of sips when the general commanding First Army came out of the kitchen and made his slow way into the parlor. His adjutant set the coffee on the arm of the sofa and heaved himself to his feet. Saluting, he said, "Good morning, General Custer."

"Good morning, Major," Lieutenant General George Armstrong Custer said as he returned the salute. For a man of seventy-seven, Custer was in fine fettle—but then, most men of seventy-seven were dead, and had been for years. Locks peroxided a brassy gold spilled out from under the hat Custer habitually wore to hide his bald head. His drooping mustache had also been chemically gilded.

With a wheeze, he sank into a chair, then produced a gold cigar case from a breast pocket of his fancy uniform. Dowling had a match ready to light the cigar he took from it. "Here you are, sir," he said. Custer drew on the cigar, coughed wetly a couple of times, and then settled down to happy puffing.

He blew out a cloud of fragrant smoke—as a general, he could get hold of far finer tobacco than the average U.S. citizen. No sooner had he done so than his wife came into the parlor. "That miserable thing stinks, Autie," Elizabeth Bacon Custer snapped.

"Now, Libbie, it's a fine cigar," Custer said in placating tones. Around his wife, if nowhere else, he took a soft line. Dowling understood that down to the ground. Libbie Custer intimidated him more than the Confederate Army did, too—and he thought she thought well of him.

"Cigars," she said with a scowl on her round face. "Taking the name of the Lord in vain." The scowl got deeper. "Liquor." Now she looked ready to bite nails in half.

" 'Scuse me, Miz Custer, ma'am." Cornelia swept by, round hips working under the skirt. "Here's that coffee you asked for, General." She laid the cup on the table in front of Custer, then left the room with that rolling stride. Custer's eyes followed her, hungrily. So did Dowling's; he couldn't help it.

And so did Libbie Custer's. When Cornelia was out of sight, Libbie glared at her husband even more fearsomely than she had when she spoke of spirits. She didn't speak now, maybe because she couldn't find a word a lady could say that would express her feelings. Instead, short and plump and determined, she stomped out of the room herself.

Custer sighed. "She *will* come up toward the front," he said. That made it harder for him to do what he wanted to do with Cornelia. Dowling didn't know if he'd done anything with the housekeeper before Libbie arrived. For that matter, Dowling didn't know if he *could* do anything with the housekeeper, being, after all, seventy-seven.

The only answer the adjutant gave was a shrug. No matter what sort of crimp having Libbie around put in Custer's plans, Dowling didn't mind it a bit. He'd noticed First Army fought better when she cohabited with her husband. The conclusion he'd drawn—that she owned more than half the family's brains—he kept to himself.

Looking around to make sure he was not overseen, Custer drew a flat silver flask from a hip pocket and poured some of its contents into his coffee. Magnanimously, he held it out to Dowling. "Want an eye-opener, Major?"

"Don't mind if I do, sir—just a wee one." Dowling tasted the improved coffee. "Ahh. That's mighty good brandy."

"Isn't it, though?" Custer gulped down half his cup. "Well, let's get down to business, shall we? Soonest begun, soonest done."

"Yes, sir," Dowling said. Custer didn't like minutiae, which made Dowling take a certain acerbic pleasure in giving him a bellyful: "Our trench raids by Cotton Town brought in twenty-seven prisoners last night, sir. The Rebs tried to raid us near White House. We beat them back pretty smartly; only lost a couple of men, and machine-gunned a couple of theirs retreating through no-man's-land. They threw some gas shells at us farther west, north of Greenbrier. That could be trouble; they've brought fresh troops into the area, and they're liable to be planning a spoiling attack."

"God damn them to hell," Custer growled, thereby making a clean sweep of Libbie's shibboleths. "God damn the whole Entente to hell. And God damn President Theodore goddamn Roosevelt to hell, too, for sticking me here against the Rebs when he knows I'd sooner pay the limeys and Canadians back for what they did to Tom."

"Yes, sir," Abner Dowling said resignedly. He wondered how many times he'd heard that from the general commanding First

Army. Often enough to be sick of it, anyhow. Custer's brother was thirty-five years dead now, slain in Montana Territory during the Second Mexican War. Custer and Roosevelt hadn't got along with each other in the past thirty-five years, either, each suspecting the other of stealing some of his glory. He tried to steer Custer back to the front where he commanded, not the one where he wished he led: "If we could return to planning, sir . . ."

"Planning? Faugh!" Custer made a disgusted noise. "Once we smash through this line, Nashville falls, because we'll be able to shell it to kingdom come. One more push—"

"They've stopped all the pushes we've tried so far, sir," Dowling reminded him: a sentence that covered thousands of dead and wounded, and burning barrels by the score. Custer's favorite strategy, now as always in a career that stretched back to the War of Secession, was the headlong smash.

Now the general commanding First Army looked sly, which alarmed Abner Dowling. "I think I've finally found a way to break through," Custer said.

"Really, sir?" Dowling hoped he kept all expression from his voice because, if he didn't, the expression that would have been there was horror. Generals on both sides in America—and on both sides in Europe, too—had been chasing breakthroughs since the war began, with the same persistence and same success as men dying of thirst chasing mirages in the desert.

Custer beamed, which made his cheeks sag and his jowls wobble. "Yes, by jingo." He leaned forward and set a liver-spotted hand on Dowling's knee, much as he would have liked to do with Cornelia. "And you're going to help me."

"You'll give me a combat assignment, sir?" Dowling asked eagerly. He'd longed for one since the war began. The War Department thought he was more useful as Custer's adjutant. It was a nasty job, but someone had to do it, and Dowling, from long practice, had got good at it. But if Custer himself wanted to put his adjutant into action . . .

Evidently, Custer didn't. He shook his head, which made those lank locks of hair flip back and forth. Dowling coughed a little at the stink of the cinnamon-scented hair oil Custer liked. Nobody else Dowling knew had used the nasty stuff since the turn of the century. "No, no, no," Custer said. "You're going to help me keep things straight with Philadelphia."

"I'll be happy to edit your correspondence, sir," Dowling said.

The general's correspondence needed editing—more than it commonly got. Custer was a firm believer in a variation on the Ptolemaic theory: he was convinced the world revolved around him. Anything good that happened anywhere near him had to redound to his credit and no one else's; nothing bad was ever his fault. In that as in few other things, Libbie aided and abetted him.

He was shaking his head again. "No, no, no," he repeated. "I have something important in mind, and I don't want those dunderheads with gold and black piping on their caps to get wind of it and tell me I can't do it because it runs against the way they read the Bible."

"Exactly what is it you have in mind, sir?" Dowling asked with a sinking feeling. Gold and black were the branch-of-service colors of the General Staff. Whatever Custer was thinking about, it was something he already knew the War Department brass in the City of Brotherly Love wouldn't love one bit.

"I'll tell you what I have in mind, Major," Custer said. "I have in mind the biggest goddamn barrel roll the world has ever seen, that's what."

Well, I might have guessed, Dowling thought. The tracked, armored, motorized forts called barrels were the best thing anyone had yet found for breaking the deadly stalemate of trench warfare. They could smash barbed wire, clearing paths for infantry, and they could bring machine-gun and cannon fire down on the enemy from point-blank range. They also broke down about every five minutes and, even when they were working, didn't move any faster than a man could walk.

The adjutant chose his words with care: "Sir, doctrine specifically orders that barrels be spread out evenly along the front, to assist infantry attacks wherever they may be carried out."

"And what a lot of poppycock that is, too," Custer declared, as if he were the Pope speaking *ex cathedra.* "The right way to use them is to build a whole great whacking column of them, smash a hole in the Rebs' line you could throw a cow through, and send in the infantry on their heels—a breakthrough. Q.E.D."

"When Brigadier General MacArthur came up with a similar plan, sir, you cited doctrine," Dowling reminded him. "You wouldn't let him do as he'd planned."

"Daniel MacArthur cares for nothing but his own glory," Custer said, which was true but which applied in even greater measure to Custer himself. "He knew the attack was weaker than it should have been, but went ahead anyhow. He deserved to fail, and he did."

"Yes, sir," Dowling said resignedly. Custer had done more than his share to weaken MacArthur's attack because he did not want the youngest division commander in the whole Army getting credit for the victory he might have won.

"Besides," Custer went on, "I aim to launch an army-scale assault, not one on the scale of a division. I intend to concentrate all the barrels in First Army and hurl them like a spear at the Confederate line. It will break, by God."

"Sir, the War Department will never let you get away with flouting doctrine like that," Dowling said. "If you try, they'll confiscate your barrels and ship 'em to other fronts where the commanders are more cooperative."

"I know." The sly look returned to Custer's face. "That's where you come in."

"Me?" Whatever was coming next, Dowling didn't think he'd like it.

He was right. "In the reports First Army sends to Philadelphia," Custer said, "all the barrels will be lined up exactly as the idiots with the high foreheads say they should be. You'll vet corps and divisional reports, too—'in the interest of greater efficiency,' you know. Meanwhile, we shall be readying the blow that will wreck the Confederate position in Tennessee once and for all."

Abner Dowling stared at him in dismay. "My God, sir, they'll courtmartial us both."

"Nonsense, my boy," Custer told him. "You're safe as houses any which way, because you're acting under my direct orders. But even I need fear only if we lose. If we win, I shall be forgiven no matter what I do. Victory redeems everything. And we *shall* win, Major."

"My God, sir," Dowling said again. But then he paused. He'd dreamt for years of seeing Custer ousted from the command of First Army and replaced by someone competent. Now Custer was greasing the skids of his own downfall. And the general was right—his adjutant would only be obeying orders. Slowly, thoughtfully, Dowling nodded. "All right, sir, let's see what we can do."

"Stout fellow!" Custer exclaimed. He winked at Dowling. "Stout fellow indeed." Dowling forced a smile.

* * *

The big White truck rumbled through the streets of Covington, Kentucky, toward the loading area by the Ohio River wharves. Cincinnatus knew the streets of Covington as well as he knew his name. He'd driven a delivery truck through them, back in the days before the war started. Covington had changed since U.S. forces wrested it from its Confederate defenders, but its streets hadn't.

One symbol of the change was the flag flying from the city hall as the Negro drove past it. For the past two and a half years, the Stars and Stripes had fluttered there, not the Stars and Bars. If the USA won the war, the Stars and Stripes would fly there forever. Kentucky—less a few small chunks in the south and southeast still in Confederate hands—had been readmitted to the United States after more than half a century out of the Union.

Guards in green-gray stood guard in sandbagged machine-gun positions in front of the city hall. Not everyone in Kentucky was happy with its separation from the Confederate States. Not even close to everyone in Kentucky was happy with that separation. Cincinnatus sighed. He knew that only too well.

"Damn, I wish I never would've got sucked into all this crazy shit," he muttered as the truck jounced over a pothole and his teeth clicked together. Confederate diehards, black Reds—were Kentucky still in the CSA, they would have been at each other's throats. As things were, they both hated the occupier worse than they hated each other. Cincinnatus cursed his luck and his own generosity for making him part of both groups. If only he hadn't hidden Tom Kennedy when the Yankee soldiers were after his old boss. But he had, and so . . .

A soldier playing traffic cop held up a hand. Cincinnatus trod on the brake and shifted the White into neutral. An officer in a chauffer-driven motorcar rolled past. The soldier waved the truck convoy on again.

Cincinnatus drove on up to the riverside, pulled into the loading area, and stopped the truck. The engine ticked as hot metal began to cool. He opened the door and climbed down onto the paving stones. The air was thick with the exhaust of a lot of trucks in a small space. He coughed a couple of times at the harsh stink.

More trucks rolled south on the bridge over the Ohio between Covington and Cincinnati. The Confederates had dropped it into the river as soon as the war began, but it was long since not only rebuilt but widened. A stream of barges crossed the river, too, carrying the sinews of war from U.S. factories toward the fighting front. Negro laborers unloaded the barges and hauled their contents over to the truck-transport unit of which Cincinnatus was a part.

He'd been one of those laborers till the head of the transport unit discovered he could drive. Since then, he'd made more money for less physical labor, but his hours were longer and more erratic than they had been. Now that the front reached down into Tennessee, it was most of a day's drive from Covington. He didn't like sleeping in a tent away from Elizabeth and their baby boy, Achilles, but nobody cared what he liked.

"Come on!" Lieutenant Straubing shouted. "Get yourselves checked off. You don't get checked off, you don't get paid."

That blunt warning from their boss got the drivers moving into the shed to make sure the payroll sergeant put a tick by their names on his sheet. About half the drivers were white, the other half colored. If a man could do the job, Straubing didn't give a damn what color he was. For a while, Cincinnatus had thought that meant Straubing had a better opinion of blacks than did most whites from either the USA or the CSA. He doubted that now. More likely, Straubing just grabbed the tools he needed without worrying about the paint job they had.

Even that attitude was an improvement on what most whites in the USA and the CSA thought about blacks.

The line in front of the payroll sergeant formed solely on the basis of who got there first. Cincinnatus fell in behind a white driver named Herk and in front of another white who, because he wore his hair cropped close to his skull, got called Burrhead a lot. They chatted amiably enough as the queue moved forward; black or white, they had work in common.

"God only knows when poor Smitty gonna get in," Cincinnatus said. "Saw him pull off with *another* puncture. That man go through more patches'n a ragpicker."

"He ain't lucky, and that's a fact," Herk said.

"He'd be a hell of a lot luckier if the damn Rebs didn't keep throwin' nails in the road," Burrhead added. "'Course, we'd all be a hell of a lot luckier if the damn Rebs didn't keep throwin' nails in the road."

"I'll tell you who's lucky." Herk pointed at Cincinnatus.

"Here's the lucky one." Cincinnatus had rarely heard a white man call him that. But Herk went on, "You and me, Burrhead, we'll sleep in the barracks tonight. He's going home to his wife."

"That ain't bad," Burrhead agreed.

Cincinnatus collected five dollars—two days' pay. Herk got the same. Burrhead, who hadn't been in the unit so long, got four and a half. Some of the white drivers had grumbled because experienced blacks got more than they did. Some had tried to do more than grumble. They were spending time at hard labor; Lieutenant Straubing tolerated nothing that got in the way of his unit's doing its job.

A trolley line ran from the wharves to the edge of Covington's Negro district, over by the Licking River on the east side of town. Cincinnatus set a nickel in the fare box without hesitation. When he'd been working on the wharves, making a dollar or a dollar and a half a day, he'd almost always walked to and from his house. By his standards of comparison, being able to sit down in the colored section at the back of the trolley was affluence.

The trolley ran past the charred ruins of a general store. Cincinnatus wondered if Conroy had been able to rebuild somewhere else. The white storekeeper was one of the stubborn Confederates still working against the U.S. occupiers. If he did get back in business, Cincinnatus expected he'd hear from him. He looked forward to that as much as he did to smallpox.

He might hear from Conroy even if the storekeeper didn't get back into business. He looked forward to that even less than he did to smallpox. The fire that had gutted the store hadn't been an accident.

When he got off the trolley car, he did not immediately hurry home as he'd thought he would. Instead, he paused and sniffed. A delicious, spicy odor hung in the air. Sure enough, around the corner came the horse-drawn delivery wagon from the Kentucky Smoke House, Apicius' barbecue palace. Apicius' son, Lucullus, was driving the wagon. He waved to Cincinnatus. "Sell you some ribs tonight?" he called, white teeth gleaming in his black face.

"No thanks," Cincinnatus answered. "Elizabeth's got some chicken stew waitin' for me when I get home."

Lucullus waved again and drove on. Cincinnatus let out a small sigh of relief. Had Lucullus asked him if he wanted red-hot ribs, that would have been an instruction to show up at Apicius' place. All sorts of red-hot things went on there, Apicius and his sons being Reds themselves.

But not tonight. Tonight Cincinnatus was free to be simply a man, not a political man. As neighborhoods in the colored part of town went, his was one of the better ones. The clapboard house in which he lived was neat and well kept. As best he could, given his color, he'd been a man on the rise before the war. As best he could, given a great many complications, he remained a man on the rise now.

When he opened the door, he grinned. The chicken stew smelled as good—well, almost as good—as the barbecue Lucullus hadn't called red-hot tonight. In the kitchen, Elizabeth exclaimed, "That's your pa!"

"Dadadadada!" Achilles came toddling out toward him on stiff legs spread wide. An enormous grin spread over his face, wide enough to show he had four teeth on top and two on the bottom.

Cincinnatus picked him up and swung him around. Achilles squealed with glee, then squawked indignantly when Cincinnatus set him on the floor again. His father swatted him on the bottom, so softly that he laughed instead of crying.

Elizabeth came out, too, and tilted her face up for a kiss. "You look tired," she said. She was still in the shirtwaist and skirt in which she cleaned house for white Covingtonians.

"So do you," he answered. They both laughed—tiredly. "Ain't life bully?" he added. They laughed again. He had a pretty good notion of how the rest of the night would go. They'd eat supper. She'd wash dishes while he played with the baby. They would sit and talk and read for a little while—they both had their letters, unusual for black couples even on what had been the northern edge of the Confederate States. Then they'd get Achilles to bed, and then they'd go to bed themselves. Maybe they would make love. Odds were better they'd fall asleep as soon as their heads hit the pillows, though.

Through the first half of the evening, things went very much as he'd expected. The stew was delicious, and Cincinnatus said so. "Your mother gits half the credit—she kept an eye on it and the baby while I was workin'," Elizabeth said. After dinner, Cincinnatus chased Achilles around the house hoping to tire him out so he'd fall asleep in a hurry. Sometimes it worked, sometimes it didn't.

Elizabeth was just drying the last dish when somebody knocked on the door. "Who's that?" she asked, frowning. "Curfew's comin'."

"I'd better find out." Cincinnatus strode to the door and opened it.

Tom Kennedy stood there, as he had on the horrible night when his mere presence dragged Cincinnatus, all unwilling, into the Confederate resistance against U.S. forces in Kentucky. As his former boss had then, he gasped, "You got to hide me, Cincinnatus! They're right on my heels, the sons of bitches."

"Who?" Cincinnatus demanded. Christ, if Kennedy had led the Yankees to him—

Before the white man could answer, a rifle shot rang out. "My God! I am hit!" Kennedy cried. He clutched at his chest. Before he could fall—as he surely would have fallen—the rifle cracked again. The left side of his head exploded, spraying Cincinnatus with blood and brains and bits of bone. Behind him, Elizabeth screamed. Tom Kennedy went down now, like a sack of peas. Blood poured from him in a wet, sticky flood over Cincinnatus' front porch.

In the barrel yard behind the U.S. First Army's front in northern Tennessee, mechanics swore sulfurously as they worked in the twin White engines that sent their enormous toys rumbling forward. Other mechanics were on their knees in the mud, tightening the tracks that let the barrels go down into shell holes and trenches and climb out the other side.

Armorers carried belts of machine-gun ammunition and crates of two-inch shells for the guns of the traveling fortresses. Each one mounted not only a cannon but also half a dozen machine guns on a chassis twenty-five feet long and more than ten feet high. They needed a lot of ammunition to fill them up.

Lieutenant Colonel Irving Morrell walked slowly along a path through the mud corduroyed with fence posts and house timbers and whatever other scraps of wood the folks who had made the path had been able to come up with. He was a lean, fit man in his mid-twenties, with a long face, pale eyes, and sandy hair he wore short. When he wasn't paying attention to the way he walked, he limped a little, a reminder of the leg wound he'd taken not long after the start of the war. Whenever he caught himself doing it, he stopped and made himself walk straight.

The farther he went into the barrel yard, the slower he walked and the more noticeable the limp became. Finally, he stopped altogether, and stood and stared in complete fascination. He might have stood there for quite a while, had a soldier coming up the path with a roll of tent cloth on his shoulder not found him in the way and, in lieu of cursing him, inquired, "May I help you, sir?"

Thus recalled to himself, Morrell said, "Yes, if you please. I'm looking for Colonel Ned Sherrard."

"That tent right over there, sir," the soldier answered, pointing to one erection of green-gray among many. "Now if you'll excuse me—"

More slowly than he should have, Morrell realized he'd been given a hint. "Sorry," he said, and stepped aside. The soldier trudged on. He was shaking his head and muttering under his breath. Morrell had no doubt what sorts of things he was muttering, either.

No corduroyed track ran toward the tent to which the soldier had directed Morrell. Without hesitation, he stepped off the path and tromped through the mud. A couple of mechanics looked up as he squelched past them. He caught a snatch of what one of them said to the other: "—ficer not too proud to get his boots dirty." He had been walking straight before he heard that. He walked straighter afterwards.

As he neared the tent, the flap opened and an officer came out: a medium-tall, wide-shouldered fellow with a graying Kaiser Bill mustache and, Morrell saw, eagles on his shoulder straps. "Colonel Sherrard, sir?" he asked.

"That's right," the other officer answered. "And you'd be Lieutenant Colonel Morrell, eh?"

"Yes, sir." Morrell saluted. "Reporting as ordered, sir." Among the other service ribbons above Sherrard's left breast pocket, he noticed a black-and-gold one showing the colonel had been on the General Staff. Morrell had that same ribbon on his tunic. Sherrard's service badge, though, was not the General Staff's eagle on a star. Instead, he wore a barrel pierced by a lightning bolt.

He was scanning the fruit salad on Morrell's chest as Morrell looked over his. Morrell got the idea that what he saw didn't altogether please him, and had trouble figuring out why. Without false modesty, he knew he had a good record. Along with General Staff service, he'd fought in Sonora (where he was wounded), in eastern Kentucky, and in the Canadian Rockies. He'd distinguished himself in each of the latter two theaters, too. So why did Sherrard look as if he smelled sour milk?

With what looked like a deliberate effort of will, Sherrard made his face altogether blank. "Come inside, Lieutenant Colonel," he said. "Let's get you settled in and see how we can best use you."

"Yes, sir." Morrell ducked through the tent flap ahead of Colonel Sherrard, who introduced him to his adjutant, Captain Wallace, and his clerk typist, Corporal Norton. Either one of them might have been a power behind the throne. Off his first impression of Sherrard, Morrell was inclined to doubt that. The colonel to whom he'd been ordered to report seemed to need no one to prop him up.

Morrell accepted a tin cup full of muddy coffee, then sat down with Colonel Sherrard to drink it. Sipping from his own cup, Sherrard asked, "So how did you happen to come down from General Staff headquarters just now?"

The question was so elaborately casual, Morrell knew it held more than met the eye. For the life of him, though, he couldn't figure out what. As he would have anyway, he answered with the simple truth: "The more I've looked at things, sir, the more important barrels have looked to me. I thought I ought to see some action with them. Besides"—his grin made him look even younger than he was—"running down the enemy in something as big as a house sounds like a hell of a lot of fun."

That got him the first smile he'd seen from Sherrard. "As a matter of fact, it is, when the damn things feel like running and when the Rebs don't have a cannon handy and don't chuck a grenade or a whiskey bottle full of burning gasoline through one of your hatches."

"If you knew beforehand who'd win, you wouldn't have to fight the war," Morrell replied with a shrug. "Since you don't, you take your chances."

That got him another smile, a wider one. "You'll have studied barrels some, then, I take it, even if you haven't served in them?" Sherrard said. After Morrell nodded, the older officer asked, "What's your opinion of our current doctrine on barrel deployment?"

"Spreading them out widely along the line, do you mean, sir?" Morrell said. Now he waited for Sherrard to nod. When the colonel did, Morrell went on, "Sir, I don't like it for beans. The barrels give us a big stick. As long as we've got it, we ought to shellack the Rebels with it."

Ned Sherrard set down his cup and folded his arms across his chest. "Lieutenant Colonel, I will have you know that I was one of the people involved in designing barrels, and that I am also one of the people responsible for formulating the doctrine in use for most of the past year. If I ask you that question again, will you give me a different answer?"

"No, sir," Morrell said with a small sigh. "You asked my opinion, and I gave it to you. If you want to transfer me out of this unit, though . . . well, I won't be happy, but I'll certainly understand." Sometimes he wished he didn't have the habit of saying just what he thought.

Sherrard kept his arms folded, as if he'd forgotten they were. "Isn't that interesting?" he said, more to himself than to Morrell. "Maybe I was wrong."

"Sir?" Morrell said.

"Never mind," Colonel Sherrard told him. "If you don't get it, you don't need to know; if you do get it, you already know and you're sandbagging."

"Sir?" Morrell said again. Now, though, he didn't really expect to get an answer. He had a notion of what he'd stumbled over: an argument among the brass about how best to use barrels. But doctrine was doctrine, and the Army clung to it as tightly as the Catholic Church did.

Sherrard, though, turned out to be more forthcoming than Morrell had thought he would. "You may be interested to learn that you and General Custer have similar views about how barrels should be employed."

"Really, sir?" That *was* interesting. Custer was . . . Morrell didn't know how old he was, but he had to be older than God. Surprising he had any ideas of his own. Off what Morrell had seen in Philadelphia of his performance, he didn't have many. He just went straight at the Rebs and slugged till someone eventually had to take a step back.

"I'll tell you something else you may find funny," Sherrard said. Morrell raised a questioning eyebrow. In a half-shamefaced way, the colonel who'd served on the General Staff went on, "God damn me to hell if I haven't started thinking he's right, too. Which also means I think *you* may be right, Lieutenant Colonel. As you put it, if we've got a big stick, we ought to clout the bastards with it."

"Really, sir?" Morrell knew he was repeating himself again, but couldn't help it. That eyebrow—both eyebrows—went up again, this time in astonishment. "Have you let the War Department know you've changed your mind?"

"I've sent them more memoranda than you can shake a stick at." Sherrard sighed. "Have you ever dropped a small stone off a tall cliff and waited for the sound it makes when it hits the ground to come back to your ears?"

"Yes, sir," Morrell replied. "The sound never comes back, not if it's small enough and the cliff is high enough." He paused. "Dealing with the War Department can be a lot like that."

"Ain't it the truth?" The colloquialism from Sherrard surprised Morrell yet again. "That's one of the reasons I've stayed in the field since I shepherded the first barrels down to this front. The cliff isn't so tall here in the field. There's less space between me and the enemy, if you know what I mean."

"Oh, yes, sir, I know exactly what you mean," Morrell answered. "Sometimes I think our boys in the field have worse enemies in Philadelphia than they do in Richmond."

Again, he wished he hadn't been so forthright. Again, it was too late. He waited to see how Colonel Sherrard would respond. Sherrard didn't show much; he got the distinct impression Sherrard seldom showed much. After a thoughtful pause, the colonel said, "Well, you were crazy enough to want to serve in barrels, Lieutenant Colonel. Now that you're here, don't you think you ought to go for a ride in one so you can see how big a mistake you made?"

"Yes, sir!" Morrell said enthusiastically. "I hear it's quite something."

"So it is. A kick in the teeth is quite something, too." Sherrard's voice was dry. "General Custer calls it the biggest sockdologer in the history of the world. My father, God rest his soul, used to use that word. I think it fits here. Come on. You will, too."

They left the tent and squelched through the mud to a barrel Sherrard happened to know was in running order. Along the way, the colonel commandeered a driver and a couple of engineers. "In case it doesn't feel like staying in running order," Sherrard explained. "In a real fight, we'd have two men on each machine gun—they're from the infantry—and two artillerymen at the cannon."

With the barrel commander, that made a crew of eighteen, from three different branches of the Army. "Not efficient," Morrell remarked.

"I know that, too—now," Sherrard said. "Here we are." He stopped in front of a barrel done up in camouflage paint except for a fierce eagle's head on the side and the name or motto *Remembrance* above it. One of the hatches was open. "Climb on up into the cupola," Sherrard told Morrell. "You will be the commander. Drive around a square and come back here."

Morrell scrambled up into the small metal box atop the barrel. He took the seat forward and to the right, the one unencumbered by controls. The driver sat in the other one. When the engineers shouted that they were ready, the driver stabbed the red button of the electric starter. The engines grumbled, then came to roaring life. The driver yelled something to Morrell. He had no idea what.

The din was terrific, incredible. If the engines had mufflers, they didn't work. Exhaust fumes promptly filled the barrel. Morrell coughed. His eyes smarted. What combat would be like in here, with the machine guns and cannon blazing away, adding their racket and the stink of burnt smokeless powder, he didn't want to think. *Hell* seemed a reasonable first approximation.

After checking to make sure both reverse levers behind his seat were in the forward position, the driver got the barrel moving by stepping on the clutches to both engines, putting the beast in gear, and opening the throttle on the steering wheel. He knew the course he was supposed to steer. If he hadn't, hand signals would have been the only way to give it to him; he couldn't have heard shouted orders. The barrel rode as if its springs—if it had any—were made out of rocks. Morrell bit his tongue twice and his lower lip once. With the window slits open, he could see a little. With them closed, he could see next to nothing.

A cough. A groan. A wheeze. Silence. Into it, the driver said, "We're back, sir. What do you think?"

Get me the devil out of here sprang to mind. Morrell suppressed it. He had, after all, volunteered for this. He said, "We need better controls and signals in the barrel." The driver nodded agreement. Only a maniac would have disagreed. On the other hand, only a maniac would have wanted to climb into a barrel in the first place.

* * *

For the first time since the summer of 1914, the Army of Northern Virginia was fighting in northern Virginia, not in Pennsylvania or Maryland. These days, instead of threatening Philadelphia, the fighting force whose ferocious onslaught had brought the Confederacy more glory than any other was reduced to defending the state for which it was named against the endless grinding pressure of the U.S. Army.

Sergeant Jake Featherston had his battery of the First Richmond Howitzers well positioned just in front of the little town of Round Hill, about fifteen miles south of the Potomac. The hill on which Round Hill sat had looked out on prosperous farming country all around. Prosperous farming country still lay to the south. To the north lay the infernal landscape of war: shell holes and trenches and barbed wire in great thick rusting belts and shattered trees.

A scrawny, fiercely intent man, Featherston stalked from one of the half-dozen quick-firing three-inch guns—copies of the famous French 75s—he commanded. Every other battery commander in the regiment was a lieutenant or captain. As far as Jake knew, every other battery commander in the C.S. Army was a lieutenant or captain. He'd die a sergeant, even if he died at the age of 109.

"Bastards," he muttered under his breath as he relentlessly checked guns and carriages and limbers and stored ammunition and horses and men. "Fucking bastards." He'd warned against Captain Jeb Stuart III's Negro body servant. His former superior had protected the colored man, whose main color turned out to be Red. The War Department had never forgiven Jake for being right. Now that Stuart had thrown his life away in battle to atone for the disgrace, the War Department never would, not when Jeb Stuart, Jr., Jeb III's father, sat behind a Richmond desk with a general's wreathed stars on his collar.

Featherston had taken command of the battery when Jeb Stuart III died. He'd kept it because he was obviously better at the job than the officers who led the rest of the batteries in the regiment. But was that enough to get the stripes off his sleeve and a bar, or two, or three, on his collar? He spat in the mud. Not likely.

He went back to his own gun, the one whose crew he'd led since the First Richmond Howitzers got word of the declaration of war and started throwing shells across the Potomac into Washington, D.C. It was the same gun only in the sense that George Washington's axe was the same axe after four new handles and three new heads: it had gone through several barrels, a new breech block, and even a new elevation screw. He didn't care. It was his.

All the men who served it were new except for him, too. A devastating Yankee barrage up in Pennsylvania had killed or maimed everybody in the original crew but him. Nobody here was green, though, not any more. The loader, the gun layers, the shell heavers had all had plenty of time to get good at what they did—plenty of time and the not so occasional prod of the rough side of Jake's tongue.

Michael Scott, the loader, looked up from a cigarette he was rolling. "How's it going, Sarge?" he asked.

"It ain't ever gonna be what you call great," Featherston answered. Even in his own ears, he sounded harsh and uncultured. That was yet another reason he hadn't been promoted: he sounded like a man whose father had been an overseer till the CSA manumitted its Negroes. A proper officer, now, had an accent almost as fancy as an Englishman's. *That's what the War Department thinks, anyway.* He scowled. *Far as they're concerned, how a man sounds is more important than how he acts. Bastards.*

Scott got the cigarette rolled and struck a match. He'd been a fresh-faced kid when he came into the battery. He wasn't a fresh-faced kid any more; he had hollow eyes and sallow cheeks and he hadn't shaved for a couple of days. Pointing north, he said, "Looks like the damnyankees are building up for another go at us."

Featherston looked in that direction, too. "I see what you mean," he said slowly. He couldn't see as much as he would have liked, not without the fancy field glasses that were in such chronically short supply in the C.S. Army. But the naked eye was plenty to catch the bubble and stir behind the Yankee lines. Something was going on, sure as hell.

Scott sucked in smoke. The inhalation made him look even more gaunt than he really was. "Heard anything?" he asked.

"Nary a word." Featherston shook his head. "You got to understand, they ain't gonna tell me first no matter what. Only way I hear about it first is if there's shit on the end they give me to grab."

"Yeah, Sarge, I know about that," Scott allowed. The whole battery knew about that. "Still and all, though, you've got that pal over in Intelligence, so I was just wondering if he'd said anything."

"Nary a word," Jake repeated. "And Major Potter isn't a pal— not exactly, anyhow." As far as he could see, the only thing he and the bespectacled major had in common was an unbounded contempt for the bluebloods who, because of who their grandfathers had been, got higher rank and a bigger arena in which to display their blunders than they deserved.

"All right." The loader eased off. The whole battery also knew not to get Featherston started, or he was liable to go on for hours. Scott looked around. "What worries me is that it doesn't look like we're building up to match 'em. Sure, the defense has an advantage, but still—"

"Yeah." Featherston's voice was rough. "We kill two damnyankees for every one of us they get, that's bully, but if they send three or four at us for every one we've got holdin' 'em back, sooner or later they run us out of our position."

"That's the truth," Scott said. "They got more o' those damn barrels than we do, too, and they scare the infantry fit to shit themselves."

"Wish I could see some barrels over yonder," Jake said. "If I could see 'em, we could try hittin' 'em, or, if we couldn't reach, we could send word back to division HQ and let the big guns have a go at 'em." He spat again, then asked, "Your gas helmet in good shape?"

"Sure as hell is." Scott slapped the ugly hood of gas-proofed canvas he wore on his left hip. "Yankees fight dirty as the devil, you ask me, throwing gas shells at us when they start a barrage and making us fight while we're wearing these goddamn things."

"I ain't gonna argue with you, on account of I reckon you're right," Jake said. " 'Course, now that they went and thought of it for us, we do the same to them every chance we get. If we had any brains back there in Richmond, we'd've figured it out for our own selves, but you look at the way this here war's been run and you'll see what a sorry hope that is."

He would have gone on—the idiocy of the War Department roused him to repeated furious tirades—but the sound of marching men heading north up the dirt road from Round Hill toward the front made him break off and look back over his shoulder. Michael Scott looked up toward the crest of the hill, too, relief on his face. "They *are* giving the line some reinforcements," the loader said. "I thank you, Jesus; I'll sing hallelujah come Sunday."

Over the hill and down toward the guns of the battery came the head of the column. Jake started to look away; he'd seen any number of infantry columns moving up toward the battle line. Here, though, his head snapped back toward the oncoming soldiers. He stared and stared.

That the troops were new and raw, that their uniforms were a fresh butternut as yet clean, as yet unfaded and unwrinkled from too many washings in harsh soap and too many delousings that didn't work—that didn't matter. He'd seen raw troops before, and knew the edges would rub off in a hurry. But these men, all save their officers and noncoms, had skins darker than their uniforms: some coffee with cream, some coffee without, some almost the black of midnight or a black cat.

On they tramped, tin hats on their heads, Tredegars on their shoulders, packs on their backs, gas helmets bouncing against their hipbones. They were big, rugged men, and marched well. A couple of them turned their heads for a better look at Featherston's field gun. Noncoms screamed abuse at them, the same sort of abuse they would have screamed at raw white troops foolish enough to turn their heads without permission.

Only when the whole regiment had marched past could Jake bring himself to speak. Even then, he mustered nothing more than a whisper hoarse with anger and disbelief: "Jesus God, we're going to have nigger infantry in front of us? What in blazes are they gonna do the first time a barrel comes at 'em? Shit on a plate, barrels scare white troops. Niggers'll run so fast, they'll leave their shadows behind, and then there won't be nothin' between the barrels and *us*."

"I don't know, Sarge," Scott said. "I don't reckon they would've put 'em in the line if they didn't reckon they'd get some fighting out of 'em."

"*I* don't reckon they would've put 'em in the line if they had any white men they could use instead," Jake retorted, to which his loader gave a rueful nod. He went on, "Oh, some of 'em'll fight—I expect you're right about that. Some of 'em, not so long ago, they was fightin' under red flags. So yeah, they'll fight. Only question is, whose side will they fight on?"

"Do you reckon the Yankees want those black sons of bitches any more'n we do?" Scott asked.

That gave Featherston pause, but not for long. "Anything that'll take us down a peg'll be fine by the Yanks, I expect," he answered. "If we'd known it'd come down to this, we never would've gotten into the war in the first place, I reckon. After it's done, those niggers'll have the right to vote, I tell you. Did you ever imagine, in all your born days, that niggers in the Confederate States of America would have the right to *vote*?"

"No, Sarge, never once," Scott said. "War's torn everything to hell."

"The war," Featherston agreed. "The war, and the boneheads down in Richmond running the war. Oh, and the niggers, too—talk about tearing things to hell, when they rose up, they almost tore the CSA to hell. And now the boneheads in Richmond are putting rifles in their hands and saying, 'Yeah, you're as good as white men. Why the hell not?' Well, there'll be a reckoning for that, too." He sounded eerily certain. "You mark my words—there'll be a reckoning for that, too."

Shivering in a trench outside Jonesboro, Arkansas, a U.S. soldier grumbled, "Where in the goddamn hell did I leave my gloves?"

"Thou shalt not take the name of the Lord in vain, Groome," Sergeant Gordon McSweeney said sharply.

"Uh, right, Sergeant," Groome answered. "Sorry, Sergeant." He was eighteen, a big, tough, beef-fed kid from the plains of Nebraska. Rank, though, had very little to do with why he backed down from McSweeney.

"You need to make your peace with God, not with me," McSweeney answered, his voice still stern. Groome nodded hastily, placatingly. Had he been a dog, he would have rolled over on his back to expose his throat and belly.

With a grunt, McSweeney went back to making his flame-thrower's trigger mechanism more sensitive. That he took a flamethrower into combat was not the reason he got instant, unthinking obedience from the soldiers in his section. That he was the sort of man who carried a flamethrower into battle with not a thought in his mind but the harm he could wreak on his enemies had more to do with it.

He scowled as he worked. His face was made for scowling, being almost entirely vertical lines: a narrow rectangle with a hard chin, a long nose, and a vertical crease between pale eyes that didn't seem to blink as often as they should. His hands, large and knobby-knuckled, manipulated a small screwdriver with surprising delicacy.

A shadow fell on the disassembled trigger mechanism. He looked up with a deeper scowl—who presumed to stand in his light? When he saw Captain Schneider, he relaxed. The company commander could do as he pleased, at least when it came to Gordon McSweeney. "Sir?" McSweeney asked, and started to get to his feet.

"As you were," Schneider said.

McSweeney obediently checked himself. As far as he was concerned, Captain Schneider was too lenient with all the men in his company, McSweeney himself included. But the captain had ordered him not to come to attention, and so he did not.

"Division headquarters wants some captured Rebs tonight for interrogation," Schneider said.

"Yes, sir, I'll go," McSweeney said at once.

Captain Schneider frowned. "I didn't mean you in particular, Sergeant," he said. "I meant for you to tell off a party to go into no-man's-land and come back with prisoners."

"Sir, I'll go," McSweeney repeated. "The men Gideon took with him to fight the Midianites chose themselves. I shall do the same. The Lord will protect me—or, if it be His will that I fall here, I shall go on to my glory, for I know in my heart that I am numbered among the elect." He was every bit as uncompromisingly Presbyterian as his features suggested.

Schneider's frown did not go away. "I don't want to lose you, Sergeant," he said. "You're too valuable a fighting man. And your courage is not in question. It hardly could be, with that on your chest."

Even on his combat uniform, McSweeney wore the small, white-starred blue ribbon of the Congressional Medal of Honor. He'd earned it the year before, destroying a Confederate barrel with his flamethrower and then slaying Rebel foot soldiers who'd sought to follow the barrel into the U.S. lines. "Sir," he said now, "snaking out prisoners is a job I'm better suited for than anyone else in the company. Why endanger somebody else when I can do it right?"

"How many times have you done it, though, Sergeant?" Schneider persisted. "How long can you go on being lucky?"

"As long as God wants me to be," McSweeney answered. He did get to his feet then, so he could look down at the company commander, whom he overtopped by several inches. "Sir, you must understand: I *want* to do this. How better can I help the Lord punish the Confederate States for their iniquities?"

Had Schneider had a good response to that, he would have given it at once. When he didn't, McSweeney smiled at him. McSweeney knew most men did not find his smile delightful. Schneider was no exception; he flinched away from it as from the screech of an incoming Confederate shell. "Have it your way, then, Sergeant," he muttered, and went walking down the trench in a hurry.

McSweeney's smile changed to the somewhat softer one any successfully stubborn soldier might have worn. He squatted down and got back to work on the trigger mechanism. By the time Ben Carlton shouted that he had supper ready, the trigger was nearly as smooth as McSweeney wanted it.

He made a horrible face at his first mouthful of stew. "What is it?" he demanded. "Is it donkey or cat?"

"Dammit, it's beef," Carlton said, offended.

"Don't blaspheme," McSweeney told him. "How is it that you've been a cook since the war started and still do no better than this?"

"Because Paul Mantarakis did it till he got killed last summer, and he was a better cook than I'll be if I live to be ninety-five, which ain't what you'd call likely," Carlton retorted. "Stinkin' shame he's dead, too."

"He was a good man, for a Papist," McSweeney admitted: from him, no small concession.

"He weren't no Cath-o-lic," the company cook said. "He was Greek whatever the devil you call it."

"The Devil has him now, I fear," McSweeney said. Mantarakis had fiddled with beads, so what else could he have been but a Papist? With grim resolution, McSweeney finished his bowl of stew. With luck, the Confederates he captured would have rations worth taking.

He didn't crawl out over the parapet of the trench till a little before midnight. Before he went, he blacked his face and hands with mud, so that he looked like a performer in some disastrous minstrel show. He had an officer's pistol on his belt, but hoped he wouldn't have to use it; he put more faith in his knife and entrenching tool.

Getting under and through the few strands of barbed wire in front of the U.S. trenches was easier than it should have been. The United States didn't take the war west of the Mississippi so seriously as he thought they should have. The U.S. advance south from the Missouri line had proceeded at a snail's pace because too many resources went into the fighting closer to Philadelphia.

A parachute flare went off overhead, bathing the hellish chaos of no-man's-land with a pure white light that might have come straight from heaven. McSweeney froze. As the light slowly sank and dimmed and reddened, Confederate and U.S. gunners blazed away at what they thought were targets. Bullets whined and occasionally screamed as they ricocheted from rocks. None came close to him.

McSweeney waited till darkness was complete before moving again. When he did move, he moved fast, or as fast as he could, taking advantage of the little while before men's eyes forgot the light. By the time he flopped down in a shell hole not far from the Confederate wire—which was hardly thicker than that protecting his line—he was filthy and wet. He was also satisfied. He settled down to listen and to wait.

The Rebs were far noisier than he let the men in his charge get. They would have pickets up near the line; he knew about where the foxholes were. If all else failed, he would go in there and bring a couple of those men back through. He didn't want to do that, being cold-bloodedly aware of the risk it entailed. But he'd been ordered out to return with prisoners, and he would.

He waited a while longer. Maybe the Confederates would send out a wiring party—although they had as much trouble getting supplies as did their U.S. opponents, so they might not have any fresh wire to string up. Wiring parties made easy meat; they were so intent on what they were doing, they paid less attention than they should have to whoever might be sneaking close to them.

Above McSweeney, stars slowly spun, now in plain sight, now hidden by scudding clouds. At about half past two, several Rebs crawled northwest toward the U.S. lines. They passed within twenty feet of him, never knowing he was there.

In a thin thread of whisper, one of them told the others, "Remember, we catch ourselves a damnyankee or three, then we get the hell back home. This ain't the mission for foolin' around."

McSweeney's smile was enormous, predatory. *The Lord hath delivered them into my hands,* he thought. They were very quiet as they slid toward the position he'd left. He was silent as he followed them.

Or so he thought, till their rearmost man hissed, "Hush! What's that?" McSweeney froze, as he had for the parachute flare. After a couple of minutes in which no one seemed to breathe, the Rebel said, "Must have been a rat. Christ, I hate them fat-bellied sons of bitches. I know what they eat." With a faint rustle of cloth, he crawled on. Again, McSweeney followed, trying to be even more quiet than before.

The Confederate raiders took up a position almost identical to the one he'd used in front of their trenches. Before they could scatter along the line, McSweeney spoke in quiet but conversational tones: "Hold it right there, boys. We've got you dead to rights. If you want to keep breathing, throw down your toys, throw up your hands, and go on through the wire."

That *we've* had the desired effect: it made the Rebels think they were outnumbered by their captors instead of outnumbering their captor. One of them started to whirl. Another one grabbed him and said, "No, you goddamn fool!" Weapons clunked and thudded to the ground.

"Coming in with prisoners!" McSweeney called.

Captain Schneider was awake and waiting for him. He stared when he saw the half-dozen men coming in ahead of McSweeney. "God damn me to hell, Sergeant, but you've done it again," he said. McSweeney nodded, though he disapproved of the blasphemous sentiment. When the Confederates found out one man had taken them, their curses were far fouler than Schneider's. Gordon McSweeney smiled.

III

"Do you see?" Lucien Galtier asked his horse as he drove the wagon into the town of Rivière-du-Loup on the southern bank of the St. Lawrence. The Quebecois farmer gestured to the macadamized road along which the wagon traveled. "Had this been an earlier year, you would have labored through ice and mud, and you would have complained even more than you do now."

The horse snorted. A paved road, even a paved road largely free of snow, impressed it very little. One of the reasons the road was largely free of snow was that it was an important highway for the U.S. forces who occupied that part of Quebec south of the St. Lawrence. A big, square, ugly White truck came growling up behind the wagon. The driver squeezed the bulb on his horn. Just enough shoulder—frozen hard here—had been cleared to let Lucien pull off for a moment so the truck and three more in its wake could roll past, kicking up little spatters of ice.

"Hey, Frenchy!" called one of the soldiers huddled under the green-gray canvas top on the last truck. He waved. After a couple of seconds' hesitation, Galtier touched the brim of the thick wool cap he wore.

He flicked the reins. "Do not think you can rest here all day, you lazy creature," he told the horse, which flicked its ears to let him know it would think whatever it pleased, and needed no advice from the likes of him.

A green-gray ambulance with red crosses on the sides and roof sped south past Galtier. The military hospital to which it was going was built on land that had been his till the Yankees appropriated it because he'd politely declined to collaborate with them. How fury had burned in him at the injustice! And now . . .

"And now the eldest of my daughters assists at the hospital," he said to the horse, "and one of the American doctors, by no means a bad fellow, is most attentive to her. Life can be most peculiar, *n'est-ce pas?*" He patted his own leg. Dr. O'Doull had sewn that up, too, when he'd tried to chop it instead of wood. It had healed well, too, better and faster than he'd thought a wound of twenty-one stitches would.

The breeze shifted so that it came out of the north. It brought to Lucien's ears the rumble of artillery from the other side of the broad river. The Americans, having forced a crossing in better weather the year before, had bogged down in their drive south and west toward Quebec City.

"Tabernac," Galtier muttered under his breath; Quebecois cursing ran more to holy things than to the obscenity English-speakers used. But he'd learned English-style swearing in his stint as a conscript more than twenty years before, while the Americans here sometimes seemed to go out of their way to curse. Experimentally, he let an English swear word roll off his tongue: "Fuck." He shook his head. It lacked flavor, like rabbit cooked without applejack.

A handful of fresh, muddy craters just outside of Rivière-du-Loup marked a bombing raid the night before by Canadian and British aeroplanes. He didn't see that they'd done any particular damage. They did keep trying, though. Pockmarks in the snow cover showed where other, earlier, bombs had fallen. So did a couple of graveled patches in the paving of the roadway.

In town, Galtier drove the wagon to the market square near the church. He quickly sold the potatoes and chickens he'd brought from the farm, and got better prices than he'd expected.

Angelique, the prettiest barmaid at the Loup-du-Nord, who for once did not have an American soldier on one arm, or on both arms, bought a chicken. His eyes traveled her up and down as they dickered. Marie, his wife, would not have approved, but she hadn't come with him. Because Angelique was so pretty, he might have given her the chicken for a few cents less than someone else would have paid. Marie would not have approved of that, either.

In her breathy little voice, Angelique said, "Have you heard the wonderful news?"

"How can I know until you tell me?" Lucien asked reasonably.

"Father Pascal is to be consecrated Sunday after next!" Angelique exclaimed. "Rivière-du-Loup, after so long, is to be a bishopric, an episcopal see. Is it not marvelous?"

"Yes," Galtier said, though what he meant was, *Yes, it is not marvelous.* Father Pascal was plump and pink and nearly as clever as he thought he was. He had welcomed the Yankee invaders with arms as open as Angelique's. Had he been a woman, he would no doubt have welcomed them with legs as open as Angelique's.

And here he came now, perhaps drawn by the sight of Angelique (even if a priest, even if a collaborator, he was a man—of sorts) or perhaps by that of poultry. The latter, it proved. He did not haggle so well as his housekeeper; Lucien roundly cheated him. Angelique, bless her, stood by and said never a word.

Feeling mellow with an extra thirty cents in his pocket, Galtier said, "Do I understand you are to be congratulated, Father?"

The priest looked too modest to quite convincing. "They honor me above my humble deserts."

"How did it happen that you were raised to this dignity?" Lucien asked.

Before Father Pascal answered, his eyes flicked for a moment to the sidewalk close by the market square. Then, still smooth, still modest, he said, "My son, in truth I have no idea. I felt, when I heard the news, as if a thunderbolt had struck me, I was so astonished."

But that brief glance had given him away. Along the sidewalk, his green-gray uniform neat as if it had just been issued, strode Major Jedediah Quigley, who administered Rivière-du-Loup and the surrounding area for the U.S. Army. Somehow or other, Lucien was sure, Quigley had pulled the wires behind Father Pascal's promotion. That might even have involved moving Rivière-du-Loup and the rest of eastern Quebec south of the St. Lawrence out of the ecclesiastical jurisdiction of the archbishop of Quebec City, who assuredly would never have raised a collaborator to the episcopal dignity.

Major Quigley saw Lucien look toward him. The American officer waved, as if he had not been the man who confiscated the land that had been in Lucien's family for more than two hundred years to build the military hospital on it. "I hope all goes well with you, *Monsieur* Galtier," he called in fluent, Parisian-accented French that seemed almost as out of place in Rivière-du-Loup as English did.

"Assez bien," Galtier answered grudgingly. Quigley waved again and walked on.

"You will excuse me," Father Pascal—soon to be Bishop Pascal—said. Off he went, carrying the chicken by its feet. Angelique went off with him. Their heads were close together as they chatted. Watching her walk away was more interesting than eyeing Father Pascal's backside, even if she too was a collaborator of sorts—*a horizontal collaborator,* Galtier thought, and smiled at his own wit.

He looked longingly at the Loup-du-Nord. Beer or whiskey or applejack would have helped chase away the cold. But no. The Loup-du-Nord, these days, was an American soldiers' saloon. He might get his drink and get out without trouble. On the other hand, a tableful of drunken Yanks might decide to stomp him into the floor. "When I get home," he told the horse, "I can have a drink."

On his way back to the farmhouse, down the fine paved road the Americans had built, he had to pull off a couple of times to let ambulances race past. Far more than that of the big, stolid trucks, their speed made him wonder what traveling in a motorcar was like. He'd taken train rides, but this seemed as if it would be different—as if he would be riding in a wagon somehow equipped with wings.

When he got to the farm, he drove the emphatically unwinged wagon into the barn. He unharnessed the horse, brushed it down, and fed it before going into the farmhouse. He did not begrudge the delay; it gave him the chance to think of more uncharitable things to say about Father Pascal's elevation.

And then, when he went inside, he found he could not say most of them. Nicole had brought Dr. Leonard O'Doull home for supper. O'Doull, a skinny, sandy-haired man with eyes as green as a cat's, was a good fellow, but he was also, to some degree, an outsider.

"Your leg, it goes well?" he asked Galtier after they shook hands. He spoke Parisian French like Major Quigley; unlike the major, he tried to adapt his tongue to that of the folk among whom he found himself.

"It goes very well, thank you." Lucien walked around to show how well he could move. "I have not even a limp, not unless I am on it for the whole day. When I went into Rivière-du-Loup today,

I did not take the stick you gave me, and the leg held me as if it had never been hurt. I am in your debt."

"Not for that," O'Doull said. "It is I who am in your debt for your friendship to me when, after all, my country occupies yours."

"You speak straight," said Galtier's elder son, Charles. "That is good."

"Of course he does," Nicole said indignantly. Lucien and Marie exchanged an amused look. Nicole defended Dr. O'Doull because of who he was, not because of what he said.

"Dr. O'Doull, you're so wonderful." Georges, Lucien's younger son, spoke first in worshipful tones and then wickedly imitated his sister: "Of course he is." He let out a sigh full of longing and molasses.

He'd been an imp since he was a toddler. That was the only reason Lucien could find for Nicole's letting him live. Even in the ruddy light of the kerosene lamps, O'Doull's flush was easy to see.

"I think supper is about ready," Marie said, which distracted everyone better than anything else might have done. Like Galtier himself, his wife was small and dark and a good deal more clever than she often let on.

Supper was a chicken stew enlivened by dried apples. Over it, Lucien told the story of Father Pascal's promotion. He told it dispassionately, out of good feeling for the American who shared the table with him. His family showed less restraint. "That man knows nothing of shame!" exclaimed Denise, who was only twelve and wore her feelings on her sleeve.

"He comes to the hospital sometimes, to visit the soldiers who are Catholic," Leonard O'Doull said. "Don't much care for him. If he were an American priest in Vermont, say, and the British occupied it, he'd suck up to them the same way he sucks up to Americans here. Have I reason, or not?"

"Oui, vous avez raison," Galtier said emphatically. "Which side he is on, that matters nothing to Father Pascal. Whether he is on top, that matters a great deal."

O'Doull hefted his glass of applejack. Applejack, especially this homemade stuff Galtier had got from a neighbor, was dangerously deceptive—sweet and mild and with a kick like a mule's. "And you, *Monsieur* Galtier, what of you?" the young doctor asked, as he might not have were he more sober.

Galtier thought about that for a while; he was a few knocks into the applejack himself. "My country has been made not my country," he said, one word at a time. "Should I be happy at that?"

Marie gave him a warning glance. Too late: the words were said. Dr. O'Doull considered them. At last, he replied, "If you think you were free as a chunk of the British Empire, no. If you do not think so, you may wish to see what you become after the war. What do you think, if it does not bother you that I ask?"

"Why should it bother me?" Galtier said lightly. "I need not answer." And the reason he did not answer, not that he would ever have admitted it, was that he was no longer sure what to think.

Nellie Semphroch went outside the coffeehouse in the bitter cold of early morning and flipped the sign on the boards that covered the space where her plate-glass window had been from CLOSED to OPEN. She had connections among the Confederates who occupied Washington, D.C., who could have got her more glass, but saw no point in using them. The next U.S. bombing raid, or the one after that, would only shatter the new window, as three—or was it four?—windows had been shattered already.

"Mornin', Ma," Edna Semphroch said when Nellie went back inside. The two women—one in her early twenties, the other in her early forties—looked very much alike, with long, oval faces and high foreheads that seemed higher because they both wore their hair pulled back. Edna painted her face; Nellie didn't. With a sneer on her red lips, Edna added, "Good morning, Little Nell."

Although Nellie had been cold, her face heated and congealed like an egg left too long on a frying pan. "Don't you ever call me that again," she said in a low, furious voice. "Ever, do you hear me?"

Edna's sneer got wider. "I hear you—" She visibly debated throwing kerosene on the fire, but decided against it. "I hear you."

With grim determination, Nellie took what was left of the previous day's bread off the icebox and started slicing it for the toast and sandwiches she'd be serving. Every stroke of the serrated bread knife made her wish she were drawing it across Bill Reach's throat.

Reach had been an annoyance from her past for a couple of years. A former reporter, he had, in Nellie's much younger days, been in the habit of putting a price down on a nightstand in a cheap hotel and partaking of her services. She'd escaped that life and attained modest respectability. Edna had never known she'd been in it—till Reach, hideously drunk, lost a quarter of a century in what passed for his mind and tried to buy her in the coffeehouse when it was packed with Confederate officers.

Edna started whistling, not too loud. Nellie ground her teeth and sliced even more viciously than before. The tune Edna was whistling had come up from the Confederate States the year before. It was called "I'll Do as I Please."

Edna had largely done as she pleased before that night, but Nellie had been able to enforce some respect for the proprieties on her. Now—now Edna lived as fast as she chose, and laughed when Nellie protested. Nellie couldn't protest much. Edna, at least, had a fiancé. What had Nellie had? Customers.

"Ain't seen that Reach character since that one night," Edna remarked. "Wonder what the devil happened to him?"

"I hope he's dead," Nellie said grimly. "If he's not dead, he ought to be. If he ever shows his face in here again, he will be, too, fast as I can kill him."

"He didn't do anything but tell the truth," Edna said. She was still very young, too young, perhaps, to realize how deadly dangerous incautious doses of truth could be.

The door opened. The bell above it jangled. Resplendent in butternut, in strode Lieutenant Nicholas H. Kincaid. The big, handsome Confederate officer planted a kiss on Edna's smiling mouth. His hands tightened greedily on her. "Mornin', darling," he said when they broke apart. Her lipstick branded him like a wound. He turned to Nellie. "Mornin', ma'am." He was polite. Very few Confederate officers were anything but. It did little to make her like him better.

"Good morning," she said, her own tone grudging. Edna looked daggers at her. Kincaid was not a man to notice subtleties. His smile reminded Nellie of a happy, stupid dog's. She sighed. Against such an amiable idiot, what hope had she? Sighing, she asked, "What can I get you today?"

"Couple of scrambled-egg sandwiches with Tabasco on 'em and a big cup of coffee," he answered.

Nellie made the eggs and toasted the bread while Kincaid and Edna sat at a table and gazed into each other's eyes. Nellie was convinced that, had Edna gazed into one of his ears, she could have gazed out the other, there being nothing but empty space between the two. But she did not want him for his brains. Nellie knew that. She wanted him for the bulge he'd had in his pants when they'd separated after their embrace.

Nicholas Kincaid's eyes widened when he took his first bite— Nellie had plied the Tabasco bottle with vigor. He gulped scalding coffee. Nellie smiled. But then, enthusiastically, he wheezed, "Good!" The smile vanished.

Edna said, "Ma, he wants us to tie the knot on the twenty-fifth of March. It's the first Sunday of spring. Ain't that romantic?"

"Are the Confederates still going to be in Washington on the twenty-fifth of March?" Nellie asked. "Fighting sounds closer every day."

"You'd best believe we'll still be here, ma'am." Kincaid sounded positive. "Yankees won't have any luck, not even a little, knockin' us out again. Just to help make sure they don't, we're gettin' more troops, whites and niggers both. This here is our town, and we aim to keep it."

The bell above the door rang again. Kincaid was usually the first customer, but then, he had an ulterior motive. He rarely stayed alone with Edna and Nellie for long. In came a couple of field-grade Confederate officers. As they ordered breakfast, they chatted about the fighting off to the west, in northern Virginia. Edna had taken everything Kincaid said as gospel (which was a devil of a thing for a woman bent on marriage to do), but Nellie added together what she had heard from many different people. Her picture of the way the war was going didn't match his optimistic words.

After the morning rush of soldiers and collaborators and their sleek, expensive women ebbed, Nellie said, "I'm going across the street to say hello to Mr. Jacobs."

"Have fun, Ma," Edna answered.

In another tone of voice, the remark would have been harmless. Nellie felt her face heat. "He's a gentleman, Edna. I know it's a word you may not understand, but it's so. We don't do what you and that overgrown side of beef most assuredly *do*."

"That makes you the fools, not Nick and me," Edna shot back.

Nellie went outside without answering. It was still chilly, but not savagely cold. As it had at dawn, as it did around the clock, artillery rumbled to the north. Every so often now, Nellie could hear individual shells screaming in on Confederate fortifications defending the Rebels' grip on the capital of the United States.

The bell above Hal Jacobs' door jingled instead of jangling. The cobbler looked up from the Confederate officer's riding boot he was resoling. "Widow Semphroch—Nellie," he said, and smiled a smile that made him look young in spite of gray mustache and thinning gray hair. "How good to see you."

"And you, Hal," she answered, closing the door behind her to keep the heat inside. She looked around. Almost all the shoes in Jacobs' shop these days belonged to Confederate soldiers. Some awaited his attention, some their owners' return. Nellie sighed and said, "The Rebs have been here a long time."

"That they have," Jacobs agreed. "That they have." He sighed, too.

Casually, she went on, "They're going to try to hold on here, too. They're bringing in reinforcements—whites and niggers both, matter of fact."

"Is that so?" the shoemaker said. "How interesting." Nellie always passed him the gossip she picked up in the coffeehouse in that easygoing, conversational way. He always responded in kind, and then sent the information on so the United States could get some use from it.

"I thought so," she answered now. After a moment, she went on, "My daughter and that Rebel lieutenant are planning to get married here, a few days after the start of spring."

For one of the rare times since she'd begun letting Hal Jacobs know what she heard, she was looking for information from him. He understood that, and did not look very happy about it. At last, grudgingly, he said, "I do hope their plans won't have to be changed, as could happen."

He wasn't going to say anything more. She could see it in his eyes. He'd told her something, anyhow. She nodded brusque thanks. Then, even more brusquely, she asked, "What do you hear from Bill Reach?"

Jacobs knew Bill Reach. Along with being a humiliating piece of Nellie's past, along with drinking like a fish, he had also been the cobbler's superior among the U.S. spies in Washington. Jacobs said, "Since that unfortunate evening, Widow Semphroch, I have not heard from him at all. Perhaps the Confederates have again jailed him as a thief."

"Perhaps he's frozen to death in a gutter." Nellie's voice was full of fierce hope.

"I never knew what he did to offend you so greatly," Jacobs said.

"Never mind, but he did." Nellie thought Jacobs was lying about his ignorance. If he wasn't, she didn't intend to enlighten him.

"I'm sorry," he said. "I'm sorry because, since you have been angry at him, you have not brought so many pieces of useful information to me—and you must hear a great deal, because your coffeehouse is so popular with the Confederates and those who deal with them."

Jacobs and his friends—about whose identities Nellie had carefully not inquired—had helped keep her coffeehouse in coffee and food, when both were in short supply in occupied Washington. She probably would have gone out of business without their help. "I am sorry, too," she said. "I do pay my debts, or try to. But that man . . . I want to pay him back—oh, yes, very much."

The cobbler held up a hand. "I had not finished. I am also sorry because, with you angry at Bill Reach, I don't get to see you as often as I would like. I've missed you, you know."

Nellie's mouth fell open. She wasn't used to having men say such things to her. Edna's father had been decent enough to marry her when she found herself in a family way. It was one of the few decent things he'd ever done. After he died, she'd been content—more than content—to live as a widow. Now—

"How you do go on, Hal," she said, trying to make light of it.

He didn't want to make light of it. "I meant what I said," he told her, and she could hear the truth in his voice. "You are a fine woman—a finer woman, I think, than even you know. Maybe you have been a widow too long to remember these things, but you must believe me here, for I know what I am talking about."

"Well, good day, Mr. Jacobs," Nellie said. "I really have to get back to the coffeehouse now." She fled from the shoemaker's shop as if a hundred Confederate spycatchers were on her trail. Her heart thudded. A man who said he missed her, a man who thought her a fine woman, was to her a more frightening apparition than all the Confederate spycatchers in the world.

Commander Roger Kimball let out a long, lugubrious sigh as the CSS *Bonefish* sailed away from Habana. Standing atop the submarine's conning tower, he peered back toward the red tile roofs and brightly painted plaster walls of the capital of the Confederate state of Cuba.

"Damn," he said with all due respect. "That sure as hell is one fine town for a shore leave, isn't it?"

"Yes, sir," agreed Senior Lieutenant Tom Brearley, his executive officer. Both men were recently promoted, after their successful raid on New York harbor. The fresh gold stripes on the sleeves of their dark gray uniform coats were easy to tell apart from the duller ones they'd worn for a while. Brearley went on, "I thought I was a whiskey-drinking man, but I expect I could get used to rum." He grinned. "I expect I *did* get used to rum."

"Hot and cold running whores, too," Kimball said with a reminiscent leer. "Black ones, brown ones, white ones—whatever you happen to feel like. Cheap, too. Cuba's a damn sight cheaper than Charleston, and you can have a better time, too—although I had me some pretty fair times in Charleston, now that I think about it."

Anne Colleton naked on a bed had been worth a dozen Habana whores. His blood heated at the memory. She'd been a tigress between the sheets—and she'd wanted him for himself, not for the money he laid down. And she was a rich lady, an influential lady. To a man who'd gone from a backwoods Arkansas farm to the Confederate Naval Academy at Mobile, a connection like that was worth its weight in rubies. Kimball didn't intend to go back to that miserable farm when his Navy days were over. The only direction he intended to head was up.

"Weather's a lot better here than up in the North Atlantic," Brearley said. "Sea's a lot calmer, too. I'm just as glad they sent us down here."

"Far as the *Bonefish* goes, so am I," Kimball agreed. "Hell of a lot easier, hell of a lot more fun where the sea doesn't try to throw your boat away or tear it in half whenever you're on the surface. But I don't care for what the move south says about the way the war is going."

Brearley shrugged. "If England doesn't get the bread and meat she needs from Argentina, she's out of the war. If she's out of the war, the Kaiser runs roughshod in Europe and the damnyankees do the same thing in America. If the United States are starting to try and take a bite out of the route from Pernambuco to Dakar, we've got to stop 'em."

Kimball clicked his tongue between his teeth. His exec was a good kid, but you needed to give him the C and the A if he was going to spell CAT. "Yeah, Tom, we've got to stop 'em. But if things were going better farther north, they wouldn't be able to turn ships loose to go after this shipping route."

"Oh, I see what you're saying, sir," Brearley answered. No doubt he did, too; he wasn't stupid, only a little slow. "We've got them beat hollow when it comes to logistics."

"Good thing, too," Kimball said. "Otherwise, this war would be within shouting distance of over. But they'll need coal and fuel oil if they're going to operate for long in those waters from out of Boston or New York or Philadelphia. We want the supply ships as much as we want the warships."

He took his binoculars out of their leather case and scanned the horizon for plumes of smoke. He knew that was foolish. If he spotted enemy ships less than an hour out of Habana, the war wouldn't just be within shouting distance of the end. It would be history.

"Anything, sir?" Brearley asked. He had to be jumpy, too, if he thought there might be something so close to the Cuban coast.

"Damn all," Kimball told him. He put the binoculars back in the case. "I'm going below."

Tropical sun, calm water, and a mild breeze smelling of the salt sea made the top of the conning tower a pleasant, even a delightful, place to stand and pass the time. Going down into the long steel tube of the *Bonefish* was like descending into another world, perhaps one found in the infernal regions.

Instead of the illimitable confines of the ocean, Roger Kimball found himself in confines as severely limitable as any in the world, confines where space for machinery was a *sine qua non* and space for men a distinct afterthought. He banged his head on a pipe fitting he hit about every other day, and he was not an especially tall man.

Dim orange-tinted electric lamps replaced bright sun. Slowly, slowly, Kimball's eyes adjusted. He knew he would squint like a blind thing when he went topside again.

Hardest of all, though, was the transition from fresh sea air to the horrible stuff inside the *Bonefish*. Even with the hatches open, even with a refit in Habana, she stank: an unforgettable mixture of bilgewater and diesel fuel and food and sweat and the reek of the heads. Kimball knew what she would be like when she came back from her cruise: like this, only magnified a hundredfold. A landlubber boarding a submersible just into port was like as not to add vomit to the reek. Kimball didn't like the stink, but held it in wry affection. It was the smell of home.

Ben Coulter had the helm. "Steady on 075, sir," the veteran petty officer said in response to Kimball's unspoken question. "Listen to her. Doesn't she sound good? Those greaser mechanics did a hell of a job."

Kimball cocked his head to one side. The engine *did* sound unusually smooth. "Greasers are loyal," he said. "It's the goddamn niggers you got to watch out for."

"Not in Cuba," Coulter said. "Niggers didn't hardly rise up at all in Cuba, what I hear tell. Never was so many Reds in Cuba like there is back home." The unlit cigar he clenched between his teeth twitched as he talked.

"Sad state of affairs when the greasers keep their niggers quiet and white men can't do it," Kimball said. "Sad state of affairs when they think they've got to give niggers guns or the whole country goes under, too. Anybody wants to know, President Semmes is out of his goddamn mind."

Ben Coulter nodded. So did most of the other crewmen within earshot. And then Kimball remembered that Anne Colleton had favored creating Negro military units, and also favored making Negroes Confederate citizens after their service. He thought as much of her brains as he did of her body, which said a great deal. If, after what she'd gone through at the hands of the Reds, she still thought the CSA needed Negro troops . . . *She's still wrong, dammit,* Kimball thought.

The *Bonefish* moved steadily east toward the rectangle on the chart through which the submersible was supposed to sweep till her patrol was done. Kimball drilled the crew hard, regaining whatever edge they'd lost in the fleshpots of Habana. When the boat slid below the surface of the Atlantic in less than thirty seconds, he pronounced himself satisfied—privately, to Tom Brearley. As far as the crew was concerned, he was never satisfied.

Navigating aboard a submersible wasn't easy, but repeated sights and hard work with the tables—much of it by Brearley, who had a fine head for mathematics—brought the *Bonefish* into the box between fifteen and seventeen degrees north latitude, thirty and thirty-three degrees west longitude, her assigned area for this patrol. Kimball chafed at working a set zone instead of hunting freely. Back and forth, back and forth the *Bonefish* prowled, like a shark in a tank.

"This isn't what war is supposed to be about," Kimball grumbled to his executive officer. "This is hide-and-seek, nothing else but."

"Orders," Brearley said placidly. As far as he was concerned, that made everything right. He had more imagination than a fence post, but not a whole lot. If he ever got his own boat, Kimball was sure he would command it competently. He was also sure his exec would never do anything spectacular.

Kimball was frustrated not least because he doubted whether any Yankee ships would come into his search zone. A patrol with a log book essentially empty of action was not what he had in mind.

He was in his bunk—which, however tiny and cramped, was the only one the *Bonefish* boasted, everyone else sleeping in hammocks or in odd places amongst the gear and machinery in the pressure hull—when the lookout on the conning tower spotted a plume of smoke to westward. Roused by the shouts, he put on his shoes and cap (the only items he'd taken off) and hurried up for a look of his own.

His first order was to bring the *Bonefish* up to fifteen knots so he could approach and get a better idea of what he was hunting. He could do that with little or no risk, because the submersible's diesels produced less exhaust than the coal-burner up ahead. He shouted a course change down to the helmsman, one that would put the *Bonefish* in front of whatever ship had presumed to steam south through the territory he patrolled. Submerged, the boat was slow. He needed to be in front to close for an attack.

He peered through the binoculars, willing himself to get a clear look at the vessel making that smoke. If it was a warship, it was dawdling through the water; it couldn't be making more than eight or nine knots. As he drew near, he made out the dumpy superstructure of a freighter.

Tom Brearley came up alongside him. When he told the exec what he'd found, Brearley asked, "Shall we sink her with the gun, sir?"

Kimball was tempted. The *Bonefish* carried far more three-inch shells than torpedoes. Gunfire was the cheap, easy way to sink enemy shipping. After a moment, though, he shook his head. "No, we'll feed her a couple of fish. She's liable to be one of those gunboat freighters the Yankees fit out to slug it out with submarines on the surface. Why take a chance?"

He shouted the order to dive to periscope depth. Brearley scrambled down the hatch. Kimball was right behind him. The captain of the *Bonefish* dogged it shut. If he'd waited more than a few seconds longer, he would have let the sea in with him.

He raised the periscope and peered through it. One of the prisms had condensation on it; the image was foggy. "Give me five knots," he said, and crawled closer on the electric engines that powered the submarine underwater. The freighter had no idea he was there, or that any submersibles might be nearby. It didn't change speed. It didn't zigzag. It went on its way, so resolutely normal it made Kimball suspicious as hell.

As he got inside a mile, he and Brearley and Coulter were all working out the torpedo solution: the *Bonefish*'s course, the freighter's course, the sub's speed, the freighter's, the torpedo's, and the distance at which he'd shoot all went into calculating the angle at which to shoot. "A couple of degrees to port," he murmured at about 1,200 yards, and then, murmuring no more, "Fire one! Fire two!"

Compressed air hurled the fish out of the forward torpedo tubes. They took about half a minute to reach the freighter. It tried to turn away from them, but far too late. One struck near the bow, the other near the stern. The rumble of the explosions filled the *Bonefish*.

The crew cheered. Kimball watched the freighter capsize and sink like a stone. The sailors aboard it had no time to launch boats. A couple of heads bobbed in water unnaturally calm. "She's leaking a hell of a lot of oil there," Kimball said. "Likely she was carrying it for the U.S. goddamn Navy. Well, they'll go hungrier now, and have to go home sooner."

"Easiest one we've had in a while," Brearley said. "Just like practice."

"Tom, they won't make us throw it back on account of it was easy," Kimball answered. After a moment, he went on with a grim certainty: "Besides, odds are the next one won't be. Nothing in this goddamn war stays simple long."

Captain Jonathan Moss' unit of fighting scouts was doing what it had done through most of the late fall and winter outside the hamlet of Arthur, Ontario: not much. The weather was too bad for flying about six days out of seven, and marginal the seventh. He'd run up an astonishing bar tab at the officers' club.

Beside him at the table there, First Lieutenant Percy Stone looked down into his whiskey-and-soda. "Nothing in this god-damn war stays simple long. The aeroplanes I trained on are as obsolete as last year's newspaper, and it wasn't that long ago."

Moss had a whiskey-and-soda, too, only the soda being omitted from the recipe. "Next time you want to keep a sense that things do go on steadily instead of by jerks, try not to get shot so you have to spend the better part of a year on the sidelines."

"That's good advice. I'll make a note of it." Stone really did make as if to write it down.

"You're a good fellow, Percy," Moss said, laughing. Stone, a photographer in civilian life, had been his observer when he was piloting a reconnaissance aeroplane in 1915. They'd been put together as much because of the way their names matched as for any other reason, but they'd always got on famously—till Stone stopped a machine-gun bullet. For a long time after that, Moss had thought he was dead, but he'd proved to be very much alive, and wearing a pilot's two-winged badge instead of the one wing that marked the observer.

He raised his glass on high. "To hell with the Sopwith Pup!" he declared now.

Everyone who heard him drank with him. Only a handful of the new British machines had got to this side of the Atlantic, but they made every American who met them wish that handful were none at all.

Having lost friends who flew outmoded Martin one-deckers against Pups that could outclimb, outdive, outrun, and out-maneuver them, Moss poured down his own drink. He'd flown a Martin one-decker himself, from the day he'd gone from obser-vation aeroplanes to fighting scouts until he came here to train on the new machines that were supposed to be able to contend on even terms with the best the limeys and Canucks had to offer. He got up, walked rather unsteadily to the bar, and bought himself another drink. With the glass of whiskey in his hand, he lifted it and said, "Here's to the new biplanes that'll tie tin cans to the Pups' tails."

That toast drew both cheers and laughs. He went back to the table. When he sat down, Percy Stone's long-jawed, handsome face was thoughtful, even worried. In a low voice, Stone asked, "Do you think they'll really be able to do the job? They're a hell of a lot peppier than anything I ever flew before, but I've been out of circulation for quite a while."

He patted his side. What with the entry and exit wounds of the bullet that had got him and the incisions the surgeons made to patch him up, he owned as spectacular a collection of scars as anyone could want—a more spectacular collection of scars than anyone in his right mind would want.

"We ought to have a good fighting chance," Moss answered with a ponderous deliberation fueled by both thought and alcohol. "This new two-decker can climb with anything ever made, and it's maneuverable as all get-out. I don't think it's quite as fast a bus on the straightaway as the Pups are, but damn close. How fast you can turn counts for more in a dogfight a lot of times, anyhow."

"That's what everybody's saying, sure enough." Stone nodded. "Now the next interesting question is, will we get a chance to fly our birds before they're obsolete, too, and the War Department decides to train us up on the next new model, whatever that turns out to be?"

"Take that one up with the chaplain, or maybe take it straight to God. Weather's not my department," Moss said. Then he slowly started thinking again. "Wouldn't be surprised if these two-deckers are damn near obsolete in Europe. That's where the real air action is. Our new buses are just copies of the ones Albatros makes for the Germans."

That had been true through most of the war. Maybe because they were in a tougher fight in the air, German manufacturers kept cranking out new and improved models, of which the Albatros biplane was but one. Some of the plans made the journey by submersible to the USA (some got sunk trying to make the journey, too, which was why the new fighting scout was slower getting out of the blocks than it should have been), just as the British did their best to keep the Canadians in aeroplanes and fresh plans.

A lot of fliers wore their pocket watches on wrist straps when in the air; bulky flying clothes made a watch impossible to check otherwise. Like some others Moss knew, Percy Stone had taken to wearing his on his wrist all the time. Looking at it now, he yawned and said, "I think I'm going to hit the hay. I'll pretend tomorrow will be a bully day for flying, even though I know damn well it'll snow and it'll be colder than a witch's tit."

"Duty," Moss said approvingly. "Responsibility. Remembrance." He looked down into his own glass. "And whiskey. Don't forget whiskey." He made sure the glass had no whiskey left in it to forget, then rose and accompanied Stone to the tent they shared with the other two men in the flight, Pete Bradley and Hans Oppenheim.

An iron stove glowed red-hot in the middle of the tent. That meant the four cots, all piled high with thick, green-gray wool blankets, were cold to sleep in, but didn't quite feel as if the North Pole had moved down to a couple of miles north of the aerodrome. This was Moss' third winter in Ontario. So far as he knew, nobody in the world could strip down to his drawers and slide under the covers faster than he could.

Reveille came at half-past five, which was, in his opinion, a couple of hours too early. His head pounded. He dry-swallowed a couple of aspirins—American imitations of aspirins, actually. They worked well enough. And, when he poked his head out of the tent, he blinked and whistled in surprise.

It was cold. The breath he exhaled whistling made a little frosty cloud in front of his face. But it was clear. In the east, the sky glowed salmon. Before too long, the sun would rise. In December, it hardly showed its face. Now that February was here, it began to remember it did have some business up in Canada after all.

He stuck his head back inside. "I think we may be able to get some flying in after all."

"That would be good," Oppenheim said seriously. He seldom was anything but serious. "When they sent us up from London after they trained us on these new two-deckers, the idea was that we should fly them. We are, after all, an operational squadron." His parents had come from Germany. He didn't have an accent, but the language he'd spoken around the house as a kid influenced the way he put his sentences together.

The fliers went to the mess tent and shoveled down bacon and eggs and pancakes and bad coffee. The squadron commander, Major Julius Cherney, nodded to them. "Can we go up along the line, sir, and see if the limeys send anyone out against us?" Moss asked.

"Well, why the hell not?" Cherney said. "Meteorology says everything looks good for the next few hours." He grunted.

"Yeah—I know—that and five cents buys you a beer." He clapped Moss on the back. "Good hunting."

Men with shovels and horses and mules with scoops made the airstrips usable. Bigger aerodromes had tractors with blades mounted in front of them to clear snow. Arthur boasted no such amenities.

Moss reveled in the way his aeroplane leaped from the ground. The streamlined fighting scout from the Wright works in Ohio—a copy of the Albatros D.II—climbed at close to a thousand feet a minute, a hell of a lot faster than his old Martin could have managed.

And all the sky in front of him was empty. He led the flight now, with Percy Stone behind him on the right and Oppenheim and Bradley on the left. They flew east till they came to the trench line that scarred Ontario between Lake Ontario and Lake Huron. West of the trenches, the snow could not hide the devastation of the land the Canadians and their British allies had fought so bitterly to hold. East of them—or, at least, east of artillery range from them—it was simply snowy country in winter. The dazzle of sun off endless miles of white made Moss blink back tears behind his goggles.

Here and there, down in the Canucks' trenches, muzzle flashes showed that soldiers were taking potshots at him and his flightmates. He laughed, and the chilly slipstream blew his mirth away. Rifle and machine-gun fire reached up to about two thousand feet. He was high above that danger.

Then Canadian antiaircraft guns opened up. Black puffs of smoke appeared in the sky, as if by magic. When one burst a couple of hundred yards below Moss' fighting scout, the aeroplane bucked like a restive horse. He began changing his speed and course and altitude more or less at random, so the gunners could not calculate just where to place their shells. The sky, thank heaven, was a big, wide place. He respected antiaircraft fire without fearing it.

He led his flight south and east along the line, in the direction of Toronto, daring enemy aeroplanes to come up and fight. Every so often, he would glance at his fuel gauge and his watch. Like most other fighting scouts, the new Wright machines could stay in the air for about an hour and a half. If he and his comrades found no challengers, they would have to go home.

When more antiaircraft shells burst in the sky south of Moss, they drew his eye toward the aeroplane at which they were aimed: one of the Avro two-seat biplanes the Canadians had been using for reconnaissance work since the beginning of the war.

Moss sped toward the Avro, followed close by his flightmates. The Canuck pilot hadn't changed course despite the Archie bursting around him; he was letting his observer take the photos he needed. Moss knew about that from his work with Stone. Having four U.S. fighting scouts on this tail was a different business for the Avro driver. He corkscrewed away from the Wrights in a spinning dive.

Sometimes speed did matter. Moss and his comrades had better than twenty miles an hour on the Avro. They closed quickly. The observer started shooting at them. They shot back from four directions at once. Four streams of tracers converged on the desperately dodging Avro.

Then it dodged no more, but plunged toward the ground. One of those streams of machine-gun bullets must have found the pilot and left him dead or unconscious. The observer kept firing till the American fighting scouts pulled away from their stricken foe. A moment later, the Avro slammed into the frozen ground and burst into flame.

We only get to claim a quarter of an aeroplane apiece, Moss thought: *no way to tell whose bullet nailed the Canuck.* He didn't care. He needed a moment to get his bearings after the dizzying action. When he knew which way was which, he waggled his wings and pointed northwest, back toward the aerodrome. The flight headed for him. Moss looked back at the burning wreck of the Avro. *We've earned our pay today,* he thought.

Confederate soldiers tramped glumly south through the mud that clogged the roads of the state of Sequoyah. The Red River, which marked the boundary between the former Indian Territory and Texas, was only a couple of miles away.

Private First Class Reginald Bartlett pointed. "What's the name of that little town there?" he asked. He was a big, fair fellow with a comic turn of phrase that let him get away with saying outrageous things that would have got other men into trouble or into fights.

"That there's Ryan," Sergeant Pete Hairston answered. The veteran's harsh Georgia drawl was far removed from Bartlett's soft, almost English Richmond accent.

Reggie grinned. "Well, I want to tell you something, Sarge," he said, making his voice as deep and authoritative as he could. "We've got to hold this town. The whole Confederacy is depending on us to hold this town."

Hairston let out a strangled snort of laughter. "You go to hell, Bartlett, you goddamn smartmouth son of a bitch."

"Sarge, why you cussin' out Reggie?" Private Napoleon Dibble asked. "What did he say that was so bad?"

A moment later, First Lieutenant Jerome Nicoll, the company commander, spoke up in deep, authoritative tones of his own: "I want to tell you something, boys—we've got to hold Ryan. The whole Confederacy is depending on us to hold Ryan."

"You *son* of a bitch," Hairston said admiringly, and made as if to throw a punch at Bartlett.

"What did he say, Sarge?" Nap Dibble repeated, his eyes wide and puzzled. "He said the same thing the lieutenant said, so why are you getting steamed at him?"

Hairston and Bartlett shared a moment of silent amusement. Dibble was a pretty good fellow, brave and good-natured, but not a fireball when it came to brains. "Don't worry about it, Nap—everything's fine," Bartlett said. He turned back to Hairston. "We've got to hang on to any chunk of Sequoyah we can, you know. The Germans still don't have all of Belgium."

A moment later, Lieutenant Nicoll delivered the same sentiment in almost identical words. "See?" Dibble exclaimed. "Reggie said just what the lieutenant said, so how come you're givin' him a hard time about it?"

"The lieutenant said the same damn thing in front of Duncan, too, an' we got run out of Duncan," Hairston said. "He said the same damn thing in front of Waurika, and we got run out of there. Just on account of we got to do somethin' don't have to mean we *can* do it."

As if to underscore that point, a shell screamed down and burst a few hundred yards off to one side of the road. It threw up a fountain of dirt. A few of the Kiowas and Comanches who'd attached themselves to the C.S. army in its grinding retreat through southern Sequoyah jumped and exclaimed. Most of them took no more notice of the explosion than did the white soldiers.

"I hear some of these Indian tribes have their own little armies in the field, fighting alongside ours," Reggie said.

Pete Hairston nodded. "That's a fact. But those are the Five

Civilized Tribes, and they pretty much run their own affairs any which way. They did, anyhow, till the damnyankees landed on 'em. God knows what's happening to the poor miserable red-skinned bastards now."

"These Indians here seem civilized enough," Bartlett said.

Lieutenant Nicoll overheard that (fortunately, he'd missed Reggie's impersonation of him). "It's a matter of law, Bartlett. The Creeks, the Choctaws, the Cherokees, and whatnot have legal control over their own internal affairs. The redskins here-abouts don't."

Ryan, when they trudged into it, might have once boasted a thousand people. Then again, it might not have. It certainly didn't have a thousand civilians in it now: most of them had fled across the Red River into Texas. Ryan lay on the edge of the Red River bottomland, with forests of mesquite and tamaracks and swamps with endless little streams winding through them taking the place of the prairie over which Bartlett had been marching for so long.

At Lieutenant Nicoll's shouted order, his company joined the rest of the Confederate soldiers retreating from Waurika in en-trenching in front of Ryan. Flinging dirt out behind him, Reggie said, "Wasn't like this on the Roanoke front. There, if you went forward or back a quarter of a mile, that was something to write home about. When we pulled out of Waurika, we had to pull back maybe ten miles."

"Yeah, well, this here's the next town south of Waurika, too. Ain't nothing to speak of between there and here," Hairston said. "The Yankees run us out of the one place, what the hell's the point in stoppin' till you got somewheres else worth holding on to?"

"Mm, maybe you've got something there," Bartlett admitted. "Lot of built-up land in the Roanoke valley, and what isn't built up is good farm country. Here, there's a lot of land just lying empty, not doing anything in particular. Seems kind of funny, when you're used to the way things are on the other side of the Mississippi."

"Yeah," Hairston agreed. A couple of three-inch field guns came by, pulled through the mud by laboring horses. "And that's our artillery. That's all the artillery we got, for miles and miles. Ain't like that on the Roanoke front, is it?"

"Lord, no," Reggie answered. "There, the Yankees and us'd

line 'em up hub to hub and whale away at each other till it didn't seem like there was a live man anywhere the guns could reach."

He wished there were barbed wire to string in front of the entrenchments he and his comrades were digging. Confederate forces had been able to use some farther north in Sequoyah, but had had to abandon it when the Yankees forced them out of their positions. Nothing new had come up from Texas. From what Reggie'd heard, the defenders of Texas had their problems, too.

He was still digging when the U.S. field guns opened up on his position. He had to throw himself down in the mud a couple of times because of near misses. After each one, he got up, brushed himself off, and went back to work.

Joe Mopope, one of the Kiowas who'd been fighting alongside the Confederates since Waurika, asked, "How can you do that? I can fight with a rifle"—he carried a Tredegar now, not the squirrel gun he'd started with—"but it's different when the big guns start shooting. They are too far away for me to shoot back at them, so they make me afraid."

Admitting fear took a kind of nerve of its own. Bartlett studied Mopope's long, straight-nosed, high-cheekboned face. "All what you're used to, Joe," he said at last, more careful of the Indian's pride than he'd thought he might be. "I've been under worse shellfire than this since 1914. I know what it can do and what it can't. First few times, it damn near scared the piss out of me."

"Ah." Mopope was usually a pretty serious fellow. Now he tried out a smile, as if to see whether it would fit his face. "This is good to know. A warrior can learn this kind of fighting, then, the same as any other kind."

"Yeah," Reggie said. Joe Mopope's father might have been a warrior of the traditional Indian sort, sneaking across the U.S. border on raids up into Kansas. That sort of thing had gone on for years after the Second Mexican War, finally petering out not long before the turn of the century.

Bartlett shrugged. He came from a family of warriors, too. Both his grandfathers had served in the War of Secession. His father hadn't fought in the Second Mexican War, but Uncle Jasper sure as hell had—and wouldn't shut up about it, either, not to this day.

From in back of the trenches, the Confederates' field guns opened up. They fired faster than their Yankee counterparts. Joe Mopope's smile got wider. "Ah, we give it back to them. That is good. Hurting them is better than sitting here and letting them hurt us."

"Yes, except for one thing." Reggie set down his entrenching tool and unslung his rifle. "If we're opening up on the damnyankees, that means they're close enough for the gunners to spot 'em. And if they're close enough for the gunners to spot 'em, we're going to have company before long."

He looked north. Sure enough, here came the men in green-gray. They advanced much more openly than they would have in the Roanoke valley, where any man outside a trench risked immediate annihilation. That aside, the Yankee commander hereabouts seemed to assess danger by how many men the Confederates in front of him knocked over on the approach. Some generals in butternut were like that, too. Bartlett was glad he didn't serve under any of them.

Rifle and machine-gun fire forced the Yankees to go to earth. Dirt flew as the U.S. soldiers dug themselves in. Any man who hoped to live through the war was handy with the spade. Stretcher-bearers carried a few wounded Confederates back into Ryan. On the other side of the line, stretcher-bearers in U.S. uniforms were no doubt doing the same thing with injured damnyankees.

"We stopped 'em!" Napoleon Dibble said happily.

Even Joe Mopope rolled his black eyes at that. As gently as he could, Reggie said, "We stopped 'em for now, Nap. We stopped 'em for a while at Duncan, and for a while at Waurika, too. Question is, can we stop 'em when they bring up everything they've got?"

"We have to," Dibble answered. "Lieutenant Nicoll said we have to. If we don't, the Yankees get Sequoyah, and they'll fill it up with Germans." He'd made that mistake before; nobody bothered correcting him about it any more.

Dusk fell. Reggie gnawed stale cornbread and opened a tin of beans and pork. That was enough to quiet the growling in his belly, though it didn't make much of a meal. Cold drizzle started falling. Rifle fire spattered up and down the lines, muzzle flashes looking like lightning bugs.

When Bartlett wanted somebody to dig a trench forward toward a good post for a picket that he'd spotted, he looked around for Joe Mopope, but didn't spot him. He wondered where the hell the Indian had got to. The Kiowas and Comanches were good enough in a fight, but they didn't like the drudgery that went with soldiering for hell.

He set Nap Dibble digging instead. Nap did the job without complaint. He never complained. He probably wasn't smart enough to complain. Because he didn't, he got more than his fair share of jobs nobody else wanted.

Sergeant Pete Hairston launched a fearsome barrage of curses. Reggie hurried over to see what was going on. There stood Joe Mopope, knife in one hand, a couple of objects Bartlett couldn't see well in the other. In tones somewhere between disgust and awe, Hairston said, "This red-skinned son of a bitch just brought us back two Yankee scalps."

Reggie stared. Then he blurted, "No wonder he wasn't around when I needed him to dig."

Very quietly, Joe Mopope laughed.

As she rode the streetcar to her job at a mackerel-canning plant, Sylvia Enos went through the inner pages of the *Boston Globe* with minute care. As far as she was concerned, the paper never talked enough about naval affairs. A battle on land that didn't move the front a quarter of a mile in one direction or the other got page-one coverage. Sometimes she thought ships got mentioned only when they were torpedoed or blown to bits.

She saw nothing about the USS *Ericsson*. Not seeing anything about the destroyer made her let out a silent sigh of relief. It meant—she devoutly hoped it meant—her husband George was all right.

Most of the people on the trolley were women on the way to work, many of them on the way to jobs men had been doing before the war pulled them into the Army or the Navy. Many of them were scanning the newspaper as attentively as Sylvia was doing. Some of the ones who weren't wore mourning black. They no longer had any need to fear the worst. They'd already met it.

Sylvia left her copy of the *Globe* on the seat when the trolley came to her stop. She wished George were home. She wished he'd never gone to war. And she hoped the *Ericsson* was far out to sea, nowhere near a port. She loved her husband, and she thought he loved her, but she wasn't sure, as she had been once, she could trust him out of her sight.

She walked the short distance to the canning plant, which was no more lovely than it had to be. It wasn't far from the harbor, and stank of fish. A skinny cat looked at her and gave an optimistic meow. She shook her head. "Sorry, pussycat. No handouts from me today." The cat meowed again, piteously this time. Sylvia shook her head again, too, and walked on.

She grabbed her time card and stuck it in the clock. The money wasn't good—it wasn't as if she were a man, after all—but, with it and her monthly allotment from George's pay, she managed well enough.

"Good morning, Mrs. Enos," the foreman said as she hurried toward the machine that stuck bright labels on cans of mackerel.

"Good morning, Mr. Winter," she answered. He nodded and limped on past her: as a young man, he'd taken a bullet in the leg during the Second Mexican War.

A couple of minutes later, Isabella Antonelli took her place on the machine next to Sylvia's. She wore black; her husband had been killed fighting in Quebec. She nodded shyly to Sylvia, set down her dinner pail, and made sure her machine was in good working order.

With a rumble of motors and several discordant squeals of fan belts, the line started moving. Sylvia had to pull three levers, taking steps between them, to bring bare, bright cans into her machine, squirt paste on them, and affix the labels—which made the mackerel whose flesh went into the cans look remarkably like tuna. Being a fisherman's wife, she knew what a lie that was. People who bought the cans in Ohio or Nebraska wouldn't, though.

Some days, stepping and pulling levers could be mesmerizing, so that half the morning would slip by while Sylvia hardly noticed any time passing. This was one of those mornings. The only time she got jolted out of her routine was when her paste reservoir ran dry and she had to refill it from the big bucket of paste under the machine before she could put on more labels.

As it did sometimes, the lunch whistle startled her, jerking her out of the world in which she was almost as mechanical as the machine she tended. The line groaned to a stop. Sylvia shook herself, as she might have done coming out of the bathtub at the end of the hall in her apartment building. She looked around. There was her dinner pail, of black-painted sheet metal like the one a riveter might have carried to the Boston Navy Yard.

Isabella Antonelli's dinner pail might have been identical to her own. The two women sat on a bench near a wheezing steam radiator. Sylvia had a ham sandwich in her dinner pail, leftovers from the night before. Isabella Antonelli had a tightly covered bowl that also looked to hold leftovers: long noodles that looked like worms, smothered in tomato sauce. She brought them to the factory about three days out of five. Sylvia thought they were disgusting, though she'd never said so for fear of hurting her friend's feelings.

Mr. Winter limped by, a cigar clamped between his teeth. He was carrying his own dinner pail, looking for a place to sit down. His eyes lingered on Isabella as he walked past. "You can go with him, if you'd like," Sylvia said.

"I will sit with you today," the Italian woman said. She smiled, which made her look younger and not so tired. "He should not take me too much for granted, don't you think?"

She and the foreman—a widower for years—had been lovers for a couple of months. They were discreet about it, both at the factory and with their own families. Winter had aimed a few speculative remarks at Sylvia since she'd started working at the canning plant; she was just as well pleased to see him attached to someone else. To his credit, he hadn't aimed any of those remarks at her since taking up with Isabella.

Sylvia said, "Anybody who takes anybody else for granted is a fool."

She didn't realize with how much bitterness she'd freighted the remark till Isabella Antonelli, a worried look on her face, asked, "But all is well with your Giorgio, yes?"

"He's well, yes," Sylvia replied, which was by no means a complete answer. Isabella obviously realized it wasn't a complete answer. She also obviously realized it was all the answer she would get. The rest of the half-hour lunch passed in uneasy silence.

For once, Sylvia was glad to go back to her machine, to lose herself in the routine of pulling and stepping, pulling and stepping, of watching cans bright with their tinning go into the machine and cans gaudy with their labels stream out. The machine asked no questions she would sooner not have answered. The machine asked no questions at all.

As she had at the lunch whistle, Sylvia started when the quitting whistle screamed. It was dark when she clocked out and walked to the trolley stop, but not quite so dark as it had been earlier in the year. Twilight lingered in the west, a harbinger of spring ahead. It was the only harbinger of spring she could find; the wind cut like a knife.

She had to stand almost all the way back to the stop by her apartment building. Except for lunch, she'd been standing since she got to the plant. Now that she'd returned from that mechanistic world, she felt how tired she was. Her legs didn't want to hold her up any more. When she finally did get to sit down, she nearly fell asleep before the streetcar got to her stop. She'd done that once, and walked back more than a mile. This time, she didn't, but getting up and getting off the trolley were more mind over matter than anything else.

She checked her mailbox in the entrance hall to the apartment building. No letter from George, which meant he hadn't come to port as of a few days before, which meant he hadn't had the chance to get into trouble in a port. He might have got into trouble on the sea, but that was a different sort of trouble, and one over which she worried in a different sort of way.

Circulars from the Coal Board, the Scrap Metal Collection Agency, the Ration Board, the Victory Over Waste Committee, and the War Savings and Tax Board helped fill the mailbox. So did one from an agency new to her, the Paper Conservation Authority, which informed her in the portentous bureaucratic tones of any government outfit that paper was an important war resource and should not be wasted.

"Then why do I get so much worthless paper every day?" she muttered, tossing the multicolored sheets into the battered wastebasket there. The answer to that was only too clear: "Because one board writes this and none of the others read it, that's why."

She went upstairs to reclaim her children from Brigid Coneval, who, after her husband was conscripted, had decided to take in the children of other women who got jobs in factories instead of getting a factory job herself. Each flight of stairs seemed to have twice as many as the one before, and each step twice as high.

When she came out into the hallway, she walked down the hall to Mrs. Coneval's flat to get George, Jr., and Mary Jane and take them back to her own apartment, where she would make supper and let them play till they were ready for bed—or, more likely, till she was ready for bed and managed to persuade them that they should lie down, too.

They were getting harder to persuade. George, Jr., was six

now, heading toward seven, and Mary Jane nearly four. Sylvia needed more sleep these days, while they needed less. It hardly seemed fair.

With so many children in Brigid Coneval's flat, shrieks and cries as Sylvia came up were the order of the day. But the shrieks and cries that Sylvia heard now did not come from the throats of children. Fear shot through her, sharp as if she'd seized a live electric wire. She had to will herself to knock, and then had to knock twice to make anyone inside notice her.

The woman who opened the door was not Brigid Coneval, though she looked very much like her. Seeing Sylvia, George, Jr., and Mary Jane came running up and embraced her. Above them, Sylvia asked the question she dreaded, the question that had to be asked: "Is she—? Is it—?"

"It is that." The woman, doubtless Brigid's sister, had a brogue like hers, too. "Less than an hour ago, the telegram came. Down in Virginia he was, poor man, and never coming back from there again."

"That's dreadful. I'm so sorry," Sylvia said, feeling the inadequacy of words. She knew what Brigid Coneval was feeling. She'd twice thought George lost, once when his fishing boat was captured by a Confederate commerce raider and once when his river monitor was blown out of the water. The only thing that had saved him then was that he hadn't been aboard, but on the riverbank, drunk and about to lie down with a colored strumpet.

She couldn't even say she understood, for Brigid's sister would not believe her. Then she found a new worry, different but in its own way no less urgent: while Brigid Coneval mourned, who would take care of the children when she had to go to work?

IV

Sam Carsten swabbed the deck of the USS *Dakota* with a safety line tied round his waist. The battleship pitched like a toy boat in a rambunctious boy's bathtub, chewing its way over and through waves that put to shame any others he'd ever known.

He shouted to his bunkmate, Vic Crosetti, who plied a mop not far away: "Everything they say about Cape Horn is true!"

"Yeah," Crosetti shouted back, through the howl of the wind. "Only trouble is, they don't say near enough, the tight-mouthed sons of bitches."

There was nothing tight-mouthed about him. He was a voluble Italian, little and swarthy and hairy and ugly as a monkey. Carsten, by contrast, was tall and muscular, with pink skin and hair so blond, it was almost white.

Crosetti leered at him. "You sunburned yet, Sam?"

"Fuck you," Carsten said amiably. He'd burned in San Francisco. Christ, he'd burned in Seattle. Duty in the Sandwich Islands and the tropical Pacific had been a hell of burning and peeling and zinc oxide and half a dozen other ointments that didn't do any good, either. "I finally find weather that suits me, and what do I get? A scrawny dago giving me a hard time."

Had some men called him a scrawny dago, Crosetti would have answered with a kick in the teeth or a knife in the ribs. When Sam did, he grinned. Carsten had a way of being able to talk without ticking people off. He even had trouble starting brawls in waterfront saloons.

Another enormous swell sweeping along from west to east lifted the *Dakota* to its crest. For a moment, Sam could see a hell of a long way. He spotted another battleship from the U.S. force that had set out from Pearl Harbor for Valparaiso, Chile, the autumn before—except autumn meant nothing in the Sandwich Islands and was spring down in Chile. Farther off, he made out a U.S. armored cruiser and a couple of the destroyers that guarded the big battlewagons from harm.

He also spied a Chilean armored cruiser. But for the different flag and different paint job—the Chileans preferred a sky blue to the U.S. gray—it looked the same as its American counterpart. It should have; it had come out of the Boston Navy Yard.

Pointing to it, Carsten said, "We sold the Chileans their toys, and England sold the Argentines theirs. Now we get to find out who's a better toymaker."

"Hell with all of 'em," Crosetti said. "If Argentina was on our side, Chile'd be in bed with the limeys. But Argentina's keeping England fed, so Chile ends up playin' on our team. Big deal, you ask me."

"Hey, listen, if Argentina was on our side, we'd be sailing east to west, straight into all these damn waves and this stinking wind instead of riding with 'em. How'd you like that?"

"No thanks," Crosetti said at once.

Carsten got a faraway look in his eyes. "How'd you like to try sailing east to west through here in a ship without an engine—I mean *really* sailing through here?" he said. Crosetti crossed himself. Sam laughed. "Yeah, that's how I feel about it, too."

"They were tough bastards in the old days," Vic Crosetti said. "Stupid bastards, too, to want to come down to such a god-forsaken corner of the world."

Before Carsten could answer that, klaxons started hooting, a noise hideous enough to cut through the raging wind. Everyone on deck undid his safety line and ran for his battle station. Sam had no idea whether it was a drill or whether some destroyer up ahead had spotted British or Argentine or maybe even French ships. He knew he had to treat the noise as if shells would start dropping around—or on—the *Dakota* at any moment.

The battleship sank into the trough between waves, plunging her bow steeply downward. Sam's foot skidded on seawater. He flailed his arms wildly, and somehow managed to keep from falling on his face. Then his shoes rang on metal rungs as he went below.

His battle station was loader on the forwardmost starboard five-inch gun. He flung himself into the cramped sponson and waited to see what would happen next.

There ahead of him—he would have been astonished were it

otherwise—was the commander of that five-inch gun, a chief petty officer and gunner's mate named Hiram Kidde and more often than not called "Cap'n." He'd ditched his habitual cigar somewhere on the way to the sponson. He couldn't have been too far from it; he wasn't breathing hard, and he was a roly-poly fellow who'd been in the Navy for years before Sam got his first pair of long pants.

"Is this practice, or for real?" Sam asked.

"Damned if I know," Kidde answered. "Think they tell me anything?"

In scrambled the rest of the crew: gun layers and shell jerkers. They were all at their stations when Commander Grady, who was in charge of the starboard secondary armament, stuck his head into the sponson. Grady nodded approval; he was a pretty decent sort. "Well done, men," he said.

Hiram Kidde asked the same question Carsten had: "What's the dope, sir? Is this just another drill, or have we got trouble up ahead?"

"We've got trouble up ahead sure as the sun comes up to-morrow," Grady answered. "Sooner or later, if they don't stop us, we *are* going to be in position to disrupt shipments of wheat and beef from Argentina to England. If we can do that, the limeys starve, so they'll move heaven and earth to keep us away."

"I understand that, sir," Kidde answered patiently. "What I meant was, have we got trouble up ahead right now?" Grady would know. Whether he would tell was liable to be a different question.

He started to answer, but then somebody in the corridor spoke to him. "What?" he said, sounding surprised. He hurried off.

"Damn," said Luke Hoskins, one of the shell haulers. He was the right man for his job, being both taller and thicker through the shoulders than Carsten, who wasn't small himself. Nobody the size of, say, Vic Crosetti could have handled five-inch, sixty-pound shells as if he were about to load them into his shotgun. Also, shell-jerker wasn't the sort of job that called for much in the way of brains.

"I think it's—" Kidde began, just as the klaxons signaled the all-clear.

"You were going to say you thought it was the real thing, weren't you?" Carsten said as they started filing out of the cramped sponson.

He expected Kidde to deny everything, but the gunner's mate nodded. "Hell yes, I did. We should have done this months ago, instead of wasting time in Valparaiso and Concepción like we did. Shit, we were ready, but the Chilean Navy ain't what you'd call a fireball."

"How do you say *tomorrow* in Spanish?" Carsten said. "*Mañana,* that's it. I wonder how many times we heard *mañana* up there."

"Too damn many, however many it was," Kidde said positively. "Wasted time, wasted time." He shook his head, a slow, mournful gesture. "Seas wouldn't have been near so heavy if we'd got moving in the middle of summer hereabouts instead of waiting till we were heading down toward fall. I still don't trust our steering, either. Wish I did, but I don't."

Carsten's laugh was a noise he made to hold fear at bay. "What's the matter, 'Cap'n'? You don't want to do a circle toward the limeys and Argentines, the way we did toward the limeys and Japs in the Battle of the Three Navies?"

Kidde swore loudly and sulfurously for a couple of minutes before calming down enough to say, "We were lucky once, which is how come we ain't on the bottom of the Pacific. You can't count on being lucky once. You sure as hell can't count on being lucky twice."

"I expect you're right." Carsten went up onto the main deck, made his way back to where he'd been working, and reattached his safety line. He might as well have been starting over from scratch; plenty of seawater had splashed up since he'd dashed to his battle station.

Vic Crosetti resumed his place a minute or so later. They were jawing back and forth when a starched young lieutenant, junior grade, came up and said, "Seaman Carsten?" When Sam admitted he was himself, the officer said, "The force commander will see you in his cabin immediately."

"Sir?" If Sam's heart didn't skip a beat, he couldn't guess why. He hadn't thought Rear Admiral Bradley Fiske knew he existed. Like any other sensible sailor, he'd hoped that pleasant condition would continue indefinitely. In a choking voice, he asked, "What does he think I've done, sir?"

"Come with me, Carsten," the j.g. answered, and Sam, a lump of ice about the size of the nearby Antarctic continent in his belly, had to obey.

Out of the corner of his eye, he noticed another officer bringing Vic Crosetti along. *God damn that little dago,* he thought. *What's he done, and how in hell did I get in hot water for it?*

He seldom had occasion to go up into officers' country. He'd never had occasion to visit the force commander's quarters, nor imagined that he would. Sure as hell, Vic Crosetti was heading there, too. Carsten cursed under his breath.

The lieutenant, j.g., went in ahead of him, then came back out and said, "The admiral will see you—both of you—now." As they went in, Crosetti gave Sam a venomous glare. *Christ,* Sam thought, *does he figure he's in trouble on account of something I did? What kind of foul-up have we got here?*

There stood Rear Admiral Fiske, a sturdy man of about sixty, in the middle of a cabin that could have held half a dozen three-level bunks. So much space inside the *Dakota* was amazing. Even more amazing was the bottle of medicinal brandy Fiske held, and that he poured three glasses from it, handing one to Sam and one to Crosetti and keeping the third for himself. "Congratulations, you men!" he boomed.

Carsten and Crosetti stared at each other, then at Rear Admiral Fiske. Sam felt as if he'd been up and down too fast on the Coney Island roller coaster. He had to say something. He knew he had to say something. "Sir?" His voice was a hoarse croak.

Fiske looked impatient. He knew what was going on, which struck Carsten as an unfair advantage. "Some time ago, you two men reported your suspicions that a certain native of the Sandwich Islands, one John Liholiho, used his position and good nature to spy for England after the USA took the said islands from her at the outbreak of the war. Investigation has confirmed those suspicions, I am informed by wireless telegraph. Liholiho has been arrested and sentenced to death."

"Sir?" Sam and Crosetti said it together now, in astonishment. Sam had almost forgotten about the affable, surf-riding Sandwich Islander. He'd long since assumed Liholiho wasn't in fact a spy, because no one had said anything to the contrary.

Fiske was saying that now. He was also saying something else: "You men are both promoted from Seaman First Class to Petty Officer Third Class, effective the date of your report. Back pay in your new rank will also accrue from the said date." He raised his glass in salute. "Well done, both of you!" He drank.

Numbly, Carsten raised his own glass. Numbly, he drank, and

discovered the rear admiral got a much better grade of medicine than did the men he commanded. After the stuff went off like a bomb in his stomach, he wasn't numb any more. He tried on a smile for size. It fit his face like a glove.

As Scipio walked down the road toward the swamp, he knew he was a dead man. Oh, his lungs still moved air in and out, his heart still beat, his legs still took step after step. He was a dead man even so. The only questions left were who would kill him, how soon, and how long he'd hurt before he finally died.

He looked back over his shoulder. Somewhere back there, Anne Colleton was liable to have a scope-mounted Tredegar aimed at his spine. She'd had one slung on her back when she sent him out on his way to the swamps by the Congaree. By the way she handled it, she knew just what to do with it, too.

She'd started following him. He didn't know if she still was. He'd caught glimpses of her once or twice, but only once or twice. He got the idea she'd wanted him to get those glimpses, to remind him she was on his trail. When she wanted him not to see her, he didn't. He'd never dreamt she could stalk like that.

Was she good enough to stalk Cassius? Scipio found that hard to believe. Cassius had been Marshlands' chief hunter for years. What he didn't know about the swamps of the Congaree, no one did. He'd been able to keep the raiders who were the hard core of the Congaree Socialist Republic a going concern in the swamp for most of a year after the Socialist Republic was crushed everywhere else.

And Cassius and the rest of the Red holdouts were about as likely to kill him as Anne Colleton was. If they found out he was acting as her bird dog, they *would* kill him. They might kill him simply for abandoning the cause and trying to live what passed for a normal life in the CSA after the black uprising went down to defeat.

Something rose from the roadside marsh in a thunder of wings. Scipio's heart rose, too, into his throat. But it was only an egret, flapping away from his unwanted company. When he was a boy, the big white birds had been far more common than they were today. The demand for plumes on ladies' hats had all but caused their extermination. Only a shift in fashion let any survive.

Here where—he hoped—no one could hear him, he trotted

out the educated white man's voice he'd used while serving as butler at Marshlands: "And what shift in fashion will let *me* survive?" For the life of him—literally, for the life of him—he could think of none.

He looked around. Water, rushes, trees. The road was turning into a muddy track. Everything seemed prosaic enough. Of course, he was only on the edge of the swamp as yet. The Negro field hands back at Marshlands had peopled the wet country with monsters with sharp teeth and glowing yellow eyes.

Those stories were nothing but superstitious twaddle. So claimed the part of him that had been so carefully educated. The little boy who had listened round-eyed to the stories the grannies told wasn't so sure. He looked around again, more nervously this time. Nothing. Only swamp. Of course, that meant cougars and gators and cottonmouths and rattlers and—he slapped—mosquitoes and the no-see-'ems that bit and vanished. He slapped again.

The road forked, and then forked again, and then again. It went in among the trees now, and the oaks and willows and pines made the sun play hide-and-seek. The road divided yet again. Every turn Scipio took was one leading deeper into the swamp.

If he didn't find the men of the Congaree Socialist Republic, he wondered if he'd be able to find his way out. If Cassius didn't kill him, and if Anne Colleton didn't kill him, the swamp was liable to do him in.

No sooner had that thought crossed his mind than three Negroes with Tredegars stepped silently out into the roadway. They wore red bandannas on their left arms. "Nigger, you ain't got no good reason to be here, you is one dead nigger," one of them said. Two of their rifles were bayoneted. They wouldn't even have to risk the noise of a gunshot to dispose of them.

He licked his lips. The bayonets looked very long and sharp. "I wants to see Cassius, or maybe Cherry," he answered in the broad patois of the Congaree. "I is on de business o' de Socialist Republic."

None of the three fighting men was from Marshlands or any nearby plantation. They didn't know him by sight, as many of Cassius' men would have. "Who you is?" their spokesman asked.

"I's Scipio," he said.

Their eyes went wide in their dark faces. They knew the name, if not the man who went with it. "Maybe you is, an' maybe you ain't," said the one who had spoken first.

"Take me to Cassius. Take me to Cherry," Scipio said. "You ask they who I is an' who I ain't."

The fighters put their heads together. After a minute of low-voice argument, the one who seemed to lead handed his Tredegar to a comrade, took the bandanna off his arm, and walked up to Scipio. "Maybe you is, an' maybe you ain't," he repeated. "An' maybe you is, an' you is a spy nowadays. You see Cassius an' Cherry, but you don' see how to get to they." He efficiently blindfolded Scipio with the square of red cloth.

"You insults me," Scipio said with as much indignation as he could simulate. Had he been rejoining the forces of the Congaree Socialist Republic in truth, he would have protested being blindfolded. Since he was a spy (and since he was Anne Colleton's spy, which, he suspected, made him more dangerous to Cassius than if he'd merely been a spy for the Confederate government), he had to do his best to seem as if he weren't.

"Come on." The man who covered his eyes grabbed him by the arm. "We takes you."

He had no idea by what route they took him. It might have been the straightest one possible, or they might have spent half their time walking him around in circles. He wondered if Anne Colleton was still following him. He wondered what sort of watchers the survivors of the Congaree Socialist Republic had posted through the swamp. He wondered whether she could get past them if she was still following him. That he did not know the answer to any of those questions did not keep him from wondering about all of them.

After about an hour, his guide said, "Stop." Scipio obeyed. The man who'd led him for so long took the blindfold off him. Standing side by side in front of him were Cassius and Cherry. She wore a collarless men's shirt and a torn pair of men's trousers. Scipio suppressed a shudder. Anne Colleton had worn men's trousers, too, though hers were elegantly tailored.

Cassius hurried up and clasped Scipio's hand. "Do Jesus, Kip," he exclaimed. "Why fo' you here? Las' I hear, you is up in Greenville, an' de buckra, dey forget you was ever borned."

Scipio was anything but surprised Cassius had kept tabs on where he'd gone. He *had* dropped out of sight of the Confederate authorities, but the Negro grapevine was a different matter altogether. With a sigh, he answered with most of the truth: "Somebody rec'nize me up dere. Dey 'rested me, take me to St. Matthews."

"To Miss Anne." Cherry's voice was flat and full of hate. Scipio nodded, more than a little apprehensively. She went on, "I reckon we done baked dat white debbil bitch las' Christmas, but she git away."

"She good." Cassius spoke with reluctant respect. "She a damn 'pressor, but she good. We cain't kill she, no matter how hard we tries." His rather foxy features grew sharp and intent. "Why fo' she send you in after we? She ask a truce? I don' trust no truce wid she. She break it like de overseer break de stick on de back o' de field hand fo' to get he to pick de cotton."

"She say, de war 'gainst de United States mo' 'portant than de war 'gainst de Congaree Socialist Republic," Scipio replied, nodding. "She say, if de damnyankees licks de CSA, dey comes an' licks de Congaree Socialist Republic, too. She say, we kin wait till de big war done, an' den we fights our own."

Cassius and Cherry and all three men who'd brought Scipio to this place burst out laughing. "She say dat?" Cherry said. With high cheekbones that told of Indian blood, Cherry's face was made for showing scorn. She outdid herself now, tossing her head in magnificent contempt. "She say dat? Mighty fine, mighty fine. We let de 'pressors git rid o' de big war, an' den dey puts all dey gots into de little war 'gainst we."

"You go back to Miss Anne," Cassius added, "an' you tell she dat when she dead, den we can have a truce wid she. Till den, we fights. She ain't licked we yet, an' she ain't gwine lick we, on account of we gots de dialectic wid we. She go on de rubbish heap o' history, 'long wid de rest o' de 'pressors." Hearing Marxist revolutionary jargon in the dialect of the Congaree never failed to strike Scipio as bizarre.

Cherry's eyes narrowed. "She have somebody follow you?" she demanded. "Dat white debbil, she have bloodhounds wid guns on your trail?"

Scipio spread his hands. "Don' know," he answered, though he had a pretty good idea. "I ain't no huntin' man. Back at Marshlands, I was de butler, you recollects. I ain't hardly been in this swamp befo'."

"Oh, we recollects," Cassius said, grinning like a catamount.

He had a flask on his belt. He freed it, swigged, and passed it to Scipio. "See if you recollects dis here." Scipio drank. As butler, he'd sampled fine wines and good whiskey. This was raw corn likker, with a kick like a mule.

When he exhaled, he was amazed he didn't breathe out fire and smoke. He took another pull. There was a roaring in his ears. After a moment, he realized the corn likker hadn't caused it. It was real. It grew rapidly, and turned to a scream in the air. He'd heard that sound in the uprising the year before.

He threw himself flat. He wasn't the first one on the ground, either. Artillery shells rained down. Explosions picked him up and flung him about. Shell fragments and shrapnel balls tore up the landscape. Blast from a near miss yanked at his ears and his lungs. Someone was screaming like a damned soul—the man who'd blindfolded him, his belly laid open like a butchered hog's.

At last, the shelling ended. Scipio thanked the God he still trusted more than Marx that he was still in one piece. Also in one piece, Cassius took the bombardment in stride. "Miss Anne, she do have you followed," he said, brushing mud from his shirt. "You want to go back to she now?" Numbly, Scipio shook his head. Cassius grinned. "Den we welcomes you to de Congaree Socialist Republic agin."

Not having wanted to join the uprising in the first place, Scipio wanted even less to join this sad ghost of it. What possible fate could he have but being hunted down and killed? After a moment, he realized Anne Colleton couldn't have had anything else in mind. *You are mine,* she'd told him. Now it pleased her to amuse herself with her possession.

As Major Abner Dowling was making his way from his tent to the farmhouse where General Custer and his wife were staying, an enormous Pierce-Arrow limousine came snarling up the road, raising an even more enormous cloud of dust. It pulled to a stop alongside of Major Dowling. "Excuse me, is this First Army headquarters?" the driver asked.

Dowling was about to give him a sarcastic answer—what the devil else would this be?—when he saw who was riding in the back of the limousine. Gold-rimmed spectacles, graying roan mustache, a big grin that showed an alarming number of teeth . . . He was so busy staring at President Theodore Roosevelt, he almost forgot to answer the driver's question.

When Custer's adjutant admitted the fellow had brought Roosevelt to the right place, the president said, "And you're Dowling, aren't you?" He got out of the motorcar and pointed at the portly soldier. "You come with me, Major. I'll want to speak with you also."

"Yes, Mr. President." Dowling could scarcely have said anything else when his commander-in-chief gave him a direct order. He did not like the way Roosevelt had shown up unannounced at Custer's headquarters. The likeliest explanation he could think of for Roosevelt's unannounced appearance was one that put Custer in hot water—and himself, as well.

He moved his bulky frame as fast as he could, to get into the farmhouse ahead of the president. He hoped that would look as if he was escorting Roosevelt, not warning General Custer of his arrival.

Custer and Libbie were in the parlor. Instead of studying matters military, they were diligently going over newspapers. Intent on that, neither of them had noticed the Pierce-Arrow outside. Dowling said, "General, President Roosevelt is here to consult with you." That was the best face he could put on the president's arrival.

"Is he?" Custer said with a distinct sneer in his voice. Sure as hell, he and Roosevelt had loathed each other since the Second Mexican War, each convinced to the bottom of his stubborn soul that the other had nabbed more credit in that mostly sorry fight than he deserved.

"Yes, General, I am here," Roosevelt said, stepping into the farmhouse on Dowling's heels. Awkward with age, Custer got to his feet and saluted his commander-in-chief. In Montana, he'd been a Regular Army brevet brigadier general and Teddy Roosevelt a cavalry colonel of Volunteers. Now their relative ranks were reversed. Dowling knew how much Custer detested that.

"How good to see you, sir," Custer said, looking and sounding like a man with a toothache.

"A pleasure, as always." Roosevelt was manifestly lying, too. He nodded to Libbie. "And a pleasure to see you, Mrs. Custer. I hope you will excuse me for taking your husband away, but I do have some business to discuss with him and with Major Dowling here."

"Of course." Libbie shot him a look full of loathing. Dowling had never seen her so neatly outflanked. Without the tiniest doubt, she wanted to stay, not only to protect General Custer but also because she knew at least as much about what the First Army was doing as he did. But she could not stay, not after Roosevelt's blithe dismissal. Long black skirt flapping about her ankles, she swept out of the parlor.

"Cornelia!" Custer called. When the pretty Negro housekeeper came out of the kitchen, the general went on, "Coffee for me, coffee for Major Dowling—and coffee for the president of the United States." He might not care for Roosevelt, but he was not above using his acquaintance with him to impress Cornelia.

And he did impress her. Her eyes widened. She dropped Roosevelt a curtsy before dashing away for the coffee. The president, affable enough, dipped his head in reply. He sat down in the chair across from the sofa where Custer and his wife had been checking the papers, and waved Dowling to Libbie's place beside the general commanding First Army. Again, Custer's adjutant could only obey.

Roosevelt did not wait for Cornelia to come with the coffee. "Let's get right down to brass tacks," he said—like Custer, he did not have patience as his long suit. "General, the War Department is of the opinion that you have not been entirely candid in the reports you have been submitting in recent weeks. I have asked Major Dowling here to discuss this with us today, as he has prepared many of these reports under your direction."

Cornelia did come in with the coffee then—Custer's and Dowling's as they liked it, Roosevelt's black with cream and sugar on the side to let him fix it as he would. The brief respite while the president fiddled with the cup did nothing to ease Dowling's mind. *Christ, they've got me cold,* he thought, and wondered if his Army career was about to end here because he'd been so foolish as to obey his superior. Only discipline learned at the poker table kept him from showing his dread.

If Custer knew dread, he didn't show it, either. "The War Department has all sorts of opinions," he said, sneering as he had when Dowling announced that Roosevelt was there. "A few of them bear a discernible relation to the real world—but only a few, mind you."

"Have you, then, or have you not been less than candid in your description of how you are deploying the barrels under your command?" Roosevelt asked.

There it was, the question without a good answer. Sweat broke out on Dowling's forehead, though the parlor was cool verging on chilly. Now Custer would lie, and now Roosevelt would crucify him—and, as small change in the transaction, would crucify Dowling, too.

Custer laughed. "Of course I've been less than candid, Mr. President," he answered, his tone inviting Roosevelt to share a secret with him. "So has Major Dowling, at my direct order. The lads with the thick glasses in Philadelphia must have been more alert than usual, to notice."

"I hope you have some good explanation for your extraordinary statement, General," Roosevelt said. Dowling devoutly hoped Custer had a good explanation, too. From long acquaintance with the general commanding First Army, though, he knew that hope was liable, even likely, to be disappointed.

Not this time. Laughing again, Custer said, "I have reason to believe the Rebels are somehow getting their hands on the reports I forward to the War Department, and so I have been carefully feeding them false information for the past several weeks. I hope they are less astute than our own people, and fail to notice the deception."

Roosevelt rounded on Dowling. "Major, is what General Custer says true?"

If he wanted to, Dowling could break Custer here. He could not only break him, he could break him and come out, in the short run, smelling like a rose as he did it. The old fool had served himself up with an apple in his mouth, and all Dowling had to do was carve. He'd dreamt of a chance like this for years—and, now that he had it, he discovered he couldn't stick the knife in. That was what it would be: a stab in the back. He might escape Custer with it, but, afterwards, who in the Army would trust an officer who laid his superior low?

"Answer me, Major," Roosevelt said.

"I'm sorry, your Excellency," Dowling said. "General Custer did not tell me why he wanted the reports to appear as if they were disguising the concentration of barrels." That was a lie, but no one could ever prove it was a lie. "I presume, though, that it was for reasons of security."

If Roosevelt felt like seeing for himself how the barrels were deployed, everything could still cave in, like a trench with a mine touched off below it. The president didn't go charging off to do that, not right away, anyhow. Rubbing his chin, he asked, "Why, General, do you believe the Confederates may have been reading your dispatches to Philadelphia?"

"Just by way of example, sir, how could General MacArthur's attack over by Cotton Town have failed last fall if the Rebs had no advance warning of it?" Custer asked—reasonably. "Daniel MacArthur is as fine a brigadier general and division commander as the U.S. Army possesses, but he failed. The Rebs must have prepared in advance to withstand him."

MacArthur's attack had failed, among other reasons, because Custer didn't give his fine brigadier general the—admittedly extravagant—artillery support and number of barrels he'd requested. Custer didn't want MacArthur gaining glory, any more than he'd wanted Roosevelt gaining glory in the Second Mexican War. Dowling had watched Custer outmaneuver MacArthur. Could he outmaneuver Roosevelt, too?

Maybe he could. The president coughed. "Why have you not presented these suspicions to the War Department?" he asked, and Dowling realized he was witnessing something few men had ever seen: Theodore Roosevelt in retreat.

Custer smiled. When he heard that question, he knew he had the game in hand. "Your Excellency, since I have not been able to determine how the Confederates are obtaining their information, I did not wish to run the risk of informing them that I knew they were doing so. Letting them have information that is not true struck me as being more profitable."

"More profitable, you say?" Roosevelt perked up. He set a finger by the side of his nose. "And you have a plan to make them pay, so you can reap the profit?"

"Mr. President, I do," Custer answered, telling the truth, as far as Dowling could see, for the first time in the interview.

"Very well, General," Roosevelt said. "Till the mare drops her foal, no one can tell what the creature will look like. I shall judge your plan—and whether you were wise to conceal it not only from the foe but also from your countrymen—by the result." He got to his feet. "I thank you for your time, General. Major Dowling, thank you also for your part in explaining what has occurred here. Good morning, gentlemen." Without waiting for a reply, Roosevelt walked out to the limousine.

Dowling stared out the window, hardly daring to believe the Pierce-Arrow was really rolling away. When it was out of sight, he let out a long, heartfelt sigh of relief. "My God, sir, you got away with it."

Custer looked disgracefully smug. "Of course I did, Major."

"That was an inspired explanation you gave him." Dowling was not used to admiring Custer's wits. Doing so felt strange and wrong, as if he were dabbling in some unnatural vice.

"So it was, if I do say so myself." The vain, pompous old fool looked more smug still. Dowling fought down the urge to retch.

Libbie Custer came downstairs in a rustle of skirts. "I saw him leave," she said. "Did he swallow it, Autie?"

"Every morsel, my dear." Some of the smugness hissed out of Custer, as if he were an observation balloon with a leak. He turned back to Dowling. "Major, now that the president has gone . . ." Had it been a complete sentence, he would have finished it with something like, *Get the hell out of here yourself.*

"Yes, sir." Dowling left in a hurry. *So Libbie was the one who came up with the second line of defense,* he thought. Slowly, he nodded. He should have known Custer wouldn't have the brains to do it on his own. He nodded again, his faith in his own sense of how the world worked in large measure restored.

But Custer, even if he hadn't planned the deception, had carried it off. If he could deceive the Confederates, too . . . He hadn't had much luck doing that in any of the fighting up till now. But then, he hadn't tried very hard, either. If he did, if he could . . .

It made a man hope. In this war, too much hope was dangerous. "I'll believe it when I see it," Abner Dowling said.

Arthur McGregor rode the wagon toward Rosenfeld. Whenever U.S. trucks came up behind him, he delayed a little before moving off to the shoulder to let them roar past. It was a tiny bit of resistance, but all he could muster. He had to clench the reins tightly to keep from shouting abuse at the Americans. When the time came, he would try to take his revenge. Till then, he had to seem as conquered, as beaten down, as the rest of his countrymen.

Outside Rosenfeld, the occupiers had a checkpoint. They were meticulous in searching the wagon, and even more meticulous in searching his person. They found nothing out of the ordinary. There was nothing out of the ordinary to find. "Pass on," one of them said.

"Thank you, sir," McGregor answered, abject as a kicked dog. He scrambled back up into the seat, flicked the reins, and rolled on toward the little town where he bought what he couldn't raise for himself.

Rosenfeld, Manitoba, these days, was more nearly an American town than a Canadian one. Most of the men on the streets wore green-gray. Most of the talk McGregor heard was in sharp American accents, sour to his ears. Most of the money that changed hands was American money: boring green banknotes, coins full of eagles and stars and thunderbolts instead of bearing the images of George and Edward and Victoria. Most of the money in McGregor's pocket was American money. He hated that, too.

He had to tie up his wagon on a side street. American motor-cars and trucks and wagons and even bicycles dominated Main Street. As he came round the corner, a green-gray Ford whizzed past him.

He had to work hard to keep his face straight, to show none of what he was thinking. Major Hannebrink was at the wheel of that Ford. Unusually, he had none of his Springfield-carrying bully boys with him. *Probably isn't out to murder anyone this morning,* McGregor thought. *Maybe he waits till after lunch to do his murdering.*

The post office was only a few doors away. When McGregor went inside, the familiar spicy smell of Wilfred Rokeby's hair oil greeted his nose. The postmaster used the aromatic stuff to keep his hair pasted down at either side of the precise part that ran back along the middle of his scalp.

"Good day to you, Arthur," Rokeby said, his voice as prim and precise as that ruler-drawn part. "How are you today?" He asked that question cautiously, as he was in the habit of doing since Alexander's death.

"I've been better, Wilf, and that's the truth, but I've been worse, too," McGregor answered. He sniffed in an exaggerated fashion. "Haven't you run out of that damned grease of yours yet? Sure as hell, the plant that made it must be turning out poison gas these days."

Rokeby glared, then stared, and then chuckled quietly. "First time I've heard you make a joke in a while, Arthur, even if it is aimed at me. What can I do for you this morning?"

"Let me have twenty-five of those stamps the Yanks are making us use," McGregor said.

"Here you are," Rokeby said. "That'll be a dollar even." Letter rate remained two cents, as it had been before the war. But people in occupied Canada also paid a two-cent surcharge for every stamp, the extra money going into a fund for entertainers who amused U.S. soldiers.

McGregor had complained about the surcharge ever since it was initiated. He kept quiet now, save for a low sigh as he set a silver dollar on the table. It was a U.S. coin, and had a bust of Liberty on one side, which struck him as ironic. The other side showed a fierce eagle and the word REMEMBRANCE.

Rokeby quickly scooped the dollar into the cash box, as if afraid leaving it where McGregor could see it might inflame him. But McGregor seemed unable to rise to inflammation today. "Saw Hannebrink driving out of town when I was walking over here," he remarked.

"Did you?" At the mention of the security officer, Wilfred Rokeby grew wary again. Then his own expression changed—to, of all things, amusement. "Was he heading out by his lonesome, without any wolfhounds along?"

"Matter of fact, he was," McGregor said. He turned and looked out the window. "You see him as he went by?"

Rokeby shook his head. "I did not," he said, and his voice compelled belief. "But I have heard—don't know for certain, mind you, but they do say it—I have heard, like I was tellin' you, he's got himself a cutie-pie somewheres outside of town."

"Hannebrink?" Arthur McGregor stared. Until this moment, the idea that any Canadian woman might be friendly—might be more than friendly—to the Yank who had murdered Alexander had never entered his mind. But for strumpets, for whom such matters were business arrangements, he hadn't heard of any of his countrywomen showing friendship—or something more than friendship—toward the hated occupiers. That, of course, did not mean such things failed to happen. "You wouldn't know who she is, would you?"

Rokeby quickly shook his head. Silent curses echoed through McGregor's mind. Had he been too obvious? Perhaps not, for the postmaster answered, "Not sure anybody here in town does.

Whoever the gal is, don't expect it's something she'd want to brag on, you know what I mean?"

"That I do, Wilf," McGregor answered. Pretending he didn't know what Rokeby was talking about would have been an obvious lie, and so more dangerous than agreeing with him. The farmer picked up the stamps, folded them over themselves, and put them into an overcoat pocket. "Obliged to you. See you again next time I come to town, I expect."

"Take care of yourself," Rokeby said. "Take care of your family." Was that an oblique warning, of the sort Maude made? McGregor didn't know. He didn't worry about it, either. With a nod to the postmaster, he left the post office, went back to the wagon for the kerosene tin, and strode down the street to the general store.

Anyone who needed a storekeeper for a vaudeville show could hardly have done better than Henry Gibbon, who looked the part from bald head to leather apron over a belly that remained comfortable despite hard times. Storekeepers shared with farmers the ability to keep themselves fed no matter how hard times got.

"How are you today, Arthur?" Gibbon asked, the same wariness in his voice as had been in Rokeby's.

"Not too bad, not too good," McGregor said: a variation on the reply he'd given the postmaster. He set a couple of cents on the counter. "I'm going to raid your pickle barrel." Gibbon nodded and plucked up the little copper coins. McGregor lifted the lid, picked out a plump pickle, and took a bite. He chewed thoughtfully. "That's not bad, but it doesn't taste quite the same as the ones you usually have in there."

"Can't get those any more," Gibbon answered. "These here pickles, they come up out of Michigan. Like you say, they aren't bad."

McGregor stared at the pickle in his hand as if it had turned on him. He almost threw it down. But, even if it came from the United States, he'd already bought it, and he was a man who hated waste. He ate it and licked the last of the vinegar off his fingers.

"Didn't come to town just for pickles," Gibbon said. "Go on—tell me I'm wrong."

Before McGregor could tell him anything, a couple of soldiers in green-gray walked into the general store and looked around as if they owned the place. They were occupying this part of the province, so in effect they did. McGregor bought another pickle and diligently ate it, finding that preferable to having to talk to the Yanks. One soldier bought a spool of thread—Gibbon had a good-sized display of stuff that made a fair match for the U.S. uniform. His pal bought a tin-plated potato peeler. Out they went.

"You'll be rich, Henry," McGregor remarked.

"Oh, yeah," the storekeeper said. "I'm going to take this here and retire on it to the south of France—unless the damn Germans get there first. Now what can I do for you today?"

"Need some beans," McGregor answered, "and my kerosene ration, and white thread for Maude—she ain't got any uniforms to mend—and five yards of calico for her, too, and a new bobbin for the sewing machine."

"You've got to give me your ration coupon for the kerosene," Gibbon reminded him. "Never seen people like the Yanks for dotting every *i* and crossing every *t*. If you get the kerosene without I get the coupon, roof falls in on me, near as I can tell. Life's hard enough without that."

"Life's hard enough." McGregor said no more. "Here you are." He pulled the coupon out of his pocket and handed it to Gibbon. "Yanks sold it to me. They're willing to let me have lights in my house this month, long as I haven't got too many."

Chuckling, Gibbon got a funnel and a bucket and filled the kerosene tin from the barrel he kept not far from the ones that held pickles and crackers. "You sound a mite better these days."

"Maybe a mite," the farmer allowed. After a short pause, he went on, "That Hannebrink almost ran me over when I was coming round the corner to the post office. Things must be a mite better for him, too, or more than a mite: Wilf Rokeby said he was in a hurry to get down to Elsie Kravchuk's place and see how bad her bed linen's rumpled." Rokeby hadn't said any such thing. But if anyone in town knew where Major Hannebrink really was going, Henry Gibbon was the man.

And, sure enough, Gibbon looked disgusted. "That damn Rokeby. All I can say is, it's a good thing he ain't got a cold, on account of he'd blow out his brains if he was to bring a hanky up to his nose. It ain't Elsie that Hannebrink's laying pipe for, it's Paulette Tooker, three farms over."

"He seemed pretty sure," McGregor said doubtfully.

"Only holes Wilfred Rokeby knows a goddamn thing about

are the ones between his stamps," the storekeeper said. "Christ on His Cross, Arthur, when have you ever known Wilf to have his gossip straight?"

"Well, you're right about that," McGregor said. "Damn shame. I don't know the Tookers what you'd call well, but I never heard anything bad about Paulette till now. I'd still sooner believe it was Elsie. She hasn't been right since her husband went into the prisoner camp."

"Believe what you want." Gibbon's voice showed his indifference.

"What other gossip have you got?" McGregor asked. "Spin it out and let's see how much of it I believe." Gibbon was happy to oblige. He knew something scandalous about almost all the Canadians in town, about half the Canadians on the farms, and about maybe one American in three. Whether what he knew bore any relation to the truth was a different question.

When the storekeeper finally ran down like a phonograph that needed winding, McGregor went out, brought his wagon around to the front of the store, and loaded his purchases onto it. He was very quiet and thoughtful all the way home. When he was almost there, he smiled.

Dirt fountained up as U.S. artillery pounded a Confederate machine-gun position in front of Jonesboro, Arkansas. "That'll teach the goddamn sons of bitches," Ben Carlton said gleefully as the barrage went on and on.

"Don't blaspheme." Sergeant Gordon McSweeney had lost track of how many times he'd warned the company cook about that. Carlton was as stubborn in sin as he was in reproof.

"Blow 'em to hell and gone," Carlton said. McSweeney did not reprove that sentiment. He agreed with it. He expected Carlton would go to hell, too, but that had nothing to do with his hatred for the Confederates in their nest of sandbags and concrete. They were a good crew and they were brave and they had cost the U.S. troops across from them too many casualties.

At last, the guns fell silent. They'd been going on so long, McSweeney imagined he still heard them roaring for a few seconds after they'd quit. He didn't put his head up over the parapet to see what they'd done to that position. If they hadn't done enough, that was asking for a bullet in the face.

And they hadn't. Defiantly, cockily, the Confederate machine gunners squeezed off a few quick bursts to let their foes know they were still in business at the same old stand.

"Bastards," Ben Carlton snarled. "God damn those bastards to the hottest fire in hell for the next million years, and then think up somethin' really bad to happen to 'em."

"For the million years after that, they could eat your cooking every day," McSweeney said, "for you will surely go down to that place of eternal torment yourself unless you leave off taking the name of the Lord in vain every time you open your mouth."

Carlton glared at him. "Fine. I'm just tickled pink them brave, upstanding Confederate gentlemen lived through everything we flung at 'em. I'm dancin' in the daisies that they get the chance to blow off the tops of some more of our heads. There. You satisfied, Mr. Holier-than-Thou?"

"No," McSweeney said in a flat voice. "I am not satisfied. Bombardment by artillery is the wrong way to put a machine-gun nest out of action. You might as well try to kill a mosquito with a shotgun."

"When the mosquitoes start bitin' around here, we'll kill 'em any which way we can," Carlton said.

"You misunderstand," McSweeney said. Carlton smirked. McSweeney fixed him with a pale-eyed glare that made the smirk drip off his face. "Not only that, you misunderstand on purpose. If that isn't sinful, it is insubordinate. Shall we talk this over with Captain Schneider?"

Carlton visibly considered it. Whatever Schneider did to him was liable to be milder than what he'd get from McSweeney. Finally, he shook his head and ate crow. "No, Sarge. I'm sorry, Sarge."

He didn't sound sorry. McSweeney reluctantly decided not to press the point. He had other things on his mind anyhow. "Artillery, I tell you, is the wrong tool to use. I know the right tool."

His eyes blazed. That was metaphorical, not literal, but Ben Carlton followed his thoughts even so. "How in . . . blazes you going to get close enough to those Confederate . . . bums to toast 'em before they put about a belt's worth of bullets through you and your gaslight there?"

"It would have to be at night," McSweeney thought aloud. "It would have to be at night, and I would need a diversion."

"You need your head examined, that's what you need." Carlton went off down the trench line shaking his head.

McSweeney, on the other hand, went off and found his company commander. "Permission to stage a raid on the enemy's trenches tonight, sir?" he asked. Captain Schneider nodded. McSweeney saluted. Sometimes things were very easy to arrange.

But, to his annoyance, Schneider came up to the forwardmost trench while the men who would take part in the raid were scrambling over the parapet. The company commander frowned. "It's usual for raiders to take along an extra sack of grenades or two," he remarked.

"Yes, sir, so it is," McSweeney agreed. "We have them. You must have seen."

"I saw," Schneider said grimly. He pointed to McSweeney. "It is highly unusual, however, for a man to go on a trench raid festooned with a flamethrower."

"I suppose it may be, sir." When McSweeney shrugged, the heavy tank of jellied gasoline on his back dug into his kidneys. His voice sounded more innocent than it had any business being. "Of course, there aren't that many flamethrowers in action."

"There aren't that many people crazy enough to want to use the damned things, either," Schneider said. "What the hell have you got lurking at the back of your mind this time, Sergeant?"

"Sir, if we always do the same thing when we fight the Rebels, they'll catch on and lick us. If we do something different every now and again, that will keep them guessing," McSweeney answered. "If they're guessing, even the same old thing will work better, because they won't be looking for it so much."

Captain Schneider gave him a fishy stare. "If I'd wanted strategy, Sergeant, I'd have talked with the General Staff." He waited to see if that would squeeze any more details out of McSweeney. When it didn't, he grimaced. "Sergeant, if you go and get yourself killed, I shall be annoyed with you."

"I am in God's hands, sir," McSweeney said. "So long as He bears me up, I shall not fall. I do not believe He is ready to abandon me yet. May I go now? I don't want the rest of them to get too far ahead of me."

"And why is that?" Schneider asked. McSweeney stood mute. The captain raked him with a glance almost as hot as the flame that sprang from the nozzle of his flamethrower. When that failed to have any effect, Schneider said, "Go, then." He turned his back, as if, like Pilate, washing his hands of the whole affair.

McSweeney climbed the sandbag steps out of the trench,

scrambled over the parapet, and crawled toward the Confederate lines. He could hear, or thought he could hear, the rest of the raiders ahead. Their course swung a little to the right of being a straight line. His swung a little to the left.

Getting through his own wire was harder with the flame-thrower on his back. Being quiet was harder, too. The tank rattled on his shoulders and banged and clanked whenever it hit a rock. He wished he would have thought to wrap it in a blanket before he set out, but he hadn't, and it was too late.

He made his slow, cautious way toward that machine-gun position. As he crawled forward, he chuckled silently. He had plenty of new shell holes in which to conceal himself. That was an advantage, if a small one—the bombardment had revised the landscape so that it didn't look as familiar to the Confederate gunners as it would have before.

Rifle fire erupted, perhaps half a mile to the south: by the sound, the Confederates were raiding U.S. trenches there. Machine guns on both sides opened up. The position toward which McSweeney was advancing fired in the direction of the U.S. line. The muzzle flashes from the machine guns were stuttering bayonets of flame. Tracers scribed brief orange lines of death through the night.

None of those tracers was aimed in McSweeney's direction. He chuckled again as he scuttled forward. He'd sent out his party to keep the machine gunners from noticing his approach, and now the Rebs' own raiding party was doing part of the job for him.

Slithering under and through the Confederate wire was a longer and tougher piece of work than getting through the sorry entanglements in front of his lines had been. For one thing, the Confederates had a little more wire than his side did. For another, moving silently was much more important here than it had been when he was several hundred yards farther away.

He inched forward. The concrete blockhouse that held the firing slits for the Confederate machine guns was only a hundred yards off . . . fifty . . . thirty . . . twenty. He stopped. He could incinerate it from here, but this was not the moment. He wanted some chance of getting back to his own lines again. If God chose not to give him one . . . well, that was God's affair. Meanwhile, McSweeney would wait and hope and pray.

Off to his right, two grenades banged. Several others followed in short order. Rifles barked, Springfields and, with a slightly different note, Tredegars. Shouts erupted, and a high shrill scream that had to burst from the throat of a desperately wounded man.

Through the din, McSweeney heard the machine guns scrape against the rims of their firing slits as their crews traversed them. He heard the gunners curse his country. He shook his head. The Lord punished those who did such things. "And I am His instrument," he whispered.

The machine guns opened up. More screams rose. McSweeney hoped Confederates were doing all the screaming, but doubted that was so. He felt sorry that some of the raiders he'd sent out would be hurt or killed, but only so sorry. God had made the world so some things simply could not be done without loss.

He got to his feet, pointed the nozzle of the flamethrower in the direction of the firing slits, and pulled the trigger. The action, after he'd worked on it, was smooth as glass. Flaming gasoline leaped the gap. The machine guns fell silent. The men who had served them, though, screamed like damned souls.

McSweeney shook his head. Torments of this world were brief, not eternal, and Satan surely had fires hotter than any of mortal devising. The Scotsman dropped back into the shell hole. Bullets creased the air. Half a minute later, he rose again and gave the machine-gun nest another taste of the lash of fire.

Cartridges inside the blockhouse began cooking off. No more screams came from it; the men inside were already cooked. McSweeney dropped down once more. He thought about standing again for a third dose of flame, but in the end thought better of it. The Confederates were howling with fury. Bullets buzzed overhead, thick as bees. He wondered if the Rebs would come out of the trenches after him. They didn't. He smiled his alarming smile. Few men in his section would have been happy about going after a foe with a flamethrower, either.

He made his slow way back across no-man's-land to his own lines, commending his soul to God all the way. If a bullet chanced to strike the fuel tank on his back—if God willed that a bullet should strike the fuel tank on his back—he would learn what sort of death he dealt out to others.

God did not so will. He scrambled over the parapet and down into his own trenches. Hunting down Captain Schneider, he said, "Sir, I can report that that machine-gun position will not trouble us again for some time to come."

Schneider said nothing at all. He stood there in the dark,

shaking his head. Ben Carlton happened to be standing not far away. "Goddamn but you're a crazy son of a bitch, Sergeant," he declared.

"Don't blaspheme," McSweeney answered automatically, and then, when he really heard what the company cook had said, "Thank you."

Till his latest troubles started, Cincinnatus had never set foot in the Covington, Kentucky, city hall. Before the war started, a Negro in the CSA saw the inside of a city hall only if he was in some kind of trouble. Before the war, Cincinnatus had always stayed out of trouble. But he hadn't stayed out since, and now the Yankees were grilling him.

Actually, Luther Bliss wasn't quite a Yankee. He was the chief of the Kentucky State Police in the readmitted administration— head of the secret police, in other words. "Now, then, boy," he said in a mild voice, "tell me again how that Kennedy son of a bitch happened to get himself shot dead on your doorstep."

The only thing Cincinnatus had going for him was that the authorities didn't really know how much trouble he was in. "I tol' you an' tol' you, suh," he answered, sounding as stupid as he could, "I don't rightly know. I used to work fo' the man, is all."

A muscle in Bliss' right cheek jumped. A scar, as from a knife, cut that cheek, which made the tic more noticeable. "Lots of people used to work for the Rebel son of a bitch," he said, mildly still. "How come he chose *you*?" His eyes, a peculiar pale brown, were very intent.

"I ain't got a clue, suh," Cincinnatus said. "Could I please go back to workin' reg'lar again, suh? If I can't do my job on account o' you folks askin' me questions all the time, things git hard back home fo' my wife an' my little boy an' me."

Bliss steepled his fingers and leaned across the table toward him. "Now let's just talk about your job, shall we? Lieutenant Kennan gives you a good character from the days when you were working on the docks, and Lieutenant Kennan, I happen to know, doesn't hardly give niggers good characters a-tall." His own accent thickened. Was he trying to lull Cincinnatus into thinking him a fool?

If he was, he failed. Cincinnatus could tell how good at his job he was, stubborn as a hound and sneaky as a snake. "I worked hard for the man," Cincinnatus said. "I work hard every place I work."

"That's what Lieutenant Straubing says, too," Bliss agreed with a nod. "He says you work as hard as any man he ever saw. But he also says there've been a hell of a lot of fires and explosions in units his outfit has resupplied. You want to tell me about that?"

"Only thing I know is, a couple times last year the lieutenant said we should all keep an eye on each other on account of trouble like that," Cincinnatus said. "Don't know what ever came of it."

He did know they hadn't found the ingredients for the cigarshaped firebombs he'd got from Tom Kennedy. As soon as Straubing made worried noises about such things, he'd made sure not to keep them in or near his house. Had the U.S. authorities discovered them, Luther Bliss wouldn't be asking him questions now. He'd be taking him apart with a hacksaw and pliers and cutting torch.

Bliss kept tiptoeing around the edges of the truth: "Kennedy had a pal, storekeeper named Conroy. His place burned down last year, too—hell of a fire. Conroy hasn't been seen much since. Folks saw you goin' into that store."

"Yes, suh, I did that, every now and then," Cincinnatus said— no point denying something where the denial could be proved a lie. "It was on the way home from the riverside. But I didn't do it a lot—he had high prices, an' he didn't fancy black folks much."

"Black folks," Bliss said musingly. "It'll be different for niggers now that Kentucky's back in the USA. Not so hard like it was before."

"Hope so, suh," Cincinnatus said. The law probably would be different. But, from what he'd seen, most whites in the USA had little more use for Negroes than did most whites in the CSA. And he didn't see white Kentuckians changing their ways because a new flag flew over them.

Bliss clicked his tongue between his teeth. "Won't be illegal for niggers to be Socialists, even, long as they're peaceable about it." He paused. "Of course, niggers likely won't get to vote right away. It's not like this was New England or somewhere like that."

"No, suh," Cincinnatus said with a sigh. Black Kentuckians

wouldn't get to vote till a majority of white Kentuckians decided they should. Cincinnatus didn't plan on holding his breath.

He just hoped that oblique reference meant Luther Bliss was still tiptoeing around his connections with the Reds, too, and not seeing it plain. Bliss glared at him with those disconcerting eyes, as a coon dog might look at a raccoon it had treed in a crowded part of the woods, suddenly realizing the quarry might escape from tree to tree. The secret policeman looked intent. Cincinnatus didn't like his expression. He'd come up with something nasty.

Before he could ask it, the door to the room in which he was questioning Cincinnatus opened. Bliss whirled angrily. "Dammit, I said I wasn't to be disturbed in here," he said.

"Sir," said the man who'd bearded him in his den, "the president is outside, and he wants to talk with you."

Bliss' pale brown eyes widened. Before he could say anything, Theodore Roosevelt strode into the interrogation chamber. That made Cincinnatus' eyes go wide, too. "I don't have time for shilly-shallying and foolishness, Bliss," Roosevelt snapped. "We need to purge this state of Rebs."

"Get the trains, Mr. President," Bliss answered. "Get the trains and ship about two people out of three somewhere else, because that's the only way you're going to purge Kentucky. If we're lucky, we can keep most of the Rebs from raising too much Cain behind our lines till we've won the war. I think I can do that much. The other? Go talk to a preacher, because I'm not in the miracles game."

Cincinnatus knew a certain reluctant respect for Luther Bliss. Telling Teddy Roosevelt he couldn't have all he wanted seemed much the same as telling a tornado it couldn't go where it wanted. The president of the United States glared at Bliss, who looked back imperturbably.

Roosevelt seemed to respect him, too. "It will have to do," he said, "though I hate half measures." He paid attention to Cincinnatus for the first time. "What's this Negro here gone and done?"

Cincinnatus spoke for himself: "I haven't done anything, sir." Where he'd wanted to impress Bliss as being ignorant and shiftless, he wanted Roosevelt to see him as a bright, intelligent innocent wronged.

The only trouble with that stratagem was Bliss' noticing his shifting style. The secret policeman's hunting-dog eyes widened, just for a moment. To Roosevelt, he said, "Hard to say, your Excellency. Fugitive Confederate underground man named Kennedy got his head blown off on this boy's front porch. Cincinnatus here drove for Kennedy before the war. Been a fair number of suspicious fires clustered around him, too."

Thinking fast, Cincinnatus said, "Mr. President, sir, one of these suspicious fires he's talking about was to Conroy's general store. Mr. Bliss told me Conroy was one of Mr. Kennedy's friends. If I was workin' for Mr. Kennedy, why would I burn out one of his friends?"

"That strikes me as a fair question," Roosevelt said. "How about it, Bliss?"

Bliss had not an ounce of retreat in him. "Mr. President, we're also looking at his connections with the Reds."

"Have you found any?" Roosevelt demanded.

"Not yet," the secret policeman said stolidly.

"And I'm not a bit surprised, either," Roosevelt said. "How in the blue blazes do you expect a man to be simultaneously aiding the Confederate resistance and the Marxist resistance, when the Marxists came as close to overthrowing the CSA as we've managed ourselves?"

"Sir, this is Kentucky," Bliss said. "Everything's topsy-turvy here."

"Poppycock!" Roosevelt snorted. "Drivel! Things either make logical sense or they don't, and that's as true in Kentucky as it is in New Hampshire. If you're trying to make out that this Negro is a Reb and a Red at the same time, and if you haven't got any solid evidence he's either one, I suggest—no, I don't suggest, I order—that you let him go on about his lawful occasions."

It wasn't poppycock. It wasn't drivel. Cincinnatus knew it wasn't poppycock or drivel. So did Luther Bliss, who, being a Kentuckian, understood his home state better than Theodore Roosevelt could ever hope to do. But the president of the United States had just given Bliss a direct order. With a sigh, he said, "All right, Cincinnatus, you are free to go. You keep your nose clean and you won't have any more trouble from me."

"Thank you kindly, suh." Cincinnatus didn't think Bliss meant that, but he had said it and could be reminded of it at need. "Suh, could you give me a letter to Lieutenant Straubing, to let him know I'm in the clear so as I can go back to makin' an honest livin'?"

Bliss plainly didn't want to, but had no choice. "I'll see to it," he said.

"Back pay!" Roosevelt exploded, so vehemently, Cincinnatus jumped. "Pay for all the days this man has not been able to work. What's your daily rate, Cincinnatus?"

"Two and a half dollars, sir," Cincinnatus answered.

"If that's all you make, and you've missed considerable work because of this folderol, you must be feeling the pinch," Roosevelt said. "Bliss, pay this man one hundred dollars, and pay it out of your own pocket, for harassing someone who's done nothing wrong."

Cincinnatus expected the chief of the Kentucky State Police to do some exploding of his own at that, but Bliss, after another moment of surprise, nodded. He said, "I'll have that and the letter ready for him when he goes. Now if we can send him out so we can talk about a couple of things without him listening—"

To Cincinnatus' disappointment, Roosevelt didn't object to that. A couple of hard-faced guards led Cincinnatus away and put him in what had probably been a small meeting room before the war but now served as a holding cell. They didn't do anything but sit him down. He knew how easily that might have been otherwise.

He waited for what had to be a couple of hours. He wondered what Roosevelt and Luther Bliss were talking about. He wondered if Bliss would wait till Roosevelt was gone and then go back to sweating him. Finally, a guard said, "Come along, you," and led him out to the city-hall steps.

There stood Luther Bliss. "Here's your letter," he said. Cincinnatus checked it. It was what it was supposed to be. "And here's your money." Bliss took his wallet from his hip pocket and peeled off five twenty-dollar bills. Only after Cincinnatus had the money in his own pocket did he wonder who was watching and why they thought he was getting it. And only after that did he realize how clever and dangerous Luther Bliss really was.

V

Flora Hamburger wished she were somewhere, anywhere, else than at Theodore Roosevelt's second inauguration. She wished, most particularly, that she were at the inauguration of President Eugene V. Debs. But Socialist Senator Eugene V. Debs of Indiana felt no qualms about attending the inauguration of the man who had defeated him, so Flora supposed she could get through it, too.

The ceremony was held in an enormous briefing room in one of the many War Department buildings that sprawled through downtown Philadelphia. In a normal year, it would have been outdoors. (In a normal year, of course, it would have been in Washington, D.C., but that was another story.) To keep Confederate bombers from disrupting it now, it was not only indoors but also secret; Flora had found out where to come only the day before.

Someone tapped her on the shoulder. She turned. Sitting behind her was Hosea Blackford of Dakota. "Tell me what kind of bargain we can make to get your vote on that immigration bill," he said.

She shook her head. "Ask me something else. Half the people in my district have relatives in Europe, and that bill would strand them there forever. If I vote for it, they'll throw me out, and I'll deserve it."

He frowned. "The party leadership backs it, you know."

"The party leadership backed the war, too, right from the start," Flora answered. "Were they right then?" Before Blackford could say anything, she waved him to silence. "Here come the president and the chief justice." She smiled down at the floor. Here she was, glad to see Theodore Roosevelt after all.

He wore cutaway, white tie, top hat, and gloves: all the trappings of capitalist power. With him strode Chief Justice Oliver Wendell Holmes, his big fierce white mustache a fitting ornament for his proud hawk face. Holmes was only a few days away from his seventy-fifth birthday, but moved like a much younger man. He was, without a doubt, a class enemy; reckoning him an honest man, Flora granted him grudging admiration for that.

He and Roosevelt took their places behind a podium more often used to let officers know the upcoming plan of attack. After Vice President Kennan took the oath for his second term, Roosevelt did the same in a loud, firm voice.

Once the applause had died down, Justice Holmes stepped away from the podium. President Roosevelt stared out over it at the senators and representatives and other assembled dignitaries. The electric lights flashed off the lenses of his spectacles, giving his face a curiously mechanical appearance, as if a device had taken almost human form and were running the United States.

"Without the fighting edge," he said, "no man and no nation can be really great, for in the really great man, as in the really great nation, there must be both the heart of gold and the temper of steel." His gestures were stiff, adding to the industrial impression those blank, shining disks that seemed to replace his eyes created.

"In 1862 England and France said it was the duty of those two nations to mediate between the United States and the Confederate States, and they asserted that any Americans who in such event refused to accept their mediation and to stop the war would thereby show themselves the enemies of peace.

"Even Abraham Lincoln regarded this as an unfriendly act to the United States, but he had not the strength to withstand it. And in so regarding it, as in few other things, Lincoln was right. Looking back from a distance of more than fifty years, we can clearly see as much. Such mediation *was* a hostile act, not only to the United States but to humanity. The nations that forced that unrighteous peace upon us more than fifty years ago were the enemies of mankind.

"Very many of the men and women who are at times misled into demanding peace, as if it were itself an end instead of being a means of righteousness, are folk of good will and sound intelligence who need only seriously to consider the facts, and who can then be trusted to think aright and act aright. Well-meaning folk who always clamor for peace without regard as to whether peace brings justice or injustice should ponder such facts, and then should still their clamor."

Ponder the facts, and then think my way, Flora thought scornfully. President Roosevelt pounded on: "England and France and the cuckoo's egg they planted in the American nest of freedom humiliated our great nation again a generation later, and have sought to encircle us on our own continent ever since, just as they and the Russian tyrants have sought to encircle our partner, friend, and ally, the German Empire, on the European continent.

"They have tried. And they have failed." Roosevelt could not go on then; thunderous applause interrupted him. He basked in it before raising his hands to ask for quiet. "I promise you this: my second term will show us the victory we have longed for since those now old were young. The debt we owe is old, too, and has accumulated much interest through the years. We shall repay it in full, and more besides." More applause echoed from the ceiling of the briefing room.

"We must stand absolutely for the righteousness of revenge," Roosevelt finished, "and we must remember that to do so would have been utterly without avail if we had not possessed the strength and tenacity of spirit which back righteousness with deeds and not mere words. Until we complete our vengeance, we must keep ourselves ready, high of heart and undaunted of soul, to back our rights with our strength."

He stepped back from the podium. The torrent of applause that rose up made everything that had gone before seem like a whisper in a distant room. Flora Hamburger joined in the applause, though tepidly and for politeness' sake. She looked around and saw that most of her fellow Socialists and the handful of Republicans still in Congress were doing the same. It mattered little. The Democratic majority made plenty of noise on their own.

Roosevelt took his time leaving the hall. He paused in the aisles to chat with soldiers and politicians and functionaries who came crowding up to him, eager to be recognized. Flora's lip curled at their fawning sycophancy . . . till she saw Senator Debs talking amiably with the president. The cooperation she'd already seen between Socialists and Democrats in Congress had surprised her. This shook her. It was as if a long-familiar picture, turned upside down, yielded another image altogether.

Then Roosevelt caught sight of her. She was easy to spot. The audience held only a handful of women, and she was the youngest by at least fifteen years. The president smiled in her direction. "Miss Hamburger!" he called, and beckoned her to him.

She could either go or, staying in her place, seem rude. What ran through her mind as she approached Theodore Roosevelt was, *My parents will never believe I'm talking with the president of the United States.* She might not share his politics, but the USA had never yet had a Socialist chief executive. "I'm honored to meet you, Mr. President," she said, *honored* being true because of his office where *pleased* would have stretched a point.

"And I am honored to meet you, Miss Hamburger—Congresswoman Hamburger, I should say," Roosevelt answered, and surprised her by sounding as if he meant it. "You showed great pluck in the campaign that won you your seat; I followed it with interest and no little admiration. And, by all accounts, you seem to be shaping well in the House."

"Thank you, Mr. President," she said. "You surprise me, since I am not of your party and"—she couldn't resist the jab—"I don't see much point to this war, even if I know a good many of the facts about it."

He surprised her again by not getting angry. "The point is that winning it will at last let our country take its rightful place in the sun, a place wrongly denied us since the War of Secession."

"My question is, what price do we pay for our place in the sun?" Flora replied. "How many young men will never see that place in the sun, some because they are blind, most because they are dead? How many young working men will die so the capitalists who own the steel mills and the coal mines and the weapons plants can buy new mansions, new motorcars, new yachts with the profits they make selling munitions to the government?"

Now Roosevelt frowned, but still did not explode. "If the capitalists can afford new toys after the war tax we've slapped on 'em, they've got better bookkeepers and lawyers than I think they do. You have a fine stump speech there, Congresswoman, and I think you are sincere in it, but it doesn't altogether match the way the world works. A pleasure to meet you, as I said. If you'll excuse me—" He shook someone else's hand.

Flora found herself more impressed with him than she'd

thought she would be. Part of that was the office he held. Part of it was realizing that what she had taken for political bombast were in fact his true beliefs. And part was the force with which he expressed those beliefs, a force mocked in her own party but, she discovered, not one to be taken lightly.

Hosea Blackford came up to her in Roosevelt's wake. His expression was somewhere between amused and curious. "Well, what do you think of the earthquake that walks like a man now that you've met him in the flesh?" the congressman from Dakota asked.

"He's—formidable," Flora answered. "He's easy to caricature, but I have the idea that taking the caricature for the man would be a mistake."

"A dangerous mistake," Blackford agreed. "Roosevelt has made a lot of people pay for doing that. When he goes charging straight at something, he seems to have no more brains than a bull moose, but anyone who thinks they aren't hiding behind that smirk ends up regretting it."

Flora sighed. "He does argue better than I thought he would."

"He met Lincoln during the Second Mexican War, I gather, the same as I did," Blackford answered. "They quarreled, so he was less impressed than I was."

"There's only one kind of person Roosevelt doesn't quarrel with, as far as I can see," Flora said. The congressman from Dakota raised a questioning eyebrow. She explained: "Someone who already agrees with every word he says."

Hosea Blackford laughed. "You *are* dangerous, aren't you? Did you get your invitation to the inaugural ball at the Powel House?"

She nodded. "Yes, I did. I hate to admit it, but I thought the president was generous to invite the whole Congress to his residence, Socialists and Republicans along with the Democrats."

"Stinginess isn't one of Teddy's besetting sins," Blackford said. "He has enough besides that. Are you going?"

"I was thinking of it, yes," Flora said. Only weeks out of the Lower East Side, she knew her fascination with the glamour she was encountering was un-Socialist, but she couldn't help it. "Are you?"

"Oh, no, and I wish you wouldn't, either," he said. Alarm stabbed through her: was she committing some dreadful *faux pas*? Stone-faced as a judge, he went on, "The Socialists should boycott it. That way, if the Confederate bombers get through and level the place, we'll be ready and waiting to take over the government."

She stared at him, then laughed so loud, Roosevelt looked back over his shoulder to see what was funny. "Let me ask you again," she said, her voice dangerous: "Are you going to the inaugural ball?" A little sheepishly, Blackford nodded. So did Flora, with the air of having won a victory. "Good. As I said, so am I. I'll see you there."

Sergeant Jake Featherston sat on an upended barrel of flour atop Round Hill, Virginia. He'd bought a Gray Eagle scratchpad in the Round Hill general store, and his pencil scraped over the paper. He knew he wasn't the best writer ever born, or anything close to it. He didn't care. So many things he hadn't been able to say to anybody—so many things he had said that nobody would hear. If he got them down, he would, at least, be able to prove he'd been right all along.

"Got any makings, Sarge?" Michael Scott called as he walked up to Featherston. "My pouch is empty as Teddy Roosevelt's head."

"Yeah, I got some," Jake answered. Before he pulled his own leather tobacco pouch out of a pocket, he slammed the notebook shut and put a hand over the cover. What was in there was *his*, no one else's. Only after he'd made sure it was safe did he toss Scott the pouch.

"Thanks," the loader said, and rolled himself a cigarette. He gave the tobacco back to Featherston. "You been writin' up a storm there, past couple days." He lit a match. His cheeks hollowed as he sucked in smoke.

"Somethin' to pass the time," Featherston said uncomfortably. It was much more than that to him, but he wouldn't admit as much, not to Scott, not to anybody else, barely to himself. He wondered how he'd managed to get through so much of the war without trying it before. If he'd gone much longer without setting down what he thought, what he felt, he was sure he'd have gone crazy.

Scott didn't seem to notice anything out of the ordinary, which eased Jake's mind. "Yeah, we've had some time to pass lately," Scott said, taking another drag on the handmade cigarette. "Yankees got down here into Virginia, and they haven't done a whole hell of a lot since."

"I know it." That didn't make Featherston any happier, though. Nothing made Featherston very happy these days. Every silver lining had its cloud. "Last time they were quiet like this, back in Pennsylvania, they were building for the push that threw us back to where we're at now. If they hit us another lick like that one there, where the hell will we end up?"

"I don't reckon it's that bad, Sarge," Scott said. "Remember how you were all up in arms about the niggers going into line in front of us? They haven't done so bad, and the damnyankees haven't exactly given 'em a big kiss on the cheek to say good morning, neither."

"Rifles," Jake said scornfully, and then, a little less so, "Well, hell, all right, machine guns, too. But they ain't seen real artillery, and they ain't seen gas, and they ain't seen barrels. Till they do, God damn me to hell if I think they'll make anything like proper soldiers."

"You're a stubborn cuss, Sarge," the loader said with a laugh.

"Bet your ass I am," Featherston said. "If I wasn't, I'd have given up long since. But I pay all my bills, and I got a hell of a lot of bills to pay."

"Uh-huh." Scott took a last drag on the cigarette, threw it down, and crushed the butt under his heel. He headed off, perhaps a little faster than he had to.

Featherston sighed with relief to see him go. He opened the tablet and began to write again: —*officers are fools because they won't see what's in front of their faces. The country doesn't need officers like that, but what other kind has it got? They can't see that the n—*

"Featherston." The voice was sharp and precise, so much so that it almost seemed a Yankee voice. Jake jumped and slammed the tablet shut.

He whirled, jumped to his feet, and saluted. "Major Potter, sir!" he said. "I'm sorry, sir. I didn't hear you come up." He would have had to show respect for any officer. He actually felt some for Clarence Potter.

"At ease, Sergeant," the bespectacled major from Intelligence said. He pointed north, toward the U.S. lines, the lines that still bubbled and seethed like a pot boiling atop a stove but that, to

Featherston's surprise, had not yet boiled over. "What do you make of the quiet?"

"Funny you should ask, sir," Jake said. "My loader and I were just talking about that very same thing. Last time they were this quiet this long was before they hit us that first big lick up in Pennsylvania."

"So it was." Potter rubbed his chin. "That's very well reasoned— reasoned like an officer, I would say, if I didn't think it'd make you pick up that barrel and break it over my head."

"Sir, I reckon your head is harder than this barrel ever dreamed of being," Featherston answered, intending it as a compliment. "Reckon your head is as hard as one of the damn-yankees' iron barrels with treads."

"Heh," Potter said. "No, those really hard heads are the ones down in the War Department in Richmond. It'd take about an eight-inch gun, maybe a twelve-inch, to blow a hole through one of them and let in some light."

"Yes, sir," Jake said. One of the reasons he thought Potter superior to the general run of officer in the Army of Northern Virginia was the boundless contempt they shared for the hidebound aristocrats who held so many important posts in Richmond.

Potter said, "Now that the colored troops have been in the line for a bit, what do you think of them?"

"Don't like 'em for hell," Featherston said promptly. "Not for hell. They're in the line, yeah, but what happens when they really get hit? We haven't seen it yet. Like I told Scott, I'll believe they can stand it when I see 'em do it."

Potter's jaws worked as if he were chewing tobacco, but he didn't have a plug in one cheek. "Here's another question for you, then, Sergeant—which would you rather have in front of you, those full colored units or white units somewhere between a quarter and half strength? Those are your choices. We've squeezed out about all the white manpower in the CSA there is to squeeze."

"I don't know the answer to that," Jake said. "I just don't know. I have a notion of what understrength white units can do. These niggers—who can guess? Might be better. Might be a hell of a lot worse."

In musing tones, Major Potter said, "Some white units without the proper experience will break and run the first time they come under truly heavy fire, or the first time they have to face barrels. If the black soldiers don't perform as well as veteran troops, you need to remember it may be because they're raw, not because they're black."

"Yes, sir, I understand what you're telling me," Featherston said. "But then again, it may be because they're niggers, too. Hell of a choice we've got, ain't it, sir? We can lose the war without 'em, or we can put 'em in the line and pray to Jesus they don't turn their guns on us or go over to the damnyankees in droves."

Fussily neat, Potter took out a clasp knife and scraped dirt from under a thumbnail. He said, "You know, the United States have a holiday called Remembrance Day coming up next month. They've been keeping a list of everything we've done to them since we fired on Fort Sumter to start the War of Secession. By now, it's a long list. If they do lick us, they're going to pay it all back and make us start a list of our own."

"You're saying they'd better not lick us," Jake said slowly.

"We won't be happy if they do," Clarence Potter agreed. Behind his spectacles, his eyes missed very little. He pointed to Featherston's Gray Eagle notebook. "Are you keeping a list of your own, Sergeant?"

Jake's ears got hot. He was indeed keeping a list of his own. If anyone besides him saw it, he'd be lucky to escape hard labor. If Major Potter asked—or demanded—to see it, he didn't know what he'd do. Keeping his voice as light as he could, he answered, "Maybe I'll do me up a book once the war is over. *Over Open Sights,* I'll call it, or somethin' like that. What do you think, sir?"

"Better be a good book," Potter said. "They'll be a drug on the market when the fighting's done—provided anyone's left alive to read them." He had on a tin hat, and tipped it as if it were a real felt derby. "Good morning to you, Sergeant." On down toward the front he went, a businesslike man who might have been a businessman were it not for his helmet and puttees.

Featherston let out a silent sigh of relief. He'd got away with not having to show what he was writing. Not only that, he'd found a title for what he was setting down in the tablet. OVER OPEN SIGHTS, he printed above the writing on the first page.

He wished he had the War Department over open sights, close enough to blast them all without even having to bother reading the range. He wished he had the Negro troops in front of him over open sights, too. He scowled. If they did run like rabbits, the way he figured they were likely to do, he would have them over open sights. He'd blast them, too.

The only trouble was, that would be too late.

Something buzzed like an early mosquito, but the sound came from farther away than a mosquito's infernal whine. Jake looked up. Tiny as a mosquito in the sky, an aeroplane sauntered along above the defensive line of the Army of Northern Virginia. Featherston knew what that meant: the damnyankees were taking photographs. When they had all they wanted, when everything was set up the way they wanted, hell would break loose.

No Confederate aeroplanes rose to challenge the Yankee spy. Belatedly, antiaircraft guns over toward Purcellville, east of Round Hill, opened up on the intruder. The hammering of the guns—the only cannon in the Confederate arsenal that were quicker-firing than the three-inchers Jake served—shattered the quiet of the late-winter morning.

Puffs of smoke, round and black as iron soup pots, flecked the sky like smallpox scars on the face of an unvaccinated man. The observation aeroplane flew through them, straight as if it were on rails. From his own observations, Jake knew what that meant: the photographer was taking his pictures.

He knew the exact instant when the photographer was through taking pictures, too. At that instant, the aeroplane stopped behaving like a locomotive on rails and started acting like a staggering drunk, lurching every which way through the air to throw off the aim of the gunners on the ground.

Wearily, Featherston cursed as the U.S. observation aeroplane escaped. He'd seen too many others escape to be more than a little disgusted. His sole consolation was that the Yankees had every bit as much trouble hitting C.S. observation aeroplanes.

As if the aeroplane's getaway were some kind of signal, firing from the U.S. trenches, which had been very light, suddenly picked up. Rifles and machine guns hammered away. And then, as Jake was about to call his men to ready themselves for the Yankee onslaught, the small-arms fire slackened again. He let out a sigh of relief and went back to filling pages of the Gray Eagle tablet.

Leading a charging column of barrels would have been more impressive if Lieutenant Colonel Irving Morrell could have seen the column he was leading. He could see next to nothing. The louvered vision slits were shut as tight as they could be and still let any light at all into the interior of the barrel. Had they been open any wider, they would have let in bullets along with the light.

Morrell kept wondering if he'd died and gone to hell. The reek wasn't of fire and brimstone; it was fire and automotive exhaust, which struck him as a reasonable approximation. The two roaring truck engines in the compartment below let out enough bellows and screams and groans for an entire regiment of lost souls. It was hot as hell in the barrel, too. This was March. What the inside of the barrel would be like on a muggy August afternoon was something Morrell did his best not to contemplate.

Nor was he alone, or even close to alone, in his mechanical damnation. Along with the driver and the two engineers who labored to keep the hot metal parts working as they should, he had for company the dozen machine gunners and the two artillerymen at the nose cannon: an apartment building's worth of people jammed into an ugly metal box half the size of a small flat.

He peered ahead. He stuck his nose too close to the louvers, and tried to flatten it against them when the barrel lurched over the scarred and battered ground. He clutched the wounded member, which, fortunately, was neither bleeding nor broken.

He peered again, as closely as before. If his nose got smashed again, it got smashed, that was all. Peering was rewarded. "Shell hole!" he screamed. "Big shell hole! Steer right!"

What with the din of the two engines and the rattle and clanks of the tracks and all the other ancillary racket inside the barrel, the driver never heard him. He cursed himself for an idiot; he'd found out, the very first time he got into a barrel, that nobody could hear anything inside.

He remembered to use hand signals just as the barrel nosed down into the crater. The driver shifted to his lowest gear. The engines screamed even louder than they had before. Morrell wondered if the barrel's pointed nose would get stuck in the dirt at the bottom of the shell hole. That was its worst disadvantage when set against its British and Confederate counterparts, which were tracked around their entire rhomboidal hulls: those babies could climb out of anything, and a U.S. barrel couldn't, quite.

This particular U.S. barrel, though, could and did climb out of this particular shell hole. Beyond it stood a fat man waving a large blue flag. Morrell held up his right hand, palm out, to the driver. Obediently, the man hit the brakes, took the barrel out of gear, and turned off the motors. Everyone inside the steel hull who could reach the handle of an escape hatch opened it, to let in air and light—and the rumble of other barrels behind Morrell.

One by one, the rest of the machines in the column also halted. Hatches and louvers also came open on them. More than a few started disgorging their crews, as the men seized the first chance they got to escape.

Irving Morrell wasted very little time in getting out of his barrel, either. He clambered down to the ground. The fat man stabbed the flagpole into the ground. "That wasn't so bad," he said. "Looked like the end of the world, coming straight at me." He stuck a finger in one ear. "Sounded that way, too."

"You had a better view of it than I did, Major Dowling," Morrell answered. He outranked General Custer's adjutant, but treated him as he would have treated a superior officer. His oak leaves might have been silver while Dowling's were gold, but the major more than made up in influence what he lacked in rank. Morrell went on, "It's noisier inside a barrel than outside, though. Far as I can tell, it's noisier inside a barrel than anywhere."

"Yes, I think so, too," Dowling said. "Astounding experience, riding in one of those damn things. Appalling experience, too." He looked over his shoulder. "Here comes the general. Let's see what he thought of the exercise."

Lieutenant General Custer picked his way through the mud with slow, mincing steps. He wore fancy black cavalry boots, and plainly didn't want to get them dirty. With him came Colonel Ned Sherrard. Sherrard had served for a good while on the General Staff, and General Staff officers were notorious among their counterparts in the field for their aversion to filth. But Sherrard looked to be turning into a real, live field soldier himself, for he took no more notice of the chewed-up terrain than he might have if he'd been in the field since 1914.

"Bully!" Custer said. "This column—or rather, an even grander column than this—will simply pulverize the defenses the Confederates have in front of Nashville. When they do, the infantry goes forward, sweeps up what the barrels have broken loose, and we have ourselves a breakthrough."

"Yes, sir," Morrell said. "I think that's exactly what will happen. I want to be at the sharp end of the wedge."

"I think we'll break through, too," Sherrard said. "I really and truly do." He sounded surprised at himself, as if still unsure how Custer had managed to seduce him away from the doctrine he himself had helped formulate.

"And once the barrels have broken the way," Custer went on, "we can also send in the cavalry, to complete the enemy's demoralization and sweep up his shattered, flying remnants."

Morrell, Dowling, and Sherrard looked at one another. None of them said a word. Every army east of the Mississippi had a division or two of cavalry based a little behind the front, waiting to exploit a breakthrough. The few times the horsemen got into action, they and their mounts died in droves. They were up above the level of the trenches, and their horses made big targets. Morrell didn't think that would be any different even after the barrels went in.

By the looks on their faces, neither did Sherrard nor Dowling. Under his breath, Dowling said, "That'll be a fine plan—when they invent a bulletproof horse."

"They did," Morrell murmured, also *sotto voce*. "It's called a barrel."

"What's that?" Custer said. "What's that? Speak up, dammit. People around me are always mumbling."

"Sorry, sir," Morrell said. Custer wasn't deaf as a post, but he didn't hear all that well, either, so nothing sounded loud to him. Moreover, Morrell got the idea that people needed to mumble around Custer, to make horrified comments about the outrageous things he said.

Stubborn old fool, Morrell thought. A man like that commonly found himself plowing ahead with bad ideas because, having got them, he was too pigheaded to give them up. Now, for once, Custer had got a good idea—one that fit in with the aggressive way he thought generally. He was too pigheaded to give that one up, too, but he also wanted to hang some of his bad ideas on it.

Major Dowling said, "Sir, of course we will have the cavalry in place, ready to take advantage of whatever opportunities arise for using it."

"Of course we will," Custer said. "Pity so many men these days carry the carbine instead of the saber. I put the saber to good use in the War of Secession. 'Go in, Wolverines!' " he called reminiscently. " 'Give 'em hell!' And we did."

"But, sir, weren't you carrying a carbine yourself during the Second Mexican War?" Dowling asked.

"Well, yes," Custer admitted with a frown. "Even so, gleaming steel terrifies in a way that bullets can't match."

Morrell studied Dowling in open admiration. Custer's adjutant was plainly very good at guiding the general commanding First Army away from courses that held no profit (to say nothing of guiding him out of the nineteenth century) and toward things that needed doing or needed doing in a particular way. Morrell commonly dealt with superior officers who proved difficult by ignoring them as much as he could. Learning other ways of handling the problem could be useful.

"When do we move, sir?" Morrell asked. He was aggressive, too, and wanted to lead the barrels into battle.

"Ground's still damper than I'd like," Colonel Sherrard said. "We'll lose a lot fewer machines to bogging if we wait till the countryside dries out a bit more. That could matter."

"We'll have to move in more artillery support, too," Dowling added. "That will also get easier as the roads dry out."

"From what I've seen up in Philadelphia, the bombardments that go on for a week or so don't do as much good as everyone thought they would when we started using them," Morrell said. "The Rebs dig in like moles, and the shelling only shows right where we're headed."

"They've come up with something new," Sherrard said. "It's particularly good against enemy artillery. You give them an opening barrage of phosgene gas shells, make them put on their gas helmets. Hell of a lot of fun to try and serve a piece in a gas helmet, you know."

"They've been harassing gunners like that as long as we've had gas shells," Morrell said.

"I know," Ned Sherrard said. "But they've got a new wrinkle on it. After that first round of phosgene, they saturate the area with puke-gas shells; the antigas cartridges that protect against phosgene don't do a thing to stop it. Then, when the Reb gunners yank off their helmets so they can heave, they hit 'em with another phosgene barrage."

Morrell considered. Having considered, he said, "That's . . . devilish, sir. Whoever thought of it was probably the Marquis de Sade's cousin." He paused. "It's also going to tie the Rebs into knots."

"And, a day and a half later, it'll give your artillery fits, because the Rebs will do it to us, too," Abner Dowling said. "That's the way this war has gone, right from the start."

"I don't think we'll be able to move till next month," Sherrard said. "When we do, we'd better hit hard."

"That's true," Dowling agreed. "If we don't break through this time, we'll never get another chance. Everyone will be watching how we do. Teddy Roosevelt said as much. If we don't measure up—" He pointed a thumb at the ground, a gesture straight from a Roman amphitheater.

"We'll smash them." Custer sounded sublimely confident. Had his performance matched his confidence, he would have been in front of Mobile, not Nashville. But confidence was never wasted. "On Remembrance Day, if the weather is good, we'll smash them."

"On Remembrance Day," Morrell repeated. Major Dowling and Colonel Sherrard both nodded. Morrell said it again, softly: "On Remembrance Day."

Nellie Semphroch had seldom felt more out of place than she did on dismounting from a hired carriage in front of St. John's Church. Looking south across Lafayette Square, she could see the White House, still battered and sad-looking from the shell hits it had taken when the Confederate States captured the capital of the USA. Presidents worshiped at St. John's; it was not normally for the likes of her. But these were not normal times.

She turned to Hal Jacobs, who sat beside her on the seat behind the driver. "Well, here we are," she said.

"Let us make the best of it, then," he answered. He looked like what he was: a dignified man without a great deal of wealth. His somber black suit, black derby, and wing collar with four-in-hand tie were correct enough for a wedding, but in no way stylish. Smiling at Nellie, he said, "You look lovely today—but then, I think that of you every day."

"Foosh," she said; his compliments never failed to make her nervous. She ran her hands down the pleated skirt of her peach silk dress.

"Edna was very kind to ask that I be the one to give her away," Jacobs said. "I know it is only because she has no men who are close kin, but it was very kind."

"So it was," Nellie said, and hoped the subject would drop—with a thud. She knew why Edna had asked the favor of Hal Jacobs: her daughter was doing some heavy-handed match-making. She also knew Jacobs had accepted not least for the spying he could do among the Confederate officers who made up the bulk of the wedding party.

They stood around in front of the white-painted church, their dress butternut uniforms shining with gold braid, their kepis almost as fancy as those French officers would wear, many of them with ceremonial swords belted on their hips. As the driver handed Nellie down from the chariot, she listened to them chatting about the war. No doubt Hal Jacobs was listening, too—intently.

But, as he offered her his arm and she, despite misgivings, had to accept or be rude in public, she knew the chance to spy was not the only reason he'd so readily accepted Edna's invitation. He was glad of her matchmaking; he wanted a match with Nellie.

No one seemed to care what Nellie herself thought. Nellie could not remember the last time anyone had cared what she thought.

As if to prove that, here came Lieutenant Nicholas H. Kincaid, his uniform as gaudy as a lieutenant's could be, the creases sharp as razors. "Good morning, ma'am," he said, beaming at her. "Isn't it a lovely day?"

"It will do," she answered. If he'd cared what she thought, he would have let her daughter alone. All he cared about, though, was stretching Edna out naked on a bed. He was a man. What point to expecting anything else of him?

He turned to Hal Jacobs. "Sir, when you give her away, you can be sure I'll take her, and you can be sure I'll take good care of her, too."

"That is very good, Lieutenant," Jacobs said. "That is as it should be."

Kincaid pointed into the church. "They must have put Edna inside somewhere when she got here a couple of minutes ago. My pals hustled me off, though, so I don't know for certain: bad luck to see the bride before the wedding, you know."

"Yes," Nellie said. Shabby Washingtonians—and, except for collaborators, there was no other kind of Washingtonians—walking by paused to stare at the wedding party. The Rebs could have public gaiety in the middle of the war. For anyone else, it was a distant memory.

"I hope everything goes as it should," Jacobs said in his deliberate way. "I hope everything goes very well."

"Yes." Nellie sounded abstracted. One of those shabby Washingtonians on the other side of H Street . . . She lowered her voice to the next thing to a whisper: "Mr. Jacobs—Hal. Is that Bill Reach over there?"

"Why—" Jacobs raised his bushy eyebrows. "Why, I believe it is. What can he be doing here? I must go over and—"

Now Nellie took hold of his arm with great firmness. "You must do nothing of the sort. What you must do is come in with me and help me marry my fool of a daughter to this great Rebel oaf she's chosen. If you do anything else"—she played what she devoutly hoped was a trump—"I'll never speak to you again."

"But, Nellie—" He also spoke in low tones, and in a voice full of anguish. "Our beloved country relies upon—"

"It does no such thing," Nellie broke in. "That skunk hasn't had anything to do with you for months, and our beloved country is doing just fine. The war's going better than it has since it started. And if that Reach . . . person makes trouble," she added, "I will kill him."

Still feebly protesting, Jacobs let himself be led into the church. Edna, dressed and veiled in white (*white she doesn't deserve,* Nellie thought, forgetting she'd worn white on her wedding day after a past far more maculate than her daughter's), sat in a waiting room. Behind the veil, her expression was the one the Confederate General Staff would have worn had the Army of Northern Virginia captured Philadelphia.

Grudgingly, trying for peace with her daughter, Nellie said, "I do hope it turns out well, Edna."

"Of course it will, Ma," Edna said with the unselfconscious confidence of youth. "We'll live happily ever after, just like in the fairy tales."

Nellie burst out laughing. She was sorry the moment she did it, but by then it was too late. Edna glared at her in fury burning as vitriol. And then, bless him, Hal Jacobs started laughing, too. He said, "I beg your pardon, Miss Edna, truly I do, but it is not so simple. I wish it were. My own life would have been much easier, believe me."

"We'll do it," Edna said. "You wait and see. We will."

Jacobs did not argue with her. Neither did Nellie. What was the use? If Edna didn't know a human being couldn't go through life without sorrow and anger and fear and boredom and jealousy and bitterness—if she didn't know that, she would find out.

"It's gonna be fine, Ma," Edna said. "Isn't everybody gorgeous out there? What would Pa think if he could see it?"

He'd think you were marrying a damned Rebel. But Nellie didn't say that, either. Again, what point? The die was cast here. "He'd think it was quite a show, so he would," she answered.

"I hope it is a show that goes well," Hal Jacobs said. Nellie looked at him sharply. He knew something. She didn't know what, but he knew something. Before she could find a way to ask him what it was, the organist began to play. The lower notes seemed to resound deep within her; she felt them in her bones rather than hearing them.

Edna got to her feet and smiled at Hal Jacobs. "Let's go," she said, and then turned to Nellie. "Is my veil on straight?" Without waiting for an answer, she adjusted it minutely.

The procession formed up in the back of the church. Like an army, the wedding had a defined order of march. Nicholas Kincaid's eyes lit up when at last he was permitted to see his bride-to-be. *Animal,* Nellie thought, having seen too many men's eyes light up in dingy rooms. *Nothing but a filthy animal.*

Up at the altar, the minister waited, looking almost like a Catholic priest in his vestments. An usher—a lieutenant who was one of Kincaid's friends—spoke in brisk, businesslike tones: "The bride and the gentleman who will be giving her away take the lead."

With a smirk, Edna gave Hal Jacobs her arm. They started up the aisle together. But they had taken only a few steps when Bill Reach burst into the church, shouting, "People had better get the hell out of here, because—"

Nellie outshouted him: "Get this man—this robber, this thief—out of here this instant!" She shrieked straight at Reach: "Haven't you done enough to ruin me, you son of a bitch?"

Words, even words no lady should ever have said, were nowhere near enough to satisfy her. The little handbag she carried did not have much room, but she'd made sure she'd included a stout hatpin, just in case any of the Confederate officers tried putting their hands anywhere they didn't belong on her. She wished she'd brought a knife instead, but the pin would have to do. Snatching it out, she rushed at the man who'd done so much to wreck her life.

Ushers and guests—Confederate officers all—were rushing toward him, too. But they would throw him out, no more. She wanted to hurt him. She wanted to kill him. "He's mine!" she shouted furiously. "Mine, do you hear?"

They didn't hear, or didn't pay any attention. They had just seized him when the first big shell landed across the street in Lafayette Square. At the scream in the sky, at that ground-shaking roar, half the officers in the church—likely the half that had seen action, as opposed to the half made up of occupying authorities—threw themselves flat between the pews.

Another shell landed somewhere off to one side. Nicholas Kincaid ran down the aisle toward Edna, shouting, "Come on! We've got to get out of here!" More shells were falling. One crashed through the roof of St. John's Church and exploded just behind the altar.

Blast picked Nellie up, flung her through the air, and slammed her down, hard. The hatpin bit into her own leg. She squealed. She couldn't hear herself squeal. She wondered if she would ever hear anything again. She had trouble breathing. When she wiped at her nose, her hand came away bloody. The explosion had tried to tear her lungs out by the roots.

Her dress was rumpled and ripped. The handbag was gone, she had no idea where. She scrambled to her feet. One ankle didn't want to bear her weight. She looked down. It wasn't bleeding. She could move her foot, though that hurt, too. That must have meant it wasn't broken, or so she hoped. She'd walk on it now and worry about it later.

The church looked as if a bomb had gone off inside it, which was true, or near enough. Edna and Hal Jacobs stumbled toward her, both of them bleeding, red smirching the white of the wedding dress. They stepped over a body in the aisle. The body's head lay in the aisle, too, a few feet closer to Nellie. Lieutenant Nicholas H. Kincaid stared up at the ceiling that was starting to smolder. His eyes would never see anything again.

Edna saw the body, saw the great pool of blood that had welled from it, and then saw and recognized the head. Her mouth opened in a scream that was for Nellie silent. Nellie ran to her, took her by both hands, and pulled her out of the church, Jacobs staggering along beside them.

More shells kept falling, each one a small earthquake. Some people in the streets were up and fleeing—fleeing in all directions, for no one path seemed safe. Others were down, some wounded or dead, others sheltering against fragments and blast. On the far side of Lafayette Square, the White House burned.

Nellie did not see Bill Reach. He must have known this was coming from the U.S. guns, as Hal Jacobs might have. He'd tried to save people. At risk to himself, he'd tried to save people. Nellie wondered if that meant she couldn't hate him any more. Savagely, she shook her head. She owed him too much for that.

Anne Colleton glared at the men who served the three-inch guns she'd managed to pry loose from an armory where they'd been gathering dust. "You haven't got rid of Cassius and his fighters," she said, her voice suggesting that that was a sin incapable of forgiveness. In her mind, it was.

Captain Beauregard Barksdale, the militiaman commanding the little artillery unit, said, "We're doing the best we can, Miss Colleton. We aren't so handy with these here guns as we might be."

She withered him with a glance. "I've seen *that*." Her voice dripped scorn. She was being unfair, and knew it, and couldn't help it. Beauregard Barksdale had undoubtedly been named for the famous Confederate general right after the bombardment of Fort Sumter, and might well be more familiar with the brass Napoleons the Little Napoleon had fired than he was with the modern artillery pieces Anne had obtained for him.

"Ma'am, we are doing what we can," Barksdale repeated stolidly. He took a deep breath, then let it wuffle out through his thick gray mustache. "And I'm still not even slightly sure it's legal for you to be ordering the militia of the sovereign state of South Carolina around in the first place."

Anne's voice was sweet as ant syrup, and no less deadly: "Shall I wire the governor up in Columbia and ask him whether he's sure? Shall I telephone him so he can tell you he's sure?"

She meant it. The militia captain could see she meant it. Behind his bifocal spectacles, his eyes went wide. She stared at him, unblinking and implacable as a hawk. He wilted. She'd been sure he would wilt. "Well, no, ma'am," he said. "I don't reckon you've got to go so far as to do that. We'll take your orders—

won't we, boys?" None of the other old men and youths serving the guns dared say no.

"You'd better," Anne said. "I haven't the time to waste going through this nonsense. If I have to go through it twice, I'll be sorry—and so will you. I am going to be perfectly plain with you: yes, I have to squat when I piss. That does not mean I can't blow your heads off with a rifle at a range beyond any at which you could hit me, and it does not mean I know nothing of war and am unfit to give you orders."

If she couldn't get them to obey her any other way, she'd fluster them into doing it. She'd never seen such a collection of red faces in her life. These men and boys had gone through their whole lives never imagining a woman would remind them *that* she pissed, let alone how she went about it.

"If you're going to give orders, just give 'em, for God's sake," Captain Barksdale said, now not daring to meet her eye. "Don't go on about . . . other things." He shuffled his feet like an embarrassed schoolboy.

"That is what I was trying to do," Anne said briskly. "I have some reason to believe I know where the Red bandits will strike next. You'll have to hit them harder than you did last time to do any good."

"Put us where we can hit 'em and I reckon we'll do it," Barksdale replied. The gunners—many of whom, Anne was convinced, could not have hit the ground if they fell off a horse—nodded.

"I will," Anne said. *I hope,* she added to herself. Scipio was not to be trusted, not any more, not after shells had come crashing down around him. Had the shells killed Cassius and Cherry, she would have reckoned it worthwhile. As things were . . . as things were, she contemplated Scipio the exacting perfectionist huddled in the swamps, and knew she had a measure of revenge with every breath he took.

Captain Barksdale said, "We'd be even likelier to hit, ma'am, if you could get us some more shells to practice with."

Anne rolled her eyes. "I count myself lucky if I'm able to pry loose enough shells for you to use in combat." That was an understatement. From the start of the war till now, the three-inch field gun had been the workhorse of the Confederate Army. It served on every front, and every front screamed for shells. Detaching any had taken every wire she could pull.

The militia gunners hitched limbers and guns to horses and

drove back to St. Matthews. In town, she saw two women on the street in trousers: not so fine as hers, but trousers. She accepted that as no less than her due. She'd been a leader in style and fashion before the war began. It was only natural that she should continue to lead now.

She was about to go up to her room when a messenger boy halted his bicycle with the heels of his boots. "Telegram for you, ma'am," he said. She took the envelope. He hurried away after pocketing a ten-cent tip.

Ripping apart the flimsy paper was not an adequate substitute for settling Cassius and Cherry for good, but it had to do. When Anne was done reading the wire, she tore it to shreds, threw them in the air, and let the wind blow them away. None of the news from her brokers had been good lately. The markets in Richmond and London and Paris were faltering; the investments that had sustained her even after the ruin of Marshlands faltered, too.

She could not imagine when Marshlands would recover. She had trouble imagining when her investments would recover, either. If they didn't . . . If they didn't, she wouldn't be the leader around these parts much longer. She had trouble imagining that, too, but less trouble than she would have had in the spring of 1916 and ever so much less than she would have had in the spring of 1915.

A train pulled into the station a couple of blocks away. The fire engine might not have been replaced after the Red uprising, but labor gangs, some working at gunpoint, had put the railroads back together in a hurry. Those iron rails bound the CSA together as nothing else could.

From the direction of the station, someone called her name. Her head turned. Coming her way was a tall man in a butternut uniform. "Tom!" she yelped in glad surprise, and ran toward her older brother.

Lieutenant Colonel Tom Colleton stared at Anne as she drew near. "Good God, Sis, what *are* you wearing?" he said.

She put her hands on her hips and glared at him. He didn't flinch, as he would have before the war. In a way, that made her proud: he'd gone from an overage boy, a useless drone, to a man on the battlefield. In another way, it irked her more than ever: even as a man, he thought women should be useless toys.

With precision that showed how tightly she was holding her

temper in check, she replied, "I am wearing the clothes I need to wear to go hunting bandits in the swamps of the Congaree—or did you want that rifle you sent me to gather dust in the closet?"

Tom took a deep breath, then decided not to make a scene. "All right," he said. "You sure as the devil took me by surprise, though. I never would have reckoned the day would come when women showed off their shapes that way."

"Really?" she asked, as if in innocence. "What sort of joints do you go to when you're on leave but you don't come home?" She had the satisfaction of watching a blush climb from his throat to his hairline. Deciding to let him down easy, she asked, "How are things at the front?"

He grimaced, but in an impersonal sort of way. "Not so well. We've lost just about all the ground we took back from the Yankees in the counterattack last fall. We're shoved away from Big Lick and the Roanoke River, back toward the Blue Ridge Mountains. Dammit, it's not that they're better soldiers than we are. The trouble is, there are more of them than there are of us."

"What about the black troops?" Anne asked.

Her brother shrugged. "They're starting to come into the line. They're raw. God only knows how they'll do when push comes to shove. And even with 'em, there are still more damnyankees than there are of us. Defending is cheaper than attacking, thank God. If we're lucky, sooner or later the USA will get tired of throwing away men against us and against the Canucks, and they'll make some kind of peace we can stand."

"And if we're not lucky?" Anne said quietly.

Tom didn't answer for a while. When he did, it was obliquely: "We've made the USA eat a lot of crow since South Carolina stopped flying the Stars and Stripes. I wonder what the bird tastes like, and how they'd serve it up. They remember every morsel, and that's a fact." He dug in his pocket, found a coin, and tossed it to Anne.

It was a U.S. quarter-dollar. On one side, it bore a bust of Daniel Webster, whom Confederate schools vilified for opposing secession. Anne turned it over. The other side showed arrows and lightning bolts superimposed on a star, with the word REMEMBRANCE stamped across it.

She handed the coin back to her brother. "Till this war, we hadn't fought them for more than thirty years," she said. "Foolish for them to keep on harping on things when the last war was over and done with so long ago—before either one of us was born."

"When you lose, Sis, the last war's never over and done with," Tom answered, scratching the scar that seamed his cheek. "I've questioned a lot of prisoners. The Yankees remember ever single slight from the day this state seceded all the way up to the day they're captured."

"The thing to do, then, is to make sure they don't have the chance to make us eat crow," Anne said, as if stating an axiom of geometry.

"Yes, that would be the thing to do," Tom Colleton said.

Anne chose to ignore the incompleteness of his agreement. As she would have before the war, she took charge of him. She took him to St. Matthews' only functioning hotel, checked him in, and then led him to the better of the town's cafés. With only two open in St. Matthews, it rated merely the comparative, not the superlative. It wasn't that good, either; a third one likely would have been the best.

With an air of big-brotherly amusement, he let her do all that. He didn't depend on her to do it, though, as he would have before the war. He ordered a beefsteak that proved less tender than it might have, stuck a fork in it, and let out several piercing brays. Anne was chewing a bite, and almost choked from laughing.

He gave her a peck on the cheek after supper, saying, "We'll talk more in the morning, Sis."

They did, and had plenty to talk about: the night was enlivened when the Reds brought a machine gun out of the swamp and fired several belts of ammunition into St. Matthews from long range before melting away under cover of darkness. Anne had a window shot out, and was nicked on the hand by flying glass.

"Is it like this all the time?" Tom asked.

"They haven't done that in a while," Anne said, "but they can, till we hunt down the last of them. We're having trouble with that, though, because so much of everything goes straight to the front."

"We'd have worse trouble yet if it didn't," Tom replied. Anne's mouth twisted in something less than a smile. She had no good answer for that.

* * *

Sam Carsten peered out of the narrow vision slit in the sponson that housed his five-inch gun as the USS *Dakota* inched her way forward. What he saw was endless choppy ocean. The South Atlantic swells were slapping against the battleship's full armored length, which made her roll unpleasantly.

As if also noticing the motion, Hiram Kidde said, "Don't nobody puke in here. Anybody pukes in here, he's in big trouble with me. You got that?"

"Aye aye, 'Cap'n,' " the gun crew chorused.

"I wish we'd put some more turns on the engines," Carsten said. "That would help smooth things out."

"Oh, that it would, by Jesus—that it would," the chief of the gun crew answered. "What's the matter with you, Sam? You think you could stash your brains in your bunk once they promoted you to petty officer? That ain't how it works, much as I hate to tell you."

Carsten's ears heated. "Have a heart, 'Cap'n.' That's not what I meant, and you know it."

"It's what you *said*, goddammit," Kidde said. "Sure, bend some more turns on the engines. Why the hell not? What the hell we got better to do than charge right into the mine belt the limeys and the Argentines laid between Argentina and the Falklands? What's it cost us so far? Just a cruiser and a destroyer. Why the hell not put a battleship on the list?"

"Maybe we should have swung wide around the goddamn Falklands." Now Sam's voice was an embarrassed mumble.

Hiram Kidde, having scented blood, wasn't about to let him off the hook. "That'd be good, wouldn't it? Tack an extra six or eight hundred miles onto the cruise. We don't have that much margin ourselves, and our supply ships have even less. Shit, the Argentines who didn't dare stir out of harbor against us are going to come right after our tenders and their escorts even now."

"Look, 'Cap'n,' why don't you forget I ever said anything?" Sam suggested. *And believe me,* he thought, *it'll be a cold day in hell—a damn sight colder than this—before I open my mouth again.* He retreated from the vision slit and went back toward the breech of the cannon. As long as he stayed at his station and kept his mouth shut, nothing too bad could happen to him—he hoped.

To his relief, Kidde started peering out at the Atlantic. Every-body kept doing that, although there wasn't anything to see but gray-green ocean. The mines hid below the surface. No one would see them till too late.

Luke Hoskins spoke to Sam in a low voice: "Don't let Kidde get you down. We're all edgy these days. We've been torpedoed, and we came through it, and we've been shelled, and we came through that, too. But if we hit a mine, likely we can't do nothin' about it—except sink, I mean."

"Yeah. Except sink," Carsten said sourly. "You do so ease my mind, Luke."

But Hoskins was right. The ship was engaged in hard, slow, dangerous work, work in which the men who served the sec-ondary armament could take no direct part. If all went well, they would live. If not, they would die—and which it would be was not in their hands. No wonder tempers flared.

Kidde turned away from the vision slit. "Things could be worse," he said, perhaps trying to make amends for ripping into Sam. "We could be in one of those destroyers up ahead of us."

"Amen." Everyone in the sponson spoke at the same time, more smoothly than the sailors would have responded to the chaplain of a Sunday morning. Sooner or later, somebody was going to say something more than that. Usually, that somebody would have been Carsten. Not this time. Sam, having been raked once, sulked in his metaphysical tent.

Luke Hoskins said what the whole gun crew had to be thinking: "You've got to be crazy to clear mines in a destroyer."

"Nope." Hiram Kidde shook his head. "All you've got to do is get your orders. Then you say 'Aye aye, sir!' and do as you're told."

"Crazy," Hoskins repeated. "Only way to clear the mines you're supposed to get rid of is to steam past 'em without blowing yourself out of the water."

"You do lose points if that happens, Luke," Kidde agreed. "Can't argue with you there."

"Goddammit, 'Cap'n,' it isn't funny," the shell-jerker said. "That damn weighted cable between the four-stackers is sup-posed to catch on the mines' mooring cables and yank 'em up to the surface so we can shoot the hell out of 'em. But if they find the mines the hard way, or if they miss 'em . . ."

His voice trailed away. Nobody said anything for a while after that. Sam knew what kind of pictures he was seeing inside his own mind. The rest of the crew couldn't have been imagining anything much different.

Turn and turn about: four hours on, four hours off. When the other crew replaced Carsten and his comrades, he hurried to the galley and shoveled down pork and beans and fried potatoes and sauerkraut and lemonade and coffee. He was amazed how much he ate these days, to hold cold and exhaustion at bay. The coffee wouldn't keep him from sleeping. Nothing would keep him from sleeping, not even the highly charged air in the cramped bunkroom after everybody had been messing on pork and beans and sauerkraut.

Climbing out of his bunk was more like an exhumation than anything else. He shook his head in bewilderment. Hadn't he just lain down? He put on his shoes and cap, grabbed the peacoat he'd set on top of his blanket, and staggered blank-faced toward the galley for more coffee to help him remember who he was and what the hell he was supposed to be doing.

He went up on deck to let the chilly breeze clear some more cobwebs from his poor befogged brain. Walking forward, he nodded to the two mine-hunting destroyers that cleared the way for the *Dakota*. So far, they'd done their job perfectly: they hadn't blown up, and neither had the battleship.

That thought had hardly made its slow way through Sam's still-fuzzy thoughts when one of the destroyers did go up, in a great dreadful gout of smoke and fire. Across half a mile of water, the roar was loud enough to stagger him.

"Oh, sweet Jesus!" he moaned. Half of that was simple horror. The other half was guilt for jinxing the destroyer by thinking how well she'd been doing her job.

She was sinking fast now, going down by the bow, her stern rising higher and higher until, only a couple of minutes after she was hit, she dove for the bottom of the sea. She never had a chance to lower boats. A handful of heads bobbed in the cold, cold water. In water like that, a man might stay alive for an hour, maybe even a little more if he was very strong.

"Rescue party to the boats!" a lieutenant shouted.

Sam stood not twenty feet from one. He was in it, along with several other men, and dangling his way down toward the surface of the Atlantic less than two minutes later. He plied an oar with a vigor that made him sweat even in that nasty weather. His was not the only boat in the water; the *Dakota* had launched several others, as had the destroyer's partner. They all raced to pick up the scattered survivors.

"Back oars!" Sam called as the boat drew near one feebly paddling man. He dropped his own oar, leaned out, and caught hold of the sailor's hand. The fellow almost pulled him into the water, but a couple of other men in the boat grabbed him around the waist and also helped him pull in the survivor.

"Thank you," the sailor said through chattering teeth. "Christ, I reckoned I was dead."

"I believe you," Sam said. "Saw you go up. Godawful thing. One second you were just going along, and the next one—"

"Felt just like somebody took a two-by-four and hit me in both feet," the sailor said. Grimacing, he went on, "Bet something's busted in there, 'cause they sure as hell hurt. Saw we didn't have a prayer. Everybody was screaming, 'Abandon ship!' Made it to the rail—I was half walking, half crawling. Made it over the side and started swimming hard as I could, on account of I didn't want to get sucked under when she went down. And I didn't, not quite. Figured my ticket was punched, but you've got to keep trying, you know what I mean?"

"Here, pal. Try this." Somebody pressed the bottle of brandy the boat carried—nothing near so fine as what Rear Admiral Fiske drank—into the sailor's hands.

He took a long pull. "Marry me!" he exclaimed blissfully. His rescuers laughed.

He raised the dark bottle to his lips again. "Don't drink it all," Sam warned. "We're going to try and get some of your pals, too." He pointed toward a man floating on his back not far away, then grabbed up his oar and helped pull the boat toward the other sailor.

The man wasn't moving. When they got to him, they saw he was dead. "Poor bastard," somebody said quietly. It was all the memorial service the sailor got.

Sam stood up in the boat to see farther. One of the boats from the other destroyer was already heading toward the last swimming man he spied. The others had either been picked up or had sunk beneath the waves forever.

"Well, we got one," he muttered—a tiny victory, snatched from the jaws of death. He sat on the bench again, then spoke once more to the sailor he'd pulled out of the South Atlantic: "I take it back, pal. You might as well get drunk."

"God bless you," the man from the destroyer said. Instead of drinking, he stuck out his hand. "You ever need anything, I'm your man. Name's Gus Hardwig."

"Sam Carsten," Carsten said, and shook the proffered hand. "Believe me, I was glad to do it. We were all glad to do it." The men in the boat with him nodded. He pointed back toward the *Dakota*. "Now we'd better take you home."

They rowed over alongside the battleship, whose cranes effortlessly lifted the boat out of the water. Gus Hardwig put a cautious foot on the *Dakota*'s deck, then jerked it away as if the steel were red-hot. "Can't make it," he said.

Orderlies whisked him away in a stretcher. Carsten stood on the deck, staring north. Only a few floating bodies and an oil slick showed where the mine-clearing destroyer had gone down. Sam's shiver had nothing to do with his wet tunic and the sharp breeze. The mine could have blown up the *Dakota* as readily as it had sunk the escort vessel. That could have been him floating in the water as readily as Gus Hardwig, or more likely him going down with the ship. He shivered again.

VI

Going home. Going home. Going home. The rails sang a sweet song in Jefferson Pinkard's ears as the wheels of the train clicked over them. He'd been away too long, too far. He couldn't wait to see Emily's smiling face now that he'd finally got himself enough leave time to escape the front and travel back to Birmingham for a few days.

He couldn't wait to see all of her, every inch, stretched out bare on their bed. He couldn't wait to feel her underneath him on that bed, or on her hands and knees as they coupled like hunting hounds, or on her knees in front of him, red-gold hair spilling down over her face as she leaned forward and—

He shifted on the hard second-class seat. He was hard himself, and hoped the little old lady reading a sentimental novel next to him didn't notice. He couldn't help getting hard when he thought about Emily. Christ, she loved to do it! So did he, with her. When he'd got short leaves in Texas, he hadn't felt any great urge to visit the whorehouses that did not officially exist. But Emily—Emily was something very special in the line of women.

She'd probably kick his legs out from under him as soon as he walked in the door. She'd gone without as long as he had. From her letters, she might have missed it even more than he did. "Very special," he muttered. The woman beside him looked up from her novel, realized he hadn't been talking to her, and began to read again.

Pinkard had the seat closer to the window. He found the Mississippi countryside more interesting than a book. Here, away from the front, the war seemed forgotten. He'd seen that as soon as the first train he'd boarded got more than an hour's travel away from the trenches. Farmers were plowing in the fields. Actually, more farmers' wives were in the fields than he would have seen before the war. That was a change, but only a small one when set against the absence of trenches and shell holes and artillery pieces. Everything was so green and fresh-looking, the way a landscape got to be when it wasn't drastically revised every few days or every few minutes.

When the train rolled through a town, factory smokestacks sent black plumes of smoke into the air. The first time Jeff saw those plumes, he was alarmed; they put him in mind of fires after bombardments. But he quickly stopped worrying about that: industry got to seem normal in a hurry.

Past Columbus, Mississippi, and into Alabama the train rolled. Here and there, Pinkard did note scars on the landscape in this part of the countryside, half-healed ones from the Negro uprisings the year before. This was cotton country, with many Negroes and few whites.

Somebody a couple of rows in front of Pinkard said, "I hear tell the niggers is still shootin' at trains every now and again."

"Ought to do some shootin' at them with the biggest guns we got," the stranger's seatmate answered.

Remembering his own train ride into Georgia and the bullets that had slammed into the cars from out of the night, Pinkard understood how that fellow felt. He'd been a new, raw soldier then, his uniform a dark, proper butternut, not faded to the color of coffee with too much cream. The fire from the Red Negroes had seemed intense, deadly, terrifying. He wondered what it would seem like now. Probably not so much of a much.

Darkness fell as the train rattled through the central-Alabama cotton fields. Jeff revised his thinking. If black diehards had fired a couple of belts of ammunition at this train, he would have been terrified all over again. If somebody was shooting at you and you couldn't shoot back, terror made perfect sense.

He leaned back in the hard, uncomfortable seat and closed his eyes. He was only going to relax for a little while. So he told himself, but the next thing he knew, the conductor was shouting, "Birmingham! All out for Birmingham!"

He pushed past the gray-haired woman, who was going on farther east. As soon as he stepped out on the platform, he knew he was home again. The smoky, sulfurous air that poured from the foundries mingled with the fog that so often stole through Jones Valley to yield an atmosphere with density and character: damp and heavy and smelly, a mud bath for the lungs.

Flame poured from the tops of the chimneys of the Sloss Works, out toward the eastern edge of town. Back before the war—back before the Conscription Bureau had dragged him out of the foundry and into the trenches—he'd thought of that sight as hell on earth. Now that he'd seen war, he knew better, but the memory lingered.

Before he could get off the platform, he showed his papers to a military policeman who had to be counting his blessings at having a post hundreds of miles from the real war. The fellow inspected them, then waved him on. Trolley lines ran close by the station, taking travelers wherever they needed to go in the city. Pinkard stood at the corner and waited for the Sloss Works car he could ride out to the company housing—yellow cottages for white men and their families, primer-red for Negroes—surrounding the Sloss Works themselves. He yawned. He was still sleepy despite the nap, but figured the sight of Emily would wake him up in short order when he got home.

The trolley driver—who'd leaned crutches behind his seat and had one empty trouser leg—worked the brake and brought the car squealing to a halt at the edge of the company town. He nodded to Jefferson Pinkard as the soldier got off. Jeff nodded back. He felt the driver's eyes on him as he walked away. Did the fellow hate him for his long, smooth strides? How could anyone blame him if he did?

Everything was quiet as Jeff headed home. Most of the cottages were dark, with men away for the war or working the evening shift or asleep if they worked days or nights. Here and there, lamplight yellow as melted butter spilled out of windows. A couple of dogs barked as Pinkard passed their houses. One of them, chained in the front yard, rushed at him, but the chain kept the big-mouthed, skinny brute from reaching the sidewalk.

Jeff turned onto his little lane. He felt swept back in time to the days before the war. How many times he'd walked this way with Bedford Cunningham, his next-door neighbor and best friend, both of them tired and hot and sweaty in their overalls after a long day's work. Alabama had been dry for a few years, but home-brew beer never got hard to come by. A couple of bottles out of the icebox went down sweet, no doubt about it.

There stood the Cunningham house, dark and still. Pinkard sighed. Bedford had gone to war before he did, and had come back without an arm, as the trolley driver had come back without a leg. A one-armed man could do a lot of things, but going back on the foundry floor probably wasn't one of them. Bedford and Fanny had hard times. Jeff wondered how long they'd be able to stay in company housing if Bedford wasn't in the Army and couldn't work for the company any more.

Lamplight shone from the curtained window of Pinkard's own house, just past the Cunninghams'. He kicked at the sidewalk in mild disappointment. He'd expected Emily would already be asleep; come morning, she'd have to head downtown toward her munitions-plant job. He'd hoped he could take off his uniform in the front room, slip naked into bed beside her, and startle her awake the best way he knew how.

Even knowing she was awake, he went up the walk on tiptoe. If he couldn't give her the best surprise possible, he'd still give her the biggest surprise he could. His thumb and palm closed on the doorknob. Gently, gently, he turned it. The door swung open without a squeak. He was glad Emily had kept the hinges oiled. In Birmingham, anything that didn't get oiled rusted.

The lamplight glinted off Emily's shining hair. Seeing that before he saw anything else, Jeff began, "Hey, darlin', I'm . . . home." What had started as a glad cry ended as a hiss, like air escaping from a punctured inner tube.

Emily half sat, half knelt on the floor in front of the divan. On the divan, his legs splayed wide, lolled Bedford Cunningham. Neither of them wore any more than they'd been born with. Her face had been in his lap till she pulled away at the sound of Jeff's voice. A thin, bright line of saliva ran down her chin from a corner of her lower lip.

"Oh, Jesus Christ," Cunningham said. "Oh, Jesus Christ. Oh, Jesus Christ." The short stump of his right arm jerked and twisted, as if he'd tried to make a fist with a hand he'd forgotten he didn't have. "Oh, Jesus Christ."

"Close the door, Jeff," Emily said. Her eyes were wide and staring. She sounded eerily self-possessed, like somebody who'd just staggered out of a train wreck.

Mechanically, Pinkard did. He was stunned, too, and said the first thing that popped into his mind: "You sneak out of Fanny's bed to come over here, Bedford?"

Cunningham shook his head. "She's workin' second shift these days." His face was pale as skimmed milk. Before he was hurt, he'd been as big and strong and ruddy and bold as Pinkard.

Now he looked thinner, older, his face lined as it hadn't been when he was a whole man.

Jeff's wits began to work. "Get your clothes on. Get the hell out of here. I ain't gonna lick a crippled man." He didn't say a word about what he'd do, or wouldn't do, to Emily.

Bedford Cunningham put on drawers and trousers and shirt one-handed with a speed that showed both practice and desperation. He hadn't been wearing shoes. He darted out the door. A few seconds later, the door to his own cottage opened and closed.

"Why?" Jefferson Pinkard asked the age-old question of the husband betrayed.

Naked still, Emily shrugged. Her breasts, firm and pink-tipped, bobbled briefly. She was, Jeff saw, over the jaundice that troubled some munitions workers who handled cordite too much. "Why?" she echoed, and shrugged again. "You weren't here. I missed you. I missed *it*. Finally, I missed it so much I couldn't stand it any more, and so—" Yet another shrug.

"But Bedford—" *My best friend!* was another husbandly howl as old as time.

Emily got to her feet in a smooth, graceful motion Jeff couldn't possibly have imitated. She walked up to him and took his hands in hers. He knew what she was doing. He could hardly have helped knowing what she was doing. "He was here, that's all, darlin'," she said. "If you'd been here, too, I never would've looked at him. You know that's so. But you was in Georgia and Texas and all them damn places, and—" She shrugged one more time. Her nipples barely brushed the breast of his tunic.

No, he could hardly have helped knowing what she was doing. That didn't mean it didn't work. His breath caught in his throat. His heart thuttered. He'd missed it, too, but he hadn't realized— he hadn't had the faintest notion—how much till she stood bare before him.

She took a step backwards, still holding his hands. He took a step forward, after her. She took another step, and another, leading him back to the divan. When he sat, it was where Bedford Cunningham had sat before him. She sprawled beside him. She had two hands to undo his belt buckle and the buttons of his fly.

She didn't kiss him on the lips. That might have reminded him where her mouth had just been. Instead, she leaned over and lowered her head. He pressed her down on him, his hands tangling in her thick hair. She gagged a little, but did not pull away.

Moments later, he exploded. He let Emily pull back far enough to gulp convulsively. Then, unasked, she returned to what she'd been doing. He stiffened again, faster than he would have believed he could. When he was hard, she got up on her knees and swung her right leg over him, as if she were mounting a horse. She impaled herself on him and began to ride.

Her cries of joy must have wakened half the neighborhood. Then, throatily, she added, "I *never* made noise like that for Bedford." Jeff's hands clutched her meaty buttocks till she whimpered in pain and pleasure mixed. He drove deep into her, again and again. And, as he groaned and shuddered in the most exquisite pleasure he'd ever known, he wished with all his soul he were back in a muddy trench in Texas, under artillery bombardment from the Yankees.

Sweat ran down George Enos' face. The sun stood higher in the sky than it had any business doing at this season of the year, at least to his way of thinking. The USS *Ericsson* was down in the tropics now, nosing around after the submarines making life miserable for the warships and freighters that were trying to strangle the trade route between Argentina and England.

"What do you think?" he asked Carl Sturtevant. "Are we after English boats, or are the Rebs out here giving their pals a hand?"

"Damned if I know," answered the petty officer who ran the depth-charge launcher. "Damned if I care, either. Knowing who they are doesn't change how I do my job. We keep them too busy either going after us or trying to get away from us, they aren't going to be able to do anything else."

"Yeah," Enos said. "Just between you and me, I'd sooner see 'em trying to get away than going after us."

Sturtevant looked him up and down. "Any fool can see you ain't a career Navy man," he said after a brief pause for thought.

"Screw you and the destroyer you rode in on," Enos returned evenly. "I've been captured by a Confederate commerce raider, I've sailed on a fishing boat that was nothing but a decoy for Rebel subs and helped sink one of the bastards, I was on the bank of the Cumberland when my river monitor got blown sky-high, and I was right here when the damn *Snook* damn near torpedoed us. To my way of thinking, I've earned a little peace and quiet."

"Everybody's earned a little peace and quiet, and in the end everybody gets it, too," the petty officer said: "nice plot of ground, about six feet by three feet by six feet under. Till then, I want my time lively as can be."

Enos grunted, then went back to what he'd been doing: watching the ocean for signs of a periscope or anything else suspicious. Everyone who didn't have some other duty specifically assigned came up on deck and stood by the rail, scanning the ocean for the telltale feather of foam following a submersible's periscope.

A shadow on the water—George's pulse raced. Was that the top of an enemy conning tower, hiding down there below the surface of the sea? He relaxed, for the shadow was far too small and far too swift to be any such thing. He raised his gaze from the ocean to the sky. Sure enough, a frigate bird with a wingspan not much smaller than that of an aeroplane glided away. Several sea birds—gulls and terns and more exotic tropical types Enos had had to have named for him—hung with the *Ericsson*, scrounging garbage. They seemed perfectly content hundreds of miles from land in any direction.

George peered and peered. A man could only watch the ocean for a couple of hours at a stretch. After that, his attention started to wander. He saw things that weren't there, which wasn't so bad, and didn't see things that were, which was. Miss a periscope and the sea birds would pick meat from your bones after your corpse floated up to the surface.

What was that, there off the port bow? More likely than not, far more likely than not, it was just a bit of chop. He kept watching it. It wasn't moving in the same direction as the rest of the chop, nor at quite the same speed. He frowned. He'd spent as much time on the ocean as any career Navy man. He knew how far from smooth and uniform it was. Still—

He pointed. "What do you make of that?" he asked Sturtevant.

The petty officer had been looking more nearly amidships. Now his gaze followed Enos' outthrust finger. "Where? Out about a mile?" His pale eyes narrowed; he shielded them from sun and glare with the palm of his right hand.

"Yeah, about that," George answered.

"That's a goddamn periscope, or I'm a Rebel." Sturtevant started pointing, too, and yelling at the top of his lungs. An officer with binoculars came running. He pointed them in the direction Sturtevant gave him. After a moment, he started yelling like a man possessed.

At his yells, klaxons started hooting. George Enos and Carl Sturtevant sprinted for their battle stations at the stern of the *Ericsson*. The destroyer shuddered under them as the engines suddenly ran up to full emergency power. Great gouts of smoke belched from the stacks.

"Torpedo in the water!" somebody screamed. The *Ericsson* had begun a turn toward the submersible, which meant that George could not see the wake of the torpedo as it sped toward the destroyer. He couldn't have done anything about it had he been able to see it, but being ignorant of whether he would live or die came hard.

Time stretched. The torpedo couldn't have taken more than a minute—a minute and a half at the most—to speed from the submersible to the destroyer. But how long was a minute or a minute and a half? With his heart thudding in his chest, every breath a desperate gasp, Enos had no sure grasp.

Tom Sturtevant pointed, as Enos had when he spotted the periscope. "There it goes, the goddamn son of a bitch!" Sturtevant shouted. Sure enough, the pale wake of the torpedo stretched out across the blue, blue water of the tropical Atlantic. Sturtevant stepped over to George beside his one-pounder and slapped him on the back hard enough to stagger him. "If you hadn't spotted the 'scope, the bastard would've been able to sneak in closer for a better shot. You made him fire it off too quick."

"Good." Enos patted the magazine of nicely heavy shells he'd loaded into the one-pounder. He remembered what they'd done to the conning tower of the *Snook*, and to a couple of Confederate sailors who'd got in the way of them. "Now we've got the ball."

"Yeah," Sturtevant said as the *Ericsson* slowed not far from the point whence the torpedo had been launched. "Now we start dropping ash cans on his head, and see if we can put him out of business for good."

At the side of the depth-charge launcher, Lieutenant Crowder said, "Let's give him a couple, shall we, Mr. Sturtevant? Set them for a hundred and fifty feet."

"A hundred and fifty feet. Aye aye, sir," the petty officer answered. He commanded the rest of the men at the launcher with effortless authority. A depth charge flew through the air and splashed into the Atlantic. A moment later, another followed.

Somewhere down under the ocean, a boatful of men who'd just done their best to sink the *Ericsson* were listening to those splashes. George felt a weird sympathy for the submersible's crew. The only thing a submersible had going for it was stealth. It couldn't fight on the surface against a warship. It couldn't outrun a warship, either. All it could do was sneak close, try for a kill, and then try to sneak away if that didn't work.

Sympathy had nothing whatever to do with whether George hoped the submariners would be able to sneak away after trying to kill him (and, in his own mind incidentally, everyone else on the *Ericsson*). He didn't. "Come on, you bastards," he said while the depth charges sank. "Come on."

Fifty yards below the surface of the Atlantic, the depth charges went off, one after the other, a few feet apart. Water on the surface bubbled and boiled. After the explosions, though, nothing more happened: no rush of air bubbles proclaiming a ruptured pressure hull, no oil slick telling of other damage, no boat hastily surfacing before it sank forever.

Turning, the *Ericsson* moved slowly to the southeast. "Hydrophone bearing," a sailor called back to Lieutenant Crowder. The underwater listening device had two drawbacks. Where along that bearing the submersible lay was anybody's guess. Also, when the destroyer's engines were running, they drowned out most of the noise the submarine was making.

Nevertheless, after a couple of minutes, a messenger hurried back to Crowder from the bridge. The young lieutenant listened, nodded, and spoke to Carl Sturtevant. "Two more depth charges. Set the fuses for a hundred feet."

"A hundred feet. Aye aye, sir," Sturtevant said. Off flew the charges, two bangs in quick succession. The wait, this time, wasn't so long. The Atlantic bubbled and boiled again. No evidence that the charges had done any good appeared.

"Is the launcher in proper working order?" Crowder demanded. It had damaged a submersible the last time they used it. Enos thought along with the officer. If it didn't force a boat to the surface this time, something surely had to be wrong with it . . . unless the skipper down below was laughing up his sleeve, which struck George as a hell of a lot likelier.

"Yes, sir." Carl Sturtevant gave the distinct impression that he'd talked with a hell of a lot of young officers in his day. No doubt the reason he gave that impression was that he had. He went on, "It's working fine, sir. It's just that there's a hell of a lot of ocean out there, and the ash cans can't tear up but a little bit of it at a time."

"We got good results—damnation, we got outstanding results—the last time we used it," Crowder said fretfully.

"Yes, sir, but life ain't like a Roebuck's catalogue, sir," Sturtevant answered. "It don't come with no money-back guarantee."

That was good sense. As a fisherman, Enos knew exactly how good it was. Lieutenant Crowder pouted, for all the world like George, Jr. "Something must be wrong with the launcher," he said, confirming George's guess.

Sturtevant sent another pair of depth charges flying into the ocean, and another, and another. And, after that last pair, a thick stream of bubbles rose to the surface, as did a considerable quantity of thick black oil that spread over the blue, blue water of the Atlantic. "That's a hurt boat down there, sir," Carl Sturtevant breathed. "Hurt, or else playing games with us." He turned to the launcher crew. "Now we hammer the son of a bitch." Ash can after ash can splashed into the water.

More air bubbles rose. So did more oil. The boat from which they rose, however, remained submerged. "I wonder how deep the water is down there," Crowder said musingly. "If we've sunk that submersible, we're liable to never, ever know it."

"That's so, sir," Sturtevant agreed. "But if we think we've sunk him and we're wrong, we'll find out like a kick in the balls." George Enos nodded. A fisherman who wasn't a born pessimist hadn't been going to sea long enough.

The *Ericsson* held her position till sundown, lobbing occasional depth charges into the sea. "We'll report this one as a probable sinking," Lieutenant Crowder said. No one argued with him. No one could argue with him. He was the officer.

Commander Roger Kimball's head pounded and ached as if with a hangover, and he hadn't even had the fun of getting drunk. The air inside the *Bonefish* was foul, and getting fouler. In the dim orange glow of the electric lamps, he struck a match. It burned with a fitful blue flame for a few seconds, then went out, adding a sulfurous stink to the astonishing cacophony of stenches already inside the pressure hull.

He checked his watch: two in the morning, a few minutes past. Quietly, he asked, "How much longer can we stay submerged?"

"Three or four hours left in the batteries, sir, provided we don't have to gun the engine," Tom Brearley answered, also quietly, after checking the dials. He inhaled, then grimaced. "Air won't stay good that long, though, I'm afraid."

"And I'm afraid you're right." Kimball shifted his feet, which set up a faint splashing. The pounding the boat had taken had started some new leaks, none of them, fortunately, too severe. "Damnyankee destroyer was throwing around depth charges like they were growin' their own crop on deck."

"Yes, sir," Brearley said. The exec looked up toward the surface. "Next interesting question is—"

"Have they stalked us?" Kimball finished for him. "I'm hoping they think they sank us. We gave 'em enough clues before we slunk away. Only way we could have been more convincing would have been to shoot a couple of dead bodies out the forward tubes, and since we didn't have any handy—"

"Yes, sir," Brearley said, and a couple of sailors nodded. "But if they're anywhere close when we surface, we're done for."

"That's a fact," Kimball agreed. "But it's also a fact that we're done for if we don't surface pretty damn soon." He came to a sudden, abrupt decision. "We'll bring her up to periscope depth and have a look around."

Even that was risky; if the U.S. destroyer waited close by, bubbles on the surface might betray the *Bonefish*. The submersible rose sluggishly. Kimball had expended a lot of compressed air in feigning her untimely demise. When the periscope went up, he peered through it himself, not trusting anyone else with the job. Slowly, carefully, he went through a complete circuit of the horizon.

Nothing. No angular ship silhouette far off against the sky— nor menacingly close, either. No plume of smoke warning of a ship not very distant. Kimball went through the circuit again, to make sure he hadn't missed anything.

Still nothing. "All hands prepare to surface," he said, adding a moment later, "Bring her up, Mr. Brearley. We'll get fresh air into the boat, we'll fire up the diesels and cruise for a while to recharge the batteries—"

"We'll flush the heads," Ben Coulter said. Everyone in earshot fervently agreed with the petty officer as to the desirability of that. The pigs on the Arkansas farm where Kimball had grown up wouldn't have lived in a sty that smelled half as bad as the *Bonefish*.

After the boat had surfaced, Kimball climbed up to the top of the conning tower to undog the hatch. Ben Coulter climbed up behind him to grab him around the shins and keep him from being blown out the hatch when it was undogged: the air inside the hull was under considerably higher pressure than that on the outside, and had a way of escaping with great vigor.

Out streamed the stinking air, like the spout of a whale. Somehow the stench was worse when mingled with the first fresh, pure breezes from outside. When altogether immersed in it, the nose, mercifully, grew numb. After the first taste of good air, though, the bad got worse.

Still, a few lungfuls of outside air went a long way toward clearing Kimball's fuzzy wits. His headache vanished. From below came exclamations of delight and exclamations of disgust as fresh air began mingling with the nasty stuff inside the *Bonefish*.

The diesels rumbled to life. "All ahead half," Kimball called down; Tom Brearley relayed the command to the engine crew. The wake the *Bonefish* kicked up glowed with a faint, pearly phosphorescence.

Brearley mounted to the top of the conning tower. He looked around and let out a long sigh that was as much a lung-clearer as a sound of relief. "We got away from them, sir," he said.

"I didn't want to get away from them," Roger Kimball growled. "I wanted to sink the Yankee bastards. I would have done it, too, but they must have spotted the periscope. Soon as I saw 'em pick up speed and start that turn, I launched the fish, but the range was still long, and it missed."

"We're still in business," Brearley said.

"We're in the business of sending U.S. ships to the bottom," Kimball answered. "We didn't do it. Now that destroyer's either going to go on south and try to strangle the British lifeline to South America, or else he'll hang around here and try to keep us from going after his pals. Either way, he wouldn't be doing it if we'd sent him to the bottom like we were supposed to."

Kimball kept on fuming. His exec didn't say anything more. The darkness hid Kimball's smile, which was not altogether pleasant. He knew he alarmed Tom Brearley. It didn't bother him. If he didn't alarm the Tom Brearleys of the world, he wasn't doing his job right.

When the sun rose, he halted the boat and allowed the men to come up and bathe in the warm water of the Atlantic, with lines tied round the middles of those who couldn't swim. They put on their old, filthy uniforms again afterwards, but still enjoyed getting off some of the grime.

And then the *Bonefish* went hunting. Kimball had got used to patrolling inside a cage whose bars were lines of latitude and longitude. He supposed a lion would have found cage life tolerable if the keepers introduced a steady stream of bullocks on which it could leap.

Trouble was, he wasn't a lion. Battleships were lions. He was a snake in the grass. He could kill bullocks—freighters. He could kill lions, too. He'd done it, even in their very lair. But if they saw him slithering along before he got close enough to bite, they could kill him, too, and easily. They could also kill him if he struck and missed, as he had at that nasty hunting dog of a destroyer.

So much of patrol duty was endlessly, mind-numbingly boring. More often than not, Kimball chafed under such boredom. Today, for once, he welcomed it. It gave the crew a chance to recover from the long, tense time they'd spent submerged. It gave the diesels a chance to recharge the batteries in full. If that damned destroyer had stumbled across the boat too soon, she couldn't have gone underwater for long or traveled very far. A submarine that had to try to slug it out on the surface was a dead duck.

A quiet evening followed the quiet day. The crew needed to recharge their batteries, too. A lot of them spent a lot of time in their hammocks or wrapped in the blankets they spread next to or, more often, on top of equipment. The odor of fried fish jockeyed for position among all the other smells inside the pressure hull—Ben Coulter had caught a tuna that had almost ended up dragging him into the Atlantic instead of his being able to pull it out.

"You know what?" Kimball asked his exec. They'd both had big tuna steaks. Kimball wished for a toothpick; he had a shred of fish stuck between a couple of back teeth, and couldn't work it loose with his tongue.

"What's that, sir?" Tom Brearley asked.

"You know the Japs?" Kimball said. "You know what they do? They eat tuna raw sometimes. Either they dip it in horse-radish or bean juice or sometimes both of 'em together, or else they just eat it plain. Don't that beat hell?"

"You're making that up," Brearley said. "You've told me enough tall tales to stretch from the bottom of the ocean up to here. I'll be damned if you'll catch me again."

"Solemn fact," Kimball said, and raised his hand as if taking oath. His exec still wouldn't believe him. They both started to get angry, Kimball because he couldn't convince Brearley, the exec because he thought the skipper kept pulling his leg harder and harder. At last, disgusted, Kimball growled, "Oh, the hell with it," and stomped back down to the solitary albeit cramped splendor of his bunk.

He and Brearley were wary with each other the next morning, too, both of them speaking with military formality usually ig-nored aboard submersibles in every navy in the world. Then the lookout let out a holler—"Smoke off to the east!"—and they forgot about the argument.

Kimball hurried up to the top of the conning tower. The lookout pointed. Sure enough, not just one trail but several smudged the horizon. Kimball smiled a predatory smile. "Either those are freighters, or else they're warships loafing along without the least little idea we're anywhere around. Any which way, we're going to have some fun." He called down the hatch: "Give me twelve knots, and change course to 135. Let's get in front of the bastards and take a look at what we've got."

The *Bonefish* swung through the turn. Kimball peered through his binoculars. "What are we after?" Brearley asked from below.

"Looks like supply ships," Kimball answered. "Can't be sure they haven't got one of those disguised auxiliary cruisers sneaking along with 'em, though. Well, I don't give a damn if they do. We've still got plenty of fish on board, and I'm not talking about that damned tuna."

Skippers who paid attention to nothing but what was right in front of their noses did not live to grow old. While Kimball guided the *Bonefish* toward her prey, he kept another lookout up on the conning tower with him to sweep the rest of the horizon.

He jumped when the sailor tapped him on the shoulder. Apologetically, the fellow said, "I hate to tell you, sir, but there's smoke over on the western horizon, and whatever's making it looks to be heading this way in a hell of a hurry."

"Thanks, Caleb." Kimball turned, hoping the sailor was somehow mistaken. But he wasn't. Whatever was making that smoke was heading in the general direction of the *Bonefish*, and heading toward her faster than anything had any business traveling on the ocean. He raised the binoculars to his eyes. Almost as he watched, the ship crawled over the horizon. He counted stacks—one, two, three . . . four. Cursing, he said, "Go below, Caleb," and then bawled down the hatch: "All hands prepare to dive! Take her down to periscope depth."

The *Bonefish* had no trouble escaping the U.S. destroyer. Depth charges roared, but far in the distance. Tom Brearley said, "We spotted her in good time."

"That's not the point, goddammit," Kimball growled. "The point is, she made us break off the attack on those other Yankee ships. They'll get away clean while we're crawling along down here. She did what she was supposed to do, and she kept us from doing what we're supposed to do. Nobody does that to me." His voice sounded the more menacing for being flat and quiet. "*Nobody* does that to me, do you hear? I hope that destroyer hangs around this part of the ocean, 'cause if she does, I'll sink her."

Sylvia Enos felt like a billiard ball, caroming from one cushion to the next. She got off the trolley not by her house, but by the school a couple of stops away. After Brigid Coneval's husband stopped a bullet with his chest, Sylvia had had to enroll George, Jr., in kindergarten. He was enjoying himself there. That wasn't the problem. Neither was his staying on the school grounds till she got out of work. A lot of boys and girls did that. The school had a banner out front: WE STAY OPEN TO SUPPORT THE WAR EFFORT.

The problem was . . . "Come on, George," Sylvia said, tugging at his hand. "We've still got to pick up your sister."

George didn't want to go. "Benny hit me a while ago, and I haven't hit him back yet. I've got to, Mama."

"Do it tomorrow," Sylvia said. George, Jr., tried to twist free. She whacked him on the bottom, which got enough of his attention to let her drag him out of the schoolroom and back toward the trolley stop.

They missed the trolley anyhow—it clattered away just as

they hurried up. Sylvia whacked George, Jr., again. That might have made him feel sorry. Then again, it might not have. It did make Sylvia feel better. Twilight turned into darkness. Mosquitoes began to buzz. Sylvia sighed. Spring was here at last. She slapped, too late.

Fifteen minutes after they missed the trolley, the next car on the route came by. Sylvia threw two nickels in the fare box and rode back in the other direction, to the apartment of the new woman she'd found to watch Mary Jane. "I'm sorry I'm late, Mrs. Dooley," she said.

Rose Dooley was a large woman with a large, square jaw that might have made her formidable in the prize ring. "Try not to be late again, Mrs. Enos, if you please," she said, but then softened enough to admit, "Your daughter wasn't any trouble today."

"I'm glad," Sylvia said. "I am sorry." Blaming George, Jr., wouldn't have done any good. She took Mary Jane's hand. "Let's go home."

"I'm hungry, Mama," Mary Jane said.

"So am I," George, Jr., agreed.

By the time they got back to the apartment building, it was after seven. By then, the children weren't just saying they were hungry. They were shouting it, over and over. "If you hadn't dawdled on your way to the trolley, we've have been home a while ago, and you would be eating by now," Sylvia told George, Jr. That got Mary Jane mad at her big brother, but didn't stop either of the children from complaining.

They both complained some more when Sylvia paused to see if any mail had come. "Mama, we're *starving*," George, Jr., boomed. Mary Jane added shrill agreement.

"Hush, both of you." Sylvia held up an envelope, feeling vindicated. "Here is a letter from your father. You wouldn't have wanted it to wait, would you?"

That did quiet them, at least until they actually got inside the flat. George Enos had assumed mythic proportions to both of them, especially to Mary Jane, who hardly remembered him at all. One corner of Sylvia's mouth turned down. She wished her husband had mythic proportions in her eyes.

"If you read it to us, Mama, will you make supper right afterwards?" Mary Jane asked. Her brother's bluster hadn't worked; maybe bargaining would.

And it did. "I'll even start the fire in the stove now, so it will be getting hot while I'm reading the letter," Sylvia said. Her children clapped their hands.

She fed coal into the firebox with care; people at the canning plant said the Coal Board was going to cut the ration yet again, apparently intent on making people eat their food raw for the rest of the war. Glancing in the coal bin, she thought she probably had enough to keep cooking till the end of the month.

As soon as she walked back into the front room from the cramped kitchen, George, Jr., and Mary Jane jumped on her like a couple of football tackles. "Read the letter!" they chanted. "Read the letter!" Some of that was eagerness to hear from their father, more was likely to be eagerness to get her cooking.

She opened the envelope with a strange mixture of happiness and dread. If George had come into port to mail the letter, who could guess what he was doing besides mailing it? As a matter of fact, she could guess perfectly well. The trouble was, she couldn't know.

When she saw a scrawled line at the top of the page, she let out a silent sigh of relief. *A supply ship bound for home came alongside just after I finished this,* George had written, *so it will get to you soon.* That meant he hadn't set foot on dry land. She could relax, at least for a while.

" 'Dear Sylvia,' " Sylvia read aloud, " 'and little George who is getting big and Mary Jane too—' "

"I'm getting big!" Mary Jane said.

"I know you are, and so does your father," Sylvia said. "Shall I go on?" The children nodded, so she did: " 'I am fine. I hope you are fine. We are down here in the—' "

"Why did you stop, Mama?" George, Jr., asked.

"There's a word that's all scratched out, so I can't read it," Sylvia answered. *Censors,* she thought. *As if I'm going to tell anybody where George's ship is.* She resumed: " 'We are doing everything we can to whip our enemies. A sub tried to torpedo us, but we got away with no trouble at all.' "

"Wow!" George, Jr., said.

Sylvia wondered how much more dangerous that had been than George was making it out to be in his letter. Like any fisherman, he was in the habit of minimizing mishaps, to keep his loved ones from worrying. " 'We went after him and we'—oh, here are more words scratched out," she said. " 'They say we either damaged him or sunk him, and I hope they are right.' "

"What does *damaged* mean?" Mary Jane asked.

"Hurt," Sylvia answered. " 'I have chipped more paint than I ever thought there was in the whole wide world. The chow is not half so good as yours or what Charlie White used to make on the *Ripple* but there is plenty of it. Tell little George and Mary Jane to be good for me. I hope I see them and you real soon. I love you all and I miss you. George.' "

She set the letter on the table in front of the sofa. "Now make supper!" George, Jr., and Mary Jane yelled together.

"I've got some scrod, and I'll fry potatoes with it," Sylvia said. Even though George was in the Navy, she still had connections among the dealers and fishermen down on T Wharf. The transactions were informal enough that none of the many and various rationing boards knew anything about them. As long as she was content to eat fish—and she would have been a poor excuse for a fisherman's wife if she weren't—she and her family ate pretty well.

Fisherman's children, George, Jr., and Mary Jane ate up the tender young cod as readily as Sylvia did. And they plowed through mountains of potatoes fried in lard and salted with a heavy hand. Sylvia wished she could have given them more milk than half a glass apiece, but she didn't know anybody who had anything to do with milk rationing.

After she washed the supper dishes, she filled a big pitcher from the stove's hot-water reservoir and marched the children down to the end of the hall for their weekly bath. They went with all the delight of Rebel prisoners marching off into captivity in the United States.

They were as obstreperous as Rebel prisoners, too; by the time she had them clean, they had her wet. In dudgeon approaching high, she marched them back to the apartment and changed into a quilted housecoat. They played for a while— Mary Jane was alternately an adjunct and a hindrance to George, Jr.'s, game, which involved storming endless ranks of Confederate trenches. When he pretended to machine-gun her and made her cry, Sylvia called a halt to the proceedings.

She read to them from *Hiawatha* and put them to bed. But then, it was nearly nine o'clock. She'd have to get up before six to get George, Jr., off to kindergarten and Mary Jane to Mrs. Dooley's. Silently, she cursed Brigid Coneval's husband for getting shot. If he'd had any idea how much trouble his death was causing her, he never would have been so inconvenient.

Twenty minutes—maybe even half an hour—to herself, with no one to tell her what to do, seemed the height of luxury. Had George been here, she knew what he would have wanted to do with that time. And she would have gone along. Not only was it her wifely duty, he pleased her most of the time—or he had.

After a long day at the canning plant, after a long day made longer by missing the trolley when she was trying to retrieve Mary Jane, *wifely duty* didn't have a whole lot of meaning left to it. If she felt like making love, she would make love. If she didn't . . .

"I'll damn well go to bed, that's what," she said, and yawned. "And if George doesn't like it—"

If George didn't like it, he'd go out and find himself some strumpet. And then, one day, he'd drink too much, and he'd let her know. And then—

"Then I'll throw him out on his two-timing ear," she muttered, and yawned again. If she didn't intend to fall asleep on the sofa, which she'd done a couple of times, she needed to get ready for bed.

She made sure she wound and set the alarm clock. If she didn't, she wouldn't wake up on time, not tired as she was. She put on her nightgown, went and brushed her teeth at the sink by the toilet, and then walked into the bedroom, turned off the lamp, and lay down.

Despite weariness, sleep did not want to come. Sylvia worried about what would happen on the sea, and about how much George hadn't told her. She worried about what would happen if he didn't come home. And, almost equally, she worried about what would happen when he did come home. He would expect things to be the same as they had been before he went into the Navy and she went to work, and she didn't see how that was possible. She saw trouble ahead, with no more effort than she needed to see snow ahead in a boiling gray sky in February.

She writhed and stretched and wiggled and, at long last, went to sleep. When the alarm clock exploded into life beside her head, she had to clap a hand over her mouth to keep from screaming. Only after that did she recover enough to turn off the clock.

"Oh, God," she groaned, "another day." She got out of bed.

* * *

Lucien Galtier stared at the envelope in some perplexity. It bore no postage stamp, not even one of the peculiar sort the United States had prepared for occupied Quebec. Where the stamp should have been was a printed phrase in both English and French: UNDER THE PERMIT OF THE U.S. OCCUPYING AUTHORITY. PENALTY FOR UNAUTHORIZED USE, $300.

Marie had not opened the envelope. Instead, she'd sent Denise to get Charles, and Charles to bring Lucien to the farmhouse from the fields. "What sort of trouble are you in?" his wife demanded, glaring from the envelope to Lucien and back again as if unable to decide which of them she despised more.

"In the name of God, I do not know," he answered. "I have done nothing to make the occupying authorities dislike me, not for some time."

"Then why do they send this to you?" Marie said, confident he had no answer, as indeed he had none. Having reduced him to silence, she snapped, "Well, why do you hesitate? Open it, that we may see what sort of injustice they aim to inflict on us now."

"This I will do," Galtier replied. "Once I open it, at least I will know what the trouble is, and no longer be plagued by wild guesses." Marie ignored that, as beneath her dignity. When Charles, who had accompanied his father, presumed to smile, she froze the expression on his face with a glance.

Muttering under his breath, Galtier tore the envelope open. Inside was a single sheet of paper, again printed in both English and French. Marie snatched it out of his hands and read it aloud: " 'All citizens of this occupation district are cordially invited to gather in the market square of Rivière-du-Loup at two in the afternoon on Sunday, the fifteenth of April, 1917, to hear an important announcement and proclamation. Attendance at this festivity is not required, but will surely prove of interest.' "

"There! Do you see? I am not in difficulty with the authorities for any reason whatsoever," Lucien said triumphantly. "It is not a letter to me or even about me. It is a general circular, like a patent-medicine flyer."

Marie took no notice of his tone. She'd had more than twenty years' practice taking no notice of his tone when that suited her purposes, as it did now. She said, "For what reason do they send this out? They have never done anything like it before." She regarded the paper with deep suspicion.

Charles nodded vigorously. "They cordially invite us," he said. "They call this a festivity. They say we do not have to come to it. They have never done anything like this since they overran our country." Galtier's elder son was probably the quietest member of the family, and also the least reconciled to the U.S. occupation.

"It could be," Lucien said, "that Nicole will know more of this, working as she does at the hospital with so many Americans. For now, and until she comes home, I do not intend to worry about it, as I have plenty to do in the fields if we are to put in any sort of crop this year."

"Yes, go on, get out of the house," Marie said. "I also have plenty to do."

"And who called me to the house?" he asked, but he might as well have been talking to the air.

Even as he worked, though, he wondered about the peculiar announcement from the U.S. occupiers. It was the most nearly civil thing they had done in the nearly three years since they'd invaded Quebec. Up till now, civility had not been their long suit. He wondered why they were changing course. Like Marie, like most Quebecois, he was suspicious of change, as likely being for the worse.

Despite that suspicion of change, he would have been glad if Nicole had brought Dr. O'Doull home for supper. But she returned to the farmhouse by herself, and proved to be as startled by the flyer as the rest of the family.

"How are we to find out what it means?" she asked.

Georges spoke up, as innocent-sounding and sarcastic as usual: "It could be—and I know it is only a foolish notion of mine—we might even stay in town after we go to Mass, and hear this announcement and proclamation for ourselves."

His older sister glared at him. He beamed back, mild as milk, which only made her more furious. Before the row could go any further, Lucien said, "That is exactly what we shall do." Marie gave him a look that was anything but altogether approving. Once he had made his intention so plain, though, not even she saw any chance of getting him to change his mind.

The highway up to Rivière-du-Loup was more crowded than usual that Sunday morning, as many families from the outlying farms came in to the town to go to church and then stay. The big, snorting U.S. trucks always on the road had to use their horns again and again to clear the slow-moving wagons from their path. Many of the men in the wagons took their own sweet time about getting out of the way, too.

Splendid in his new vestments, Bishop Pascal officiated at the Mass. "Please stay for the afternoon's announcements," he urged his flock. "You will find it of interest, I assure you." He said no more than that, which both surprised Lucien and set him scratching his head. The Pascal he knew could hardly open his mouth without falling in. It was another change to mistrust.

When Galtier emerged from the church with his family, he found one more change: the market square had been draped with bunting, some red, white, and blue, some simply white and blue, the colors of Quebec. "What are they going to say?" he asked the air. "What are they going to do? Are they going to say we are now a part of the United States? If they say this, I say to them that we shall be a troubled part of the United States."

"We are here," Marie said. "Let us wait. Let us see. What else can we do?" There, Lucien found nothing with which to disagree.

They waited, and chatted with neighbors and with folk who did not live close by the farm and whom they saw but seldom. At precisely two o'clock, Major Jedediah Quigley and Bishop Pascal ascended to a bunting-draped platform a squad of U.S. soldiers had set up not far from the church.

An expectant hush fell. Into it, Major Quigley spoke in his elegant—his too-elegant—French: "My friends, I should like to thank all of you for coming here today and becoming a part of this great day in the history of your land. As others are announcing elsewhere at this very same moment, the government of the United States from this time forth recognizes the sovereignty and independence of the Republic of Quebec."

"The what?" Lucien frowned. "There is no such thing."

"There is now," someone behind him said. He nodded. He did not know what to feel: joy, fury, bewilderment? Bewilderment won. Quebecois were a separate people, yes, assuredly. Were they a separate nation? If they were, what sort of separate nation would they be?

Quigley was continuing: "I am pleased to announce that the sovereign and independent Republic of Quebec has already been accorded diplomatic recognition as a nation among the nations of the world by the German Empire, the Empire of Austria-Hungary, the Ottoman Empire, the Kingdom of Bulgaria, the

Kingdom of Poland, the Republic of Chile, the Republic of Paraguay, the government of the Republic of Liberia, and the government-in-exile of the Republic of Haiti in Philadelphia. Many other governments, I am certain, will soon recognize your new and thriving nation. From this, citizens of the Republic of Quebec, you can see that your well-deserved independence from the British creation of Canada is popular throughout the world."

From this, Lucien thought, *we can see that the United States and their allies recognize this so-called Republic, and that no one else does.* That left him anything but surprised: the Entente powers would hardly acknowledge that one of their own would be, could be, torn asunder. The Entente powers did not recognize the Poland the Germans had erected on soil taken from Russia, either.

As if on cue—afterwards, but only afterwards, Galtier wondered if it *was* on cue—a soldier came running up to the platform waving a pale yellow telegram. Quigley took it, read it, and stared out at the buzzing crowd. A wide smile spread across his narrow face. He waved the telegram, too. "My friends!" he cried, his voice choked with emotion either genuine or artfully portrayed. "My friends, word has just reached me that the Kingdom of Italy and the Kingdom of the Netherlands have also recognized the Republic of Quebec."

That made the buzzing even louder, and changed its note. Lucien did not buzz, but he did raise an eyebrow. Italy was a member of the Quadruple Alliance with the USA, Germany, and Austria-Hungary, but a backsliding member: she had been neutral since the war began. And the Netherlands, though bordered on her entire land frontier by Germany and German-occupied Belgium, still carried on what trade with England she could. She was a true neutral, and she had recognized this republic.

"I am greatly honored to congratulate Quebec on achieving her independence, even if it was far too many years delayed by British contempt," Major Quigley said, "and I am privileged to offer this salute to you, Quebecois free at last: *vive la République de Québec!*"

"Vive la République!" Not everyone in the square shouted it. Not even a majority of the people in the square shouted it. But a surprising number—surprising, at any rate, to Lucien, who kept silent with his family—did shout it. Everyone looked around to

see who shouted and who did not. Would feuds start because some had shouted and some had not?

Jedediah Quigley stepped back and Bishop Pascal stepped forward. *"Vive la République de Québec!"* he echoed, not inviting anyone else to shout the phrase but making clear where he himself stood. "I say to you, it is long past time that we should be free, free from the indignities the British have heaped on us for so long. How many of you men, when you were conscripted into the Army of the Canada that was, and when you tried to speak your beautiful French language, were told by some ugly English sergeant, 'Talk white!'?"

He dropped into English for those two words, which doubled their effect. Galtier chuckled uncomfortably. He'd heard sergeants say that, plenty of times. He was not the only man chuckling uncomfortably, either—far from it. Bishop Pascal knew how to flick where it was already raw.

He continued, "How many times have we had our sacred faith mocked by the Protestants in Ottawa, men who would not know piety and holiness if they came knocking on their doors? How many times must we be shown we are not and cannot be the equals of the English before we decide we have had a sufficiency? Soon, I pray, the Republic of Quebec will embrace all the Quebecois of *la belle province de Québec*. Until that time comes, though, which God hasten, we have begun. Go with God, my friends, and pray with me for the success of *la République de Québec*. Go in peace," he finished, as he had finished the Mass not long before.

"What do we do now, Father?" It was Georges who asked the question, his voice and his expression both unwontedly serious.

"I do not know," Lucien answered, and he could hear that he was far from the only man saying *Je ne sais pas* in the square at that moment. Slowly, he went on, "It is plain to see that this Republic, so-called, is to be nothing but a creature of the United States. But we were not altogether our own men in Canada, either. So I do not know. We shall have to see what passes."

"It is too soon to tell what this all means." Where Lucien had groped for words, Marie spoke with great finality. They both said the same thing, though. In the end, they usually did. Seeing as much, their children for once forbore to argue.

* * *

"Remembrance Day soon," Captain Jonathan Moss remarked to Lieutenant Percy Stone as the two fliers rode battered bicycles along a dirt road not far from the aerodrome near Arthur, Ontario. Both men wore .45s on their hips; trouble wasn't likely hereabouts, but it wasn't impossible, either. Ontario remained resentful about occupation.

"It'll be a good one," Stone answered. His breath still steamed when he spoke, though spring, by the calendar, was almost a month old. It didn't steam too much, though; it wasn't the great cloud of frost it would have been at the equinox. Here and there, a few green blades of grass were poking up through the mud, though snow might yet put paid to them.

"A good one? It'll be the best one ever," Moss said. "Everything we've remembered for so long, we're finally paying back."

But Stone shook his head. "The best Remembrance Day ever will be the one after the war is over and we've whipped the Rebs and the Canucks and the limeys. Everything till then is just a buildup."

Moss considered, then nodded. "All right, Percy. You've got me there."

Stone looked around. "This road could use some building up. Come to that, this whole countryside could use some building up."

"Well, you're right about that, too," Moss said. "Of course, you could say the same thing about just about any piece of Ontario we're sitting on. If we haven't ironed it flat to use it for something in particular, it's had the living bejesus shot out of it."

As if to prove his point, he had to swerve sharply to keep from steering his bicycle into a shell hole that scarred the road as smallpox scarred the face. And, as smallpox could scar more than the face, shell holes and bomb craters scarred more than the road; they dotted the whole landscape.

By what had to be a miracle, a twenty-foot stretch of wooden fence still stood next to the road not much farther on. Moss dug his heels into the dirt to stop his bicycle. He studied the fence with astonished fascination. "How many bullet holes do you suppose that timber's got in it, Percy?" he asked.

"More than I feel like counting, I'll tell you that," Stone answered at once. "We should have brought Hans along. He'd count 'em, and tell you how many were our .30 caliber and how many the .303 the limeys and Canucks were shooting back at us."

"You only think you're joking," Moss said. His friend shook his head. He wasn't joking, and they both knew it. Hans Oppenheim *would* do the counting, and was liable to try to figure out how many men on each side were firing captured weapons, too.

Then Jonathan Moss stopped worrying about bullet holes and, for that matter, about Hans Oppenheim, too. Moving slowly across a battered field by the side of the road was a fair-haired woman of about his own age. She led a couple of scrawny cows toward a little creek that meandered through the field.

Percy Stone was also eyeing the young woman. He and Moss stopped their bicycles at the same time, as if they had turned their aeroplanes together up above the trench line. "You're a married man," Moss murmured to Stone.

"I know that," his flightmate answered. Then he raised his voice: "Miss! Oh, Miss!"

The woman's head came up, like that of a deer when a hunter steps on a dry twig. She looked back toward the distant farmhouse from which she'd come, then toward the much closer Americans. Plainly, her every urge was to flee, but she didn't quite dare. "What do you want?" she demanded, her voice, like her face, wild and wary and hunted.

And what will Percy say to that? Moss wondered. *Something like, Will you take a couple of dollars for a roll in the hay?* Moss didn't think that approach would work. Moss didn't think any approach would work, not with a woman who had trouble even holding still in their presence.

Percy Stone didn't even smile at her. He said, "If you'd be so kind, could we buy some milk from you?"

"You're a genius," Moss breathed. Stone did smile then, one of his little, self-deprecating grins.

The young woman stared at the cows as if she'd never seen them before, as if they betrayed her merely by being there. Visibly gathering her courage, she shook her head. "No," she said. "I haven't anything—not one single thing—that I'd sell to you Yanks."

Moss and Stone looked at each other. That was the reaction the U.S. occupiers got from almost all the Canucks in Ontario. From everything Moss had heard, it wasn't like that everywhere in Canada. If it had been, the USA never could have set up the Republic of Quebec farther east.

"We don't mean you any harm, Miss," he said, "but my friend

is right. Some fresh milk would be good, and we'd gladly pay you for it."

"If you don't mean any harm," the woman said, "why don't you get out of my country, go back to yours, and leave us alone?" Her head came up in defiance; if she wasn't going to run away from a couple of Yanks, she'd give them a piece of her mind instead.

"If you want to argue like that, why did England invade my country from Canada during the Second Mexican War?" Moss returned.

"Why did you Yanks try invading us during your Revolution, and again during the War of 1812?" she said. "You can't blame us for not trusting you. You've never given us any reason to trust you, and you've given us plenty of reason not to."

"Did we invade Canada back then?" Moss whispered to Stone.

Stone shrugged. "Don't know. If we did, we didn't win, so you can't expect the history books to say much about it."

Moss grunted. "In that case, the history books wouldn't have much to say about anything that's happened since the War of Secession." But it wasn't the same thing, and he knew it. Since the War of Secession, the USA had been put upon. Everybody knew that. If the United States had been trying to do the muscling in the earlier days and had got licked, too, that wasn't just defeat. It was embarrassment, which was worse.

"You don't even believe me," the young woman jeered. "Your schools have filled you so full of lies, you don't believe the truth when you hear it. If you want to know what I think, that's pretty sad."

"What makes you so sure you're preaching the Gospel?" Moss said, getting angry in turn. "I never once heard of a Canuck who wouldn't lie."

He didn't care about milk any more. He wanted to wound the young woman. To his surprise, she laughed. "How do I know I'm telling the truth? Because my maiden name is Laura Secord, that's how. I'm named after my four-times-great aunt, who went through twenty miles of woods in the dark to let the British soldiers know you Yanks had invaded. And do you know what else? Laura Secord was born in Massachusetts. Up here, any school child knows about her."

"Like Paul Revere," Stone muttered, and Moss ruefully nodded.

"Maybe you won that time," he said to Laura who had been born Secord, "but we're here to stay now. You may as well learn to like it."

"Go on your way, Yank," she said, tossing her head. "You'll be older than Methuselah before we learn to like it. And don't be too sure you're here to stay, either. We're still in the fight." The slight Scots burr that distinguished the Canadian accent from the American made her sound very determined indeed.

"Where is your husband?" Percy Stone demanded, his voice suddenly harsh, too.

"Where? Where do you think? In the Canadian Army, where he belongs," the young woman answered. "I told you once—now I tell you again, go on your way." She spoke with an odd authority, as if she owned the land and were entitled to give commands on it.

The breeze picked up her yellow hair, which hung uncurled and unconfined, and threw it out behind her like a flag. Her eyes, granite gray, blazed. If her husband was anywhere near as formidable as she, Moss thought, he'd be one dangerous Canuck with a rifle in his hands. Just for a moment, she put the flier in mind of a Viking, and made him wonder, only a little less than seriously, if she'd charge down on him and Stone.

She did take a step toward the two Americans. It was not a charge, though. Her face crumpled; tears ran down her cheeks. Her voice choked, she said, "Go on. Can you not have at least the simple human decency to let me be? Is that too much to ask?"

Without answering her, without looking at Percy Stone, Moss started riding again. A moment later, the former photographer from Ohio joined him. "Quite a lot of woman there," Stone remarked after a bit.

Jonathan Moss nodded. "Quite a lot of lady there, too," he said. "After a while, you forget the difference between the one and the other, till it up and stares you in the face."

Stone nodded. "A woman like that—" He sighed. "She makes you wish she liked the USA better. If we could win over that kind of people, we'd win the war and the peace both."

"I wonder what they do in Canada instead of Remembrance Day," Moss said. "They've been on top so long, they don't know what it's like to be on the bottom. And"—he tried to forestall his friend—"I don't give a damn about what the first Laura Secord did a hundred years ago."

"Why not?" Stone said, not about to be forestalled. "If she hadn't made it through those woods back then, maybe Canada would have been part of the USA the past hundred years, and we wouldn't have to worry about beating the Canucks now."

"If I'm going to play the game of might-have-beens, I'd sooner play it with the War of Secession, thanks. If we'd won that and kept the damn Rebs in the United States with us, maybe—"

"Fat chance," Percy Stone said. "They had England and France on their side, and Lee and Jackson for generals. Jackson licked us again twenty years later, too. And what did we have? President Abraham Lincoln!" His lip curled contemptuously.

Moss sighed and nodded. Might-have-beens was a stupid game, when you got right down to it. Look back on things, and you couldn't help but see they'd come out the way they had to come out.

VII

Everything squelched. That was Private First Class Reginald Bartlett's overwhelming impression of the Red River bottomlands. If you put a foot down on the boggy ground, it squelched. If you dug a spade into it, threw away the dirt, and turned your back for a minute, the hole would be half full of water when you turned around again.

"We have to dig in, men," First Lieutenant Jerome Nicoll said, over and over, as he was in the habit of saying things over and over. "We have to hold on to whatever corners of Sequoyah we can, same as the British and the Belgians are keeping some of Belgium free from the Hun's boot. They're entrenched in the muck of Flanders, same as we are here. We have to hold on."

"Good thing the British and the Belgians are helpin' us keep the Huns out of Sequoyah, ain't it?" Napoleon Dibble said.

"Sure as hell is," Reggie agreed gravely. "And it's just as much a fact—God damn me to hell if it's not—that what we're doing right here, Nap, is keeping the damnyankees from pouring troops into Belgium."

"For true?" Nap Dibble's eyes got big and round. "I didn't know that." He started digging like a man with a mission, dirt flying from his entrenching tool as if from a steam shovel. "Then this here's important business, I reckon."

Sergeant Pete Hairston coughed a couple of times, then pinned Reggie under his gaze as an entomologist might have pinned a butterfly to his specimen board. "God damn you to hell is right," the veteran grunted in a low voice, so Bartlett would hear and the still furiously digging Dibble wouldn't.

"Have a heart, Sarge," Reggie said, also quietly. "I wasn't telling him anything that wasn't so, now was I?"

"Maybe not," Sergeant Hairston answered. "But you sure as

hell weren't telling him anything he could use, neither." He slapped at himself and cursed. "I'll tell you what *I* could use. I could use one of those goddamn flame-throwing gadgets they're starting to issue, that's what."

"You don't want to just shoot the damnyankees?" Reggie asked. "You want to toast 'em instead?"

"Fuck toasting the damnyankees," Hairston answered. "You got to be crazy to want to get up close enough to 'em to use one o' them flamethrowers. Nah, what I want to do is, I want to wave that damn thing around and toast me about a million billion mosquitoes." He slapped again.

"Ah. Now I get you, Sarge." Reggie Bartlett was slapping, too, and not having much luck. "And after you toasted that million billion, there'd only be about a jillion million billion of the sons of bitches left, and that doesn't count the chiggers or the ticks or the leeches."

"Don't remind me." Not only did Hairston slap, he scratched, too. "And fleas and cooties and all the other little bastards."

"Back in Richmond, I was a druggist's helper," Bartlett said wistfully. "Seems like a hundred years ago now. This time of year, we'd sell camphor candles by the dozen, to keep the mosquitoes away, and zinc-oxide ointment, and little bottles of kerosene with perfume in it to kill lice and nits. Some pretty high-class folks would buy that stuff, too."

"Always knew there was a bunch of lousy bastards runnin' things in Richmond," Hairston said. "Just goes and proves things, don't it?"

Joe Mopope came mooching along. What he was looking to see, Reggie knew, was whether the entrenchments had got big and deep enough for him to scramble down into them without doing any digging of his own. The Kiowa was a hell of a fighting man. He enjoyed fighting. What he didn't enjoy was the work that went into making sure you stayed alive in between fights.

"Hey, Joe," Reggie called, "you got any secret Indian tricks for keeping the mosquitoes and things off you?"

"You got to do two things," the Kiowa answered. His long face was serious to the point of being somber. All the white men in earshot leaned forward to hear his words of wisdom. Seeing that he had everybody's attention, he gave a dramatic pause as good as anything on a vaudeville stage, then went on, "You got to slap like hell, and you got to scratch like hell."

"And *you* got to go to hell, Joe," Sergeant Hairston said, but he was laughing. Joe Mopope never cracked a smile. Hairston added, "You got us good that time, but I'm gonna get you back. I know just how, too: hop down here, whip out a spade, and set yourself to diggin'."

"Damnyankees wouldn't treat me this way," Mopope said. He did start entrenching, although without much enthusiasm. "Maybe I should have stayed in town and let them come along."

"Oh, yeah." Hairston's nod was venomously sarcastic. "That would have been really great, Joe. The CSA's let you Indians do pretty much like you please up here in Sequoyah. Ain't been like that in the USA. After we licked 'em in the War of Secession, they took out after the Sioux, and they been takin' out after their redskins ever since. They purely don't fancy your kind of people, and I don't reckon they'd give you a big kiss now."

Joe Mopope exhaled through his nose: not quite a snort, but close. "Oh, yeah. The president in Richmond treats us halfway decent 'cause he likes us. Come on. It's 'cause he can use us against the Yankees, and everybody knows it."

Hairston stared at him. So did Reggie Bartlett. Little by little, the Kiowa was making him realize a red skin didn't mean the fellow wearing it was stupid. Reggie glanced over at Nap Dibble, who was still working away like a machine. A white skin didn't turn somebody into a college professor all by itself, either.

Maybe, if he'd had the chance to think about it, he would have wondered what having a black skin meant. He might even have wondered if it meant anything more than a red one or a white one. But, at that moment, rifle fire broke out to the north: U.S. troops, prodding at the Confederate position. He stuck his entrenching tool in his belt, grabbed his Tredegar off his shoulder, and squatted down on the damp ground to see how bad it would get.

The soldiers in green-gray didn't come swarming and rampaging toward him. Only mosquitoes swarmed hereabouts. Machine guns started hammering. Reggie watched the Yankees who were on their feet go flat, some wounded, some prudent enough to try to make sure they wouldn't be. He fired a couple of rounds, but had no idea whether he hit anyone.

One of the U.S. field guns opened up. The shells tore up the swampy bottom country, but not so badly as they would have had the ground been harder and drier. And much of their explosive force went down into the muck or straight up, rather than out in all directions.

All the things that made Reggie glad when the U.S. troops were shelling the Confederates made him sorry when his own gunners returned the fire. They didn't hurt the damnyankees nearly so much as he thought they should.

But the U.S. soldiers did not press the attack. Instead, they began to dig in where they lay. Maybe that was all they'd intended to do: push their own lines a little farther forward with this attack so they could try pushing the Confederates back with the next one or the one after that.

"If they had a lot of artillery, they'd ruin us or drive us down into Texas," Pete Hairston said gloomily. "They'd shoot up all the river crossings so we couldn't move supplies into Sequoyah any more, and that'd be that. But they haven't got much more in the way of supplies than we do, so we'll hang on a while longer. Damned if I know how to push 'em back, though."

"Mebbe they'll all drown in the mud an' never be seen no more, Sarge," Nap Dibble suggested.

Had anyone else said it, it would have been a joke, and everyone would have laughed. The trouble was, Nap meant it, and that was painfully plain to his comrades. In a more gentle voice than he would have used to speak to most of his soldiers, Hairston said, "Only trouble with that is, Nap, we're down here in the mud with 'em, and we'd likely drown first."

"Oh, that's right, Sarge." Dibble nodded brightly. "I wonder how come I didn't think of that."

"Funny thing about that, ain't it?" Hairston said. He wasn't mocking Dibble, not in the least. He got the most he could from a man who was willing without being very bright. Reggie Bartlett admired the way the sergeant handled Nap. He doubted he would have had the patience to match it.

Lieutenant Nicoll came by, inspecting the part of the line his company was digging. He nodded. "This is how you do it, men. Dig in well and the Yankees can never dislodge you."

"Dig in well, men," Reggie echoed after Nicoll had gone on his way. "Dig in well and they can't drive you out of Waurika. Dig in well and they can't drive you out of Ryan. Dig in well and you'll have your own grave all nice and ready for those damnyankee sons of bitches to plant you in it."

Joe Mopope's grunt was evidently intended for a laugh. "You

face this the way one of my people would," he said. "What will be, will be. Whatever it is, you move toward it. You cannot help moving toward it. It is there. It waits for you. You cannot escape it."

"I joined up as soon as the war started," Bartlett answered. "I've spent too damn much time in the trenches since. A lot of time when I wasn't in the trenches, I was in a damnyankee prison camp because the bastards nabbed me when I was up at the front. I've seen enough now that nothing I see from here on out is going to surprise me a whole hell of a lot."

The other soldiers nodded. They were grimy and unshaven and tired and wet and full of bites. Pete Hairston said, "Whatever happens, I reckon I'm ready for it." The soldiers nodded again.

Joe Mopope studied them. "You are warriors, all of you," he said at last. "You are not just soldiers. You are warriors."

"Whatever the hell we are, it isn't worth gettin' into an uproar about it," Bartlett said. More nods. He fished through his pockets and found a scrap of paper that had stayed dry. More fishing revealed a tobacco pouch, but it was empty. "Anybody have some makings? I'm plumb out."

"I got some," Sergeant Hairston said. Reggie held out his hand with the paper in it. Hairston poured tobacco onto the paper. Nodding his thanks, Reggie rolled the cigarette. After a couple of drags, he felt better.

Sergeant Chester Martin envied U.S. Army engineers. They always seemed to know exactly what they were doing. He knew that wasn't always so, but it was so often enough to leave him impressed. His own part in the war, he strongly felt, he was making up as he went along.

He also envied the engineers because they were cleaner than he was. A lot of them wore boots that almost reached their knees—cavalry boots—which kept their trousers from getting as filthy as his. They worked now with fussy precision, laying out lengths of white tape from one stick to another.

"What's all this about?" David Hamburger asked. "They laying out the route for the Remembrance Day parade?"

"Couple days too early for May Day," Martin said with a grin, needling the private with a Socialist congresswoman for a sister. "Besides, if it was for that, the tape'd be red, and then you'd get up and march along it and get yourself shot."

"Funny, Sarge," the Hamburger kid said. "Funny like a crutch." But he was grinning, even laughing a little. He hadn't seen much action—things had been quiet since Martin crossed the Potomac to join B Company of the 91st—but he fit in as well as if he'd been wearing green-gray since 1914.

Tilden Russell said, "If he was paradin' for May Day, the Rebs wouldn't shoot at him, not with all the colored troops they've got in their trenches. Those smokes are better true-blue Reds than any Socialist from outta New York City, even if he does have his sister in Congress tellin' Teddy Roosevelt how to run things."

"I don't know why you expect Roosevelt to listen to Flora," David Hamburger said. "He hasn't listened to anybody else since he got elected."

Martin laughed. Corporal Reinholdt, on the other hand, scowled. "Shut up," he said in a flat, hostile voice. "Nobody's gonna make fun of the president of the United States while I'm here to kick his ass."

"Hey, take it easy, Bob," Martin said. "Nobody's getting in an uproar about this."

"Oh, now you're gonna undercut me, are you, Sarge?" Reinholdt growled. "Must be another goddamn Red yourself."

Had he left off the adjective and smiled, he might have got by with it. As things were, Martin couldn't ignore it. He'd been waiting for this moment since he got here. It had held off longer than he'd expected, but it wouldn't hold off any more. His right hand went into a trouser pocket and came out in a fist. "Get up," he snapped at Reinholdt, who was hunkered down over a tin coffeepot.

"Yeah?" the corporal said as he got to his feet. He was shorter and stockier than Chester Martin; they probably weighed within five pounds of each other. By the way Reinholdt leaned forward, he knew the time was here, too. He took a step toward Martin. "Come in here and take the slot that shoulda been mine, will you?" A season's worth of resentment boiled in him. "I ought to—"

"Oh, shove it up your ass, or I'll—" In the middle of the sentence, without warning, Martin threw a left. Reinholdt ducked with a scornful laugh. Martin laughed, too. He hadn't expected much from that left. The arm still wasn't so strong as it should have been, not after the wound he'd taken.

His right, though ... The uppercut caught Bob Reinholdt

square on the point of the chin. Reinholdt didn't fall over; he was made of stern stuff. But the punch he had on the way ran out of steam before it got near Martin, and was hardly more than a pat when it connected with his ribs. Reinholdt's eyes stayed open, but they weren't seeing much.

Martin had the luxury of deciding whether to kick him in the crotch. He kicked him in the belly instead, with precisely measured viciousness. Reinholdt folded up like a sailor's concertina. Martin hit him in the face again for good measure as he was going down.

"He didn't need that last one," Tilden Russell said, sudden respect in his voice over and above that to which Martin's three stripes entitled him. He studied Reinholdt, who lay unmoving. "He wasn't going anywhere anyway."

"Maybe not." Martin shrugged. "You ever get in a saloon brawl, though, one of the first things you learn is, never let the other guy think he could have licked you if you hadn't got lucky."

"Sarge, I don't think you need to worry about that," David Hamburger said.

Martin wondered whether the kid was right. When the real fighting started, would he be able to trust Reinholdt behind his back with a rifle? He'd have to do some thinking there. For now, though, he'd taken care of what needed taking care of. "Throw some water in his face," he told Hamburger. "He's got no business sleeping on the job."

His hand went back into his pocket. The short, fat steel cylinder he stashed there was just about as good as a set of brass knuckles, and a hell of a lot less conspicuous. Such toys were commonplace in the saloon fights among steelworkers in Toledo; Martin gave hardly more thought to having one than he would have to a box of matches.

Reinholdt groaned and spat blood when David Hamburger flipped water on him. After a while, the battered corporal sat up. His eyes still didn't want to focus. He spat again. This time, the red had a couple of white flecks in it. He looked up at Martin. "What the hell you hit me with?"

"This." Martin showed him his right fist. He didn't show him the steel cylinder he'd had in it. He went on in a pleasant tone of voice: "You better pay attention to what I'm telling you now, Bob. You try messing around with me again and one of us is

liable to end up dead. I'm going to tell you one other thing, too—
it won't be me. Now, you got all that?"

"I got it," Reinholdt said. Maybe he was even convinced.
Martin couldn't tell. The battered corporal tried to get to his feet.
On the second try, he made it. His legs were still wobbly. He
rubbed his jaw. "Shit, feels like I got bounced with a rock." He
spoke like a man with considerable knowledge of such things.

"Just remember that next time, is all," Martin said.

Reinholdt nodded, then winced. Martin had caught a couple
on the buzzer in his time, too; he knew Reinholdt had what felt
like the world's worst hangover, without even the fun of getting
drunk first. "Oh, yeah," the corporal said. "I'll remember. Shit,
tomorrow's Remembrance Day." He turned and walked down
the trench. Privates made a point of getting out of his way as fast
as they could.

Later that day, Captain Cremony summoned Martin to the
dugout where he was filling out ammunition requisition forms.
The company commander looked up from the forms and said, "I
hear you and Reinholdt had a little talk about the weather this
morning."

"Sir?" Had Martin looked any more innocent, a halo would
have sprung into being above his head. "I don't know what
you're talking about, sir."

"Of course you don't—and if pigs had wings, we'd all carry
umbrellas," Cremony said with heavy irony.

"If pigs had wings, they'd be generals, sir," Martin answered.
"And you're right, we'd all carry umbrellas."

Cremony stared at him, then started to laugh. "If you'd said
'captains,' you'd be on your way back to the guardhouse this
minute." His eyes narrowed. "But you're not going to distract
me with a joke." Since that was what Martin had hoped to do, he
stood still, a serious expression on his face, as if the idea had never
entered his mind. He'd had plenty of practice looking opaque for
officers. Captain Cremony grunted. "Dammit, Martin, I understand why this happened, but the timing was very bad."

"Yes, sir. I'm sorry, sir," Martin said. "I couldn't really take
care of that as well as I might have, though. If a fellow wants to
talk about the weather right then and there, sometimes you just
have to listen to him."

"Sergeant, if there's no more talk of the weather between the
two of you, I will forget this discussion," the company com-

mander said. "If there is, I'll have to remember it. After all, tomorrow is Remembrance Day, and we'll have all sorts of things to remember then."

"Oh, yes, sir," Martin said. "I know that, sir. In a way, I'm just as glad Bob and I had this little talk now instead of waiting till later. We might have said sharper things to each other later, if you know what I mean."

"As I said, I'm not remembering any of this. And I'd better not have a reason to remember it. I'm telling that to you, and I'll tell it to Reinholdt. If I do have reason to remember it, you'll both be sorry. Dismissed, Sergeant."

Martin tromped over boards and through mud back to his section. When he got there, he found Bob Reinholdt drinking coffee out of the side of his mouth. He didn't say anything to Reinholdt about Captain Cremony's warning; that would have made him into the teacher's pet. He'd seen that Cremony knew what he was doing. The company commander would get the message across.

Reinholdt didn't say anything to him, either. That suited him fine.

An engineer came along the trench. Every so often, he would pause, get up on the firing step, and peer through binoculars south toward Round Hill, Virginia, and the Confederate lines in front of it. Then he'd scribble something in a notebook, go on a little farther, and look south again.

"You don't mind me saying so, sir, that's a hell of a good way to get yourself shot," Chester Martin remarked.

"Do tell?" the engineer said, as if the notion had never crossed his mind. "Chance I take, that's all. Have to hope the niggers in those Rebel trenches over yonder can't shoot."

"Haven't seen any sign of that, sir, have to tell you," Martin said. "They don't seem much different than white troops, far as that goes. They throw a lot of lead around, and every so often somebody gets hit. The bullet doesn't care who shot it, only where it's going."

"Chance I take," the engineer repeated, and worked his way down the trench line, not making a fuss, just doing his job. No cries of alarm rose, nor shouts for stretcher-bearers, so Martin supposed he got away with it.

Dusk fell. Martin rolled himself in a blanket, against the chill and against mosquitoes both. He fell asleep right away. He almost always fell asleep right away. He woke up every bit as fast, too, commonly grabbing for a weapon.

Sometime in the middle of the night, a horrible clatter and rumble had him on his feet with his Springfield halfway to his shoulder before he realized that, whatever else it was, it wasn't gunfire. It wasn't C.S. bombing aeroplanes overhead, either. "What the hell?" he said. "What the hell?"

"It's the barrels coming up, Sarge," David Hamburger said in the darkness. "Remembrance Day today."

"That's right," Martin breathed. "Remembrance Day today."

In Philadelphia, Flora Hamburger discovered she'd had only the vaguest notion of what Remembrance Day meant. Up till then, she'd lived her whole life in New York City. Her home town observed Remembrance Day, of course. How could it be otherwise? April 22, the day marking the end of the Second Mexican War, had been a national day of mourning ever since. But New York City did not observe Remembrance Day the way the rest of the United States did.

Oh, there were always military parades and speeches, the same as there were elsewhere in the country. But there were also always Socialist counter-demonstrations and hecklers in New York City; Flora had been caught up in the Remembrance Day riots of 1915. The Socialist Party was not about to let Remembrance Day steal its May Day thunder.

In Philadelphia, though, the Socialist Party maintained a much smaller presence. Philadelphia was a city of government, and therefore, overwhelmingly, a city of Democrats. It was also, far more than New York, a city of soldiers.

No one mocked here. No one heckled here. People crowded along the parade route to cheer the soldiers and the Soldiers' Circle men of prewar conscription classes—not so many of them left, not with the guns so hungry these past nearly three years—and the graying veterans of the Second Mexican War and the aged veterans of the War of Secession and even, riding along in a motorcar, a pair of ancient veterans of the Mexican War, the last war against a foreign power the United States had won.

Church bells pealed. Flora knew the churches were packed, too, packed with people lamenting past U.S. defeats and praying for future victory. Someone in the crowd on the far side of

Chestnut Street from the platform where Flora sat with the rest of Congress and other government dignitaries held up a placard that seemed to sum up the mood as well as anything: IT'S OUR TURN THIS TIME.

Aeroplanes buzzed overhead—U.S. fighting scouts, flying in swarms to make sure the CSA did not interrupt the day's observances. Flora craned her neck to watch them. They put her in mind of dragonflies, and were far more interesting than the endless parade of soldiers and marching bands and veterans.

As he had a way of doing at functions, Hosea Blackford sat close to her. Seeing her looking up into the sky, he said, "It was even more interesting a couple of years ago, when the Confederates stood on the Susquehanna. Then there were dogfights above the parade, and the C.S. bombers dropped their toys not far from the parade route."

"It was more interesting in New York City, too," Flora said. "I was there for the riots that year."

Blackford frowned. "I wish they had never happened. They did the Party a great deal of damage around the country, damage from which it has not entirely recovered even now."

Flora said, "Nobody knows to this day who threw the bomb that started the riot, whether it was a Socialist or a Mormon who sympathized with the rebellion in Utah."

"That's true," the congressman from Dakota said. "But it's also true that Socialists did most of the rioting, no matter how the trouble started."

"What if it is?" Flora said. "What if it is? We were trying to do something to stop this useless, senseless war. It's more than anyone else in the country was doing. It's more than anyone else in the Socialist Party was doing, too," she added pointedly.

"How could anyone stop the war by then?" Hosea Blackford said. "We were fighting the Confederate States from the Gulf of California to the Atlantic, against Canada heavily from Winnipeg east and here and there farther west, too, and against England and France and Japan on the high seas. It was too big to stop. It still is."

"It should never have started," Flora said. "A Hapsburg prince wasn't reason enough to throw the world on the fire."

"Maybe you're even right," Blackford said. "But when Roosevelt called on us to vote for war credits, what would have happened if we had said no? I would not be in Congress now, you would not be in Congress now, none of us would be in Congress now."

"My brother would not be in Virginia now," Flora said. "My sister would not be a widow now. My nephew would not be growing up without ever having the chance to know his father now. If you think I would not go back to New York and make that bargain, Mr. Blackford, you are mistaken."

"You shame me," he said quietly.

"I think the Party needs shaming," Flora answered. "I think the Party—especially outside of New York City—has become too bourgeois for its own good, and forgotten the oppressed workers and peasants of the world. If the Socialist Party in the USA goes to war against the Labour Party in England and the Socialist Party in France, where is the international solidarity of Socialism? I'll tell you where—down in the trenches with a rifle, that's where."

Blackford did not reply. Instead, he made a small production out of lighting a cigar. Before he had to say anything more, a rumbling, clanking rattle and ecstatic shouts from the crowd farther up the parade route made Flora forget about the conversation, at least for a little while. Like everyone else, she was staring at the enormous mechanical contraptions lumbering along Chestnut Street.

President Theodore Roosevelt's voice rose above the racket from the snorting monsters. "Bully!" Roosevelt shouted, as enthusiastic as a small boy over a tin motorcar. "By George, what a bully pack of machines they are!"

They were impressive, if size and noise were the criteria for impressiveness. Each had a cannon at the snout and bristled with machine guns. They were the deadliest-looking things Flora had ever seen. The fighting scouts in the sky were killing machines, too, but graceful and elegant killing machines. The barrels were as graceful and elegant as so many rhinoceri.

Each of them had in it a man standing up so that the top half of his body was outside the square cupola in the middle of the machine's roof. Each of those soldiers saluted the platform, and Roosevelt in particular, as his barrel waddled past.

"Now go into the fight!" Roosevelt shouted to one barrel after another. "Now go into the fight, and teach all those who dare trifle with the might of the United States the error and folly of their ways!"

He was indeed like a boy playing with tin motorcars and lead soldiers and aeroplanes carved from balsa wood. But his toys really burned and bled and crashed—and made other, similar toys with different markings and colors burn and bleed and crash. He seemed not to understand that.

Flora wondered how such a blind spot was possible. She turned to Hosea Blackford with a question that had, on the surface, little to do with their previous argument: "Roosevelt fought in war. How can he take it so lightly?"

"Because he is what he seems, I suppose," Blackford answered. "Because he really does believe everything he preaches. And, not least, I suppose, because he enjoyed himself and won glory when he went to war."

"But he's been in the trenches now," Flora persisted. "He knows there is no glory in fighting against cannon and machine guns. My brother's sergeant helped him take cover when the Confederates shelled the part of the line he was visiting—David has written me about it. How can he not see?"

"He sees the country going forward. He doesn't see the suffering he's creating to make it go in the direction he wants," Blackford said slowly. "That's the best answer I can give you, and I doubt he could give you a better one."

Flora wondered about that. Roosevelt was a good deal more eloquent than she'd expected him to be. But he was hardly an introspective man, so perhaps Blackford had a point after all.

The clank and rattle and rumble of the barrels faded in the distance. So, more slowly, the noise of the crowd faded, too. A sort of muted thunder remained. Flora had heard it whenever things grew quiet along the parade route. She wondered what it was. It put her in mind of the roar of the sea by the oceanside, but more by its steadiness than by the sound itself.

Up at the front of the platform, President Roosevelt approached a microphone—which was, Flora thought irreverently, like a fat man approaching a chocolate cake, for the president had no more need of the one than the fat fellow did of the other.

"Listen!" Roosevelt called to the crowd. Pointing to the south, he went on, "Do you know what that is?" Flora realized the low reverberations were coming from that direction.

"Tell us!" somebody—probably a paid shill—called from the crowd.

"I will tell you," Roosevelt said. "That is the sound of our heavy guns, shelling the forces of the Confederate States still on U.S. soil. We are also shelling them on their own territory, and the Canadians and British opposing us in the north. This is a Remembrance Day they shall remember forever, yes, remember with fear and trembling."

How the people cheered! Listening to them sent a chill through Flora. The war was not popular in her home district, nor anything about it. The war itself was probably unpopular in Philadelphia, too. But victory, and what victory would bring—those were popular. Flora's district was full of immigrants, newcomers to the United States, who didn't bear the full weight of a half century's resentment and hatred and humiliation on their shoulders.

It was different here. The Army of Northern Virginia had occupied Philadelphia at the end of the War of Secession, as it had come so close to doing in this war. The government had fled here in the Second Mexican War and the present struggle. Philadelphians didn't merely want peace—they wanted revenge, wanted it with a brooding desire frightening in its intensity.

Lost in her own thoughts, she'd missed some of what Roosevelt was saying. "And if we have suffered," he thundered now, "our foes have suffered more. If they have overrun some of our sacred soil, we stand in arms on more of theirs. If our cities have suffered from their bombing aeroplanes, their cities have suffered more from our mighty bombers. And we advance, my friends. We advance! Everywhere on the continent of North America, the foe is in retreat.

"So I say to you, stand fast! The enemy's hope is that our resolve will falter. They pray in Richmond, they pray in Canada, that we shall weary of the struggle. They pray that we shall throw in our hand, our winning hand, and give them at the table what they cannot win on the field of battle. Will we fall into their trap, my fellow citizens of the United States?"

"No!" the crowd cried, a great and angry roar.

Hosea Blackford leaned toward Flora. "Now you see the danger of opposing the war effort too strongly."

"No, I don't," she answered. "I only hear a lot of wind."

Blackford shook his head. "It's worse than that. Suppose we do everything we can to end the war . . . *and Teddy Roosevelt goes ahead and wins it anyhow?* Who would ever take us seriously again? If Lincoln had somehow won the War of Secession, don't you think the Republicans would have tarred the Democrats with the brush of peace? Don't you think Roosevelt would do the same to us—and enjoy every minute of it?"

That was a larger political calculation than Flora had ever tried to make. "Do you really imagine a victory like that is possible?" she asked as the president reached another rhetorical crescendo.

Through the bellowed applause of the crowd, Congressman Blackford gave an answer that chilled her though the day was warm and sunny: "I begin to think it may be."

Lieutenant Colonel Irving Morrell's barrel rumbled and clattered south across no-man's-land toward the Confederate defenses east of White House, Tennessee. It bucked and bounced over the broken ground like a toy boat in a stormy sea, or perhaps more as if Morrell were riding a three-legged horse no one had ever bothered breaking for the saddle.

Now he used hand signals almost as automatically as he breathed. *Right, then straight,* he ordered the driver, and the ungainly vehicle steered around a shell hole that might have made it bog down.

There just ahead stood the first barbed-wire belt in front of the enemy's trenches: an obstacle as deadly to infantry as flypaper to flies. *Straight,* Morrell signaled, and the barrel crushed the barbed wire under better than thirty tons of metal.

With a noise like heavy hail on a tin roof, machine-gun bullets started slapping the armored front of the barrel. Some of them ricocheted off the cupola, too. None, fortunately, hit the armored vision louvers. Even with those louvers closed down tight, lead splash was dangerous.

There, straight ahead, was the reinforced-concrete box from which the machine gun was spitting death. *Halt,* Morrell signaled to the driver, and the barrel stopped. "Take it out!" Morrell screamed to the two artillerymen at the nose cannon. He didn't know whether they heard him or not. What he wanted, though, was plain enough.

The cannon bellowed. Inside the barrel, the report was hard to hear over the noise of the two White truck engines. The cordite fumes from the explosion made Morrell cough. But, peering through the vision slits, he watched the machine-gun position crumble to rubble. *Straight,* he signaled to the driver, and the barrel crushed another belt of wire.

By hook or by crook, General Custer had managed to assemble a striking column of more than three hundred barrels. Every one of them—every one of them that hadn't broken down or bogged down before it got this far—was chewing a path through the wire for the infantry that was following.

Another, last, belt of wire surmounted, ground down into the mud, and nothing more stood between the barrel and the foremost Confederate trench. Here and there, a few brave men who had withstood the short, fierce preliminary bombardment and who were not overwhelmed by fear of the oncoming barrels popped their heads above the parapet and blazed away with their Tredegars.

Morrell needed to give no orders there. The two machine guns on either side of the barrel started chattering. They could not bear straight ahead, but the nose cannon could. And other barrels were advancing side by side with Morrell's; their machine guns helped sweep out the space in front of his traveling fortress, just as his swept the space in front of them.

As he bore down on the Confederate soldiers, some of them broke and fled. Bullets sent most of those spinning and writhing to the ground. The rest fought on in place till they too were slain.

Over the parapet climbed the barrel. The machine gunners inside pounded enfilading fire up and down the trench, as far as each traverse. The advance had given them a target of which men of their trade could normally but dream.

Then the barrel was over the trench, almost falling into it, crushing the ground underneath the tracks, helping to level its own way down and forward. Shells had damaged the far wall of the trench. Engines screaming, the barrel climbed over onto the ground between the first trench and the second.

One of the machine gunners was holding a hurt wrist from that awkward descent. He kept feeding ammunition into the gun for his partner to fire, though. All six machine guns, even the pair in the rear, were blazing away now, making things lively for any Confederate soldiers unlucky enough to be nearby.

"Keep moving!" Morrell shouted to the driver. "We've got to keep moving." The young fellow at the barrel's complicated controls raised both eyebrows to show he didn't understand. *Straight,* Morrell signaled resignedly. But he couldn't keep from talking, even if he couldn't hear himself, let alone make anyone else hear: "We've got to keep driving them. If we hit them hard enough now, we can crack this line, and if we crack this line, Nashville isn't worth anything to them any more, because we'll shell it flat."

Left, he signaled the driver, waggling his hand to show he didn't need a whole lot of left. He saw a way over the next trench line, one not quite so drastic as the barrel had used in its first descent. They went down a ways, they came back up, and the machine guns kept hammering.

He wondered how the rest of the barrels were doing, and the U.S. infantry moving forward with and after them. He couldn't tell, not stuck inside the way he was. *Wireless telegraph,* he thought. *We need barrels with wireless telegraph sets inside, so we can keep track of what's going on all over the field.* He shrugged. If it didn't happen in this war, it would in the next, whenever that came along.

Meanwhile, he realized he did have a way to find out what was going on around him. He undogged the roof hatch, threw it open, stood up, and looked ahead and to the rear. "Bully," he said softly. "Oh, bully."

A few of the barrels had bogged down in trenches and shell holes. Others had taken hits from artillery or were otherwise disabled, some pouring pillars of greasy black smoke into the sky to mark their pyres. But most, like his, were still rumbling forward—rumbling forward and driving all before them.

The artillerymen fired the barrel's nose cannon. Out here in the open air, the noise was terrific, like a clap of doom. The high-explosive shell exploded in front of a knot of Confederate soldiers and knocked them flying. Some, Morrell saw, were colored men. That confirmed intelligence reports. The shell didn't care. It did its damage most impartially.

He took another look over his shoulder, and pumped a fist in the air in delight. In the wake of the barrels, and coming up even with the slower ones, were infantrymen in green-gray, swarming forward and out to the flanks to take possession of the ground the barrels cleared.

Not all the Confederate troops, white or Negro, were breaking. Morrell rapidly discovered that, while standing up so his head and torso were out of the barrel gave him a far better view of the field than he could have had inside the machine, it also made him a far better target. Bullets cracked past his head. Others clanged and ricocheted off the cupola with assorted metallic sounds of fury.

After half a minute or so, he decided he'd be tempting fate if he stayed out there any longer. He ducked back into the infernal gloom and fumes inside the barrel, and slammed the hatch shut after him. The driver and the rest of the crew stared at him as if convinced he'd gone utterly mad. His grin was compounded of excitement and triumph. He stuck up a thumb to show how things were going on the battlefield as a whole, then signaled to the driver. *Straight,* his hands said. The driver, eyes wide, saluted before pressing on.

The crew cheered loud enough to be heard over the roar and rumble of engines, tracks, and guns.

How far had they come? Morrell was sure they'd made better than a mile, maybe even a mile and a half, and noon was—he checked his watch—still more than an hour away. If they could keep it up, they'd have a hole miles wide and three or four miles deep torn in the Confederate line by the time the sun set on this most spectacular Remembrance Day of all time.

"Keep going," he muttered. "We've got to keep going."

Plenty of men in butternut were inclined to disagree with him. The C.S. soldiers defending the line above Nashville understood its importance every bit as well as did the U.S. attackers. The roar off to his left was a barrel taking a direct hit from a shell. Another shell struck in front of his own machine, showering the armored chassis with fragments and lumps of earth.

Speed up, he signaled the driver, and the barrel rattled forward. As if he were in an aeroplane, he went through random right and left turns to throw off the enemy gunners' aim. Hitting a moving, dodging target was not something the crews of field pieces practiced. Shells burst near the barrel, but none hit. This was not like shelling infantrymen: a miss, here, was as good as a mile.

One of the two artillerymen at the nose cannon waved to him and pointed. He nodded, then signaled the driver to halt. They fired their gun once, twice in quick succession. Peering through his louvers, Morrell watched men tumble away from the carriage of one of the CSA's nasty three-inch guns. They did not get up again. *Straight,* he signaled the driver.

A moment later, he caught sight of another barrel, a little off to the right and several hundred yards ahead. He snarled something he was glad no one else could hear. He thought he'd been one of the leaders of this assault. How had that other bastard got so far ahead of him? He was green with jealousy, greener than his uniform.

Then he took another, longer, look. Jealousy faded, replaced by hot anticipation. That wasn't a U.S. barrel—it was one of the rhomboids the CSA built, copying the design from the British. Barrels had seldom met other barrels in combat. His mouth stretched wide in a grin. A new encounter was going onto the list.

He got the driver's attention, then pointed southwest till the fellow spotted the Confederate barrel—*tanks,* the Rebels sometimes called them, which struck Morrell as a silly name. He clenched his fist to show the driver he wanted to engage the enemy machine. The youngster nodded and turned toward it.

The Confederate barrel had spotted him, too, and began making a ponderous turn of its own to bring both its sponson-mounted cannon to bear on him. Since neither machine could move at anything much above a walking pace, the engagement developed with the leisure, though hardly with the grace, of two sailing ships of the line.

Flame burst from the muzzle of one of the Confederate barrel's guns. Uselessly, Morrell braced himself for the impact of the shell. It missed. The artillerymen waved to him. He signaled the driver to halt. They fired. They missed, too. *Straight,* he signaled the driver. *Speed up.*

Perhaps unnerved by his lumbering charge, the crew of the Confederate barrel's other cannon also missed their shot. His own gunners waved again. The barrel halted. They fired. Smoke and flame spurted from the enemy. "Hit!" Morrell screamed. "We got him!" Hatches on the sides and top of the Confederate machine flew open. The crew began bailing out. Morrell swung his own barrel sideways, so his machine gunners could give them a broadside.

And then the command was *Straight* again. He stood up once more to look around, this time for only a moment. Fewer U.S. barrels were near than before. More had been hit or bogged down or broken down. But the survivors—and there were many—still advanced, and the U.S. infantry with them.

Maybe they would go on all the way to the Cumberland.

Maybe the Confederates, with the advantage of moving on un-wrecked ground, would patch together some kind of line and halt them short of the river. In a way, it hardly mattered. The big U.S. guns would move forward, miles forward. From their new position, they'd pound Nashville to pieces.

"Breakthrough," Irving Morrell said, and ducked down into the barrel again.

Gas shells didn't sound quite like shrapnel or high explosive. They gurgled as they flew through the air, and burst with a report different from those of other rounds. "Get your gas helmets on!" Sergeant Jake Featherston screamed as the shells began raining down around the guns of his battery.

He threw on his own rubberized-burlap gas helmet and stared through its murky glass windows toward the line above Round Hill, Virginia, the line that had been quiet for so long but was quiet no more. Here came barrels, a few, widely spaced, rumbling toward and then through the belts of barbed wire in front of the trenches of the Army of Northern Virginia. Yankee machine guns blazed away, making the soldiers in those trenches, black and white, keep their heads down. Men in green-gray swarmed like ants in the barrels' wake, and between them as well.

"Range is 4,500 yards, boys," Featherston shouted, the gas helmet muffling his voice. "Now we make 'em pay their dues."

Normally, the three-inch field guns fired half a dozen rounds a minute. In an emergency, they could triple that for a little while. They could triple it for a little while with the gun crews unencumbered, anyhow. In the stifling gas helmets, they didn't come close. Even keeping up the normal rate of fire was a strain while wearing the helmets. Featherston felt he couldn't breathe. His head pounded. Sweat fogged the glass portholes through which he had to watch the world.

All the guns in the battery were firing, though. Jake got a blurrier view than he wanted, but he shouted with glee to watch shells rain down on the damnyankees now that they'd come out of their trenches. The range was too long for him to be able to see individual U.S. soldiers ripped and torn and thrown aside like rag dolls, but he could watch the shells burst and imagine the butchery they were meting out. He had seen enough battlefields to know all too well what artillery did to soft human flesh.

He could also see that his battery and the rest of the Confederate guns on Round Hill and farther to the rear were not going to be able to keep the damnyankees from going forward. Already, barrels were in among the trenches of the Army of Northern Virginia, lashing them with machine-gun fire at close range. Hitting something as small as a barrel at a range of two and a half miles wasn't a matter of precise aiming. Dumb luck had a lot more to do with it.

Reserves started going forward to help stem the tide. But Yankee artillery was chewing up the ground behind the trenches, too. Reinforcements took casualties long before they got close enough to the front to do any good. Featherston couldn't tell whether they were white troops or colored. Whoever they were, they suffered.

And the U.S. artillery hadn't forgotten about Round Hill, either. Along with the gas shells, the Yankees flung around high explosive and shrapnel as if they'd have to pay for what they didn't use up. One of Jake's shell-jerkers collapsed with a shriek, clutching at his belly.

The leftmost piece of the six-gun battery fell silent. Featherston dashed over to its emplacement to find out why. If a hit had taken out the crew but left the gun intact, he'd yank a man or two off the rest of the guns in the battery and keep all of them in action.

He discovered the crew was down, but so was the gun. The carriage was wrecked; it had taken a direct hit from what, by the size of the crater, had to be a six- or eight-inch shell. Cursing fate—and the U.S. heavy artillery that overmatched its Confederate counterpart—he dashed back to his own gun.

Stretcher-bearers had carried away the wounded crewman. Jake had to stop and rest before he could do anything else. His heart pounded like a sledgehammer in his chest. He wanted to yank off the gas helmet, but didn't dare; gas shells were still falling, releasing their deadly contents in bursts of oily vapor.

Like furious machines, the gun crews of his battery kept hitting the Yankees as hard as they could. They shortened the range again and again, as the green-gray infantry forced its way into and past one trench line after another.

"Bastards are going to be coming up the hill at us," Jake snarled, trying to suck enough air into his lungs to satisfy him.

"We'll give 'em shrapnel, Sarge," Michael Scott said, slamming home another shell. "Hell, we've got a few rounds of case shot. We'll give 'em that." The thin-walled shells of case shot were filled with lead balls. In effect, they converted a field piece to a giant shotgun.

A great roar off to the right meant a Yankee shell had found the limber that carried ammunition for one of the guns there. Jake was a stickler for making sure his crews didn't park the limbers too close to the guns, and also that they built sandbag barricades between the ones and the others. In case the shells went up, such precautions did only so much good.

He hurried over, panting like a dog. The gun remained intact. So did the loader and the assistant gun layer. The rest of the crew was down, dead or wounded. "We've still got enough men to fight this piece, even if we have to haul ammo from the dump." He looked around. "Where's the niggers who take care of the horses and do your cookin'? They can carry shells."

"Titus!" the gun layer shouted. "Sulla!" No black men emerged. He shook his head. "Maybe they got it, too, or maybe they're hidin' somewheres and they ain't comin' out, or else they took off runnin' when the shelling started."

"Worthless bastards," Featherston snarled, ignoring the possibility that the black men might be hurt or dead. He pointed north, toward the front. "Niggers up there'll run, too. You wait."

He would have elaborated—it was a theme on which he was always ready to elaborate—but more gas shells came in just then. He smelled something horrible. Whatever it was, the absorbent cartridge in his gas helmet did absolutely nothing to keep it out. His guts knotted. He gulped. A moment later, he tore off the gas helmet and was down on his hands and knees heaving as if he'd drunk too much bad whiskey.

He wasn't the only one, either—both the loader and the gun layer from the shattered crew vomited beside him. "Puke gas," the loader moaned between spasms. "Damnyankees are shootin' puke gas at us."

Featherston's reply meant, *Really? I hadn't noticed,* but was rather more pungently phrased.

Another salvo of gas shells burst on Round Hill. Jake spat foul-tasting slime from his mouth, then sucked in a long, painful breath. The breath proved painful not only because he'd just puked his guts up and felt as if he'd heave some more. His lungs burned. He coughed and gagged and started to choke.

"That's phosgene!" he wheezed, and yanked the gas helmet

over his head again. But then he did have to vomit again. He couldn't do it inside the gas helmet, so he took it off. If he inhaled enough phosgene to kill him while he was heaving . . . well, he felt like dying, anyhow.

He might have smoked a hundred packs of cigarettes in a minute and a half. He gasped and choked and wondered if he would fall over right there. The gun layer had. His eyes were wide and staring; his face went from purple toward black as he fought for air his lungs couldn't give him.

Jake threw on the gas helmet. He started to puke again, but made himself keep things down even though he thought he would explode. The gas helmet did hold out the phosgene, and the Yankees didn't send over any more shells full of vomiting gas, or none that hit near him.

The loader on the gun with the wrecked limber was also down, choking. He wasn't so bad off as the gun layer, but he was in no shape to fight, either. Slowly, staggering as he walked, Jake went back to his own piece.

A couple of its crewmen were heaving and choking, too, but the rest, no matter what sort of anguish in which they found themselves, kept on fighting the gun. The range had shortened again, too; if the Yankees hadn't gained a mile of ground since the attack started, Featherston would have been astonished.

And they were still coming on, too. Some of their barrels had bogged down. Some were on fire. But the ones that survived still moved like broad-shouldered behemoths among the advancing infantry, hunting out pockets of resistance and blasting them out of existence. U.S. artillery kept on pounding not only Confederate guns but also the ground across which C.S. reserves had to come.

Here and there along the line, men in butternut were moving back, not forward. Flesh and blood could bear only so much. As the Confederate troops retreated, they entered the zone the U.S. artillery was pounding behind the line. They took casualties there. "Serves you right, you bastards," Featherston growled. But the disorder and fear spreading through the retreating soldiers also infected the reserves who had been going forward. Whatever chance there might have been for a counterattack dissolved.

In growing horror and fury, Jake realized the front was not going to hold. The Army of Northern Virginia wouldn't lose a few hundred yards of ground, to be regained later with bayonet and grenade. This was going to be a bad defeat, so bad, probably, that the battery would not be able to stay on Round Hill.

He went over to the two guns that were out of action and removed their sights and breech blocks, which he threw into the limber for his own gun. The Yanks would get no use from the weapons they captured. Then he checked the horses that would have to pull away the four surviving cannon. They'd come through everything better than he'd dared hope. If they'd gone down, he would have had to disable all six field guns in the battery before withdrawing.

Up Round Hill came the Confederates who'd run farthest and fastest. Most of those faces, close enough now for him to see the fright on them, were black. Behind the shield of the gas helmet, his own face twisted into a savage grin. "Canister!" he shouted.

Scott loaded the round into the gun. Jake twisted the elevation screw to lower the piece as far as it would go. He peered over open sights at the men in butternut heading his way.

"What are you doing, Sarge?" Scott asked.

"Fire!" Featherston screamed, and the loader obediently yanked the lanyard. Jake whooped to watch the colored cowards blown to bits. "Another round of the same!" he cried, and then, "Fire!" He shook his fist at the black soldiers still on their feet in front of him. "You won't fight the damnyankees, you shitty coons, you got to deal with me!"

He brought out the four surviving guns from the battery, brought them out and brought them back to the new line the Army of Northern Virginia was piecing together behind Round Hill. As the day ended, he shelled the first Yankees coming over the hill. He set two barrels on fire. The U.S. infantry drew back. When fighting ebbed with the light, he sat by a little fire, too keyed up to sleep, writing and writing in the Gray Eagle notebook.

Lieutenant General George Custer stood at the top of the ridge in front of White House, Tennessee, the ridge the Confederates had defended so long and so tenaciously. Back in the distant days of peace, the ridge had been wooded. Now . . . now God might have intended it as a toothpick and splinter farm. Custer struck dramatic poses as automatically as his heart beat. He struck one now, for the benefit of the military correspondents who hovered close to hear what pearls of wisdom might drop from his lips.

"From here, gentlemen, I can see the waters of the Cumberland, and Nashville across the river from them," he declared bombastically. "From here, gentlemen, I can see—victory."

The correspondents scribbled like men possessed. Major Abner Dowling turned away so no one would have to see his face. *From here, gentlemen,* he thought, *I can see a fat, pompous old fraud who's ever so much luckier than he deserves and who hasn't the faintest inkling how lucky he is.*

He turned back toward the general commanding First Army. He still felt little but scorn for Custer's generalship, but he was having a certain amount of trouble holding on to that scorn. For the sake of his own peace of mind, he worked at it, but it wasn't easy.

Truth was, Custer had gone far out on a limb—and taken Dowling with him—backing a doctrine directly contrary to the one coming out of the War Department. Truth was, he had won a sizable victory here by going his own way. Truth was, he *could* see Nashville from where he stood, and the guns of First Army could hit Nashville from near where he stood. Truth was, the CSA had left on this side of the Cumberland only battered units falling back toward their crossings.

Truth was, Custer, as he had done in the War of Secession and the Second Mexican War, had somehow managed to make himself into a hero.

"General, we've been using barrels for a year now," a reporter said. "Why haven't they done so well for us up till this latest battle?"

"They are a new thing in the world," Custer answered. "As with any new thing, figuring out how best to employ them took a bit of doing." He strutted and preened, like a rooster displaying before hens. "I came up with the notion of using them as a mass rather than in driblets, tried it out, and the results were as you have seen."

Dowling turned away again. The really infuriating thing was that, in boasting thus, Custer was for once telling the exact and literal truth. From the minute he'd first set eyes on barrels, he'd wanted to line them up in a great column and send them plowing straight into the enemy. Everyone had told him he couldn't do that—doctrine forbade it. He'd gone ahead and done it anyhow—and he'd forced a breakthrough where there had been no such creature in going on three years of war.

There would be considerable wailing and gnashing of teeth in Philadelphia on account of what he'd done. There already had been, in fact. Custer had rubbed the War Department's nose in the fact that it hadn't had the faintest idea what to do with barrels once it got them. The only way a man got away with committing such a sin was to be proved extravagantly right. Custer had done that, too.

Another reporter spoke up: "Having beaten the Rebels once in this way, General, can we lick them again?"

"We *are* licking them," Custer said. "Not only did First Army smash them here in Tennessee, but I understand the fighting also goes well in Virginia, and that our forces may soon regain our nation's capital from the enemy's hands." He struck another pose. "This was a Remembrance Day we and our enemies shall long remember."

Dowling listened to that in something close to amazement. Custer must indeed have had a surfeit of glory if he was willing to share some with generals operating on other fronts. He was, in his own way, a patriot. Maybe that accounted for it. Dowling couldn't think of anything else that would.

"Not quite what I meant, sir," the reporter said. "Can we here in western Tennessee strike the Confederates another blow as strong as the one we just dealt them?"

"Well, why the devil not?" Custer said grandly. The correspondents laughed and clapped their hands.

Without trying hard, Dowling could come up with half a dozen reasons why the devil not, starting with the need to refit and reinforce the barrels and ending with the geography. Breaking through on the other side of the Cumberland would be anything but easy. It wasn't so great a river as the St. Lawrence, which had bedeviled U.S. strategy throughout the war, but it was by no means inconsiderable, either. Dowling wished Custer wouldn't be so damned blithe and breezy. Custer's adjutant wished any number of things about him, none of which looked like coming true.

With a sigh, Dowling turned away from Custer. In doing so, he bumped into a U.S. officer of less exalted rank. "Beg your pardon, sir," he said. "Didn't see you were there till too late."

"No damage done, Major," Lieutenant Colonel Irving Morrell said. Dowling nodded his thanks. Having led the column of barrels that made the breakthrough, Morrell was in very good odor at First Army headquarters. "I'm glad I found you," he went on now. "I have an idea I want to put to you."

"Yes, sir. I'm listening," Dowling said. Even though Morrell stood perfectly still before him, the man seemed to quiver slightly, as if he were a telegraph wire with a great many messages speeding back and forth on it. Dowling suspected he didn't have *an* idea—odds were he had a whole great flock of them, each struggling against the others to be born.

"Major," Morrell said, "I think I know how we can secure a bridgehead on the far side of the Cumberland."

"You have my attention, sir," Dowling said. That was surely the problem Custer would face when he was done celebrating the victory he'd just achieved. "Tell me how you would go about it." Dowling did not say he would give Morrell Custer's ear if he liked the idea. A man full of so many ideas would be able to figure that out for himself.

And Morrell started to talk. He wasn't a particularly fluent talker, but he was extraordinarily lucid. He had no bluster in him. After years at General Custer's side, that in itself made listening to him a pleasure for Dowling. It was no wonder, the adjutant thought, that *Custer* and *bluster* rhymed.

Morrell also knew what he was talking about. Again, Dowling suppressed any invidious comparisons with the general commanding First Army. Morrell knew what resources First Army had, and what reinforcements it was likely to receive. He knew what part of those could be committed to his scheme, and he had as good a notion as a U.S. soldier could of what the CSA could bring to bear against them.

When he was through, Dowling paid him a high compliment: "This is no humbug." He followed it with one he reckoned even higher: "Anyone would think you were still on the General Staff."

But Morrell pursed his lips and shook his head. "I enjoy serving in the field too much to be happy in Philadelphia, Major."

That he had in common with Custer, at least before Custer had got old and plump and fragile. Dowling had questioned a great many things about Custer, but never his courage. That courage was one of the things that led him to go after the enemy piledriver fashion. It had led Lieutenant Colonel Morrell in a different direction.

Abner Dowling glanced back toward Custer. His illustrious superior had begun to run out of bombast; some of the correspondents were drifting off to write up their stories and wire them to their newspapers or magazines. Dowling didn't feel any great compunction about leading Morrell through the knot of men around Custer and saying, "Excuse me, General, but this officer would like your opinion on something."

Custer looked miffed; he hadn't been completely finished. But then he recognized the man at Dowling's side. "Ah—Lieutenant Colonel Morrell, who so valiantly headed the column of barrels." Again, he shared glory: no matter how brightly a lieutenant colonel might be burnished, he would never outshine a lieutenant general. Custer waved to the reporters. "Go on, boys. Business calls. Any time so gallant a soldier as this brave officer seeks my ear, you may rest assured I am pleased to give it to him."

That made the gentlemen of the Fourth Estate pay more attention to Morrell than they would have otherwise. A photographer snapped his picture. A sketch artist worked on a likeness till Custer waved again, imperiously this time. The fellow closed the notebook and went off with Morrell only half immortalized.

"Now, then," Custer said, "what can I do for you, Lieutenant Colonel? I trust it is a matter of some importance, or Major Dowling would not have interrupted me in the course of my remarks." He gave his adjutant a veiled stare to let him know that was not forgotten.

Dowling had no trouble bearing up under Custer's stares, veiled or not. Sometimes he did have trouble not laughing in Custer's face, but that was a different story. Anyhow, veiled stare notwithstanding, he thought Custer would forget his pique this time. With a nod to Morrell, he said, "Go ahead, sir."

Morrell went ahead. Even more precisely than he had for Dowling, he set forth his idea for Custer. Dowling intently watched the general commanding First Army, wondering how the old boy would take it—it wasn't his usual cup of tea, nor anything close.

Custer didn't show much while Morrell was talking. How many hours on garrison duty here and there in the West had he spent behind a pile of poker chips? Enough to learn to hold his face still, anyway.

When Morrell was done, Custer stroked his peroxided mustache. "I shall have to give this further consideration, Lieutenant Colonel, but I can say now that you have plainly done some hard thinking here. Some solid thinking, too, unless I am much mistaken."

"Thank you, sir." Morrell had the sense to stop there, not to push Custer for a greater commitment.

"Shall I begin converting this to a plan of operation, sir?" Dowling asked.

"Yes, why not?" Custer said, artfully careless.

VIII

"All the news is bad these days," Arthur McGregor complained to his wife over a supper plate of fried chicken and fried potatoes.

"More Yankee lies, I expect," Maude answered. "They don't let any of the truth get loose. Remember how many times their papers have said Toronto has fallen, or Paris to the Germans?"

"I don't think it's like that this time," McGregor said. "Those other stories, you could tell they were made up. What we hear now—that Nashville place getting knocked to bits, and the Americans pushing ahead on the border farther east . . . those are the kinds of things that really do happen in a war. They're the kinds of things you have to believe when you read them."

"But if you do believe them, it means we're losing the war," his daughter Julia said.

"It means our allies are in trouble, anyhow," McGregor said gravely. He bit at the inside of his lower lip before going on, "I don't think we're doing any too well here in Canada, either. You can hardly hear the cannon fire up north toward Winnipeg these days."

Ever since the Yanks had overrun his farm, McGregor had used the sound of the guns to gauge how the fighting was going. When they were far away, the Yankees were making progress. A deep rumble on the northern horizon meant an Anglo-Canadian counteroffensive. He wouldn't have minded in the least had shells fallen on his land; that would have meant the Yanks were pushed most of the way back toward Dakota. But it hadn't happened. He was beginning to wonder if it ever would.

Mary, his younger daughter, spoke with great certainty: "We *can't* lose the war. We're *right*. They invaded us. They had no business doing that." She was only eight years old, and still confused the way things should have been with the way they were.

McGregor and Maude looked at each other. They both knew better. "They can, Mary," her mother said. "We have to hope they don't, that's all."

"No, they can't," Mary repeated. "They shot Alexander. If they win, that means—that means—" She cast about for the worst thing she could think of. "That means God doesn't love us any more."

"God does what He wants, Mary," McGregor said. "He doesn't always do what we want. If He did, your brother would still be here, and the Yanks would be down in the USA where they belong."

"If they win, they'll try to turn us into Americans," Julia said angrily. "They're already trying to turn us into Americans."

With American coins in his pocket, with American stamps on his letters, with American lies in the schools—so many American lies, neither Julia nor Mary went any more—McGregor could hardly disagree with her. Instead, he said, "What we have to do is, we have to remember who we are and what we are, no matter what happens around us. That may be the best we can do."

He felt Maude's eyes on him again. He needed a moment to understand why. When he did, his mouth tightened. Though he'd spoken indirectly, he'd never come so close to admitting Canada and her allies were losing the war.

His wife looked as grim as he did. So did Julia, who now had nearly a woman's years and had been thinking like an adult for a long time, anyhow. If Mary didn't follow—maybe that was just as well. Of them all, McGregor thought she was the fiercest one, even including himself. No matter how old she got, he doubted she would ever slow down to count the cost before she acted. He had to. He hated himself for that, but he had to.

After supper, and after the girls had gone to bed, he said to Maude, "I'm going out to the barn. I've got some work to take care of."

The only question Maude asked was, "Shall I wait up for you?" When he shook his head, she came over and kissed him on the cheek. He blinked; they seldom showed affection for each other outside the bedroom.

He slapped at mosquitoes on the way to the barn. Crickets chirped. Frogs croaked and peeped in ponds and creeks and puddles. Spring was here. He shook his head again. Spring was here, and with it shorter nights. He could have used the long blanket of dark winter gave. But winter also gave a blanket of snow, and snow, unless it was falling hard or unless the wind was howling, meant tracks. He could not afford tracks. The family had already lost Alexander. He knew how hard a time they would have if they lost him, too.

"Counting the cost," he muttered. He did not fear death, not for himself. He feared it for the sake of those he loved. Mary would not have feared, period. He felt that in his bones. It shamed him. It drove him on.

He did not light a lantern in the garage. The wooden box he sought was hidden, but he knew where. No Yankees on the road would see any light and wonder about it. He had to be careful.

He had to be careful about that road, too. He couldn't travel on it, not unless he wanted to be challenged. The box under his arm, he approached the road. He didn't approach too closely, not till nobody was coming in either direction. Then he crossed in a hurry.

His neighbors' farm had a path leading to the road, just as his did. His neighbors' farm also had a path leading southeast toward another road, an east-west one not so frequently traveled by Americans. If the dog stayed quiet, it would not disturb anyone in the dark, quiet farmhouse. The dog was quiet. It had known him for years, and knew him as well as it knew anyone outside its own family. Down that southeastern path he strode, and onto that east-west road.

"East," he muttered. He had the road to himself. Alone with his thoughts: not a safe place to be, not with the thoughts filling his mind. If he set the box down and stomped on it, he would be alone with his thoughts forever. That was tempting, but he was not the sort of man to leave a thing half done.

Whenever he passed a farmhouse, he tensed, making sure it had no lamps burning. He did not want any wakeful soul noting the presence of a lone man on the road. No one could recognize him, not from those houses, but someone might note the time at which he walked by or the direction in which he was going. Either could prove dangerous.

He heard a distant rattle on the road behind him. Looking back over his shoulder, he saw tiny headlamps rapidly getting larger. He stepped into the field by the roadside and lay down. A Ford whizzed past, a Ford painted some light color, not the usual black: a light color like green-gray, for instance.

"Christ, let me be lucky," he whispered. "Let me catch the whore and the murderer both." He waited till the motorcar had gone a good way down the road before getting up and following it. The Americans installed rearview mirrors on most of their motorcars; he did not want whoever was in this one—Major Hannebrink's name burned in his mind—spotting him.

On he walked, gauging time by the wheeling stars. If he could keep on, if he did not flag or falter, he might do what he had come to do.

The next interesting question, and one of whose answer he was not quite sure, was whether the Tooker family owned a dog. He didn't really think so. If he was wrong, the best thing that could happen would be a long walk in the dark for nothing. Possibilities went downhill in a hurry from there.

A lamp went out downstairs. Lamplight showed a moment later in a room upstairs. *A bedroom,* McGregor thought. *Paulette Tooker's bedroom.* That she would do such a thing with an American major was bad enough. That she would do such a thing and watch, or even let him watch, was depravity piled on depravity. What if one of her children woke in the night? Her son, if McGregor remembered rightly, was not far from Julia's age—old enough and to spare to despise what his mother did . . . unless he was a collaborator, too.

Where was her husband? Was he dead? Was he captured? Was he still fighting for his country farther north? McGregor didn't know. He wondered if Paulette knew, or cared.

That light would not go out. McGregor muttered under his breath. What the devil was Hannebrink doing in there, driving railroad spikes? McGregor didn't dare approach the house, as he'd intended doing. Hannebrink had parked the Ford a good distance away from the place, though, no doubt for discretion's sake. McGregor wanted the man who'd ordered his son killed far more than he wanted that man's Canadian whore.

Cautious as a man could be, he went up to the motorcar. The night smelled of fresh, damp earth. He took a trowel from his belt and began to dig in the fresh, damp earth in front of the Ford's left front tire. When he'd dug enough, he set the box in the hole, covered it over, and scattered the leftover dirt its volume had displaced. Then he headed home himself.

He got back just ahead of morning twilight. A light was burning in a room upstairs in his farmhouse, too. When he went in, he found Maude sitting up in bed sewing. Breath gusted from her when she saw him. "Is everything all right?" she demanded sharply.

"Everything is fine," he answered. "You should have slept."

"I tried," she said. "I couldn't." She shrugged. "About time to get up now, anyhow. One way or another, we'll stagger through the day. So long as everything's all right."

"Yes," he said again. Even as he said it, though, he wondered. He should have been able to hear the explosion, even if the bomb—and the Ford—blew up when he was almost back here. What the hell had Hannebrink and Paulette Tooker been doing back at her house? How long could they keep doing it?

He did get through the day, moving like a man of ice only slightly thawed. When night came, he slept as hard as he had since he was Mary's age.

He wanted to go into Rosenfeld, to learn what, if anything, he'd accomplished. He refrained, not wanting to draw notice to himself. To how many people had Henry Gibbon given the name of Hannebrink's paramour? The more, the better.

Gossip brought word before he couldn't hold back any more and made a trip to town. After supper, while the girls were up-stairs playing with dolls, Maude said, "Della from across the road tells me Lou Tooker stepped on a bomb, and there isn't going to be enough of him left to bury. He was—what?—fifteen, maybe sixteen."

"A bit younger than Alexander." McGregor nodded. "That's going to be hard for Paulette to bear, eh?"

Almost as hard as it was for me, when the Yanks murdered my son, he thought. He wondered how Hannebrink had missed set-ting off the bomb. Maybe he'd backed the Ford up to get back onto the road. McGregor shrugged. However the U.S. major had escaped, Paulette Tooker wouldn't be inclined to open her legs for him, not any more she wouldn't. And, sooner or later, McGregor would get another chance at Major Hannebrink. He was in no hurry. Doing it right counted for more than doing it. No, he was in no hurry at all.

The U.S. bombardment had been short but ferocious. Now, engines bellowing, several barrels waddled forward toward the barbed wire the men of the Army of Northern Virginia had strung out to protect their positions in front of Aldie, Virginia.

The wire shone in the early-morning sun; it was so newly in place, it hadn't even started to rust.

Whistles blew in the U.S. trenches. "Come on, boys!" Captain Cremony shouted. "Time to give the Rebs another dose of medicine." He was the first one out of the trench and heading toward the Confederate lines.

Sergeant Chester Martin nodded approval as he gathered his section by eye and led them up the sandbag staircase, out of the protection of their hole in the ground, and onto the stretch of open country where bullets could easily find them. Cremony hadn't made it sound like fun, and it wouldn't be. But he had made it sound like something that needed doing, and he was leading the way. Hard to ask more than that of an officer.

"Come on!" Martin shouted, echoing the company commander. He pointed to one of the barrels ahead. "Form up behind that bastard. You know the drill. You'd damn well better, by now."

"That's the truth, Sarge," Tilden Russell said. "Wasn't for those big, ugly things, there'd be a hell of a lot fewer of us left after we went over the top in front of Round Hill."

Martin nodded, double-timing despite heavy gear to get as close to the barrel as he could. He'd seen too much hard fighting on the Roanoke front to have any doubts how much barrels were worth. With them, the unit had taken casualties, yes. Casualties were one of the things war was about. Without barrels, though—without them, the advance wouldn't have got a quarter as far, and would have cost four times as much.

Not all the Confederates in those new trenches had been silenced. Rifle bullets whipped past Martin. He wasn't afraid. He didn't know why, but he wasn't. Before he went over the top, yes. When he had a chance to rest, he'd be afraid again. For the time being, he just went on, like most infantrymen. Whatever was going to happen to him would happen, and that was all there was to it.

Confederate machine guns started yammering, too. The barrels opened up on them with cannon fire and their own machine guns. The C.S. machine guns concentrated most of their fury on the barrels. They always did that, and it was a mistake. They had very little chance of hurting the great armored machines, and withheld their fire from the soft, vulnerable men they could have harmed.

Barbed wire underfoot—barbed wire crushed into the dirt by the barrel ahead. Since the opening days of the war, since U.S. forces first pushed their way down into the Roanoke valley, Martin had watched friends and comrades—and enemy soldiers, too, in Confederate counterattacks—trap themselves on wire like flies in a spiderweb and writhe and twist till bullets found them . . . and then, briefly and painfully, afterwards. That would not happen here. It would not happen now.

There was the battered parapet, just ahead. A black man with a rifle in his hands popped up onto the firing step, ready to shoot at Martin. Martin shot first, from the hip. It was not an aimed shot, and he did not think it hit. But it did what he wanted it to do: it made the Confederate soldier duck down again without shooting at him from short range.

A moment later, Martin was down in the trench himself. The black man wasn't there. He'd fled from the firebay into a traverse. Martin did not charge after him. He and who could guess how many pals were waiting, fingers on the triggers of their Tredegars. Charging headlong into a traverse after the enemy was anything but smart.

Martin pulled a potato-masher grenade off his belt, yanked off the cap at the end of the handle, and tugged on the porcelain bead inside. That ignited the fuse. He flung the grenade up over the undug ground and into the traverse.

At the same time as his grenade went into the air, a Reb in the traverse threw one of their egg-shaped models at him and his comrades. Someone behind him yelled in pain. More grenades flew. More shouts rose. He and the men of his section couldn't stay where they were. The attack had to move forward. That meant—

He scowled. Even when it wasn't smart, a headlong charge was sometimes the only choice left. "Follow me!" he shouted.

His men did. If they hadn't, he would have died in the next minute. As things were, that next minute was an ugly business with rifle and entrenching tool and bayonet and a boot in the belly or the balls. More U.S. soldiers came around the corner than the Rebs in the traverse could withstand. The men in butternut went down. Most of the men in green-gray went on.

Through a zigzagging communications trench they ran, deeper into the Confederate position. Somewhere not far from the far end of that trench, a machine gun stuttered out death. The barrels had taken out a lot of machine-gun positions, but not all of them. The guns that survived could wreak fearful havoc on advancing U.S. soldiers.

With one accord, Martin and his section went hunting that machine gun and its crew. The only soldiers who didn't hate machine guns were those who served them. Martin's lips skinned back from his teeth. There was the infernal machine, blazing away toward the front from a nest of sandbags. One white man fed belts of ammunition into it, the other tapped the side of the water jacket every little while to change the direction of the stream of bullets.

The sandbags kept the Confederates from bringing the gun to bear on Martin's men, who approached from the side. The gun crew kept firing till the last second at the U.S. soldiers they could reach. Then they threw their hands in the air. "You got us," the trigger man said.

"Sure as hell do," the Reb who'd been feeding ammunition agreed.

Chester Martin shot one of them. Corporal Bob Reinholdt shot the other one at the same instant. As the Confederates crumpled, the two men who despised each other both stared in surprise. Reinholdt found words first: "Those sons of bitches can't quit that easy."

"Sure as hell can't," Martin agreed. Machine-gun crews rarely made it back to prisoner-of-war camps. For some reason, they always seemed to want to fight to the death.

Up ahead, the barrel leading the U.S. infantry exploded into flames and smoke: a shell from a Confederate field gun had struck home. Hatches flew open. Some of the machine gunners tried to bring out their weapons and fight on the ground. Most of them, though, went down as every C.S. soldier anywhere nearby turned his rifle on the stricken traveling fortress. The Confederates loved barrel crewmen every bit as much as ordinary infantrymen on both sides loved the men who served machine guns.

After brief but heartfelt curses, Martin said, "Things get tougher now. I wonder where the hell the next barrel is at."

"Not close enough," David Hamburger said. "We should do it like they did in Tennessee, put all the barrels together, smash on through the Rebs' lines, and then let us tear the hole wide open."

"Thank you, General," Tilden Russell said. He was ragging the kid, but not too hard; Hamburger had given a good account of himself since the offensive opened. He didn't have a veteran's bag of tricks, but he was brave and willing and learned in a hurry.

But Russell had left the obvious line unused. Martin used it: "Listen, David, you don't like the way we're doing things, you write your congresswoman and give her an earful." He laughed.

"I am doing that," David Hamburger said. Martin hadn't been serious, but he was. "We've pushed the Rebs back here, but we haven't broken through. If it hadn't been for the river they're hiding behind in Tennessee, they'd be running yet."

Shells started landing around them. They dove for cover. "Jesus," Tilden Russell shouted, holding his helmet on his head with one hand. "God damn Rebs still have soldiers of their own in this part of the trench. What the hell are they doin', shelling us like this here?"

"Trying to kill us, I expect," Martin answered.

"I bet their artillery don't care a fuck if they kill a few of their own foot soldiers," Bob Reinholdt added. "They're all white men back there"—he pointed south, toward the Confederate guns—"but half the bastards up here in the trenches are niggers. Probably just as glad to be rid of 'em. Hell, I would be."

"Makes sense," Martin agreed, after a moment adding, "The other thing to remember is, there's no guarantee those were Rebel shells. They might have been ours, falling short."

Nobody said anything for a few seconds. All the men in filthy green-gray huddled there knew only too well that such things happened. You were just as dead if a shell fragment from one of your own rounds got you as from Confederate artillery.

Whoever had fired it, the salvo ended. "Come on," Martin said. "Even if the barrel's dead, we've got to keep going."

They had almost reached the far end of the network of trenches when Confederate reserves—black men with white officers and noncoms—brought them to a standstill. Some of the black soldiers in butternut fired wildly and ran. Some—more than would have been true of white troops—threw down their Tredegars and surrendered first chance they got. Counting on either, though, was risky—no, was deadly dangerous. Most of the black Confederates fought as hard as white Confederates.

With the Rebel reinforcements in place, Martin didn't need long to figure out that he and his pals weren't going to push much farther forward today. He got the men busy with their entrenching tools, and got busy with his own, too, turning shell holes and bits of north-facing trench into south-facing trench.

Sighing, he said, "We took a bite out of their line, but we didn't slam on through it."

"We need more barrels," the Hamburger kid said. "They can really smash trenches. What else can?"

"Bodies," Martin answered. "Lots and lots of bodies." Anyone who'd fought on the Roanoke front, whether in green-gray or butternut, would have said the same thing.

"Barrels work better," David Hamburger said, and Martin did not disagree with him. He'd seen too many piled-up bodies.

Anne Colleton read through the *Columbia Southern Guardian* with careful thoroughness over her morning eggs and coffee. Breakfast wasn't so good as it might have been. She'd made it herself. After having servants cook for her almost her entire life, her own culinary skills were slender. But for the time while she'd languished in a refugee camp during the Red uprising, she'd have owned no culinary skills at all.

She hardly noticed she'd got the eggs rubbery and the coffee strong enough to spit in her eye. The *Southern Guardian* took most of her attention. Despite censors' obfuscations and re-porters' resolute optimism, the war news was bad. It had been bad ever since the damnyankees opened their spring offensives in Tennessee and Virginia and Maryland.

"Damn them," she whispered. Then she said it out loud: "*Damn* them!" The paper wasn't printing maps of the fighting in Maryland and Virginia any more. Anne had no trouble under-standing why: maps would have made obvious how far the Army of Northern Virginia had fallen back. Unless you had an atlas, you couldn't tell where places like Sterling and Arcola and Aldie—which had just fallen after what the *Southern Guardian* called "fierce fighting"—were.

But Anne did have an atlas, used it, and didn't like what she was seeing. What had her brother Tom said? That there were too many damnyankees to hold back? Virginia looked to be the USA's attempt to prove it.

Nashville, though, Nashville had been something different. The paper went on for a column and a half about the horrors the city was suffering under Yankee bombardment. Anne scowled at the small type. What was in there might well be true, but it wasn't relevant. If the line that held U.S. guns out of range of the city hadn't collapsed, it wouldn't *be* under bombardment now.

But that line, which had held even under the heaviest pressure since the autumn before, went down as if made of cardboard when the Yankees hammered it with a horde of their barrels. That hammering worried Anne more than it seemed to worry the Confederate War Department. U.S. forces weren't using their barrels like that anywhere else. But if they did . . .

"If they do, they're liable to break through again, wherever it is," Anne said. She could see that. Why couldn't they see it in Richmond?

Maybe they could see it. Maybe they simply didn't know what to do about it. That possibility also left her unreassured.

She looked at her plate in some surprise, realizing she'd finished the eggs without noticing. She sighed. Another day. She'd never felt so useless in all her life as she did here in St. Matthews now. Were she back at Marshlands, she would be fretting about the year's cotton crop. But there would be no cotton crop this year. She dared not go back to the plantation that had been in her family for more than a hundred years.

Her back stiffened. No, that wasn't true. She dared to go back, even if she would not have cared to spend the night there. In fact, she *would* go back—with militiamen, and with a Tredegar slung over her shoulder. The plantation was ravaged. It was ruined. But it was hers, and she would not tamely yield it to anyone or anything.

No sooner decided than begun. She did not officially command the St. Matthews militia, but she had enough power in this part of the country—enough power through most of South Carolina, as a matter of fact—that within an hour she and half a dozen militiamen were rattling toward Marshlands in a couple of ramshackle motorcars.

Some of the militiamen wore old gray uniforms, some new butternut. Some of the men were old, too—too old to be called into the Army even during the present crisis at the front. One, a sergeant of her own age named Willie Metcalfe, was a handsome fellow when viewed from the right. The left side of his face was a slagged ruin of scars. He wore a patch over what had been his left eye. Anne wondered why he bothered. In that devastation, who could have said for certain where his eye socket lay? A couple of his comrades were surely less than eighteen, and looked younger than Anne's telegraph delivery boy.

Half a dozen miles made a twenty-minute ride along the rutted dirt road between St. Matthews and Marshlands. It would have been twice that long if one of the motorcars had had a puncture, but they were lucky. When Willie Metcalfe—who, predictably, was driving in the lead automobile, to avoid displaying his wrecked profile for a while—started to pull into the driveway that led to the ruins of the Marshlands mansion, Anne spoke up sharply: "No, wait. Stop the motorcar here and pull off to the side of the road."

"Yes, ma'am." Sergeant Metcalfe's voice was mushy; the inside of his mouth was probably as ravaged as the rest of that side of his face. But he said the words as he would have said *Yes, sir* to a superior officer, and obeyed as promptly, too. The other motorcar followed his lead.

Because she hadn't had to shout at him, as she'd had to shout at so many men in her life, she deigned to explain: "The only motorcars likely to come here will have white people in them— probably white soldiers in them. What better place to hide a bomb than in the driveway there?"

Metcalfe thought for a moment, then nodded. "That makes sense," he said. "That makes a lot of sense."

Linus Ashworth, who with his white beard looked a little like General Lee and was almost old enough to have fought under him, said, "We ain't likely to be bringing niggers into the militia any time soon, not when we're chasin' 'em, and I don't give a . . . hoot what the Army does." He got out of the automobile and spat a stream of tobacco juice into the lush grass. A brown drop slid down that white beard. A yellow streak in it said that sort of thing happened to him all the time.

Anne and the militiamen advanced on the wreckage of the Marshlands mansion in what Metcalfe called a skirmish line. He unobtrusively took the left end. They all had a round in the chamber of their Tredegars. Anne didn't expect any trouble. The Red rebels shouldn't have known she was on the way to Marshlands. She herself hadn't known she would be till not long before she was. But taking chances wasn't a good idea.

Linus Ashworth spat again. "It's a shame, ma'am," he said,

"purely a shame. I seen this place when it was like what it's supposed to be, and there wasn't no finer plantation in the state of South Carolina, God strike me dead if I lie."

"Yes," Anne said tightly. Ashworth had seen Marshlands before the war, but she'd lived here. Coming back after the men of the Congaree Socialist Republic were driven back into the riverside swamps had been hard enough. Coming back now . . .

Now the Marshlands plantation wasn't ruined, as it had been then. Now it was dead. The cabin where she'd lived after the mansion burned was itself charred wreckage. The rest of the cabins that had housed the Negro field hands were deserted, glass gone from the windows, doors hanging open because nothing inside was worth stealing. One door had fallen off its hinges and leaned at a drunken angle against the clapboard wall. White bird droppings streaked the door's green paint.

Anne looked out to what had been, and what should have been, broad acres of growing cotton. Weeds choked the fields. No crop this year. No chance of getting a crop this year, even if she could find hands who would work for her and not for Cassius and Cherry and the rest of the Reds—and good luck with that, too. No money coming in from Marshlands this year. But the money would keep right on bleeding out. War taxes . . . *outrageous* wasn't nearly a strong enough word. Her investments had kept her afloat so far, but they were tottering, too.

"This here is sad, ma'am," Sergeant Willie Metcalfe said. "This here is really sad." Just for a moment, he raised a hand to the black cord that held his patch. "This here place got hurt the same way I did."

"Yes, it did," Anne said. She would not—she *would* not—let him hear the tears in her voice.

And then she forgot about tears, because something moved up ahead. She was on the ground, her rifle aimed, before she knew how she'd got there. A couple of the young militiamen stood gaping for a few seconds. The others, the men who had seen combat of one sort or another, were on their bellies like her, offering targets as small as they could.

"Come out!" Metcalfe shouted. "Come out right now or you're dead!"

Anne wasn't even sure she'd seen a human being. Motion where nothing had any business moving had been plenty to send her diving to the ground. She wondered if they'd have to go hunting through the field hands' cottages. If the Reds had come back for some reason, that might not be any fun at all.

But why would the Reds come back to Marshlands? she thought, trying to reassure herself. It wasn't as if she had any treasure buried on the plantation to tempt them. If she'd had anything like that, she would long since have dug it up herself.

Then anticlimax almost made her burst out laughing. From around the corner of the nearest cabin came a pickaninny, a Negro girl ten or eleven years old. After a moment, Anne recognized her. "What are you doing sneaking around this place, Vipsy?" she demanded. "You almost got shot."

"I's jus' lookin' fo' whatever I kin find," Vipsy answered artlessly—so artlessly, Anne's suspicions kindled.

"Where are you staying these days, Vipsy?" she asked. "There's nothing for your father and mother to do at Marshlands now."

Vipsy pointed northward, toward the Congaree: "Over yonder where I's at," she answered.

How far over yonder? Anne wondered. *All the way into the swamp? Are your father and mother Reds?* If they were . . . She looked down at the ground so the colored girl would not see her smile. "All right, go on your way," she said when she looked up again. "I'm just glad you weren't coming around sniffing after the treasure. If you were, we would have had to shoot you."

"Don' know nothin' 'bout no treasure," Vipsy said, and strolled off with as much dignity as if she wore a gingham frock rather than a dress cut from a grimy burlap bag.

The next trick, of course, would be convincing the militiamen she had no treasure buried here at Marshlands. If she couldn't do that, half the people in St. Matthews would be out here by day after tomorrow at the latest, all of them armed with picks and shovels. But if she could persuade the militiamen—well, something useful might come from that.

Gordon McSweeney walked up to Captain Schneider. After saluting the company commander, he said, "Sir, I wish you wouldn't have done what you did."

Schneider frowned. "I'm sorry, McSweeney, but I don't see that you left me any choice in the matter."

"But—" Except when discussing matters of religion, McSweeney was not a particularly eloquent man. He touched the top of his shoulder, and the new shoulder strap sewn onto his tunic. No insigne marked the strap, but its mere presence disturbed him. "Sir, I don't *want* to be an officer!" he burst out.

"Believe me, second lieutenants barely deserve the name," Captain Schneider answered with a wry chuckle.

"I was comfortable as a sergeant, sir," McSweeney said. "I was—I was happy as a sergeant." It was, as far as he could recall, the first time in his life he'd ever admitted being happy about anything.

"If you go on with this, *Lieutenant* McSweeney"—Schneider bore down on the title—"you will make me angry—but not angry enough to bust you back to sergeant, if that's what's on your mind." He paused to roll a cigarette. Once he'd sucked in smoke, he went on, "God damn it, McSweeney, look at it from my point of view. What the hell am I supposed to do with you?"

"Sir, you could have—you should have—left me where I was," McSweeney answered. "That was all I expected. That was all I wanted."

For some reason he did not fathom, Captain Schneider looked exasperated. Seeing he did not fathom it, Schneider spelled it out in words of one syllable: "You are wearing the ribbon for one Medal of Honor. God knows you deserve an oak-leaf cluster to go with it for what you did to that machine-gun position, but the War Department would think I was shell-shocked if I put you up for it twice, no matter how much you deserve it. Any lesser medal fails to do you justice. What choice did I have but promoting you?"

"I didn't do what I did for glory, sir," McSweeney answered, deeply embarrassed. "I did it because it was my duty."

Schneider studied him. Slowly, slowly, the company commander blew out a long, gray cloud of smoke. "You mean that," he said at last.

"Of course I do." McSweeney was embarrassed again, in a different way. "I always mean what I say."

After another long pause, Captain Schneider said, "You may be the most frightening man I have ever met."

"Only to the enemies of God and the United States of America, sir."

Schneider suddenly snapped his fingers. "I know part of what's troubling you, damn me to hell if I don't." If he kept talking like that, McSweeney was sure God would damn him to hell. But, however harsh he was to those under him, McSweeney could not and never would reprove his superiors. Schneider continued, "You don't want to give your flamethrower to anybody else."

McSweeney looked down at the muddy ground under his feet. He hadn't thought Captain Schneider would be able to read him so well. Now it was his turn to hesitate. Finally, he said, "When I carry it, I feel myself to be like the fourth angel of the Lord in Revelations 16, who pours out his bowl on the sun and scorches the wicked with fire."

"Hmm." Schneider scratched his chin. Stubble rasped under his fingernails. "Tell you what, McSweeney. Think of it like this: you're not the only one in this war. We're all scorching the Rebs together, and it doesn't matter whether we've got rifles or .45s or flamethrowers. How's that?"

"Sir, when the Good Book speaks of searing those who curse God's name, I believe it means what it says—no more, no less," McSweeney replied.

"Of course you do," Schneider muttered. He paused to sigh and to stamp the butt of his cigarette into the dirt. "Well, we're going to make it hot for the Rebs, all right. They're going to take us out of the line here and put fresh troops in our place, to hold. We shift to the right, about five miles over."

"And do what, sir?" McSweeney asked.

"There's about a square mile of woods there—it's called Craighead Forest on the map," Schneider answered. "If we can push the Confederates out of it, we outflank 'em and we may be able to shove 'em clean out of Jonesboro."

"So long as we're fighting, sir, it suits me," McSweeney said.

"Well, it doesn't suit me, not for hell it doesn't," the company commander told him. "We haven't got the barrels to go in there and do the dirty work for us, the way they do on the other side of the Mississippi. We have to take that forest the old way, the hard way, and it's going to be expensive as the devil."

"Where I go, my men will follow, and I will go into that wood," McSweeney said positively. Schneider looked at him, shook his head, and went off down the trench still shaking it.

Replacements began filing into the line that afternoon, under desultory Confederate shelling. They were clean-faced, neatly shaven men in clean uniforms. They seemed present in preposterous numbers, for action had not thinned their ranks faster than replacements could refill them. They stared at the lean, grimy veterans whose trenches they were taking over. Gordon McSweeney was far from the only veteran to stare back in cold contempt.

He led the platoon he did not want down a series of winding tracks shielded—but not too well—from enemy observation. A few shells fell around them. A couple of men were wounded. Stretcher-bearers carried them back toward dressing stations. But for the wounded men, nobody thought it anything out of the ordinary.

Up through the zigzags of communications trenches they went. McSweeney stared ahead, toward the wood of pine and oak. Fighting there hadn't been heavy, not till now. Most of the trees were still standing, not lying smashed and scattered like a petulant giant's game of pick-up-sticks. Under those trees, men in butternut waited in foxholes and in trenches much like these. Between the U.S. line and the edge of the wood lay a few hundred yards of low grass and bushes, all bright green. Tomorrow morning . . .

"Tomorrow morning, uh, sir," Ben Carlton said to McSweeney, "a lot of us are going to end up dead."

McSweeney gave the cook a cold look. "Take it up with the Lord, not with me. I am going forward. So are you. God will choose who lives and dies." Carlton went off muttering to himself. McSweeney checked his rifle, read his Bible, rolled himself in his blanket, and slept the sleep of an innocent man.

The U.S. bombardment blasted him awake a little before dawn. He nodded his approval. Short and sharp—that was the way to do it. A week-long bombardment only gave the Rebs a week to get ready, and didn't kill nearly enough of them to be worth that.

Whistles blew, up and down the line. "Come on, you lugs!" McSweeney shouted. "Follow me. I'll be the one they shoot at first, I promise you."

With that encouragement, he led his platoon over the parapet and through the grass toward the edge of the now more battered wood, from which little winking lights—the muzzle flashes of machine guns and Tredegars—began to appear. Bullets clipped leaves from bushes and stirred the tall blades of grass almost as a stick might have done.

"By sections!" McSweeney yelled. "Fire and move!"

Half the men he led went down, though only a few had been

shot. The ones on their knees and bellies blazed away to cover the advance of the rest. After a rush, the men ahead hit the dirt and fired while the former laggards rose and dashed past them.

They took casualties. Had it not been for their tactics—and for the artillery still falling in the woods, knocking over trees fast enough to make Paul Bunyan jealous—they would have taken more. But the survivors kept going forward in ragged waves. Several bullets cracked past Gordon McSweeney close enough for him to feel the wind of their passage. One brushed at his sleeve, so that he looked over to see if a comrade close by was tugging his arm. Seeing no one close by, he realized what must have happened. "Thank you, Lord, for sparing me," he murmured, and ran on.

Then he was in among the trees. The covering barrage moved deeper into Craighead Forest, leaving it up to the men in green-gray to finish dealing with the men in butternut it had not killed or maimed. The Confederates were there in distressing numbers; they knew, as U.S. soldiers knew, how to lessen the damage artillery did.

That left hard, hot work to do. Many—not all—of the C.S. machine-gun crews stayed at their guns even after U.S. soldiers had got by them on either flank, lingering to do their foes as much harm as they could before they were slain. They were brave men, brave as any in green-gray.

McSweeney knew as much. He'd known as much since the day he crossed the Ohio into Kentucky. "The Egyptians who followed Pharaoh into the opening in the Red Sea after the children of Israel surely were brave men," he muttered. "The Lord let the Red Sea close on them even so, because they were wicked."

Confederates fired from behind and from under trees. Snipers fired from in the trees. The Rebels fought from their trenches. They popped up out of foxholes. Sometimes they hid till several U.S. soldiers had passed them, then turned around and fired at their backs.

McSweeney had blood on his bayonet before he was a hundred yards into the woods. He'd been changing clips when a Confederate soldier lunged at him. How the Reb had screamed when the point went into his belly! He would scream like that forever in hell.

"Schneider's down!" somebody shouted. McSweeney waited for one of the other lieutenants, all of them senior to him, to start directing the company. None of them did. Maybe they were down, too. He shouted orders, driving the men on. He was loud and sounded sure of what he was doing, the next best thing to being sure of what he was doing.

Forming any firm line in the forest was impossible. The Confederates kept filtering past the U.S. forward positions and raising Cain. They knew the woods better than their foes—some of them had probably hunted squirrels and coons through these trees—and did not mean to lose them.

"Here!" McSweeney threw aside the bodies of two Rebs from the machine gun at which they'd fallen. He grabbed a couple of his own men and turned the machine gun around. "If you see any of those miscreants, shoot them down."

"Miscre-whats, sir?" one of them shouted at him.

"Confederates," he answered, which satisfied the soldier. He and his pal wouldn't be so good as a properly trained crew, but they would be better than nothing for as long as their ammunition held out. McSweeney did that several more times, getting firepower any way he could.

U.S. machine guns started coming forward into Craighead Forest, too. By nightfall, most of it was in U.S. hands, though Confederate cannon kept shelling the woods their side had held when day began. Maybe the men in green-gray would be able to mount a flank attack on Jonesboro afterwards, maybe not. McSweeney couldn't tell. He didn't care, not too much. He'd done his job, and done it well.

Scipio squatted on his heels in the mud by the Congaree River, reading a newspaper one of the black fighters of what still called itself the Congaree Socialist Republic had brought back from a Fort Motte park bench. Going into a town was dangerous; actually buying a newspaper from a white man would have been suicidally dangerous.

"Do Jesus!" Scipio said, looking up from the small print that gave him more trouble than it had a few years before. "Sound like the Yankees is kickin' we where it hurt the most."

Cassius was gutting catfish he'd pulled out of the muddy river. When they were fried, they would taste of mud, too. Cassius threw offal into the river before cocking his head to one side and giving Scipio a glance from the corner of his eye. "Them Yankees ain't kickin' we, Kip," he said at last.

Scipio snorted. "Don' tell me you believes we gwine lick they any day now, an' we jus' fallin' back to fool they. De papers prints de lies like that to keep de stupid buckra happy."

"I knows it," Cassius answered calmly. "De lies makes de buckra mo' and mo' stupid, too. But, Kip, you gots to recollect— de Congaree Socialist Republic ain't at war wid de United States. The Confederate States, they is at war, but you ain't no Confederate citizen, now is you? Never was, ain't, never gwine be. This here the onliest country you gots, Kip."

Instead of answering, Scipio buried his nose in the newspaper again. He did not trust himself to keep from saying what he really thought if he spoke at all. Since he would surely be shot the moment he did, shot and tossed in the river like catfish guts, he thought silence the wiser course.

A country! A country of mud and weeds and muddy water and stinks and furtive skulking and shells falling out of the sky whenever the militia managed to lay their hands on some ammunition. A country surrounded by a real country intent on wiping it from the face of the earth. A country that existed more in Cassius' imagination than in the real world.

"We is the free mens," Cassius said. "The 'pressors o' de world got no power here." Methodically, he gutted another fish.

Cherry came striding up in her tattered trousers. She moved like a free woman, or perhaps more like a catamount, graceful and dangerous at the same time. Scipio could readily understand how she'd enthralled Jacob Colleton. She didn't just smolder. She blazed.

Now she squatted down beside Cassius and said, "What you think o' dis story Vipsy bring back from Marshlands?"

"Woman, you knows what I thinks," Cassius answered impatiently. "I thinks Miss Anne bait a trap fo' we. I thinks I ain't gwine be foolish enough to put this here head"—he tapped it, almost as if to suggest he had another one stored somewhere not far away—"in de noose."

Cherry's lips skinned back from her white teeth in a hungry smile. "But if it so, Cass, if it so an' we can git our hands on de treasure—"

"But it ain't, an' you knows it ain't, same as I knows it ain't," Cassius said, his voice still good-natured, but with iron underneath.

"How you know that for a fac'?" Cherry demanded. "You was a hunter. You wasn't into the mansion all de time, no more'n me."

Cassius pointed at Scipio, as Scipio had known he would. "Dis nigger here, he know if anybody do. Kip, you tell Cherry what you done tol' her before. See if maybe she listen dis time, damn stubborn gal."

Scipio found himself longing for the polite, precise formality of the English he'd spoken as Anne Colleton's butler. He could have disagreed without offending much more readily in that dialect than in the speech of the Congaree. "Cassius, he right," he said, as placatingly as he could—he might have been more afraid of Cherry than of Cassius. "Ain't no treasure."

"How you know dat?" Cherry snapped. "How *kin* you know dat? Miss Anne, she one white debbil bit of a 'pressor, but she one *sly* white debbil bitch, too. Couldn't never git away from we las' Christmas, she weren't one sly white debbil bitch."

In the other English, the English he spoke no more, Scipio would have talked about probabilities, and about the impossibility of proving a negative. He could not do that in the dialect of the Congaree. Instead, at last losing his temper, he answered, "I knows Miss Anne's business better'n any other Marshlands nigger, and I says there ain't no treasure. You wants to go lookin' fo' what ain't dere, go on ahead. An' if de buckra wid de guns blows yo' stupid head off 'cause they layin' fo' you like you was a deer, don' you come back here cryin' afterwards."

Cherry's eyes blazed. Her high cheekbones and narrow, delicate chin told of Indian blood; now she looked as if she wanted to take Scipio's scalp. Her voice was deadly: "An' when I comes back wid de money, drag you down an' cut your balls off—or I would, if I reckoned you gots any."

"Easy, gal, *easy*," Cassius said. Sometimes Scipio thought Cherry alarmed the hunter who led the Reds, too. Cherry had not an ounce, not a speck, of give anywhere about her splendidly shaped person. Cassius went on, "You make a man 'fraid to tell you de truth, or what he reckon de truth, sooner o' later you gwine be sorry you done it."

Cherry tossed her head in a gesture of magnificent contempt Scipio had seen from her many times before. Pointing to him, she said, "He don' need me to make he afraid. He wish he was still Miss Anne's house nigger, still Miss Anne's lapdog." She spat on the ground between Scipio's feet.

Scipio violently shook his head, the more violently because she told nothing but the truth. He'd never wanted anything to do with the revolutionary movement, partly because of a suspicion— an accurate suspicion, as things turned out—the Red revolt would fail, partly because he had indeed been comfortable in the life he was living at Marshlands. He'd always assumed that, if anyone in power among the revolutionaries learned as much, he was a dead man.

But then Cassius said, "I knows dat. We all knows dat. De lap dog like de sof' pillow an' de fancy meat in de rubber dish. He cain't he'p it."

Right then, Scipio was glad of his dark, dark skin. No one could see the flush that made him feel he was burning up inside. He schooled his features to the impassivity required of a butler. *Let no one know what you are thinking.* He'd had that beaten into him in his training. It served him in good stead now.

Cassius went on, "But Kip, he keep he mouf shut. He don' never say boo to Miss Anne 'bout we. De proletariat, dey gots nuffing to lose in de revolution. Kip, he gots plenty to lose, an' he wid us anyways. If dat don' make he a hero o' de revolution, you tell me what do."

Cherry tossed her head again. "Shit, he jus' too 'fraid to betray we. He know how he pay fo' dat."

She was right again. Fortunately for Scipio, Cassius didn't think so. The hunter said, "He have plenty chances to give we away an' git away clean, an' he never done it. He *wid* us, Cherry."

"He *ain't*," Cherry said positively. "Miss Anne spread she legs, he come runnin' to lick dat pussy wid de yellow hair, same as he always done."

"Liar!" Scipio shouted now, a mixture of horror, embarrassment, and fury in his voice. Only after that anguished cry passed his lips did he realize she might have been using a metaphor, if a crude one. Part of the embarrassment, he realized with a different kind of horror, was that Anne Colleton *was* beautiful and desirable. But a black man who was found out looking on a white woman with desire in the CSA was as surely dead as one who betrayed the revolutionary movement.

Even Cassius looked distressed. "Enough, Cherry!" he said sharply. "You gots no cause to rip he to pieces dat way."

"Got plenty cause," Cherry retorted. "An' when I comes back

with the treasure, Cass, we see who am de gen'l sec'tary o' de Congaree Socialist Republic after dat." She stalked off.

Cassius sighed. "Dat one hard woman. Ain't nobody gwine stop she—she gwine try an' fin' dat treasure, an' it don't matter if it ain't there. She try anyways."

"She gwine get herself killed," Scipio said. "She gwine get whoever go wid she killed, too."

"I knows it," Cassius said unhappily. "I ain't no fool, an' I weren't borned yesterday. But how is I s'posed to stop she? If I shoot she wid my own gun, she dead, too—an' dat bitch liable to shoot first. I done told her, don' go. But she don' listen to what I say." He sighed again, a leader hard aground on the shoals of leadership. "I brings her up befo' de revolutionary tribunal, they liable to do like she say, not like I say. Dere some stubborn revolutionary niggers on de tribunal. I oughts to know. I put 'em dere my ownself."

"Maybe you jus' let she go, then," Scipio said. "Maybe you jus' let she go an' get herself killed." His voice turned savage. "Maybe dat jus' what she deserve." If he could find a way to get a message to Anne Colleton, letting her know when Cherry was going to try to plunder Marshlands, he would do it, and it would be a true message, too. Letting—helping—one of the women who'd made the past year and a half of his life a nightmare dispose of the other had a sweet ring of poetic justice to it.

But Cassius was watching him with those hunter's eyes. Somebody was watching him all the time. The surviving revolutionaries did not altogether trust him. They had good reason not to trust him. Casually, as if he weren't thinking at all, he took from his belt a tin cup that had once belonged to a Confederate soldier now surely dead. He dipped up water from the river and drank. The water tasted of mud, too. Only because he'd grown up in a slave cabin not far away could he drink it without having his guts turn inside out.

Cherry and half a dozen men went treasure hunting the next day. Cassius watched them go with a scowl on his face. If by some accident Vipsy had been telling the truth, if by some accident Miss Anne had done something of which Scipio was ignorant, Cassius' place at the head of the Congaree Socialist Republic was indeed in danger. Could the Red rebels survive a leadership struggle? Scipio had his doubts.

But Cherry came back after sundown, empty-handed. Scipio

had hoped she wouldn't come back at all. The glower she aimed at him almost made her return worthwhile, though. He concentrated on his bowl of stew—turtle and roots and other things he ate and tried not to think about.

"I knows dat treasure there," Cherry said. "I's gwine find it. I ain't done. Don't nobody think I's done." She glared at Scipio, at Cassius, at everyone but the men who'd followed her. Scipio wore his butler's mask. Behind it, he kept on trying to figure out how to get a message to Anne Colleton.

Marie Galtier held out a tray loaded with stewed chicken to Dr. Leonard O'Doull. O'Doull held up both hands, palms out, as if warding off attack. "*Merci,* Mme. Galtier, but mercy, too, I beg you," he said. "One more drumstick and I think I'll grow feathers."

Marie sniffed. "I do not see how you could grow feathers when you do not eat enough to keep a bird alive."

"Mother!" Nicole said reprovingly, and Marie relented.

Dr. O'Doull looked over to Lucien Galtier. "Seeing how she feeds you, it is to me a matter of amazement that you do not weigh three hundred pounds."

"Our father is very light for his weight," Georges said before Lucien could answer.

"In the same way that you, my son, are very foolish for your brains," Galtier said, and managed to feel he had got a draw with his son, if not a win over him.

Serious as usual, Charles Galtier asked, "Is it true, *monsieur le docteur,* that U.S. forces continue their advance against Quebec City?"

"Yes, from what I hear at the hospital, that is true," Dr. O'Doull told Galtier's elder son.

"Is it also true that fighting alongside the forces of the United States is a corps from the *soi-disant* Republic of Quebec?" Charles asked.

"Charles . . ." Lucien murmured warningly. Speaking of it as the so-called Republic of Quebec before an American, one of the people who called it that, was something less than the wisest thing his son might have done.

But Leonard O'Doull, fortunately, took no offense. "Not a corps, certainly, for there are not nearly enough volunteers for a

Quebecois corps," he replied. "But a regiment, perhaps two regiments of Quebecois from the Republic—yes, I know they are in the line, for I have treated some of their wounded, being called upon to do so because I am lucky enough to speak French."

It was a straightforward, reasonable, matter-of-fact answer. Lucien waited with some anxiety to hear how his son replied to it. If Charles denounced the Republic, life could grow difficult. But Charles said only, "I do not see how Quebecois could volunteer to fight Quebecois."

"In the War of Secession, brother fought brother in the United States—what was the United States," O'Doull said. "It is not an easy time when such things happen."

"But no one outside created the Confederate States, *n'est-ce pas*?" Charles said, doggedly refusing to let go. "They came into being of themselves."

To Lucien's relief, his son once more failed to get a rise out of Dr. O'Doull. "Perhaps at the beginning, yes," the American said, "but England and France have helped prop them up ever since. Now, though, the props begin to totter."

Charles could have said something like, *Just as the United States prop up the Republic of Quebec*. But O'Doull made it plain he was likely to agree with a statement like that, not argue with it. That took half—more than half—the fun away from making it. To his father's relief, Charles kept quiet.

After Marie, Nicole, Susanne, Denise, and Jeanne cleared the plates away from the supper table, Lucien got out a bottle of the homemade apple brandy that helped keep nights warm in Quebec. "Is it possible, M. Galtier, that I might talk to you alone?" Dr. O'Doull asked, staring at the pale yellow liquid in the glass in front of him as if he had never seen it before.

Lucien's head came up alertly. Charles and Georges looked at each other. "Well, I can tell when I am not wanted," Georges said, and stomped upstairs in exaggerated outrage. Charles said nothing. He simply rose, nodded to O'Doull, and left the dining room.

"And for what purpose is it that you desire to talk to me alone, Dr. O'Doull?" Galtier said, also examining his applejack with a critical eye. He could without much difficulty think of one possible reason.

And that proved to be the reason Dr. Leonard O'Doull had in mind. The American physician took a deep breath, then spoke rapidly: "M. Galtier, I desire to marry your daughter, and I would like your blessing for the match."

Galtier lifted his glass and knocked back the applejack in one long, fiery gulp. No, O'Doull's words were not a surprise, but they were a shock nonetheless. Instead of answering straight out in brusque, American fashion, the farmer returned a question: "You have, I take it, had somewhat to say of this matter with Nicole."

"Oh, yes, I have done that." Dr. O'Doull's voice was dry. "I will tell you, sir, she likes the idea if you will give your approval."

"And why would she not?" Galtier replied. "You are a personable man, you are a reasonable figure of a man, and you are skilled in your profession, as I have reason to know." He patted the leg O'Doull had sewn up. "But even so, before I say yes or no, there are some things I must learn. For example, suppose that you marry her. Where would you live when the war ends? Would you take her back to the United States?"

"As a matter of fact, I was thinking of setting up shop in Rivière-du-Loup," O'Doull answered. "I've been asking around when I go up into town, and you folks here can use a good surgeon. I *am* a good surgeon, M. Galtier; any doctor who works in a military hospital turns into a good surgeon because he has so many chances to practice his trade." He gulped down his own applejack, then muttered in English: "Damn the war."

"You would speak French, then, and mostly forget your own language, except"—Galtier's eyes twinkled—"when you need to swear, perhaps?"

"I would," O'Doull said. "I speak French better than many people who come to the United States speak English. They do well enough in my country. I should be able to do well enough in yours."

"I think you have reason there," Galtier said. "That you can do this, I do not doubt. The question I was asking was whether you were willing to do it, and I see you are. And you are a Catholic man. That I have known for long and long."

"Yes, I am a Catholic man," O'Doull said. "I am not a perfectly pious man, but I am a Catholic."

"The only man I know who believes himself to be perfectly pious is Bishop Pascal," Galtier said. "Bishop Pascal is surely very pious, as he is very clever, but he is neither so pious nor so clever as he believes himself to be."

"There I think *you* have reason, M. Galtier," Leonard O'Doull said, chuckling. He blinked a couple of times; if a man drank apple brandy when he was tired, it hit even harder than usual. After a moment's thought, he went on, "May I now tell you something to help you decide?"

"Speak," Galtier urged. "Say what is in your mind."

"No—what is in my heart," O'Doull replied. "What I want to tell you is that I love your daughter, and I will do everything I can to take care of her and make her as happy as I can."

"Well," Lucien Galtier said, and then again: "Well." He picked up the bottle of applejack and poured a hefty dollop for Dr. O'Doull and another for himself. He raised his glass in salute. "I look forward to my grandchildren."

O'Doull's long face was normally serious almost to somberness. Galtier had not imagined such a wide smile could spread over it as happened when the doctor understood his words. Still smiling that broad smile, Dr. O'Doull reached out and shook his hand. The doctor's skin was soft, uncallused from manual labor, but not smooth—poisons to kill germs had left it rough and red.

"Thank you, my father-in-law to be," O'Doull said. "Thank you."

"Now you make me feel old," Galtier said in mock severity. He raised his glass. "Let us drink, and then let us tell the rest of the family—if Nicole has not already done as much in the kitchen."

Only as the brandy slid warmly down his throat did he reflect on how, after the United States had overrun his country, he had been certain—he had been more than certain; he had been resolved—he would hate the invaders forever. And now his daughter was going to marry an American. He had just given permission for his daughter to marry an American. He shook his head. Life proved stranger than anyone could imagine.

When he called, his wife and daughters flew out of the kitchen and his sons came leaping down the stairs like mountain goats. They might not know what he would say, but they knew what he was going to talk about. He got up, walked over to Leonard O'Doull, and set a hand on his shoulder. "We are going to have in our family a new member," he said simply. "Our friend, *monsieur le docteur* O'Doull, has asked of me permission to marry Nicole, and I have given to him that permission and my blessing."

He remembered then that O'Doull had not asked for permission, only his blessing. He wondered what would have happened had he refused it. Would O'Doull have done something foolish? Would Nicole? He had no way of finding out now. Perhaps—no, probably—that was just as well.

And then he forgot about might-have-beens, because Nicole squealed with joy and threw herself into his arms, her three little sisters squealed with excitement and started jumping up and down, Charles and Georges went over to O'Doull and pounded him on the back (that Charles did so rather surprising Lucien), and Marie squeezed between them to kiss the American doctor on the cheek.

"Thank you, Papa. Thank you," Nicole said over and over.

He patted her on the back. "Do not thank me now, my little one," he said. "If you thank me ten years from now, if you thank me twenty years from now, if *le bon Dieu* permits me to remain in this world so that you may thank me thirty years from now, that will be very good."

"If I want to thank you now, I am going to thank you now," Nicole said. "So there!" To prove it, she kissed him.

He glanced over to O'Doull, one eyebrow upraised. "See how disobedient she is," he said. "You should know what you are getting into."

"I'll take my chances," O'Doull said with a laugh.

"And we will at last get our older sister out of the house!" Georges said. If the dance he and Charles danced wasn't one of delight, it made an excellent counterfeit.

Galtier waited for Nicole to explode into fury. It didn't happen. She said, "This is the happiest day of my life, and I am not going to let my two foolish brothers ruin it for me."

The happiest day of my life. When the USA first invaded Quebec, Galtier had never imagined those words in connection with an American. Now Nicole spoke them altogether without self-consciousness. And now he did not explode into fury on hearing them. He poured himself more applejack, to serve as a shield against strangeness.

quite what it meant or where. God alone knew they walked a fine line in the capital. One had one well-to-do. She wouldn't be happy if the mother decided it was merely a different face in a different century

"Well, Edna," Nellie Semphroch said with a groan, "I wish you'd married that Rebel officer and moved away from here, the way you were talking about."

"So do I, Ma," her daughter moaned. "Oh, Jesus Christ, so do I." They were not angry at each other, not for the moment. What sounded like a thunderstorm raged outside.

It was not a thunderstorm. It was worse, much worse. "If you'd gone somewhere far away, you'd be safe now," Nellie said. "You ain't safe here. Nobody's safe in Washington, not any more."

Two candles lit the cellar under the coffeehouse from which Nellie had made so much during the war. Every few seconds, another U.S. shell would crash down, and the candlesticks would shake and the flames jerk. Every so often—far more often than Nellie's frazzled nerves could readily bear—a shell would land close by or a round from a big gun would hit a little farther off. Then the candlesticks would jump, and the flames leap and swoop wildly. A couple of times, Nellie had to move like lightning to keep the candlesticks from falling over and the candles from starting a fire.

If a big shell came down on the coffeehouse . . . If a big shell came down on the coffeehouse, it would pierce the roof and then the ceiling of the first story and then the floor, every one of them as if it weren't there at all. Those shells, she'd heard, had special hard noses to smash their way even into concrete installations. If one of them exploded in the cellar—well, she and Edna would never know what hit them, and that, she had seen, was in its own way a mercy.

A heavy shell thudded home. The ground shook, as if in an earthquake (or so Nellie imagined; she'd never felt a real earthquake). Edna started to cry. "God, God, Ma," she wailed. "This here is the capital of the United States. What the hell is the U.S. Army doing, blowing the capital of their own goddamn country to pieces?"

"If the Rebs would have left, if they would have said Washington was an open city and pulled back over the Potomac into Virginia, this never would have happened," her mother answered. "But they keep going on about how Washington is theirs, and they built all those forts on the high ground north of town—built 'em or took over the ones we made—and so this is what happens on account of it."

Edna was not inclined to argue politics. She'd wanted to marry Lieutenant Nicholas H. Kincaid for his personal charms, not out of sympathy for the Confederate States of America. Falling in love with him (that was what Edna called it, though to Nellie it had never looked like anything but an itch in the privates) had made her more sympathetic to the CSA, but not all that much more.

One of the candles burned out, making the cellar even gloomier and filling it with the greasy stink of hot tallow. Edna lighted a fresh candle from the one still burning and stuck it in its candlestick. The flickering flames filled her face with shadows, making her look far older than her years. "Ma . . . ?" she began, and then hesitated.

"What is it?" Nellie asked warily. These days, that kind of stuttering led only to trouble.

Sure enough, when Edna resumed, it was to ask, "Ma, why do you suppose that Bill Reach yelled for everybody to get out of the church just when the Yanks—uh, the Army—were gettin' ready to start shooting at Washington?"

"I don't know." Nellie's voice was tight. "I don't care. I wish I'd never set eyes on Bill Reach, not a long time ago and not now, either."

She waited for her daughter to bait her about the strumpet's life she'd led. But Edna's mind, for once, turned in a different direction. "How do you suppose he knew, Ma? How could he have known the Army was going to open up on us right then?"

"I couldn't begin to tell you," Nellie answered. That didn't mean she didn't know, as she hoped Edna would think it would. It meant only what it said: that she couldn't tell.

But Edna, despite being wild for life, was not a fool in matters unrelated to large, handsome, empty-headed men. "He *couldn't* have known, Ma," she insisted, "not if he's just a drunken bum. Only thing a drunken bum cares about is his next bottle. Only way he could have known . . ." She drew in a sharp, excited breath. "Ma, the only way he could have known is if he's a spy."

Edna had hit the nail on the head. She didn't realize that hitting the nail on the head endangered not only Bill Reach—who, in Nellie's view, deserved all the danger he could find and then some—but also Hal Jacobs and Nellie herself. With a sniff, Nellie said, "Anyone who'd hire that louse to spy for him would have to be pretty hard up, if you want to know what I think."

That was true. Hal Jacobs, now, was sober and sensible—sensible enough to stay sober, too. Nellie could see him as a spy. Why Reach never started babbling about what he knew to everyone around him when he got drunk was beyond her.

Edna said, "But he couldn't be anything else, Ma. He *knew*. Somebody must have told him."

"*I* wouldn't want to tell Bill Reach anything, except where to head in," Nellie said grimly. "And anybody else who would want to is a fool, like I said before. I don't know what he might have heard while he was laying in the gutter, and I don't want to know, either."

For a wonder, Edna subsided. The bombardment didn't. The U.S. Army seemed intent on killing every Confederate in Washington, D.C. If that meant killing all the U.S. citizens left in the tortured city, too, well, fair enough. For variety's sake, perhaps, bombing aeroplanes roared overhead and dropped long strings of explosives that made the candlesticks quiver as if they were in torment along with everything else in town.

At last, hours later, a lull came. "Let's go up and cook something to eat," Nellie said. "Then, if they haven't started up again by the time we're through, I think I'll scurry across the street and see how Mr. Jacobs is getting along."

"All right, Ma, you go ahead and do that," Edna said, but without the viciousness that would have informed the words before the disaster of her wedding. Losing her fiancé on what would have been their wedding day had taken a lot of the starch out of her.

It was dark in the coffeehouse, too: night outside, with a few strips and circles of moonlight sliding through holes shell fragments had punched in the boards that covered the window opening. The gas had gone out as soon as U.S. shelling started, which was sensible of the Confederate authorities but made life no easier. Edna scooped coal into the firebox of the stove and got a fire going.

"I hope this beefsteak is still good," Nellie muttered, sniffing at it as she took it out of the icebox. She sighed. "You may as well cook it up, because it won't be any better tomorrow. God only knows when we'll have the chance to get ice again."

Edna fried it in an iron spider. It tasted a little gamy, but not too bad. But when Edna turned the tap to get water to make coffee, nothing came out. "The Rebs wouldn't have shut off the water," she said. "They couldn't put out any fires if they did."

"A shell must have broken a pipe somewhere not far away," Nellie said. "If the water doesn't come back on soon, we'll have to carry it back from the river in a bucket and boil it. That will be dangerous, if the shelling keeps up like this."

"Oh, well." Edna tried to make the best of things: "If there ain't no water, I can't very well do dishes, now can I?"

"I'm going across the street," Nellie said, and her daughter nodded. When Nellie opened the door and inhaled, she coughed. The air was thick with smoke. A lot of the things that could burn in Washington were burning. Here and there in the near and middle distance, orange flames flickered and leaped.

Nellie was not supposed to be on the street after dusk. A Confederate patrol that spied her was as likely as not to shoot first and ask questions later. But she didn't think she would be spotted, and she wasn't.

When she opened the door to Hal Jacobs' cobbler's shop, the bell over it jangled, as if cheerily announcing a customer. Jacobs looked up, candlelight exaggerating the surprise on his face. The two men huddled with him also looked startled. One was Lou Pfeiffer, a pigeon fancier who used his birds to carry messages out of Washington. The other, to Nellie's horrified dismay, was Bill Reach.

"I came to check and make sure you were all right, Mr. Jacobs," Nellie said in a voice that might have been carved from ice. "I see you are. Good evening." She turned and started back across the street.

"Widow Semphroch—Nellie—please wait," Jacobs said. "Mr. Reach has something he would like to say to you—don't you, Bill?" He bore down heavily on the last three words.

Reach, for once, wasn't obviously drunk. That did not make his tone any less raspy and rough when he said, "I'm sorry as he—as anything for all the trouble I caused you, Lit—uh, Nellie, and I sure as—as can be won't do anything like that ever again, honest to God I won't." He took off his battered black derby, revealing a mat of unkempt gray hair beneath.

It wasn't enough. It wasn't nearly enough. But it sufficed to bring Nellie back into the shop. Lou Pfeiffer's round head went up and down on his fat neck. "That's good," he wheezed. "That's very good."

And then the thunder from the north that had died away started up again, not only started up again but was, impossibly, louder and fiercer than ever. Shells began crashing down, some very close by. Fragments whined off brick and stone and bit into and through rough wood. "To the cellar!" Jacobs shouted.

Nellie hesitated. Crossing the street to get back to her own cellar in the middle of the bombardment was nothing but madness. Going down into the cellar here, with a man who, she thought, loved her; a man who had used her; and a man about whom she knew next to nothing . . .

She hesitated, and was lost. "Come on! To the cellar!" Jacobs bawled again. He grabbed her by the arm and half dragged her down the stairs.

Meant for one, his cellar was obscenely crowded for four. Nellie sat in one corner of the tiny, stifling chamber, her skirts pulled in tight around her, willing no one to come near. And no one did. But they all kept looking at her in the flickering light of the candle flame. And they were all men, so she knew—she was sure she knew—what went through their filthy minds.

And then, to her horror, Bill Reach pulled from his pocket a flask and began to drink. She sprang to her feet and was up the stairs and shoving the cellar door open before Hal Jacobs could do anything more than let out a startled bleat. She slammed the door down on top of the three U.S. spies and fled.

When she got back to the cellar under the coffeehouse, she discovered flying fragments had sliced her skirt to shreds. Not one of them had touched her flesh. "You all right, Ma?" Edna asked. "I heard you at the cellar door right in the middle of all the guns—before that, I was afraid you were a goner, and then I thought you were nuts, coming out in that."

"With where I was, I'd go out among the shells again in a

minute." Nellie spoke with great conviction. "In a second, believe me." Edna shot her a quizzical glance. She shuddered but did not explain.

Far in the distance, off somewhere on the west Texas plains, a coyote howled, a wail full of hunger and loneliness and unrequited lust. Hipolito Rodriguez let out a soft chuckle. "He is not very happy, I don't think. The way he sound, he might as well be a soldier, *si*?"

Before Jefferson Pinkard could answer, Sergeant Albert Cross said, "Need some men for a raidin' party on the Yankee trenches tonight."

Pinkard stuck up his hand. "I'll go, Sarge."

Cross looked at him without saying anything for a while. Then he remarked, "You don't got to kill all the damnyankees in Texas by your lonesome, Jeff. Leave some for the rest of us."

"I want to go, Sarge," Pinkard answered. He had never been a particularly eloquent man. Instead of saying more with words, he folded his big hands into fists. "What they done—" He shook his head in frustration. The words clogged in his throat.

In the end, Sergeant Cross shrugged. "Well, hell, you want 'em that bad, reckon you can have 'em. Who else?"

"I go," Hip Rodriguez said quietly.

One by one, Cross got the rest of the volunteers. "That's good," he said. "That's mighty fine. We go out half past midnight. Y'all grab yourselves some shuteye before then. Don't want any sleepy bastard yawnin' out in the middle of no-man's-land an' lettin' the damnyankees know we're comin'. See y'all tomorrow mornin'—*early* tomorrow mornin'."

After the sergeant went on his way, Rodriguez said, "Ever since you get back from leave, *amigo,* you want to go on all the raids, on all the attacks. You never used to do nothing like that before."

"What about it?" Pinkard said. "Yankees ain't gonna get out of Texas unless we grab 'em by the scruff of the neck and heave 'em on out. Somebody's got to do it. Might as well be me."

Rodriguez studied him. The little Sonoran farmer's eyes might have been black glass in his swarthy face. "You don't have such a good time like you think when you get back home?" he asked. He didn't push. He didn't raise his voice. He let Pinkard answer without making him feel he had to tell any deep, dark secrets.

But no matter how discreet he was, no matter how little pressure he applied, Jefferson Pinkard kept on saying what he'd been saying ever since he returned to the front from Birmingham: "Had a hell of a time back home."

In a certain sense, that was even true. He hadn't screwed so much on his honeymoon down in Mobile. Emily had done everything he wanted. Emily had done more than he'd imagined. He'd wakened one night to her sucking him hard and then pulling him over onto her. She'd been wet and waiting. He'd worn himself out by then, and hadn't thought he could come, but he'd been wrong.

Bedford Cunningham had made himself scarce, too. After that first dreadful moment, Jeff hadn't seen him at all. That suited Jeff fine. If he never saw Bedford again, that would suit him even better.

But now he was back here, somewhere east of Lubbock. Bedford Cunningham remained in Birmingham, remained next door to Emily. What were they doing now that Jeff was gone? Was she rubbing her breasts in his face? Was she teasing his foreskin with her tongue? Was she groaning and gurgling and urging him on, her legs folded around his back tight as a bear trap's jaws?

Every filthy picture in Pinkard's mind made him wish he were dead, and Cunningham, and Emily. And, at the same time, every filthy picture in his mind made him wish he were back in Birmingham, so Emily could do those things to *him*.

"Yeah, a hell of a time," he repeated. Rodriguez plainly didn't believe him. *Well, too damn bad, Hip,* Jeff thought.

He wrapped himself in his blanket, more to keep the mosquitoes away than for warmth, and did his best to sleep. Images of Emily naked and lewd made him sweat harder than the hot, muggy weather could have done by itself. At last, despite them, he dozed—and dreamt of his wife, naked and lewd. Whether awake or asleep, he could not escape her . . . except when he fought.

Sergeant Cross shook him awake at midnight. For a moment, he thought the hand on his shoulder was Emily's. When he realized it wasn't, he also realized he was liable to be killed inside the next hour. He scrambled eagerly to his feet. "Let's get moving, Sarge," he said.

"Keep your britches on, Jeff," Cross answered. "Some of our buddies are still sawing wood. We got to wait on the artillery, too. They're gonna lay down a box barrage for us, keep the Yanks from bringing reinforcements into the stretch of trench we hit."

"That sounds pretty good," Pinkard said. "They want us to bring back prisoners, or are we supposed to come back by ourselves?"

"Nobody told me one way or the other," Cross said. "Reckon we'll have to play that one by ear when we get over there." Seeing Pinkard yawn, he went on, "Grab yourself some coffee. Pot on a little fire just down the way."

The coffee was thick and tasted like dirt and was strong enough to strip paint, but it made Pinkard's heart beat faster and his eyes open wide. He gulped it down, swearing as it burned his mouth. Several of his comrades took cups, too. Pretty soon, the pot was empty.

Sergeant Cross passed out burlap sacks of grenades. Jeff took one. The little round bombs—British style, not the potato-mashers the Yanks and the Huns used—were fine for trench fighting. Bayonet and entrenching tool were even better, as far as Pinkard was concerned.

One by one, the men in butternut climbed out of the trench and crawled through the few pathetic lengths of wire that passed for a belt. Cross said, "This here wire reminds me of a bald fellow combin' about the last three strands he's got across his shiny old dome and pretendin' he's got hisself a whole head o' hair. He may be fooled, but ain't nobody else who is."

Several soldiers chuckled in low voices. Pinkard didn't, but he nodded at the aptness of the comparison. Because they had any barbed wire at all, the Confederate commanders in Texas often seemed to think they had great thickets of the stuff, as was true in Virginia and Tennessee—not that, from the news coming west, it had done the CSA a whole lot of good there, either.

A little to the north, a flare rose from the Yankee lines. It burned in the sky, a fierce white point of light. Under its glare, the advancing Confederate soldiers froze. Pinkard pressed his face into the dirt. It smelled of dust and of dead bodies. That stink of rotting flesh never left his nostrils; even more than cordite and coffee and tobacco, it was the definitive odor of the front, as hot iron was the definitive odor of the Sloss Foundry.

After what felt like forever, the flare finally faded. Jeff crawled on. He skirted shell holes when he could, but was always ready to dive into one if the U.S. soldiers opened up on the raiding party.

Cross muttered discontentedly: "Sure as hell, goddamn artillery's gonna open up too goddamn soon. They ain't gonna figure out we had to wait for the flare. Goddamn artillery can't figure out to grab their asses with both hands, anybody wants to know."

He was right. The Confederate soldiers hadn't reached the Yankee wire—thicker than their own, but not much—when the three-inch guns behind the C.S. line started barking. Shells rained down on the U.S. position, making the sides and back of a box that isolated a stretch of the forward trenches.

Like the rest of the men in the raiding party, Pinkard wore a wire-cutter on his belt. He could crawl under most of the wire the damnyankees had laid, and snipped his way through the few places where he had trouble crawling. Somebody in the U.S. trench fired. Jeff didn't think it was an aimed shot. He wanted to thank the Yankee for it; it told him exactly where the trench line was.

He yanked a grenade out of the sack, pulled off the ring, and chucked the bomb into the trench, as close to the Yankee rifleman as he could put it. The report was loud and hard and short. He threw more grenades. So did the rest of the raiders. Then, with a yell, he scrambled forward and leaped down into the U.S. trench.

"Hey there, you—" The words were spoken in a sharp Yankee accent. Jeff didn't reach over his shoulder for his rifle. Faster to yank the entrenching tool off his belt and swing it in a short, flat arc. The shovel blade struck flesh and bit deep. The U.S. soldier went down with a groan. Then Pinkard unslung the Tredegar and ran along the firebay.

A potato-masher grenade hurled from a traverse exploded eight or ten feet in front of him. A fragment bit the back of his hand. Another tore through his tunic without grazing him. He dashed past the place where the grenade had gone off and into the traverse. A Yankee yelled and fired. He missed. Pinkard lunged with the bayonet. He grunted as it penetrated the U.S. soldier's flesh, almost as he sometimes grunted when he penetrated Emily's flesh.

The damnyankee shrieked and crumpled. Jeff fired and

stabbed, stabbed and fired, till three or four more Yankees were down and none left on his feet in the traverse. He grunted again, an oddly sated sound.

Somebody touched him on the shoulder. He whirled, and would have spitted Hip Rodriguez if the Sonoran hadn't beaten the bayonet aside with his own rifle. "We got to go back, Jeff," Rodriguez said. "The sergeant, he blow the whistle. You no hear?"

Consumed in his orgy of killing, Pinkard hadn't heard anything. He shook his head like a man coming out of a dream. "All right, Hip," he said meekly. "I'll come back with you."

Rodriguez looked down the length of the traverse. Muttering, "Ten million demons from hell," he crossed himself. To Jeff, he said, "You fight like a crazy man, *amigo*."

"Yeah," Pinkard said. "Come on. Let's get the hell out of here."

U.S. artillery pumped shells into no-man's-land as the Confederate raiders crawled and scrambled back to their own line. One man took a splinter in the leg. One man hadn't come out of the trench. Even so, Sergeant Cross reported to Captain Connolly with considerable pride: "Sir, we whaled the stuffing out of the sons of bitches. Pinkard here, he was worth a regiment all by hisself."

"Good news, Sergeant," the company commander said. "Well done, Pinkard."

"Thank you, sir," Jeff answered. His voice was dull, far away. The red mist of slaughter had retreated from his mind. He felt spent and empty. Emily cavorted once more behind his eyes.

Four fat freighters slowly steamed south. Watching them from the deck of the USS *Ericsson*, George Enos sighed and said, "I don't know why they bother painting themselves in camouflage colors. A big bull's-eye with SINK ME alongside it in big letters would be more like the straight story."

Carl Sturtevant chuckled. "You aren't looking at the world with the proper spirit, George," he said, for all the world like a chaplain.

Enos snorted. "And you aren't looking at the world like any petty officer I ever heard of," he retorted. "You're supposed to go 'Goddamn right' when I say something like that."

The chief of the depth-charge projector crew laughed. "I never do what I'm supposed to if I can help it."

"All right." Enos chuckled, too. The ships wallowed along, painted in stripes and patches and gaudy colors that were supposed to make it hard for the skipper of a submersible to gauge either their range or their course. Whether the camouflage job did that or not, George couldn't have said. It made the freighters ugly as sin, though. There he was certain.

Stripes zigzagged jaggedly over the *Ericsson*, too, in an effort to break up her outline and make her seem to be moving in the direction of her own stern. She and a sister ship scurried around the freighter like sheep dogs around sheep, doing their best to keep the flock safe from the wolves that lurked under the surface of the sea.

"What I want to do," Enos said, "is get the bastard who almost torpedoed us a few weeks ago. Lord knows he's still hanging around; he would have chewed up that other bunch of freighters if we hadn't run him off."

Sturtevant raised an ironic eyebrow. "I swear, I don't know what the hell you're talking about. Lieutenant Crowder reported that submersible as probably destroyed, and if you don't think Lieutenant Crowder knows everything in the world, well, shit, just ask him."

"Yeah, and rain makes applesauce," Enos said. They both laughed then; laughing at the pretensions of officers was a sailors' tradition old as time.

"He's not too bad a fellow," Sturtevant allowed in an astonishing display of magnanimity, "as long as you don't take him too serious. Give him a chance, though, and he'd have half of us up in aeroplanes and the other half down under the water in deep-sea diver suits, tryin' to catch torpedoes like they were footballs the Rebs were throwing at us."

"He does like gadgets," Enos agreed. "At least the depth-charge projector is a pretty good gadget."

A veteran seaman, Sturtevant had almost as little use for new-fangled devices as he did for young officers enamored of them. When he said, "Yeah, it's not too bad," he surely meant it as high praise, and that was how George Enos took it.

Enos stared out across the blue, blue water of the tropical Atlantic, looking for anything that might alert him to the presence of the Confederate submarine that also seemed to make its home in this stretch of ocean. He'd spied the stinking thing once—why not twice?

Ocean, squawking birds, sun standing higher in the sky every day—and far higher now than Enos had ever seen, anyway. Despite that fierce and brilliant light, he didn't spot anything out of the ordinary.

He kept looking ahead of the freighters, ahead and off to one side. If the submersible did prowl in these waters, that was the direction from which it would attack. It couldn't move very fast while submerged; it had to take the lead on the surface, then go under and slowly sneak toward its intended prey.

George did his best to think like the skipper of a submersible. One thing he knew: the skipper of the boat that had almost sunk the *Ericsson* had nerve and brains both. He'd pretended to be sunk well enough to fool Lieutenant Crowder, and then he'd gone after U.S. freighters the first chance he got. That was his job, and he was going to do it come hell or high water—in fact, he'd probably prefer high water.

"There ought to be a better way to find a submersible that's hunting than bare-naked eyeballs," George said. "What we need"—he glanced over at Carl Sturtevant—"is a new kind of gadget."

"Here's what you need." Sturtevant displayed the middle finger of his right hand. "And for God's sake don't say that anyplace where Crowder can hear you. He'll either order you to invent the damn thing yourself—and by day before yesterday, too, or you'll be in Dutch—or else he'll try and do it himself, and that won't work, either."

"Yeah, but—" Enos got no further than that. The lead freighter blew up. It was a spectacular explosion; the ship must have been carrying munitions. The report slapped George in the face across a couple of miles of water. "Jesus!" he exclaimed.

Klaxons started hooting men to their battle stations. The *Ericsson*'s deck shuddered under Enos' feet as he ran. The stacks belched smoke. The destroyer picked up speed.

At the one-pounder by the stern, George peered about. He suspected—he feared—he was likelier to spot a torpedo wake heading straight for the *Ericsson* than a telltale periscope. If he didn't try to spot a periscope, though, nothing could be more certain than his failure.

A runner came up to Lieutenant Crowder at the depth-charge

projector by Enos' gun and said, "Sir, this is where the bastard—uh, the submersible—is hiding. Captain wants you to shake him up to the surface if you can."

"We'll do that," Crowder said. He turned back to Carl Sturtevant, who did the dirty work of running the projector. "We'll shake those Rebel bastards or their limey pals right out of their shoes. Give me four charges, Sturtevant; set the fuses for two hundred feet."

"Aye aye, sir. Four charges. Two hundred feet," the veteran petty officer repeated tonelessly. That tonelessness was itself a dead giveaway that he did not agree with his superior's order. Indeed, as the crew loaded the first two charges onto the projector, he went so far as to ask, "Did I hear that right, sir?" If Crowder said no, he could change the order without losing face by having a man of lower rank correct him.

But Crowder, crisply, said, "Yes. I want them deep. After he sank that freighter, the skipper down there will surely have seen us coming to the attack. He will try to place as much ocean between himself and us as he can. Two hundred feet I said; two hundred feet it shall be."

"Yes, sir," Sturtevant answered, even more woodenly than before. Two by two, the depth charges flew off the *Ericsson's* stern and splashed into the sea.

That *yes, sir* in place of *aye aye, sir* was a telling proof of how strongly Sturtevant disagreed with Lieutenant Crowder. Standing there behind the one-pounder, George Enos found himself on the petty officer's side. Whatever flag the boat somewhere under them flew, its skipper had proved himself a tough, aggressive bastard in earlier attacks. George didn't think a skipper like that would lurk in the depths, either. His guess was that the enemy captain would come up to periscope depth as soon as he could, and try to put a fish right in the *Ericsson's* engine room. In which case, sending depth charges down two hundred feet would be a waste of good explosives.

George's eyes went back and forth, back and forth, looking for the feathery plume of wake that trailed and could give away a periscope. He imagined he saw something a couple of times, but longer looks proved him wrong.

Astern of the *Ericsson*, water boiled and bubbled, the surface mark of the depth charges' explosions. Moments later, oil floated up from far underwater, flattening the waves over which it rode. "Well, dip me in shit and fry me for bacon," Carl Sturtevant said in conversational tones. "Either we've hurt the son of a bitch or else he's trying to make us think we did. Whether it's the one or the other, we didn't miss him by much." He solemnly took off his hat to Lieutenant Crowder. "Beg your pardon, sir. You were right and I was wrong, and I'm man enough to admit it."

"Never mind that." Crowder pointed back to the oil slick. "Let's get over it and pound that boat to death. I'll want half the ash cans we throw down there fused for a hundred and fifty feet, the other half for two-fifty."

"Aye aye, sir," Sturtevant said, and repeated back the order. No back talk now; his thoughts and Crowder's were running down the same track.

Like any destroyer, the *Ericsson* was an agile vessel. She quickly returned to the floating oil. Into the water splashed the new salvo of depth charges.

Explosions underwater once more roiled the surface of the sea. Enos stood at his gun, ready to pound away at the submarine if she had to surface in a hurry. He was also ready for disappointment; the submersible had tricked the destroyer before. More oil came to the surface, and air bubbles, and bits of wreckage swept up by the bubbles.

The men at the depth-charge projector cheered and beat their fists against its metal sides. "If he's shamming this time, he's a better actor than any Booth ever born," Lieutenant Crowder shouted. "Set some for two-fifty again, Sturtevant, and some for an even hundred. If we've hurt that boat bad enough, it'll have to surface. Hop to it, you men."

Hop to it they did. Depth charges rained into the Atlantic. With a kill so close, Crowder fired them off with reckless abandon. If the *Ericsson* didn't sink the submarine, she'd be all but defenseless against it. George caressed the curved metal of the one-pounder's trigger as if it were his wife's curved flesh. "Come on," he muttered. "Come on, you son of a whore."

And, like a broaching whale, up the submarine came. She rose bow-first, and was plainly in desperate straits. No sooner had the boat reached the surface than she heeled over onto her side and began to sink once more. Though it was more nearly horizontal than vertical, an officer came out of the conning-tower hatch and threw something into the water: the boat's papers in a weighted sack, George supposed.

He fired a ten-round clip of one-pounder shells at the enemy officer. One struck home; the officer's head exploded into red fog. The fellow—he was a Rebel, for he wore dark gray trousers, not Royal Navy blue—tumbled into the sea. A moment later, the submersible sank, this time for good.

Carl Sturtevant pounded George on the back. "Good shooting, snapping turtle," he bawled in Enos' ear. "You see the name on the boat there?"

"*Bon*-something," George said. "She rolled over too damn fast to get more than just a glimpse."

"*Bonefish*, had to be," Sturtevant said. "There's swarms of 'em in C.S. waters; no wonder they'd name a boat after 'em."

"We sent it to the boneyard, by God," Enos answered. Solemnly, the two men shook hands.

Cincinnatus wished he were driving his truck. Inside the cab of the rumbling, snorting White machine, nobody was watching him. Here in Covington, he wished he had eyes in the back of his head, and one on each side, too. Did that fellow with the gray mustache waiting for the trolley belong to Luther Bliss' Kentucky State Police? Was that redhead in overalls a member of the Confederate underground that kept on doing its best to disrupt Kentucky's return to the USA? When he got back into the colored part of town, he wondered whether the woman hawking apples reported to Apicius or some other Red cell leader. All those groups were intently interested in keeping an eye on him.

And things weren't simple, either. The colored woman selling apples might have reported to Luther Bliss, or even to the Confederate diehards. Cincinnatus had worked with them; other Negroes could, too. For that matter, white Reds could work with black Reds. Maybe none of those people, nor any others he passed on the street, was interested in him at all. He hoped none of those people was interested in him at all. He had trouble believing it, though.

Time was when he'd let out a sigh of relief coming up the walk to his house. When he was home with Elizabeth and little Achilles, nothing could bother him. That was what he'd thought then.

Now . . . As he went up the wooden steps onto his front porch, his eyes automatically dropped to look at the boards right in front of the door. There was nothing to see. He and Elizabeth had both worked hard to get rid of every trace of Tom Kennedy's blood. No, there was nothing to see. But he knew the blood was there.

What he didn't know was who had blown off a big chunk of Kennedy's head. He had next to no chance of finding out, either, because everyone thought he was in someone else's pocket and so didn't want to give him the time of day. But if he didn't find out who'd murdered the Confederate diehard and why, whoever it was might decide he needed killing, too. Since he didn't know whom in particular to worry about, he had to worry about everybody, which got wearing.

Elizabeth had got home ahead of him. She must have seen him coming, for she opened the door as he was reaching for the knob. Out toddled Achilles, a big smile on his face. "Dada!" he said, grabbing Cincinnatus around the leg. "Dada!"

"Sounds more like a real word now," Cincinnatus said, leaning forward over his son to kiss his wife. "Not jus' babble, babble, babble, way it used to be."

Then Achilles tugged on his trouser leg and spoke imperiously: "Up!"

Laughing, Cincinnatus lifted him. He was a lot lighter than crated rifles and munitions, and there was only the one of him, not unending loads in the back of the truck. When Cincinnatus remarked on that, Elizabeth snorted. "May only be the one," she said, "but it sure enough seems like there's about a hundred an' ten of him sometimes."

Cincinnatus carried the toddler into the house. He paused in the front hall and sniffed appreciatively. "What smells so good?"

"That beef tongue I bought at the butcher's the other day," his wife answered. "Your mother threw it in the pot with taters an' onions while she was watching Achilles. And I've got some string beans and salt pork cookin' up in there, too."

"I *knew* I married you for some reason," Cincinnatus said. Elizabeth stuck out her tongue at him. When she turned to go into the kitchen, he swatted her lightly on the backside. They both laughed.

Supper proved to be as good as it smelled, which wasn't easy. Afterwards, happily replete, Cincinnatus played with Achilles while Elizabeth cleaned up in the kitchen. Achilles liked chasing a little rubber football. Whenever he tried to kick it, he fell on his bottom. He thought that was part of the fun.

After a while, he tried something different. Cincinnatus had been tossing the ball for him to chase. He went and got it and did his best to throw it back. It went up in the air and bounced off his head. As far as he was concerned, that was pretty damn funny, too.

While he got the ball and tried again to throw it to Cincinnatus, his father laughed and said, "I wonder if that's how the Yankees got the notion of throwin' the ball forwards when they play football." In the Confederate States, passes toward the other side's goal line were against the rules. Football in the United States, though, permitted forward passes that were hurled from at least five yards behind the line of scrimmage.

When Elizabeth finished the dishes, Cincinnatus lighted a cigar (a lousy cigar—tobacco had gone downhill since Kentucky's forcible separation from the CSA) and read the evening newspaper Elizabeth had—with the white lady's permission—brought home from one of the houses she cleaned. As usual, the paper claimed extravagant U.S., German, and even Austrian victories. Had a quarter of what the papers claimed been true, the forces of the Quadruple Alliance would have conquered the world ten times over.

Someone knocked on the door. Cincinnatus and Elizabeth both looked up in alarm. Not so long before, Tom Kennedy had knocked on the door like that—and died on the doorstep a moment later. Was it a neighbor wanting to borrow some molasses, or was it a ruse to get Cincinnatus to open the door and expose himself to someone crouched in the dark with a rifle?

Only one way to find out. "Who is it?" Cincinnatus asked warily. Before the war, he would have opened the door without asking. Before the war, the door might well have been open anyhow on a warm spring night, or Elizabeth and he might have been sitting out on the front porch.

A deep voice answered: "It sure as hell ain't the Easter bunny, and it ain't Father Christmas, neither."

Cincinnatus opened the door. There stood Apicius, who was almost certainly the best barbecue cook in the USA. He might have been the best barbecue cook in the CSA, too, but the competition was stiffer there. As fit his trade, the big black man was big in all dimensions. Solid muscle lay under his fat. "You better come in," Cincinnatus said. "I don't reckon this is no social call."

"And it ain't," Apicius said, squeezing past him. "I ain't here on my business. I'm here on the business of the workers and peasants of the state of Kentucky." His chuckle was wheezy. "And why ain't you surprised?"

"Can't imagine," Cincinnatus answered, letting the cook precede him down the hall and into the front room. Apicius and Elizabeth greeted each other. Then she took Achilles back to the bedroom. As far as Cincinnatus was concerned, the less she involved herself in affairs of politics and the various undergrounds with which he was entangled, the better.

"You got the fine start to a family here," Apicius said, and nodded at his own words. "Need yourself some more young uns, but that'll come, that'll come."

"You didn't come over here to jaw about my family," Cincinnatus said. "Nothin's gonna pry you away from the barbecue pit if it ain't important."

"That's a fact," Apicius said. "You never was a fool, Cincinnatus."

"Yeah, go on and baste me with that big old long-handled brush o' yours," Cincinnatus said. "Then you put me over the fire an' turn me on the spit."

Apicius laughed, but he quickly sobered. "All right. I won't waste your time. I won't waste my time. What I got to know is this: whose man is you? I can talk with you if you is my man. I can talk with you if you is Tom Kennedy's man. I—"

"You know what happened to him," Cincinnatus broke in, his voice harsh.

"I know what. I dunno who done it, and I wish I did. But he still have folks left on his side." Apicius waved a big, thick-fingered hand, as if to make Cincinnatus' interruption disappear. "I can even talk with you if you is Luther Bliss' man."

Cincinnatus interrupted again: "I ain't, but you'd be a fool to talk with me if I was. You don' know how dangerous that Bliss is."

"Hell I don't," Apicius said. "Ain't no law says the forces of reaction can't have people on their side who know what they's doin'. But I can talk with you if you is Bliss' man. Have to watch what I say, but I can talk. But if I don't know *whose* man you is, Cincinnatus, how can I talk with you? I say somethin', how do I know who hears it?"

Apicius' point made perfectly good sense. Of all the factions still struggling in Kentucky, Cincinnatus had more sympathy for the Reds than for any other—the Reds were, after all, his own people. But a man who'd been struggling to reach what passed for the upper stratum of black society before the war didn't completely sympathize with the Reds' leveling aspirations, either.

The other side of the coin was that, if Apicius didn't like the answer Cincinnatus gave him, no insurance company in the world would put a nickel on his life. With a sigh, Cincinnatus said, "I never wanted to be nothin' but my own man. If that ain't good enough for you, don't talk with me at all—'cept to say thanks when I buy me some ribs."

Apicius sighed, too. "You know too goddamn much to be your own man and nobody else's. You is mixed up in this. Can't get yourself unmixed, any more'n you can take the sugar out of the coffee once it's in."

That was probably true, too. Cincinnatus was about to say so when another knock came from the front of the house. Apicius' had been ordinary. This one was brisk, authoritative. Whoever was out there expected to be let in right away, with no backtalk from anybody.

"Who?" Apicius whispered.

"Don't know," Cincinnatus whispered back. Apicius' hand went to a trouser pocket: a pistol in there, no doubt. Cincinnatus wished he had one, too. For the second time that evening, he went to the door and called, "Who is it?"

"Queen of the May," the man outside answered.

Everyone was giving smart answers tonight. Cincinnatus opened the door for Luther Bliss, wondering if he'd get caught in the cross fire between the chief of the Kentucky State Police and Apicius. A glance over his shoulder told him the Red leader had that pistol out and ready. But then, to his amazement, Apicius lowered it. "Evenin', Luther," he said.

"Evenin', Apicius, you damn Red," Bliss answered amiably. Cincinnatus stared from one of them to the other. They both laughed at him. Pointing to Apicius, Luther Bliss said, "I know who this son of a bitch is. I know what he stands for. Because I know that, he doesn't worry me too much. I can handle him— reckon he thinks the same about me. You, though, Cincinnatus— who the hell are you? Who are you really working for?"

Apicius laughed again, louder this time. He pointed to Cincinnatus. "I come over here to find out the same damn thing,

Luther—and I don't care if you's here or not. He still could be one o' yours."

"Only man I work for is Lieutenant Straubing, who bosses my truck unit," Cincinnatus said. "I ain't nobody's man but my own." He looked from Apicius to Luther Bliss and back again. One thing was obvious: neither of them believed him.

In the mid-Atlantic, Sylvia Enos read in the *Boston Globe* as she rode the trolley to work, *the USS* Ericsson *engaged and sank the* CSS Bonefish, *a submersible that had for some time tormented shipping in the region. The* Bonefish *had previously torpedoed the* SS Teton, *a civilian steamship in U.S. service. Our bold Navy has valiantly swept away yet another vicious scourge of the sea.*

That was George's ship. If they'd fought a Confederate submarine, he'd surely been in danger. She folded the paper and leaned back in the uncomfortable seat. He was all right now. And with this *Bonefish* sunk, he'd keep on being all right a while longer. Now that she hadn't seen him for a few months, her anger was cooling. He might have wanted to be unfaithful, but he hadn't actually gone and done it.

And he was all right. *Thank you, God,* Sylvia thought. Next to that simple fact, the war news on the front page, the mutinies in the French Army and all the rest of it, faded to insignificance. The *Ericsson* had fought again, and nothing had happened to George. The world looked good.

When the trolley came to her stop, Sylvia left the *Globe* on the seat for whoever might want it. She hoped the next person who picked it up would find as much good news as she had, and not a name he recognized in the black-bordered casualty lists.

She had a spring in her step as she went into the canning plant. It was usually missing in the morning—especially these days, when she had to get George, Jr., off to kindergarten and Mary Jane to Mrs. Dooley's before she could come to work.

She was humming a song about coal conservation when she punched in. The words were as stupid as those of most wartime patriotic songs, but she couldn't get the tune out of her mind. *Save your coal for me—Always!/ Says the sailor on the sea— Always!* She shook her head in annoyance—not just a stupid song but irritating, too, because it would not leave her alone.

Mr. Winter, the foreman, followed the war news closely, as

befit a veteran wounded in the service of his country. "That's your husband's destroyer that sank that Rebel submersible, isn't it, Mrs. Enos?" he called as she walked to the machine that put labels on cans of mackerel.

"Yes, Mr. Winter, George is on the *Ericsson*, that's right," she answered.

"Thought so," the foreman said, puffing on his cigar. "Well, good for him, by God. I'm glad he came through that safe. Those submersibles are things we didn't have to worry about in my day. I'll tell you something else, too: I'm not sorry to have missed them." He patted his gimpy leg. "I just wish the Rebs had missed me."

"I'm sure of that, Mr. Winter," Sylvia said. When she got to her machine, she checked the paste reservoir, which was full, and the label hopper, which turned out to be almost empty. She quickly filled it. That would have been just what she needed: to get caught by surprise fifteen minutes into her shift, and have to hold up the line while she fed the hopper. Mr. Winter would have made some not so polite conversation with her about that.

Isabella Antonelli came hurrying up to the machine next door. "I saw in the paper—your husband's ship, it sank a submarine," she said. "This is good news. Better news would be for the *dannata* war to end, but this is good news for you."

Before Sylvia could do anything more than nod, the line, which had shut down for shift changeover, started again with the usual assortment of groans and creaks from the belts and gearing. Into the machine went the first brightly tinned can. Sylvia pulled a lever. Three lines of paste flowed onto the can. She took a step and pulled a second lever. On went the label, with the colorful picture of the improbably tunalike mackerel on it. Another step, a third level, and the can went on its way. She went back and did it again . . . and again . . . and again.

The day went smoothly. She didn't have to think about what she was doing. The labels didn't jam in the hopper once during the whole shift. That was the machine's Achilles' heel, the most common problem that could shut down the line and bring down the wrath of Mr. Winter.

Not today. Sylvia still felt almost alarmingly fresh as she clocked out and hurried to the trolley stop to catch the next car to George, Jr.'s, school. The streetcar was right on time. A man with a white Kaiser Bill mustache stood up so she could sit down.

Everything was going so well, she wondered what would happen to break the lucky streak. She found out when she got to the school. He wasn't in the kindergarten classroom. "You'll have to get him at the front office," his teacher, Miss Hammaker, told Sylvia.

"What did he do?" she gasped. "Is he all right?"

"You'll have to get him at the office," the dyspeptic-looking spinster repeated. Sylvia snarled at her and hurried away.

When she saw George, Jr., she knew right away what the trouble was. A clerk clacking away at a typewriter spelled it out in two well-chosen words: "Chicken pox." Then she went on, "I'm afraid you're going to have to keep him home until the scabs come off the pox."

"But that will be two weeks from now," Sylvia exclaimed in horror.

"I'm sorry, Mrs. Enos, but we can't very well let him go spreading a contagious disease, now can we?" the clerk said primly.

"But my job!" Sylvia said. "What am I supposed to do about my job?"

"I really don't know what to tell you about that, ma'am," the clerk answered. "We do have the other children to look out for, too, you know."

Sylvia put a hand on her son's shoulder. "Come on, George," she said wearily. "Let's go get your sister and take the two of you home and then try to figure out what to do next." She had no idea what to do next. Once she got home, she could start worrying about it. The clerk started typing again. Now that George, Jr., was leaving, she didn't have to worry about him any more. Sylvia did.

When she got to Mrs. Dooley's, the woman looked at her with the same disapproval Miss Hammaker had shown. "Mrs. Enos," she said pointedly, "your daughter will not be welcome here—"

"Until she gets over the chicken pox," Sylvia finished for her. Mrs. Dooley's eyebrows rose. Sylvia said, "Just a wild guess, of course." She kept her arm around George, Jr. The longer he had to stay on his feet, the more pale and sick he looked—and the redder his spots got by comparison.

"I can't have her here till she's better," Mrs. Dooley said. "The other women whose children I mind would have a fit if I let her stay, and I wouldn't blame them one bit." She turned. "Go on,

Mary Jane. Go home with your mother. When you're well, you can come back again."

"All right," Mary Jane said meekly. That she offered no mischief or snippy talk was a telling indication she didn't feel right. She too was starting to break out in the red spots that would soon turn into blisters.

Cautiously, Mrs. Dooley asked, "She *is* vaccinated, isn't she?"

"What?" Sylvia needed a moment to understand what the question meant. "Oh. Yes. She and her brother both. It's only chicken pox—it can't be smallpox."

"All right." The older woman nodded. "Most children *are* vaccinated these days, but you never know. Well, that's a relief. You take them home now, Mrs. Enos, and bring your daughter back when she's well."

Nodding, Sylvia turned away and led the children back to the trolley stop. They didn't frisk ahead of her, the way they usually did. She urged them to hurry, but they lacked the energy to do it. She counted herself lucky they didn't make her miss a streetcar.

They had no appetite at supper, which also didn't surprise her. After they were done picking at their food, she gave them aspirins and put them to bed early. "This itches, Mama," George, Jr., said. "It itches a lot."

"Try not to scratch," Sylvia answered. "If you do, it'll leave scars."

"It *itches*!" he said.

Remembering her own bout of chicken pox—she'd been nine or ten—she knew how fiercely they itched. "Do your best," she said. She had a pockmark on the side of her jaw, one between her breasts, several on her arms and legs, and one or two in other places she hadn't known about till her husband found them. That had amused George no end, though she'd been embarrassed.

By the time she finished the supper dishes, the children were asleep. She went down the hall and knocked on Brigid Coneval's door. When the Irishwoman opened it, she was in mourning black. "Mrs. Enos," she said, and stepped aside. "Do come in. What might I do for you today?"

Her apartment looked more battered than Sylvia's, and smelled of cooking grease and cabbage. Her children, three boys ranging from George, Jr.'s, size on down, ran around raising hell. Through their racket, Sylvia said, "I was wondering if I could pay you enough to watch my children, just long enough to let them get over the chicken pox."

Brigid Coneval shook her head. "That I cannot, and that I will not," she answered. "For one thing, I'm taking in other people's wee ones no more, as you know. And for another, Patrick has not had the chicken pox himself, nor has Michael, nor Billy, neither. I'll be just as well pleased without them having 'em, too, sure and I will."

"But what am I going to do?" Sylvia exclaimed. She'd been saying the same thing to anyone who would listen ever since she'd first seen George, Jr., covered with spots. "How am I going to go to work?"

"Well, if you do, you do—and if you don't, you don't," Mrs. Coneval said airily. "Tell 'em you'll not be in while the babes are after being sick, that's all. What else can you do?"

"They'll fire me." Sylvia stated the obvious.

"Will you starve while you miss a couple weeks' pay?" Brigid Coneval asked. Reluctantly, Sylvia shook her head. The new widow went on, "Then be damned to the job. You'll get another soon enough—plenty to be had, with so many men off getting killed. You'll have no trouble at all, at all."

"I've worked there a long time." Sylvia sighed. "But you're right. In the end, you're right. If they fire me for staying home, then they do, that's all. I don't want to leave that job, but I can if I have to. Thank you, Mrs. Coneval. You've made me see things clear."

"Any time at all, dearie," Brigid Coneval said.

Behind Private First Class Reginald Bartlett, artillery thundered: not a lot of artillery, not by the standards of the Roanoke front, but more than he'd heard on the Confederate side of the line here in Sequoyah. "Let the damnyankees keep their heads down for a change," he said.

Pete Hairston nodded. "Only trouble is, once the guns stop, we get to go forward and push 'em out," the veteran sergeant said. He paused and shrugged. "Us and the niggers do. God-damned if I like that."

Joe Mopope said, "You people are crazy, giving niggers guns. Wouldn't never catch us Kiowas giving niggers guns."

"If those colored regiments hadn't come over the river,

we never would have got enough men to attack the Yanks," Reggie said.

Hairston nodded again. "That's a fact. We'd be holding on tooth and toenail, same as we have been. Now we got a chance to take back some of this here state. We better see that we don't waste it, on account of I don't reckon we'll ever see another one."

Whistles blew, up and down the reinforced Confederate line. Lieutenant Nicoll shouted, "Come on, boys, now it's our turn!" Out of the trenches came his company. Howling the Rebel yell, they trotted forward. "Go!" Nicoll roared to them. "Go on! They aren't doing so well back East—we've got to show them how to play the game."

"We'll get 'em!" Napoleon Dibble said. "They can't mess with the Belgians, and they can't mess with us."

Reggie said nothing. He didn't waste his breath yelling. Every time he came up above ground, he felt like a turtle coming out of its shell. He was vulnerable up here. His time in the close-quarters fighting of the Roanoke front had taught him how hideously vulnerable a man was when he came up out of his trench.

He wasn't afraid, though, not in the ordinary sense of the word. Whatever was going to happen would happen. It was largely out of his hands. If he let it worry him, he'd be letting his pals down, and he couldn't stand that, not after they'd been through and suffered so much together.

On they came. Some dropped into cover to shoot while others advanced, then leapfrogged past when the other group hit the dirt. The bombardment hadn't taken out all the Yankees; bombardments never did. Rifles and machine guns stuttered to life. Men in butternut began falling not of their own volition.

Some of those men were black, the new units going forward along with the white troops who had been in the field for years. The Negro soldiers charged straight at the U.S. trenches; they weren't skilled in the fire-and-move tactics the veterans had learned by painful experience. And they went down in gruesome numbers. When they screamed, Bartlett couldn't tell their voices from those of white men.

He lay in a shell hole, fired a couple of rounds toward the Yankee line ahead, and then got to his feet and ran by the men he'd been supporting. He dove behind a stump and started shooting again. Once his buddies had dashed past him and found cover, he scrambled up and ran on.

He was about thirty yards from the Yankee trench when a traversing machine gun turned its balefully winking eye upon him.

His first feeling was nothing but surprise. One moment, he'd been sprinting forward, his eyes fixed on the Yankees in their ugly cooking-pot helmets who were shooting at him and his countrymen. The next, he slammed to the ground on his face.

Somebody punched me, he thought. *Somebody punched me twice. God damn that Joe Mopope anyhow—this is no time for practical jokes.*

Then he tried to move. What had been impact turned to pain, stunning pain, in his left shoulder and right leg. Someone very close by was screaming at the top of his lungs. Only when Reggie needed to inhale did he realize those cries belonged to him.

Machine-gun and rifle fire kept right on stitching past him. In what was more a roll and a wriggle than a crawl, he made it into a hole in the torn-up ground, pulled out his wound dressing, and wondered what the hell he should bandage first.

Blood was turning the outside of his right trouser leg blackish red. His left arm didn't want to do what he told it to do. Awkwardly, one-handedly, he got a sort of a bandage around his thigh and stuffed a pad of gauze into the hole in his shoulder. The world kept going gray as he worked, but he persevered.

"Stretcher-bearer!" he shouted. "Stretcher-bearer!" His voice was hoarse and raw-edged. No one came. The Yanks didn't usually shoot stretcher-bearers on purpose, any more than the CSA did, but bullets weren't fussy, either.

Reggie got out his canteen and drank it dry. The day was hot and muggy. Before very long, the anguish of thirst joined the agony from his wounds. The sun beat down on him out of a brassy sky. His bandages went from white to red and soggy.

Every so often, when the pain backed off a little, he wondered how the attack was going. He occasionally saw men in butternut going forward. Nobody flopped down in his shell hole. He didn't think that was fair.

More screams rose. This time, they didn't come from Reggie. After a while, those screams stopped. They never started up again. Bartlett got the idea that the fellow who'd been making them wasn't breathing any more.

Up ahead, the firing hesitated, then broke out anew, louder

and fiercer than ever. Shells from the damnyankees' field artillery whistled overhead. Some, no doubt aimed to impede the Confederates' advance, dropped down near Reggie. He halfway—more than halfway—hoped one would land square on him. He'd never know what hit him then. He knew exactly what had hit him now. He moaned through dry lips.

Slowly, ever so slowly, the scorching sun slid across the sky. As it sank toward the western horizon, men in butternut started coming back past the shell hole where Reggie Bartlett lay. He called out to them, but his voice was a dry husk of what it had been. No one heard him. No one saw him reach out imploringly with his good hand. His comrades retreated.

In their wake, the soldiers of the U.S. Army advanced. They fired and moved, as their Confederate counterparts had done during the morning. The sun was going more orange than gold when one of them jumped down into Reggie's hole.

The Yankee had fired twice before he realized the body in there with him was not dead. He had it in his power to change that on the instant. Reggie got a good, long, close look at him: he was in his late twenties or early thirties, dark, in need of a shave, and wearing what the Yanks called a Kaiser Bill mustache. It had a couple of white hairs in it. Reggie thought it looked stupid. Two stripes on the fellow's sleeve: a corporal.

He said, "I ought to blow your fuckin' head off, Reb." Reggie shrugged a one-shouldered shrug. The U.S. corporal suddenly looked thoughtful. "If I bring you in, though," he went on, thinking out loud, "your pals miss a chance to blow my fuckin' head off, and that don't make me even a little bit sorry, I got news for you."

Reggie forced a word out through parched throat: "Water?"

"Yeah," the corporal said, and held a canteen to his lips. The water was warm and stale and tasted ambrosial. Then the Yankee heaved him up onto his back with a bull's strength, ignoring his cries of pain. The U.S. soldier started toward his own line, shouting, "Stretcher-bearers! Got a wounded Reb prisoner here!"

A couple of U.S. soldiers with red crosses on their helmets and on armbands took charge of Bartlett. "How you feelin', Reb?" one of them asked, not unkindly.

"Shitty," he answered.

"Stick him, Louie," the other stretcher-bearer said. "We don't want him yellin' at us all the way to the field hospital."

"Sure as hell don't," Louie agreed, and stuck a needle in Reggie's arm. Reggie sighed as relief washed over him. The pain remained, but now he floated over it instead of being immersed. The relief must have shown on his face, for Louie chuckled. "That morphine's great stuff, isn't it?"

"Yeah," Reggie breathed.

The stretcher-bearers hauled him through zigzagging communications trenches similar to the ones behind his own front line. Then they put his stretcher in the back of an ambulance. "Daniel brought in this here Reb," the one who wasn't Louie told the driver. "Thought he'd be worth patching. Might even be right—he ain't pegged out on us while we were lugging him back here."

"Hate to waste the sawbones' time on a Rebel," the ambulance driver said, "but what the hell?" The ambulance's motor was already turning over. He put the machine in gear and headed back toward the field hospital, whose tents were out of range of artillery from the front.

When Bartlett got there, another pair of stretcher-bearers took him out of the ambulance and laid him on the ground outside a green-gray tent with an enormous red cross on it. Most of the men there were U.S. soldiers, but a few others wore butternut. Attendants gave him water and another shot.

Presently, a doctor in a blood-spattered white coat came by and looked him over. "That leg's not too bad," he said after cutting away bandages and trouser leg. He examined the shoulder. "We're going to have to take you into the shop to repair this one, though. What's your name, Reb?" He poised a pencil over a clipboard.

"Reggie Bartlett. I broke out of one Yankee prisoner-of-war camp. Reckon I can do it again." With two shots of morphine in him, Reggie didn't care what he said.

He didn't impress the Yankee doctor, either. After recording his name, the fellow said, "Son, you're going to be a good long while healing up. I don't care whether you escaped before. By the time you think about flying the coop again, this war'll be over. And we'll have won it."

Bartlett laughed in his face—the morphine again.

Captain Jonathan Moss looked down on the tortured Canadian landscape from on high, as if he were a god. He knew better, of course. If one of the shells the Americans aimed at the Canadian and British troops who had blocked their way for so long happened to strike his Wright two-decker, he would crash. The same, assuredly, was true of the shells the enemy hurled back at the U.S. forces, and of the Archie their antiaircraft guns sent up.

Spring was at last in full spate. The land was green, where shellfire hadn't turned it to mucky brown pulp. All the streams flowed freely; the ice had melted. And the line was beginning to move, too, though it had been frozen longer than any Canadian river.

Below Moss, U.S. troopers advanced behind a large contingent of barrels that battered their way through the defenses the Canucks and limeys had built with such enormous expenditure of labor. The Canadians had barrels, too, though not so many. They dueled with the American machines in a slow, ugly, two-dimensional version of the war Moss and his friends—and his foes as well—fought in the air.

He spied a flight of enemy fighting scouts down near the deck. They were shooting up the advancing Americans, who grew vulnerable when they came up out of their trenches to attack. But the Entente aeroplanes were vulnerable, too. Moss pointed them out to his own flightmates, then took his American copy of a German Albatros into a dive better suited to a stooping falcon. Percy Stone, Hans Oppenheim, and Pete Bradley followed.

Wind screamed in Moss' face. It tried to tear the goggles off his eyes, and peeled lips back from teeth in an involuntary grin. The grin would have been on his face anyhow, though. His gaze flicked back and forth from the unwinding altimeter to the enemy aeroplanes. The British or Canadian pilots were having such a high old time shooting up American infantry, they made the mistake of not checking the neighborhood often enough. Moss intended to turn it into a fatal mistake if he could.

His thumb came down on the firing button. The twin machine guns roared, spitting bullets between the two wooden blades of the prop. If the interrupter gears didn't function properly, as, every so often, they didn't . . . but contemplating that kind of misfortune gave no better profit than thinking about one's own path intersecting that of a shell.

Tracers let him direct his fire onto the rearmost enemy fighting scout. He must have hit the pilot, for the Sopwith Pup slammed into the ground an instant later and burst into flame.

"That'll teach you, you son of a bitch!" he shouted exultantly. Pups had been machines of terror when set against the Martin one-deckers U.S. pilots had been flying for so long. *So long* was right—that was what you said when you went up against a Pup in a one-decker. But the new Wright machines had helped even the odds.

Another Pup started to burn. The pilot turned for home, but never got there. He didn't have much altitude, and rapidly lost what he had. He tried to land the aeroplane, but rolled into a shell hole and nosed over. Fire raced down the length of the fighting scout. For the pilot's sake, Moss hoped the crash had killed him.

The other two Sopwith Pups twisted away from Moss' flight. On the level, they were slightly faster than the not-quite-Albatroses the Americans flew, and succeeded in making good their escape.

Moss led his comrades up out of that part of the sky where a lucky rifle or machine-gun bullet could put paid to a fighting scout. Climbing was slower work than diving had been. Before he got out of range of small-arms fire from the ground, a couple of bullets went through his wings with about the sound a man would have made by poking a stick through a tightly stretched drumhead.

Hans Oppenheim was the pilot pumping his fist up over his head, so Moss assumed he'd brought down that second Pup. Moss couldn't imagine anything else that would have got the phlegmatic Oppenheim excited enough to show such emotion.

He looked at his watch. They'd been in the air well over an hour.

He looked at his fuel gauge. It was getting low. He oriented himself, more from the way the trenches ran than by his unreliable compass, and found northwest. "Time to get back to Arthur," he said, and let the slipstream blow the words back to his comrades.

They couldn't hear him, of course. With their engines roaring, they couldn't hear a damn thing, any more than he could. But they saw his gestures and, in any case, they knew what he was doing and why. They couldn't have had any more gasoline in their tanks than he did in his.

The aerodrome was surprisingly busy when he and the rest of his flight bumped over the rutted fields. It was the kind of activity he hadn't seen for a long time. Everybody was tearing things up by the roots and pitching them into trucks and wagons.

"We're moving up?" Moss asked a groundcrew man after he shut off the Wright's engine and his words were no longer his private property.

"Hell, yes," the mechanic answered as Moss descended from the cockpit and, awkward in his thick flying suit, came down to the ground. "Front is moving forward, so we will, too. Don't want you burning up too much gas getting where you're going."

"That sounds plenty good to me," Moss said.

"Me, too." The groundcrew man pointed to the bullet holes in the fabric covering the fighting scout's wings. "Looks like the natives were restless."

"Ground fire," Moss replied with a shrug. "But I knocked down a Pup that was strafing our boys, and Hans got another one, and we came back without a scratch."

"Bully, sir!" the groundcrew man said. "What's that bring your score to?"

"Six and a quarter," Moss answered.

"I knew you were an ace," the fellow said, nodding.

Moss laughed—at himself. "And I'll tell you something else, too: I was keeping track so well that they were able to give me a surprise party after my fifth victory, because I didn't remember which one it was. Hans gets everybody drunk tonight, though—this was his first."

His flightmates were down from their aeroplanes, too. He went over and thwacked Hans Oppenheim on the back. He hit Oppenheim a solid lick, too, but all the leather and wool his fellow flier had on armored him as effectively as anything this side of chainmail.

"Major Cherney will not be unhappy with us today," Oppenheim said. He had all his self-possession back, and seemed faintly
embarrassed to be the object of Moss' boisterous congratulations.

Percy Stone shook his head. "Cherney won't even notice
we're here, except that we give him some more things he has to
think about. He's got moving the aerodrome on his mind."

"He doesn't have to worry about moving our aeroplanes—
we'll fly 'em," Pete Bradley said. "I just wonder where the hell
we're supposed to fly 'em to."

"Don't let 'em promote you past captain," Stone advised
Jonathan Moss. "Once you get oak leaves on your shoulders,
you have to worry about too many other things to do as much
flying as you want."

"That's so," Moss said. He started to add that he would be as
happy not to have unfriendly strangers shooting at him up in the
sky. Before the words came out of his mouth, he realized they
weren't true. He never felt more alive than he did two or three
miles above the ground, throwing his aeroplane through turns it
wasn't meant to make so he could get on an enemy's tail or shake
a Canuck off his own. It was pure, it was clean, and it made
everything else in the world—fast motorcars, fast women—
seem about as exciting as solitaire.

Women . . . maybe not. After the flight had reported to Major
Cherney, the squadron commander said, "Get yourselves packed
up, boys. You're scheduled to move out bright and early tomorrow morning. New aerodrome's over by Orangeville, twenty
miles up the road. We have made some progress. And well done
to you all. Hansie, first drink's on me tonight, for losing your
cherry."

"Thank you, sir," Oppenheim said. Moss never would have
had the nerve to call him *Hansie*, not in a million years.

Back at the tent the flight shared, Moss looked over his
meager belongings and said, "I can throw this stuff in a trunk
and a duffel bag in half an hour flat. I think I'm going to take a
walk before I pack."

"I know where you're walking," Percy Stone said. Amusement glinted in his eyes. "I've walked that way a time or three.
You're wasting your time. She still hates Americans."

"All right, maybe I am wasting my time," Moss said. "At least
I'll be wasting it in better-looking company than any of you
lugs." He left the tent to the jeers of his flightmates.

When he got to Laura Secord's farm, she was on her hands and knees in the vegetable garden, weeding. When she saw him, she gave him the same greeting she usually did: "Why don't you go away, Yank?"

"That's what I came to tell you," he answered. "I am going away. The whole base is going away. I came to say I'd miss you."

She glared at him, which only made him find her more attractive. "Well, I won't miss you or any other Yank," she answered, gray-blue eyes flashing. Then she softened a little. "Where is the base going?"

"I won't tell you," he answered. "If I did, you'd probably try to imitate your famous ancestor and let the British know where we are. I don't want to wake up one night with bombs falling all over the place."

Laura Secord bit her lip. She must have been thinking about doing just what he'd said. Indeed, she admitted it, saying, "You weren't supposed to see through me. Go on, then. Go wherever you're going. I only wish you—all you Yanks—were going out of my country and never coming back."

"That isn't going to happen," he said. "In fact, I will tell you we're going forward, because you could find that out for yourself."

She looked down at the ground. When she raised her face again, it was wet with tears. "Damn you," she whispered. "Damn all of you, however too many there are."

Moss found himself with little to say after that. It was his usual condition in conversations with Laura Secord. But, for once, he did come up with something: "When the war is finally over, I hope your husband comes back here safe." Most of him even meant it.

"Thank you, Captain Moss," she said. "You make it hard for me to hate you in particular along with the United States."

"That's the nicest thing you've ever said to me," he replied with a smile.

"It's the nicest thing I'm likely to say to you, too," she told him. "Now go your way, wherever it is that you dare not let me know." With unmistakable emphasis, she returned to her weeding.

And Jonathan Moss walked back to the aerodrome and landing strips that would soon be abandoned. He'd never seen any of Laura Secord but her face, her hands, and her ankles. He'd never touched her. He'd rarely had anything but insults from her. He was whistling as he walked. He wondered why he felt so good.

The *Dakota*'s seaplane splashed down into the South Atlantic close by the battleship. Sailors on deck, Sam Carsten among them, waved to the pilot. He waved back, delighted as always to come down in one piece.

Carsten turned to Luke Hoskins and said, "I hope to Jesus he's found something worth our while to fight. Otherwise, we're going to have to turn around and head back to Chile."

"Goddamn ocean is a big place," Hoskins said, "and the limeys' convoys are hugging the shore now that they know we're in the neighborhood."

"We've got to hit 'em in Argentine waters, too," Carsten agreed unhappily. "If we sink half a dozen freighters inside Brazilian territory, it's even money whether we scare Dom Pedro IV into coming in on our side or make him so mad, he'll declare for the Entente."

"I don't want to get all that close inshore," Hoskins said. "The limeys have been selling those damn little torpedo boats to Argentina the last twenty years, and everybody and his brother's been selling 'em to the Empire of Brazil. Run up against one of those babies when you're looking in the wrong direction and it's liable to ruin your whole day."

That was more talk from the shell-heaver than Sam had heard for the past week. "Those torpedo boats are one of the reasons we've got the destroyers playing tag with us," he said.

"Come on, Sam, I know that—I didn't ride into town on a load of turnips," Luke Hoskins answered. "Here, let me ask it like this: are you happier knowing your neck is on the line if somebody on one of those goddamn pipsqueak four-stackers didn't polish his telescope when he should have? Damned if I am, I'll tell you that much."

"Well, hell," Sam said, "when you put it like that, I'm not, either." He stared over toward the nearest destroyer, as if to make certain nobody on deck was asleep at the switch.

Out swung the crane. It plucked the aeroplane out of the water and hoisted it, pilot and all, onto the deck of the *Dakota*. As usual, Sam tried to get close enough to the machine to hear what the pilot was telling the officers who crowded round him. As usual, he failed.

Frustrated, he turned away—and almost ran into Vic Crosetti. "Stickin' your nose in where it don't belong, ain't you, Sam?" Crosetti said.

"Yeah, same as you are," Carsten returned.

Crosetti laughed, altogether unembarrassed. "Hey, everybody can tell I got a big nose, right?" He put a hand on the organ in question, which was indeed of formidable proportions. "You know what they say—big in the nose means big somewhere else, too."

"In the ears, looking at you," Sam said.

"You better watch yourself, Carsten," Crosetti said, clenching a fist in mock anger. "Pretty soon we're going to sail far enough north for the sun to remember its first name, and then they'll stick an apple in your mouth, on account of the rest of you's gonna look like a roast pig that needs a little more time in the oven."

"I'd laugh like a damn loon if only that was a joke," Carsten said, warily eyeing the sky. Here below the equator, fall was heading toward winter. He favored winter, and clouds, and storms.

Before long, the *Dakota* leaned into a long turn that swung her course to the west. The rest of the joint American-Chilean fleet moved with her. Vic Crosetti clicked his tongue between his teeth. "Pilot must have spotted a convoy sneaking along the coast," he said happily. "I guess we'll go leave 'em a calling card."

"I'd say you're likely right," Sam agreed. "Using a battleship to sink freighters is like smashing a fly with an anvil, if anybody wants to know what I think, but nobody seems to."

"I sure as hell don't," Crosetti said, grinning as he planted the barb.

When the hooting horns summoned the crew of the *Dakota* to battle stations, Hiram Kidde was grinning from ear to ear as he greeted the sailors who manned the five-inch gun. "Just like shooting fish in a barrel, boys," the gunner's mate said. "Fish in a barrel, sure as hell."

"Fish in a barrel don't shoot back," Carsten said. "Fish in a barrel don't man torpedo boats."

"That's right," Luke Hoskins agreed. "That's just right. Sam and I were talking about that topside."

"It's a risk," "Cap'n" Kidde allowed. "But it ain't a hell of a big risk, I'll tell you that. I'd sooner take my chances against those damn mosquitoes than against a real live battleship any day of the week, and twice on Sunday."

Nobody quarreled with that. Carsten stepped away from the breech of the five-inch gun and peered out of the sponson through the vision slit. He needed a moment to realize the horizon wasn't smooth and unbroken, as it was farther out to sea. It had lumps and bumps on it. "We're within sight of land," he said in surprise.

"Won't be much longer before things start happening, then," Kidde predicted. "If you can see it from here, they've seen it from the observation mast for a while now. I wonder if the skipper aims to get in close enough to use the secondaries to sink the freighters, and save the wear and tear on the big guns."

"That'd be good," Sam said. "You get close enough to use the secondaries against a battleship and you're in more trouble than you really want. We found out everything we wanted to know about that and then some in the Battle of the Three Navies—oh, Lord, didn't we just?"

Heads bobbed up and down as all the men in the gun crew remembered the *Dakota*'s wild and undesired ride toward first the British and then the Japanese fleet. Hoskins said, "What I want to do is, I want to hit a torpedo boat with a five-inch shell. God damn me if there'd be anything left of the bastard but matchsticks and kindling." The gun crew nodded again. Carsten liked the picture that made in his mind.

As he usually did, Hiram Kidde thought along with the officers in charge of the *Dakota*. Commander Grady, who was responsible for the starboard secondary armament, stepped into the crowded sponson and said, "Boys, they're going to give us the fun this time. Pick your target, blow it to hell and gone, and then hit the next one. Every time you send a few thousand tons of meat and wheat to the bottom, you push the limeys that much closer to starving."

"Yes, sir!" Kidde said. "It'll be a pleasure, sir."

"Good." Grady hurried away to pass the word to the rest of the five-inch gun crews on his side of the battleship.

Kidde peered down into the rangefinder. "Inside nine thousand yards," he murmured, and worked the elevation screw. To the crew, he added, "Let's get a shell in the gun."

Hoskins jerked one out of the magazine and passed it to Sam

Carsten, handling the sixty-pound weight as if it were nothing. Sam slammed it into the breech and slid the block closed.

"Fire!" Kidde shouted.

Carsten jerked the lanyard. The gun roared and bucked. Stinking cordite fumes filled the sponson. The other guns of the secondary armament were roaring, too. Sam worked the breech mechanism. The empty brass shell casing clattered down onto the steel deck. Luke Hoskins handed him another shell. He slammed it home.

"That one was long," Hiram Kidde reported, fiddling with the elevation screw again. When he was satisfied, he let out a grunt and shouted "Fire!" again. He grunted once more when the shell hit. "Short this time. All right—we've got the bastard straddled. Give me another one."

"This one should be right on the money," Sam said as he fired the cannon.

"Hit!" Kidde screamed. "That was a hit. Bastard's burning! Pour a couple more into him, Carsten."

"Right, 'Cap'n,' " Sam said. "Feels good to do the shooting instead of getting shot at."

When the first target had taken what Kidde reckoned to be fatal damage, he turned the gun toward another hapless freighter. But before he had the gun laid, he grunted yet again, this time in surprise. "Somebody's shooting back at us," he said. "I didn't spot any flash or smoke, but a good-sized shell just splashed down forward of the bow."

"Railroad gun somewhere inland?" Carsten asked.

"That'd be sneaky, wouldn't it?" the gunner's mate answered. "You got a nasty head on your shoulders, you know?" He peered through the vision slit. "Still don't see anything, though."

Guns topside started firing: not the titanic main armament, which Sam would have thought the proper response to a big gun mounted on a flatcar, but the one-pounders that had been bolted into place here and there on deck not long before the war began. Luke Hoskins, who had less imagination than any man Carsten knew, was the one who solved the riddle: "That wasn't a shell, 'Cap'n'—bet you anything it was a bomb off an aeroplane."

Everybody in the gun crew stared at him. "Dip me in shit if I don't think you're right," Kidde said. "Jesus! What do we do about that? Only way you knock down an aeroplane is by dumb fucking luck." He shrugged. "They don't pay me to worry about it. They pay me to fight this gun, and that's what I'm going to do." He finished turning it to its new target. "Fire!"

Sam jerked the lanyard. The gun bellowed. A moment later came the bellow of another explosion, this one on deck. It was a big explosion, a frighteningly big explosion. Bombs didn't have to survive being shot out of guns the way shells did, Carsten realized. Not needing thick walls, they could carry a hell of a lot of explosive for their size.

Another blast shook the deck under Sam's feet. He kept on loading and firing to Hiram Kidde's commands. As Kidde had said, what else could he do? But then the *Dakota* turned away from the freighters he'd been shelling, away from the Argentine coast, and ran for the open sea. More bombs fell on and around her.

Hiram Kidde stared out the vision slit and then back at his gun crew. His face wore nothing but astonishment. "Aeroplanes!" he said, his voice cracking like a boy's. "Aeroplanes! And they might have sunk us. What the hell is the world coming to?"

Newspapers in Cuba were printed roughly half and half, English and Spanish. Sipping his morning coffee, puffing on a fine Habana, Roger Kimball suddenly burst out laughing. "What's funny, sir?" Tom Brearley asked.

Kimball pointed. "Look here. The damnyankees say they sank us."

His exec scanned the item. He didn't laugh. He got angry. "Those dirty, lying sons of bitches," he burst out. "You can never trust what a Yankee says—never. My granddad taught me that, and they've proved he was right time after time after time. Hell, they make Jews look honest."

"Don't blow a gasket, Tom," Kimball said. "When we came back here for refit, who took our place in the map box?"

"Hampton Ready's boat," Brearley answered at once. "He was in the class ahead of mine at Mobile."

"Ready's boat, yeah," Kimball said: "the *Bonito*."

Brearley needed a minute to take it in. When he did, he went from angry to grim in the blink of an eye. "You're right," he said. "Sure as hell, you're right. And that means they really did sink him, too. Damn. He was a good sailor, and a good fellow, too."

"Must have made it to the surface just long enough for the

Yanks to get a fast look at the name, and then straight down before they could read it all. Christ." Kimball shivered. That was a nasty way to go. There weren't any nice ways to go, not when you jammed yourself down into a tin can and went after real ships. "You all right, Tom? You look green around the gills."

Brearley didn't answer, not directly. "Hamp's wife just had a baby girl maybe six months ago. You know Katie? Little redhead; nice gal."

"I've met her," Kimball said. "Married man shouldn't skipper a submersible. Makes you think too much." But that didn't solve Brearley's problem—or Katie Ready's now. Kimball couldn't do anything about hers. About Brearley's, and, he admitted to himself, his own . . . He waved. A swarthy waiter hurried over. "Two *mojitos, pronto*."

"*Dos mojitos. Sí.* Yes, sir," the officers' club waiter said. He hurried away, not seeing anything in the least unusual about a Navy officer ordering drinks with breakfast. Prohibition might have made strides on the Confederate mainland. It was only a word in Cuba, and a seldom-used word at that.

Rum and mint over crushed ice went enormously well with strong coffee and fine cigars. Tom Brearley drank half of his, looked thoughtful, and slowly nodded. "That was the medicine I needed, all right."

"Steady you down," Kimball agreed. He took a pull from his own *mojito*. "I grew up drinking whiskey, same as everybody else in Arkansas, but I'll tell you, I could get used to rum."

Brearley nodded. "I'm the same way. It's got the kick, no two ways about it." He picked up the newspaper, then threw it down on the table, shaking his head. "Hamp Ready. That does hurt. Damn fine fellow." He poured down the rest of the drink.

Kimball picked up the paper and read further. "Says the boat was sunk by the USS *Ericsson*." He stiffened. "That's the destroyer that's been playing cat and mouse with us, all right. Ready wasn't ready enough, and they got him."

"That box on the map doesn't have a boat in it now," Brearley said. "We were going to go back and take over for the *Bonito* when she finished her tour. What do you want to bet they send us back fast as they can now?"

"You're right, goddammit." Kimball got up, slapped coins on the table, and left. Over his shoulder, he said, "If I don't have much time to enjoy myself, I'm going to make the most of what I've got."

Instead of heading for one of the many sporting houses that catered to Confederate Navy men, he walked down San Isidro Street, away from the harbor, till he came to a telegraph office. He sent a wire to his mother and the man she'd married after his father died. He hoped they'd get it; last he'd heard, the damn-yankees had been close to overrunning the farm on which he'd grown up.

He sent another wire to Anne Colleton. Both read the same: I'M NOT AS EASY TO KILL AS THE YANKEES THINK. HOPE TO SEE YOU SOON. LOVE, ROGER. To his mother, *hope to see you soon* was a polite sentiment, nothing more. With Anne Colleton . . . He hoped to see her the very soonest he could, and with the most privacy he could arrange.

Telegrams sent, he hurried back toward the *Bonefish*. A fat commander with the three oak leaves of Supply above the stripes on his sleeve stood on the wharf alongside Kimball's submersible. Longshoremen, some black, some swarthy like the waiter, streamed into and out of the boat. The officer from Supply checked off items on a clipboard.

"Good to see you here, Skipper," he said, nodding to Kimball. "We're stepping things up—as best we can, anyhow. You'll be going back to sea sooner than you might have hoped when you came into port."

"Reckoned as much." Kimball nodded back. "You all will have known about the *Bonito* a while before I worked it out." He donned an exasperated expression, half genuine, half assumed for effect. "You might have been good enough to let me know my boat would be turning around in a hurry."

"Oh, we would have gotten around to it, Commander, never fear," the officer from Supply answered breezily. He did indeed have an impressive belly. He was smoking a cigar that made the one Kimball had enjoyed with breakfast seem a stogie made from weeds. Kimball wondered when he'd last set foot in an actual working vessel of the C.S. Navy. Probably when he'd reported to Havana, whenever that was. He didn't come from Cuba; his accent said Alabama or Mississippi.

Fixing him with a gaze he might have sent toward a U.S. cruiser through his periscope, Kimball said, "I am like the fellow whose neighbor has a mean dog. I might put up with one bite, but sure as hell I won't put up with two. If I need to know something, I expect to find out the minute I need to know it, not when somebody gets around to it."

He didn't advance on the commander from Supply. He didn't clench his fist. He didn't even raise his voice. The commander staggered back as if hit in that comfortable, well-upholstered belly even so. "I'm sure you won't have any trouble like that in the future," he said, pasting a wide, placating smile on his face and taking the fancy cigar out of his mouth to make the smile even wider.

"Good." Kimball still didn't raise his voice, but the officer from Supply took another couple of steps back. Kimball strode past him and climbed down into the noisome darkness that was the interior of the *Bonefish*.

Ben Coulter had things well in hand there. After a stretch of time with the crew out and the boat cleaned up as much as it could be, the stench had diminished. It was still enough to make most sailors in the surface Navy turn up their toes, or perhaps heave up their breakfasts. To Kimball, it was the smell of home.

"Long as we can keep things fresh, sir, we'll live like kings," Coulter said. "Plenty of eggs and meat and fish and greens— some of 'em are these funny Cuban vegetables that look like God forgot what he was doin' when He was makin' 'em, but you boil 'em long enough and they all taste the same, sure as hell. Yes, sir, like kings."

"Crowded kings," Kimball remarked, and the veteran first mate nodded. Kimball and Coulter both knew perfectly well that before long they'd be eating beans and salt pork and stinking sauerkraut and drinking orange juice and lemon juice to hold scurvy at bay. As a cruise wore along, fresh-caught fish became a luxury. Dwelling on better times was more enjoyable.

"We're full up on shells again, too, sir," Coulter said. "Armorers haven't come with the fish yet, though."

"We'll get 'em. We do most of our work with 'em these days," Kimball said. "Too damn many ships with wireless. We need to sink 'em fast and sneaky."

"Yes, sir." Coulter nodded again. "Damnyankees keep pulling destroyers out of their hats, too, like magicians with rabbits. It's getting so we can't hardly take a shot at a freighter without dodging ash cans for the next week."

"I know. I'm getting damn tired of it, too." Kimball slapped

Coulter on the back. "By the way they're going at this resupply business, likely you've guessed we'll be going out sooner than we reckoned when we got into Habana."

Ben Coulter's head went up and down once more. "Sure as hell did, sir. Reckon the Yankees must have done somethin' nasty to the *Bonito*."

"They sank her," Kimball said bluntly, adding, "They thought she was the *Bonefish*; the Yankee papers are reporting us sunk." That jerked a laugh out of the mate. Kimball went on, "The *Ericsson* got her—same destroyer that's given us such a hard time. When we get back into our box on the map, Ben, I'm going to kill that bastard."

"Oh, hell, yes," Coulter said. "Can't let the damnyankees own the whole damn ocean."

"Can't let 'em get past us, either," Kimball said. "If they sit on England's supply line, she's out of the war. If England has to quit, we've lost, too, and so have the froggies."

"Whole crew understands that, sir," Coulter answered. Then he sighed. "Sure are a hell of a lot of Yankees tryin' to get south of us these days when we're cruising out there, though."

Kimball didn't reply. As far as he could see, the war was probably lost even if the U.S. Navy didn't succeed in choking off England's supply line to Argentina. It would take longer to lose if the British stayed in the fight, that was all.

He didn't care. He had a job to do, and he was damn good at it. He had very little modesty, false or otherwise. He knew how good he was. He enjoyed doing what he was doing, too. As long as the CSA stayed in the fight, he'd do it as well as he could. And if the Yankees sank him . . . well, he'd already hurt the USA a lot worse than losing the *Bonefish* would hurt his own country.

When he got back to his quarters, a telegram was waiting. He wasted no time in tearing open the envelope. "If this here is from my ma," he muttered, "I'm going to be disappointed as hell."

But it wasn't. Anne Colleton wrote, GLAD THE YANKS ARE BAD FISHERMEN. LET ME KNOW NEXT TIME. MAYBE WE'LL MEET HALFWAY. ANNE. No *love*, not from her. Not even a promise. Kimball had seen such fripperies were not her style. But a *maybe* from a woman like that was worth a lay from half a dozen of the ordinary sort. Kimball carefully tore the telegram into tiny pieces. He was smiling as he did it.

* * *

As it happened, Arthur McGregor wasn't far from the farm-house when two green-gray Fords turned off the road from Rosenfeld and onto the path that led to his home. He decided he wouldn't go out to the fields after all, but turned and walked back.

The motorcars got there before he did. U.S. soldiers with bayoneted rifles piled out of one of them. More soldiers got out of the other. Instead of a Springfield in his hands, one of those men wore a pistol on his hip. Major Hannebrink was slim and quick-moving and dapper, easy to recognize from a long way off. McGregor scowled, but did not pick up his pace.

When he reached the knot of soldiers, he looked down at the American officer, who was several inches shorter than he. "You must think I'm a dangerous character," he said slowly, "if you need to bring all these bullies along when you come to say hello."

"I don't know whether you're a dangerous character or not," Hannebrink answered coolly, "but I don't believe in taking chances, and I do aim to find out one way or the other."

"Barn first, sir, or the house?" one of the soldiers—a sergeant—asked.

McGregor's eyes went to the farmhouse. Maude was watching from the kitchen window, Julia alongside her. Mary wasn't tall enough to see out. If her mother and sister hadn't already told her soldiers were here, though, she'd know soon enough, and then she'd call them everything she knew how to call them, and she knew a surprising amount.

"House," Hannebrink answered. "Get the women out of there. We'll turn it inside out, and then we'll do the barn." He drew the pistol and pointed it at McGregor. "This gentleman won't be going in there to take out anything he doesn't fancy us seeing."

"Wasn't going to do that anyway," McGregor said stolidly. "You bastards have stuck your noses in there before, and you never found a thing, because there's nothing to find. You won't find anything this time, either—still nothing." He'd told that lie so many times, it came out smooth as the truth, though he'd never been a man who lied easily before Alexander was marched up against a wall and shot.

If they found the explosives . . . *If they find them, it's over,* he thought. He wasn't ready for it to be over, not yet. He hadn't taken nearly enough revenge yet. But the best way to keep from betraying himself was to act as if whether they found what they were looking for didn't matter.

Out came Maude and Julia and Mary, under the Yanks' guns. Sure enough, his younger daughter, the spitfire, was doing her best to scorch the soldiers. It didn't work so well as she might have hoped; one or two of the Americans, instead of getting angry, were fighting laughter.

A couple of the men in green-gray stayed with Major Hannebrink to stand guard on McGregor and his family. The rest went back into the house. Occasional crashes from within said they were indeed turning the place inside out. Hannebrink might have thought Maude was calm. McGregor knew better. He set a hand on his wife's shoulder to keep her from hurling herself at the American major. Julia looked furious, and made no effort at all to hide it.

After an hour or so, the sergeant came out and said, "Sir, the worst thing they've got in there is kerosene for the lamps."

"It's good for killing lice, too," Mary said, looking right at Hannebrink.

His lips thinned; that got home. But he said only, "We'll have a look in the barn, then." He gestured with the .45 in his hand. "Come on, McGregor. You can watch and make sure we don't steal anything."

"You've already stolen more from me than you can ever give back," he answered. He knew why Major Hannebrink wanted him along: in the hope that he'd give something away.

Hannebrink turned to the women. "You can go clean up now," he said. "That should give you something to do for the rest of the day."

In the barn, the U.S. soldiers methodically went through everything, climbing up into the loft to poke their bayonets into the hay in the hope of finding hidden dynamite and also searching all the animals' stalls. They opened every crate. They dumped the drawers set into McGregor's workbench out onto the ground and pawed over his chisels and drill bits and screwdrivers, his twine and his carpenter's rule.

He wondered if he'd somehow made a mistake, if he'd put one of the bomb-building tools in among the others. The low-voiced curses of the men in green-gray said he hadn't.

He glanced toward the old wagon wheel. There it lay, rust on the iron tire, half covered with straw. One of the soldiers strode around it to get at a box by the far wall. He used a pry bar to open the box, whose lid was nailed shut. Then he turned it upside down. A couple of horseshoes that had worn thin, a broken scythe blade, and some other scrap iron spilled out onto the ground with a series of clanks.

"Thanks," McGregor said. "Forgot I had that junk lying around. I can do something with it, I expect."

"Go to hell, you damn murdering Canuck," the Yankee soldier snapped. He took a long step over the wagon wheel and glared into McGregor's face.

McGregor neither moved back nor blinked. Evenly, he said, "You're the people who know all about murdering."

Before the soldier could reply, Major Hannebrink broke in: "Enough, Neugebauer." The private in green-gray stiffened to obedient attention. Hannebrink went on, "We don't know that McGregor here is a murderer. We're trying to find out." He turned to the farmer. "So far, we have no evidence, only a man who thinks he has a reason to be angry at us."

"You had no evidence against my son, either," McGregor said. Not lunging at the U.S. officer was one of the hardest things he'd ever done. "You didn't need any. You shot him without it."

"I had evidence I thought good," Hannebrink said. "I did my duty to my country. I would do it again."

"I believe *that*," McGregor said. "I don't know why you're bothering with this rigmarole. If you need evidence against me, you can always plant it whenever you please. Then you'll haul me off to jail and shoot me, same as you did with Alexander."

Hannebrink exhaled through his nose. "If I have no evidence against you, I have no quarrel with you. If you aren't the man who's been planting bombs hither and yon through the countryside, I don't want to waste my time on you. I want to catch the son of a bitch who is doing that and make him pay."

He sounded sincere. But then, to be good at his job he needed to sound sincere. McGregor answered, "If I was crazy enough to make bombs, I wouldn't plant 'em hither and yon through the countryside." He pointed to Hannebrink. "I'd go after you."

"One of those bombs almost did kill me," the U.S. major said.

"Really?" McGregor was calm, casual, cool. "Too bad it missed. I'd buy a beer for the fellow who got you, and then I'd hit him over the head with my mug, for doing it before I could."

"You ought to bring him in for sedition, sir," said the private—

Neugebauer—who'd stepped over and around McGregor's bomb-making supplies.

Hannebrink shook his head. Raising his voice a little, he asked, "Anything here even a little out of the ordinary?"

"No, sir," the soldiers answered, almost in chorus.

Hannebrink shook his head again. "Then I've got no reason to bring him in. He does have some reason not to be in love with me. That doesn't worry me. I did what I thought was right, and I'll live with it. Let's go back to town, boys."

When they walked out to their Fords, they discovered that each of them had a punctured inner tube. Cursing, the soldiers set about patching the punctures. McGregor wanted to smile. He didn't. He was too worried. All the soldiers had been back at the barn, and . . .

Major Hannebrink folded his arms across his chest. "If these punctures turn out to be knife cuts, Mr. McGregor, I am not going to be pleased with your family, I warn you."

Oh, Mary, McGregor thought, *what have you done?* But then a soldier at the nearer motorcar said, "Sir, we got a nail in this one."

"Don't know what did this one, sir," said Neugebauer, who was holding the inner tube from the other Ford, "but it looks like a hole, not a cut."

"Anybody see anything?" Hannebrink asked. None of the U.S. soldiers answered. McGregor realized he hadn't been breathing, and sucked in a long, ragged inhalation. The soldiers wouldn't be thinking about a little girl. Even Hannebrink, who was professionally suspicious, wouldn't be thinking about a little girl. Maude, maybe, but not Mary.

Hannebrink pursed his lips. "No evidence," he said. "Maybe we picked up those punctures on the way over here. Maybe. It could have happened. Since I can't prove it didn't happen that way, I'm going to leave it alone. But if it ever happens here again, Mr. McGregor, someone is going to be very unhappy, and it won't be me."

"Why are you barking at me?" McGregor asked. "I was in the barn with you and your hooligans." For once, he was telling the whole truth. It sounded no different from his lies.

Hannebrink didn't answer. He waited while his men fixed the punctures, which they handled with practiced efficiency. Then all the Yank soldiers piled into the motorcars and drove off.

McGregor waited till they'd left his land. Then he walked into the house. His wife was furious. "They turned everything upside down and inside out, those dirty—" She hissed like a cat with its fur puffed out, then went on, "I wish I was a man, so I could say what I think."

"Never mind," McGregor said, which made Maude hiss again. Ignoring her, he went over to Mary. He knelt down and kissed her on the forehead. "This is for what you did, and for being clever enough to use a nail and not a knife." Then he spanked her, hard enough to make her yelp in both surprise and pain. "And this is to remind you not to do it again, no matter how much you want to."

His younger daughter stared. "How did you know it was me, Pa? You were inside the barn with the Yankees. You couldn't see it."

"How did I know? Because I'm your father, that's how. This time, I'm proud of you, you little sneak. Some things you can only get away with once, though. This is one of them. Remember it."

"Yes, Pa," Mary said demurely, so demurely that McGregor could only hope she'd paid some attention—a little attention—to what he'd told her.

The big guns rumbled and roared. The bombardment of Nashville itself hadn't stopped since the U.S. guns got close enough to reach the city. Lieutenant Colonel Irving Morrell had long since got used to that rumble from the western horizon.

Closer, but still west of his position on the northern bank of the Cumberland, another bombardment lay its thunder over the more distant rumble. For the past six days, U.S. artillery had been hammering the Confederate positions south of the river with high explosives and gas. Bombing aeroplanes had added the weight of their munitions to the unending gunfire. Fighting scouts swooped low, strafing the Rebel's trenches with their machine guns.

General Custer could hardly have made it more obvious where he intended to throw First Army across the Cumberland. He had even been rash enough to let them get glimpses of the barrels he was gathering for his frontal blow.

And the Confederates, having such generosity bestowed upon them, were not slow to take advantage of it. Though the U.S. artillery hampered their movements, they brought reinforcements forward. Their own guns pounded away at the force Custer had assembled. Their aeroplanes were outnumbered, but still stung the U.S. soldiers waiting on Custer's order to cross the river.

Irving Morrell looked west with benign approval.

Beside him, Colonel Ned Sherrard pulled out his watch. Morrell imitated the gesture. Together, they said, "Five minutes to go."

Sherrard put his watch back into its pocket. He said, "How does it feel to have the whole First Army moving to a scheme you thought up?"

"Ask me in a few days," Morrell answered. "If it goes the way I hope, it'll feel great. If it doesn't, I'll be so low a deep dugout will look like up to me."

As he watched the second hand of his own watch sweep into its final minutes before the curtain went up, he realized how much he had riding on the next few days. He would soon know the answer to a question so many men ask themselves: *are you really as smart as you think you are?* If he was, he'd be wearing a colonel's eagles himself soon, or maybe even a brigadier general's single stars. If he wasn't, he'd be a lieutenant colonel if he stayed in the Army for the next fifty years, and no one would pay any attention to him during all that time.

Compared to failure, dying on the battlefield had its attractions.

"Fifteen sec—" he started to say, and then the guns behind him, the guns that had stayed hidden under canvas and branches, the guns that had remained silent for so long while their brethren pounded the Confederates to the west, opened up with everything they had against the thinned Rebel line just east of Lakewood, Tennessee. On the far side of the Cumberland, earth leapt and danced and quivered in agony.

A flight of bombers added their explosives to the attack, as they were doing farther west. Under the cover of the bombardment, Army engineers rushed to the bank of the Cumberland and began building half a dozen pontoon bridges across the river. Everything depended on the sappers. If they could get those bridges built fast enough, the rest of Morrell's plan would unfold as he'd designed it. If they failed, he failed with them.

He wanted to stay and watch them work. He knew what was riding on their shoulders. Already a few of them had fallen, from machine-gun fire and from shells falling too near. The rest kept on. That was their job.

Colonel Sherrard reminded him of his job: "Into the barrel, Irv. As soon as those bridges get across, we go." Sherrard shouted at the top of his lungs, right into Morrell's ear. Morrell barely heard him. He thought about pretending he didn't hear him so he could keep on watching the sappers, but knew Sherrard was right. He trotted off toward his barrel.

Like all the others waiting to cross the Cumberland, it had come here by night, to keep prying Rebel observation aeroplanes from spotting it. Like the artillery concentrated by similarly stealthy means, it had hidden under canvas since arriving. Now the canvas was off. The columns of barrels were ready to go forward if they could. And Irving Morrell's would go first.

He nodded to the driver, reached down and slapped the right-side engineer on the back, and then, unable to bear being cooped up in this great iron box, opened the top hatch and stood up in the cupola. He *had* to watch the engineers at work. He *had* to watch the bridges snake across the Cumberland.

If one was wrecked, he could go with five. If two were wrecked, he could go with four. If three were wrecked, he had orders not to go, but thought he might disobey them. But all six bridges still pushed forward toward the southern bank of the spring-swollen river. General Custer's ostentatious preparation had pulled the Confederate defenders closer to Nashville. Not many men, not many guns, were left to contest what would be the real crossing.

Riflemen and machine-gun crews in green-gray rushed to the ends of the extending bridges as they neared the far bank of the Cumberland. They started blazing away at the Confederates closest to the river, men who already risked their lives thanks to U.S. artillery fire.

A green flare—one of the bridges had reached the southern bank. A moment later, another one burned in the sky. The rest of the engineering crews worked like madmen. The sappers were as fiercely competitive as any soldiers God ever made. A third green flare blazed from the southern bank of the Cumberland.

Morrell ducked down into the cupola. "Fire 'em up!" he shouted. "We're going." The twin White truck engines bellowed to life. The iron deck, patterned to keep feet from slipping, shivered and rattled and shook under his boots. Maybe he was jumping the gun, but he didn't think so. One of those last three bridges would surely succeed in making it across, and even if it didn't . . . He stood up again, to stare across the Cumberland.

There! The fourth green flare. Now he could go with no reservations whatever. Some of the other barrel commanders were also standing up in their cupolas. He waved to them. They waved back. He'd also detailed a soldier with a hammer to run down each line of barrels and give the side of every machine in it a good, solid clang to signal that action was at hand.

More engines coughed and belched and caught. Even as Morrell stooped down into the cupola once more, the sixth and last green flare rose into the sky. He grinned. So far, everything was perfect. The way to keep it perfect was to push hard, never let the Confederates have a chance to build a defensive line of the sort they'd held so well for so long north of Nashville.

"Off balance," he muttered to himself, not that anyone else in the barrel could have heard him even had he shouted. "Got to keep them off balance." He pointed straight ahead, index finger extended. *Forward.*

Forward the barrel went, adding the clatter and rattle of the tracks to the engines' flatulent roar. Morrell stood up again. The driver had his louvers open. He could see as much as he ever could, which wasn't a great deal. But it was enough to let him get onto the bridge over which he would cross the Cumberland.

The bridge dipped and swayed a little under the weight of the barrel, but held. At the machine's best pace—about that of a trotting soldier in full kit—it waddled over the bridge. Barrels also crossed on two more bridges. On the other three, infantry marched at double time.

A jolt, and the barrel clattered off the bridge and onto the soft dirt of the southern bank of the Cumberland. For a bad moment, Morrell thought the dirt would be soft enough to make the barrel bog down, but, engines screaming, the machine moved ahead, and onto ground better able to support its weight.

Machine-gun bullets clattered off the barrel's armored carapace. The two left-hand machine guns returned fire. The Confederate gun fell silent. Maybe they'd knocked it out. Maybe its crew had been so busy shooting at the barrel, U.S. infantry were able to rush them. Morrell had seen that before: barrels were machine-gun magnets, attracting fire that might have been more profitably aimed against foot soldiers.

Now Morrell had the vision louvers down to slits. Through those slits, he saw Confederate soldiers moving forward now that the barrage had passed them by to punish targets farther behind the line. *Halt,* he signaled, and reached forward with a length of dowling to tap one of the artillerymen at the nose cannon on the shoulder.

They had no trouble figuring out the target he had in mind. The cannon snarled once, then again. The noise wasn't too much worse than everything else going on inside the barrel. Through the slits, Morrell watched oncoming Rebs get flung aside as if they were paper dolls. The men in butternut who came through unhurt had to dive for cover.

Forward, Morrell signaled again. Forward they went, through the Confederate defensive system. The Rebs had a lot of trench lines, but not very many men in them. The barrel crews concentrated on wrecking machine-gun positions; those guns could tear the heart from an infantry attack, and had torn the heart from many. One after another, the barrels put them out of action.

Then, quite suddenly—or so it seemed—the barrels had traversed all the Confederate trenches, and reached the level ground behind them. A few C.S. artillery pieces were still firing. More had been pulled back and out of the pits from which they had shelled U.S. forces.

And quite a few were wrecked. Morrell's traveling fortress rumbled past a quick-firing three-inch gun whose barrel had burst not far from the breech. U.S. shells had wrecked the carriage; most of the crew lay dead by the piece. At the end of the trail sat one of the gunners, his head in his hands, a picture of despair. His war was over. Soon the infantry advancing with the barrels would scoop him up.

Southwest, Morrell signaled. He stood up in the cupola again, to compare the field to the map he carried inside his head. If anything, what he saw looked better than what he had imagined and presented to General Custer.

"Open country!" he said exultantly. "We've got the Rebs out of their holes at last. They know how to fight from trenches, but now we're playing a different game."

There ahead, a railroad line ran toward Nashville. Along it chugged a train full of soldiers, the engineer blissfully unaware the United States Army had broken through. A cannon shell through the boiler brought him the news. Gleefully, the machine gunners in Morrell's barrel raked the train.

Forward, he signaled again. He intended his thrust to cut off and outflank the Rebs who were defending Nashville from the rest of First Army. "Keep going," he muttered. "We've got to keep going. You don't get what you want by doing things half-way. I don't want to scare these bastards. I want to wreck 'em."

On rumbled the barrel. For the moment, the CSA seemed to have little with which to stop it.

Cassius tossed Scipio a Tredegar. Automatically, Scipio caught it out of the air. Automatically, he checked the chamber. It had a round in it. He pulled off the clip. By its weight, it was full.

"You is one o' we, Kip," Cassius said, and tossed him a couple of more ten-round boxes. "When we fights de feudal 'pressors, you fights wid we."

The men of the Congaree Socialist Republic hadn't trusted him with a rifle in his hands since he'd returned to the swamps by the river that gave the Republic its name. He looked around. "Cherry ain't here," he remarked.

Cassius' expression turned sour. "She still huntin' dat damn-fool treasure Miss Anne never hid no kind of way."

"She kin hunt till she git all old an' shriveled up," Scipio said. "If they ain't nothin' there, she ain't gwine find it."

"She keep huntin', she don' live to git all old an' shriveled up," Cassius answered. "Miss Anne, she put de militia round Marsh-lands. Dey catch Cherry an' de poor fools she got with she."

I hope they do, Cassius thought. *Dear God, I hope they do.* Cherry knew him for the cold heart, for the weak spirit, he was. She knew he had no true revolutionary fire in his belly, knew and despised him for it. If Anne Colleton caught her, Scipio would do nothing but rejoice.

In one pocket of his tattered dungarees, he had a letter ad-dressed to Anne Colleton in St. Matthews. Getting hold of paper and pencil hadn't been too hard. Even laying his hands on an en-velope hadn't been too hard. Finding a postage stamp, though . . .

Finally, he'd seen a dice game where one of the raiders was tearing stamps off a sheet a few at a time to cover his losses. Scipio had had almost no money in his own pockets, but he got down on one knee as fast as he could. Luck was with him; he'd rolled a seven his first try out and then made his point—it was four, which made it tougher—so that, before long, several small, red portraits of James Longstreet took up residence alongside his pocket change. One of them was on the envelope now.

Cassius said, "We's gwine up to hit Gadsden a lick tonight. We ain't done no fightin' no'th o' the Congaree in a while. Them fat white bastards up there, they reckons they's safe from de force o' revolutionary justice. I aims to show they that they is mistooken."

"You goes up there, you draws the militia up there after you," Scipio said. "Not so many white sojers around Marshlands after dat. Cherry, she can dig all she like."

"I knows it," Cassius said. "Cain't be helped." He was by no means enamored of Cherry or her search for the treasure both he and Scipio were convinced did not exist. Then Cassius turned his gaze on Scipio. He still had a hunter's eyes—or maybe they were sniper's eyes. He didn't say anything. He didn't need to say anything. His expression spoke more plainly than words. *Yes, you've got a rifle in your hands,* it declared. *You don't dare use it against me or any of the other revolutionary fighters here. You'd have only one shot sent in the wrong direction, and then you'd be mine—because you and I both know that if that one shot is at me, you'll miss. And I won't.*

Scipio sighed. He'd always been a halfhearted Red at best. He wasn't even that any more. He was a man trapped in a nightmare with enemies on all sides and no way out. He saw no way to take Cassius with him when he fell, as he surely would fall. He did have hopes of bringing down Cherry—or, if Cherry got extraordinarily lucky, of bringing down Miss Anne. But Cassius? Cassius was a force of nature.

The force of nature joined Scipio and a couple of other men in a battered rowboat and glided north through the swamps of the Congaree. Several other boats followed. Cassius knew the ways through the maze of twisting channels. Starlight was all he needed. Each of the other boats carried at least one man who knew the swamps almost as well.

Something floated by overhead. Scipio's blood ran cold. The part of his mind that the Colletons had spared no trouble or expense to educate insisted it was only an owl. The part of him that had grown up in one of those clapboard cabins a world away from the Marshlands mansion by which they sat said it was something worse, something ghostly, something that would lure them all into the heart of the swamp and never let them escape.

Then it hooted, and he felt foolish. More often than not, the educated part of his mind did have some notion of what it was talking about. But the other part was older, with roots that went down deeper. Education ruled his brain. His belly, his heart, his balls? No.

"Do Jesus!" one of the oarsmen said, his voice a shaky whisper. "I reckoned that were one o' they bad hants, the kind that don't never let you come out o' the swamp no more." Scipio hadn't been the only one frightened, then.

Cassius said, "Ain't no hant can stand up against dialectical materialism." His new beliefs had overpowered the older ones. Almost, Scipio envied him for that. Almost. Cassius' new beliefs had overpowered his good judgment, too, and these tattered remnants of the Congaree Socialist Republic the Reds had hoped to establish were the proof of that.

Cassius did not, would not, see defeat, only a setback on the inevitable road to revolution. He could no more deny that inevitability than a devout Christian could the inevitability of the Second Coming.

Trees and bushes began to thin out as the boats full of Reds neared the edge of the swamp. Ahead, across fields once full of tobacco and cotton and rice that now held mostly weeds, the lights of Gadsden shone: a few houses bright with electricity, more showing the softer, yellower light of burning gas. Most of the houses showed no lights at all; most people, like most people all over the world, had to get up and go to work in the morning.

Cassius waved. The men at the oars brought the rowboat up against the bank of the creek that fed into the Congaree. It grounded softly on mud. The other boats came up alongside. Black men with rifles clambered out of them. "Let's go, comrades," Cassius said in a low but penetrating voice. "Time fo' de buckra to learn some more o' de price de 'pressors pay."

He left one man behind to guard the boats. Scipio wished he could have been that man, but knew better than to show it. The revolutionaries did not trust him enough to let him out of their sight. Cassius might have, but he did not try to override the opinion of the others. Since they were right and he wrong, that was as well for their cause, if not for Scipio's.

A motorcar chugged along the road toward town. The driver

never saw Cassius and his men, for he led them along paths he knew through the overgrown fields. They went past a couple of mansions, both dark and silent and deserted. Few great landowners around the Congaree dared live among the dozens of Negro servants and field hands needed to make a plantation and mansion live, not these days they didn't.

Militiamen—the too old and the too young—stumped along the streets of Gadsden. One of them was rash enough to carry a kerosene lantern. Cassius let out a soft chuckle. "Look at that damnfool buckra goin' roun' like he a night watchman sayin', 'Twelve o'clock, an' all's well!' It ain't no twelve o'clock, an' it ain't well, neither."

He raised his Tredegar to his shoulder in one fluid motion, aimed, and fired. The militiaman dropped the lantern with a shriek. The burning puddle of kerosene set fire to the boards of the sidewalk.

Another militiaman fired at the sound of Cassius' shot, and perhaps at the muzzle flash. His bullet didn't come close. Three Negroes fired at the flash from his rifle. He screamed, too; one of those rounds must have struck home. "Come on!" Cassius said. He advanced on Gadsden in long, loping, ground-eating strides.

Black shadows in the black night, the Reds ran after him. Scipio panted along with the rest, doing his best to keep up. The factory work he'd done had hardened him. He wasn't the swiftest here, nor anywhere close to it, but he wasn't the slowest, either.

A bell began clanging in the center of town: probably a fire alarm turned to a new purpose. Here and there, lights came on in upper stories as people got ready to come out and fight or simply tried to find out what was going on. The raiders fired whenever those lights gave them targets. More screams rose.

Slower than it should have came a cry that made sense: "Niggers! It's the Red niggers!"

Militiamen and whoever else could lay hands on a rifle or shotgun or pistol started banging away, sometimes at the Negroes who ran through the streets but as often at one another. The townsfolk had not been raided for a while, and so did not put up the kind of energetic, organized defense the whites of St. Matthews, for instance, might have shown.

Scipio darted along Market Street toward the corner of Williams. A white-bearded militiaman dashed from Williams out onto Market just as Scipio got to the corner. They both stared in horror. Scipio shot first, before the old man's rifle had quite come to bear on him. The militiaman fired as he fell. The bullet cracked past Scipio's head.

Seeing the militiaman still trying to work the bolt on his rifle, Scipio shot him again, in the head. He didn't move after that. He wasn't the first white man Scipio had killed, but Scipio hadn't wanted to shoot him. He'd got in the way; that was all. At the corner of Williams and Market stood a cast-iron mailbox. Scipio threw his note to Anne Colleton into it, then ran on.

The men of the Congaree Socialist Republic shot whomever they could shoot, started half a dozen fires, and then, at Cassius' shouted command, melted away into the night. Some of the younger and more intrepid militiamen and townsfolk tried to pursue, but the Negroes knew where they were going and the whites did not. Escape proved easy enough.

"Don't lose a man, not one!" Cassius exulted when they got back to the boats. "We tears that town to hell and gone"—he pointed back toward the leaping flames—"and we don't lose a man. Is that a great raid, or is it ain't?"

"That a great raid, Cass," Scipio said solemnly. "A great raid."

XI

"Nashville is ours, and fairly won!" Lieutenant General George Armstrong Custer exulted, standing in front of the badly damaged State Capitol of Tennessee. Correspondents again hung on his every word, and he had plenty of words to keep them hanging. "We smashed their line north of the Cumberland when no one thought we could. We crossed the Cumberland when no one thought we could. And now, more than half a century after an unjust and ignominious peace forced us to evacuate Nashville, the Stars and Stripes wave over it once more."

As he had on the other side of the Cumberland, Major Abner Dowling listened with mixed emotions to the general commanding First Army. Custer's bombast always gave him the pip. But now, by God, Custer had plenty to be bombastic about. He'd gained two smashing victories over the Confederates in the space of a month. People with greater reputations had done less.

"Where do we go from here, General?" one of the scribes asked.

"Forward against the foe," Custer said grandly. Before Dowling could spoil the proceedings by throwing up on his superior's shoes, Custer did something most unusual for him—he gave a sensible reason for one of his rhetorical flights of fancy: "More than that, I am not at liberty to say, lest the Rebels learn in our papers what their spies could not tell them."

"How long can the Rebs stand up under this kind of pounding, sir?" another reporter said.

"You need to ask that question in Richmond, Jack, not here," Custer said. Chuckling, he added, "As long as the Rebs still own Richmond, anyhow. If they start using barrels back East the way we've taught them here, the Confederate States may not keep their capital very long."

"With Russia in revolution, with France tottering and French soldiers throwing down their guns or turning them on their own officers, with England stretched to the breaking point and the CSA hammered on several fronts, how long can the Entente go on? How long can the war go on?" Jack asked.

"Until the United States and Germany win their rightful places in the sun, and until those places are recognized by all the powers in the world," Custer said. "It could be tomorrow. It could be five years hence. However long it takes, we shall persevere." He struck one of his poses.

"If the Rebs do throw in their hand, General, what sort of peace would you recommend imposing on them?" somebody asked.

Before Custer could get started on that one, Abner Dowling stepped in: "Boys, that's not the sort of question you ask a soldier. That's a question for the president or the secretary of state or for Congress." Part of his job—no small part of his job—was keeping the general commanding First Army from embarrassing not only himself but his country.

Given General Custer's nature, it wasn't an easy job. With a laugh, Custer said, "Don't worry, Major. They know I'm not one of the boys in the morning coats and striped trousers. All they asked was what I would recommend, and I'm happy to tell them that much."

"Sir, I don't really think you—" Dowling began.

It was hopeless. Custer rolled over him like a barrel smashing barbed wire into the mud. "If it were up to me, I would impose upon the Confederate States a peace that would prevent them from ever again threatening the peace and security of the United States. Twice now they have rubbed our faces in the dirt. They came too close to doing it once more in this great war. They should never, ever have another chance."

On the whole, Dowling agreed with him (which made Custer's adjutant want to reexamine his own assumptions). But there were dangers with a punitive peace, too, as one of the correspondents recognized: "What if our terms are so harsh, the Confederates would sooner take their chances on the battlefield than accept them?"

"Bully!" Custer boomed. "So much the better. In that case, I confidently believe the restoration of the Union by force of arms, which unfortunately failed when first attempted under the inept leadership of Abraham Lincoln, would now, in God's good time, at last come to pass."

He did give good copy. The newspapermen jotted phrases in their notebooks. Abner Dowling was of the opinion that his boss had to be suffering from a touch of the sun. Crossing the Cumberland had been a splendid feat of arms, no doubt about it. Even so, a hell of a lot of ground lay between Nashville and Mobile.

Dowling said, "I think that's about enough, boys. Remember that you're asking these questions inside Nashville. If that doesn't speak for itself, I don't know what does."

"I don't mind answering questions," Custer said. "I could stand here all day and enjoy every minute of it."

Dowling knew how true that was. Every question Custer answered meant another line, maybe another paragraph, in the papers. Seeing his name in print was meat and drink to the general commanding First Army. But his insistence on his own stamina reminded the correspondents that he had considerably surpassed his Biblical threescore and ten. They drifted away by ones and twos to file their stories.

Custer gave his adjutant a sour look. "I was just warming to the subject, Major. Why did you go and cut me off at the knees?"

"They already know you're a hero, sir," Dowling said. He smiled to himself, watching Custer lap that up like a kitten with a pitcher of cream. After a couple of seconds, though, that inner smile slipped. Custer really *was* a hero, and, Dowling reluctantly admitted to himself, really deserved to be. The portly major went on, "Besides, sir, we truly do have to plan the axis of First Army's next attack."

After lighting a cigar, Custer blew smoke in Dowling's face. "I suppose so, Major," he said with poor grace, "but blast me if I know why we're bothering. The geniuses in Philadelphia will tell us what to do, delivering their orders in a chariot of fire from on high, as if from the hand of God Himself—and it will work as well as their doctrine on barrels, you mark my words."

Having vented steam, he let his adjutant lead him back into the capitol. The southern wing was more nearly intact than the northern; First Army headquarters had been established there. In the map room, an enormous chart of Tennessee was thumbtacked to one wall. Two red arrows projected out from Nashville, one southeast toward Murfreesboro, the other southwest toward Memphis, better than two hundred miles away.

As far as Dowling was concerned, that second line was madness, an exercise in hubris. But it attracted Custer as much as a pretty housekeeper did. "By pushing in that direction, Major, we can lend aid to the attack on Memphis that's been developing in Arkansas," he insisted.

Keeping Custer connected with reality was Dowling's main assignment. "Sir, the Tennessee River is in the way," he said, as diplomatically as he could. "Not only that, the attack from Arkansas has been developing since 1915, and it hasn't developed yet."

"Jonesboro has fallen," Custer said.

"Yes—at last," Dowling said, certain the sarcasm would fly over the head of the general commanding First Army, as indeed it did. Stubbornly, Custer's adjutant went on, "Expecting anything from a campaign west of the Mississippi is whistling in the dark, sir. We just don't have the forces over there to do all we want. If the Rebs weren't shy of men west of the river, too, we'd be in worse shape there than we are."

"We'll draw off their defenders," Custer said. "They haven't got enough men on this side of the river, either."

That held just enough truth to make it tempting, but not enough to make it valuable. In thoughtful tones, Dowling said, "Well, you may be right, sir. I've heard Brigadier General MacArthur find some good reasons for the advance in the direction of Memphis."

He'd gauged that about right. Custer's peroxided mustache twitched; he screwed up his mouth as if he'd bitten into a lemon. "The only direction of advance Daniel MacArthur knows anything about is the one in the direction of the newspapers," he sneered.

Takes one to know one, Dowling thought. Brigadier General MacArthur, with his trademark cigarette holder, courted publicity the way stockbrokers courted chorus girls. Did Custer refuse to admit to anyone else that he did the same thing, or did he refuse to admit it to himself, too? Despite his long association with the general commanding First Army, Dowling hadn't ever been able to decide.

Custer said, "I wonder what Lieutenant Colonel—no, Colonel: you did send in that promotion, didn't you?—Morrell's view is?"

"I did send in that promotion, yes, sir," Dowling said.

"Good," Custer said. "Good. I wonder what Morrell thinks, yes I do. Now there is a man with a good head on his shoulders, who thinks of his country first and his own glory second. He's not a grandstander like some people I could name. A very solid man, Morrell."

"Yes, sir," Dowling said. Custer approved of him because his plan had brought Custer fame, but it had brought Custer fame because it worked. Dowling didn't think Morrell so unselfishly patriotic as Custer did, but he didn't mind ambition in a man if it didn't consume him.

"And," Custer muttered, more than half to himself, "I had better find out in which direction Libbie thinks we should go."

"That would be a good idea, sir," Dowling said enthusiastically— so enthusiastically, Custer gave him a dirty look. Dowling didn't care that Libbie kept the general commanding First Army from rumpling serving women. He did care that Libbie had shown herself to be the brains of the Custer family. Whenever she shared living quarters with the general, First Army fought better.

Custer said, "Whether we move against Murfreesboro or Memphis, we have to strike hard."

His adjutant nodded. Custer's one great military virtue was aggressiveness. That aggressiveness had cost the lives of thousands of men, because it meant Custer kept trying to ram his head through the stone walls the CSA kept building against him. But, when barrels finally gave him the means to do some real ramming, he made the most of them, as a more subtle general might have been unable to do.

"We have to strike hard," he repeated. "If we but strike hard, the whole rotten edifice of the Confederate States of America will come tumbling down."

A year earlier, Dowling would have reckoned that the statement of a madman. Six months earlier, he would have thought it the statement of a fool. Now he nodded solemnly and said, "Sir, I think you may be right."

Reggie Bartlett's hospital gown was of a washed-out butternut, not a pale green-gray like those of most of the inmates of the military hospital outside St. Louis. For good measure, the gown had PRISONER stenciled across the chest in bloodred letters four inches high.

He could get around pretty well with one crutch these days, which was a good thing, because the shoulder that had taken a machine-gun bullet was still too tender to let him use two crutches. The doctors kept insisting the wound infection was clearing up, but it wasn't clearing up anywhere near fast enough to suit him.

He made it to the toilets adjoining the room where he and his companions spent so much time on their backs, eased himself, and slowly returned to his bed. "Took you long enough," one of the Yankees said. "I figured you were trying to escape, the way you keep bragging that you did before."

"Pretty soon, Bob, pretty soon," Reggie answered. "Just not quite yet, is all."

"Shoot, Bob, didn't you know?" said another wounded U.S. soldier, this one named Pete. "Reggie started escaping day before yesterday, but he's so damn slow, this is as far as he's gotten."

"You go to hell, too, Pete," Reggie said. He took care not to sound too angry, though; Pete's left leg was gone above the knee, blown off by a Confederate shell somewhere in Arkansas.

Bartlett sat on the edge of his bed and leaned his crutch against the wall next to it. That was the easy part. What came afterwards wasn't so easy. He used his sound right arm to help drag his wounded right leg up onto the mattress. The leg was getting better, too. But, while it was on the way, it hadn't arrived yet.

Once he was sitting with both legs out before him, he eased himself down flat onto his back. That hurt worse; the shoulder felt as if it had a toothache in there, a dull pain that never went away and sometimes flared to malevolent heights. Sweat sprang out on his forehead at the wound's bite. After he lay still for a while, it dropped back to a level he could bear more easily.

"You all right, Reggie?" Bob asked, tone solicitous as if Bartlett had been from Massachusetts or Michigan himself. Pain was the common foe here.

"Not too bad," Reggie said. "I'll tell you, though, this whole business of war would be a hell of a lot more fun if you didn't get shot."

That drew loud agreement from the Yankees on the other beds in the room. "They made the old fools who ordered this war go out and fight it, it never would've lasted five minutes," Bob said. "Tell me the truth, boys—is that so or isn't it?"

Again, most of the wounded men in the ward agreed. But Pete said, "I don't know about that. Roosevelt fought in the Second Mexican War when he was our age."

"Well, that's a fact—he did," Bob allowed. "He fought one medium-sized battle against the limeys, licked 'em, and they went home. That was plenty to make him a hero back then. We fight the Rebs or the Canucks, do they go home with their tails between their legs on account of we lick 'em once? We all know better'n that, don't we?"

"None of us'd be here if the bastards on the other side ran away quick," Pete said. He grinned. "Well, Reggie would, I reckon, but he don't count anyway."

"You damnyankees don't run, either, the way you did the last couple of times we fought you," Bartlett said, returning verbal fire. "Wish to Jesus you did. I wouldn't have these damn holes in me, and I'll tell you, I liked life a lot better before I got ventilated."

Out in the hallway, a faint squeak of wheels and rattle of crockery announced the coming of the lunch cart. As the wounded soldiers from both sides were united in their struggle against pain, so they were also united in their loathing of what the hospital fed them.

Reggie gagged down yet another meal of medium-boiled egg, beef broth, stewed prunes, and a pudding that tasted as if it were made from four parts library paste and one part sugar. When the nurse took away his dishes, she clicked her tongue between her teeth in reproof. "How do you expect to get better if you don't eat more?"

"Ma'am, if you give me beefsteak, I will eat a slab the size of this mattress and ask you kindly for seconds. If you give me fried chicken, I will build you a new wing to this hospital from the bones. If you give me pork chops, I will gobble them down till I grow a little curly tail. But ma'am, if you feed me slops you wouldn't give the pigs you got the pork chops from, I will waste away and perish."

"That's telling her, Reb!" one of the wounded U.S. soldiers said. Several others clapped their hands.

The nurse looked furious. "You are getting a nourishing meal suited to your digestion, and you ought to be grateful the United States are giving it to you instead of letting you starve the way you deserve."

"We have Yankee prisoners, too, ma'am," Bartlett said. "They get doctors. They get food, same as I do here. If they don't get better food than I do here, why, I'm sorry for 'em, and that's a fact."

He hadn't made a friend. The nurse set hands on hips. "You are getting exactly the same meal as wounded American soldiers," she said coldly.

"I'm an American," Bartlett said. "What do you think I am, a Chinaman?"

"A troublemaker," the nurse answered. By her expression, that was worse than a Chinaman, and by a good distance, too. She rolled the cart away from Reggie's bed. Her back still radiated outrage.

"Don't nobody hook the Reb's pudding tomorrow," Pete said when she was gone, "not unless you want to eat the glass ground up in it, too."

"Only thing ground-up glass would do for that pudding is make it better," Reggie said, and nobody seemed inclined to tell him he was wrong.

The next morning, Bob got promoted to a different ward, one a step closer to eventual release. In his place, an attendant wheeled in another Confederate prisoner—a Negro with a bandaged stump where his left foot should have been. He grunted with pain as he got into Bob's bed.

Nobody knew what to do or what to say. The wounded U.S. soldiers looked in Reggie Bartlett's direction. The U.S. Army still did not allow Negroes to serve, though they'd been able to join the U.S. Navy for years. In the CSA, the very idea of black men in uniform remained strange, though the pressure of fighting a larger, more populous foe had forced it on the ruling whites.

Reggie found one question he could safely ask: "Where did you get hit?" He had trouble figuring out what sort of tone to use. A lifetime's experience had taught him he was superior to any black man ever born. But this Negro was a fellow soldier, and they were both prisoners of the Yankees: hardly an exalted status.

"Outside o' Jonesboro, Arkansas," the newly arrived black answered. He also spoke cautiously. "How about you?"

"Over in Sequoyah, in the Red River bottomlands." Bartlett hesitated, then gave his name and said, "Who're you?"

"Rehoboam, my ma and pa called me, out o' the Good Book," the Negro said. He was very, very black, with a low, flat nose and small ears. Before he was wounded, he'd probably been strong and muscular; now his skin sagged, as it did on men who'd lost a lot of flesh in a hurry. After another moment's thought, he added, "Had me a stripe on my sleeve 'fore I got shot."

He said it in a way that made Bartlett believe him. It also made Reggie smile. "Can't pull rank on me, Rehoboam," he said. "I had one, too."

"We got the same rank now," Rehoboam said. "We's prisoners."

"Yeah, I was thinking the same thing," Reggie said, nodding. When he'd been in prison camp before, over in West Virginia, the Yankees had used captured Negro laborers to lord it over their white prisoners of war, and to spy on them, too. The blacks there had taken savage pleasure in doing just that, enjoying being on top instead of on the bottom.

Rehoboam didn't seem inclined to act like that. But he didn't act submissive, either, the way he surely would have back in the CSA. Bartlett didn't know what to make of him. The idea of simple equality with a Negro had never crossed his mind.

"Outside of Jonesboro, eh?" Pete said. "Craighead Forest?"

"Sure as the devil," Rehoboam answered. He looked over toward the U.S. soldier. "You?" After Pete nodded, the Negro went, "This great big old damnyankee officer was screamin' about God and Jesus an' I don't know what all else, an' he went an' shot me. He was runnin' way the hell out in front of his men—balls like an elephant, I reckon, but he was crazy, you ask me."

"I even think I know about the guy you mean," Pete said. "McSwenson, something like that. From what I've heard about him, you're right—he's nuts. Leastways you know who got you. That's something. Me, shell went off and the next thing I knew I was shy a pin." He patted his short stump.

One of the other wounded U.S. soldiers asked Rehoboam, "Were you a Red before you put on a Confederate uniform?"

"Maybe I was," Rehoboam answered, "but maybe I wasn't, too." He gave Reggie a sidelong look. "Nobody asked me nothin' about that when I went into the Army, so I don't reckon I got to talk about it now."

"Let's say you were," the Yank persisted. "How could you try and shoot the Rebs one day and then fight for 'em the next?"

"If I was—and I ain't sayin' I was, mind you—I would have

been tryin' to make the CSA a better place for me an' black folks to live in either which way," Rehoboam said. "Maybe that's why nobody asked me nothin' about none o' that when I walked into the recruitin' office."

Pete turned to Bartlett. "How about it, Reggie? How do you like havin' a smoke like Rehoboam fightin' on your side once you Rebs ran out of white men you could throw at us?"

"Hey, I'll tell you this much," Reggie said. "I'd sure as hell sooner have him shooting at you damnyankees than at me."

Now Rehoboam gave him a measuring stare. "That's fair," the Negro said. "I ain't got no trouble with that."

He spoke as if his opinion had as much weight as Reggie's. In terms of law in the Confederate States, Reggie realized, Rehoboam's opinion did have as much weight as his, or would. The black man would surely get an honorable discharge when repatriated, and that would make him a citizen of the CSA, not just a resident.

"How you feelin'?" Rehoboam asked Reggie.

"Leg's getting better," he answered. "They say the shoulder is, too, but damned if I can see it. How about you?"

"My damn toes itch," Rehoboam said, pointing to where they would be if still attached to the rest of him. "They ain't there, but they itch anyways."

"Oh, Lord, I know what you mean," Pete said. "I reach down to scratch sometimes, and I'm scratching air."

As a Negro, Rehoboam might not have fit into the ward. As a wounded man, he fit fine. Reggie Bartlett pondered that. He had a lot of time in which to ponder it, too. He wasn't going anywhere, certainly not very fast.

General Leonard Wood appeared before the House's Transportation Committee to testify about the difficulties in civilian railroad transport caused by the enormous demands the Army was putting on the rail system of the United States. As the chief of the U.S. General Staff droned on about millions of man-miles traveled, Flora Hamburger jotted the occasional note. Wood was forceful and intelligent, but she found his subject matter distinctly uninspiring.

She wished the Speaker of the House had assigned her to some other committee, but, since she was a Socialist without seniority, nobody—least of all the Speaker—cared about what she wished. But Transportation wasn't the worst committee, because so many types of legislation involved its subject in one way or another. She could have ended up on the Forestry Committee. *That* would have been a choice assignment for a representative from New York's Lower East Side!

Being the most junior member of the committee, and of a minority party to boot, she had to wait a long time for her turn to question General Wood. When at last it came, her first question was different from those the chief of the General Staff had been getting from other congressmen: "Why are the U.S. forces in the East so slow to adopt the mass use of barrels that has proved so effective in Tennessee?"

The chairman rapped loudly for order. "That question is not germane at this time, Miss Hamburger," he said. "It falls under the purview of the Military Affairs Committee, not our own."

"Mr. Taft, the question may not be germane to you, but it is very important to me," Flora answered. "My brother is a private, and he asked me in a letter to ask that question if I ever had that chance. I can introduce the letter into the record, if you like."

William Howard Taft's round, plump face—not at all suited to the upthrust Kaiser Bill mustache he wore—turned red. Flora hid a smile. If the chairman silenced her now, he would also be silencing a man in uniform, a man whom the Democrats' policies had put into uniform. That would give the Socialists all sorts of lovely ammunition; Flora could already imagine speeches on how the Democrats, not content with starting the war, were now concealing mistakes in how it was being fought.

Taft had been in Congress almost as long as Flora had been alive; he could figure out the angles, too. He turned to Wood. "If the general pleases, he may answer the question," he said unhappily.

"I will answer," Wood said, scratching at his gray mustache. "They have pioneered a new way of using barrels out in Tennessee. We had formerly employed a different doctrine throughout the Army. Now that the western way has shown itself to give better results, we are extending its use to other fronts. These things do take a certain amount of time, though, ma'am."

"So it would seem," Flora said. "Otherwise, you wouldn't have kept the—is *mistaken* too strong a word?—doctrine for the past year. Can you estimate how many men have died because of it?"

Congressman Taft looked unhappier still that he'd allowed the first question. Having allowed it, though, he could hardly shield Wood from the question. Jowls quivering, he nodded to the chief of the General Staff. "No, I cannot give any firm answer to that, ma'am," Wood said. "I can only tell you that we have, from the beginning, prosecuted this war to the best of our ability. We are but men. We have made mistakes. When we discover a better way of using any equipment, we take advantage of it. I regret the extra casualties we surely suffered because we did not know so much then as we do now. My training was as a physician. I regret any and all human suffering, believe me."

To her surprise, Flora did believe him. His long, mournful face and slow, deep voice made her have a hard time picturing him as a liar. Still, she persisted in her own line of questioning: "How did they happen to be right in Tennessee when all the best thinkers in the War Department were gathered together here in Philadelphia to come up with . . . the wrong answer?"

"Let me give you a comparison I think you'll understand, ma'am," General Wood said. "Suppose you're in a kitchen, and—"

Patronizing Flora Hamburger was not a good idea. "I've spent most of my time in factories and offices," she snapped. "I fear I don't know so much about kitchens." That was stretching a point; she'd helped her mother every day after getting home from work. But she was not about to let him treat her like a housewife instead of a U.S. Representative. "Please answer the question without kitchen comparisons."

"Yes, ma'am," Wood said crisply. If her pinning his ears back angered him, he didn't show it. "We designed the doctrine at the same time as we were designing the machines themselves. Any time you do something like that, you take the chance of not getting everything perfectly right. General Custer tried something different, it proved to work better than anything we'd done with the doctrine we had before, and we will take advantage of that from now on."

Flora nodded reluctantly. It was a good answer. Wood had spent a lot of time testifying before Congress. Representative Taft beamed with relief. "If the distinguished lady from New York has no further questions, we can—"

"I do have one more," Flora said. Taft sighed. Since members

of his own party had droned on and on over matters less conse-
quential than those concerning barrels, he could hardly shut her
off without raising howls from the Socialists. He held out his
hand to her, palm up, fingers spread, to show she could go on.
"Thank you, Mr. Chairman," she told him. "General Wood, if all
that you say is so, why did General Custer have to violate War
Department orders against using barrels in any way except that
prescribed by Philadelphia in order to prove that his ideas were
better than yours?"

She hoped he would deny any such orders existed. She knew
they did. Not many Socialists worked in the War Department, but
the ones who did had a way of keeping their Congressional dele-
gation well informed about the department's inner workings—
and its dirty laundry.

But Leonard Wood was too canny to let himself be caught in a
lie. He said, "Ma'am, we had done the best we could in Philadelphia. Do please recall, we did win victories with barrels used as
we suggested. Maybe we would have done better using them
from the start as General Custer did, but there are many other
possible ways to use them, too, most of which are likely to have
done worse than ours. The main reason we tried to forbid all ex-
perimentation with barrels is that, by the very nature of things,
most experiments fail. General Custer's happened to succeed,
and he deserves the credit for it, as he would deserve the blame
had it gone wrong."

By his tone, he thought Custer deserved blame anyhow. But
he could have plausibly denied that, and she had no documents
to make him out a liar there. "Anything else, Miss Hamburger?"
Congressman Taft asked. Flora shook her head. The fat Democrat got in a dig of his own: "Nothing actually pertaining to
trains?"

"Mr. Chairman, if the choice is between asking questions that
have to do with how crowded trains are and how safe my brother
is, I know which questions I want to ask," Flora said.

"I hope your brother stays safe, Miss Hamburger," General
Wood said. "Despite our gains, the fighting in Virginia has been
very hard."

"Thank you," she said. For a moment, she was surprised he
knew where David had been sent, but only for a moment. Soldiers who happened to be related to members of Congress no
doubt had special files high-ranking officers could check at need.

"Any further questions from anyone?" Taft asked. No one spoke. The chairman of the Transportation Committee asked another question: "Do I hear a motion to adjourn?" He did, and gaveled the session to a close.

Later, in her office, Flora was answering letters from constituents when her secretary came in and said, "General Wood would like to see you for a few minutes, ma'am."

"Send him right in, Bertha," Flora said. "I wonder what he wants." She wondered if she'd struck a nerve with her questions about barrels. If he complained about those, she'd send him away with a flea in his ear.

Into the inner office he strode, erect, soldierly. The first words out of his mouth surprised her: "You did a good job of raking me over the coals there earlier this afternoon. One of these days, we'll sift all the Socialist sneaks out of the War Department, but it isn't likely to be any time soon."

She didn't want to thank him, but he'd succeeded in disarming some of the hostility she felt. "You didn't come here just to tell me that," she said.

"No, I didn't," he answered. "I came here to tell you again that I wish all the best for your brother. The 91st is a good unit, and they've compiled a record that will stand up against anyone's."

"I wish they'd never had to compile that kind of record—or any other kind of record, for that matter," Flora said.

"I understand," General Wood answered. Flora must have raised an eyebrow, for he went on, "I do. Soldiers fight wars; they know what goes into them. Glory is what happens afterwards, what civilians make up."

"Not much glory will come out of this war, even afterwards," Flora said. "Hard to squeeze glory out of mud and lice and bullets and shells flying every which way."

Wood surprised her again by nodding. "Maybe that means we won't fight another one for a long time. I hope to heaven it does." He paused, rubbed at his mustache, and finally went on, "Your brother—David, isn't it?—yes, David, has already made more than an honorable contribution to our cause and to our ultimate victory. If he were to request a transfer to, say, a clerical position or one of the supply services, I think that request would be likely to receive favorable attention."

"More favorable than if a seamstress' daughter put in the same request?" Flora asked. The chief of the General Staff did not answer, which was an answer in itself. Almost despairingly, Flora said, "You put me in an impossible position, you know. If I keep him safe, I take unfair advantage of who I am. If I don't, and anything happens to him . . . I think you had better go."

General Wood got to his feet. "I am sorry, Miss Hamburger," he said. "I hoped to ease your mind, not to upset you. Good day."

Out he strode, shoulders back, spine straight. Flora stared after him. She didn't believe him. He was too intelligent not to have understood every bit of what he was doing. He'd done it anyhow. Why? Just to upset her? Or to gain whatever advantage he could if she asked him to help David? "Damn you, General Wood," she muttered. "Damn you."

Anne Colleton crouched in the brush that had advanced from the woods toward the ruins of the Marshlands mansion. With her crouched not only a squad of local militiamen but also a machine-gun team from somewhere down by Charleston. She'd almost had to go down on her knees in front of the governor to get them, but they were here. If he'd asked her to go down on her knees in front of him when they were all alone, she'd have thought about doing that, too. That was how much she wanted to make sure her trap slammed shut hard.

In a back pocket of her mannish trousers, she had a torn, dirty scrap of paper with a few words written in a crisp, elegant hand that did not match its stationery. If what Scipio told her was true . . .

If it wasn't true, she was either wasting her time here or walking into a trap rather than setting one. Just for a moment, her hand fell to the barrel of the scope-sighted Tredegar beside her. Any trap that tried closing on her would take some damage first.

Off on the left of the little line, Sergeant Willie Metcalfe stiffened and let out a low hiss. As if afraid that wouldn't be enough, he turned his head so that he presented the ruined left half of his face to his comrades. "Here they come," he said in a hoarse whisper.

"Don't open up too soon," Anne ordered the militiamen. She'd said it before. She would say it again: "Let them get close. Let them get busy. And then . . ." Her voice, still soft, turned savage. "Let them have it."

She stared avidly through the brush, north toward the Congaree. The ground—the ground that should have been covered with cotton instead of overrun by weeds—steamed as the sun rose higher and burned down on it. Through that thin, shimmering mist, she too made out the Negroes heading for the mansion.

They were a ragged lot, ragged and filthy, but they carried themselves like fighting men. Their strides were quick and wary. Their heads never stopped moving. She froze whenever they looked toward her, and hoped her companions had the sense to do the same. The militiamen, she feared, weren't in the same class as the men of the Congaree Socialist Republic. If they kept the advantage of surprise, they wouldn't need to be.

Some of the Negroes carried spades, some rifles, most both. One in particular stalked along like a beast of prey in spite of the Tredegar on his shoulder. *His* shoulder? Anne took a longer look at that Red rebel.

"Cherry," she whispered. Her lips drew back from her teeth in a smile so ferocious that Linus Ashforth, who crouched beside her, involuntarily flinched away, as from a wild beast. Anne never noticed the white-bearded militiaman. Her attention remained altogether focused on the Negro woman who had been first her brother's lover and then, as the Red revolt began, the instrument of Jacob Colleton's death.

She didn't need long to realize that, as she led the militiamen, Cherry bossed the Negroes. She bossed them imperiously, bullying them into doing exactly as she required. *Bitch. Hateful bitch,* Anne thought, never noticing how much Cherry's style resembled her own.

"We done tried over yonder, dat side o' the mansion." Cherry's voice floated across a hundred yards of open ground. "Now we tries on dis side." She led the Reds over toward the side where Anne and the militiamen waited. "Dig, you damn lazy niggers. Dig!" She set down the rifle and grabbed a spade herself.

They dug with her. Few would have been bold enough to argue. Cassius would have, but Cassius wasn't here. Anne let out a silent sigh. Had Scipio handed her Cherry and Cassius both, she might even have thought about forgiving him. But Cherry by herself was no small prize.

"At my signal," Anne whispered to Linus Ashforth and to the man to her left. "Pass it along the line." They did. She picked up her rifle. She didn't aim at Cherry, not yet. The militiamen stirred, picking their own targets.

Cherry was as alert as a beast of prey, too. She caught some tiny motion in the brush and let out a cry of alarm.

At the same instant, Anne shouted, "Now!" She fired at one of the men who'd just thrown down a shovel and was turning to grab for his rifle. The turn only half completed, he slumped bonelessly to the ground, blood pouring from a wound in his flank.

All along the line of militiamen, rifles barked. The machine gun hammered away like a mad thing. A couple of the Reds managed to fall flat, get hold of their rifles, and fire back. Their fire did not last long. Methodical as factory workers, the machine gunners traversed the muzzle of their weapon back and forth. Nothing on the ground in front of them could stay unhit for long.

Seeing how things were, Cherry turned and ran. Anne had run once, too, when revolution broke out around her in Charleston. She'd escaped. Cherry was not so lucky. Anne peered through the telescopic sight, which made her target seem even closer than it was—and Cherry would have been an easy shot for someone less handy with a rifle than she was. She exhaled. She pulled the trigger. The Tredegar kicked against her shoulder. Cherry toppled with a shriek.

Anne started to break cover, then hesitated. One or more of the Negroes the militiamen had shot down were liable to be shamming. Beside her, Linus Ashforth did stand up. Sure as hell, a bullet cracked past his head. It could as easily have shattered his skull like a dropped flowerpot. He dove for cover. The machine gun hosed down the Reds. When Willie Metcalfe got to his feet, no one fired at him.

"Let's see what we've got," Anne said coldbloodedly. Now she rose.

"That one ain't finished yet, ma'am." Sergeant Metcalfe pointed in the direction of Cherry, who was still trying to crawl away with a shattered lower leg. He started to raise his own rifle.

"No!" Anne's voice was sharp. "I want her alive. You men!" She waved to the rest of the squad, then pointed in the direction of the Reds who had been digging. "See to them. If any of them are still breathing, finish them off."

She loped toward Cherry. Behind her, a couple of short, flat cracks rang out. Nodding in satisfaction, she trotted on. She had a round in the chamber of her Tredegar, and was ready and more than ready to fire if the colored woman had a pistol tucked in the pocket or waistband of her tattered dungarees.

Cherry snarled hatred at her, but made no move to reach for a weapon. "White debbil bitch," she said. "They was right all along, damn them. You never was nothin' but a goddamn liar."

"You know all about lies, don't you?" Anne said evenly. "You told enough of them, back before the rebellion."

"I ain't never told lies like you 'pressors tell de niggers and de poor stupid buckra and your ownselves," Cherry retorted. She gathered herself, though blood was puddling around her right calf.

"Don't try it," Anne advised her. "I'm too far away for you to reach me, and I won't shoot you in the head. I'll try for somewhere that hurts more and takes longer. Kidney, maybe, or one in each shoulder."

To her surprise, Cherry nodded. "Ain't a patch on what I do to you, I had you down shot on de ground."

The longing in the black woman's voice made Anne shiver, though she was the one with the rifle. She said, "After what you did to Marshlands, after what you did to my brother, you've had your turn already."

"Ain't." Cherry shook her head. "Ain't come close. Cain't pay back three hundred years o' 'pression in a day. Done whipped we and 'sploited we and sold we like we was horses and fucked we till we gots so many yaller niggers it's a cryin' shame. No, we ain't come close."

Anne heard the words. She heard the accusations. They didn't register, not in any way that mattered. She shook her head. "You rose up against us," she said. "You stabbed us in the back while we were fighting the damnyankees. And you—you—" When she tried to say what Cherry in particular had done, words failed her for one of the rare times in her life.

Despite the pain from her ruined lower leg, Cherry smiled. "I knows what I done, Miss Anne. I was fuckin' and suckin' your brother, and I was puttin' on airs on account of it. And you knows what else?" The smile got wider. "All the time that goddamn skinny little white dick was in me, Miss Anne, I never feel one thing. Never oncet."

Without conscious thought, ahead of conscious thought, Anne's finger squeezed the trigger. The Tredegar roared. The back of Cherry's head exploded, splashing blood and brains and pulverized bone over her and the ground around her. She twitched and shuddered and lay still. But, below the neat hole in her forehead, her face still held that mocking smile.

"To hell with you," Anne whispered, and two tears ran down her face, half sorry for Jacob, half fury at the black woman and the way she'd duped him and used him. And Cherry had got the last word, too, and goaded Anne into giving her a quick end at the same time. Anne kicked at the dirt. Automatically, she worked the bolt and chambered a fresh round.

Linus Ashforth came up to her. The elderly militiaman spat a stream of tobacco juice into Cherry's puddled blood. "This here was right good, ma'am," he said. "Them murderin' devils done took the bait you left 'em, and there ain't a one of 'em going back to the swamps. Yes, ma'am, this here was pretty blame fine."

"It wasn't good enough," Anne said, as much to herself as to the old man. "It wasn't enough."

"What more could you want?" Ashforth asked reasonably. "Every single nigger stuck his nose out of the swamp is dead now. Can't do much better'n a clean sweep, now can you?"

"But there are still Reds *in* the swamps," Anne answered. "When they're all hunted down and killed, that will be—" She started to say *enough*, but shook her head before the word passed her lips. That wouldn't be enough. Nothing could be enough to repair the damage the Negroes had done to the Confederate cause, the damage they had done to the Confederate States. She ended the sentence in a different way: "That will be a start, anyhow."

Linus Ashforth's whistle was soft and low and wondering. "Ma'am, don't sound to me like you'll ever be satisfied."

"I would have been," Anne said. "I could have been. God, I *was*. But it will be a long time before I'm satisfied again; you're right about that. It will be a long time before this is a country anyone can be satisfied with."

"Jesus God, Miss Anne, I'm sure as the dickens glad you ain't mad with *me*." The militiaman spat again, then wiped his mouth on his sleeve.

"You ought to be," Anne Colleton said. She weighed the words, then nodded. "Yes, you ought to be, because if I'm angry at something, I'll hunt it down and kill it." She looked north, toward the Congaree. Silently, her lips shaped a name. *Cassius*.

* * *

Like so many small, hunted creatures, Nellie Semphroch had learned to stay laired up in her burrow, and to come out at night to forage. The occupying Confederates hardly bothered to patrol Washington, D.C., any more. Hal Jacobs said they'd given up because every man they had, they needed at the front. Nellie didn't know about that. She did know that getting water from the Potomac or firewood from a wrecked building, she worried more about a chance U.S. shell than she did about men in butternut. Even at night, the bombardment from the north did not halt. It only slowed a little.

She was far from the only one prowling the night. If she passed close enough to Jacobs and a few others to recognize them, she would nod. When she saw others, she shrank back into the shadows, and that though she never ventured forth without a long, sharp kitchen knife. Still others shrank from her. That made her feel oddly strong and fierce.

Sometimes Edna would come out with her, sometimes not. When they needed water, they generally went down to the river together. Stove wood was easier to come by close to home. One of them would usually go out for it, or else the other.

"I wish we could find some coal," Nellie said, not for the first time. "The grate isn't really right for wood, and the stove pipe will get all full of soot and creosote. It's liable to catch on fire."

"If you're going to wish, Ma, don't waste your time wishing for coal, for God's sake," Edna said. "Wish for a couple days without shells falling all the damn time. That'd be somethin' really worth having."

"I think we may get that wish before too long," Nellie said. "How much longer do you suppose the Confederate lines north of town are going to be able to stand the pounding the Army is giving them? They'll have to crack pretty soon, and then the United States will have Washington back again."

"Oh, bully!" Edna loaded her voice with sarcasm. "Even if you're right, Ma, it'll only take 'em a hundred years to build it all back up the way it was. And the Rebs'll fight hard to keep the place, too."

"I know they will—it's about the only part of the line where they're still on our soil instead of the other way round," Nellie said. "But when you look at the way the war is going everywhere else, it's hard to see how they're going to be able to do it."

"Well, what if the United States do come in?" Edna said. "Then the Rebs will pound the city to pieces from the other side of the Potomac. The only difference will be which way the guns are pointed."

Nellie sighed and nodded in the candlelit dimness of the cellar under the coffeehouse. Her daughter's guess held an unpleasant feel of truth.

After it got dark outside as well as down in the cellar, Nellie went out to see what she could find and to discover what the bombardment had knocked flat since the last time she came up above ground. One of the things that wasn't flat any more was the street down the block from the coffeehouse. A big shell had dug an enormous crater in it. Time was when such wounds had been rare and the Confederates patched them as soon as they were made. Now the Rebs kept a few roads to the front open and forgot the rest.

Half a block farther along the street, another couple of shells had landed, converting several houses and shops to rubble. In among the bricks would be lumber, much of it already broken into convenient lengths. Nellie tossed them into a large canvas duffel bag.

She had the bag nearly ready to drag back to the coffeehouse when Bill Reach's voice spoke from out of the darkness close by: "Evenin', Little Nell."

Ice ran through Nellie, though the night was warm and humid. "You're drunk again," she said quietly. "If you were sober, you'd know better than to call me that." Her head went back and forth, back and forth. Where was he?

He laughed. "Maybe I am. Maybe I would. And maybe I'm not, and maybe I wouldn't. What do you think of that?"

There. Behind that pile of bricks, out of which stuck a couple of legs from an upended cast-iron stove. Her fingers closed around the handle of the kitchen knife. "Go away," she said, still looking around as if she hadn't found him. "Can't you just leave me in peace?"

"I sure as hell would like a piece," he said, and laughed again. "I liked it when I had it before, and I know I'd like it again. Oh, you were a hot number in between the sheets, Little Nell, and I don't figure God ever gave another woman in the whole wide world a nastier mouth. Things you used to do . . ."

If she'd writhed with grunting, sweating customers pounding

away atop her, it was only to make them finish faster, get off her, and leave the cheap little room where she worked. She'd always hated sucking on men's privates. It seemed filthy, even when they didn't squirt vile-tasting jism into her mouth—usually after promising they wouldn't.

"Go away," she repeated. "Those days are long gone, thank God. I'm a respectable woman now—or I was till you walked into my coffeehouse, anyways. Go back into the gutter, go back to spying, go wherever you want, just as long as you leave me alone. I don't want anything to do with you, do you hear?"

He stood up. In his black coat and black derby, he was still hard to see. He swayed a little, then brought a bottle to his lips. Oddly, the whiskey seemed to steady him instead of making him keel over. "But I want somethin' to do with you, Little Nell," he said. "You haven't given it to me, so it looks like I'm just gonna have to go and take it." He smashed the fat end of the bottle on the bricks. A little whiskey spilled out—not much. Jagged edges glittered under the stars. "Just gonna have to go ahead and take it," he repeated.

"Go away," Nellie whispered once more.

"You take what's coming to you, and everything will be fine." Bill Reach waved the bottle around. "You give me any trouble, and you'll be real sorry. Yes, you will. Real sorry. Now get down on the ground and take it. Once it's in there, you'll love it. Hell, you always did."

"No." Nellie held the knife behind her back so Reach wouldn't be able to see it.

The acrid fumes of the whiskey, some from his breath, some from the inside of the bottle, made her nostrils twitch as he came closer. "You ain't runnin'," he said. "You ain't screamin'. See? You know you want it. I'm the man to give it to you, too. If you're good, I'll even pay you, same as old times."

"No," Nellie said again. Either he didn't hear her or he didn't listen. He took a couple more steps toward her, then extended his left hand to push her to the ground.

He still held the neck of the bottle, but he didn't think he'd have to do anything with it. He'd surely made a lot of mistakes in his time, but that was the last and the worst. Nellie had no experience as a knife fighter, but Bill Reach couldn't have stopped a two-year-old swinging a wooden spoon right then. The knife went deep into the left side of his chest. Its edge grated against a rib when Nellie yanked it out and rammed it home again.

He let out a brief, bubbling shriek, then toppled. Nellie wiped the knife clean on his coat while he was still feebly kicking. "Once it's in there, you'll love it," she said. Then she grunted as she picked up the duffel full of chunks of wood, slung it over her shoulder, and headed for home.

When she got back, Edna was mixing salt pork into canned soup. "That looks like a good load, Ma," her daughter said. "You were gone a while longer than I thought you would be, though. You have any trouble out there?"

"Trouble?" Nellie shook her head. "Not a bit. That soup smells good."

"Make you thirsty as all get-out," Edna said.

"I know. It still smells good." Nellie had a big bowl. The soup did make her thirsty, so she drank a glass of boiled river water. She went down to the cellar to sleep, and had a better night than she'd enjoyed in years.

Artillery started thundering before dawn, but didn't wake her right away. Neither she nor anyone else left in Washington would have got any sleep at all if they'd let shellfire unduly disturb them. When she did wake, she gauged the bombardment with a practiced ear. So did Edna, who said, "They're pounding the front line right now."

Half an hour or so later, though, the pattern of the shelling abruptly changed. Rounds began falling inside Washington, along the routes the Confederates used to move reinforcements through the city toward the front. "I wonder if the Army is trying to break through the Rebs' trenches right now," Nellie said.

"Do you really think they can?" Edna asked. "The Confederates have been digging and putting in concrete and wire ever since they got here, and that's going on three years now."

"Would they try if they didn't think they could do it, anyway?" Nellie asked in return. Her daughter only shrugged in return, which was, when you got down to it, a reasonable enough answer. From the perspective of a coffeehouse, who could know what the U.S. General Staff had in mind?

But then, a couple of hours later, Nellie heard a rattle of small-arms fire, rifles and machine guns, off to the north. Edna recognized it for what it was, too. She let out a soft whistle. "Haven't hardly heard that since the Confederates drove the USA out of here."

"Sure haven't," Nellie agreed. "As long as we have water and fuel, I think we'd better stay right where we're at. If it was bad outside before, it's going to be worse now, with both sides shelling the city and with bullets flying around along with the shells."

They did sneak out for water one night. Other than that, they stayed inside the coffeehouse all the time for the next several days, and down in the cellar whenever they weren't at the stove. The battle for Washington raged around them. They saw almost none of it, which suited Nellie. If she'd seen the battle, the soldiers fighting it would have seen her, with consequences ranging from unpleasant to lethal.

A couple of times, barrels rumbled up the street. Nellie thought they belonged to the CSA, but she didn't go outside to look. Two days later, somebody—she didn't know who, and again didn't care to find out—set up a machine-gun post just down the street and fired off belt after belt of ammunition, the gun roaring like a demented jackhammer. Then came rifle fire and running, shouting men. After that, the racket of small arms sounded from the south, not the north.

Several hours of relative calm were shattered when somebody pounded on the cellar door with a rifle butt. "You the Semphrochs down there?" a deep voice shouted. "Nellie and, uh, Edna?" He sounded as if he might be reading the names from a list.

"Yes," Nellie said, and went up the stairs and pushed the door open.

She found herself staring down a rifle barrel. The soldier holding the rifle wore a green-gray uniform that was familiar and a pot-shaped helmet that wasn't. "Nellie Semphroch," he said—sure enough, he had a list. "You and your daughter are the ones who had the coffeehouse where the damn Rebs came all the damn time."

"But—" Nellie began.

He talked right through her: "Come out, both of you. You're under arrest. Charges are collaboration and treason."

"Come on, men," Gordon McSweeney called as his company trudged wearily down an Arkansas dirt road. "Come on. I will not have you go any place I will not go myself in front of you. What I can do, you can also do. What I can do, you *will* also do— or you will answer to me."

Nobody argued with him. Nobody had argued with him since the day Captain Schneider fell in the Craighead Forest. Schneider, McSweeney feared, had been translated to a clime warmer than this one. That was a warm climate indeed; as both summer and the edge of the Mississippi delta grew closer with every passing moment, the muggy heat made McSweeney feel as if his uniform tunic and trousers had been pasted to his hide.

He'd remained in command of the company since the fight in the Craighead Forest. He'd also remained a second lieutenant. A sergeant was commanding one of the other companies in the regiment, and nobody seemed to be making any noise about replacing him, either. Officers didn't grow on trees, especially not west of the Mississippi they didn't.

"Pick 'em up," McSweeney called to the troopers shambling along under the weight of helmet and Springfield and heavy pack and entrenching tool and clodhopper boots and however much mud clung to the boots. "If God grant that we pierce their forces but once more, we can bring Memphis and the Mississippi River under our guns. That would be a great blow to strike, and a sore hurt to the wicked cause of the Confederate States."

"You talk like something right out of the Bible, sir," said a private named Rogers who had not been in the section or platoon McSweeney led before getting the whole company.

"It is the word of God," McSweeney answered. "Is a man not wise to shape his words in the pattern of those of his Father?"

Rogers didn't answer. He just kept marching. That suited Gordon McSweeney fine. Even if he had the words of the Good Book on which to model his own, he was more comfortable doing than talking. Men could easily argue what he said. No one could argue about what he did.

Spatters of gunfire off to the right said the Confederates were trying to slow down the U.S. advance any way they could. The gunfire wasn't close enough for him to swing his men out of their line of march to respond to it, so he kept them going. After U.S. forces finally forced the Rebs out of Jonesboro, the front had grown fluid for a change. The more ground he made his men cover, the closer they would be to Memphis.

Up ahead, one of those Rebel copies of a French 75 started

banging away. McSweeney muttered something under his breath that would have been a curse had he permitted himself to take the name of the Lord in vain. Like every U.S. infantryman who had ever advanced against them, he hated those quick-firing field guns. This one, fortunately, was shooting long, over the heads of his company. Officers who hadn't pushed their men so hard would have to worry about explosives and shrapnel balls and shell fragments.

The road led out of the woods and into a clearing, near the center of which stood a farmhouse. Rifle fire came from the farmhouse. McSweeney's smile was broad and welcoming. "All right, men," he said. "If they want to play, we can play with them. Let's see how they like the game then."

Past that, he needed to give very few orders. The men knew what needed doing, and did it without undue fuss or bother. Fire-and-move tactics that had taken them through the heavily fortified forest were perhaps wasted against a farmhouse with a few diehards in it, but the U.S. soldiers used them even so. Some went left, some went right. Before long, they had worked in close enough to pitch grenades through the windows of the house.

McSweeney wished for his flamethrower. How the faded pine timbers of this place would have burned! Then a fire started anyhow, whether from grenades or bullets he could not tell. A couple of men in butternut burst out the front door. They weren't surrendering; they came out shooting. A fusillade of lead stretched them lifeless in the dust.

One of them was white, the other colored. McSweeney looked down at the Negro's bleeding corpse and shook his head. "If black men will fight for the government that for so long has mistreated their kind, they deserve whatever that government gives them," he said. "When they rose in revolt against their masters, I admired them. If they fight for those masters . . . they will pay the price, as this one has."

After the brief interruption, the company moved on. A few Confederates fired at them from out of the bushes. They hunted the Rebs, though McSweeney, to his disgust, thought a couple of them got away.

Then came an interruption of a different sort. McSweeney had long since grown used to shells from field guns screeching their way through the sky. It had been a long time, though, since he'd heard a roar of cloven air like this one. Altogether without conscious thought, he threw himself flat.

The great shell burst fifty yards off to the left. Even as dirt thudded down onto his back and fragments hissed malevolently through the air, another shell thundered home, this one striking about twenty-five yards to the right of the road.

Some men were down as McSweeney was, to gain what little shelter they could from those enormous rounds. Others were down and screaming or wailing, clutching arms or legs or bellies. Others were down and not moving at all, nor would they ever move again.

"They aren't supposed to have this kind of firepower way the hell out here!" somebody shouted. "Those have to be eight-inch, maybe ten-inch, shells." Even as he spoke, two more of the big shells thundered in. More screams rose.

Busy with his entrenching tool, McSweeney forgot to reprove the soldier for cursing. Suddenly, the answer blazed in him. "River monitors!" he exclaimed. "They shelled us when we crossed the Ohio. This must be another one. If our own boats could get down as far as Memphis, we wouldn't have been fighting our way through Arkansas all these months."

Another pair of shells burst not far away. "What can we do, sir?" a soldier cried.

"Pray," McSweeney answered. He would have said that under most circumstances. It seemed particularly fitting here. "What else can we do, when no guns of ours are able to reach those aboard the Confederate river monitor?"

As he spoke, he dug himself deeper into the soft, dark brown soil. The unwounded men in the company did the same. So did some of the wounded men. After almost three years of war, digging entrenchments was altogether natural. McSweeney had known men safe behind their own lines to dig foxholes before settling down to sleep for the night. He'd done it himself a couple of times.

Up ahead, a Confederate machine gun started barking. If the river monitor hadn't halted McSweeney's troops, they would have run into it in short order—and it would have done them about as much damage as the big guns on the Mississippi were doing.

Most company commanders would have sent scouts forward to examine the enemy machine-gun position. That never entered

Gordon McSweeney's mind. He scrambled out of the foxhole he had dug just as another pair of shells from the river monitor landed near the position his company had taken. More dirt rained down on him. Even after he stuck a finger in one ear, it didn't hear so well as it should have.

He wriggled forward. One thing was different now that the U.S. Army had finally pushed the Rebs out of their lines in front of Jonesboro: not so much barbed wire on the ground to hamper movement. Grass and shrubs gave plenty of cover, too, and his muddy green-gray uniform made him hard to spot as he scooted toward the machine gun.

No concrete emplacement here. The Rebs were set up in a nest of sandbags. All the same, McSweeney bit his lip in frustration. Even if he picked off all the gunners, who seemed to have no idea he was anywhere close by, more Confederates would take over the weapon. He shrugged a tiny shrug. That might do. The new Rebels at the machine gun wouldn't be a regular crew, and wouldn't shoot so effectively.

He was just bringing his rifle up to his shoulder when firing off to his right made the Confederates turn the gun in that direction and start blazing away at his countrymen who were trying to advance over there. With the Rebs thus distracted, McSweeney put a bullet through the head of one of them. When the other one, the one who fed belts into the machine gun, half rose to check his friend, McSweeney drilled him, too. Both Confederate soldiers slumped down. He thought they were both dead.

His member throbbed. Save for an annoyed mutter too low to make sense even to himself, he ignored it. He waited for more Confederates to come forward and take over the gun. They didn't. It sat there, silent. He muttered again, this time intelligibly: "Fools."

He crawled to within sixty or seventy yards of it, where the cover petered out. Then he wasn't crawling. He was running, in great bounding leaps. A couple of startled shouts rose. A few bullets cracked past him. None bit, though. He dove over the wall of sandbags, knocked the Confederate corpses out of the way, and manhandled the machine gun around so that it bore on the surviving Rebs farther east. Grinning from ear to ear, he gave them a taste of their own medicine.

Before long, his own men came hurrying up to support him. "Good to see you," he said, not intentionally ironic.

Ben Carlton shook his head. "When that machine gun turned around, uh, sir," the cook said, "I knew you'd got to it some kind of way. You've done it too damn often for me even to be real surprised about it any more."

"Do not blaspheme," McSweeney said, almost automatically. "I do my duty. And here, if not in your cookery, you have done yours. Let us push on against the foe. With God's help, victory shall indeed be ours at last."

XII

Sergeant Jake Featherston cursed a blue streak. The surviving guns of his battery, along with the rest of those belonging to the First Richmond Howitzers, perched on Sudley Mountain, a little east of Centreville, Virginia. From those low hills, they could have wreaked fearful havoc on the Yankees farther west, over near the small stream called Bull Run—if they'd had any ammunition.

A runner came up to Featherston. "Sir, uh, Sergeant, I mean, the wagons will be here in an hour or so, headquarters says."

Could looks have killed, the messenger would have been deader than if a twelve-inch shell from a battleship had gone off under his feet. "They should have been here this morning, God damn it," Featherston ground out. "What the fucking hell happened to them?"

The runner stared. He took a lot of abuse: a big part of his job was telling people of superior rank they couldn't have what they wanted and what they thought they were entitled to. Featherston's words were nothing out of the ordinary. The icy vitriol of the tone was. It might have come from an irate colonel, not a sergeant running a battered battery.

"Sergeant, they got tangled up with a division of infantry on the march, so after that they needed a good long while to get unraveled again."

"Do you think the damnyankees don't care that the Army of Northern Virginia doesn't know what in Christ's name it's doing?" Jake snapped. "Maybe they do care—enough to send us a big thank-you bouquet."

"I've given you the news I have, Sergeant," the runner said, and went on his way. Having other duty let him escape Featherston's fury; it wasn't as if Jake were his commanding officer.

Out came the Gray Eagle scratch pad and *Over Open Sights.* *The white-bearded fools in Richmond are doing their best to make sure that we lose this war,* Featherston wrote, *though we had victory straight ahead of us. Now they give the niggers guns to try to put their own blundering to rights, even though it was the niggers who helped stick us in this mess in the first place. And white troops would never have let themselves get fouled up with ammunition wagons like that.* The messenger hadn't said whether the troopers who'd cause his problem were white or black. He drew his own conclusions.

"When you first started keeping those notes, Sergeant," someone said behind Featherston, "I never thought you would keep on with them. I seem to have been mistaken."

Automatically, Jake closed the cover of the notebook. What he wrote in there was *his,* nobody else's. "Major Potter, sir," he said now, "I got nothing better to do than write, on account of I can't go pasting the damnyankees the way I want to, on account of God may know where the ammunition is, but I sure don't."

Clarence Potter sighed. "I wish you could paste them, but that you can't may matter less than you think. They are building up for another large push against us. If you have the ammunition you'll need to help stop that, well and good. If not . . ." He didn't go on.

"If not, we're in too much trouble for anything to matter. That's what you're saying, isn't it, sir?"

"That's what I'm saying." Potter studied him. "I never have figured out exactly how smart you are, Featherston, but you've made it plain you're shrewd enough and to spare. If you hadn't made the fatal mistake of being right at the wrong time, we might have the same rank by now."

Maybe he meant that to console Jake. It didn't; it made him furious. "Best way to save the country I can think of, sir, would be for a Yankee bomber to put three or four heavy ones right on top of the War Department. That might do it. Can't think of anything else that would."

The intelligence officer shook his head. "All things considered, they've done about as well as anyone could have expected."

"God help us if that's so," Featherston said. "We'd better make peace in a hurry, before the damn fools do something even worse than they have already. Don't know what that could be, but I reckon they'd come up with something."

"You *are* shrewd." Behind their metal-rimmed spectacles, Major Potter's eyes widened slightly. "There are people in the Army and people in the government beginning to say the same thing. If Britain is forced to leave the war, if we have to face not just the whole U.S. Army but the whole U.S. Navy, less whatever part keeps fighting Japan in the Pacific—if that happens, the odds against us grow very long."

"Odds were long during the War of Secession, too," Jake said. "We licked the Yankees twice over by Manassas Gap. We'd lick 'em again if only that damned ammunition would ever get here."

"We had help then," Potter said. "Without it, I think we should have lost."

"One way or another, we'd have licked them." Featherston didn't know whether that was likely to be true or just his own stubbornness talking. "We'd be licking them now if the damn niggers hadn't risen up and stabbed us in the back."

"I wonder," Clarence Potter said. "I do wonder. We'd be better off than we are, no doubt, but would we be winning? The last two times we fought the United States, we won fairly quickly, before they committed everything they had to the struggle. We failed to do that this time, and they are fully committed to the fight—and they have more to commit to it than we do."

As if to underscore his words, a flight of U.S. aeroplanes buzzed by overhead. No C.S. fighting scouts rose to answer them. Aeroplanes were mere annoyances, but Jake was sick of being annoyed without having the chance to return the favor. At long last, a couple of antiaircraft guns opened up on the Yankees. They scored no hits. They hardly ever did.

Potter went on, "And speaking of our colored troops, do I hear correctly that you opened up on them with canister during the re-treat from Round Hill?"

"Hell, yes, you heard that straight," Featherston said defiantly. "If they ain't more afraid of us than they are of the damn-yankees, they won't do us any good, will they? They were run-ning from the enemy, sir, and it was the only way I had to make 'em stop."

"Some of them will never run from the enemy again, that's certain—or toward him, either," Major Potter said. "Some of their white officers and noncoms sent complaints about what you did to Army of Northern Virginia headquarters. You might have faced a court-martial if others had not spoken out on your behalf."

"Surprised I didn't any which way," Jake said. "There's a big raft of officers who don't love me a whole hell of a lot."

"Really?" Potter raised an eyebrow. "I hadn't noticed." Featherston, who didn't know what to make of such understated irony, started to boil till the intelligence officer raised a hand and went on, "That's a joke, Sergeant. I am happy to be able to tell you that I was able to deflect the complaints and make sure none of them went on to Richmond."

"Thank you for that much, sir," Jake said. Potter *was* a decent sort, as far as officers went. But Featherston hated being in anyone's debt. He especially hated being in an officer's debt.

"You've had a few bad turns come your way," Potter said. "Seems only right to even things up as we can."

There he stood, smug and sweatless in the muggy heat. *Yes, you're a lord,* Featherston thought. *You can throw the poor peasant a crust of bread and never miss it.* In that moment, he might have come close to understanding what had driven the Negroes of the CSA to rise up late in 1915. But he never thought—he never would have thought—to compare his situation to theirs.

Before the comparison could have occurred to him, the first ammunition wagon arrived, too late to suit him but still sooner than the runner had said. Forgetting his resentment of Potter, he took out on the wagon driver the older anger he still felt, cursing him up one side and down the other. The driver, a lowly private first class, had to sit there and take it.

Finally having ammunition in his hands, though, let Jake work out resentment with something more than words. In mere minutes, the four guns he had left were banging away at the Yankees. The range was too long to let him see individual U.S. soldiers, but he could make out the boil and stir as shells slammed down among them. A man dropping rocks on a nest of ants below his second-story window could not see any of the individual bugs, either, but he could watch the nest boil and stir.

Clarence Potter, who spent most of the war back at the Army of Northern Virginia headquarters, also looked on with benign approval. "Make them sting," he told Jake. "The higher the price they pay, the likelier they are to let us have the sort of peace we can live with."

"I don't give a damn about a peace we can live with," Featherston snarled, adjusting the elevation screw on his field gun. "Only thing I give a damn about is killing the sons of bitches." He raised his voice to a shout: "Fire!" Michael Scott jerked the lanyard. The cannon roared. Out flew the shell casing. In went another shell.

A man dropping rocks on a nest of ants did not have to worry that the ants would try to drop rocks on him, too. The guns of Featherston's battery enjoyed no such immunity. Before long, U.S. artillery began replying. Shells did not come in so often as he sent them out, but they came from bigger pieces—four- and six-inch guns—firing from a range he could not hope to match. Since he could not match it, he ignored the fire, and continued to pepper the closer U.S. infantry, whom he could hit.

"You're cool about this business," Major Potter said. For a man unused to coming under shellfire, he was pretty cool himself. He didn't dive for cover at a couple of near misses till the crew of Jake's gun did.

Featherston shrugged. "They can't shoot for hell, sir." That wasn't true, and he knew it damn well. The Yankee artillerymen were no less skilled at their trade than their counterparts in butternut. Since the beginning of the war, they'd enjoyed an edge in heavy guns, too. Sometimes the numbers and quick firing of the Confederates' three-inchers could make up for that. Sometimes, as when trying to cave in deep dugouts, they couldn't.

In a lull, Potter said, "We have to hold them at Bull Run. If we can't hold them here, Richmond itself is threatened."

"Do my damnedest, sir," Jake answered. He didn't know if that would be enough. By the way Potter talked, he didn't think it would. Jake shrugged again. Defeat wouldn't be his fault. As far as he was concerned, the War Department and the niggers could split the blame.

Lucien Galtier had not been expecting a visit from Major Jedediah Quigley. He certainly had not been expecting a warm, cordial visit from Major Quigley. That was what he got, though. The U.S. officer even brought along a bottle of brandy far smoother and finer than the homemade applejack Galtier had grown used to drinking.

After Marie came in from the kitchen with glasses, Quigley splashed brandy into them with a generous hand. He raised his glass in salute. "To the union of our great peoples!" he declared in his elegant French.

As far as Lucien was concerned, the U.S. major was making too much of the impending marriage between Nicole and Dr. O'Doull, but the Quebecois farmer held his peace. Quigley's job seemed to entail making too much of everything that came to his notice, for ill or for good. This, at least, was for good.

It was also a toast to which Galtier could drink, even if he found it a bit more than the occasion called for. And the brandy *was* good. He hardly felt it going down his throat, but it filled his belly with warmth that quickly spread outward. *"Formidable!"* he murmured, respect in his voice.

"Glad you like it," Quigley said, and sloshed more into his glass. The American poured himself a fresh dollop, too. After sipping, he went on in thoughtful tones: "I will admit to you, M. Galtier, that I never expected to be paying a social call here. When we first came to Quebec, you seemed a man more in love with the past than with the future."

What he meant was, *You didn't act like a collaborator.* Lucien still didn't feel like a collaborator, either. He said, "When young people come to know each other, one cannot always guess ahead of time how these things will turn out."

"There you certainly have reason," Major Quigley said. "Back in New Hampshire, where I come from, my daughter married a young fellow who makes concertinas." He knocked back his brandy. For a moment, thinking about the choice his daughter had made, he looked not at all like an occupying official, but rather than an ordinary man, and a surprised ordinary man to boot.

Galtier found himself surprised, too: surprised Quigley could look and even act like an ordinary man. Politely, the farmer said, "I hope your son-in-law is safe in the war."

"He is well so far, thanks," Quigley answered. "He's out in Sequoyah, where the fighting isn't so heavy as it is east of the Mississippi—nor so heavy as north of the St. Lawrence or over in Ontario."

"The United States have stubborn neighbors to the south of them," Galtier said. "The United States have also stubborn neighbors to the north of them. I think that, before this war began, you Americans did not altogether understand how stubborn these northern neighbors of yours were."

Some of that was the brandy talking. Here, for once, Quigley had come to his house for some reason other than doing him wrong, and now he was giving the American fresh reason to suspect him. Marie would have some sharp things to say about that. Galtier had some sharp things to say about it, too. He said them, silently but with great vigor, to himself.

But Quigley did not take the comment as he might have. Instead, he nodded soberly, or perhaps not so soberly: as he spoke, he reached for the bottle of brandy again. "Well, once more you have reason," he said. "When we began the war, we thought it would soon be over. But, as you say, our neighbors were more stubborn than we thought, and also stronger than we thought. The fighting has proved harder than we ever imagined."

He held out the bottle to Lucien, who let him pour. After three big glasses of brandy, the farmer would be slow-moving and achy in the morning, but the morning was a long way away. "I did not think an American would admit any such thing," Galtier said.

Quigley tapped his long, thin nose. He had to shift his hand at the last minute to make it connect. "I admit I've got this here," he said, "and the other is every bit as plain. But that doesn't mean the United States aren't going to win this war. It just means we've had to work much harder than we thought we would. We have done the work, M. Galtier, and we are at last beginning to see the results of it."

"It could be so," Lucien said. By everything he could learn, it was so, but he knew that what he could learn was limited. Both the United States and the new Republic of Quebec made sure of that.

"It *is* so." The brandy was talking through Jedediah Quigley, too. Normally as smooth and polished as a new pair of shoes, he made a fist and thumped it against his thigh to emphasize his words.

He also spoke louder than usual. Marie stuck her head out of the kitchen to make sure no quarrel was brewing. When she'd reassured herself, she disappeared again. Galtier didn't think Quigley saw her.

The farmer said, "I will be glad when the war is over." He did not think anyone could disagree with that, or with the way he continued: "Everyone will be glad when the war is over."

And, sure enough, the American officer nodded vigorously.

"The only people who love a war are those who have never fought in one," he declared, to which Lucien could but incline his head; he had not thought Major Quigley could say anything so wise. And then Quigley spoiled it: "But you, M. Galtier, you will have come out of the war having done pretty well for yourself. Without it, you would not have gained a doctor as a fiancé for your daughter."

Even without brandy in him, Galtier would not have let that go unchallenged. With brandy in him, he let fly, saying, "Without the war, Major Quigley, I would not have had part of my patrimony . . . alienated"—even with brandy in him, he had sense enough not to say *stolen*—"from me so that the United States Army could build on it a hospital."

Major Quigley coughed a couple of times. The brandy had turned him a little ruddy. Now he went red as a brick. "I will speak frankly," he said. "I already told you that, when the war was new, I did not think you were a man the United States could trust."

"Yes, you said that," Galtier agreed. *And you were right to think what you thought.* He had sense enough to keep that to himself, too.

After coughing once more, Quigley said, "I also told you I seem to have been wrong. I do not deny I chose your land on which to build this hospital in part because I did not believe you were reliable."

"And now you know differently?" Lucien asked. He had to make it a question, not least because he remained unsure of the answer himself.

But Quigley nodded. "Now I know better," he echoed, and coughed yet again. When he went on, he seemed to be talking as much to himself as to Galtier: "Since I know better, it could be that what I did might not have been the wisest thing to do."

"Perhaps, then, you should think about how you might make amends." Galtier stared down at the little bit of brandy left in his glass. Had what he'd drunk really made him bold enough to say that?

Evidently it had. Major Quigley rubbed his nose. He fiddled with a cuff on his green-gray tunic. At last, he said, "Perhaps I should. What would you say a fair rent for the piece of ground on which the hospital was built would be?"

Galtier had all he could do not to ask if he had heard correctly.

Quigley still assumed he'd had the right to use the land regardless of whether Lucien approved or not, but an offer to pay back rent was ever so much more than the farmer had expected to hear. He scratched his chin, named the most outrageous amount he could think of—"Fifty dollars a month"—and braced himself for the haggle to come. *If I end up with half that,* he thought, *I shall be well ahead of the game.*

But Major Quigley, instead of haggling, simply said, "Very well, M. Galtier, we have a bargain." He stuck out his hand.

In a daze, Lucien Galtier took it. The daze had nothing to do with the brandy he had drunk. He did not know whether to be delighted Quigley had met his price or disappointed he hadn't tried to gouge the American officer out of more. In the end, he was delighted and disappointed at the same time.

Quigley said, "Here, I will leave the bottle with you. If I drink any more from it tonight, I shall be unable to drive back to Rivière-du-Loup."

"Here is an advantage of a wagon or a buggy over a motorcar," Galtier said. "A horse would be able to get you back to town if only you pointed him in the right direction. A motorcar is not so accommodating."

"C'est vrai, et quelle dommage," the American replied, in tones that made it a truly pitiful pity. He got to his feet and walked—steadily but very slowly—to the doorway. *"Bonsoir, Monsieur Galtier."*

"Bonsoir," Lucien said. Major Quigley went outside and cranked his Ford to life. Lucien stood in the doorway and watched him drive—steadily but, again, very slowly—north toward Rivière-du-Loup.

Marie came out of the kitchen. Nicole followed her. Astonished disbelief filled both their faces. Almost whispering, Marie said, "Did my ears tell me the truth? Can it be that the Americans will pay us rent for the land they stole for their hospital?"

"If they pay rent, we can no longer say they stole the land from us," Galtier replied. "It becomes then a matter of business. And what business!" The full weight of what he'd done began to sink in. "Not only rent, but back rent. Not only back rent, but *fifty dollars a month.*"

"We shall be rich!" Nicole exclaimed.

Her mother shook her head, denying even the possibility of such a thing. "No, we shall not be rich. Rich is not for the likes of us. It could be . . . it could be that, for a little while, we may have almost enough." Saying even so much took a distinct effort of will from her.

"That would be fine," Lucien said. "Even of itself, that would be very fine." Acid returned to his voice: "It might even let us make up for the robbery the Americans committed against us during the first winter of the war."

In a worried voice, Marie said, "But taking this money . . . I pray it shall not be as it was when Judas took his thirty pieces of silver."

"Nonsense," Galtier said. "Judas took silver for betraying our Lord. We shall take this money in exchange for what is rightfully ours, in exchange for the Americans' use of my patrimony."

"Father is right," said Nicole, who had her own reasons to want things to go smoothly between her family and the Americans.

"I suppose so." But Marie still did not sound convinced.

Lucien was not altogether convinced, either, but he had made the offer and Major Quigley accepted it. What could he do now? Like Nicole's engagement to Dr. O'Doull, the rent tied him ever closer to the United States and the interests of the United States. He clicked his tongue between his teeth. In 1914, he never would have, never could have, imagined any such thing.

Night was slowly lifting over northern Virginia. Sergeant Chester Martin hadn't got much in the way of sleep even while darkness hung over the land. Ever since midnight, U.S. machine guns had been hammering away at the Confederate line to the east and south, and the guns of the Army of Northern Virginia hadn't been shy about replying, either. The din had kept most of Martin's section awake, though Corporal Bob Reinholdt still lay wrapped in his blanket, sleeping the sleep of a man more innocent than he was likely to be.

But the din had also kept the Rebs from noticing the noise of a whole great whacking lot of barrels moving toward the front line—or so the brass hoped. So Chester Martin devoutly hoped, too.

He turned to David Hamburger. "Next time you write to your sister, tell her thanks," he bawled in the kid's ear. "Looks likely they've got a really big force of barrels here, like they've been doing it in Tennessee."

"I don't know how much she had to do with any of that,"

Hamburger shouted—in effect, whispered—back. "You've got to remember, Sarge, she hates the war and anything that has anything to do with it."

"Hey, she's not the only one," Martin said. "You think I like getting shot, you're crazy. But if we've got to have the goddamn thing, we'd better win it. The only thing worse than having a war is losing one. The United States know all about that."

Before Hamburger could reply, U.S. artillery, which had been pretty quiet, opened up with a thunderous roar. Short and sweet—that was how they did it these days. None of the week-long bombardments that Martin had seen on the Roanoke front, enormous cannonadings that did more to tell the Rebs where the attack was going in than anything else.

Artillery or no artillery, Bob Reinholdt kept right on sleeping. Martin went over and shook him, then had to leap back as Reinholdt lashed out with a trench knife. "Naughty," Martin said; the corporal always woke up at maximum combat alertness. "Show's about to start."

"Yeah?" Reinholdt said. "All right." He grunted, rolled up his blanket, and got to his feet. He hadn't given Martin any trouble since absorbing both fist and steel reinforcement with his chin. Maybe he'd learned his lesson. Maybe he was biding his time. Martin still kept an eye on him, in case he was.

Captain Cremony strode along the trench. "All right, boys," he said. "Now we're driving nails in their coffin. We've cleared 'em out of Washington. We need a buffer, so they can't shell it whenever they choose. Our granddads fought on this ground. They won some fights in Virginia, too, even if they didn't win the war. We get to make up for what they couldn't quite manage."

"*My* grandfather didn't fight here," David Hamburger said after Cremony was out of earshot, which didn't take long. "He was still on the other side of the Atlantic, wondering if the Czar would put him in the Russian Army for twenty-five or thirty years. When the Czar said *go*, he went—here."

"Conscription-dodger, eh?" Martin grinned. "Somewhere down at the roots of my family tree is a poacher who got out of England a short hop ahead of the sheriff. That's what my old man says, anyway. How about you, Bob?"

"Me?" Reinholdt seemed surprised at the question. "I'm a son of a bitch from a long line of sons of bitches. You don't believe me, ask anybody."

Martin wouldn't have argued with him for the world. He didn't get the chance, anyhow. When the barrels' engines went from low power to high, not all the machine-gun fire and artillery in the world could have concealed the racket. The traveling fortresses clanked and rumbled toward the Confederate line, their own machine guns blazing away at the enemy positions ahead.

All along the front lines of the U.S. works, officers blew whistles to urge their men over the top. Cremony tweeted away till his face turned red. U.S. soldiers scrambled up ladders and sandbag stairways and followed the barrels toward the Confederate trenches.

"Stay close!" Captain Cremony shouted.

"Stay close!" Martin echoed. "Those big iron critters may be ugly, but they're our best friends." Even as he spoke, the barrel behind which he advanced began smashing its way over and through the wire the Rebels had strung to protect their position. Between the last wire belt and their forwardmost trenches, the Confederates' Negro laborers had dug a great ditch, too wide for the barrels to cross and deep enough to be sure to bog them down.

But U.S. observation aeroplanes or balloonists must have spotted the digging, for some of the barrels bore on their forward decks great bundles of sticks and logs bound with chains and ropes. They dumped them into the ditch, then ground their way across over them.

Captain Cremony, who was fond of Shakespeare, shouted out in high glee: "Birnam Wood comes to Dunsinane!"

Martin didn't know about that. He did know the bundles of wood made it easier for him and his men to cross the ditch, too, though some of them used bites the artillery had taken out of its front and rear walls to scramble down and then up. "Stay close to your barrel!" Martin yelled again. "Stay close!"

The barrels were bludgeoning the Army of Northern Virginia into submission. These were new positions for the Rebs, hastily run up after the retreat from Aldie. They lacked much of the reinforced concrete of lines built more slowly and held longer. Machine-gun nests of sandbags could not stand up to the barrels' nose cannons. One after another, the barrels cleared them out.

Tilden Russell shouted something into Martin's ear. Martin

had trouble making out what he said amidst the rattle of gunfire, the thunder of artillery, and the dyspeptic roar of the barrels. Obligingly, the private shouted it again: "Breakthrough!" He stuffed a cigar into his mouth, got it going with a bronze-cased flint-and-steel lighter, and puffed out happy clouds of smoke.

Was it a breakthrough? Martin wasn't sure, not here, not now, though on the Roanoke front he would have been ecstatic at the ground he and his comrades were gaining. A day's advance here could be measured in miles, not yards. If that wasn't a break-through, what was it?

But, if a breakthrough required the Rebs to throw down their rifles and quit in carload lots, that didn't happen. Soldiers in butternut, white and colored, kept fighting till the barrels and the U.S. infantry rolled over them. If anything, the colored Confed-erate soldiers fought harder than they had when the U.S. troops broke out of their bridgeheads south of the Potomac. Maybe that was because the whites had given them dire warnings about what would happen to them if they didn't fight. Maybe, too, and more likely, the Negro soldiers were steadier now simply be-cause they'd seen some action.

East of the infantry trenches and the village of Centreville, the ground rose. The Rebel batteries on those hills—maps called them mountains—hadn't given up and gone home, either. Shells from U.S. guns kept falling among them, but they went right on giving the advancing men in green-gray a hell of a hard time. They reserved their chiefest fury for the barrels. The traveling forts were not easy targets, principally because they *could* travel, but every so often a shell would slam home with the noise of a man beating an iron pot with a pick handle.

Worse noises commonly followed—ammunition cooking off, engines and gas tanks going up in flames, men screaming as they cooked. Barrels' armor plate held out machine-gun bullets, but three-inch shells, when they hit, pierced it like so much pasteboard.

And the CSA had barrels of their own in the field. They were fewer and more widely scattered than those of the USA, but they were there, and some of them gave a good account of them-selves. When not fighting for his own life, Martin watched in fascination as barrel battled barrel. The fights put him in mind of the dinosaurs struggling in swamps he'd read about in the Sunday supplements.

One particular Confederate barrel—tanks, the Rebs called them, aping the British as they so often did—was altogether too good at making its U.S. opponents extinct. It set two green-gray barrels afire in quick succession. The second victory let it bear down on Martin and his section.

"Hit the dirt!" he shouted, and dove behind a pile of rubble that had been a Rebel's chimney once upon a time. Machine-gun bullets from the Confederate barrel chewed up the dirt around him and snarled off the bricks in front of him. If the barrel kept coming straight ahead, it would squash him into a redder smear in the red-brown dirt. Shouts and screams from around him said only too plainly that some of his men hadn't been so lucky in finding cover as he had.

Clang! The machine-gun fire from the Confederate barrel abruptly stopped. Wary as a wild animal, Chester Martin raised his head. The barrel was burning. Hatches flew open as crewmen tried to escape. With a fierce glee, Martin and his comrades shot them down. Out of their steel snail shell, they were easy meat.

Martin looked around and grimaced. "Stretcher-bearers!" he shouted, his voice cracking with urgency. "Stretcher-bearers!"

He ran over to David Hamburger, the closest wounded soldier. The kid was clutching his left thigh and howling like a wolf. Martin didn't think he knew he was doing it. Bright red blood trickled out between his fingers. When he saw Martin, he stopped howling and said, "I'm going to write my congress-woman about this." His voice was amazingly calm.

"Yeah, you do that," Martin said. "Let's have a look at what you caught there." Reluctantly, Hamburger took his hands away. The wound was in the middle of the thigh. Martin whistled in a minor key. A bullet to the inside, and the kid would have bled out in short order. This was better news, but it wasn't what you'd call good.

"Here, we'll take him, Sarge." A couple of stretcher-bearers paused beside the wounded man.

"Do your best. He's a good fellow, and his sister's in Congress." With the stretcher-bearers there, Martin couldn't wait around. He awkwardly patted David Hamburger on the shoulder, then hurried past the blazing hulk of the Confederate barrel and on through Centreville.

Confederate artillerymen were made to quit the high ground east of the little Virginia town only with the greatest reluctance.

Some of the gun crews stayed till they could fire at the advancing barrels over open sights. They took heavy casualties, though; splinter shields were no match for the firepower bearing down on them.

A Rebel gunner, one of the last on the field, shook his fist at the oncoming U.S. soldiers as his crew limbered up their field piece. He shook it again as they galloped away. Martin shot at him, but missed. He shrugged. One man didn't much matter. The high ground belonged to the USA.

Joe Conroy was about the last man in the world Cincinnatus wanted to see. By the look on the fat, white storekeeper's face, Cincinnatus was about the last man in the world he wanted to see, too. "Come to gloat, I reckon," Conroy said, shifting a plug of tobacco from one cheek to the other.

"Got nothin' to gloat about, suh," Cincinnatus answered. With Kentucky a state in the USA these days, he didn't have to be so deferential to a white man as he would have before the war, when the state still belonged to the CSA. But Conroy was a Confederate diehard. Cincinnatus figured using the old ways was a good idea if he hoped to learn anything.

He might not learn anything anyhow. Conroy sneered at him. "Yeah, a likely story. You go on and tell me you don't know what the hell happened to my store after me and Tom Kennedy, God rest his soul, taught you how to make those little firebombs that ain't no bigger'n cigars."

"Mr. Conroy, suh, I don't know what the hell happened to your store," Cincinnatus said evenly. "I didn't have nothin' to do with burnin' it down. That there is the truth, and you can take it to the bank."

That there was a lie, and his mother would have boxed his ears for telling a lie had she been here to listen to it. But his mother wasn't anywhere around, and he told the lie with great aplomb. "Huh," Conroy grunted, as if to say he didn't believe it for a minute. But then he went on, "If you don't know about it, who the hell does?"

Cincinnatus shrugged. "Who the hell knows about how Tom Kennedy got hisself killed, suh?"

He didn't think he'd made the question too obvious. Conroy had offered him another question on which to hang it, so he didn't seem to be pulling it in from out of the blue. The store-keeper looked down at the park bench on which they sat at opposite ends before giving an answer more oblique than useful: "Never could figure out what the hell Tom saw in you."

"Swear to Jesus, suh, never did figure out what he was doin' there outside my door," Cincinnatus said.

Conroy's eyes were narrow slits, almost hidden in folds of fat. Cincinnatus still couldn't decide whether he was clever or just sly. Now he said, "They were after him—what do you think?"

Only a lifetime of disguising his feelings toward whites and the stupid things that came out of their mouths let Cincinnatus keep from barking scornful laughter at that. Had nobody been after Kennedy, nobody would have shot him. "Who's 'they,' Mr. Conroy?" he asked. "That's what I'm tryin' to find out."

"Well, now," the storekeeper said slowly, "I don't rightly know. Could have been a whole bunch of different folks."

Cincinnatus wanted to grab him by the neck and shake him till his narrow eyes popped. "You got any notion who?" he asked, as gently as he could. "Been a lot o' different folks comin' round askin' me questions I ain't got no good answers for, 'less I talk way too much."

Unless I tell them who Tom Kennedy's friends are, was what he meant. Would Conroy be bright enough to figure that out, or would he need a more direct hint? The only more direct hint Cincinnatus could think of was a whack in the teeth. That would be satisfying, but . . .

Conroy got what he was talking about. The white man's absurd little rosebud mouth puckered up as if he'd bitten into the world's sourest pickled tomato. "Who?" he repeated, sounding like an unhappy owl. "Could have been one of those Kentucky State Police bastards. Could have been some of the Red niggers, too. You'd know more about that than I would, I reckon."

He gave Cincinnatus a stare that meant, *I can talk, too.* Cincinnatus hid a grimace. Everybody could talk about him to somebody. He said, "From what I seen, Mr. Kennedy and the Reds didn't get on too bad."

"I told him to watch out for 'em just the same," Conroy said. "Can't trust a Red. He'll yell 'Popular Front!' today and kick you in the nuts tomorrow. Tom thought he could handle it. He always thought he could handle everything."

That did sound like the Kennedy Cincinnatus had known.

Conroy's characterization of the Reds wasn't far wrong, either, though Cincinnatus wouldn't have admitted it to the storekeeper.

And Conroy wasn't through, either. He continued, "Could even have been some of our own boys. I've heard this one and that one go on about how Tom was selling us all down the river."

"That a fact?" Cincinnatus pricked up his ears. "You got names for any o' those fellows?"

Conroy looked down at his shoes, which were every bit as scuffed and battered as Cincinnatus'. He didn't say anything. After a while, Cincinnatus realized he wasn't going to say anything. Everybody played his cards close to his vest in this game. Kennedy and Conroy were the only two Confederate holdouts Cincinnatus had ever met. Conroy didn't care to give him the key to more.

In casual tones, Cincinnatus said, "Luther Bliss'd ask a lot more questions than I do, and he'd ask 'em a lot harder, too. I been down to the Covington city hall. I know what I'm talkin' about."

"Yeah, and he gave you money out of his own pocket, the cold-blooded son of a bitch," Conroy snapped.

Cincinnatus sighed. Teddy Roosevelt had done him a good turn, but Bliss had put barbs in it. Still casually, Cincinnatus said, "Maybe he'd listen if I was to tell him somethin', then."

"Maybe he would. And if you was to tell him somethin', maybe some smart nigger who wasn't quite as smart as he reckoned he was would get a bullet through the ear one day when he's drivin' that big ugly old White truck o' his that's plumb full o' shit the damnyankees're shootin' at his countrymen. Or maybe his wife'd have a little accident. Or maybe his kid."

"I ain't the only one accidents can happen to, Conroy." Cincinnatus had to work to hold his voice steady. Plenty of people had threatened him. Threatening his family was an alarming departure.

Conroy leaned back against the park bench, looking like a fat cat with canary feathers on his whiskers. "Reckon I know a bluff when I hear one."

"Reckon you don't," Cincinnatus said. "Got me a little Gray Eagle notebook. I been writin' things in it for a long time. Anything happen to me or mine, it'll get to the right place. I've made sure o' that."

The storekeeper stared at him in undisguised loathing. He *was* running a bluff, but he wouldn't be for long; the idea of having such protection was irresistibly appealing. Conroy said, "We was a pack o' damn fools to ever let any niggers learn their letters."

"Maybe so, maybe not," Cincinnatus answered with a shrug. "Too late to worry about it now, one way or the other." The USA had fewer laws against educating Negroes than did the CSA; he hoped Achilles would get more in the way of learning than he'd ever been able to acquire. But it was too early to worry about that now. He fixed Conroy with a stare that had flint in it. "Which of your pals didn't take to Kennedy dealin' with the Reds?"

"None o' your damn business," Conroy ground out. He glared back at Cincinnatus. "You want to talk to Luther Bliss, go talk to Luther goddamn Bliss. We'll see which one of us ends up happier afterwards."

Cincinnatus didn't want to talk to Luther Bliss. He never wanted anything to do with the chief of the Kentucky State Police for the rest of his life. Getting his wish there, though, struck him as unlikely. He and Conroy had reached an impasse.

He could, he supposed, ask Apicius if he knew the names of some of the other Confederate diehards. But Apicius' Reds were as likely to have killed Tom Kennedy as anyone else. And Apicius would not take kindly to questions from Cincinnatus any which way. The cook would wonder for whom he was asking them, and would never believe he was asking them for himself alone.

Conroy heaved himself to his feet. "I reckon we're done," he said, and Cincinnatus did not disagree. The storekeeper shook his finger in Cincinnatus' face. "Don't you come around there askin' after me no more, neither. I ain't got nothin' more to say to you, and I ain't gonna be—" He shook his head. His jowls wobbled like gelatin. Off he stomped.

I ain't gonna be—what? Cincinnatus wondered. *I ain't gonna be there,* was the likeliest guess. Cincinnatus wouldn't have wanted to live in the dingy roominghouse where Conroy made his home, but didn't expect the storekeeper to head on to much better lodgings. Cincinnatus sighed. He'd got something to think about, but where could he go with it? Nowhere he could see.

With another sigh, he got up and headed toward the nearest trolley stop. Elizabeth would have something sharp to say about his wasting so much of a Sunday afternoon, and she'd be right.

But he hadn't known it would be a waste till he'd gone and done it, which was too late.

The trolley stop was across the street from a saloon with a plate-glass window. As Cincinnatus came to the stop and dug in his pocket for a nickel, a man in a black homburg came out of the saloon and strode across the street to the stop. He seemed as certain the motorcars would stop for him as Moses had been that the Red Sea would part for him. The sea had parted; the motorcars did stop.

"Afternoon, Cincinnatus." Luther Bliss' pale brown eyes looked at Cincinnatus and, the Negro would have sworn, through him as well. "That damn diehard know who parted Tom Kennedy's hair with a .30 caliber slug?"

Cincinnatus was glad he was black. Had he been white, Bliss could have watched him turn pale. "How the devil did you know what we was talking about?" he demanded with almost superstitious awe.

Bliss' laugh didn't quite reach those hunting-hound eyes. "You could have been talking about a lot of things," he answered. "All the others are worse. Let's just hope that was the only one."

"If you know all the people you don't fancy in this here town, Mr. Bliss," Cincinnatus said, "why don't you throw 'em all in jail so you don't have to worry about 'em no more, 'stead of leavin' 'em run loose and raise trouble?"

"I know all the people I don't fancy in this here *state*," Luther Bliss answered, "and the reason I don't throw 'em all in jail is simple as hell: there aren't near enough jails to hold the bastards." He laughed again, but Cincinnatus didn't think he was kidding. After a moment, he dug in his pocket, continuing, "You got a hundred dollars from me on account of the president. This here is from me personal, you might say."

He handed Cincinnatus a nickel. Looking down at the coin that sat in the pale palm of his hand, Cincinnatus said, "Sure as hell you won't go broke spendin' your money like this here, Mr. Bliss."

"You're a funny one," Bliss said. "You better get on home now—here comes the trolley. And if I ever figure out how you got to be so funny, I'll come round again and see if you're still that way after I take you to pieces." He tipped his hat and went on his way, smooth as a snake. Cincinnatus threw the nickel in the trolley car's fare box. He didn't want it in his pocket. It might have been listening to him.

The SS *Pocahontas, Arkansas* lay alongside the USS *Ericsson*. Staring at the supply ship, George Enos said, "If that's not the stupidest name for a steamboat I ever saw in all my born days, I don't know what is."

Carl Sturtevant looked sly and smug. "I know why it's got that name."

"All right, I'll bite," George said. "Somebody doesn't know that Pocahontas ended up marrying a Pilgrim?"

"Hell, till this minute I didn't know she ended up marrying a Pilgrim," Sturtevant answered. "Nah, that hasn't got anything to do with it."

"Come on, then—cough it up," George said.

"Pocahontas, Arkansas, is this little no-account town a few miles south of the U.S. border," the petty officer said. "During the Second Mexican War, the Army took the place and held it for a little while. Outside of Montana, there wasn't much glory for our side in that war. Whatever there was, they pasted onto whatever would take it, and so we've got a freighter named for a Rebel whistle stop."

"All right." Enos waved a hand. "You got me there. I knew about the real Pocahontas, but not about that town down there named for her. I'll tell you something else I know, too." He looked around nervously. "I know I don't like sitting here in the middle of the goddamn Atlantic while we take on supplies. I don't like it for hell."

Sturtevant raised a mocking eyebrow. "You don't like us to have fuel so we can keep on patrolling? You don't like fresh vittles? I don't know about you, but I'm damn sick of kraut and beans. You don't like getting mail? You got a wife, ain't that right?"

"Yeah, I got a wife," George Enos answered. "Mail's fine, but I want to get home to Boston in one piece when the war's finally over, too, and if I'm sitting here not moving, that damn Rebel submarine's going to put a torpedo into our side somewhere right between the number two and number three stacks."

"We sank that damn Rebel submarine," Sturtevant said. "Wasn't one of Lieutenant Crowder's pipe dreams that time, neither. You blew the captain to pieces when he was pitching their secret papers, and then the *Bonefish* went under again, and she ain't never comin' up no more."

Enos exhaled angrily through his nose. "You should have been a lawyer, not a sailor. You figure the Confederate Navy's got only that one submersible in it? They build those bastards by the netful. If there isn't already another one out here to take the place of that boat, there will be in a few days."

Like George, Carl Sturtevant looked older than he was; sun and wind and spray had tanned his skin, turned it leather, and wrinkled it, too. He looked older still as he contemplated Enos' words. "Well, you're right, God damn it," he said at last. "Now I'm going to worry, too."

Sailors hauled sides of beef and hams and sacks of potatoes and endless cans from the *Pocahontas, Arkansas* to the *Ericsson*. They chattered at one another in English and a variety of foreign languages that seemed to consist mostly of consonants. Fuel oil gurgled through a hose connecting the hold of the *Pocahontas, Arkansas* to the *Ericsson*'s engine room.

As Sturtevant had said, it all promised that the destroyer would be able to keep on steaming and keep on feeding the crew for the next couple of weeks—provided she lived through the next couple of hours. Somewhere out there, a submersible—all right, not *the* submersible, but *a* submersible, sure as hell—was cruising along looking for something to send to the bottom. Maybe that sub was fifty miles away. On the other hand, maybe it was somewhere under the surface, trying to sneak in from a mile to half a mile to make sure it sank the *Ericsson*, which was as sitting a duck as had ever been hatched.

You couldn't outrun a torpedo. You couldn't outrun a torpedo at flank speed. A fish had at least ten knots on a destroyer. But, if you were cruising along when one of those bastards tried to shoot you in the back, you did have a chance to dodge.

How in God's name were you supposed to dodge when you weren't even moving? The answer was depressingly simple: you couldn't. Finishing this resupply depended on not being spotted while it was going on.

George stared out over the tropical Atlantic, looking for a periscope or its wake. Odds were against him. He knew it. Even if he did spot one, it was all too likely to be too late. He knew that, too.

Light chop made the surface dance. In a dead calm sea, the

wake from a periscope would have stood out against the background. Here, the background helped hide or mislead, as it did with a camouflaged ship. He wished he were down in the engine room. The only way the black gang found out about a torpedo was when one exploded in their laps.

Finally, after what seemed like forever but couldn't have been more than the couple of hours Carl Sturtevant had talked about, the *Pocahontas, Arkansas* disconnected the hose and reeled it back in, leaving a dark smear of fuel oil across the deck for an officer to have conniptions about any minute now. All the freighter's sailors were back aboard her, too.

The deck began to thrum and vibrate under George's feet. He let out a long, heartfelt sigh of relief no doubt being echoed all over the *Ericsson*. They'd got away with it. Danger didn't disappear now—danger, from everything George had seen, never disappeared—but it diminished.

Coal smoke poured from the *Pocahontas, Arkansas*' stack, too, as the freighter's wheezy powerplant also began to work harder. The only way the beamy old ship would go faster than about ten knots, Enos thought, was if someone threw her over a cliff. Sooner or later, though, she'd get where she was going. In the end, that was what mattered.

But the *Pocahontas, Arkansas* did not get where she was going. The notion that she would had hardly crossed George's mind before her bow blew off right in front of his horrified eyes. A moment later, another torpedo struck her amidships. She might as well have been a bull in a slaughterhouse hit over the head with a sledgehammer. She stopped dead in the water and started to sink.

The *Ericsson* stopped dead in the water, too, or so it seemed to George. Then he wondered if he'd lost his mind: the hulk of the freighter seemed to be moving forward once more.

While Enos was scratching his head, Carl Sturtevant let out an admiring whistle. "Skipper must have been eating his fish lately," he said. "You know—brain food. Slam us over to full power astern and we can keep the *Pocahontas* between us and whoever that son of a bitch out there is. And speaking of which—" He turned and ran toward the depth-charge projector at the stern.

George ran that way, too, toward the one-pounder by the projector. "Hadn't thought of that," he admitted. "It is pretty sly, I guess. There's only one thing wrong with it that I can think of."

Sturtevant, who wasn't young and wasn't skinny, wheezed to a stop by his post. "Yeah," he said, panting. "We ain't gonna have a shield much longer."

"That's it," George agreed. The *Pocahontas, Arkansas* was sinking fast, going down by the bow. Even as Enos watched, another torpedo hit shook the freighter. He shivered. "That one was meant for us."

"You bet it was," Sturtevant said. The *Pocahontas, Arkansas* rolled over and sank. Only a handful of men from her were bobbing in the water when she did, and the undertow she generated when she went down pulled a couple of them with her.

"What do we do now?" George asked. "If we hang around here and pick those guys up, that submersible is liable to put the next one into us. But if we don't . . . Hell, I wouldn't want to be one of those poor bastards."

"Me, neither," Sturtevant said. He lowered his voice so Lieutenant Crowder couldn't hear him before continuing, "Every once in a while—times like this, mostly—I'm glad I'm not an officer. Between you, me, and the bulkhead, I don't want to have to play God." Enos nodded without hesitation.

Up on the bridge, the *Ericsson*'s skipper made his choice, also without hesitation. Sailors hurled cork life rings toward the men still struggling in the ocean as the destroyer steamed past them. The ship did not stop or even slow to pick up survivors; as Sturtevant had said, the submarine that had torpedoed the *Pocahontas, Arkansas* was sure to be waiting, its own skipper hopefully licking his chops, for any such move.

A runner came back from the bridge to Lieutenant Crowder. "Sir, captain's orders are for you to lay down as many depth charges as you can, set for widely different depths, when we reach the position where we reckon the submersible is at. We may not sink the bastard, but we'll make him keep his head down while we pick up the men from the supply ship."

"Aye aye," Crowder said crisply. He turned to the depth-charge crew and started giving orders. Sturtevant ignored some of them as he gave his own instructions to the men who served the projector. When a signal flag waved from the bridge, the crew methodically pumped one depth charge after another into the blue water of the Atlantic. The water soon began boiling and seething from the force of the explosions under the surface.

George Enos eagerly peered astern, looking for leaking oil or a trail of air bubbles that might mark a damaged submersible. He spied nothing of the sort. Neither did anyone else. "We ought to be operating in a flotilla," Lieutenant Crowder grumbled. "If we had three destroyers after that submersible instead of just our one, we'd sink him for sure."

If I had a million dollars . . . , Enos thought.

Abruptly, the *Ericsson* broke off the attack on the submarine and raced back toward the survivors from the *Pocahontas, Arkansas*. After hauling the four or five of them aboard with lines, the destroyer hurried away from the spot where the supply ship had gone down.

Carl Sturtevant sighed. "Well, the limey or the Reb down there under the water won that one, damn him to hell and gone."

"Yeah," Enos said, his Boston accent making the word come out as *Ayuh*. "Didn't get us, though, so I reckon he's not as happy as he might be. A destroyer is worth a hell of a lot of freighters."

"I ain't gonna tell you you're wrong," Sturtevant said, "but the game's not over yet, either. He's still down there. He's trying to get us, we're trying to get him. Wonder if we'll lock horns again."

"How will we even know whether we ever fight the same boat again or some different one?" George asked.

Sturtevant chewed on that for a moment before he shrugged. "What difference does it make? Any time one of those bastards shows himself, we'll go after him, whether he's this boat or a different one."

George considered, then nodded. "I won't tell you you're wrong," he said.

Seawater from a new leak dripped down onto Commander Roger Kimball's cap. The electric motors were running on very low power, just enough to keep the prop turning over and give the *Bonefish* steering way. The roars of exploding depth charges, some well removed from the submersible, others terrifyingly close, put Kimball in mind of a summer thunderstorm back home.

Then the rain of depth charges stopped. Kimball pulled out his watch. He let one minute tick by, two, and then, reluctantly, three. When the third quiet minute had passed, he turned to his exec and said, "Take us up to periscope depth, Tom."

"Are you sure, sir?" Lieutenant Brearley said. "God only knows where the damnyankees are up there. They're liable to be waiting around to spot us so they can drop the other shoe."

Kimball growled discontentedly, deep in his throat. Tom Brearley had a point. But every instinct in Kimball cried out for attack. "I'm blind down here, dammit," he muttered. "Only way to find out where the damnyankees are is to go looking for 'em." He pulled out his watch again. After the small second hand went round its dial twice more, he spoke again, this time in tones that brooked no disagreement: "Periscope depth!"

"Aye aye, sir," Brearley said, though he sent Kimball another reproachful look. The skipper of the *Bonefish* generously failed to let himself notice it. The boat climbed out of the depths in which it had taken shelter from the pounding the Yankee destroyer had given it.

As soon as the periscope lifted above the surface of the Atlantic, Kimball started to curse. "He's hightailing it out of here," he snarled in disgust. "Might have got the lousy bastard if I'd surfaced a little faster." He glowered at his executive officer. "Some people are afraid of their own shadows."

"Sir," Brearley said stiffly, and the fetid atmosphere inside the *Bonefish* got nasty in a different way.

"Be a cold day in hell before I listen to somebody else's jim-jams again, instead of my own plain good sense," Kimball said. He was growling at Brearley, but was angrier at himself. He hadn't obeyed his own instincts, and had lost a chance to take out the Yankee destroyer.

Trying to spread oil over troubled waters, Ben Coulter said, "That Yankee four-stacker has a right smart skipper. Way he slid behind the freighter we nailed—who would have reckoned he'd be so sneaky? Never came close to giving us a good shot at him."

"All the more reason to wish the son of a bitch was down at the bottom of the ocean," Kimball said. "If that wasn't the *Ericsson*, it was another one from the same class. They still think they sank us. One day soon, I'm going to think I sank them, too. Only difference is, I'm going to be right."

He rotated the periscope through a complete circle. No other Yankee surface ships besides the destroyer were above the horizon, and she wouldn't be for long, not the way she was scooting.

The *Bonefish* would be able to surface soon. Kimball shook his head. He should have surfaced after a double triumph, the freighter and the warship both.

Presently, the *Ericsson* or whoever she was vanished from periscope view. Kimball stayed submerged a while longer all the same: the destroyer had a higher observation point and therefore a wider horizon than he did. When he judged the U.S. ship could no longer spot him, he grudged a few words toward Tom Brearley: "Bring us to the surface."

"Aye aye, sir," the exec answered. He tried to add a light note: "Time to get some fresh air, anyhow."

Kimball didn't answer. He told off Ben Coulter to hold his legs while he opened the hatch at the top of the conning tower. As always, the pressurized air rushing out seemed particularly foul. Kimball already felt like throwing up, but was too stubborn to do it.

He climbed out onto the conning tower and looked around. Nothing but ocean, as far as the eye could see. No smoke on the horizon; the wind had dispersed the plume from the *Ericsson* or her twin, and no other ship was close enough to be showing. He might have had the whole Atlantic to himself.

And then Tom Brearley came clanking up the steel rungs of the ladder. The executive officer inhaled deeply, then chuckled. "Feels good to breathe in something you can't taste."

Kimball didn't answer. He turned his back so that he stared out at a different quadrant of the ocean. Behind him, he heard Brearley shift his feet on the conning-tower roof. He pretended he didn't hear. He pretended the exec didn't exist. He wished the pretense were true.

Brearley was young and earnest and lousy at taking hints. Instead of going below, he cleared his throat. Kimball kept right on ignoring him. But when Brearley began, "Sir, I just wanted to say that—" Kimball couldn't ignore him any more.

He whirled, so fast and fierce that he plainly startled the exec, and might have frightened him, too. "You jogged my elbow," he said in a soft, deadly voice. "Because you jogged my elbow, that damn destroyer got away. If you think I am very happy about that, Mr. Brearley, you had better think again."

"But, sir," Brearley said, "if he had been sitting there waiting for us, he could have dropped half a dozen ash cans in our lap."

"Yeah, he could have." Kimball's head jerked up and down in

a single short, sharp nod. "But he didn't, on account of he wasn't sitting there. I didn't think he'd be sitting there. But you got the whimwhams, and you put my back up, too, and so we stayed down longer than we should have, and so the son of a bitch got away. If you reckon I am very happy with you, you're wrong."

Brearley got a stubborn, martyred look on his face. "Sir, it is my duty to advise you on matters concerning the welfare of the boat," he said stiffly. "I would be failing in my duty if I kept silent. If you choose not to take my advice, that is your privilege as captain. If you do take it, though, the responsibility becomes yours, not mine."

He was right. By the book, he was right. By everything Kimball had learned at the Naval Academy at Mobile, he was right. But the way things really worked, especially on a boat as cramped as a submarine, wasn't exactly the way the book said it was. Kimball snarled something sulfurous under his breath. "You think twice before you open your mouth out of turn again," he said aloud. "Do you hear me, Mr. Brearley?"

"Yes, sir," Brearley said in a voice much colder than the weather.

A low buzzing filled Kimball's ears. For a moment, he thought it was the sound of his own rage. Then he realized it was real, and coming from outside himself. He looked around, as he might have for a mosquito, till he spotted the aeroplane approaching from the northeast. Coming from that direction, it was unlikely to be off a Confederate cruiser or battleship. For as long as he could, he hoped it had been launched from a Royal Navy vessel. That hope vanished when he saw the eagle's heads on the undersides of the wings and on the fuselage.

The aeroplane had spotted the *Bonefish*, too, and came in for a closer look at her. Kimball understood that; he'd come to the surface too recently to have run up a Confederate naval jack on the conning tower or at the stern.

Kimball waved to the pilot. The fellow waved back. He was close enough for Kimball to see—and to distrust—his smile. Kimball smiled, too, as he would have at a poker table. Through that smile, he said, "Mr. Brearley, go below, but don't make a big fuss about doing it. Order the machine-gun crew topside. Tell them to act as friendly toward that goddamn aeroplane as they can—and if he gives them half a chance, even a quarter of a chance, I want them to shoot his ass off."

"Aye aye, sir," Brearley said. "Shall I have some other men come up on deck, too, to gawk at the aeroplane and keep the pilot from paying attention to the gunners?"

"Yeah, do that, Tom." Kimball nodded. Without noticing, he slipped back into the informal address common aboard submersibles. Now that the exec had made a good suggestion, he tacitly forgave him.

Brearley slipped below. If the pilot of that aeroplane didn't like it, all he had to do was turn around and fly away. He didn't. He came around for another pass close by the *Bonefish*: he was still trying to figure out to whose navy she belonged.

Out came the sailors. They pointed at the aeroplane and waved to the pilot and generally acted as much like damn fools as they could. Some of them were alarmingly good at the role. The pilot waved back. He was spiraling higher into the sky now. Maybe he'd satisfied himself that the *Bonefish* was a U.S. boat. In that case, *he* was a damn fool. Or maybe, like everybody else in this little charade, he was sandbagging.

Nobody had fired the machine gun aft of the conning tower at a real target since the *Bonefish* went up the Congaree River to help put down the Red uprising among the Negroes almost a year and a half before. It burst into noisy, staccato life now, tracers drawing hot orange lines in the direction of the U.S. flying machine.

Something fell from between the aeroplane's floats. Kimball yipped with triumphant glee, thinking the gunners had damaged the Yankee aircraft. A couple of his men cheered, too.

But someone yelled "That's a bomb!" an instant before it smashed down into the sea and exploded a few yards in front of the *Bonefish*'s bow. A great column of water and spray rose and then fell, drenching the sailors farthest up the hull and even splashing a little water into Kimball's face.

He swiped a sleeve across his eyes, then stared up toward the U.S. aeroplane with a new and startled respect. If it had another bomb . . . He was about to shout orders for a crash dive when the aeroplane flew off in the direction from which it had come.

"That son of a bitch," he said indignantly. "That *son* of a bitch. He'd hit us square there, he'd have sunk us." He shook his fist at the receding aeroplane. "I didn't know the damnyankees were putting bombs aboard those things these days. Can't trust anybody any more."

"I expect we gave him a nasty surprise, too," Tom Brearley said.

"Hope to Jesus we did," Kimball said. "But putting a bomb on one of those scout aeroplanes—war just got a little tougher. Having 'em flying around and spying on us is bad enough. If they can hurt us once they spot us instead of sending for their pals on the wireless—well, hell, if they can do that, how are we supposed to do what we're supposed to do?"

"We need a proper antiaircraft gun, sir, a one-pounder, not just the machine gun," Brearley said.

Kimball nodded. That might help. It wasn't the answer, though. For the life of him, he didn't know what the answer was.

XIII

Sylvia Enos was discovering that Brigid Coneval had been right: Boston held plenty of jobs. A lot of them paid better than the one she'd had in the canning plant, too. In the time since she last looked for work, wages had risen sharply. Her own had gone up, too, but not by so much. The more she saw what others were getting, the more she kicked herself as a fool for not quitting sooner.

She also discovered many more jobs were open to women than had been true when she got work after George went into the Navy. She didn't see any women in overalls with pickaxes and sledgehammers on road-paving crews, but that was about the only limitation she found.

"Reason for quitting previous position?" a—female—clerk asked at a shoe factory.

"Both my children came down with chicken pox at the same time," she answered, as she'd answered several times already. She looked for a sympathetic glance from the clerk, who wore a wedding band, but got nothing but the *Well, where's the rest of it?* expression a bored man might have used. A bit nonplused, she went on, "I didn't have anyone else who could watch them, and the canning plant wouldn't hold the job for me—they could hire someone without any experience and pay her less."

That still rankled. They'd used her, and then they went and threw her away with no more hesitation than if she'd been a torn label. Massachusetts, despite agitation, did not let women vote. If it had, Sylvia would have voted Socialist without a moment's hesitation.

"Except for that, will this plant give you a good character?" The clerk made as if to reach for the telephone on her desk.

"Yes, I think so," Sylvia said.

The clerk did not pick up the earpiece and ask for the operator. Sylvia smiled to herself. The woman had wanted to see if she'd been lying and could be panicked into revealing it. After scribbling a note to herself, the woman said, "You do know how to use a sewing machine?"

"Oh, yes." Sylvia nodded. "I'm like most people, I suppose. I have one at home, and I use it when I have the time. I buy some ready-to-wear, but making clothes for myself and the children saves a lot of money."

She'd done a lot of sewing while she was home with George, Jr., and Mary Jane. She'd sewn, and she'd taken care of the children, and she'd read the books and magazines in the apartment till she could have recited chunks of them from memory. She'd got out very little. She was hard pressed to remember when she'd felt more delight than that which filled her when her children's blisters got crusty and scabbed over and the scabs started falling off.

"Have you ever sewn leather with a sewing machine?" the hiring clerk asked.

Sylvia shook her head. If she lied there, she would be too easily found out. "No, I've never done anything like that," she admitted.

"Well, come try it," the clerk said. "I'm sure we'll be able to find you an empty machine." She got up from her desk. "Follow me, please."

Back in the enormous work area, little old men—too old to be conscripted—sat hunched over about a third of the sewing machines. Women of all ages used the rest. The men, with only a couple of exceptions, ignored Sylvia, so intent were they on their work. Most of the women looked her over, curious as she would have been to see who might be hired next.

"Here," the clerk said, pointing to a machine with no one at it. "Let me find you a couple of leather scraps, and you can see what it's like."

The stool behind the sewing machine had no back and was not very comfortable, but it was an improvement over standing all day, which Sylvia had been doing before. When she stretched out her right leg to set her foot on the treadle, she got a surprise.

"We have electric motors on the machine," the clerk said, seeing what must have been the startled look on her face. "It lets the operators work much faster on thick leather like this than they could with foot-powered machines. You'll see what I mean." She handed Sylvia two pieces of shoe leather. "Join these together with two straight seams about a quarter-inch apart."

"All right," Sylvia said. Sure enough, the sewing machine had a switch near the base. She flicked it, and the motor hummed to life. Before guiding the pieces of leather under the needle, she noted how sturdy it was, and how strong and thick the thread that went through the eye.

As she started to sew, her right foot went up and down, up and down, even though it wasn't on a treadle. The hiring clerk smiled. "A lot of girls do that when they first come here," she said. "Some of them keep right on doing it even after they've worked here for years."

"Do they?" Sylvia hardly noticed answering, because the needle snarled into action. The motor *was* strong as the very devil; she felt as if she were riding a poorly broken horse. The needle seemed to bite its way through the leather with every stitch the machine took. She'd hurt herself once or twice with her own sewing machine—she didn't want to think what this one would do to her hand if she slipped or got careless.

She knew nothing but relief when she turned off the machine and handed the clerk her sample work. The woman examined it, then slowly nodded. "That's very nice," she said. "Even, straight. You can do the work, no doubt about it. Starting pay is fifty cents an hour. You go up to fifty-five after three months."

That was more money than she'd been making at the cannery. "What time does the shift start tomorrow morning?" she asked.

"Eight o'clock," the hiring clerk answered. "Eight o'clock *sharp*. You're docked for every minute you're late, and for every minute you clock out early."

"I didn't expect anything different," Sylvia answered. This place looked to be like all the others. They wanted everything from the people they were generous enough to hire—that was how they'd look at it, anyhow—but what would they give back? What had the canning plant given back? Only a swift good-bye.

Still, at fifty cents an hour—fifty-five if she stayed—she'd soon make up for the time she'd lost taking care of the children. Fifty cents an hour plus the allotment she got from George's pay was pretty good money. It was more money than she'd ever imagined making for herself. It would have been more money still had prices not risen right along with, and sometimes faster than, wages.

She got reminded how prices had gone up when she stopped at the Coal Board offices on the way home from the shoe factory. Being able to go without having the children along was an unusual blessing. The Coal Board was bureaucracy at its most plodding, and George, Jr., and Mary Jane did not take well to waiting in interminable lines.

Neither did Sylvia, not when the petty functionary she finally reached told her next month's ration would be smaller but cost more. "This is the third time this year I've heard that!" she exclaimed in dismay. "It's not right."

"I'm sorry, ma'am," the fellow said, sounding not a bit sorry. *Why aren't you in the Army?* Sylvia thought resentfully. The Coal Board clerk went on, "I am not responsible for setting policy, you must understand, ma'am, only for seeing that it is carried out. Here, let me stamp your ration tickets"—he did, plying the rubber stamp with might and main—"so you can go over to Line 7C to pay for the coal. Remember, you cannot acquire it without the stamp I just gave and the pay confirmation stamp you will receive in Line 7C."

"I remember," Sylvia said. "How could I forget?" She went and stood in Line 7C, and stood there, and stood there.

At last, grudgingly, the clerk there accepted her money and added his square red stamp to the other bureaucrat's round black one. "Obtaining coal without a ration coupon showing both authorization and pay confirmation marking is a violation of law punishable by fine or imprisonment or both," he droned.

"Oh, yes, I know." Sylvia could have repeated the rigmarole back at him. She heard it every month.

"We are pleased to have been of service to you," the clerk said, just as if he meant it. Then, while she was still standing in front of him, he forgot Sylvia existed. "Next."

Luxuriating in an afternoon without the children and with a job in hand, Sylvia went out and bought a couple of shirtwaists and a skirt in the new style that daringly left the ankles bare. It was advertised as saving fabric for the war effort. That, she was convinced, had nothing to do with why only a couple were left on the rack. People finally felt victory in the air, and wanted to bust loose and go a little wild.

She took her purchases home before going out again to pick up the children. That was another small extravagance, but she would have plenty of nickels coming in to make up for the extra one she was spending on trolley fare. Both George, Jr., and Mary Jane looked forlorn, with the marks of the chicken pox still upon them, but they had been certified as noncontagious. Several of George, Jr.'s, classmates were down with the disease, as well as another girl Mrs. Dooley cared for.

After supper, the children were playing and Sylvia washing dishes when someone knocked on the door. "Who's that, Mama?" Mary Jane said.

"I don't know," Sylvia said. "I'm not expecting anyone." Apprehension filled her as she went to the door. Opening it, she breathed a silent sigh of relief to find no Western Union messenger standing there, but rather Isabella Antonelli. "Come in," Sylvia exclaimed. "Have you eaten? Can I make you coffee?"

As the children stared at the woman who was a stranger to them, Mrs. Antonelli said, "Coffee will be fine. I have eaten, yes, thank you. I am not very hungry anyhow."

The two women sat at the kitchen table and chatted. When they didn't pay much attention to George, Jr., and Mary Jane, the children gradually stopped gaping at Isabella Antonelli. Sylvia was sure she hadn't come to talk about the weather or even the high price of coal. Whatever was on her mind, she would get to it when she was ready.

Eventually, she did: "Mr. Winter asked me to marry him the other day."

"That's wonderful!" Sylvia said, at the same time thinking, *Better you than me.* "Have you set a day yet?"

"He wants it to be in about six months," Isabella answered. Slowly, deliberately, she set both hands above her navel. "That is about five months later than I would like." Her meaning was unmistakable. Sylvia's eyes widened. The widow Antonelli nodded, adding, "He does not know this yet. What do I do?"

"Oh." Sylvia understood why Isabella had not gone to her family. Even if she was a widow, they would have pitched a fit. All the Italians she'd ever met were like that. After some thought, she said, "I think you'd better tell him."

Panic filled Isabella Antonelli's face. "And what if he leaves me? I do not know if he wants a child."

"Dear, doesn't he have one whether he wants one or not?" Sylvia asked, to which Isabella gave a miserable nod. *Or you could look for an abortionist,* Sylvia thought. But she had no idea how to go about finding one; she'd never needed to, for which she heartily thanked God. She never would have advised anyone to do anything so flagrantly illegal, anyhow. And Isabella was Catholic, which would have made the suggestion worse than illegal in her eyes.

"That is so," she said now. Her fingers spread, there on her belly.

"He'd better know," Sylvia said. "It is his business, too, after all. I think he'll do what's right." She was by no means sure the canning-plant foreman would, but . . . "If he doesn't, do you want to have him around anyway?"

"With a *bambino* coming, I want someone around," Isabella said in a firm voice. "I think you are right, though. He is a good man. He will do what is right. *Grazie*. Thank you." She rose, kissed Sylvia on the cheek, and was gone before Sylvia could say good-bye—or anything else.

"Why did she come over here, Mama?" George, Jr., asked.

"To talk," Sylvia answered absently. "Why don't you and your sister get ready for bed?" She ignored the howls of protest that brought. *Better you than me, Isabella,* she thought again. *Better you than me.*

Wearily, Jefferson Pinkard and the rest of his regiment marched out of the front lines. Wearily, he groused with his buddies about how criminal it was to leave them at the front for so long without a breather. "What I reckon it is," Sergeant Albert Cross said, "is that Richmond done forgot we was even here, so of course they forgot to send anybody out to take our goddamn place."

A couple of people laughed: relatively recent replacements, most of them, who were innocent enough to think that was meant as a joke. "This Texas prairie sure as hell is the ass end of nowhere," Pinkard muttered. "Wouldn't surprise me one damn bit if everybody forgot about us."

"To me, the country does not look so bad," Hipolito Rodriguez said. Pinkard grunted; next to the chunk of Sonora Rodriguez had tried to farm, the west Texas prairie was liable to look pretty good, which, when you got down to it, was a frightening thought. The stocky little Sonoran went on, "And the Yankees, Jeff, the Yankees, they don't forget about us."

Pinkard grunted. Nobody could deny that. The U.S. advance wasn't going fast—the United States didn't have as many men in

Texas as they needed, either—but it was and remained an advance. Nobody talked about throwing them back on Lubbock any more. The most anybody would talk about was halting their advance, and talk outran reality there, too.

Sergeant Cross said, "Damn me to hell and toast my toes over the fire if it ain't gonna feel good not to get shot at for a while."

"Sí, es verdad," Hip Rodriguez said. *"Muy bueno."*

"Yeah," Pinkard said, because Rodriguez expected him to say something like that. He didn't mean it, though. He suspected his pal knew he didn't mean it. Rodriguez had enough tact for any other dozen soldiers Jeff had ever met. Jeff wanted to be in the trenches. He wanted to be in the Yankee trenches, killing Yankees. When he was doing that, he didn't have to think about anything else.

Replacements came forward to fill the trenches Pinkard and his comrades were leaving. It was a black unit, with white noncoms and officers moving the men along. *"Mallates,"* Rodriguez said, shaking his head. "You know, down where I was living, I didn't hardly never see no niggers, not till I come into the Army."

"Isn't like that in Alabama," Jeff said. " 'Bout as many of 'em back home as there are white men." *Didn't have to bring niggers down into Sonora, with greasers there already.* But he didn't say that out loud, and hoped Hip didn't know he thought it. Rodriguez was a good soldier and a good guy—a good friend—even if he was a greaser.

On they trudged, toward the tiny hamlet of Grow, Texas, whose dusty main street, all of two blocks long, made a liar of the cockeyed optimist who'd named the place. Most of the buildings along those two blocks had been turned into saloons. Texas was officially dry. Where soldiers were involved, people looked the other way.

Some of the barmaids—most of the barmaids—sold more than beer and whiskey, too. Up above every saloon were several small rooms in constant frantic use. That sort of thing did not officially exist, either. Jeff had never felt the urge to go upstairs in any place like that, of which he'd seen a good many. A few shots of whiskey, maybe some poker—that had been plenty.

He didn't know what the hell he'd do now. Along with most of his pals, he went into a saloon that called itself the Gold Nugget. When they got inside, Sergeant Cross said, "They should have named this place the Cow Pie." He didn't walk out, though. None of the other dives in Grow was any different. Sawdust on the floor, a bouncer with a bludgeon on his belt and a sawed-off shotgun by his chair, the stink of sweat and booze and the barmaids' cheap perfume . . . they all came with saloons in Grow and in any of scores of little towns behind both sides of the line from the Atlantic to the Gulf of California.

Somebody from another unit got out of a chair while Jeff was standing by it. He threw his backside into it before anyone else could. A barmaid wiggled through the crowd of soldiers trying to crowd up to the bar. Their hands roamed freely till she almost decked one of them with a roundhouse slap.

"I ain't apples, boys," she said. "You got to pay before you pinch the merchandise."

She spoke good English, but her accent reminded Pinkard of Hip Rodriguez's. So did her chamois-colored skin and black, black eyes. Most of the barmaids were of Mexican blood. A few were black. Jeff didn't see any white women at the Gold Nugget, though some did work in the other saloons in Grow.

When the barmaid finally got over to him, he ordered a double shot of whiskey and gave her a dollar, which would have been outrageous before the war and was too damned expensive now. Pinkard wasn't one of the ones who groused about that, though— what the hell else did he have to do with his money except spend it on hooch and whatever other pleasures he could find?

He knocked the whiskey back in a hurry after the barmaid— Consuela, some of the guys were calling her—brought it to him. It wasn't the sort of whiskey to sip and savor. It tasted like kerosene and went down his throat as if it were wearing shoes with long, sharp spikes. But once it got to his stomach, it made him hot and it made him stupid, and that was the point of the exercise.

He waved his empty glass, a signal that he wanted a full one to take its place. Eventually, he got one. He drank it and peered around. The Gold Nugget looked cleaner. The kerosene lamps looked brighter. He wondered what the devil the barkeep was putting in the whiskey.

When he waved the glass again, Consuela brought him another refill. She looked better, too. A moment later, she plopped herself down in his lap. Coyly, she spoke in Spanish: *"Te gustaría chingar?"*

He had a pretty good idea what it meant. *Chinga tu madre* was one of the things Hip Rodriguez yelled at the Yankees when he ran out of English. To leave Jeff in no possible doubt, Consuela wrapped her arms around his neck and gave him a big kiss. He wondered whom else she'd kissed lately—and where. After a few seconds, though, his blood heated and he stopped worrying.

"We go upstairs?" she asked, coming back to English. Then her voice got amazingly pragmatic: "Ten dollars. You have a hell of a good time."

Ten dollars was at least five dollars too much. With three doubles sloshing around inside him, Jefferson Pinkard wasn't inclined to argue. "Upstairs," he agreed, surprised at the way his tongue stumbled inside his mouth. "Ten dollars. Hell of a good time."

Going up the stairs took longer than it would have if he'd been sober. The cubicle to which Consuela led him was cramped and humid and smelled as if someone should have taken a hose to it a long time before. She held out a hand for the money, then shucked out of her clothes with nonchalant aplomb.

He had a little trouble rising to the occasion. "I'll fix," Consuela said, and started to lower her head.

"No!" Jeff exclaimed. She looked up at him in surprise; she probably hadn't had anybody refuse that offer lately. But instead of Consuela's face, Jeff saw Emily's, her eyes glowing, on the night he'd caught her with Bedford Cunningham. She'd lowered her head that same way. The mixture of pleasure and pain was too strong for him to want to repeat it.

He spat on his palm and played with himself instead till he was stiff enough to go into Consuela. She shrugged and did her best to hurry him along once he was inside her. The second after he spent himself, he wished he hadn't bothered. That was too late, of course.

Hip Rodriguez came out of a little cubicle two doors down from the one he'd used. The little Sonoran looked drunk and sad, too. "Ah, Jeff," he said, "I do this, it feels good, and I still miss my *esposa*. Maybe I miss her more than ever. Where is the sense in this? Can you tell me?" He was drunk, all right, and drunkenly serious.

"Sense?" Jefferson Pinkard shook his head. "Damned if I see any of that anywhere at all." He wondered if he missed Emily. He supposed he did. When an opium fiend couldn't get his pipe, he missed it, didn't he? That was how Jeff missed his wife. He

wanted her. He longed for her. And he wanted her and longed for
her even though he knew she wasn't good for him.

Downstairs, the bouncer and a couple of military policemen
were breaking up a brawl. The military policemen looked like
men going about their business. The bouncer looked like someone having a hell of a good time. Pinkard wouldn't have wanted
to tangle with him, and he was a big man who'd been a steelworker before going into the Army. He wondered why the
bouncer wasn't wearing a uniform himself. Maybe they didn't
make one wide enough through the shoulders to fit him. Had a
tent had sleeves, that might have worked.

Consuela didn't waste much time upstairs. Pretty soon, she
was down on the floor of the saloon again, hustling drinks. And
pretty soon again, she was going up the stairs with another
soldier.

"Look at that," Jeff said. "Just look at that. If she does that
kind of business every day, she'll end up owning half of Texas by
the time the war's over."

"Yes, and the Yankees will own the other half," Rodriguez
said. "And do you know what else, Jeff? I will not be sorry.
Sonorans have no love for Texans. More than anyone else in the
CSA, Texans treat Sonorans like niggers. Let the Yankees have
Texas. *Hasta la vista. Hasta luego.*" He waved derisively.
"Adiós."

"But you're fighting in Texas," Pinkard pointed out. "Never
heard you talk like this here before."

"Yes, I am fighting in Texas," Rodriguez agreed sadly. *"Mala
suerte*—bad luck. You never hear me talk like this?" His smile
was oddly sweet. "I am not so drunk before, I think, when we
talk of Texas."

"I don't give a damn about Texas myself any more," Pinkard
said. "Hell, we've lost the damn war. Like you say, the damnyankees are welcome to the place. All I want to do is go back
home."

"You no say, 'Go back home to my wife,' like you used to,"
Rodriguez said. "You didn't used to go up with the *putas*, neither, when they take us out of line."

"Leave it alone, Hip," Jeff said. "Leave it the hell alone.
Whatever happened back there happened, is all. It ain't anybody's business but mine."

Rodriguez looked at him with large, liquid eyes. He realized he'd never before admitted anything out of the ordinary had happened back in Birmingham. The Sonoran said, "I hope it turns out well for you, whatever it is."

"I got my doubts, but I hope so, too," Jeff said, and fell asleep in his chair.

Even out in the middle of the ocean, Sam Carsten kept a weather eye peeled for aeroplanes whenever he came out on the USS *Dakota*'s deck. He was still amazed at how much damage a bomb explosion could do; the one from the Argentine-based aeroplane had caused at least as much harm as a hit from a battleship's secondary armament.

Hastily welded sheets of steel covered the destruction the bomb had wrought; they looked as out of place as bandages covering a wound on a man's body. Because the patches were neither painted nor smooth, they drew the wrath of petty officers merely by existing. Sam laughed when he had that notion—he was a petty officer himself these days, even if he did still think like an ordinary seaman.

Hiram Kidde came up beside him. Kidde had been one of the exalted for a long time now; Carsten waited for some snide comment about the way the *Dakota* looked with a steel plate in her head, or at the least a grumble over the repairs' not having been neater.

He got nothing of the sort. What Kidde said was, "It's a good thing those limey sons of bitches didn't have an armor-piercing nose on that bomb, the way we've got armor-piercing shells. Otherwise, that one little bastard would've done even worse than it did."

Carsten considered that. After a couple of seconds, he nodded. "You're likely right, 'Cap'n,' " he said. "This was only a first try, though. I expect they'll get it right, or we will, or somebody will, pretty damn quick."

Kidde gave him a look that was anything but warm. "You know what you're saying, don't you?" he demanded. "You're saying we might as well melt the *Dakota* and all the other battlewagons in the whole damn Navy down for tin cans right now, on account of by the time the next war rolls around, aeroplanes'll sink 'em before they get within five hundred miles of where they're going."

"Am I saying that?" Sam did some more thinking. "Well,

maybe I am. But I tell you what—maybe we don't melt 'em down for cans till after this here war is over, because I don't figure the aeroplanes'll sink too many battleships this time out."

"Real white of you," the gunner's mate said. "*Real* white. You make me feel like a guy in the buggy-whip business, going broke an inch at a time because people are buying Fords instead of buggies these days."

"Hell of a big buggy whip we're sailing on," Sam observed after letting his eye run along the *Dakota* from bow to stern.

"Don't talk stupid," Hiram Kidde snapped. "You know what I'm talking about. You're a squarehead, yeah, but you never were a dumb squarehead."

"Goddamn, 'Cap'n,' you say the sweetest things," Carsten said, and they both laughed. After one more pause for thought, Carsten went on, "Maybe we'll get some use out of battleships in the next war after all." He didn't doubt there would be a next war; there would always be a next war.

Kidde got a cigar going, then held it in his mouth at an angle that made his dubious look even more dubious. "Wait a minute. You're the same guy who was just saying somebody'd have armor-piercing aeroplane bombs long about day after tomorrow, or next week at the latest. Soon as that happens, the jig is up, right?"

"Maybe," Sam said. "Maybe not, too. It's up if the aeroplanes get to drop the bombs on the ships, sure as hell. But if our side has aeroplanes, too, to shoot down the other fellow's bombing aeroplanes, the battleships can get on with the job they're supposed to be doing, right?"

Now Kidde stopped and did some thinking. "That sounds good," he said when he came out of his own study, "but I don't think it works. You squeeze enough, you might be able to mount two or three aeroplanes on a battleship, maybe one or two on a cruiser. That won't be enough to hold off all the aeroplanes the other bastards can throw at you from dry land."

"Mmm," Carsten said—an unhappy grunt. "Yeah, you're right. A fleet'd need a whole ship stuffed full of aeroplanes, and there is no such animal."

"See?" Hiram Kidde said. "You got to keep your head on your shoulders, or else you go flying off every which way." He walked down toward the stern, puffing contentedly on his cigar.

Carsten stuck his thumbs in his trouser pockets and slowly

mooched after the gunner's mate. His idea had been pretty foolish, when you got down to it. He had a picture of the Navy, whose business was ships, building a ship to take care of aeroplanes. It hung in his mental gallery right alongside the portrait of the first Negro president of the Confederate States.

The *Dakota* swung through a turn toward the west, toward the Argentine coast. Sam knew what that meant: it meant that, aeroplanes or no aeroplanes, the flotilla was going to bore in and see what they could do to the British convoys scuttling along in or near Argentine territorial waters.

He supposed that made sense. It sure as hell made dollars and cents. This attack had surely cost millions to fit out, and as surely hadn't worked near enough devastation to be worthwhile. Rear Admiral Bradley Fiske either had wireless orders from Philadelphia to do something worth doing, or else he was going to try to do something big to keep from getting wireless orders from Philadelphia telling him to sail his command back to Valparaiso and forget about marauding in the South Atlantic. Carsten had no way of knowing which of those was true, but he'd been in the Navy long enough to be pretty sure it was one or the other.

Rear Admiral Fiske was also doing everything he could to keep the *Dakota* and the American and Chilean ships with her from getting a nasty surprise of the sort they'd already had once. Long before klaxons hooted men to their battle stations, he had crews at all the antiaircraft guns on the battleship's deck.

He also sent not only the *Dakota*'s aeroplane but the other two the flotilla boasted off to the west ahead of the ships. They wouldn't be able to fight off any bombing aeroplanes, but they could at least warn of their presence. Sam wondered how much good that would do. He shrugged. It couldn't hurt.

The U.S. aeroplanes could and did do one other useful thing: they could spot convoys for the *Dakota* and her companions to attack. Down in the five-inch gun's sponson, Sam attributed a sudden shift in course to the north as likely springing from a wireless report. "Hope they haven't stuck some freighters out there to humbug us into getting too close," Luke Hoskins said.

"Now there's a nice, cheery thought," Carsten said. He turned to Hiram Kidde, who was peering out through the vision slit. "See anything, 'Cap'n'?"

"Smoke trails," the chief of the gun crew answered. "Can't spot the ships that are making 'em, though. Land behind 'em. We—"

A thunderous roar interrupted him. "That's the main armament," Sam said unnecessarily. If it weren't the main armament, it had to be the end of the world.

Kidde looked disgusted. "They must have let the big guns open up as soon as they could take the range up in the crow's nest on the observation mast. Skipper doesn't want to get in close enough to let us do any work."

"After what happened that one time, do you blame him?" Sam asked.

"Blame him? Hell, yes, I blame him. I want to be in on the fun, too, 'stead of sitting around here like some homely girl nobody wants to dance with," Kidde said. He paused. "Now if you ask me whether I think he's smart to do it this way, that's a different question. Yeah, he's smart."

"Listen," Hoskins said from behind Sam, "the best fighting is the fighting you don't have to do." As he spoke, he had both hands on the casing of a shell, ready to pass it to Carsten.

"Nope." Kidde shook his head. "What matters is winning."

"If we can win here easy enough so they don't have to squawk for the secondaries, that'll be fighting we don't have to do," Sam said. "We, this gun crew, I mean."

"Give the man a big, fat, smelly cigar and put him in the judge advocate's office," Kidde said with a snort. "Sure as hell sounds like a bunkroom lawyer to me."

"I always hated a Rebel accent," Carsten said, "but this one time when I was a kid, I heard a fellow from Louisiana going on and on about lawyers—he'd just lost a lawsuit down in the CSA, I guess—and every time he said the word, it sounded like he was saying *liars*. I liked that. The older I get, the better I like it, too."

"I remember one time I—" Luke Hoskins began. They never found out what he'd done or said or thought one time, because the main armament bellowed out another broadside. Speech was impossible through that great slab of noise, thought nearly so.

Then Kidde shouted "Hit!"—his voice sounding thin and lost after the guns spoke with twelve-inch throats. Everybody yelled after that. Carsten elbowed his way to the vision slit. Sure enough, out there far away, a British or Argentine or French freighter was burning, sending up more smoke than could ever have come out its stack.

The cruisers with the flotilla were firing, too; their guns had enough range to reach the freighters. The destroyers stayed silent, for the excellent good reason that their main armament was no match for the five-inch guns of the battleships' secondary weaponry. Battleships were fierce, proud creatures, sure as sure. Nothing that prowled the sea could beat them.

For a moment, that thought made Sam Carsten feel as large and powerful as the ship of which he was a tiny part. Then he remembered submersibles and floating mines and the gnat of an aeroplane that had carried such a nasty sting in its tail. Twenty years earlier, battleships might have been all but invulnerable, save to one another. It wasn't like that any more.

What would it be like for battleships twenty years down the road? He and Hiram Kidde had had that discussion just a little while before. He came up with the same answer as he had then: it would be tough as hell.

That was twenty years down the road, though. Now, here, the battleships and cruisers methodically pounded the convoy of freighters to bits. No one came out to challenge them: no torpedo boats, no submersibles, no aeroplanes. They had everything their own way, just as they would have in the old days before aeroplanes, before submersibles, when even torpedo boats were hardly to be feared.

Sam should have felt triumphant. In fact, he did feel triumphant, but only in a limited way. *We pounded them to bits* wasn't really what was going through his mind. It was much more on the order of, *Thank you, Jesus. We got away with one this time.*

The Canucks and the limeys were pushed back to their last line in front of Toronto. They'd been working on that line since 1914—probably since before that—and had no doubt worked on it again after barrels entered the picture. If Toronto fell, the war for Ontario was as near over as made no difference. They did not intend to let it fall.

What the Canadians and British intended was not the most urgent thing on Jonathan Moss' mind. He had been a part of the struggle since the day it opened. Thinking back on the Curtiss Super Hudson aeroplane with the pusher prop he'd flown then, he laughed. If either side presumed to put a flimsy old bus like that in the air in this modern day and age, it would last only until the first enemy fighting scout spotted it and shot it down— unless, of course, it fell out of the sky of its own accord, as such antiques had been all too prone to do.

Moss set a gloved hand on the doped-fabric skin of his fast, graceful, streamlined Wright two-decker. Here was a machine to conjure with, nothing like the awkward makeshifts with which both the Quadruple Alliance and the Entente had gone to war.

Archie from the enemy's antiaircraft guns burst a little below Moss' flight. Some of those black puffs came close enough to make his aeroplane jerk from the concussion. He started his game of avoidance, speeding up, slowing down, gaining a little altitude, losing some, swinging his course now a few degrees to one side, now a few to the other.

Along both sides of the line, tethered observation balloons hung in the sky like fat sausages. Some pilots went hunting for them with whole belts of tracer ammunition, hoping the flaming phosphorus that made the rounds visible would set the hydrogen in the balloons afire. Anyone who got forced down on the other side's territory with that kind of load in his guns was unlikely to survive the experience, even if he landed perfectly.

And some pilots hunted balloons with no more than their usual ammunition. Moss had gone after a few in his time on the front line, but he'd never really worked at being a balloon buster. To him, enemy aeroplanes and enemy troops on the ground seemed more important targets.

Here today, though, one balloon in particular caught his eye. It had to be floating close to a mile in the air, a thousand feet or so higher than the other gas-filled cylinders from which observers watched U.S. troops movements and called artillery down on the Americans' heads.

Moss grunted, a sound of discontent he could not hear over the roar of the engine and the shriek of the wind. That balloon was liable to be a trap. The enemy always had plenty of Archie around his sausages. If they'd run up a balloon there just to lure U.S. aeroplanes, they were liable to have more than plenty. But those extra thousand feet would give an observer a long, long look behind the American lines.

If the observation balloon was a trap, it was—that was all there was to it. Trap or not, it needed taking out. Moss nodded to himself as decision firmed. He swung his aeroplane toward the balloon. Percy Stone, Hans Oppenheim, and Pete Bradley followed without hesitation, though they had to know what they were liable to be getting into.

Sure as hell, heavy antiaircraft fire burst around Moss' two-decker as he approached the balloon. "Told you so," he said to no one in particular. He did settle one thing to his satisfaction, though: it *was* an observation balloon, not just a trap. He could see a man moving in the wicker basket beneath the gas bag.

Often, a balloon's groundcrew would reel it in by its cable when it came under attack. That didn't happen here. Maybe the observer thought the Archie would drive off the U.S. aeroplanes. Maybe he was a patriot. Maybe he was a damn fool. Moss neither knew nor cared. If the fellow stayed up there so temptingly high, he was going to get himself and his balloon shot to bits.

The twin machine guns mounted about the fighting scout's engine started chattering. Moss aimed the stream of bullets first at the balloon and then at the smaller, more difficult target the wicker basket made.

To his amazement, the enemy observer started shooting back. He was hideously outgunned, but he'd brought a rifle up there to keep him company, and he was taking aimed potshots at Moss and his flightmates. The son of a bitch was a good shot, too. A bullet cracked past Moss' head, close enough to scare him out of a year's growth. He jammed his thumb down on the firing button as hard as he could, trying to blow holes in that crazy Canadian or eccentric Englishman or whatever the hell he was. He'd never live it down if he got shot down by an observer in a balloon basket.

That was a joke, something to laugh at, till Hans Oppenheim's aeroplane pulled out of its run at the balloon and broke back toward the west, toward the American lines. Either the bus or Oppenheim himself was in trouble; Moss saw to his astonished dismay that his flightmate wasn't going to make it back to territory the U.S. Army controlled. Down Hans went, not far from an enemy artillery position.

Canucks and limeys came running from every direction toward Oppenheim's aeroplane. After seeing that, Moss had to look away, because he was around the far side of the balloon, with that infernal observer still blazing away at him and Stone and Bradley. The son of a bitch was a *good* shot. A bullet thrummed through the tight-stretched fabric of the fuselage, about three feet behind Moss' seat.

He whipped the Wright two-decker into a tight turn and bored in on the observation balloon, Stone behind him to the right, Bradley to the left. "There!" he shouted in savage exultation, as the hydrogen in the fabric sausage finally caught fire. "That'll teach you, you bastard."

Maybe nothing would teach the observer. Even as his crew on the ground at last began hauling down the flaming balloon, he calmly climbed over the edge of the wicker basket from which he'd fought so hard and so well and leaped off into space.

His parachute must have been connected to the basket by a static line, for the big silk canopy opened almost at once. Pilots of fighting scouts were not issued parachutes. Moss didn't know whether to be jealous or to despise the device as a sissy affectation.

The latter, he decided, and swung the nose of his aeroplane down a little. A burst from his machine gun, and the observer hung limp and unmoving beneath the 'chute. Maybe Moss wouldn't have done it had the fellow not shot down his friend. But maybe he would have, too; that Canuck or limey or whoever he was had been too damn good to let him live.

Moss swooped down below the thunderous Archie and streaked toward the spot where Hans Oppenheim's aeroplane went down. His flightmate wasn't inside the bus any more; dead or alive, the enemy soldiers had taken him away. A crowd of men in khaki were gathered around the Wright. Moss machine-gunned them, and whooped with glee to watch them scatter. Some didn't scatter—some crumpled and wouldn't get up again.

Then Moss and Stone and Bradley zoomed past the disabled two-decker and low over the front line. The Canadian and British troops in the trenches gave them a warm sendoff with rifle and machine-gun fire. And then, because they were coming out of the east, half the Americans assumed they had to be hostile and fired at them, too. More bullets pierced Moss' aeroplane.

"Now wouldn't that be bully?" he growled. "Hell of a mission to have to try and explain to Major Cherney: a balloon observer shot down one machine from the flight and our own ground fire made another one crash. He'd love that, yes he would. He'd love it a hell of a lot."

But his two-decker kept flying, and so, he saw to his relief in the rearview mirror, did those of Percy Stone and Pete Bradley. U.S. antiaircraft guns opened up on them, too, but they made it back to the Orangeville aerodrome unscathed.

As Moss had known it would be, "What happened to Lieutenant Oppenheim?" was the first question the groundcrew asked after he shut off the motor and the sounds of the outside world returned to his ears. After he answered, the silence that fell made him wonder if he'd gone deaf.

"You're joking, ain't you, sir?" asked a fitter who was walking down the length of the fuselage and examining the bullet holes Moss had picked up. "I mean to say, you guys shoot at the balloons. The guys in the balloons don't shoot back—that's Archie's job."

"You know that, Herm, and I know that," Moss said, "but nobody ever told this skunk. One thing, though—he won't ever do it again." The groundcrew man nodded at the grim emphasis he gave the words.

As they walked toward Major Cherney's tent, Stone and Bradley sounded as disbelieving as had Herm. "The nerve of that son of a gun," Bradley said, over and over. "The nerve!"

"Good thing you got him," Stone said to Moss. "If somebody didn't punch his ticket for him, he'd have ended up an ace, and he hasn't even got a motor in that damn thing."

When they told Major Cherney what had happened to Hans Oppenheim, the squadron leader looked at them for a long time without saying anything. At last, he did speak: "You really mean it." Solemnly, Moss, Stone, and Bradley nodded. Cherney shook his head. "You go into a war. You fight it for damn near three years. You think you've heard every single thing that could happen. And then . . ." He shook his head again. "Shot down by an observer in a balloon. I will be goddamned. Maybe it's just as well for him that he didn't make it back to our side of the line. Nobody would ever have let him forget it."

"I only hope he's alive *to* try and forget it, sir," Pete Bradley said. "I couldn't tell when we flew over his aeroplane."

"Neither could I," Moss and Stone said together.

"I will be goddamned," Major Cherney repeated. He let out a long, slow sigh. "Maybe the Canucks will let us know. They do sometimes when one of our boys gets forced down on their side, same as we do for them."

Two days later, an enemy aeroplane dropped a note behind the U.S. line in a washed-out jam tin made more noticeable by the small 'chute taken from a parachute flare. It duly made its way back to the Orangeville aerodrome, where Major Cherney called in Moss, Stone, and Bradley. "Hansie died of wounds," he said heavily. "The Canadians buried him with full military honors, for whatever it's worth."

"Thank you, sir," Jonathan Moss said. With one accord, he and his flightmates headed for the officers' club after they left the squadron commander's tent. After they had the first of what would be many drinks in front of them, Moss turned to the men on whom his life depended—and *vice versa*—and said, "Well, boys, I wonder what sort of bird'll join our flock next."

"Won't be long till we find out," Bradley said. Soberly—for the time being—Moss nodded.

Time hung heavy in the hospital. Lying there with a rubber drainage tube coming out of the shoulder that still stubbornly refused to heal, Reggie Bartlett had plenty of time to think and very little chance to do anything else.

One of the things he thought about—and disapproved of—was the weather. "You all sure this is really Yankee country?" he asked the wounded U.S. soldiers who filled most of the beds in the big ward. "Richmond doesn't get any hotter and stickier than this."

"St. Louis, sure as hell," Pete reminded him. The one-legged soldier winked. "You ought to feel at home, ain't that right?"

"Doesn't mean I liked the weather," Reggie said. "Anybody who likes summer in the Confederate States is crazy." He turned to his countryman for support. "Isn't that right, Rehoboam?"

The Negro was scratching toes on the foot he no longer had, as he often did. He said, "Don't know nothin' 'bout what it's like in Richmond. Out in the fields down around Hattiesburg, Mississippi, where I's from, it gets powerful hot in the summertime. This ain't a patch on that, I don't reckon."

"From what I've heard about Mississippi, I expect hell would look chilly in the summertime next to it," Reggie said thoughtfully. His shoulder twinged. He grunted and thought some more till the pain faded. Then he added, "Working in the fields down there doesn't sound like a whole lot of fun."

Rehoboam looked at him from across the aisle. "You ain't the stupidest white man I ever did see."

Pete whistled. "You gonna let him talk to you like that, Reggie? I thought a smoke who talked to a white man like that down in the CSA could go and write his will—except you wouldn't let him learn to write and he wouldn't own enough to bother leaving it to anybody."

"You're a natural-born troublemaker," Reggie told him. "If

you still had that other leg, I'd tear it off you and beat Rehoboam to death with it. That'd settle both of you. There. Are you satisfied now?"

"Minute I woke up and found out I was shy a pin, I was satisfied and then some, I'll tell you that right now," the amputee answered. "Right then, I knew I'd had all the fighting I was ever going to do."

Reggie only grunted in reply to that. He still wasn't satisfied, not in that sense. If he ever got healed up, he'd try to escape again. He'd done it once; he didn't think doing it again would be so hard. But, while his leg wound bothered him less each day, pus still dripped from that shoulder. It left him sore and weak and feverish. There were lots of things he told himself he should be doing, but he lacked the energy to do any of them. Lying here was what he was up to, and lying here was what he did.

In came the nurse with a tray of suppers. Everyone got an identical slab of chicken breast—or possibly it was baked cardboard—an identical lump of mashed potatoes with gravy that looked and tasted like rust and machine oil, and something that might have been bread pudding or might have been sponge in molasses.

After working his way through the dismal meal, Reggie said, "You Yankees are winning the damn war—or you say you are—and this is what they give you? God have mercy on you if you were losing, that's all I can tell you."

"If cooking was something they shot out of the barrel of a gun, we'd be good at it," Pete said. "Since it ain't, we haven't much bothered with it since the end of the Second Mexican War. Had more important things to worry about instead."

Rehoboam said, "The kind o' cooking you Yankees do here, y'all ought to shoot it out the barrel of a gun."

"Amen," Reggie said. "But if you shot it at our side, you'd just make the boys fight harder, for fear of having to eat like that all the time."

Pete laughed. So did the rest of the wounded U.S. soldiers. They were no fonder of the grub the military hospital doled out than were their Confederate counterparts. And so did Rehoboam. But his laugh had an edge to it, and his dark face twisted in a way that for once had nothing to do with the pain and phantom itches from his missing foot.

"What's chewing on you?" Reggie called across the aisle.

"What do you reckon?" Rehoboam returned. "When you was talkin' 'bout what the boys'd do, you didn't mean me. I ain't *the boys* to you, an' I ain't never gwine be *the boys*, neither. I's just a nigger, an' I'd be a nigger without a gun if all the whites in the CSA wasn't worse afeared o' the damnyankees kickin' 'em in the ass than they was of putting a Tredegar in my hands and callin' me a sojer."

He hadn't spoken in a loud voice, but he hadn't particularly kept it down, either. Everybody in the ward must have heard him. Silence slammed down. Everybody looked toward Reggie Bartlett, to see what he would say.

He hadn't the faintest idea what the devil *to* say. He'd seen for himself that Confederate blacks harbored a deep and abiding loathing for the whites who ruled them. Outside of the prisoner-of-war camp in West Virginia, though, none of them had ever come out and said so to his face.

Rehoboam pressed the point, too: "What you think, Reggie? Is that the truth, or ain't it?"

Bartlett had never had a Negro simply call him by his name before, either. He said, "Yeah, that's the truth. I was there in Capitol Square in Richmond when President Wilson declared war on the USA, and I cheered and threw away my straw boater, same as every other damn fool in the place. If we could have licked these fellows here"—he waved with his good arm at the men in the green-gray hospital gowns—"without giving black men guns, of course we'd've done it."

"Kept things like they always was, you mean," Rehoboam said.

"Of course," Reggie repeated. Only after the words were out of his mouth did he realize it wasn't necessarily *of course*. White Confederate public opinion was so wedded to the *status quo* that realizing other choices were possible came hard.

Then Pete stuck his oar in the water, saying, "Blacks got guns of their own any which way."

"Don't know much about that, especially not firsthand," Bartlett said. "I got captured over on the Roanoke front before the risings started, and they'd been put down by the time I got loose."

"Bunch of Reds." Pete gleefully stoked the fire.

He got Rehoboam hot, too. "You take a man and you work him like they works niggers in the CSA," the Negro growled, "and if he *don't* turn into no Red, he ain't much in the way of a man. Wasn't for the risings, I don't reckon Congress never would've done nothin' about the Army."

"Wouldn't be surprised if you're right," Reggie said. "But they did do something, you know. I was thinking about that a while ago. When you go back to Mississippi, you'll be a citizen, with all the same rights I've got."

"Mebbe," Rehoboam said through clenched teeth. "Mebbe not, too."

"It's what the law says," Bartlett pointed out.

"Ain't got no black police. Ain't got no black lawyers. Ain't got no black judges. Ain't got no black politicians." Rehoboam rolled his eyes at Reggie's naïveté. "How much good you reckon the law gwine do fo' the likes o' me?"

To Reggie, a law was a law, to be obeyed automatically for no better reason than that it was there. Seeing another side of things made him feel jittery, as if an earthquake had just shaken his bed. Still, he answered, "If there's enough of the likes of you, you'll do all right."

"You reckon the stork brings the babies, too?" Rehoboam asked acidly. "Or do you figure they finds 'em under the cabbage leaves when they wants 'em?"

The ward erupted in laughter, laughter aimed at Reggie. His ears got hot. "No," he said with venom of his own. "The Red party chairman or general secretary assigns 'em. That's how it worked in the Socialist Republics, isn't it?"

"You liable to be too smart for your own good," Rehoboam said after a pause.

"I doubt it, not if I volunteered for the Army," Bartlett replied. "And if you didn't want to be a citizen, and if you didn't think being a citizen was worth anything, what made you put on butternut?"

That made the Negro pause again. "Mebbe I was hopin' more'n I was expectin', you know what I'm sayin'?"

As a white man, as a white man living in a country that had beaten its neighbor two wars in a row, Bartlett had seldom had to worry about hope. His expectations, and those of his white countrymen, were generally fulfilled. He said, "I wonder what the Confederate States will look like after the war's over."

"Smaller," Pete put in.

Both men from the CSA ignored him. Rehoboam said, "We don't get what's comin' to us, we jus' rise up again."

"You'll lose again," Reggie said. "Aren't enough of you, and you still won't have enough guns. And we won't be fighting the damnyankees any more."

"Mebbe they give us a hand," Rehoboam said. "Mebbe they give us guns."

"Not likely." Now Reggie's voice was blunt. "They don't much fancy black folks themselves, you know. If we deal with you, that'd suit them fine."

And Rehoboam, who had answered back as boldly as if he were a man who had known himself to be free and equal to all other men since birth, now fell silent. His eyes flicked from one of the wounded U.S. soldiers with whom he shared the ward to the next. Whatever he saw there did not reassure him. He buried his face in his hands.

Pete said, "I guess you told him."

"I guess I did," said Reggie, who had not expected the Negro to have so strong a reaction over what was to him simply a fact of nature. He called to Rehoboam, "Come on, stick your chin up. It's not that bad."

"Not for you." Rehoboam's voice was muffled by the palms of his hands. "You're white, you goddamn son of a bitch. You got the world by the balls, just on account of the noonday sun kill you dead."

"If I had the world by the balls, none of these damnyankee bastards would have shot me," Bartlett pointed out.

Rehoboam grunted. Finally, he said, "You had the world by the balls when you wasn't in the Army, anyways. It's the rich white bastards who don't never have to fight got the world by the balls all the time."

"See? I knew you were a Red," Reggie said.

"Maybe he's just a good Socialist," Pete said.

"What the hell's the difference?" Reggie demanded.

Rehoboam and Pete both got offended. They both started to explain the difference. Then they started to argue about the difference, as if one of them were a Methodist preacher and the other a hardshell Baptist. Reggie lay back and enjoyed the show. It was the most entertainment he'd had since he got wounded.

Bertha came back into Flora Hamburger's private office. "Congresswoman, Mr. Wiggins is here to see you. Your two o'clock appointment."

"Thank you," Flora told the secretary. "Send him in."

She put away the Transportation Committee report she'd been reading and wondered again whether she should have made the appointment with Mr. Edward C.L.—he'd insisted on both middle initials—Wiggins. Over the telephone, he hadn't described his reason for wanting to see her as anything more specific than "a matter of possible common interest." Well, if that was a polite way of leading up to offering her a bribe, she'd show him out the door one minute and put the U.S. marshals on his trail the next.

In he came. He proved to be a chunky little man in his late forties, sweating in a wool tweed suit and vest and fanning himself with a straw hat. "Very pleased to make your acquaintance in person, ma'am," he said, giving Flora a nod just short of a bow. His manner was courtly, almost stagily so.

"Pleased to meet you, too," Flora answered, wondering if she was lying. She did not believe in beating around the bush: "Now that we *are* meeting in person, I hope you will tell me what you have in mind."

"I certainly aim to," Edward C.L. Wiggins replied. "I want you to know, I truly do admire the way you've spoken out against the war, both before you got elected to Congress and since. I think it does you great credit."

Flora had not expected that tack. "Thank you," she said. "But I don't quite see what that has to do with—"

"I'll tell you, then," Wiggins broke in. "You are not the only one who thinks this war was a mistake from the beginning and has gone on far too long already. I do hope your brother is doing well."

"As well as you can with one leg," Flora said tightly. Then she stared at her visitor. "How do you know about David and what happened to him? Are you connected with the War Department, and coming around here to gloat because I wouldn't play along with you?"

"No, ma'am." Edward C.L. Wiggins raised his right hand, as if taking an oath. "I have nothing to do with the U.S. government, nothing whatsoever. The people I have to do with don't want this war to go on any more. They want to end it as soon as may be. That's why I'm here: because you've been bold enough and brave enough and wise enough to want the killing stopped, too."

"Thank you," Flora repeated. "Who *are* the people you have

to do with?" He was not a Socialist. She was sure of that. He behaved like a prominent man in his own circle, whatever that was, and it was not hers. Were the remnant Republicans approaching her with some kind of deal? Was he a renegade Democrat? A capitalist who'd grown a conscience?

"You must understand, this is at present highly unofficial, ma'am," Wiggins said. Flora did not reply. In another moment, she was going to ask her visitor to leave. He must have sensed that, for he sighed and went on more quickly than he'd spoken before: "Very well, ma'am; I rely on your discretion. Unofficially, I have to do with President Gabriel Semmes, down in Richmond. The Confederate States are looking to see if there might be an honorable way to put an end to this ghastly war."

Flora Hamburger gaped. That was among the last answers she'd expected. "Why me?" she blurted. "If President Semmes wants peace, why not go straight to President Roosevelt, who can give it to him?"

"Because President Roosevelt has made it plain he does not want peace, or peace this side of subjugation," Wiggins replied. "Sooner than accept that, the CSA will go on fighting: I was instructed to be very clear there. But a fair peace, an equitable peace, a peace between equals, a peace that will let both sides rebuild after this devastation—that, President Semmes will accept, and gladly."

"I see," Flora said slowly. She had no great love for President Gabriel Semmes, reckoning him as much a class enemy of the proletariat as Theodore Roosevelt. His unofficial emissary had approached her in defense of no principle save his country's interest. Still . . . "I will take what you have said to President Roosevelt. I can urge him to accept the kind of peace you are talking about, though you have given me no details. Kentucky has rejoined the USA, for instance. How do you stand on that?"

"We would accept the results of plebiscites as binding, there and elsewhere," Wiggins answered. Flora nodded in understanding and some admiration. That not only had a fine democratic ring to it, it was likely to favor the CSA. Edward C.L. Wiggins went on, "We are also ready to negotiate all other matters standing in the way of peace between our two great American nations."

"If President Roosevelt wishes to reach you, how may he do so?" Flora asked.

"I am at the Aldine Hotel, on Chestnut Street," Wiggins said. Flora nodded again and wrote that down, though she had not taken notes on any other part of the conversation. Wiggins rose, bowed, and departed.

Flora stared down for a long time at the address she'd written. Then she picked up the telephone and told the switchboard operator she wished to be connected with the Powel House. "Congresswoman Hamburger?" President Roosevelt boomed in her ear a couple of minutes later. "To what do I owe the honor of this call?" *Why does a radical Socialist congresswoman want to talk with me?* was what he meant.

She gave him the gist of what Wiggins had told her, finishing, "In my opinion, Mr. President, any chance to end this horrible war is a good one."

Roosevelt was silent for a while, a novelty in itself. Then he said, "Miss Hamburger, your brother-in-law lost his life in the service of his country. Your brother has been wounded in that service, and my heart goes out to him and to you and to your family. I am going to speak plainly to you now. In a fight, if you have a man down, you had better not let him up until you have finished beating him. Otherwise, he will think he could have beaten you, and he will try to beat you again first chance he sees. If the Confederate States want to say 'Uncle,' they shouldn't come pussyfooting up to you and whisper it. Let them cry 'Uncle!' for the whole wide world to hear."

"Haven't you seen enough fighting yet, Mr. President?" Flora asked.

"As for seeing it, I've seen a great deal more than you have," Roosevelt answered. "I've seen enough that I don't want to see more in a generation's time. And that is why, before I make peace with Confederate States, I aim to lick them till they don't dream about getting up any more, and Canada right along with 'em."

"If the Confederate States are seeking terms of peace, don't you think they've seen enough war?" Flora said.

"If they want peace, Miss Hamburger," Roosevelt told her again, "let them come right out and say so instead of sneaking around behind my back. Can *you* grant them peace, pray tell?"

"Of course not," Flora said, "though I would if I could."

"*I* would not," Roosevelt said, "most especially not if they go about it in this underhanded way. And, since I was comfortably returned as president of the United States, defeating Senator

Debs who shares your views, I must conclude that my views on the subject are also the views of the large majority of the American people."

That was probably true. Because of it, Flora did not have a good opinion of the political wisdom of the large majority of the American people. Nationalism kept too many from voting their class interests. She said, "Mr. Wiggins—Mr. Edward C.L. Wiggins—is staying at the Aldine Hotel. I think you should hear him out, to see if the terms Richmond proposes are acceptable to you."

"Not bloody likely," Roosevelt said with a snort. "What did this fellow with the herd of initials have to say about Kentucky, for instance?"

Roosevelt might be a class enemy, but he was no fool. Flora reminded herself of it again: he went straight for the center of things. Reluctantly, she answered, "He spoke of a plebiscite, and—"

"No," Roosevelt broke in. "Kentucky is ours, and stays ours. And I need hear no more. When the Confederate States are serious, they will let us know. Good day, Miss Hamburger." He hung up.

So did Flora, angrily. Slighted was the least of what she felt. Her first instinct was to call or wire half a dozen good Socialist newspapers and break the story of the president's refusal to negotiate with the CSA. But, before she picked up the telephone once more, she had second thoughts that had nothing to do with Socialism and everything to do with the ghetto from which her family had escaped to the United States. *Don't do anything to make things worse* was the eleventh commandment of the ghetto, at least as important as the original ten.

And so, when she did pick up the telephone, it was not to call the newspapers: not at first, at any rate. Instead, when her call was answered, she said, "May I please speak with Mr. Blackford? This is Miss Hamburger."

"Hello, Flora," Hosea Blackford said a moment later. "To what do I owe the pleasure of this call?"

Flora felt her face heat at Blackford's cordial—maybe even more than cordial—tone. As baldly as she could, she told him of the approach from Edward C.L. Wiggins, and of President Roosevelt's response to it. When she was through, she said, "I want to expose Roosevelt for the bloodthirsty rogue he is, but at the same time I don't want to do anything that would hurt the Party."

Blackford was silent even longer than Roosevelt had been when she put Wiggins' proposal to him. She heard him sigh, start to speak, and then stop. At last, he said, "Much as I regret admitting it, I would advise you to keep Mr.—Wiggins', was it?—visit to yourself. You might embarrass Teddy if you thunder what he did from the rooftops. You might, I say, but I wouldn't want to bet on it. You're too much likelier to embarrass us instead."

Flora made automatic protest: "This is a capitalists' war. If we can keep the workers and farmers of one country from slaughtering those of another in the sacred name of profit, how can we hold back?"

"Because the workers and farmers of the United States will be perfectly happy to slaughter those of the Confederacy and Canada as long as they win in the end." Was Blackford mournful or cynical or both at once? Flora couldn't tell. The congressman from Dakota went on, "A year ago, I would have told you to take it to the papers as fast as you could. A year ago, the war was going nowhere."

"And because it was going nowhere, the Confederate States wouldn't have come to anyone in Congress looking for a way out," Flora said.

"Exactly." Blackford paused for a moment, perhaps to nod. "But if you go to the papers now, with the war on the edge of being won, Roosevelt will crucify us and say we're jogging his elbow—and I'm afraid people will believe him."

"But—" Flora didn't go on right away, either. She sighed instead; it seemed to be her turn. Then she said, "All right, Hosea; thank you. You may be right." Only then did she realize she'd called him by his first name.

"I am right. I wish I weren't, but I am," he said, and changed the subject: "How is your brother doing?"

"He's not going to die," Flora answered. "He's out of the woods, as far as that goes. He's only going to be crippled for life, in this war that Teddy Roosevelt has brought to the edge of being won, this war where we don't dare jog his elbow, this great, grand, glorious, triumphant war." She hung up the telephone and, very quietly, began to cry.

XIV

When Luther Bliss unhappily released him from the Covington, Kentucky, city hall, Cincinnatus had devoutly hoped he would not see the inside of the building again. That hope failed. Here he stood outside the city hall, soon to be inside once more, and, very much to his surprise, he was not filled with panic.

One thing he had seen since the USA drove the CSA from Kentucky: bureaucrats were far more numerous and far more thorough than their C.S. counterparts. That had a great deal to do with why he was standing in front of the Covington city hall in the middle of a long line of Negroes. He and they laughed and gossiped as the line moved forward. Why not? They were friends and neighbors; the new government of Kentucky had been summoning Covington's Negroes to the city hall a few square blocks at a time.

"I tell you," somebody behind him said, "this here gonna make the passbooks we had to put up with look downright puny alongside it. You step out of line now and they kin step on your whole blame family, wherever they be in the USA."

"Ain't doin' nothin' with us the white folks ain't done to themselves," somebody else answered.

"And they reckon they's free," the first speaker said, and shook his head.

"They ain't free," Cincinnatus said. "All the taxes they got to pay, they're powerful expensive. And now we get to be just like them. Ain't that bully?"

Nobody answered, not straight out. A couple of people let their eyes flick toward a white policeman who was standing not far away. Cincinnatus looked his way, too, then nodded ever so slightly. He'd pitched his words about right. The people he wanted to hear had heard, while the cop with his billy club and permanent tough expression hadn't noticed a thing.

As the line snaked forward, the man right behind Cincinnatus murmured, "Don't want to let the white folks know you's a Red."

"Ain't against the law, not like it used to be," Cincinnatus answered, but the fellow had a point. Cincinnatus glanced at the white cop again. He wondered if the bruiser had been a policeman when the CSA ruled Covington, or if he was one of Luther Bliss' men. If he belonged to Bliss' Kentucky State Police, he was liable to be more dangerous than he looked.

Once Cincinnatus got inside the city hall, he found himself face-to-face with white petty officials whose faces said they were disgusted at having to show up for work of a Sunday. That he and his fellow Negroes might also be unhappy at having to come to the city hall on Sunday never seemed to enter their minds. That surprised Cincinnatus not a bit.

"What's your name, boy?" a clerk snapped when he got to the head of the line.

"Cincinnatus, suh," Cincinnatus answered. Kentucky might be part of the USA again, but the clerk, by his accent, had likely served the Confederate States far longer than his new country. Long and sometimes bitter experience warned Cincinnatus to walk soft.

Not soft enough. "Cinci—what?" the clerk demanded, even though Cincinnati was just across the Ohio River. He gnawed at the top of his fountain pen. Toothmarks showed that was a habit of his. "I don't reckon you can spell that for me, can you?"

"Yes, suh, I can," Cincinnatus said, as quietly and submissively as he could. He spoke the letters one by one, slowly enough so that the clerk had no trouble writing them down. Then he gave his address. Reading upside down, he saw that the clerk had misspelled the name of his street. He did not correct the man; being literate gave him a leg up on being thought uppity, and he was already in enough hot water with enough different people.

"Family?" the clerk asked.

"My wife Elizabeth, my son Achilles," Cincinnatus answered. He had to spell *Achilles*, too.

As if taking some small revenge for that, the clerk shook his head. "Not enough, boy. You got any other kin in town, any other kin at all, who haven't been registered yet? Names and addresses both, mind you—you reckon I'm gonna let you waste my time, you can think again."

"My pa's called Seneca. My mother's name is Livia." Cincinnatus gave their address, too.

"*Now* we're gettin' somewhere," the clerk said in sour satisfaction. He gnawed the pen some more, scribbled on the form in front of him, and went on, "All right, boy, what surname are you choosing for this lot of people here?"

Having hashed that out with his family ahead of time, Cincinnatus answered without hesitation: "Driver, suh."

"Driver," the clerk repeated. He seemed to weigh it on some mental scales, which finally came down on the side of approval. "Well, that's not too bad. Anybody would've asked me, I'd've told him letting niggers own surnames was a pack of damnfoolishness, but nobody asked me. Even niggers have surnames in the USA, and we're in the USA, so . . ." He shrugged, as if to show he wasn't responsible for the policy he had to carry out.

"Makes it easier to keep tabs on us," Cincinnatus said, not altogether without bitterness.

"Did fine with passbooks for a hell of a long time," the clerk said, but he brightened, if only fractionally. "Maybe you're right." He wrote some more, reading as he wrote. "Cincinnatus Driver. Elizabeth Driver. Achilles Driver. Seneca Driver. Livia Driver. Wherever any of you go in the United States, that there last name goes with you."

When you got right down to it, that was a pretty large thought. "You don't mind me sayin' so, I'd sooner carry around a name than a passbook."

The clerk looked at Cincinnatus as if he emphatically did mind his saying any such thing. "Cards for all you people will be coming in the mail in the next few days. From now on, if it has to do with you, it has to do with Cincinnatus Driver, whatever it is. You got that, boy?"

"Yes, suh," Cincinnatus answered.

"Then get the hell out of here," the clerk said, and Cincinnatus—Cincinnatus Driver—took his leave. Behind him, the clerk called "Next!" and the black man in back of Cincinnatus stepped forward to take his place.

He got out of the Covington city hall as fast as he could; he kept expecting Luther Bliss to pop out of nowhere and start grilling him. Had the Kentucky State Police chief known what all Cincinnatus had done instead of merely suspecting him because of the company he kept, he would have been in a different line, a line where his ankles were shackled to those of the prisoners in front of and behind him.

When he got outside, he let out a sigh of relief. He also felt a surge of pride that surprised him. Somebody might actually call him *Mr. Driver* now, a form of address impossible before. In the form of his name—if in very little else—he had become a white man's equal.

He spotted Apicius in the line snaking its way toward the building. The barbecue cook saw him, too, and waved. As he waved back, he wondered what the local Red leader would think of this small measure of equality. Nothing much, he suspected; *mystification* was one of Apicius' favorite words.

Apicius waved again, more urgently this time. With a certain amount of reluctance, Cincinnatus approached. "What are you callin' yourself?" the fat black man asked him.

"Driver," Cincinnatus answered. "How 'bout you? You gonna be Cook?"

"Hell, no." Apicius' jowls wobbled as he scornfully shook his head. "I'm gonna call me an' my boys Wood. You ain't got the right wood in the fire, you ain't got no barbecue."

"Apicius Wood." As the clerk had before, Cincinnatus tested the flavor of the new surname. As the clerk had, he decided he approved. "Sounds pretty good, you want to know what I think."

"Don't care much," the Red answered, "on account of it don't matter a hill of beans any which way. Just one more tool of the oppressors to do a better job of exploitin' us. Hell of a lot easier to keep track of Apicius Wood than it is to keep track of Apicius the barbecue king."

He made no particular effort to keep his voice down. Most Kentucky Negroes, like most down in what was still the CSA, had at least some sympathy for the Marxist line. Cincinnatus felt that way himself. Grinning at Apicius, though, he said, "They ain't gonna have much trouble keepin' track o' you."

Apicius set his hands on his hips, which only made him look wider than ever. "I ain't sayin' you're wrong, mind you, but I ain't sayin' you're right, neither," he said. "Other thing is, ain't a whole lot o' niggers stand out in a crowd like I do." He snapped his fingers. "In a crowd—that reminds me, goddamn if it don't."

"Reminds you of what?" Cincinnatus asked.

"Reminds me of why Tom Kennedy got his head blown off," Apicius replied.

Cincinnatus stiffened. "I think maybe you better tell me whatever it is you reckon you know."

"Wonder if I ought to," Apicius said thoughtfully. "I still don't know whose game you're playin'."

"I'm playing my own game, goddammit," Cincinnatus replied in a low, furious voice. "And I'll tell you somethin' else, too—I know how to play rough. You don't reckon I'm tellin' you the truth, you remember what happened to Conroy's store and you reckon it up again."

"You come prowlin' round my place, you ain't goin' home again," Apicius told him. "Catfish on the river bottom git hungry this time o' year." Cincinnatus looked back at him and said not a word. The barbecue cook was the first to shift from foot to foot. "Dammit, I do recollect about Conroy's."

"Tell me what you know, then."

"Think about it like this," Apicius said. "Think about how come Kennedy came round your place. Think about how come he didn't go to Conroy or any o' them Confederate diehards."

Cincinnatus duly thought about it. His first thought was the one Apicius no doubt wanted him to have: that Kennedy had fallen foul of the diehards and was trying to escape them. But Cincinnatus' ex-boss could as easily have been fleeing Luther Bliss or the U.S. Army. Or, for that matter, the Reds might have been after him while trying to make him—and Cincinnatus—think someone else was.

Letting Apicius see any of those thoughts but the first one was dangerous. "Uh-*huh*," Cincinnatus said, as if to tell the Red leader he was with him and had not gone one step beyond him.

A broad, friendly grin spread over Apicius' face. Cincinnatus trusted it no further than he would have trusted a smile from Luther Bliss. Apicius said, "That's the way the money goes."

Pop goes the weasel, Cincinnatus thought. *Popped right between the eyes, most likely. And I'm the weasel.* He took up his new surname and carried it off toward his home.

"We've grabbed 'em by the nose!" Lieutenant General George Custer said in the map room of what had been the Tennessee state capitol. "Now we have to kick 'em in the pants."

"Yes, sir," Major Abner Dowling said resignedly. Custer was a great one for mouthing slogans. He was a great one for inspiring his men, too. He'd had a lot of practice at that, having fed so many of them into the meat grinder. But, now that he'd come up with what was admittedly the great military idea of his career, he seemed disinclined to think about any other military ideas.

He had reasons, too, or thought he did. "The War Department is run by morons," he growled, "and expects everyone else to be a moron, too."

"Sir, as I've said before, in my opinion it's just as well that First Army doesn't advance on Memphis," Dowling answered. "We're too distant for the thrust to do much good. Murfreesboro is a better choice all the way around."

Custer muttered something into his gilded mustache. It sounded like, *If the War Department orders it, it must be wrong.* But, since he hadn't said it quite loud enough to compel Dowling to notice it, his adjutant didn't. He made such a point of not noticing, in fact, that Custer had to say something intelligible: "So long as we kick 'em in the pants hard enough, maybe it won't matter which direction we go in."

"Yes, sir," Dowling said, more enthusiastically than before. "We truly may have them on the ropes. All we need to do is finish them off."

Was he really talking like that? He was. Did he really believe what he was saying? He did. That he believed it still astonished him. The Rebs were fighting hard—nobody had ever accused Confederate soldiers of having any quit in them—but there weren't enough of them, white or black, and they didn't have enough guns or barrels to hold back the United States, not any more.

Custer said, "The Barrel Brigade will put a crimp in the CSA—you wait and see if it doesn't."

"Yes, sir." Abner Dowling didn't know whether to be pleased he was thinking along with the general commanding First Army or appalled Custer was thinking along with him. After momentary hesitation, the latter emotion prevailed.

With a chuckle that struck Dowling's ear as evil, Custer went on, "I'm going to make sure the Barrel Brigade doesn't smash the Rebel line anywhere near General MacArthur's division, too. And do you know what else, Major? I'll have MacArthur thank me for doing things that way, too, because I'll extend his men the great privilege of feinting against the Rebels to draw their attention away from the main axis of my attack."

"That's very—clever, sir," Dowling said. No wonder Custer had sounded evil. He might not be a great soldier (on the other hand, despite everything, he might be, a realization that never failed to unsettle Dowling), but more than half a century in the Army had made him a nasty schemer. Daniel MacArthur could no more help putting his heart into any attack he made than a trout could help rising to a fly. But an attack meant as a feint would be foredoomed to failure, and not all his brilliance could change that. *Poor bastard,* Dowling thought—not that he was fond of the arrogant MacArthur, either.

"Colonel Morrell, now, Colonel Morrell is a proper officer," Custer said. "That young fellow will go far."

Since Morrell had made himself so prominent in Custer's eyes, Dowling had done some checking on the officer who led the barrels. Morrell's record *was* impressive; the only thing that could possibly be construed as a blemish was trouble getting along with the General Staff back in Philadelphia. Dowling didn't hold that against a man, and Custer, no doubt, would look on it as virtue rather than vice.

Off in the distance, antiaircraft guns began to pound. First Army had driven the CSA out of artillery range of Nashville, but the Confederates never stopped trying to hit back as best they could. Their aeroplanes were finishing the job of pounding the town to bits that U.S. artillery north of the Cumberland had begun so well.

Larger explosions started mingling with the barking thunder of the guns. Dowling frowned. "Archie can't hit the broad side of a barn," he complained. "It's a good thing the Rebs aren't any better at it than we are, that's all I have to say."

The explosions came closer to the state capitol as the Confederates' bombing aeroplanes penetrated one ring of U.S. antiaircraft guns after another. Dowling wondered how much damage the bombers were liable to do. In the early days of the war, bombing raids had been pinpricks, annoyances. Now more and bigger aeroplanes carried more and bigger bombs. They could hurt.

"Sounds like they're heading right toward us," Custer remarked. He didn't sound afraid, or even particularly concerned, only interested. No one had ever challenged his courage. His good sense, perhaps, but never his courage.

As the antiaircraft fire grew more frantic, the drone of the bombers' motors provided a swelling background to it. The ground quivered under Dowling's feet from bombs slamming into Nashville one after another, marching ever closer to the already-battered building in which he stood.

His urge was to dive under a table. The only thing he personally could do about the bombers was try to keep them from killing him. Being under fire, so to speak, without being able to do anything about it galled him.

It galled Custer, too, far more. He went to a south-facing window, yanked his pistol from its holster, and blazed away at the Confederate aeroplanes overhead. Abner Dowling knew how utterly futile that was, but sympathized with it nonetheless. And then Custer shouted, "One of them's coming down, by God!"

Dowling stared. Custer couldn't possibly have—

Custer, no doubt, hadn't. The Confederate bomber had to have been in trouble long before the general commanding First Army opened fire on it. Otherwise, it would have crashed beyond the state capitol instead of coming down not far in front of the building Custer was using as his headquarters.

It must have had most of its bomb load still on board, too. The blast sounded like the end of the world. Custer reeled away from the window, both hands clapped to his ears. One of his elbows caught Dowling in the belly. "Uff!" his adjutant said. They both sat down, hard.

Custer yelled something. Dowling had no idea what it was. He hoped his ears would start working again one of these days. They weren't working for the time being.

Bombs kept falling, too. Dowling heard them, and felt them as well. One of them blew the glass out of the window Custer had thrown open. Dowling yipped as a little fragment bit the back of his neck. He clapped a hand to the wound. His palm came away red, but not too much worse than if he'd cut himself shaving.

"Get up!" Custer screamed in his ear. "We've got to make sure this headquarters is still a going concern."

Grunting, Dowling struggled to his feet. Custer was up ahead of him, even though the general commanding First Army carried twice his years. That shamed Dowling, although every part of his corpulent body—his right ham in particular—seemed one great bruise.

Custer's right trouser leg was out at the knee. He had a cut on his face and another on the back of his hand, each about the same as the small wound Dowling had taken. He seemed to notice none of that. Spry as a new recruit, he ran back to the window and fired some more at the Confederate aeroplanes. Only when his pistol clicked instead of roaring did he bellow what had to be a curse and shove the weapon back into the tooled leather sheath in which it had sat idle for so many years.

Dowling wondered if he would reload. Instead, he ran for the door. Limping, his adjutant followed. Dowling had never actually seen Custer under attack till now. Lieutenant generals seldom approached the front: the last time Custer had been there was during the first chlorine gas attack against the CSA, two years before.

Now, all at once, Dowling understood how Custer's shortcomings had failed to keep him from advancing to his present eminence. In combat, the general commanding First Army was a man transformed. Nothing fazed him. He threw open the door and charged down the hall, Dowling in his wake.

"General Custer! General Custer!" Officers and enlisted men yelled Custer's name loud enough to penetrate the cotton wool some unknown malefactor seemed to have stuffed into Dowling's ears. "What do we do, General Custer?"

"Come with me!" Custer shouted, and they came. They obeyed without question. Dowling was very impressed. He was even more impressed at the stream of orders Custer threw out. Wherever the general saw a fire or a pile of rubble, he set men to attacking it. They went in with a will, too, just as they'd gone in with a will against the Confederates in so many expensive attacks.

Steam pumps played water on the fires closer to the Cumberland, from which they could easily draw a good supply. Other fire engines struggled against those here close by and in the state capitol, but pressure in the mains wasn't all it should have been; Dowling wondered if some of the bombs had damaged the water works. He sighed. The USA had finally got them running again, and now . . .

But Custer, far more than in an office or conferring with his subordinates around a map, took charge. "Don't worry, pal," he called to a soldier whom other men in green-gray were digging out from under bricks and stones. "If you think this is bad, just wait till you see what we do to those Rebel sons of bitches."

"That's bully, sir," the wounded man answered. By the blood soaking his leg and by the way he held it, he wouldn't be doing any more fighting any time soon, but he was smiling as his comrades carried him away. Dowling shook his head in amazement. He wouldn't have been smiling with a broken leg. He would have been screaming his head off. Would listening to Custer have made him shut up? He didn't think so, but it had sure as hell done the job for the wounded soldier.

Custer turned and said, "Major, get on the telegraph to Philadelphia. Let the War Department know I am well and tell them First Army has just begun to fight."

Dowling, whose ears were still stunned, had to get him to repeat that several times before he had it straight. Custer gladly repeated himself: the only thing he liked better than hearing his own voice was seeing his name in the newspapers. But the men he'd been directing listened avidly, no matter how pompous he sounded.

"Sorry, sir," said the telegrapher to whom Dowling brought the message, "but the lines north are all down right now."

"They had better be fixed soon, for the future of the nation may ride on them," Dowling boomed. He was appalled at how much he sounded like Custer. A moment later, he was appalled again, this time by the telegraph operator's fervent apology. It made him blink and scratch his head. Damned if the old boy didn't have something after all.

Barrels crawled north up the road past Arthur McGregor's farm. They chewed the dirt to hell and gone, kicking great clouds of dust into the air. McGregor wouldn't have wanted to be one of the Yankee soldiers marching behind the noisy, smelly barrels. But then, he wouldn't have wanted to be a Yankee soldier under any circumstances.

He looked out across his fields. They were beginning to go from green to gold. He would have a fine crop this year if the weather held—and the only way he would be able to dispose of it was to the U.S. authorities. He grimaced. Almost better to touch a match to the wheat than sell it to the USA.

The barrels passed—*like a kidney stone,* he thought, remembering a torment of his father's. More men in green-gray slogged north on foot. Watching them, McGregor thought of ants swarming round spilled molasses. You could smash some, but more kept coming. How many columns of U.S. soldiers had he watched trudging up that road? How many men did the United States hold, anyway? One answer fit both questions: *too many*.

Southbound traffic was sparser. The farm near Rosenfeld was a long way from the front these days; few Americans needed to withdraw this far. Gloomily, McGregor headed for the barn to muck out and to get in a little work on his latest bomb. He thought he had a way to get it into town, but he wasn't sure yet.

Here came a U.S. Ford, painted green-gray as Army motorcars often were. McGregor paused, wondering if it was Major Hannebrink trying to catch him in the act. If so, the Yank would be disappointed. McGregor had nothing out now, and would have nothing out ninety seconds after he stopped work. He did not believe in taking foolish chances with his revenge.

When the Ford stopped just outside the lane that led to his farmhouse and barn, he laughed quietly, sure he'd pegged things aright. "Not today, Major," he murmured. "Not today."

But then the automobile sped up again, rolling south toward the border. McGregor scratched his head, wondering why it had stopped in the first place. He got his answer a moment later, when a great exultant shout ripped from the throats of the marching American soldiers: "Winnipeg!"

McGregor took two quick steps to the barn and leaned against the timbers by the door. He didn't think he could have stood up without that support; he felt as punctured, as deflated, as the inner tubes on the motorcars that had come with Hannebrink after Mary got through with them.

"Winnipeg!" the U.S. soldiers cried, again and again. "Winnipeg!" Every repetition felt like a fresh kick in the belly to Arthur McGregor. Since the war began, the city through which passed the railroads linking Canada's east and west had held out against everything the United States threw at it. McGregor knew fresh train lines had been built north of Winnipeg, but if the Yanks had broken into it, could they, would they, not move past it as well?

Slowly, grimly, he walked back toward the farmhouse. The bomb would wait. The bomb would wait a long time. The United States looked to be in Canada to stay.

When he went inside, Julia gave him a severe look and said,

"Don't you dare slam the door, Father. Don't you dare stomp around the way you usually do, either. I've got bread in the oven, and I don't want it to fall."

"All right," McGregor said meekly, and shut the door with care. The last time he could remember sounding meek, he'd been about eight years old. He shook his head like a bear bedeviled by dogs and wondered what the devil to do next. He had no idea. With Winnipeg lost, what did anything matter?

His older daughter noticed that he sounded strange. "What's wrong, Father?" she asked.

He cocked his head to one side. With the door closed, with the windows closed, he had trouble hearing the Yankees yelling. If Julia had been busy with the bread, she probably hadn't even noticed them. "Winnipeg's fallen," he said baldly. "I think the Americans mean it this time."

Julia stared at him as if he'd started spouting gibberish. "But it can't have," she said, though she had to know perfectly well it could. Then she burst into tears and threw herself into his arms. He held her and stroked her hair as if she were a little girl and not turning ever more into a woman day by day.

Hearing Julia start to cry was enough to bring Maude and Mary at a run. McGregor knew what was in his wife's mind, at least—Maude had surely feared the Yanks were seizing him. Seeing him there, she stopped dead. "Dear God in heaven, what is it?" she demanded.

"Winnipeg," he said. The one word was plenty. It made Julia cry harder than ever. Maude turned away, as if she could not bear to hear such news—and if she could not, who could blame her?

Mary's mouth fell open. "God *doesn't* love us," she whispered, no doubt the worst thing she could think of. Then, as a grown man might have done, she gathered herself. Over Julia's shoulder and bent head, McGregor watched the process with nothing but admiration. A word at a time, Mary went on, "I don't care if God loves us or not. I *won't* be a Yankee, and there's nothing they can do that will make me be one."

"I won't be a Yankee, either," Julia said, and stood straighter. McGregor affected not to notice the dark tear stains on the front of his denim overalls. "I won't be a Yankee," Julia repeated. But she, more than anyone else in the family, had a way of looking at things over the long haul. "I won't be a Yankee," she said for the third time, and then added, "but what will my children be, if I ever have children? What will *their* children be?"

McGregor, thus prodded, thought of those distant, hypothetical great-grandchildren he probably wouldn't live to see, since they'd be born around 1950, a year that seemed impossibly distant from mundane 1917. What *would* they be like?

Try as he would, he couldn't see them as much different from himself and his own family. He supposed that was foolish. His great-grandfather, whom he'd never known, would have been astonished at the modern conveniences to be found in Rosenfeld, just a few hours away by wagon. Maybe, when the century had halfway run its course, such conveniences would reach farms, too.

That wasn't really what he wanted to think about. If the United States won this war, as they looked like doing, how would those great-grandchildren think of themselves? Would they be contented Americans, as the Yanks would try to make them?

"They have to remember," he said, more to himself than to anyone else. "They have to remember they're Canadians, and the USA stole their country from them. They have to try to take it back one day."

"Can they do that?" Maude asked the ruthlessly pragmatic question. A farm wife who was anything but ruthlessly pragmatic had a long, hard, rocky road ahead of her.

But McGregor, to his own surprise, had an answer ready: "Look at Quebec. The Frenchies there are still mad that we licked them on the Plains of Abraham a hundred and fifty years ago. As soon as the Yankees gave them their chance, they jumped on the idea of this Republic of theirs, and to the devil with whatever went before it. If somebody gives us the chance, we can do the same."

"Who would give us a chance, with the United States smothering us the way a bad sow smothers her piglets?" Maude said.

"I don't know," McGregor admitted. "But the Quebecers didn't know before the war, either. Sooner or later, something will turn up."

"My bread!" Julia exclaimed. "I forgot the bread!" She fled back into the kitchen. The oven door clanked open. Julia let out a sigh of relief.

"It smelled fine," Maude called after her. "I didn't think you had anything to worry about."

Mary looked at her mother in astonishment. "Don't you think turning into a Yankee is something to worry about?"

"Well, yes," Maude said, "but it isn't something Julia can fix by taking it out of the oven on time." Her younger daughter thought that over. At last, reluctantly, Mary nodded.

McGregor said, "Maybe they can make us stand up in front of the Stars and Stripes. Whatever they do, though, they can't keep us from spitting on it in our hearts, and from staying loyal to the King."

"God save the King!" Mary said, and McGregor and Maude each put a hand on her shoulder. She caught fire, as she had a way of doing. "We'll make it our secret," she breathed. "We'll all make it our secret. I don't mean all of us—I mean all of us Canadians. We'll do what the Yanks tell us, but inside we'll be laughing and laughing, because we'll know what we really think."

Arthur and Maude McGregor looked at each other over their daughter's head. "Some of us will," McGregor said. "Some of us will keep the secret. Some of us will want to. Some of us won't care, though—remember how things were in your school? Some people will believe the Americans' lies."

"We'll make them pay," Mary said fiercely. Her parents looked at each other again. McGregor didn't know how much she knew about his bombs. She did know Major Hannebrink kept coming around—and she knew her father hated him. McGregor might have taken her out of school because the teacher mouthed the Yanks' lies, but Mary knew how to add even so.

"What happens next?" Maude asked.

McGregor blew air out through his lips, making a whuffling noise a horse might have produced. "I don't know. I don't know enough to know. If we can stop them *in* Winnipeg and keep them from getting at the new railroads farther north, the fight goes on a while longer."

He was trying to find the bright side, and that was the most hopeful thing he could say. If the Americans kept driving, if the Canadians and the British were able to stop them no more . . . in that case, the fight wouldn't go on a while longer. It would be over in a matter of weeks.

"Whatever happens, *we* have to go on," he said.

"Whatever happens, we have to pay the Americans back," Mary said. "We have to pay them back for Alexander."

"We will," Maude said. "I don't know how, but we will."

"You can count on that, Mary," McGregor added. His daughter nodded. She had confidence in him even if he had none in himself, even if the war was as good as lost. He looked up at the ceiling. He seemed to look right through the ceiling, to look on the naked face of God. The war might be as good as lost, but all his confidence came flooding back.

As she'd done every day she could since the war began, Nellie Semphroch opened the coffeehouse for business. The morning was fine and bright. Before long, it would get impossibly hot and impossibly muggy, the way it did every summer in Washington. Nellie stood on the sidewalk, enjoying the freshness while it lasted.

She had little else to enjoy. The view was one to inspire horror, not delight, even if a robin did trill from a tree that had been broken only into table legs, not into matchsticks. Most of her own block had come through pretty well, which is to say it hadn't been smashed flat and then burned. Even so, bullet holes pocked storefronts, shells had bitten chunks out of them, and the only glass in sight was not in the windows but drifted in the street to puncture motorcars' inner tubes.

Off to the south, on the far side of the Potomac, artillery boomed. It was U.S. artillery, pounding the Confederates still farther south. Confederate forces had retreated out of artillery range of Washington, driven not so much by the U.S. troops who had retaken the capital as by U.S. successes off to the west, which had left the Rebels afraid of being cut off. Not having to worry about shellfire for the first time in weeks felt good, though C.S. bombers did still make nocturnal appearances overhead.

Hal Jacobs threw wide the boarded-up door across the street to show his cobbler's shop was open, too. He waved and called, "Good morning, Nellie."

"Good morning, Hal," Nellie answered. She didn't like giving Jacobs the encouragement of using his Christian name, but didn't see she had much choice, either. As she did every morning she saw the shoemaker these days, she said, "Thank you for getting me and Edna out of that military jail."

Jacobs waved his hands. "I have told you before, do not thank me for this. It was my duty. It was my pleasure. People saw Confederate officers in your coffeehouse—naturally they thought you were collaborating. They didn't know you were passing what you heard on to me."

"You could have let me rot," Nellie said. *I didn't come across for you, so you didn't have any reason to come across for me.* That was how things worked in the world from which she'd escaped, and, for the most part, in the more decorous world she'd managed to enter, too. They didn't seem to work that way for Hal Jacobs, which made Nellie intensely suspicious.

He waved again, this time in rejection of the idea. "You bravely served your country. How could I do such a wicked thing? If Bill Reach turns up again—no, I will say *when* Bill Reach turns up again—I know he would—*will*—feel the same."

"That's nice," Nellie answered. She had to make herself not look in the direction of the wreckage where, she presumed, Bill Reach still lay. Jacobs might talk about his turning up, but she knew he wouldn't turn up again till the Last Trump blew.

With a final wave, Jacobs went back inside and got to work. Nellie went inside, too. While she was opening up, Edna had come downstairs. Her daughter's face bore a look of sullen discontent, as it often did lately. "Jesus, this town is dead nowadays," Edna complained. "We did a hell of a lot better when the Rebs were running things."

"We wouldn't have, if it hadn't been for the help we got from Mr. Jacobs and the rest of the people who worked for the United States," Nellie said.

Edna's discontented look went from sullen to angry. "And you never told me about it, not a word," she said shrilly. "I even said that crazy Bill Reach was a spy, and you went, 'Pooh-pooh! The very idea!' You would have let me marry Nick and then taken my pillow talk straight across the street."

Since that, while unkind, was not altogether untrue, Nellie did not rise to it. She did say, "You know I never wanted you to marry him at all."

"But that wasn't because he was a Reb," Edna said. "That was just because he was a man. He could have been on the U.S. General Staff, and you would've felt the same way." That also had a good deal of truth in it. Edna went on, "You just don't want a girl to have any fun, and look at what all you done when you was my age and even younger."

"That's wasn't fun," Nellie replied. "That was hell, is what that was." But Edna didn't believe her. She could see as much in her daughter's eyes. Edna was convinced she was acting like a dog in the manger. What Edna wanted was to screw herself silly, not having a clue how silly she was already. With a sigh, Nellie said, "Get a pot of coffee going, why don't you? I could use a cup, and I bet you could, too."

"Might as well make it for us," Edna said. "Ain't nobody else likely to come in and drink it. Most of the folks left here in town don't have the money, and most of the ones who do still think we was a pack of traitors."

"I know." Nellie sighed again, this time over lost business unlikely to return. "Good thing I put aside as much as I did, or we'd be in worse shape than we are." One more sigh. "Only thing that Rebel scrip we got is good for now is blowing our noses on it, I'm afraid."

"We haven't got that much of it, though," Edna said, lighting the fire in the stove. "The Rebs liked us. Why not? We always had good coffee and good food, so no wonder they liked us and mostly paid us real cash." As she started measuring grounds for the pot, she gave her mother another sour stare. "Now I know how we got all that good stuff. I never did before, on account of you never told me."

Before Nellie could answer, a motorcar stopped outside. She was amazed anyone had even tried to negotiate the shell-pocked, glass-strewn roadway. "Got a puncture, I'll bet," she said.

A moment later, the door opened. Nellie started to say, *See? Told you so,* but the words clogged in her throat. Into the coffeehouse walked Theodore Roosevelt. He pointed a finger at her. "You are Mrs. Nellie Semphroch," he said, as if daring her to disagree.

"Y-Yes, sir," she said, and dropped a curtsy. "And this here is my daughter Edna." She didn't know whether she ought to be introducing Edna to the president of the United States. She didn't know whether she should have admitted her own name, either. If Roosevelt was inclined to believe most of her neighbors and not Hal Jacobs, he was by all accounts capable of ordering her dragged out and shot on the spot.

"Now that our capital is in our own hands once more," he said, "I decided to come down from Philadelphia and see what was left of this city that was once so wonderful. The Rebs haven't left us much, have they?"

"No, sir," Nellie answered. On the stove, the pot began to perk. "Would you care for some coffee, sir?"

"Bully!" Roosevelt said. A couple of hard-faced men in green-gray—bodyguards, by the look of them—came into the coffeehouse after him. "Cups for Roland and Stan, too, if you please. I have something for you here, Mrs. Semphroch, and also for your lovely daughter."

Edna simpered as she poured the coffee. Nellie wished the cups that had survived the recapture of Washington were all from the same set. She supposed she should have been grateful any cups had survived. One direct hit and they wouldn't have. One direct hit and she might not have, either.

After taking a sip, Roosevelt set down his cup and reached into his pocket. His hand came out not with a derringer but with a dark blue velvet box, the sort of box in which a ring might have come. He opened the box. Nellie gaped at the big golden Maltese cross on a red, white, and blue ribbon. Roosevelt lifted the medal out of the box. The ribbon was long enough to go around Nellie's neck.

"The Order of Remembrance, First Class," Roosevelt boomed. "Highest civilian honor I can give. I argued for a Distinguished Service Cross myself, but the stick-in-the-muds at the War Department started having kittens. This is the best I could do. Congratulations, Mrs. Semphroch: a grateful country thanks you for your brave service."

He slipped the medal over Nellie's head. Dazedly, she watched him put a hand in his pocket again and produce another velvet box. When he opened it, the Maltese cross inside was of silver, with inlaid gold stripes. The ribbon attached to it was also of the colors of the national flag, but not quite so wide as the one on Nellie's medal.

"Order of Remembrance, Second Class," he said, putting the decoration over Edna's head. "For you, Miss Semphroch, for helping your mother gather information from the foe and pass it on to the United States."

Edna gaped. So did Nellie. Maybe Roosevelt didn't know Edna had been on the point of marrying Confederate Lieutenant Nicholas H. Kincaid—would have married him if the U.S. bombardment hadn't turned the ceremony into a bloody shambles. Maybe he did know and didn't care.

No sooner had that thought crossed Nellie's mind than, as if on cue, a photographer strode into the coffeehouse. President Roosevelt put one arm around Nellie, the other around Edna, and Nellie realized the photographer's appearance wasn't *as if* on cue at all. It *was* on cue. The fellow touched off his tray of flash powder. *Foomp!* As a glowing purple smear made hash of Nellie's eyesight, the shutter clicked.

"Can we do one more?" the photographer asked, beginning to set up again.

"I'm standing here with my arms around two lovely ladies, and you ask me a question like that?" Roosevelt said. "By all means, sir, by all means. Take all day if you need to—but make sure you do the job right."

Edna laughed at the president's joke. Had Roosevelt shown any interest in more than her laugh, she probably would have given him that, too. Nellie did not like being touched without having invited it, but she endured it. She'd endured worse in her time, and Roosevelt took no undue liberties.

Of one thing Nellie was very, very sure: he had no more idea than did Hal Jacobs of how Bill Reach had died. Nor did she intend to let either of them ever learn.

Thinking that, she was smiling when the flash powder went *Foomp!* again. So was Theodore Roosevelt. So was Edna. "Great!" the photographer said. "The newspapers'll eat this one up."

"Bully!" Roosevelt said again. He let the women go and then turned to them. "Now I must depart, I fear. I have to look over this poor tormented town and try to decide how we can set it to rights once more. But now that I have had a cup of your excellent coffee and given you some small portion of the reward you so richly deserve, I do hope any and all slanders against you on the part of your neighbors shall cease forthwith. A very good day to you both."

And he was gone, a human hurricane in a black suit and straw boater. His bodyguards followed him out. So did the photographer, who had the grace to tip his hat. Nellie felt as if she'd survived yet another bombardment.

As soon as that feeling faded even a little, though, she went to a counter and pulled out a can of red paint and a brush. Roosevelt's limousine was still making its slow way around the corner when she painted a message on the boards covering her shattered window: OUR COFFEE IS FINE ENOUGH FOR THE PRESIDENT OF THE UNITED STATES. HOW ABOUT YOU?

"Oh, that's good, Ma," Edna said, the medal still around her neck.

"It's better than good," Nellie said. "It's *bully*!" Mother and daughter smiled, at ease with each other for one of the rare times since the shooting started.

A horse-drawn cab driven by a white man whose right arm ended in a hook carried Anne Colleton across the bridge from the Georgia mainland to Jekyll Island. "I hope the weather at the hotel will be a little nicer than this," she said; down near the Florida border, Georgia could give South Carolina lessons in heat and humidity.

"Which hotel were you at again, ma'am?" the driver asked.

"The Laughing January, it's called," she answered.

"Oh, yes, ma'am, that's on the ocean side. It's always cooler there. Place got the name on account of, before the war, rich Yankees'd come down here to get away from winter. I had to live up in Yankee country and I had the money, reckon I'd do the same thing."

The road did not go directly to the Laughing January, but meandered around the rim of the island. Most of the interior was swamp and salt marsh and, on the rare ground that rose slightly higher, woods of pine and moss-draped oak. Egrets and herons, their wings as broad as a man was tall, rose from the marshes and flew off with ungainly haste. A cardinal perched on a branch outthrust from an oak added a splash of brightness.

It caught the driver's eyes, too. "My blood was about that color when the damnyankees blew up my arm," he remarked, and then, "You got any kin in the war, ma'am?"

"They gassed one of my brothers," Anne answered. "He's dead now. The other one's an officer on the Roanoke front. He was well, last I heard." If the driver had been on the point of making any cracks along the lines of *a rich man's war and a poor man's fight*, that forestalled him. He kept quiet the rest of the way to the hotel.

Not all the rich—Yankee and Confederate—had stayed at hotels. Their villas had crushed-shell driveways leading off from the road. Some of the fancy houses were in fine shape, with servants bustling about. Some looked abandoned, forlorn, weather-beaten: men from the United States had probably wintered in them. And some, these days, were charred ruins like Marshlands. She wondered how bad the Red risings had been here. She didn't ask. She didn't really want to know.

"Here we are," the cab driver said at last. "The Laughing January." The place seemed more like a village than a hotel, with individual cottages surrounding a larger building to the north, the south, and the east, toward the ocean. The driver had been right about the weather. Even inside the cab, Anne could feel as much. It wasn't cool. It wasn't dry. It was better than it had been.

After hitching the horse, the driver carried her bags into the lobby. He was handy with his hook but used his right arm only for the lighter pieces. Inside, a colored bellhop took charge of them all. *And what were you doing, there toward the end of 1915?* Anne thought, looking at him. He was all deference now. Under that deference, who could guess what went through his mind? Anne had once thought she could. She didn't any more.

At the desk, the clerk—a woman—confirmed that her reservation was in order and handed her a shiny brass key with a large 8 stamped onto it. "You'll have a grand sea view from that cabin, ma'am," she said, "and the netting on the porch is fine enough to keep out the mosquitoes and the nasty little no-see-'ems, too."

"That's good," Anne said. She got directions on how to find cabin 8, then headed off down the walk with the colored attendant pushing her bags on a little wheeled cart behind her.

"You jus' here by your lonesome, ma'am?" he asked. "You didn't bring no servants or nothin'?"

"No," she said tightly. After folk who had been her servants tried to kill her, she neither wanted anything to do with them nor wanted to acquire new ones, lest they prove to have similarly unfortunate habits.

She gave the attendant half a dollar once he set the bags down on the floor of the front room of her cottage. It would have been an extravagant tip before the war, and was still a good one; he went back toward the main building whistling and with a spring in his step Anne didn't think was assumed. Would that save her if the Negroes planned another uprising? Her laugh had broken glass in it. She knew better.

She was hanging up a white tennis dress when someone knocked on the frame to the screen door. Maybe it was the bellhop again. Had she dropped or forgotten something? Or maybe—

A Navy officer in tropical whites stood there, his cap under

one arm, a cigar dangling from his mouth at a deliberately rak-
ish angle. "Why, Commander Kimball," Anne drawled, exaggerating her accent to the point of burlesque. "What a pleasant
surprise."

To her genuine rather than assumed surprise, Roger Kimball
glared at her instead of grinning. "I didn't get interested in you
because you were cute and sweet and helpless," he growled. "If I
want that, I can buy it on a streetcorner any time I please. I got
interested in you because I think you're the only woman I ever
met who's every bit as ornery and uppity as I am. You don't like
that, I'll head back to Habana."

He meant it. She could see as much. She almost did send him
packing; if there was one thing she couldn't stand, it was being
upstaged. But he was one of the few men she'd ever met who
came close to being as ornery and uppity as she was. She didn't
think he matched her, but he did come close.

And so, when she spoke again, it was in tones she might have
used with her brother: "All right, Roger. It takes one to know
one, I expect. Come in. How long do you have in Georgia?"

"Four days," he answered. "Then back on the train and the
boat to Cuba, and then back to sea. No rest for the weary." He
stepped past her into the cottage and closed the door. "You have
any whiskey in this place? Plenty in mine if you don't."

"I don't know," Anne said. "I haven't had a chance to look."

Kimball nodded. "Saw you on the way over here, with the
coon hauling your bags. I usually like a little water in my
whiskey, but not here. Jekyll Island water tastes like swamp.
They say it's safe to drink, but it's nasty."

"Thanks for letting me know," Anne answered as they made
their way back toward the little cottage's kitchen—if you came
to the Laughing January with a cook and a housekeeper, you
could do some very handsome entertaining. "I haven't tried that
yet, either."

Kimball stopped, so suddenly that she almost ran into him.
Voice lazy and amused, he asked, "What else haven't you tried
here?"

Afterwards, she couldn't sort out which of them grabbed the
other first. What followed was as much a brawl as lovemaking.
He tore a couple of hooks and eyes from her gauzy summer
frock as he got her out of it; she sent one of the gold buttons from

his uniform jacket spinning across the room when she yanked it open instead of bothering to undo all the fastenings.

They didn't even look for the bedroom. For the rough coupling they both wanted, the floor seemed better. Kimball's weight pinned Anne half against rug, half against polished hardwood. He slammed himself into her as if he wanted to hurt her and please her at the same time.

And he did, both. Her nails clawed stripes down his back as she bucked under him. "Come on, damn you, come on," she said, her own excitement mounting. She bit his shoulder and tasted blood.

He grunted, drove even deeper into her—she would not have thought it possible—and spent himself. Only a couple of quick heartbeats later, she cried out, too, a noise any cat prowling along a fence would have recognized.

Suddenly, he was heavy upon her. Before she could push him away, he rolled off and to one side. She felt a small pang of regret as he pulled out of her. "*Hell* of a woman," he muttered to himself, and then spoke directly to her: "You don't believe in taking prisoners, do you?" He set a hand where she'd bitten, stared at the red smear on his palm, and shook his head. "I was wondering if I'd come out of that one alive."

Anne rubbed her backside in a fashion no properly refined lady would have used—but then, no properly refined lady would have got rugburn on the area in question by screwing her brains out on the floor. "I thought you were trying to ram me down into the basement," she replied, not without admiration.

"These places don't have basements," Roger Kimball said.

"I knew that," Anne told him. "The way you were going there, I didn't think you cared." Her stretch was an odd blend of satisfied lassitude and abraded posterior.

One appetite for the moment slaked, Kimball remembered another. "We were coming in here for some whiskey, weren't we?" He got to his feet and searched the cabinets. Curtains covered the windows, but they weren't thick. A dedicated snoop would have had no trouble spotting his nudity. He didn't care. Anne admired him again, this time for brazenness—not that she didn't already know about that. She also admired the red lines on his back . . . and the back itself.

He grunted again, on a different note from when he'd shot his seed into her, and held up a bottle three-quarters full of amber liquid. "If this cottage is like mine, the bedroom should be . . . over here," he said, and sure enough, it was.

He bothered with glasses no more than he'd bothered with clothes. Anne followed his lead, something she was unused to doing. He yanked the cork from the bottle with his teeth when it would not yield to his fingers. "What shall we drink to?" Anne asked.

She wondered if he would say *victory*. She thought he started to, but the word did not pass his lips. Instead, he answered, "To doing our jobs the best way we know how while the world goes to hell around us," and took a long pull at the bottle.

"Leave some for me," Anne said. She had to pull it out of his hand. It wasn't the best whiskey she'd ever had, nor anywhere close, but, if she drank enough of it, it would get her drunk. After she'd swallowed and her eyes stopped watering, she said, "We're going to lose, aren't we?"

"Don't see how we can do anything else," Kimball said. "Scuttlebutt is, we've already started sniffing around for terms."

"I hadn't heard that," Anne said. "I'd have thought President Semmes owed me enough to let me know such things, but maybe not." Maybe, with her plantation in ruins and her investments in hardly better shape, she wasn't rich enough to be worth cultivating any more.

"Well, he hasn't told me about it, either. I don't know if the stories are true or not," Kimball said. "Ones I've heard say that damned Roosevelt turned us down flat, so it doesn't matter any which way." He drank again, then stared at the bottle. "What are we supposed to do after we lose the war? How are we supposed to get over that?"

"The damnyankees did. They did it twice," Anne said. "Anything those people can do, we can do, too. We have to figure out where we went wrong in this fight and make sure we don't go wrong that way again."

"Because there *will* be another round," Kimball said, and Anne nodded. She reached for the whiskey bottle. He handed it to her. She drank till her eyes crossed. Anything, even oblivion, was better than thinking about spending so many lives and so much treasure—and losing anyhow.

She discovered Roger Kimball's hand high up on her bare thigh. As she stared at it, it moved higher still. She set the bottle on the floor by the side of the bed and clasped Kimball to her.

Love, or even fornication, was better than thinking about what might have been, too.

An aeroplane buzzed high over the line east of Lubbock. Jefferson Pinkard stared up at it. He thought about firing a few rounds—by the way it had come, it was plainly a U.S. machine—but decided not to waste the ammunition. It was so high up there, he had no chance of hitting it.

"Why we don't got no aeroplanes to shoot down that *puto*?" Hipolito Rodriguez asked. "The Yankees, they got aeroplanes all the time. They look at us like a man peeking at a woman taking a bath in a river."

Jeff thought of Emily. He couldn't help imagining her naked. That was all right, when he didn't imagine Bedford Cunningham naked beside her or on top of her. He answered, "Guess they don't reckon this here front's important enough to send us much in the way of flying machines. Yankees always have had more'n us."

Something fell from the U.S. aeroplane. Pinkard's first reaction was to hit the dirt, but he checked himself—that wasn't a bomb. No: those weren't bombs. They drifted and fluttered in the air like the snowflakes he occasionally saw in Birmingham. Rodriguez stared at them in blank wonderment. Jeff guessed he never saw snow down in Sonora, even if he'd made its acquaintance here this past winter.

"Papers!" Sergeant Albert Cross said. "The bastards are dropping leaflets on us."

"Rather have 'em drop leaflets than bombs any old day, and twice on Sunday," Pinkard said.

"Sí." Hip Rodriguez nodded enthusiastic agreement. "With papers, too, I can wipe my ass. This is *muy bueno.*"

"Probably be scratchy as hell," Cross said after a judicious pause for thought. "But hey, Hip, you're right—damn sight better'n nothin'. It's a fucking wonder all the flies in Texas don't live in this here trench."

"You mean they don't?" Jeff said, kidding on the square. "Could have fooled me." As if to make him pay for his words, something bit him on the back of the neck. He swatted, but didn't think he got it.

By then, the fluttering papers had nearly reached the ground. A few drifted back toward the Yankees' trenches. Others fell in no-man's-land. Still others came down in and behind the Confederates' forward line.

Had Pinkard stabbed up with his bayoneted Tredegar, he could have spitted one of the descending leaflets. He didn't bother. He just grabbed one out of the air. Cross and Rodriguez crowded close to see what the devil the United States thought it worthwhile to tell their foes.

At the top of the leaflet was a U.S. flag that looked to have too many stars in the canton crossed with another one Pinkard hadn't seen before, a dark banner with the light silhouette of a tough-looking man's profile on it. The headline below explained: THE UNITED STATES WELCOME THE STATE OF HOUSTON INTO THE UNION.

"Wait a minute," Cross said, "Houston's *in* Texas, God damn it. I been through there on the train."

"Here, let me read it," Jeff said, and did: " 'When Texas was admitted to the United States in 1845, it retained for itself the right of forming up to four new states within its boundaries. The people of the state of Houston have availed themselves of the opportunity to break free of the evil and corrupt Richmond regime and found a new political body: in the words of the immortal John Adams, 'a government of laws and not of men.' The new state takes its name from Governor Sam Houston, who so valiantly tried to keep the whole of Texas from joining the Confederate States of America. The United States are delighted at this return to the fold of so many upstanding citizens who repent of their grandfathers' errors.' "

Pinkard crumpled up the paper and stuck it in his pocket. "It's an ass-wipe, sure as hell." He went down the trench, gathering more leaflets.

Rodriguez and Sergeant Cross also picked up several copies of the announcement, no doubt for the same purpose. Rodriguez peered west, toward the enemy lines and what was presumably the territory of the new state of Houston. "How do they do this?" he asked. "Make a new state where there was no state before, I mean."

"Same way they did when they stole part of Virginia from us during the War of Secession and called it West Virginia, I reckon," Pinkard answered with a snort of contempt.

Sergeant Albert Cross added, "Then they went and found themselves enough traitors and collaborators to make themselves a legislature out of, like they done in Kentucky when they went and stole that from us. Wonder how many soldiers they got to use to keep the people from hanging all those bastards from the closest lamp poles."

"Probably enough so that, if we start ourselves a counterattack, the Yankees won't have enough reinforcements left to be able to hold us back," Jeff said.

Sergeant Cross laughed louder than the joke deserved. "That's good, Pinkard, that's right good," he said, but then gave the game away by adding, "Ain't heard you say nothin' that funny in a while now."

"World hasn't been a funny place lately, and that's a fact," Jeff said. "The Yankees have been pushin' us back every place there is to push, and livin' in the trenches wouldn't be my notion of a high old time even if we was winnin'. Other thing is, way it sounds is that everybody else on our side is about to fall over dead, too. Don't know about you, Sarge, but none of that makes me want to do a buck and wing."

Hip Rodriguez looked at Pinkard with his large, dark eyes and didn't say anything. He was still convinced Jeff had more urgent reasons for not making jokes these days. He was right, of course, but also too polite to push it.

Sergeant Cross lacked Sonoran manners. Not only that, he outranked Pinkard, which Hip didn't. He said, "I don't reckon it's fretting over whether we're goin' to lose the damn war that's made you try to get yourself killed every time we sent raiders out the past couple months."

"Haven't been trying to get myself killed," Pinkard protested, which, at least as far as the top part of his mind went, was true. "Want to kill me as many damnyankees as I can, is all."

"You used to have better sense than to volunteer to do it all the damn time," Cross said. "You go across no-man's-land often enough, sooner or later you don't come back."

If he could have shot Emily and Bedford first, Pinkard might have been content to turn his Tredegar on himself. One of the reasons he shook his head now was that he hadn't shot the damned bitch. Give her the satisfaction of outliving him? He shook his head again.

Then, from the other side of no-man's-land, the Yankees started firing trench mortars. The bombs whistled cheerily as they fell. As he'd almost done for the leaflet, Pinkard threw himself flat. *"Hijos del diablo!"* Hip Rodriguez shouted as he dove down to the bottom of the trench, too.

Sons of the devil, that meant, and Pinkard couldn't have agreed more. Mortar bombs flew right down into a trench, as conventional artillery, with its flatter trajectory, often could not. Along the line, somebody shrieked as fragments pierced him.

Machine guns started to rattle, both from the Yankees' entrenchments and from the Confederate line under attack. "They're coming!" someone yelled.

Cursing, Jeff scrambled up. That made him more vulnerable to the mortar bombs, which kept on falling. Lying down and waiting for damnyankees to jump into the trench and shoot him or bayonet him was the worse side of that bargain, though.

Just as he gained his feet, a soldier in green-gray did leap down into the trench. Jeff thought he shot him before the Yankee's feet hit the dirt. As the fellow crumpled, Jeff shot him again. He groaned. His Springfield slipped from fingers that could hold it no longer. Blood poured from the wounds in his chest and from his mouth and nostrils. He was a dead man, even if he didn't quite know it yet.

His pals were intent on making Jefferson Pinkard a dead man, too. Jeff shot another Yankee just before the man could shoot him. The U.S. soldiers shouted to one another in their sharp accents. They seemed dismayed that the Confederates should be so alert and ready to fight. "How the hell we supposed to bring back prisoners like the lieutenant wants?" one of them called to another.

"Shit, I don't know," his friend answered. "I only hope to Jesus I bring myself back in one piece."

Here and there, parties of damnyankees were getting into the Confederate trenches. Then it became a stalking game, rushing out of traverses and into firebays, flinging grenades, and fighting vicious little battles with bayonet and entrenching tool.

Jefferson Pinkard didn't think he was trying to get himself killed. But he was at the fore of the party that swarmed out of a traverse to beat down the last U.S. squad still holding a length of firebay. He swung an entrenching tool with savage abandon, reveling in the resistance the flesh and bones of a Yankee's head gave to the edge of the tool, reveling also in the way the soldier in green-gray moaned and dropped his rifle and clutched at himself and toppled, all in the space of a couple of seconds.

Then the Yankees, those few who hadn't been shot or stabbed or otherwise put out of action, were fleeing over the parapet and back toward their own lines. "Have fun in the state of Houston, boys!" Pinkard shouted, taking a couple of potshots at the retreating U.S. soldiers. He thought he hit one of them; the others kept on running.

A couple of U.S. soldiers still lay groaning and wounded in the trench. Sergeant Albert Cross examined their injuries with experience gained in a lot of war. "They ain't gonna make it back to field hospitals still breathing," he said. "Christ, Pinkard, looks like you took off half this poor bastard's face with that damn shovel of yours."

"He wasn't there to give me a kiss, Sarge," Jeff answered.

"Didn't say he was," Cross replied equably. He pointed down the length of the firebay. "Might as well put these sons of bitches out of their misery."

Nobody moved for a few seconds. There wasn't a Confederate soldier in the trench who didn't hope somebody, regardless of whether friend or foe, would do him that favor if he ever lay in agony, horribly wounded. That didn't mean many men were eager to do the job. Killing in cold blood, even for the sake of mercy, was different from killing in battle.

"I'll take care of it," Pinkard said at last. He loaded a new clip into his Tredegar and walked slowly down the trench line. Whenever he came across a U.S. soldier who was still breathing, he shot him in the head. One of the Yankees, whose guts spilled out onto the ground from a dreadful bayonet wound, thanked him as he pulled the trigger.

"They didn't buy anything cheap today," Sergeant Cross said.

"No," Jeff answered, "but they're in Texas and we ain't in New Mexico. What the hell have we bought?" Cross didn't say another word.

XV

Lieutenant Gordon McSweeney peered across the Mississippi from the bushes on the low, swampy Arkansas bank to the bluffs on which sat Memphis, Tennessee. U.S. guns, painfully moved forward over roads that would have had to improve to be reckoned miserable, pounded away at the Confederate bastion.

Nor were the Confederates in the least shy about pounding back. They had a lot of guns in Memphis, and a lot of shells, too. Rail lines up from Mississippi made it easy for them to keep those guns supplied with munitions. Farther east, the course of the Tennessee River shielded Memphis from attack by the U.S. First Army.

And C.S. river gunboats dominated not only the course of the Tennessee but also this stretch of the Mississippi. The mines upstream remained too thick for U.S. monitors to make their way down and challenge the Confederate boats. That meant that, wherever the CSA wanted large-caliber guns to deliver their fire, they could—and they did. They'd hurt U.S. forces on the west bank of the river too many times already.

A U.S. field gun down by the riverbank not far from where McSweeney was standing presumed to fire on one of the river monitors flying the Confederate naval ensign. It hit the monitor square on the turret. The C.S. boat, though, was armored to withstand the shells of others of its kind. A hit from a three-inch gun got its attention but did no damage to speak of—the worst of both worlds.

Ponderously, the turret swung so that the pair of eight-inch guns inside bore on the field piece. Flame and great clouds of gray smoke belched from the muzzles of those eight-inch guns. A couple of seconds later, McSweeney heard the roar as the sound traveled across the water to his ear. An instant after that—

or perhaps an instant before—the two shells launched from the guns blew the U.S. field piece and its crew to kingdom come. On steamed the gunboat, smug in its invulnerability.

"God have mercy on their souls," Gordon McSweeney murmured. He said not a word about the bodies of the brave but foolhardy U.S. gun crew. After those shells struck home, the gunners were fit for burial in jam jars; coffins would have been wasted on their remains.

He'd watched that sort of thing happen too many times before. The United States might have finally reached the bank of the Mississippi, but the Confederate States still ruled this stretch of river. Some U.S. mines had gone into the muddy brown water, but McSweeney hadn't seen them do any good.

"If you want something done properly, do it yourself," he muttered under his breath. He was no expert with the mines both sides used in ocean and river warfare, but that did not worry him. The methods that sprang to his mind for disposing of a river monitor were considerably more direct.

He wished one of them involved his beloved flamethrower. He could not figure out how to use it without destroying himself along with the monitor, though. He sighed. God did not grant anyone everything he wanted.

If he asked permission to attack a Confederate river monitor, his superiors would surely tell him no. Accordingly, he asked nothing of anyone, save only the Lord. And the Lord provided . . . with a certain amount of help from Gordon McSweeney.

He already knew how to swim. He knew how to make a raft, too. After a little thought, he figured out that he would be wise to make the raft well upstream, to ensure that the current did not sweep him past the river monitor instead of toward it. If he came out of the Mississippi without having done what he intended to do, he would be in trouble with the U.S. Army. If he came out on the wrong bank of the Mississippi, he would be a prisoner of war—unless the Rebs chose to shoot him, for he would certainly be out of uniform.

"Where are you going, sir?" a sentry asked as McSweeney left the company perimeter.

"To reconnoiter," he answered, a response that had the virtue of being true and uninformative at the same time.

Another sentry, a man who did not know McSweeney, asked him the same question when he left the battalion perimeter. He gave the same answer, and got by the same way he had with the soldier from his company. The sentry was not inclined to quarrel with an obvious U.S. officer who sounded short-tempered and was armed to the teeth.

McSweeney would have shown just how short-tempered he was had anyone come across the raft he'd hidden behind bushes and underbrush. But there it was when he pulled the brush aside. He stripped off his clothes, loaded his weapons aboard the raft, and pushed off into the river. No one paid any attention to the small splashing noises he made.

The Mississippi was warm. The mud it carried didn't keep a couple of fish from finding him and nibbling at him. What he would have done if an alligator or snapping turtle had come up to investigate him was a question he was glad he did not have to answer.

He kicked hard, propelling the raft out toward the middle of the Mississippi. One thing he had not taken into account was his small circle of vision with his eyes only a few inches above the water. If he drifted past the C.S. river monitor without spying it, he would feel worse than just foolish.

There it was! That long, low shape, with almost no freeboard, couldn't be anything else. Someone had described the original *Monitor* as a cheese box on a raft, which also fit its descendants, both U.S. and C.S., to a tee—although the Confederates billed theirs as river gunboats, refusing to name their kind after a U.S. warship.

McSweeney hung onto the raft with his fingertips, letting as little of himself show as he could. His scheme would have been impossible had the C.S. vessel's deck been higher above the waterline. As things were, it was just insanely foolhardy. Gordon McSweeney had been doing insanely foolhardy things since the war began. If God willed that he die doing one of them, die he would, praising His name with his last breath.

He wondered what sort of watch the Confederate sailors kept on deck. He knew they didn't patrol with electric torches. Had they been foolish enough to do so, U.S. sharpshooters on the western bank of the Mississippi would have made them regret it.

He had to kick hard to keep the raft from gliding past the Confederate monitor and down the river. Grabbing the .45 and the sack of rubberized canvas he'd carried on the raft, he scrambled up onto the monitor's deck. His bare feet made not a sound on the riveted iron. Somewhere aft, a sentry was pacing; his shoes clanked on the deck.

And here he came. He moved without any particular urgency, but as much on his appointed rounds as a postman might have done. McSweeney had no trouble keeping the turret between himself and the man who strode on through the darkness, never expecting trouble could come on his watch when the Confederate States so dominated this stretch of the Mississippi River.

Whether he expected it or not, trouble shared the deck with him. McSweeney undid the sack and drew from it two one-pound blocks of TNT, twenty seconds' worth of fuse for each, and a match safe that had stood up to all the rain and mud nearly three years in the trenches had thrown at it. The matches inside rattled. He glared at them, willing them to be silent, then crimped the fuses to the explosive blocks.

Silent himself, he scuttled round the turret to the openings from which the barrels of the monitors' big guns projected. Once he got there, he reluctantly set down the .45 so he could take a match out of the trusty safe and strike it.

The hiss of the match as it caught was tiny. So was the light that came from it. One or the other, though, alerted the sentry. "Who goes there?" he demanded, his voice suddenly sharp and alert.

"Damnation," McSweeney muttered, and only saved himself from the blasphemy he so despised by hastily adding, "to the enemies of the Lord." He lit the fuses attached to the explosive blocks, tossed them inside the monitor's turret, as far to the back as he could, and snatched up the pistol once more.

"Who goes there?" the sentry repeated. Now his shoes rang on the deck as he hurried to investigate.

McSweeney fired three quick rounds at him. One of them must have hit, for the Reb let out a shriek. McSweeney didn't care, except insofar as the fellow didn't get a chance to shoot at him. He threw away the pistol and dove into the Mississippi. He'd cut things too fine, both metaphorically and, with the fuses, literally as well.

He swam away from the monitor as fast as he could. He tried to go as deep as he could. His ears ached in protest. He ignored them, knowing better than they what was about to happen.

No matter how muddy the Mississippi was, suddenly the surface of the water, high over his head, lit up bright as day, bright as hellfire. The explosion behind him sent him tumbling through the water, more than half stunned. Why he didn't open his mouth and breathe in half the river, he never knew. Either the Lord watched over him or he was simply too stubborn to drown.

After a while, his lungs told him he had to breathe or die. By then, the chunks of iron—some of them bigger than he was—had stopped raining down out of the sky. When he broke the surface, he was amazed he'd swum so far from the Confederate monitor—till he remembered the explosion had given him a big push.

He'd hoped his explosives would touch off the magazine inside the turret, and had they! Had they ever! *Bombs bursting in air,* he thought as one explosion followed another. God had wanted him to live, and so he lived. Surely no one aboard the monitor did, not now. He struck out for the Arkansas bank of the river. His slow backstroke let him rest whenever he needed.

Alarm tingled through him when he finally splashed up onto the bank of the Mississippi. What if the current had swept him beyond the limits of U.S.-held territory and into land the Rebels still controlled? Then he would have to make his way north, that was all. As long as he was on the right side of the river, being captured never entered his mind.

The sentry who challenged him when he came up onto the land was a pure Yankee, from Maine or New Hampshire. He didn't believe McSweeney's explanation of who he was or why he was naked. Neither did his superior, nor that fellow's superior, either.

Calm as could be, McSweeney kept explaining who he was, what he'd done, and how he'd done it. They gave him clothes. Eventually, they got hold of his service record. That made them argue less and gape more. Then they found out he wasn't with the company where he was supposed to be, which made them begin to wonder if he might not be in front of them after all.

It was mid-morning before they brought Ben Carlton down to identify him. When Carlton did, they stared and stared. "Oak-leaf cluster," they kept muttering. "Medal of Honor with an oak-leaf cluster. Who would dare write up the citation, though? Who would believe it?"

"Can you please send me back to my unit?" McSweeney asked. "I've had a long night, and I'm very tired." Everyone kept right on staring at him.

* * *

Scipio wished he were anywhere but trapped in the swamps by the Congaree River. He'd wished that ever since Anne Colleton sent him here. He'd never wished it so intensely as now.

From out on the perimeter, the fighters of the Congaree Socialist Republic kept up a continuous crackle of fire. The Confederate militiamen were not nearly so good, man for man, as the Reds, but they had more men and, finally, what looked to be a determination to press the fight.

Cassius looked worried. Scipio had never before seen Cassius look worried, not even when the CSA put down the larger version of the Congaree Socialist Republic, the version that had tried to carry the Red revolution to a wide stretch of South Carolina.

"*Damn* that Cherry!" he burst out now. "She don' listen to nobody but her ownself, an' she weren't as smart as she reckon she were. An' now she ain't here no more, an' I feels like I's missin' my lef' hand."

"Maybe you is," Scipio said, "but maybe you is just as well off without it, too. If she was your left hand, you was always watchin' it to make sure it don't stab you in the back."

"Now I knows that ain't a lie, but I misses she all de same," Cassius answered. "What she do, she do for the sake o' the revolution. Anything gits in the way o' the revolution, she sure as hell push it off to de side." He sighed. "She sure as hell try and push me off to de side, you right about dat. But even so, I misses she. She hate de 'pressors more'n anything in the whole wide world."

Scipio remained not the least bit sorry he'd mailed that letter to Anne Colleton. "Kin hate too much," he said.

"Mebbe." Cassius shrugged. "Sure as hell wish she was shootin' at de damn buckra, though."

"Yeah, she do dat good," Scipio allowed, as if making a great concession. " 'Course, she shoot at anything that strike she fancy. She shoot at de buckra, or else she shoot at you or me or anything else."

"She committed to de revolution," Cassius repeated. "She shoot anybody, she reckon dey gets in de way o' de revolution. She screw anybody, she reckon dat help de revolution. She screw Miss Anne's gassed brother till he don't know up from Tuesday." He scowled at that. He might have recognized the revolutionary need for it while it was going on, but he hadn't liked it then. He still didn't.

"Marse Jacob, he dead," Scipio said quietly, reminding the leader of the Congaree Socialist Republic. Off in the distance, the crackle of gunfire increased. "All o' we gwine be dead, too, we don't figure out what the devil we do 'bout they buckra pretty damn quick."

Cassius didn't even disagree with him, not directly. He said, "Even if we's dead, de revolution go on widout we."

Scipio would sooner have gone on without the revolution than the other way round. Saying as much struck him as highly inexpedient. Just then, a series of rending crashes off to the northwest made him peer in that direction. "The militia find some shells for they artillery again," he said, and then, "Do Jesus! Ain't we got a camp over yonder, 'bout where that stuff come down?"

"We does—or maybe we done did." Cassius frowned. "I don't reckon de buckra knowed about dat place. I don't reckon nobody who don't live in de swamps could know about dat place."

Traitors. The word hung in the air as clearly as if the Red leader had spoken it aloud. Any talk of traitors inevitably became talk of Scipio, too. He knew it. For once, though, he was innocent. He had betrayed Cherry, but not the camp. But somebody was liable to jump to the wrong conclusion in this particular case, which would also put him in trouble.

Before Cassius could so much as turn his eyes toward Scipio in speculation, both men looked up at a noise in the sky. Scipio, for a wonder, spotted the aeroplane before Cassius did. It was, as far as aeroplanes went, an antique: an ungainly biplane with a pusher propeller, all struts and booms and wires. Against the swift, sleek fighting scouts the USA put in the air these days, the ugly machine wouldn't have survived five minutes. But it was plenty good for spying on the men of the Congaree Socialist Republic.

Cassius figured that out as fast as Scipio did. "Ain't fair!" he shouted furiously. "Shitfire, Kip, it ain't fair. If the buckra looks down on the swamp like a man look through the cabin window when a pretty woman take off she dress, how we gwine stay hid?"

That was a good question. As far as Scipio could see, that was *the* good question. He shook his head. No, there was one other. He asked it: "You reckon that pilot got one o' they wireless telegraph machines up there with he?"

"Don't rightly know," Cassius answered. "Do Jesus, though, I hope he don't."

That hope, like so many hopes of the Congaree Socialist Republic, was shortly to be dashed. The aeroplane flew back and forth, back and forth, over the encampment. A few of Cassius' men fired rifles and machine guns at it. It was too high for any of that to damage or even alarm it. Back and forth, back and forth.

Cassius cursed horribly for the next couple of minutes. That did no good, either. He had no more than a couple of minutes to curse. After that, shells started falling on the encampment where he and Scipio had been talking.

The first few explosions were long, and off to Scipio's right. The next couple were short, and off to his left. Sure as hell, the pilot must have had a wireless telegraph in his flying machine, and used it to correct the aim of the gunners firing at the encampment. The first correction had been excessive, but he'd seen where those shells fell, too. After that—

"Do Jesus!" Scipio screeched through the wail of falling shells. "These ones is comin' down right on top o' we!"

Cassius must have said something by way of reply. Whatever it was, though, Scipio didn't hear it. He'd been right and more than right—the shells were coming down on top of him and on top of the biggest encampment the men of the Congaree Socialist Republic had maintained in the swamps by the river that gave them their name.

Scipio threw himself flat. He had seen enough of war to have learned that lesson. Cassius sprawled on the ground a few feet away from him. Mud rained down on them as shell fragments chewed up the landscape all around. Through the explosions, men screamed like lost souls. More shell fragments and shrapnel balls hissed through the air. Something that was not mud fell almost harmlessly on Scipio's back. Almost harmlessly—it was hot enough to burn. With an oath, he knocked away the hunk of brass.

Overhead, the aeroplane kept circling and circling. The pilot could spot exactly how much damage the artillerymen were doing, and let them know where to send the next few shells. The Confederate States had been doing that sort of thing against the United States since 1914. Now the men of the Congaree Socialist Republic were getting a taste of how effective it could be.

"Scatter!" Cassius shouted. "Git out o' de camp. Git under the trees an' de bushes. Dat buckra pilot up dere cain't see we, he cain't tell de buckra at the guns where to put they shells. Scatter!"

Along with the rest of the Negroes in the encampment, Scipio fled into the forest. He paid no attention to which way he was running, so long as it was away from the unending thunder of the Confederate militia's cannon. A man not twenty feet in front of him was blown to red rags when a shell exploded between his legs. There wasn't enough left of him to scream. Scipio shuddered and kept running. If he'd run faster, that might have been him.

No one paid him any special attention as he blundered through the lush woods and the mud. For the first time since Anne Colleton's machinations had forced him back into the shrunken Congaree Socialist Republic, he was on his own. Running for his life from the bombardment, he needed a while to figure out what that meant. He wasn't thinking so clearly as he might have been had unfriendly strangers not been doing their best to kill him.

Only when he paused to lie panting under a pine did he realize the bombardment gave him an opportunity the likes of which he had not known since entering the swamp. If he was lucky enough, he might escape. If he wasn't lucky and he tried it, he'd end up dead, of course. Sometimes he told himself he would sooner die than go on living in the swamps by the Congaree. Unfortunately, he knew what a liar he was.

Still, if he never tasted scrambled turtle eggs again, he wouldn't shed a tear. Now that he was farther from the artillery bombardment, he noted that the small-arms fire was heavier and closer than it had been. The Confederate militiamen really were doing their best to hammer the Congaree Socialist Republic flat this time. Maybe they would.

If they saw him, he'd be just another Red nigger to them, just another rebel to shoot or bayonet so their vision of what the Confederate States should be could go forward. If they saw him . . . The problem, then, was to make sure they didn't see him.

Had he been the woodsman Cassius was, it would have been easy. Even being the poor excuse for a woodsman he truly was, he'd got beyond most of the firing before a white man snapped, "Halt! Who goes there?"

Scipio peered through the brush that screened him. The militiaman pointing a Tredegar his way might have been handsome once, but some disaster had ruined the left side of his face. He was going to shoot if Scipio didn't satisfy him right away. Scipio tried, using his best butler's tones to say, "Carry on, Sergeant. The sooner we rid these nasty swamps of the Goddamned Red niggers who infest them, the better off our beloved country shall be."

Had he laid it on too thick? Sometimes, when he used that voice, he sounded more like an Englishman than an educated white Confederate. But the militiaman with the slagged face was satisfied. "Yes, sir!" he said, and plunged deeper into the swamp. He couldn't possibly have known who Scipio was, but assumed anyone who talked the way he did had to be an officer.

"Thank you, Miss Anne," Scipio whispered as he made his way farther and farther from the Congaree. Teaching him how to talk like an educated white man hadn't been for his benefit—having a butler who could talk like that had given Marshlands more swank. It had also made him a white crow, one who couldn't fully fit in with the rest of the Negroes on the plantation. He'd hated it while it was going on. Now it just might have saved his life.

If he kept going straight away from the swamp, he'd emerge somewhere near the ruins of the Marshlands mansion. He didn't want to do that. Too many people around there were liable to recognize him. He swung to the west, guiding himself by the sun as best he could.

He came out in a cotton field that was, like so many others in this part of the country, untended and overrun with weeds. He was filthy and exhausted. He didn't care. He didn't care even a little bit. He'd escaped Anne Colleton and Cassius, too. He was, for the time being, a free man again.

Chester Martin was not the only U.S. sergeant commanding a company in Virginia these days. They might eventually get around to promoting him or bringing in an officer to take over. On the other hand, they might not. They might just keep putting more young privates under him, sending them forward, and seeing what the hell happened next. Somewhere not far away, there was supposed to be a regiment led by a first lieutenant, the outfit's senior officer who was alive and in one piece.

Even a year before, rank would have worried him more than it did today. Today, all he wanted to do was get on with the attack, however it went in. He had trouble believing he was actually eager to go forward. Nor was he the only one. Corporal Bob Reinholdt, who had been furious at not getting a section but was now commanding one, looked up from the Springfield he was cleaning and said, "One more good push and these bastards are going to roll over and play dead."

"That's about the size of it, I think," Martin agreed. "Never thought I'd say it, but they don't snap back the way they used to."

Tilden Russell remained a private, too, but he was leading a squad in Martin's shrunken company. He might lack rank, but he had experience. He said, "The Rebs are like an inner tube with a little tiny leak. They look fine till you press on 'em, but then they give."

Martin whistled, a low, respectful note. "That's not half bad, Tilden. You ought to think about writing for the newspapers when the war's done."

When the war's done. The words hung in the air. For a long time—from the minute the fighting started up to his own getting shot and beyond—the war had seemed to stretch out forever ahead of Martin. If he wasn't still fighting thirty years from now, his sons or grandsons would be, if he found time to marry and beget any on his infrequent leaves. The only way out he'd seen was getting killed—and he'd seen a lot of that.

Now . . . now it was different. As he rolled himself a cigarette, he thought about how. Reinholdt and Russell had defined the difference as well as he heard it defined. "If we keep pressing on 'em, sooner or later they'll go flat. I'm finally starting to think it'll be sooner."

It hadn't happened yet. Confederate artillery south of Manassas started banging away at the U.S. lines threatening the town. Those lines weren't so deeply entrenched nor so well furnished with dugouts as many of the ones in which Martin had previously served: they were too new to have acquired what he'd come to think of as the amenities of trench life. He threw himself down in the dirt and hoped he wouldn't be like Moses, dying before he entered the promised land of peace. Of course, no one had promised that land to him.

After a while, the barrage eased. He braced for a Confederate counterattack to follow it, but none came. The Rebs still fought ferociously on defense, but they didn't hit back so hard or so often as they once had—another sign, as Tilden Russell had said, that their inner tube had sprung a leak. Martin wished the Army could have pinned them against the Potomac from the west before they could pull out of Washington. That might have ended the war right there.

As things were, he was glad to get to his feet. He was glad to have feet to get to, and arms, and everything else he'd had before the shelling started. Here and there, wounded men and their pals were shouting for stretcher-bearers. He gauged the cries with practiced ears. The company hadn't been hurt too badly, not as a group. The unlucky soldiers who were the exceptions wouldn't have seen things the same way.

A couple of hours later, as afternoon drifted toward evening, a fellow who looked no older than Martin but who had gold oak leaves on his shoulder straps came down the trench. "I'm looking for the company commander," he called.

"You've found him, sir," Martin said, and jabbed a thumb at his own chest.

The major looked surprised, but only for a moment. "All right, Sergeant. Looks like you got your job the same way I got mine."

"Yes, sir: I'm still breathing," Martin answered.

"Fair enough," the major said with a laugh. "I'm Gideon Adkins. Happens that I'm the senior officer still breathing in this regiment, so the 91st is mine till they send somebody to take my place—if they ever get around to that."

"We're in the same boat, all right, sir," Martin said. "Let's get down to business. What do you need from B Company?"

Adkins studied him. He knew what was in the major's mind—the same thing that would be in a brigadier general's mind when he studied Adkins: can this man do the job, or do we need to replace him? If they did replace Martin, he hoped he wouldn't be as resentful as Bob Reinholdt had been when he first joined the company.

Well, Major Adkins couldn't complain about the question he'd asked. Indeed, the young regimental commander said, "That's the spirit, Sergeant . . ."

"Oh, sorry, sir. I'm Chester Martin."

"Thanks, Sergeant Martin. Wish I didn't have to ask, but I'm still learning the ropes, too, no doubt about it. All right, here's what you need to know: in three days, we go over the top. First objective is Manassas. Second objective is Independent Hill."

Adkins drew a much-folded map from his breast pocket and pointed the hill out to Martin.

After he glanced at the scale of miles, Martin raised his eyebrows. "Sir, that looks to be eight or ten miles past Manassas. If they're setting that as an objective for this attack, they do think the Confederate States are ready to throw in the sponge."

"If they aren't, we're going to make them throw it in anyhow," Gideon Adkins declared. "That's what this attack is all about. We'll have plenty of barrels to throw at them, and plenty of aeroplanes, and they'll be bringing forward some new light machine guns that'll do a better job of keeping up with a rapid advance."

"That all sounds good, sir." Martin gave a wry smile. "And there'll be plenty of us old-fashioned, garden-variety infantrymen around, to do whatever the barrels and the aeroplanes and the machine guns can't."

"Infantrymen?" Major Adkins made as if he'd never heard the word. Then he laughed and slapped Martin on the back. "Yes, I expect there'll be something or other for old-fashioned critters like us to do."

Martin spread the word to the other sergeants who commanded the platoons in his company. They had all seen a lot of fighting. One of them said, "Well, it's been going better lately, but ain't a one of us'd have the job he's doing right now if it'd been going what you'd call good." That summed up the course of the war so well, nobody tried to improve on it.

Barrels came forward under cover of night. They went into position behind the front line, shielded from snoopy Confederates by canvas when the sun rose. Even so, they were about as hard to hide as a herd of elephants in church. U.S. aeroplanes did their best to keep Rebel observers in the sky from flying over territory the United States held.

As had the other recent offensives, this one opened with a short, sharp artillery barrage, designed more to startle and paralyze than to crush. Nobody had bothered to issue Chester Martin a whistle—even if he was commanding a company, he wasn't an officer. "Come on, boys!" he shouted. "A couple more kicks and the doors fall down."

A lot of soldiers would fall down, too, fall down and never get up again. Martin wondered how many times he'd gone over the top now. The only answer he came up with was, *too many*. As machine-gun and rifle bullets whipped around him, he wondered why the hell he'd done it even once. For the life of him—literally, for the life of him—he came up with no answer.

The barrels behind which the infantry advanced forced their way through the Confederates' forward line. U.S. fighting scouts buzzed low overhead, adding their machine-gun fire to that from the barrels—and that from the light machine guns Major Adkins had talked about. Having along firepower more potent than that which Springfields could provide felt very good to a veteran foot soldier.

Here and there, Rebel machine-gun nests and knots of stubborn soldiers in butternut, some white men, some colored, held up the U.S. advance. Martin's bayonet had blood on it before he got out of the trench system. Rebel artillery, though outgunned, remained scrappy. And the Rebels had barrels of their own, if not so many as those that bore down on them.

Yet, even though resistance was heavy in spots, the Army of Northern Virginia yielded its forward positions more readily than Chester Martin had ever seen it do before. As the soldiers in green-gray broke out of the trenches and into open country, he spotted Bob Reinholdt not far away. "This is too damn easy," he called. "The Rebs have to have something up their sleeve."

"Reckon you're right," Reinholdt answered, "but to hell with me if I know what it is. I'm going to enjoy this while it lasts."

"Yeah, me, too," Martin said. He didn't enjoy it long, because the Army of Northern Virginia did have something up its sleeve. It had put fewer men into the forward trenches than usual, its generals perhaps aware that, no matter what they did, they could not withstand the first U.S. blow.

Once the first line was pierced, though . . . The Confederates had machine guns cunningly concealed in every cornfield. They had snipers in every other pine and oak. The ground south of their front line was more stubbornly defended than Martin remembered from earlier fights. He tried to think strategically. In those earlier fights, the Rebs defending open country had been men forced from their trenches. Here, the Confederates had planned from the beginning to fight in the open, and they showed a nasty talent for it.

Martin got to hate cornfields in a hurry. The plants stood taller than a man. You couldn't see more than one row at a time. Anything might be lurking among them. All too often, it was. Machine guns, trip wires, foxholes . . . anything at all.

His company managed to bypass the fighting for Manassas it-self, skirting it to the west. Before long, by the sound of things, the town was cut off and surrounded, but the Confederates inside showed no signs of quitting: they kept banging away at the U.S. soldiers with whatever they had.

"Come on!" Martin yelled as a Wright two-decker, which could see better than he could, poured fire on the Rebs in a field ahead. The objective lines on Major Adkins' map had seemed insanely optimistic. They were. The soldiers weren't going to reach those set for the first day, even if Manassas would fall soon. Martin rolled himself in a blanket when night came and wearily thanked God he was still breathing.

The next day was another grim blur, as the Rebs brought reinforcements forward and tried to counterattack. The U.S. soldiers, glad to play defense for a little while, took savage pleasure in mowing them down. By that evening, the Confederates couldn't find any more troops who would press home a counterattack. Their raw recruits would make a halfhearted lunge, then fall back in disorder and dismay when rifle and machine-gun bullets began to bite.

By noon the next day, a day behind the preordained schedule but far ahead of Chester Martin's fondest dreams, he stood atop Independent Hill—a knob barely deserving the name—and peered south, wondering where the next push would take him.

Somewhere north of Independent Hill, Jake Featherston and what was left of his battery—what was left of the First Richmond Howitzers, what was left of the Army of Northern Virginia—tried to hold back the tide with bare hands. He was filthy; he couldn't remember the last time he'd had leisure even to splash in a creek. His butternut uniform, aside from being out at the knees and elbows, had enough green splotches on it to make him look halfway like a damnyankee.

The real damnyankees were forcing their way across Cedar Run. He'd expected they would be any time now, and had taken the range for his guns. "Let's give it to them, boys," he shouted, and the four surviving guns of the battery began banging away. Peering through field glasses, he watched the explosions a couple of miles to the north. The shells were falling right where he wanted them to: on the leading Yankees and trailing Confederates.

He was the man with the binoculars. The rest of his gun crews couldn't tell exactly where the rounds were coming down. That wasn't their job; it was his. If the Confederate stragglers caught a little hell from their own side, too damn bad. *Odds are they're niggers anyway,* he thought.

Retreating infantry streamed past the battery to either side. Some of the men falling back were indeed colored. Others, to Jake's disgust, were white. "Why don't you fight the goddamn sons of bitches?" he shouted at them.

"Fuck you," one of the infantrymen shouted back. "Got your damn nerve yellin' at us when you lousy bastards ain't never been up in a trench in all your born days. Hope the damnyankees run right over you, give you a taste of what real for-true soldierin' is like."

Featherston's temper went up like an ammunition dump. "Canister!" he shouted, fully intending to turn his gun on the infantryman who'd talked back to him—and on the fellow's pals, too. "Load me a round of canister, damn your eyes. I'll teach that asshole to run his mouth when he don't know what he's talkin' about."

"Sorry, Sarge, don't reckon we got any more canister," Michael Scott said. That was a damn lie, and Featherston knew it was a damn lie. He cussed his loader up one side and down the other. By the time he was through, the offending soldiers were around a stand of trees and out of sight. Scott probably thought that meant they were forgotten, but he underestimated Jake, who never forgot a slight, even when he could do nothing about it.

This was one of those times. Regardless of his shelling, the Yankees kept right on crossing Cedar Run. A few aeroplanes emblazoned with the Confederate battle flag swooped down on them. But more U.S. fighting scouts raked the soldiers in butternut who were trying to hold them back.

Despite the aeroplanes, despite the Yankees' numbers, Featherston thought for a while that the Army of Northern Virginia would be able to hold them not too far south of Cedar Run. From his own position on slightly higher ground, he was able to watch U.S. assaults crumple in the face of fire from the machine guns the Confederates had posted in cornfields and woods.

"Those fields'll raise a fine crop of dead men," he said with a chuckle, turning the elevation screw to shorten the range on his own field piece.

But the men in green-gray did not give up, despite the casualties they took. In almost three years of war, Jake had come to know the enemy well. The Yankees made more stolid soldiers than the men alongside of whom he'd gone to war. They weren't quite so quick to exploit advantages as were their Confederate counterparts. That coin had two sides, though, for they kept coming even after losses that might have torn the heart out of a C.S. attack.

As usual these days, they had barrels leading the way, too. Featherston whooped with glee when one of the guns from his battery set a traveling fortress on fire. "Burn now and burn in hell, you sons of bitches!" he shouted. He hoped they did burn. That would hurt the damnyankees, for every barrel carried inside it a couple of squads' worth of men.

For every U.S. barrel Confederate artillery or Confederate tanks—Jake still sneered whenever the term crossed his mind—knocked out, though, two or three more kept waddling forward. And the Yankees' front-line troops seemed to have an ungodly number of machine guns, too. Featherston recognized the muzzle flashes that went on and on as the guns fired burst after burst at the C.S. troops resisting them.

In disgust, he turned to Michael Scott. "There's somethin' else we'll get around to trying in six, eight months—maybe a year—or we would, 'cept the goddamn war'll be lost to hell and gone by then," he said.

"Those can't be regular machine guns," the loader replied. "They're keeping up with the rest of the damnyankee infantry way too good for that. Yankees must've turned out some lightweight models."

"So why the hell ain't we?" Featherston asked, a good question without a good answer. Not long before, he'd reckoned U.S. soldiers stolid in the way they fought. There was, unfortunately, nothing stolid about their War Department. He spat in disgust. "Those white-bearded fools down in Richmond shouldn't ever have started this here fight if they didn't reckon they could whip the USA."

"They did reckon that." Steady as if he were attacking New York instead of defending Richmond, Scott loaded yet another shell into the breech of the quick-firing three-inch. Featherston made a minute adjustment to the traversing screw, then nodded. Scott yanked the lanyard. The gun bellowed. Scott opened the breech. Out fell the shell casing, to land with a clank on one of the many others the piece had already fired. As he placed the next shell in the breech, the loader went on, "Maybe they weren't quite right this time."

"Yeah—maybe." A rattlesnake might have carried more venom in its mouth than Jake Featherston did, but not much more. He fiddled with the traversing screw again—the Yankee machine gun at which he'd aimed the last shell was still blazing away. When he was satisfied, he yelled, "Fire!" The field gun roared again. He took off his tin hat and waved it in the air when that lightweight gun—Scott had made a shrewd guess there—abruptly fell silent.

Darkness slowed the carnage, but didn't stop it. Featherston slept by his gun, in fitful snatches when the firing died down for a while. Ammunition did come forward to his guns, but U.S. bombing aeroplanes kept thundering by low overhead and dropping their loads deep behind the Confederate line. Troops and munitions would have a harder time moving up in the morning.

When the skirmishing along the front line picked up, he fired a few rounds at where he thought the damnyankees were. Michael Scott wasn't so sure. "Haven't you shortened the range so much, those'll be dropping on our own boys?" he asked.

"Don't reckon so," Jake answered. "Yanks'll likely have moved up a bit since we could see where they were at. And if they haven't, well, what the hell? Odds are I'm just blowing up some coons."

Fighting grew heavy before sunrise. As soon as black turned to gray, the two armies started going at each other—or rather, the U.S. forces started going at the Army of Northern Virginia, which fought desperately to hold back the onslaught. The damnyankees had brought soldiers and supplies forward during the night, too, and threw everything they had into the fight.

For a couple of hours, in spite of his gibes about the fools in Richmond and his contempt for the Negroes surely manning a large part of the line in front of him, Featherston dared hope that line would hold. The Yankees crept within a couple of thousand yards of his position—close enough that occasional rifle and machine-gun bullets whistled by—and stalled.

But then, no doubt saved for just such an emergency, fifteen or twenty barrels painted green-gray rumbled over pontoon bridges thrown across Cedar Run and straight at the outnumbered, out-gunned men in butternut. Jake looked wildly in all directions. Where were the Confederate barrels that could blunt the slow-moving charge of the U.S. machines?

He saw none. There were none to see. He shouted to his gun, to his battery: "It's up to us. If we don't stop them fuckers, no-body does."

They did what they could do. Three or four barrels went up in flames, sending pillars of black smoke high into the sky to mark their funeral pyres. But the rest kept coming, through the woods, through the fields, straight at him—and straight through what was left of the Army of Northern Virginia's line.

And the line gave way. He'd seen that up at Round Hill: a sea of panic-stricken men in butternut streaming back toward him. He'd hoped he'd never see anything like it again. But here it was. These soldiers—some white, more colored—had had all the fighting they could stand. The only thing left in their minds was escaping the oncoming foe.

They might have had a better chance if they'd stayed and tried to hold back the U.S. soldiers. Infantrymen in green-gray and barrel crews were not the least bit shy about shooting fleeing Confederates in the back.

Featherston would cheerfully have shot them in the back, too. He didn't have that choice, since they were coming his way. "Fight!" he shouted to the infantrymen. "Turn around and fight, God damn you!" They didn't. They wouldn't. As he had at Round Hill, as he had when the soldier cursed him the day before, he shouted, "Canister! If I can't do it any other way, I'll send 'em back on account of they're more afraid of me than they ever dreamt of being afraid of the damnyankees."

Michael Scott objected again: "Sarge, God only knows how come we didn't get crucified the last time we did that. If we do it again—"

Featherston did not intend to let his loader balk him, not now. He drew his pistol. "I'll load and fire it myself if I have to," he snarled. Then, over open sights, he aimed the gun at the Confederate soldiers heading his way. Scott could have drawn his own weapon. Instead, white-faced, he loaded the round Jake had demanded. Jake pulled the lanyard himself. He shrieked out a Rebel yell when the worthless, cowardly scum in butternut vanished from before the gun as if swept aside by a broom. He might have hit some of the Yankees close on their heels, too.

But the canister rounds—he fired several—did not, could not, stem the rout, any more than they had at Round Hill. The infantry *would* run, and he could not stop them. Save for the ones he killed and maimed, the men in butternut fled past him. Black soldiers and white cried out in amazement that he did not flee, too.

"Cowards!" he shouted at them in turn. "Filthy, stinking, rotten cowards! Stand and fight, damn you all. You're stabbing your country in the back."

And then the Yankees were well within canister range. He gave them several rounds, too, to make them go to ground. That bought him time to limber up his guns and abandon his own position. He could not hold if everything around him fell. All four guns got out.

"Backstabbers," he muttered as he trudged south past Independent Hill. "Nothing but filthy backstabbers. I'll pay them all back one day, every goddamn one of them, so help me Jesus I will."

Sam Carsten shoveled in beans and smoked sausage and sauerkraut alongside dozens of other men in the galley. The USS *Dakota* rolled as he ate, but the tables were mounted on gimbals. The rolling wasn't nearly enough to make his food end up in his lap.

Across the table from him, Vic Crosetti grinned and poured down coffee. "Well, you were right, you lucky son of a bitch— we're still down here and it's turning into winter. You don't toast for a while longer yet."

"Oh, come on," Sam said mildly. "Yeah, it's winter, but it's not *winter*, if you know what I mean. Just kind of gray and gloomy, that's all. It's like San Francisco winter, kind of. That's not so bad."

"Yeah, that's not so bad," Crosetti said, with the air of a man granting a great and undeserved favor, "but it ain't so goddamn good, neither. If we was back in the Sandwich Islands now, I'd be laying under a palm tree with one of those what-do-you-call-'em flowers in my hair—"

"Hibiscus?" Carsten said.

"Yeah, one of them," Crosetti agreed. "With a hibiscus flower in my hair and with my arm around a broad. I'd be suckin' up a cold drink, or maybe she'd be suckin' up somethin' else. But no, it's winter out in the goddamn South Atlantic, and you, you son of a bitch, you're *happy* about it."

"You bet I am," Carsten said. "For one thing, back at Pearl Harbor we might get leave once in a while, yeah, but they'd work our tails off the rest of the time, harder'n they're working us now when we aren't fighting. That's one thing, mind you. You know damn well what the other one is."

"Sure as hell do." Crosetti cackled like a hen just delivered of an egg. "Layin' under a palm tree wouldn't do you one single, stinking, solitary bit of good. Everybody'd reckon you were the roast pig they was supposed to eat for supper, 'cept maybe you wouldn't have an apple in your mouth. God help you if you did, though."

"Jesus!" Sam had been swigging coffee himself. He had everything he could do to keep it from coming out his nose. "Don't make me laugh like that again. Especially don't make me laugh like that and want to deck you at the same time." He put down the coffee mug and made a fist—a pale, pale fist.

Vic Crosetti grinned again, no doubt ready with another snappy comeback. *Damn smartmouth wop,* Carsten thought with wry affection, bracing himself to laugh and get furious at the same time again. But instead of sticking the needle in him one more time, Crosetti jumped from his seat and sprang to attention. So did Sam, wondering why the devil Commander Grady was coming into the galley.

"As you were, men," the commander of the starboard secondary armament said. "This isn't a snap inspection."

"Then what the hell is it?" Crosetti mumbled as he sat down again. Carsten would have said the same thing if his bunkmate hadn't beaten him to it. Several sailors let out quiet—but not quite quiet enough—sighs of relief.

"I have an announcement to make," Grady said, "an announcement that will affect the *Dakota* and our mission. We have just received word by wireless telegraph that the Empire of Brazil has declared war on the United Kingdom, the Republic of France, the Confederate States of America, and the Republic of Argentina." He grinned now, an expression of pure exultation. "How about that, boys?"

For a few seconds, the big compartment was absolutely still.

Then it erupted in bedlam. At any other time, a passing officer would have angrily broken up the disturbance and assigned punishment to every man jack in there. Now Commander Grady, showing his teeth like a chimpanzee in the zoo, pounded on the bulkhead and whooped louder than anybody else.

"Dom Pedro knows whose ship is sinking, and it isn't ours!" Carsten shouted.

"Good-bye, England!" Crosetti yelled, and waved at Sam as if he were King George. "So long, pal! Be seein' you—be seein' you starve."

"Hell of a lot longer run from Buenos Aires to west Africa than it is from Pernambuco," Sam said through the din, as if he were seeing things from Rear Admiral Bradley Fiske's cabin. "And with Brazil in the war on our side, we'll be able to use their ports, and they'll have some ships of their own they'll throw into the pot." As he weighted the sudden, enormous change, his smile got wider and wider. "Near as I can see, the limeys are a lobster in the pot, and the water's starting to boil."

"Near as I can see, you're right." Vic Crosetti nodded emphatically. Then he leered at Carsten. "And you know what else?"

"No, what?" Sam asked.

"Near as I can see, you're a lobster in the pot, and the water's starting to boil, too," Crosetti answered. "If we go up into Brazilian waters, buddy, that might as well be Pearl Harbor." He pantomimed putting on a bib. "Waiter! Some drawn butter, and make it snappy."

"You go to hell," Carsten said, but he was laughing, too.

"Maybe I will," the swarthy Italian sailor answered, "but if we head to Brazil, you'll burn ahead of me, and that's a promise."

He was right. Sam knew only too well how right he was. All at once, the big, fair sailor dug into the unappetizing dinner before him. "I better eat quick," he said with his mouth full, "so I can get to the pharmacist's mate before I have to go back on duty."

"First sensible thing I've heard you say in a long time," Crosetti told him. With Commander Grady still there celebrating along with the sailors, Sam couldn't even think about punching his bunkmate in the nose . . . very much.

The pharmacist's mate behind the dispensary window was a wizened, cadaverous-looking fellow named Morton P. Lewis. On a day like today, even his face wore as much of a smile as it had room for. "Ah, Carsten," he said, nodding rather stiffly at

Sam. "Haven't seen you for a while, but I can't say I'm surprised to see you now." His Vermont accent swallowed the *r* in Sam's last name and turned *can't* into something that might have come from an Englishman's mouth.

"Heading up toward sunny weather," Carsten said resignedly. "You want to give me a couple of gallons of that zinc-oxide goop?"

"It's dispensed in two-ounce tubes, as you know perfectly well." Lewis' voice was prim, proper, precise.

"Oh, don't I just," Sam said. "Don't I just." He sighed. "Damned if I know why I bother with the stuff. I burn almost as bad with it as without it."

"Your answer, I would say, boils down to the word *almost*," the pharmacist's mate replied.

"Yeah." Carsten sighed again. "Well, let me have a tube now, would you? Sooner I start using it—" He broke off and stared at Morton P. Lewis. "*Boils down to* is right. You do that on purpose, Mort?"

"Do what?" said Lewis, a man whose sense of humor, if he'd ever had one, must have been amputated at an early age. His blank look convinced Carsten he hadn't done it on purpose. But, even if humorless, the pharmacist's mate wasn't stupid. "Oh. I see what you're asking about. Heh, heh."

"Listen, can I have the stuff, for God's sake?" Sam asked.

"You don't require a doctor's prescription for zinc-oxide ointment," Lewis said, which Carsten already knew from years at sea. "You don't require authorization from a superior officer, either." Carsten knew that, too. The pharmacist's mate finally came to the point: "You do require the completion of the required paperwork." He didn't notice he'd used the same word twice in one sentence, and Sam didn't point it out to him.

He did say, "Mort, if we get men wounded during an action, I hope you don't make them fill out all their forms before you give 'em what they need."

"Oh, no," Lewis said seriously. "Unnecessary delay in emergency situations is forbidden by regulation." He went back in among his medicaments before Carsten could find an answer for that.

When he returned, he was carrying a tinfoil tube and a sheaf of papers. In ordinary situations, delay seemed to be encouraged, not forbidden. Sam checked boxes and signed on lines.

What it all boiled down to was that he wouldn't use the zinc oxide for anything illegal or immoral. Since the stuff was too thick and resistant to be any fun if he wanted to jack off with it, he couldn't imagine anything illegal or immoral he *could* use it for.

Wading through the paperwork meant he had to hustle to make it up on deck without getting chewed out. That was the way life in the Navy worked: you hurried so you could take it easy a few minutes later. It had never made a whole lot of sense to him, but nobody'd asked his opinion. He wasn't holding his breath waiting for anyone to ask, either.

No sooner had that thought crossed his mind than Hiram Kidde came by, puffing on a fat cigar. He asked Sam's opinion: "How about Dom Pedro, eh?" But he didn't wait for an answer, giving his own instead: "Took the wall-eyed little son of a bitch long enough."

"Yeah," Carsten said; he agreed with that opinion. "But he's gone and done it. He sees the writing on the wall."

"He'd better," the chief gunner's mate said. "Train was almost out of the station before he decided to jump on board." He sneered, an expression that could turn a junior lieutenant's bones to water. "Doesn't cost him anything, either—just his name on four pieces of paper. Not like Brazil's gonna do any fighting."

"Maybe a little against Argentina," Sam said. "But yeah, not much. Jesus, though, closing that coast to England and opening it up to us . . . doesn't cost Dom Pedro much, like you say, but it does us a hell of a lot of good."

"Uh-huh." Kidde gave him almost the same leer Vic Crosetti had. "Does us a hell of a lot of good, but you're going to be fried crisp when we head up that way."

Wearily, Sam reached into his pocket and displayed the tube of zinc-oxide ointment. Hiram Kidde laughed so hard, he had to take the cigar out of his mouth. When he started to flick the long, gray ash onto the deck, Carsten said, "Whoever swabs that up ought to swab your shoes, too."

Kidde looked down at his feet. He could have seen himself in the perfectly polished oxfords. Three steps put him by the rail. The ash went into the Atlantic. "There. You happy now?" he asked.

"Sure," Sam answered. "Why not? Way I see things, world's looking pretty decent these days. Yeah, I'm going to burn for a while, but the *Dakota*'s home port is San Francisco. War ever ends, I figure we'll go back there for a spell."

"You burn in Frisco, too," Kidde pointed out, "and that ain't easy."

"I know, but I don't burn so bad there," Sam said. "I'll tell you one more thing, too: Brazil jumping into the war may make me burn, but it makes the limeys sweat. You come right down to it, that's a pretty fair bargain."

"Well, *mon vieux,* how is it with you?" Lucien Galtier asked his horse as they made their way up toward Rivière-du-Loup. A U.S. Ford didn't bother to honk for them to pull over, but zoomed around the wagon and shot up toward town at what had to be close to thirty miles an hour. "I wonder why he is in such a hurry," Galtier mused. "I wonder why anyone would be in such a hurry."

The horse did not answer, save for a slight snort that was likelier to be a response to the stink of the motorcar's exhaust than to Galtier's words. But the Ford kicked up hardly any dust from the fine paved road. The Americans had extended it for their own purposes, not for his, but he was taking advantage of it. Jedediah Quigley had told him he would. Jedediah Quigley had told him quite a few things. A good many more than he'd expected had turned out to be true.

His mind couldn't help doing a little of the arithmetic the good sisters had drilled into him with a ruler coming across his knuckles. If he had a motorcar capable of thirty miles an hour—oh, not today, not tomorrow, but maybe one of these days—he could get to town in . . . could it possibly be so few minutes?

"My old," he said to the horse, "I begin to see how it is that the Americans have put so many of your relations out to pasture. I mean no offense, of course."

A flick of the ears meant the horse had heard him. It dropped some horse balls on the fine paved road. Maybe that was its opinion of going out to pasture. Maybe that was just its opinion of the road. Behind him, some chickens made comments of their own. He never paid attention to what the chickens had to say. Their first journey into town was also their last. They did not have the chance to learn from experience.

Outside Rivière-du-Loup, the snouts of antiaircraft guns poked into the sky. The soldiers who manned them wore uniforms of American cut, but of blue-gray cloth rather than green-gray. Galtier cocked his head to one side to listen to them talking back and forth. Sure enough, they spoke French of the same sort as his own. *Soldiers of the Republic of Quebec,* he thought. Dr. O'Doull had said there were such men. Now he saw them in the flesh. They were indeed a marvel.

"What do you think?" he asked the horse. Whatever the horse thought, it revealed nothing. Unlike the chickens, the horse was no fool. It had come into town any number of times. It knew how much trouble you could find by letting someone know what was in your mind.

Lucien drove the wagon into the market square. Newsboys hawked papers whose headlines still trumpeted Brazil's entry into the war, though Galtier had heard about it several days before from Nicole, who had heard it from the Americans at the hospital. The newspapers also trumpeted Brazil's recognition of the Republic of Quebec. That was actually news.

He tried to outshout the newsboys and all the other farmers who'd come into the market square to sell goods from their farms. His chickens had a solid reputation. They went quickly. He made good money. Soon he was down to one last ignorant fowl. He waited for a housewife to carry it off by the feet.

But the chicken was not to go to a housewife and her tinker or clerk or carpenter of a husband and their horde of hungry children. Here came Bishop Pascal, plump enough to look as if he could eat up the whole bird at one sitting. Galtier hid a smile. The bishop was being a good republican—ostentatiously being a good republican—and shopping for himself again, instead of letting his housekeeper do the job. How she would scold if she found out how much a rude farmer had overcharged him! Lucien had no compunctions whatever. Bishop Pascal could afford it, and then some.

"Good day, good day, good day," he said now with a broad smile. "How does it go with you, my friend?"

"Not bad," Lucien said. "And yourself?"

"Everything is well. I give thanks to you for asking, and to *le bon Dieu* for making it so." Bishop Pascal crossed himself, then held his right forefinger in the air. "No. Not quite everything is perfectly well." He pointed that finger at Lucien Galtier as if it were a loaded gun. "And it is *your* fault." As best he could with his round smiling face, he glowered. He sounded very severe.

"*My* fault?" Lucien's voice was a startled squeak, like Georges' when his son was caught in a piece of tomfoolery. "What have I done?" What *had* he done to offend Bishop Pascal? Offending the bishop could be dangerous.

"What have you done? You do not even know?" Bishop Pascal sounded more severe yet. He wagged that forefinger in Lucien's face. "Do I understand correctly that I am not to officiate at the wedding of your lovely Nicole to Dr. O'Doull?"

"I am desolated, your Reverence, but it is so," Galtier replied, doing his best to imply that he was desolated almost to the point of hurling himself into the St. Lawrence. That was not so; he felt nothing but relief. "You must comprehend, this is not my fault, and it is not meant as an insult to you. Dr. O'Doull is the closest of friends with Father Fitzpatrick, the American chaplain at the hospital, and will hear of no one else's performing the ceremony."

Only the truth there. That it delighted Galtier had nothing to do with the price of chickens. He wanted as little to do with Bishop Pascal as he could; the man had got too cozy with the Americans too fast to suit a lot of people, even those who, like Lucien, had ended up getting closer to the Americans themselves than they'd ever expected.

"One can hardly go against the express wishes of the bridegroom, true. Still—" Bishop Pascal always looked for an angle, as his quick collaboration proved. "I must confess, I do not know Father Fitzpatrick as well as I should. I am certain his Latin must be impeccable, but has he also French?"

"Oh, yes." Galtier most carefully did not smile at the disappointment in the bishop's eyes. "I have spoken with him several times. He is not so fluent as Major Quigley or Dr. O'Doull, but he makes himself understood without trouble. He also understands when we speak to him. I have seen many an English-speaker who can talk but not understand. I have some of the same trouble myself, in fact, when I try to use English."

"Ah, well." Bishop Pascal sighed. "I see there is nothing more to be said in that matter, and I see also, to my great joy, that this choice has not come about because I am diminished in your eyes." Galtier shook his head, denying the possibility with all the more vigor because it was true. Bishop Pascal turned his forefinger and his attention in another direction. "Since this is so, perhaps you will do me the honor of selling me that lovely fowl."

Lucien not only did Bishop Pascal the honor, he did him out

of about forty cents for which the bishop, being a man of the cloth, had no urgent need. If Bishop Pascal proved unwise enough to mention to his housekeeper the price he'd paid to Galtier, he would indeed hear about it. He'd hear about it till he was sick of it. Odds were, he'd heard enough of similar follies often enough to try to keep quiet about this one.

"I thank you very much, your Reverence," said Galtier, who could think of several useful purposes to which he might put forty cents or so. He waved at the empty cages behind him. "And now, since that was the last of the birds I brought to town today, I think I shall—"

He did not get the chance to tell Bishop Pascal what he would do. Three newsboys ran into the market square, each from a different direction. They all carried papers with enormous headlines, a different edition from the ones Galtier had glanced at coming into Rivière-du-Loup. They were all shouting the same thing: "France asks for armistice! France asks Germany for armistice!" Over and over, the words echoed through the square.

"*Calisse.* Oh, *maudit calisse,*" Lucien Galtier said softly. He needed time to remember that the Germans who were the enemies of France were allied to the United States, the supporters of the Republic of Quebec and, much more to the point, the homeland of his soon to be son-in-law. He wished he had not cursed such news where Bishop Pascal could hear him.

The bishop waved to the newsboys, who raced to get to him. He bought a paper from the one who ran fastest. He blessed them all: some consolation, but probably not much. As they went off, one happy, two disappointed, he turned to Galtier. "I understand how you feel, my friend," he said, "and I, I feel this pain as well. It is the country from which our forefathers came, after all, and we remain proud to be French, as well we should. Is it not so?"

"Yes. It is so," Galtier said. To hear that his homeland had gone down to defeat at the hands of the *Boches* was very hard, even when the *Boches* were friendly to the United States.

But Bishop Pascal said, "The France that is beaten today is not the France that sent our ancestors to this land. The France that was beaten today is a France that has turned its back on the holy mother Catholic Church, a France that embraced the godless Revolution. This is a France of absinthe-drinkers and artists who paint filthy pictures no sensible man can understand or would want to understand, a France of women who care nothing for their reputations, only that they should have reputations. It is not ours. If it is beaten, God has meant for it to be beaten, that it may return to the right and proper path."

"It could be that you are right." Lucien spread his hands. "I am but an ignorant man, and easily confused. Right now I feel torn in two."

"You are a good man—that is what you are. Here, let us see what has happened." Bishop Pascal read rapidly through the newspaper, passing sentences to Galtier as he did so: "The Republic of France, unable any longer to withstand the weight of arms of the Empire of Germany, requests a cease-fire. . . . All English troops to leave France within seven days, or face combat from French forces. . . . The German High Seas Fleet and the U.S. Navy to have fueling and supply privileges at French ports, the Royal Navy to be denied them. . . . The new border between France and Germany to be fixed by treaty once the war ends everywhere. Thus the atheists and their mistresses are humbled and brought low."

No doubt there were some in France who met Bishop Pascal's description. But, since France was a nation of men and women like any other, Lucien was sure it also held a great many more folk who did not. And they too were humbled and brought low. A meticulous man, Galtier had trouble seeing the justice in that.

Had Germany been conquered instead of conquering, what would have happened to the ordinary Germans? Much the same, he suspected. Did that make it right? Was he God, to know the answers to such questions?

Bishop Pascal said, "How much longer can the war on this side of the Atlantic go on now? How much longer before all of Quebec joins our Republic of Quebec? I assure you, this cannot now long be delayed."

"I think you are likely to be right." Lucien recalled the men in blue-gray uniforms at the antiaircraft guns outside of town.

"The killing shall cease," Bishop Pascal said. "Peace shall be restored, and, God willing, we shall never fight such a great and mad war again."

"I hope we do not," Galtier said. "I shall pray that you are right." But he spent a lot of time talking to his horse on the way home from Rivière-du-Loup. When he got there, he still felt torn in two.

Colonel Irving Morrell stood up in the cupola of his barrel as it pounded through the rough and hilly country just north of Nolensville, Tennessee. He did that more and more often these days, and more and more of the commanders in the Barrel Brigade were imitating him. Some of them had stopped bullets. The rest were doing a better job of fighting their machines.

He grinned. He had a toy the other fellows didn't, or most of them didn't, anyhow. When First Army infantry got light machine guns to give them extra firepower as they advanced, he'd commandeered one and had a welder mount the tripod in front of the hatch through which he emerged. When the Rebels shot at him now, he shot back.

They were shooting. They'd been shooting, hard, ever since the drive on Murfreesboro opened two days before. But First Army had already come better than ten miles, and the advance wasn't slowing down. If anything, the barrels were doing better today than they had the day before.

A bullet ricocheted off the front of the barrel. Just one round—that meant a rifleman. A moment later, another one snapped past Morrell's head. His lips skinned back from his teeth in a ferocious grin. He'd spotted the muzzle flash from the middle of a clump of bushes. He swung his own—his very own—light machine gun toward the bushes and ripped off a burst. No one shot at the barrel from that direction again.

"We've got them!" he said. Once, playing chess, he'd seen ten moves ahead: a knight's tour that threatened several of his opponent's pieces on the way to forking the fellow's king and rook. It had been an epiphany of sorts, a glimpse into a higher world. He was at best a medium-good player; he'd never known such a moment before or since . . . till now.

He'd had a taste of that feeling when First Army crossed the Cumberland. This was different, though. This was better. There, the Confederates had been fooled. Here, they were doing everything they could do, as the soldier across the chessboard from him had done everything he could do—and they were losing anyhow.

They did not have enough men. They did not have enough aeroplanes. No sooner had that thought crossed his mind than a U.S. fighting scout zoomed past the waddling barrel. Morrell waved, though the pilot was gone by then. He almost wished it had been a Confederate aeroplane; he longed to try out the light machine gun as an antiaircraft weapon and give some Reb a nasty surprise.

The Confederate States did not have enough barrels, either, nor fully understand what to do with the ones they had. Every so often, a few of their rhomboids would come forward to challenge the U.S. machines. Individually, theirs were about as good as the one Morrell commanded. But what he and Ned Sherrard and General Custer had grasped and the Confederates had not was that, with barrels, the whole was greater than the sum of its parts. A mass of them all striking together could do things the same number could not do if committed piecemeal.

A shell whine in the air sent Morrell ducking back inside his steel turtle's shell. Even as he ducked, a shell burst close to the barrel. Fragments hissed past him and clattered off its plating. None bit his soft, tender, vulnerable flesh, though.

More shells burst close by. A battery of C.S. three-inchers was doing its best to knock out his barrel and any others close by. Except at very short range, field guns hit barrels only by luck, but the hail of splinters from the barrage forced Morrell to stay inside for a while.

It was like dying and going to hell, except a little hotter and a little stickier. July in Tennessee was not the ideal weather in which to fight in a barrel. The ideal weather, for men if not for engines, would have been January in Labrador. The barrel generated plenty of heat on its own. When its shell trapped still more . . . Morrell was coming to understand how a rib roast felt in the oven.

And the rest of the crew suffered worse than he did. When he stood up, he got a breeze in his face: a hot, muggy breeze, but a breeze even so. They got only the whispers of air that sneaked in through louvered vision slits and the mountings of the cannon and machine guns. The engineers, down below Morrell in the bowels of the barrel, got no air at all, only stinking fumes from the twin truck engines that kept the traveling fortress traveling.

Morrell stood up again. Shells were still falling, but not so close. There was Nolensville, only a few hundred yards ahead. Infantrymen and machine-gun crews were firing from the houses and from barricades in the street, as they did in every little town. As Morrell watched, a shell from the cannon of another U.S. barrel sent chunks of a barricade flying in all directions. A moment later, that barrel started to burn. Soldiers leaped from it. Morrell hoped they got out all right. He sprayed a few rounds in front of them to make the defenders keep their heads down.

Infantrymen in green-gray and barrels converged on Nolensville. U.S. aeroplanes strafed the Confederates in the town from just above chimney height. Morrell did not order his barrel into Nolensville, where it might easily come to grief moving along any of the narrow, winding streets. He poured machine-gun fire and cannon shells onto the Rebels from just outside, where the barrel could move as freely as . . . a barrel could move.

Some of the defenders died in Nolensville. Some, seeing they could not hold the town, broke and ran. Morrell's barrel rumbled past Nolensville. He took potshots at fleeing men in butternut, some white, some colored. Some of them, probably, had been brave for a long time. Under endless hammering, though, even the hardest broke in time.

Another Confederate came out from behind a large, dun-colored rock. Morrell swung the light machine gun toward him. He was on the point of opening fire when he saw the man was holding a flag of truce.

Bullets from one of the barrel's hull machine guns stitched the ground near the Confederate officer's feet. He stood still and let the flag be seen. The machine gun stopped firing. All over the field, firing slowed to a spatter and stopped.

Morrell ducked down into the cupola. *Halt,* he signaled urgently. Then, like a jack-in-the-box, he popped up again. Even before the barrel had fully stopped, he scrambled down off it and ran toward the Confederate with the white flag. "Sir, I am Colonel Irving Morrell, U.S. Army. How may I be of service to you?"

Courteously, the Rebel, an older man, returned the salute. The three stars on each side of his stand collar showed his rank matched Morrell's. "Harley Landis," he said. He said nothing after that for close to half a minute; Morrell saw tears shine in his eyes. Then, gathering himself, he resumed: "Colonel, I—I am ordered to seek from the U.S. Army the terms you will require for a cease-fire, our own forces having proved unable to offer effectual resistance any longer."

Joy blazed in Morrell. To let his opposite number see it would have been an insult. Sticking to business would not. "How long a cease-fire do you request, sir, and on how broad a front?"

"A cease-fire of indefinite duration, along all the front now being defended by the Army of Kentucky," Landis answered. Again, he seemed to have trouble finding words. At last, he did: "I hope you will forgive me, sir, but I find this duty particularly difficult, as I was born and reared outside Louisville."

"You have my sympathies, for whatever they may be worth to you," Morrell said formally. "You must understand, of course, that I lack the authority to grant a cease-fire of any such scope. I will pass you back to First Army headquarters, which will be in touch with our War Department. I can undertake to say that troops under my command will observe the cease-fire for so long as they are not fired upon, and so long as they do not discover C.S. troops improving their positions or reinforcing—or, of course, unless I am ordered to resume combat."

"That is acceptable," Colonel Landis said.

"A question, if I may," Morrell said, and the Confederate officer nodded. Morrell asked, "Are the Confederate States requesting a cease-fire along the whole front, from Virginia to Sonora?"

"As I understand it, no, not at the present time," Harley Landis replied.

Morrell frowned. "I hope you see that the United States may find it difficult to cease fighting along one part of the front while continuing in another?"

"Way I learned it, fighting in the War of Secession went on a while longer out here than it did back East, on account of the United States kept trying to hold on to Kentucky," Landis said.

That was true. Whether it made a binding precedent was another question. Morrell shrugged. "Again, that's not for me to say, sir. Let's head back toward Nashville till I can flag down a motorcar and put you in it. The sooner the fighting does stop, the better for both our countries."

"Yes, sir. That's a fact." As Landis stalked past the barrel from which Morrell had emerged, he glowered in its direction. "You Yankees hadn't built these damn things in carload lots, we'd have whipped you again."

"I don't know," Morrell said. "We'd stopped you before we began using them. Breaking your lines would have been a lot harder without them, though; I will say that." Landis didn't answer. He kept on glaring. But he kept on walking, too, north and west toward Nashville and First Army headquarters. The white flag in his hand fluttered in the breeze.

Every soldier in green-gray who saw the Confederate officer inside U.S. lines with a flag of truce stared and stared, then burst into cheers. Off in the distance, gunfire still rattled here and there. It fell silent, one pocket after another. The Rebels had to be sending more men forward under flag of truce to let U.S. forces know they were seeking a cease-fire.

Before Morrell spotted a motorcar, he found something even better: a mobile field-telephone station, the men still laying down wire after them as their wagon tried to keep up with the advance. "Can you put me through to Nashville?" he demanded of them. They nodded, eyes wide with wonder as they too gaped at Harley Landis and the flag he bore. Morrell said, "Then do it."

They did. In a few minutes, Morrell and General Custer's adjutant were shouting back and forth at each other through the hisses and pops and scratching noises that made field telephones such a trial to use. "They want what, Colonel?" Major Abner Dowling bawled.

"A cease-fire on this front," Morrell shouted back.

"On this front? This front only?" Dowling asked.

"That's what Colonel Landis says," Morrell answered.

"The general commanding won't like that," Dowling predicted. "Neither will the War Department, and neither will the president."

"I think you're right, Major," Morrell said. "Shall I turn him back?" He watched Landis' face. At those words, the Rebel officer looked like a man who'd taken a bayonet in the guts.

At the same time, Dowling was shouting, "Good God, no! Send him on! If they give so much without being pushed, we'll get more when we squeeze, I wager. And come yourself, too. Only fitting you should be in at the death."

"Thank you, sir," Morrell said, and hung up. He turned to Colonel Harley Landis. "They will be waiting for you, sir. If I had to make a prediction, though, I would say they will not find acceptable a proposal for a cease-fire on one front only."

"Sir, I have my orders, as you have yours," Landis replied, to which Morrell could only nod.

A Ford came picking its way up the battered road toward the front. Morrell gave a peremptory wave. The courier who had been in the automobile soon found himself on shank's mare, while the Ford turned around and carried Landis and Morrell back through the wreckage of war toward Nashville.

Boston was going out of its mind. The trolleyman kept ringing his bell, but inside the trolley Sylvia Enos could hardly hear it through the din of automobile and truck horns, wagon bells, church bells, steam whistles, and shouting, screaming people. The trolley had a devil of a time going forward, for people were literally dancing in the streets.

"Rebs ask for cease-fire!" newsboys shouted at every other streetcorner. They were mobbed. "Rebs ask for peace!" newsboys shouted at the corners where the Rebs weren't shouting for a cease-fire. They were mobbed, too. Sylvia watched a fistfight break out as two men struggled over one paper.

Mostly, though, joy reigned supreme. Only the oldest grand-dads and grandmas remembered the last time the United States had beaten a foreign foe. Sylvia saw more men and women kissing and hugging in public during that slow streetcar ride to the shoe factory than she had in her life before.

A man got on the trolley drunk as a lord before eight o'clock in the morning. He kissed two women who seemed glad to kiss him back, then tried to kiss Sylvia, too. "No," she said angrily, and pushed him away. He might have fallen over, but the trolley was too crowded to let him. "The war's not over yet," Sylvia told him and whoever else might listen. As far as she was concerned, the newsboys shouting *Peace!* were out of their minds.

As far as the drunk was concerned, Sylvia was out of her mind. His mouth fell open, giving her another blast of gin fumes. "Of course"—it came out *coursh*—"the war's over," he said. "Rebs're quitting, ain't they?"

She'd already read the *Globe*. She hadn't just listened to the boys yelling their heads off. "No," she answered. "They haven't surrendered, and there's still fighting in places. And the Cana-dians haven't quit fighting anywhere, and neither has England."

And George was out there somewhere in the Atlantic, and no indeed, the Royal Navy had not quit fighting, and nobody'd said anything about the Confederate Navy quitting, either.

"So what?" the drunk said. "We'll lick 'em. We'll lick all them bastards." He paused and leered. "Now how about a kiss?"

Sylvia wondered if she would have to use a knee in a most unladylike fashion. Her expression, though, must have been fierce enough to get the message across even to a lush. He turned away, muttering things she was probably lucky not to be able to understand.

She also wondered if she was the only person anywhere in the United States *not* convinced all the shooting was over as of this moment. By all appearances, she was the only person on the streetcar who thought that way. People avoided her and patted the drunk on the back. One of the women he'd kissed now kissed him in turn. She didn't look like a slattern. She looked like a schoolteacher.

At last, after fighting its way through endless traffic jams, the trolley got to Sylvia's stop. Two more men, one drunk, one sober, tried to kiss her before she got to the shoe factory. She dodged the drunk and stepped on the sober man's foot, hard. He hopped and cursed and cursed and hopped. She hurried to work.

She clocked in almost twenty minutes late. When she went in from the front hall where the time clock stood to the great cave of a room where she worked, she expected the foreman to descend on her with fire in his eye. Despite being only an inch or so taller than she was, despite a snowy mustache, Gustav Krafft was not a man to trifle with.

But he only nodded and said a guttural "Good morning" as she went to her sewing machine. A good third of the workers hadn't yet made it to the factory. Sylvia let out a silent sigh of relief.

Women and more little old men drifted in as the morning wore along. Some of them, like the drunk on the trolley, were visibly the worse for wear. Sylvia would not have wanted to come to work that way, not when she was working at a machine that could bite if she was careless. She sewed pieces of upper together and tossed them into a box. When it got full, a feeble-minded young man carried it away to the workers who would join uppers to soles.

Halfway through the morning, one of the men who looked as

if he'd been born at his sewing machine let out a horrible yell and held up a hand that poured blood. Gustav Krafft dashed to his aid at a speed that belied the foreman's years. "*Ach,* Max, *Dummkopf!*" he shouted, and then a spate of German Sylvia could not understand at all.

After wrapping his own handkerchief around the wound, Krafft led Max out of the chamber toward first aid. The worker was still yelling, and emitting hot-sounding gutturals of his own between yells.

Sylvia turned to the woman at the sewing machine next to hers and said, "I wouldn't have thought he'd be one who let himself get hurt."

"Neither would I. Max has been here since this place opened up, I hear," replied the other woman, whose name was Emma Kilgore. She was plump, a few years older than Sylvia, and had curly hair two shades darker than a carrot. "It's the war news—everybody's going crazy now that things are over."

"But they *aren't*," Sylvia protested. "There's still fighting, and plenty of it."

"My husband's down in that Tennessee place," Emma said. "As long as they aren't shooting at Jack, the war's over as far as I'm concerned."

"George is in the Navy, out in the Atlantic," Sylvia said. "It's not over for him, not by a long shot, and that means it's not over for me, either."

"That's a tough one, dearie." Emma's sympathy was real but perfunctory. As she'd said, her own worries were gone. Few people, Sylvia had seen, really cared about the troubles of others unless they shared them.

Gustav Krafft came back into the cavernous room. Max's blood stained the front and side of his shirt. He looked around, saw how many machines weren't working, and scowled fiercely. "Even if the war is over, the work is not," he said. "The devil loves idle hands. I do not."

"If you loved milk, it'd curdle," Emma Kilgore muttered. Sylvia let out a strangled snort of laughter, but her head was bent over her machine, which was snarling before Krafft's eyes could pick out from whom the sound had come. The foreman's gaze swept on. Sylvia laughed again, this time silently. She felt as if she'd been naughty in class and got away with it.

In a couple of hours, Max came back, his hand wrapped in

bandages that had turned red here and there. "He's crazy," Emma Kilgore whispered.

"Maybe he needs the money," Sylvia whispered back.

Emma shook her head, which made those copper curls fly about. "I hear tell he owns an apartment house, and I know for a fact he's got one son who's a cop and another one who's a cabinetmaker. He ain't broke."

As if to offer his own explanation, Max said, "It is not the first time the machine gets its teeth in me. It is probably not the last, either." He sat down and went back to work. Now that he was paying attention to what he was doing, he was more deft with one good hand and one bandaged than Sylvia could dream of being with both of hers. But an absentminded moment had given him a nasty wound.

Krafft came over, thumped Max on his bent back, and said something to him in German. He answered in the same language. The foreman thumped him again, careful not to disturb him while he was guiding leather under the needle. Then Krafft spoke in English: "Max says he is like the United States. He has been hurt many times, but he wins at the last."

Several people clapped their hands: on this day of all days, patriotic sentiment won applause. Sylvia kept right on working, with doggedness similar in kind if not in degree to that which Max showed. Emma muttered, "Christ, he didn't cut his hand off." Her patriotism, plainly, was limited to getting her husband back in one piece. Sylvia was ready to settle for having George home safe, too.

She clocked out as slowly as she could after the closing whistle blew, to make up a couple of the minutes she'd lost in the morning because the trolley hadn't got her to work on time. It was late coming to pick her up, too. The celebration on the streets of Boston hadn't slowed down since she'd last seen it. If anything, crowds were thicker, louder, and better lubricated than they had been earlier in the day.

When at last she got to George, Jr.'s, school, she found it festooned with red, white, and blue bunting. George, Jr., came pelting over to greet her when she stuck her head into his room. "We won, Ma!" he shouted. "We licked the dirty Rebels, and that means Pa can come home!" He jumped up and down in excitement.

"I wish it was that simple," she answered. "Your father's not home yet, and I don't know when he's going to be. For that matter, we're not home yet, and I don't know when we're going to be, either. We still have to get your sister, and everything's a little crazy today."

"We won!" George, Jr., repeated. He wasn't old enough to know any better. But plenty of people who were old enough to know better were saying the same thing.

Sylvia led George, Jr., up to Mrs. Dooley's to get his little sister more than half an hour late. She resigned herself to another lecture from the woman about tardiness. But Mrs. Dooley opened the door with a smile on her face. She smelled of what Sylvia recognized after a moment as cooking sherry. "Hello, Mrs. Enos," she said. "Isn't it a grand and glorious time to be alive?"

"Yes, I suppose it is," Sylvia said. "I am sorry I'm late. Everyone seems to be in the streets today."

"Nobody will blame anybody for anything today," Mrs. Dooley said. She turned. "Mary Jane, your mother is here." By the noises from within, Mary Jane wasn't the only child whose mother was late today.

When she came around Mrs. Dooley's billowing black skirt, she chirped, "We won the war, Mama!"

"Well, we're certainly winning," Sylvia said. That let her state her own opinion without sounding too much as if she was disagreeing with what seemed to be the whole world but for her. "Now we, the three of us, need to go home." There was an opinion on which she would put up with no disagreement at all.

They were late getting home, too, of course, which meant they had a late supper. The children were too excited to want to go to bed when they should. Sylvia had known they would be. At last, she got them settled. Then she had to settle herself, too. The trouble she had going to sleep made her wonder whether, down deep, she was exulting over victory, too.

Lieutenant Brearley stowed the code book in the locked drawer and turned the key. "Here's what it means, sir," he said, handing the decoded wireless message to Roger Kimball. "It's—important."

"Give it here," the commander of the *Bonefish* said. "I'll decide how important it is." He wished the exec hadn't said anything to draw the crew's attention to the message. Sailors were curious enough without encouragement.

He unfolded the paper, read it, and then read it again to make sure his eyes weren't playing tricks on him. It still said the same thing the second time: SEEKING CEASE-FIRE ON LAND. END OF-FENSIVE ACTIVITY. IF ATTACKED, DEFEND SELF. ACKNOWLEDGE RECEIPT.

"You're sure you decoded it right?" he demanded of Brearley.

"Yes, sir," the executive officer said. "Here are the groups they sent." He made as if to open the drawer again and get out the code book.

"Never mind," Kimball said wearily. "I believe you. I believe it. We were getting hammered the last time the *Bonefish* went into port. It's just that . . . aah, God damn it to hell." His left hand closed into a fist and struck his left thigh, hard enough to hurt. Then, slowly and deliberately, he tore the message into tiny, in-decipherable shreds and threw them away.

"What do we do, sir?" Brearley asked.

"We acknowledge receipt, as ordered," Kimball said. "Then we keep right on with the patrol. We weren't ordered to hold in place. I don't see a surrender order or anything like it, do you?"

"Well, no, sir, not when you put it like that," Brearley ad-mitted. He looked even unhappier than he had already. "I wish they'd have told us more, so we'd have a better idea of what we're supposed to do."

Kimball reveled in commanding a submersible not least be-cause the Navy Department had very few chances to tell him what to do. "The more code groups they send, the better the odds the damnyankees'll figure out what they mean," he answered. "Now, you get clicking on the wireless telegraph and acknowl-edge that we got that order." He lowered his voice but raised the intensity in it: "And for God's sake keep your mouth shut after-wards. I don't want the crew to hear one word about what kind of shape the country's in. You got that, Tom?"

"Yes, sir," Brearley answered, and then, "Aye aye, sir," to show he not only understood but would willingly obey.

Gloomily, Kendall climbed back up to the conning tower and peered out over the Atlantic. It was a hell of a big place. As far as he could tell, the *Bonefish* might have been alone in the middle of it. If he spotted no plumes on the horizon, he didn't have to worry about following the order from the Navy Department.

But he *wanted* to spot a smoke plume, there on the edge of visibility. He *wanted* to send more Yankee ships to the bottom, the same way a hunting dog *wanted* to tree a possum or a coon. It was what he'd been trained to do, and it was what he enjoyed doing. And, he knew without false modesty, he was damn good at it.

As he raised the binoculars to his eyes, he knew the secret wouldn't keep forever. It probably wouldn't even keep very long. He wished he could blame Brearley for calling him down from the conning tower to read the decoded message, but he couldn't. It was too important to allow delay. The crew would already be wondering what it was all about, though. One way or another, they'd learn, too. Somehow or other, they always did.

And what would they do then? Would they cause trouble, saying peace was at hand and they didn't want to fight any more? Or would they want to keep fighting no matter what happened on land? *They* hadn't lost the war, regardless of the failures of the fools in butternut.

"Miserable bastards," Kimball muttered, meaning the soldiers, not the crew of the *Bonefish*. But then a long, grim sigh burst from his lungs, followed by more muttering: "Shit, it doesn't hardly matter anyhow, not with Brazil in the war on the wrong side."

With the Empire of Brazil in the war on the wrong side, all the shipping routes from Argentina that had kept England fed for so long didn't work any more. And with France out of the fight across the Atlantic, the German High Seas Fleet was liable to pick off any freighters the U.S. Navy missed.

In that case, why go on fighting? he wondered. The only answer he could come up with was that the C.S. Navy, though battered, did remain unbeaten. As long as he could strike a blow against the enemies of his country, he would do it.

He scanned the horizon, turning slowly through 360 degrees. Nothing. And then, as he'd learned to do in the past few weeks, he scanned the rest of the heavens, too. Any aeroplane he spotted through his field glasses would belong to the United States.

Experience paid off, as experience has a way of doing. The aeroplane was too far away for him to hear its engine. Without the binoculars, he might not have seen it at all, or might have taken it for a distant soaring albatross. He started to scramble down the hatch and order a quick dive, then made himself watch and wait. If the aeroplane came closer, he would dive before it could drop a bomb on the *Bonefish*. If it didn't, if it turned away . . .

Slowly, he smiled. If it turned away, it would be turning away for a reason, or he hoped it would. Sure enough, a minute later the moving speck swung off toward the north. Looking more satisfied than he had any business being, given the state of the war and the state of his orders, Kimball paced the steel roof of the conning tower. The aeroplane had spotted the *Bonefish*. He was sure of that; it wouldn't have changed course so abruptly if it hadn't. And Kimball didn't think the pilot thought anyone on the *Bonefish* had noticed him. No reason he should. Nothing aboard the submersible had changed while he looked it over.

Kimball kept watching the whole round of the horizon. He would have been a fool to do otherwise, and he had not stayed alive for almost three years in a submarine by being a fool. But he would also have been a fool not to pay particularly close attention to the north. When not one but three smoke plumes came into view, he nodded to himself. He waited till he was sure the ships were destroyers, then waited a little more. Let them think he was a little on the slow side.

Then he did go back down into the fetid steel tube that was the *Bonefish*, the real *Bonefish*, dogging the hatch after him as he did. "Take her down to periscope depth," he called to the crew. "We've got some damnyankees coming to pay us a call."

They were coming hard, too, in the hopes of sending the *Bonefish* to the bottom. Kimball had loitered on the surface a good deal longer than he would have otherwise, to make them think he'd be easy pickings. He slid toward them at five knots, easing the periscope above the surface every minute or two to keep an eye on them.

Ben Coulter spoke quietly: "Beg your pardon, sir, but we ain't headin' toward those sons of bitches so as we can surrender, are we?"

"Hell, no," Kimball answered, hiding how appalled he was at the speed with which rumor spread. "You ever hear of submerging before you give up?"

"No, sir," the veteran petty officer answered. "I never heard of any such thing, and I'm damn glad of it." He went back to his post.

"Sir, our orders—" Tom Brearley began.

Kimball silenced him with a glare. "I am obeying our orders,

Mr. Brearley," he snapped. "Now you see that you obey mine." Brearley bit his lip and nodded.

One of the trio of destroyers went straight for the spot where they'd seen the *Bonefish*. One went to the southeast of that spot, one to the southwest. Coulter let out a quiet chuckle when Kimball relayed that news. "They reckon we're runnin' away, don't they, sir?"

"That's how it looks to me," Kimball said. He let out a sigh that might have been annoyance. "All these years of fighting somebody, and they don't know him at all. I bet they don't know who's screwing their wives, either." In the dim lamplight, his sailors grinned at him.

Just for a moment, he wondered if anybody was screwing Anne Colleton right now. If anybody was, he'd never find out about it, not unless she wanted him to. There in the middle of the stinking steel tube, he nodded respectfully. Say what you would, that was a woman with balls.

Splash! The sound was very clear inside the pressure hull: a depth charge flying into the Atlantic, followed by several more at short intervals. They were still splashing into the sea when the first one exploded. As best Kimball could judge, it had been set to burst deep.

He turned to his executive officer. "I'd say we are being attacked," he remarked. Brearley nodded; a depth charge was not the prelude to an invitation to tea. Grinning, Kimball said, "And now, by Jesus, I aim to defend myself."

"Yes, sir," the exec said. Tom wasn't stupid; after a while, he was liable to wonder whether his skipper had dawdled on the surface on purpose, to provoke the damnyankees into attacking the *Bonefish*. But that would be later. For now, they had a fight on their hands.

Kimball crept closer to the nearest destroyer. Watching ash cans flying off her stern, he grinned again. "Yeah, keep it up," he muttered. "Good luck with your damn hydrophones while you're throwing those babies around." He ordered the two forward tubes flooded; an exploding depth charge covered the noise of inrushing water. Then it was just a matter of sliding in to within eight hundred yards and shooting the fish.

The destroyer had barely started an evasive maneuver when the first torpedo hit her amidships. A moment later, the second struck the stern. With two fish in her, the destroyer shuddered to a stop and began to sink. The other two U.S. warships turned in the direction of their stricken comrade, and in the direction from which the *Bonefish* had launched the torpedoes.

"Dive deep and evade, sir?" Brearley asked.

"Hell, no," Kimball answered. "That's what they'll be looking for me to do. I want an approach at periscope depth—but only at four knots, because I want to save the batteries as much as I can. I don't aim to come up for air till after sunset, when the ships and the aeroplanes can't spy me."

He got a good shot at one of the two Yankee destroyers, but her skipper turned tight into the path of the fish, and it sped past her bow. After that, it was the surface ships' turn. Kimball still refused to dive deep, but staying at periscope depth, where his boat might be spotted from the surface—and from overhead, if that damned aeroplane was buzzing around again—was too foolhardy even for him to contemplate. By the time he'd sneaked far enough away from the depth charges that sent endlessly repeated thunder through the boat to take another look with the periscope, he was too far away to fire off any more fish.

"Well, we hurt 'em," he said in no small satisfaction. "If they think we're giving up and going home, they can damn well think again."

That had a salutary effect on the sailors. Rumors of a surrender would be a lot harder to believe now. Kimball noticed Tom Brearley watching him, there in the orange-lit, stinking gloom. He grinned at his exec: a tiger's smile, or a hammerhead's. Brearley stayed sober. He was drawing his own conclusions, all right. *Too damn bad,* Kimball thought. *I don't aim to quit till I have to—and maybe not then.*

Captain Jonathan Moss had flown over Lake Ontario in the early days of the war, when the U.S. Army was slowly—so slowly—battering its way through one fortified belt on the Niagara Peninsula after another. Now here he was again, flying down from the northwest instead of up from the south. As it had then, Archie from Canadian guns filled the sky around his aeroplane with puffs of black smoke. The Wright-built Albatros copy bucked in the turbulence of near misses.

Now, though, the antiaircraft fire came from inside Toronto, from the city the United States had confidently thought they would overrun in a few short weeks. Moss' grimace had only a little to do with the wind tearing at his face. "Nothing in this damn campaign has gone the way it should," he muttered.

He'd said the same thing out loud—sometimes drunkenly loud—with his flightmates and in the officers' club. Seeing the slate-blue water of the lake below him brought it to mind again. Nothing in Lake Ontario had gone as it should have, either. Even at the start of the war, a man could probably have walked from shore to shore on the mines laid there. Along with them, the Canucks' submersibles had meant U.S. Great Lakes battleships— they would have been coast-defense ships on the ocean—hadn't done a quarter of what they were supposed to.

Down below him, thunder of a different sort roared, along with huge tongues of fire and clouds of gray smoke. The Canadian Navy still had a couple of Great Lakes battleships in working order behind their mine fields; the ships, these days, were earning their keep by pouring shells from their big guns onto the U.S. infantrymen pushing their way into Toronto.

"Let's see how you like this," Moss said, diving on the behemoth below. Percy Stone, Pete Bradley, and Charley Sprague, who had replaced unlucky Hans Oppenheim on the flight, followed him down.

He wished he were carrying a bomb fixed to his landing gear, so he could hope to do some real damage to the armored warship below, but consoled himself by remembering that real bombers hadn't been able to sink her, either. He'd do what he could, that was all.

Men scurried on the deck of the Great Lakes battleship. It carried its own Archie: guns very much like those used on land. They started hammering away at him. So did machine guns, the long spurts of flame from their muzzles very different from the intermittent flashes from the antiaircraft guns proper.

His thumb came down on the firing button on top of the stick. The twin machine guns atop the engine chattered into life. He raked the deck from bow to stern, buzzing along no higher than the warship's stack. He was past the ship before he could see how much damage he'd done—but not before a couple of machine-gun bullets pierced the fabric covering his fighting scout.

He clawed for altitude; if any enemy aeroplanes had spotted his dive, they'd be stooping on him like so many falcons. As he did, he also swung back toward the Great Lakes battleship for another run. His flightmates formed in line behind him. They'd come safe through the heavy antiaircraft fire, too, then.

Sailors were dragging wounded or dead men to shelter. "Give up, you stupid bastards," Moss growled. "You and the limeys are the only ones left fighting, and you can't last long."

Strictly speaking, that wasn't true. Out in the Pacific, the Japanese had given as good as they'd got. But that part of the war was a sideshow for the United States. Down below Jonathan Moss, Toronto lay at its bleeding heart.

As he started his second pass at the Canadian warship, he thought of Laura Secord, back on her farm near Arthur. Had her ancestor not imitated Paul Revere, Toronto might have belonged to the USA for the past hundred years and then some. He shook his head. If he got to worry about what might have been, he was liable not to worry enough about what was going on, and to lose the chance to worry about what would go on in the future.

A hail of bullets and shells greeted him when he went into that second dive. He fired back. The sailors on deck were a stationary target, and he wasn't. There were a lot of them, too, and only one of him. They didn't do him any harm. He hoped he hurt them.

The Great Lakes battleship almost shot him down without meaning to. The big guns roared out another broadside, the shells aimed at foot soldiers far away. But blast sent Moss' flying scout flipping through the air. He had only moments to straighten out before he ended up in Lake Ontario. Shouting curses he hardly even noticed, he fought for control and won it just in time.

Anxiously, he looked back for Stone and Bradley and Sprague, wondering if the warship's main armament had accidentally done what the antiaircraft guns could not do on purpose. To his relief, he spied all three of them. He also saw that he was beginning to run low on fuel, and was not in the least sorry to discover it. When he waved back toward the aerodrome by Orangeville, his flightmates followed his lead with what seemed like relief of their own.

They were up above ten thousand feet by the time they crossed the front line just outside of Toronto. That didn't stop the Canucks and limeys from blazing away at them, nor did it keep some overeager idiots on the American side of the line from sending some Archie their way. Fortunately, the U.S. gunners were no better at what they did than their counterparts on the other side.

Moss bumped his fighting scout to a stop on the rutted grass landing strip outside the little Ontario town. As usual, the groundcrew men clucked at the fine assortment of punctures he'd picked up. "The idea, sir, is to fly an aeroplane, not a patchwork quilt," Herm said.

"As long as they don't puncture me or the motor, I'm not going to worry about it," Moss said.

"Well, well." Charley Sprague came up to him as he was descending from the cockpit to the ground. "That's not the sort of instruction you can get in flying school, is it, sir?" Sprague was tall and lean and good-looking, with expressive eyebrows and a Kaiser Bill mustache waxed to a pointed perfection not even the slipstream could ruffle. He had the indefinable manner of coming from a moneyed family.

"Not more than once," Moss answered, which made Sprague break into a wide grin. More seriously, Moss went on, "After that, the War Department sends your family a wire they'd sooner not have."

"After what?" Percy Stone asked, his goggles pushed up on top of his head. "After you strafe a Great Lakes battleship? I bet they do. The only thing I can think of that was less fun was when I got shot."

"Actually, I was thinking of after you train to strafe a Great Lakes battleship," Moss said.

Stone considered that, then nodded. "You've got something there. I knew about as many people who got killed learning as I did fliers who went down against the enemy. Nobody ever talks about it, but it's true."

Charley Sprague nodded. "You're right about that, sir," he said: even in brief acquaintance, Moss had seen that he punctiliously observed the rules of military courtesy. "I saw half a dozen fellows die while I was learning the game. Some of them were better fliers than I was, but they thought they were better than they were, too, if you know what I mean. And some fell out of the sky for no reason anyone could see." He spread his hands. " 'Time and chance happeneth to them all,' is what the Bible says about that."

Last of the flight, Pete Bradley came up in time to hear Sprague's last couple of sentences. "Ain't it the truth?" he said, a sentence unscriptural but most sincere. "When your number's up, it's up, that's all." He wiped his forehead with the back of his hand. "I thought all our numbers were up when we made the second run at that damn boat."

"Worst of it is, they can go right on mounting more machine guns on it, too," Moss said. "Pretty soon strafing it *will* be suicide, nothing else."

"Have to bomb at high altitude, then," Lieutenant Sprague said. "We'll need better bombsights for that; we couldn't hit the broad side of a barn with the ones we have now. And the bombers will need more guns, to hold off the foe's fighting scouts. Regular flying fortresses, that's what they'll have to be."

Moss looked at him in admiration. "You've got all the angles figured, don't you, Charley? Sounds like you're ready for the next war right now."

"Poppycock!" Sprague said. "What wants doing is plain enough—plain as the nose on my face, which is saying something." He touched the member in question, which, though long and thin, was not outstandingly so. "How to get from where we are to where we need to be: ay, there's the rub."

"That's Shakespeare," Percy Stone said, and Sprague nodded. Stone slapped him on the back. He stiffened slightly, as at an undue familiarity. Either not noticing that or ignoring it, Stone went on, "Good to have you in the flight, by God. First the Bible, now this—you give us a touch of class we sure don't get from our flight leader here." He jerked a thumb at Jonathan Moss.

Lieutenant Sprague turned toward Moss, and turned pink at the same time. "Sir, I don't want to offend or—"

"Don't worry about it, Charley," Moss said easily. "I was good enough to bring Percy's carcass back home when he got himself a puncture a couple of years ago, and now I'm good enough for him to insult. That's the way the world goes, I guess."

He made sure Stone understood he was kidding. Both Sprague and Bradley looked worried; they weren't sure he meant it for a joke till Stone laughed and said, "Well, it's not like I asked you to do it. I was too busy bleeding for that."

"I know." Thinking about what the observer's cockpit had looked like after he and the groundcrew got Stone out of it made Moss' stomach do a slow loop. He fought the memory with another gibe: "You gave me so much trouble, I figured you'd make yourself a nuisance to the limeys and the Canucks, too."

"Indeed." Charley Sprague trotted out another tag from

Shakespeare: " 'But when the blast of war blows in our ears, / Then imitate the action of the tiger.' "

"I can't do that, Charley," Stone said. "I'm not limber enough to lick my own balls."

All four men from the flight laughed like loons, more because they were young and alive when they could easily have died than because Percy Stone had said anything so very funny. "Come on," Jonathan Moss said. "Let's go tell Major Cherney what we did on our summer holiday."

The squadron commander listened to their report, then said, "I'm glad you're all back in one piece, but don't go sticking your heads in the lion's mouth like that again, and that's an order."

"But, sir—" Moss began.

Cherney held up a hand. "No buts, Captain. Even if that ship had no antiaircraft guns at all, you couldn't sink her or hurt her big guns. Don't waste yourself on targets like that, not with the war so close to won. Do what you *can* do. Fight the enemy's aeroplanes and balloons. Shoot up his men on the ground. If you take on a Great Lakes battleship, you're fighting out of your weight."

"But—" Moss said again. Then he remembered Charley Sprague's words: *some of them were better fliers than I was, but they thought they were better than they were, too.* And they'd ended up dead, and they hadn't helped the war effort a bit. Slowly, reluctantly, Moss nodded. "Yes, sir."

"I've been thinking," George Enos said between gulps of air as he stood beside the one-pounder at the stern of the USS *Ericsson* after yet another dash to battle stations, this one a drill.

Beside him, Carl Sturtevant was panting more than a little. "Probably won't do you any lasting harm," he said, and then, presently, "Yeah? What were you thinking about?"

"That son of a bitch who sank the *Cushing* yesterday and almost put a fish into us," Enos answered.

"Yeah, well, I can see how that'd be on your mind," the veteran petty officer allowed. "So what about it?"

"Whoever the skipper of that boat is, he fights mean," George answered, to which Sturtevant could only nod. George went on, "He comes at us, and he comes hard, and he doesn't like to dive deep for hell."

"That's all true," Sturtevant agreed. "Like I said, though, so what?"

"He fights like the skipper who almost sank us before we sank the *Bonefish*," Enos persisted. "Whoever he is, whether he's a limey or a Reb, I don't think we got him when we got that boat."

Sturtevant screwed up his face as he thought that over. "That other bastard dove deep and tried to hide after he took a shot at us, didn't he?" He smacked his lips a couple of times, tasting an idea instead of soup. "Maybe you've got something there." He glanced over toward Lieutenant Crowder, who was talking with another officer. Lowering his voice, Sturtevant said, "You ain't gonna make him your bosom buddy if you tell him, though."

"But if I don't tell him, and we go on doing what we've been doing, and he goes on doing what he's been doing, we're all liable to end up dead," Enos said.

Sturtevant didn't answer. His expression made plain what he was thinking: that Lieutenant Crowder wouldn't listen even if he did get told. Crowder was convinced he'd sunk the submersible that had come so close to putting the *Ericsson* on the bottom for good. Telling him otherwise would make him unhappy, which was liable to make George's life miserable.

Not telling him, though, was liable to make George's life short. He went over and positioned himself so Lieutenant Crowder would have to notice him sooner or later. It was later, not sooner, but George had been sure it would be. Eventually, the lieutenant said, "You wanted something, Enos?"

George saluted. "Yes, sir," he said, and proceeded to set out for Crowder the same chain of reasoning as he'd given Carl Sturtevant. As he spoke, he watched Crowder's face. It was not encouraging. He sighed silently. He hadn't expected it to be.

When he was through, the officer shook his head. "I don't believe it for a minute, sailor. That the Rebs or the limeys have put a new boat into this area—that is possible. In fact, it's more than possible. It's certain, as recent events have shown. That it would be the boat we battled before—no. We sent that one to the bottom, and that's where he richly deserves to be."

"But, sir, the way this fellow operates—" Having begun the effort, George thought he ought to see it through.

Crowder did not give him the chance. "Return to your battle station at once, Enos, or I'll put you on report."

"Yes, sir." Stiff and precise as a steam-powered piece of machinery, George did an about-face and strode back to the one-pounder. Once there, he could look over at Lieutenant Crowder, who'd gone back to talking to the other officer. Enos let out another silent sigh. He really should have known better.

Carl Sturtevant caught his eye. *Told you so,* the petty officer mouthed. George shaped the beginning of an obscene gesture with a hand his body shielded from Lieutenant Crowder. Sturtevant laughed at him. In spite of that laughter, or maybe because of it, Sturtevant was a pretty good fellow. A lot of petty officers were as stuffy as real officers about ordinary seamen giving them a hard time.

After a couple of minutes to let Crowder get involved in his conversation again, Sturtevant said, "Hell, it probably won't matter for beans, anyway. Rebs are on their last legs—they're doing their damnedest to get out of the fight. Pretty soon, it'll just be us and the limeys, and they won't last long, either."

"For all we know, it's a limey boat we're talking about. One we sank belonged to the Confederates, yeah, but that's not the one with the nasty skipper no matter what Lieutenant Crowder thinks."

"Mm, that's true," Sturtevant admitted, "but you've got to figure the odds are whoever was patrolling this stretch probably kept right on doing it. It'd be harder to work if things went back and forth between two different countries."

George thought about that. "All right, you've got something there," he said at last. "Does make sense. If we sank one Rebel boat, that means there's probably another one prowling around—which means it's even more likely this is the same skipper who almost got us before."

"That sounds logical," Sturtevant said. He nodded over toward Lieutenant Crowder. "You feel like taking another shot at convincing *him*?"

"No thanks," Enos answered. "He already knows everything there is to know—and if you don't believe me, just ask him."

Without apparently moving a muscle, Sturtevant made his face into a mask of contempt. "I don't need to ask him. I already know what he knows." By the tiniest twitch of an eyebrow, he got across how little he thought that was.

"Well, then, shouldn't we—?" George began.

"I don't reckon we've got to worry about it, on account of it ain't gonna matter worth a hill of beans anyway." Sturtevant waved out across the Atlantic. "Look. The Rebs won't bother keeping a boat around these parts that much longer anyway, because the shipping route they were guarding went to hell and gone when Dom Pedro finally figured out which side his bread was buttered on."

As if to underscore his words, a flotilla of U.S. cruisers steamed past, heading south. They looked enormous alongside the destroyers that cruised to either side of them, protecting them from submarines as sheepdogs protected their flocks from wolves. Battleships were yet another size up; to George, who was used to going to sea aboard fishing boats, they resembled nothing so much as floating cities.

He said, "Haven't seen so many of our freighters passing through these parts lately, especially northbound."

"Probably won't, either," Sturtevant answered. "They'll come down from the USA to supply our warships, yeah, but for a lot of things they won't have to head back to the States any more. They can load up in one of the Brazilian ports—hell of a lot quicker trip that way."

"Son of a bitch, you're right." Enos shook his head, disgusted with himself. "I should have thought of that."

"Hey, nobody can think of everything." Sturtevant glanced over at Lieutenant Crowder again. Crowder, still chattering away with the other officer, tapped his forefinger against his own chest, so he was talking about his favorite subject: himself. The veteran petty officer rolled his eyes. "Jesus Christ, some people can't think of anything."

Enos snorted. "I'm not going to argue with you about that." He made himself cheer up, almost as if a superior officer had given him an order. "And odds are you're right about the other, too. Once the fellows with the high foreheads back in Philadelphia figure it out, too, they'll probably call us back to port."

Carl Sturtevant laughed in his face. "You fisherman, you! It'd be cheaper to do things that way—sure it would. But do you think the Navy gives a fart in a hurricane about cheap? In a pig's ass they do, especially during a war. We don't go home till the whole Quadruple Entente's waving white flags at us—and maybe we don't go home then, either. Maybe we go around the Horn and teach the Japs they picked the wrong side." He eyed Enos. "You ever been on the other side of the Equator before?"

"You know damn well I haven't," Enos said. "This is further south than I ever figured I'd come before the war started."

"Just a damn polliwog." Sturtevant shook his head and clicked his tongue between his teeth. "Well, old Father Neptune will settle *your* hash."

Enos had heard about those rituals from sailing men who'd gone through them, some in the Navy, some as merchant seamen. They'd shave his head or put him in a dress or maybe both at once, and he and the rest of the polliwogs on the *Ericsson* would have to do whatever Father Neptune told them. Something in the way Sturtevant's eyes gleamed made George ask, "Have you ever been Father Neptune?"

"Who, me? What could have given you that idea?" The petty officer might have been the soul of innocence. Then again, he might not have.

The all-clear sounded then. Lieutenant Crowder kept right on talking with the other officer. As Enos drifted away from his battle station, he quietly asked, "Is *he* a polliwog, by any chance?"

"I don't know," Sturtevant said. "I really don't know. I may have to go and ask a few questions, because that would be worth finding out. An officer polliwog is just another damn polliwog, as far as Father Neptune's concerned." He slapped George on the back. "That could be a lot of fun, couldn't it?"

"Couldn't it, though?" George said dreamily. "It's not that he's dumb—more that he thinks he's so smart."

Chipping paint was easier to take after that, somehow; instead of thinking about himself going through the antics Father Neptune would require of him, he thought about Lieutenant Crowder going through them. When someone else was the victim, the joke got a lot funnier.

The petty officer supervising the never-ending job of stopping rust stared at Enos when he strolled by. "Damn me to hell if you haven't pulled your weight today," he said. "Well done."

When George looked back to see what had impressed the petty officer, he discovered he'd chipped twice as much paint as he usually would have done in so much time. Thinking about Lieutenant Crowder making an ass of himself in front of the whole crew had been so entrancing, he hadn't kept his work pace to the usual just enough to get by. He shook his head. Now they'd expect him to work this hard all the time—and it was Lieutenant Crowder's fault.

Everything was Lieutenant Crowder's fault. "If I get killed, I'll never forgive him," George muttered.

Lieutenant Straubing paced among the big White trucks as colored roustabouts hauled supplies from the Covington wharves and loaded them into the green-gray machines for the drive south. Straubing spoke to the men, some white, some black, who would be in the cabs of those trucks: "What you've got to remember, boys, is that the war's not over. Yes, there's a cease-fire in Tennessee, and it's still holding pretty well. But the shooting could start up again any day, and there's still fighting in Virginia and out in the West. Besides, God only knows there are Rebel diehards loose in Kentucky. Don't do anything stupid like dropping your guard this late in the war. It'd be a shame to get yourself killed now."

Cincinnatus—Cincinnatus Driver, as he was learning to think of himself these days—turned to the driver nearest him and said, "The lieutenant don't give two whoops in hell if we get ourselves killed. If the cargo don't get through to where it's supposed to go, that's a different story. That ticks him off plenty."

Herk chuckled. "You got that one right." He was as white as Lieutenant Straubing, and Cincinnatus, despite spending a lot of time on the road with him, even getting shot up by some of those diehards with him, still had no idea what his last name was, or even if he owned one. He'd always just been Herk. Now he went on, "The lieutenant treats the cargo like he was paying for it out of his own pocket."

"Yeah," Cincinnatus said. He watched the roustabouts load more trucks. He'd done that work himself, before he'd convinced the U.S. forces to let him drive instead—and to pay him more money for doing it. Despite his own experience at their job, he muttered, "I wish they'd move faster, damn it."

Herk didn't make any cracks about lazy niggers. Lieutenant Straubing would have given him seventeen different kinds of hell if he had. Men of one color giving men of another a hard time about it interfered with getting matériel down to the front, so he refused to tolerate it. What Herk did say was, "You've been itchy to get on the road lately, haven't you? Kid givin' you a hard time at home?"

"Nah, it ain't that so much," Cincinnatus answered. "When I'm movin', though, nobody's botherin' me, you know what I'm sayin'? There's just me and the truck and the road, that's all."

"Yeah, sure—unless somebody's layin' in the bushes with a goddamn machine gun like happened before," Herk said.

"Happen inside Covington easy as it can outside," Cincinnatus said. "Had a man shot dead on my own front stoop, remember. Could have been me shot dead out there, easy as that other fella."

When he was on the road, he didn't have to worry about whether every stranger he passed on the sidewalk would carry tales about him to Luther Bliss . . . or to Apicius—no, Apicius *Wood*—and his Red friends . . . or to Joe Conroy and however many other Confederate diehards still operated in Covington. When he was on the road, he was free. Oh, he had to obey Lieutenant Straubing's orders, but his spirit was free. That counted for more than he'd ever imagined.

At last, the cargo bay in his truck was full. Whistling under his breath, he cranked the White's engine to loud, flatulent life. When it was going, he jumped into the cab and fed it more gas. Other trucks rumbled awake, too. With Lieutenant Straubing in the lead, they headed south.

More of the road down to Tennessee was paved every time Cincinnatus drove it. He suspected that wasn't true only of the road that went through Covington. The United States would need to move supplies down every highway they could. When the war ended, Kentucky would have a pretty fine network of paved roads, or at least the north-south strands of such a network.

A man in the trucking business—a man like Cincinnatus Driver, say—might do well for himself. There were some rich Negroes in the USA: not many, but a few. That put the USA a few up on the CSA. "A chance," Cincinnatus muttered. No one sitting beside him in the cab could have heard the words, but that didn't matter. He knew what he was saying. "All I want is a chance. I ever get it, I'll make the most of it."

He wasn't going to hold his breath hoping he would get it. Laws against blacks weren't so tough as they were in the CSA, though that varied from state to state. What didn't vary was that most whites in the USA would have been just as well pleased if they could have readmitted Kentucky without its Negroes.

He rolled past a truck by the side of the road, the driver, a black man, out there with a jack and a pump and a patch, repairing the puncture. Cincinnatus hoped it was only one of those things that happened now and again, and that the diehards hadn't gone and strewn the road with nails or broken glass or specially made four-pronged inner-tube biters. That would make a lot of trucks late, and *that* would make Lieutenant Straubing unhappy. Very little else would, but that was guaranteed to do the trick.

Parts of the country were very much as they had been before the war began: prosperous farmlands raising wheat and corn and tobacco and horses. More, though, looked as if a mad devil had lost his temper and spent twenty years kicking it to pieces. That wasn't even so far wrong, except that war had done the job faster than any devil could have managed.

Near Covington, almost three years had passed since U.S. forces overran the countryside. Grass had grown over trenches; rain had softened their outlines; some of the rubble and wrecked buildings had been cleared away; some had even been rebuilt. The farther south Cincinnatus went, the fresher the scars of war got. The Confederate States had fought as hard as they could to keep Kentucky one of their number—the tormented landscape told of their effort. But it spoke even more loudly of their failure.

Cincinnatus' luck held: he got through the day without a puncture. After a stop for fuel for the truck and a bowl of pork and beans from an Army kettle at midday, he rolled on steadily until, toward evening, he crossed from Kentucky into Tennessee. He started passing bands of soldiers heading toward the front. They got off onto the soft shoulder for the truck convoy and smiled and waved as the big, square, clumsy machines passed them. They even smiled and waved at Cincinnatus. They had the world by the tail, and they knew it.

He also steered the truck past columns of men coming away from the front. A few of them, a very few, showed the same high spirits as the soldiers who were replacing them. Most simply trudged along toward the north, putting one foot in front of the other, their faces and no doubt their minds far away. They'd seen so much hell, they didn't yet realize they'd escaped it—or perhaps they'd brought it with them.

They'd converted the White from acetylene lamps to electric ones not too long before; Cincinnatus enjoyed being able to throw light on the dimming road ahead at the turn of a knob, without having to stop and get out. He'd liked it even better the first time he'd done it in the rain.

At last, about nine o'clock, they pulled into the supply depot. "We expected you an hour ago," complained an officer with a quartermaster's badge: crossed sword and key over a wheel on which perched an eagle. Cincinnatus had never known a quartermaster with a good word to say to or about the men who fetched him the supplies he then grudgingly disbursed.

"Sorry, sir," Lieutenant Straubing said. "We made the best time we could." He had to give a soft answer: the other man outranked him.

"Likely story," the quartermaster sniffed. "Well, you're here now, so we'll unload you." He made it sound as if he were doing the truck convoy an enormous favor.

"That's good, sir," Straubing said equably. "I can certainly see you've been ready for us this past hour."

In the cab of his truck, Cincinnatus chuckled. Nobody was waiting to unload the trucks. Plenty of people should have been. Straubing knew just how to place the dart to get the most damage with it. "Lieutenant . . ." the other officer began, doing his best to make Straubing wish he'd never been born. But the truth was too obvious for him to bluster his way past it. He seemed to deflate like a punctured observation balloon that hadn't caught fire. Then he started shouting for soldiers to get off their lazy backsides and come unload the trucks.

Lieutenant Straubing, having got what he wanted, turned into the soul of helpfulness, offering all sorts of suggestions so the soldiers could do the job quicker and more efficiently. He seemed to be everywhere at once. When he passed Cincinnatus' truck, he tipped him a wink. Cincinnatus grinned and winked back.

Straubing used the quartermaster's embarrassment to get him to order his men to run up tents in which the drivers from the truck convoy could spend the night. More and more trucks kept rattling into the depot, as those that had had punctures or breakdowns on the road down from Covington caught up with the rest.

Straubing also arranged for bedrolls and hot meals for the men in his charge. Spooning up greasy stew full of meat that might have come from an elderly cow or a fairly tender mule, Herk said, "The lieutenant, he looks out for his people, no two ways about it."

"He does that," Cincinnatus agreed, talking with his mouth

full. He'd seen as much before, when Lieutenant Straubing placed under arrest soldier-drivers who tried to refuse to work alongside Negroes from Covington. He didn't mention that to Herk, because he wasn't sure the white driver would take it as supporting his point of view. "I ain't worked for many bosses as good as he is like that. Don't know if I ever worked for any, now as I think about it."

Tom Kennedy had come pretty close. Like Lieutenant Straubing, though not to the same degree, he'd been more interested in the work he could get out of Cincinnatus than in what color he was. For a white citizen of the Confederate States, he'd been as good a boss as a colored resident—not citizen—of the CSA could hope for. If he hadn't been, Cincinnatus would have turned him over to the Yankee soldiers, that night they came looking for him.

His life probably would have been simpler if he had. Too late to worry about that, though. Too late to worry about Tom Kennedy, too, except to wonder who had put a bullet through his head. Shaking his own head, Cincinnatus went back to get more stew and a tin cup full of coffee.

"Come on, boys—eat up and get some sleep," Straubing called, like a father telling a houseful of children what to do. "We're heading back to Covington before it gets light; they'll need us again soon as we can be there. I told you before, the war's not done till the Rebs roll over and play dead along the whole line."

The men in the convoy obeyed as children would obey their father, too. Cincinnatus gulped down his coffee—he was tired enough, he knew it wouldn't keep him awake long—and ducked into one of the tents. He took off his shoes, wrapped himself in a blanket as much to hold bugs at bay as for warmth, and drifted toward sleep.

Outside the tent, the officer from the depot spoke: "Lieutenant, I will say you have yourself a pretty fair batch of men there."

"I've spent a lot of time getting them to where I want them, sir," Lieutenant Straubing answered. "I must say, I'm not altogether displeased with them now myself. By whatever means necessary, they get the job done. They took a while to learn that from me, but now they've got it down solid. They get the job done, and that's what counts."

XVII

In Augusta, Georgia, Scipio didn't turn around every few seconds, as if afraid his own shadow were about to rise up and stab
him in the back. It wasn't that a price didn't remain on his head.
It did. It probably would, as long as he lived: certainly as long as
Anne Colleton lived. However unenthusiastically, he'd played
too big a role in the Congaree Socialist Republic for that to
change.

But, with the Confederate States tottering on the brink of
losing the war against the USA—actually, the war *was* lost, but
the CSA hadn't yet been able to persuade the USA to stop advancing on the fronts where fighting went on—earlier victories
over the Socialist Republics were forgotten. Whites on the
streets in Augusta went around with stunned, dazed expressions
on their faces. They'd never lost a war before. They'd never
imagined they *could* lose a war. The Confederacy had gone from
one triumph to another. Now the whites here were learning what
the United States had learned half a century before: what defeat
tasted like. Next to that, chasing Reds was of small import.

The other side of the coin was that Scipio had got to Georgia.
Whatever he'd done in South Carolina, he might as well have
done in a foreign country. Confederate states often seemed
proud of paying no attention to what went on in their neighbors'
backyards. Georgia had reward posters up for its own Red Negro
rebel fugitives, but none for those from South Carolina. Here,
Scipio was just one more anonymous black man looking for work.

He was looking harder than he'd expected, too. Factories
weren't hiring the way they had been a year before. "We're already letting people go," a clerk told Scipio. "What's the point of
bringing more onto the lines when the war orders are gonna dry
up and blow away any minute now?"

"I understands that, suh," Scipio said, "but I gots to eat, too. What is I s'posed to do?"

"Go pick cotton," the white clerk answered. "Reckon that's what you were up to before the war started. Won't hurt you to get on back. When the Army shrinks, the soldiers'll need their own jobs back again."

White men will need their old jobs back again, Scipio thought. *And the Negroes who were doing those jobs? Well, the hell with them. They might have been good enough to help out for a little while, but now they're going to have to learn their place again.*

He'd got rebuffs from every factory he tried. For a while, he'd wondered if he would have to work in the fields. The money he'd earned from odd jobs as he made his way across South Carolina was almost gone. His life at Marshlands had convinced him of one thing: he did not want to be a field hand. But he did not want to starve, either.

And then he passed a little restaurant on Telfair Street with a sign in the window: WAITER WANTED. He started to go in, then shook his head. Reluctantly, he spent a couple of quarters on a shirt and a pair of pants that, if long past their salad days, were not ragged and falling to pieces. Then he went back to his flophouse in the Terry, the Negro district in the southeastern part of town, and bathed in a tin tub that plainly hadn't been used as often as it should have. Only after his clothes and he were as fresh as he could make them did he head back toward the restaurant.

Inside, a colored fellow was setting cheap silverware on a table. "What you want?" he asked in neutral tones as he slowly put down the last couple of pieces.

"I seen the sign in the window," Scipio answered. "I's lookin' for work. I works hard, I does." He wondered if the proprietor had already hired the other man, in which case he'd parted with money he couldn't afford to lose.

But the other Negro just shrugged and asked, "You wait tables befo'?"

"I's done that." Scipio nodded emphatically. He pointed to the place setting the fellow had just finished laying out. "De soup spoon belong on the udder side o' de teaspoon."

Smiling now, the fellow reversed them. "You *has* waited tables." He raised his voice: "Hey, Mistuh Ogelthorpe! I think we got you a waiter here."

A white man in his late fifties came out of the back room. He walked with the aid of a stick. Scipio wondered if he'd been wounded in this war or the Second Mexican War. More likely the latter, by his age—or, of course, he might just have been in a train wreck or some other misfortune. He looked Scipio over with gray eyes that were far from foolish. "What's your name, boy?" he asked.

"I's called Xerxes, suh," Scipio replied. He'd been called a lot of different things lately. He was glad he could keep them straight and remember who he was supposed to be at any given moment.

Ogelthorpe turned back to the other waiter. "How come you reckon he's a waiter, Fabius?"

"On account of he knows the difference 'tween a soup spoon and a teaspoon, and where each of 'em goes on the table," the other Negro—Fabius—said.

"That a fact?" Ogelthorpe said, and Fabius nodded. The white man who owned the restaurant turned to Scipio and asked, "Where'd you learn the business, Xerxes?"

"Here an' dere, suh," Scipio answered. "I been doin' factory work since de war start, mostly, but de factories, dey's shuttin' down."

"Here and there?" Ogelthorpe rubbed his chin. "You tell me you got anything like a passbook, I'm liable to fall over dead from the surprise."

"No, suh," Scipio said. "Times is rough. Lots o' niggers ain't got none dese days, on account of we's moved around so much."

"Or for other reasons." No, Ogelthorpe wasn't stupid, not even close. A frown twisted his narrow mouth. "Wish you didn't talk like you been pickin' cotton all your born days."

Had Scipio wanted to, he could have talked a great deal more elegantly than Ogelthorpe. He'd used that ability to speak like a polished white man to help escape from the swamps of the Congaree. But, if he didn't speak like a polished white man, speaking like a field hand was all he could do. He'd never before missed his lack of a middle way. Now he did, intently.

"I's powerful sorry, suh," he said. "I tries to do better."

"You read and write and cipher?" Ogelthorpe looked as if anything but a *no* there would have surprised him, too.

But Scipio read the names and prices of the soups and sandwiches and stews and meat dishes on the wall. He found a pencil and a scrap of paper on the counter and wrote his name and Fabius' and Ogelthorpe's in his small, precise script. Then he handed Ogelthorpe the paper and said, "You write any numbers you wants, an' I kin cipher they out fo' you."

He'd wondered if his demonstration would make Ogelthorpe not bother, but the white man scrawled a column of figures—watching, Scipio saw they were the prices of items he served—and thrust back the sheet and the pencil. "Go ahead—add 'em up."

Scipio did, careful not to make any mistakes. "They comes to fo' dollars an' seventeen cents all told," he said when he was done.

Ogelthorpe's expression said that, while they did indeed come to $4.17, he rather wished they didn't. Fabius, on the other hand, laughed out loud. "You got anything else you want to give him a hard time about, boss?"

"Don't reckon so," Ogelthorpe admitted. With a sigh, he turned back to Scipio. "Pay's ten dollars a week, an' tips, an' lunch an' supper every day you're here. You play as good a game as you talk, I'll bump you up a slug or two in a month. What do you say?"

"I says, yes, suh. I says, thank you, suh," Scipio answered. He wouldn't get rich on that kind of money, but he wouldn't starve, especially not when he could feed himself here. And he'd be able to get out of the grim Terry flophouse and into a better room or even a flat.

Ogelthorpe said, "You can tell me I'm crazy if you want, but I got the idea you ain't got a hell of a lot of jack right now. You're clean enough, I'll say that, but I want you to get yourself black trousers an' a white shirt like Fabius is wearin', and I want you to do it fast as you're able. You don't do it fast enough to suit me, back on the street you go."

"I takes care of it," Scipio promised. He thought Fabius was dressed up too fancy for the kind of food the place dished out, but realized his own tastes were on the snobbish side. *One more thing I can blame on Miss Anne,* he thought. Maybe, now that he was outside of South Carolina, she wouldn't be able to track him down. He hoped to Jesus she couldn't.

Outside, a clock started chiming noon. A moment later, two steam whistles blew. "Here comes the lunch crowd," Ogelthorpe said. "All right, Xerxes, looks like you get baptism by total immersion. Me, I got to get my ass back to the stove." He disappeared into the rear of the restaurant.

Fabius just had time to hand Scipio a Gray Eagle scratch pad before the place filled up. Then Scipio was working like a madman for the next hour and a half, taking orders, hustling them back to Ogelthorpe, carrying plates of food to the customers, taking money and making change, and trading dirty china and silverware for clean with the dishwasher, an ancient black man who hadn't bothered to come out and see whether he'd be hired.

Some of the customers were white, some colored. By their clothes, they all worked at the nearby hash cannery or the ironworks or one of the several factories that made bricks from the fine clay found in abundance around Augusta. Whites and Negroes might come in together, sometimes laughing and joking with one another, but the whites always sat at the tables on one side of the restaurant, the blacks at those on the other.

Scipio wondered if Fabius would wait on the whites and leave the Negroes for him. The whites would undoubtedly have more money to spend. Scipio presumed that would translate into better tips. But the two waiters split the crowd evenly, and Scipio needed less than half an hour to find out his idea wasn't necessarily so. The idea of tipping a colored waiter had never crossed a lot of white men's minds. When they did tip, they left more than their Negro counterparts, but the blacks were more likely to leave something, if often not much. Taken all together, things evened out.

By half past one, after the last lunch shift ended, the place was quiet again, as it had been before noon. Panting like a hound, Fabius said, "Reckon you see why Mistuh Jim hired hisself a new waiter. We got more business'n two can handle, let alone one like I was doin'."

"You one busy nigger 'fore today, sure enough," Scipio said.

"You done pulled your weight," Fabius said. "Never had to hustle you, never had to tell you what to do. You said you know about waitin' on tables, you wasn't lyin'."

"No, I weren't lyin'," Scipio agreed. "We git our ownselves somethin' to eat now? Plumb hard settin' it in front o' other folk wif so much empty inside o' me."

"I hear what you say." Fabius nodded. "I done et 'fore the rush started, but you go on back there now. Mistuh Ogelthorpe don't feed you good, you take a fryin' pan and whack him upside the head."

Ogelthorpe also nodded when Scipio did head back to the cooking area. "You know what you were doin', sure as hell," he said.

"Yes, suh," Scipio said. Compared to the fancy banquets Anne Colleton had put on, this was crude, rough, fast work, but the principles didn't change.

"Chicken soup in the pot," Ogelthorpe said. "You want a ham sandwich to go along with it?"

"Thank you, suh. That be mighty fine." Scipio had carried a lot of ham sandwiches out to hungry workers. He knew they were thick with meat and spears of garlicky pickle and richly daubed with a mustard whose odor tickled his nose. He'd just ladled out a bowl of soup when Ogelthorpe handed him a sandwich of his own.

The first bite told him why people crowded into the restaurant. Miss Anne would have turned up her nose at such a rough delicacy, but she wasn't here. Scipio was. He took another big bite. With his mouth full, he said, "Suh, I's gwine like this place jus' fine."

"Here you are, ma'am," the cabbie said to Flora Hamburger as he pulled to a stop at the corner of Eighth and Pine. "Pennsylvania Hospital."

"Thank you," she answered, and gave him half a dollar, which included a twenty-cent tip. That was enough to make him leap out of the elderly Duryea and hold the door open for her with a show of subservience that made her most uncomfortable. Socialism, to her, meant equality among all workers, no matter what they did.

But she had no time to instruct him, not now. She hurried past the statue of William Penn toward the front entrance to the hospital, whose cornerstone, she saw, bore an inscription dating from the reign of George II.

A soldier walked past her, smiling and nodding as he did so. By his stick and the rolling gait he had in spite of it, Flora knew he was using an artificial leg. Because of what he'd gone through, she smiled back at him. Without that, she would have ignored him, as she was in the habit of ignoring all the young men who smiled and nodded at her.

She went up the stairs to the second floor. One wing had private rooms; the best doctors gave the patients in them the best care they could. That was an advantage David Hamburger would not have had without his sister's being in Congress. Using it went against every egalitarian instinct she had, but family instincts were older and deeper.

She almost ran into a nurse coming out of her brother's room. The woman in the starched gray and white uniform with the red cross embroidered on the breast gave back a pace. "I'm sorry, Congresswoman," she said. "I didn't realize you were coming in."

"It's all right, Nancy." Flora knew a lot of the nurses who helped take care of David. She came to the Pennsylvania Hospital as often as she could. She felt bad about not coming more often than she did, but sitting in Congress and handling the endless work that went along with sitting in Congress was a trap with huge jaws full of sharp teeth.

David lay quietly in the bed, his face almost as pale as the white linen of sheets and pillowcases—being at war with the CSA and the British Empire had made cotton scarce and hard to come by. Under the covers, the outline of his body seemed unnaturally small—and so it was, with one leg gone above the knee. But the rest of him seemed shrunken, too, as if losing the leg had made him lose some of his spirit. And if it had, would that be so surprising?

He managed a smile. "Hello, Flora," he said. He sounded very tired, even now. Flora was glad he sounded any way at all. Loss of blood and an infection had almost killed him. If the infection had been a little worse . . . How would Flora ever have been able to show her face to her family? She had enough trouble showing her face to her family now. They didn't condemn her. She condemned herself, which was far harder to bear.

"How are you?" she asked, feeling foolish and useless.

"Not too bad," he answered, as he did whenever she asked—which meant she couldn't take the words seriously. He'd lost a lot of flesh; parchmentlike skin stretched tight over the bones of his face. His dark eyes were enormous. Then he did seem to pick up a little energy, a little life, as he asked, "Are the Rebs really and truly trying to surrender?"

Back in New York City, he'd never called them Rebs; he'd picked that up in the trenches. Flora didn't like it. It made him sound as if he endorsed the war even after what it had done to him. She said, "Pieces of the cease-fire are in place, but Roosevelt won't give them all of it. He's still driving in Virginia and the West. I wish he weren't, but he has the bit between his teeth."

"Bully," David said, as if he were Roosevelt. "After everything it's cost us, we'd better get the most we can out of this war. If we stop too soon, why did we go and fight it in the first place?"

"Because we were mad," Flora replied, staring at her brother with a new kind of horror: he *did* sound like the president, where he'd been growing up a Socialist like everyone else in the family. She asked, "How can you say that, after what happened to you?" Only after she'd spoken the words did she notice she'd slipped from English into Yiddish.

David answered in the same language: "How can I say anything else? Do you want me to lose my leg and the country to have nothing to show for it?"

"I never wanted you to lose your leg at all," Flora said. "I never wanted anyone to lose his leg, or his arm, or his eye, or anything. Even if we win, we have nothing to show for it. We never should have fought at all."

"Nu?" David said. Even raising an eyebrow seemed to cost him no small physical effort. "Maybe you're right, Flora. Maybe we shouldn't have gotten into it. But once we did decide to fight, what can we do but fight as hard as we can to win?"

That dilemma had dogged the Socialist Party from the beginning. Cutting the war short once a treasure of money and an even greater treasure of lives had been spent had proved not just impossible but, worse, unpopular, as the majorities Roosevelt and the Democrats brought in showed.

As David had learned new ways of talking and thinking in the trenches, so Flora had on the floor of Congress. Being without a good answer, she changed the subject: "Have they said anything more about fitting you with an artificial leg? As I was coming in, I saw a man walking very well with one." She was stretching a point, but not too far.

"They'll have to wait a while longer," he said. "The stump's not healed well enough yet, and the amputation was pretty high." His mouth twisted. "Maybe I'll be a one-crutch cripple instead of a two-crutch cripple." Flora's expression must have betrayed her, for her brother looked contrite. "It's better than being dead, believe me."

Reluctantly, Flora nodded. Her sister's husband, Yossel Reisen, had been killed in Virginia bare days after he married Sophie; he had a son he'd never seen and never would see now.

A doctor came in. "Congresswoman Hamburger," he said, polite but not obsequious: he'd dealt with a lot of important people. "If you'll excuse me—" He advanced on David.

"Maybe you'd better go," David said to Flora. "The stump looks better than it used to, but it's still not pretty."

She was glad of the excuse to leave, and ashamed of herself for being glad. Here was her baby brother—or so she remembered him, at any rate—dreadfully mutilated, and here he was, too, wanting the fighting to go on so others could suffer a like fate or worse. He obviously meant every word he said, but he might as well have started talking Persian for all the sense he made to her.

She went downstairs. A soldier with no legs was moving along in a wheelchair. He was whistling a vaudeville tune of some sort, and seemed happy enough with his world. Flora didn't understand it. Flora couldn't understand it. And, had she asked him, she was sure he would have told her the war had to go on, too. She didn't understand that, either, but she was sure of it.

She went back to her office, but accomplished little that truly resembled work. She'd expected nothing different; seeing David always left her the worse for wear. After a while, realizing she'd read a letter three times without having the faintest idea what it was about, she put it away, got up, and told her secretary, "Bertha, I'm going over to my apartment."

"All right, Miss Hamburger," Bertha answered. "I hope your brother is better. I pray for him every night." She crossed herself.

"Thank you," Flora said. "He's doing as well as he can, I think." She'd said that so many times. It was even true. But *as well as he can* was a long way from *well*. And still he thought the United States should keep on with the war. Flora shook her head till the silk flowers on her hat rustled and rattled. She could live another hundred years without having it make sense to her.

She was standing in front of the Congressional office building waiting to flag a taxi when someone in a Ford called to her: "Where are you going, Flora?"

It was Hosea Blackford. "To my apartment," she answered.

The congressman from Dakota pushed open the passenger-side door. "I'm heading that way myself," he said. "Hop in, if you've a mind to." She did hop in, with a word of thanks. She had very little to say on the short trip back to the apartment building. Blackford glanced over at her. "You've been to see your brother, or I miss my guess. I hope he hasn't taken a turn for the worse?"

"No," Flora said, and then she burst out, "He *still* thinks we have to go on pounding the Confederate States!"

Blackford drove in silence for some little while before finally saying, "If your own brother feels that way after he was wounded, you begin to get an idea of what the Democrats would have done to us if we had tried hard to cut off funds for the war after it began. This country thirsts for revenge the way a drunk thirsts for rotgut whiskey."

"But it's all mystification!" Flora exclaimed. "The capitalists have tricked the workers into going to war against their class interest, and into being thankful while they're getting slaughtered. They've even tricked someone like David, who ought to know better if anyone should." To her dismay, she began to cry.

Congressman Blackford parked the Ford across the street from the apartment building where they both lived. "Mystification is a notion that sounds more useful than it is," he observed as he got out and went around to open her door for her. "What people believe and what they'll do because they believe it is a big part of what's real, especially in politics."

"It's one of the planks in the platform," Flora said, taking his arm as she got out of the motorcar. "The capitalists and the bourgeoisie mystify the proletariat into going along with their desires." She raised an eyebrow; he'd shown before that his ideology wasn't so pure as she would have liked.

He shrugged now. "If you run a campaign that doesn't do anything but shout 'They're tricking you!' over and over, you're going to lose. That's one of the things the Socialist Party has proved again and again. The other thing the Democrats have proved for us—or against us, rather—is that, right now, anyhow, nationalism is stronger than class solidarity." He shrugged again. "I'd say the whole world has proved that for us."

"What about the Negroes in the Confederate States?" Flora asked.

"What about them?" Blackford returned. "They rose up and they got smashed. You're still learning the difference between being an agitator and being a politician. Listen to me, Flora." He sounded very earnest. "Compromise is not a dirty word."

"Maybe it should be," she answered, and strode into the apartment building ahead of him. She could feel his eyes on her back, but she did not turn around.

Gordon McSweeney prowled along the west bank of the Mississippi, looking for Confederate soldiers to kill. He didn't find any. The United States had this stretch of the riverbank under firm control these days. He felt frustrated, as a lion might feel frustrated looking out of its cage and seeing a cage full of zebras across the walk in the zoo.

Not even the new, shiny captain's bars he wore made him feel any easier about the world. He knew he'd been lucky to wreck one Confederate river monitor. Asking God to let him be that lucky twice was pushing the limits of what He was likely to grant.

Across the Mississippi lay Memphis. It might as well have lain across the Pacific, for all McSweeney could do to it. U.S. artillerymen still pounded the city; the cease-fire did not hold west of the Tennessee River. McSweeney was glad of that. Watching smoke rise from the foe's heartland gave him a certain amount of satisfaction, but only a certain amount. He hadn't caused any of that devastation himself, and acutely felt the lack.

Ben Carlton came up alongside him. Carlton wore new sergeant's chevrons on his sleeve. He was a sergeant for the same reason McSweeney was a captain: the regiment had gone through the meat grinder taking Craighead Forest, and not nearly enough new officers and noncoms were coming up to replace the dead and wounded. Very few veterans were still privates these days.

"Pretty damn soon, the Rebs'll pack it in here, too, I expect," Carlton said.

"Every blasphemy that passes your lips means a hotter dose of hellfire in the world to come," McSweeney answered.

"I've seen enough hellfire right here on earth," Carlton said. "The kind the preachers go on about don't worry me as much as it used to."

"Oh, but it must!" McSweeney was shocked out of anger into earnestness. "If you do not repent of your sinful ways, the things you have seen here will be as nothing beside the torments you will suffer there. And those torments shall not pass away, but endure for all eternity."

Instead of giving a direct answer, Carlton asked, "What are you going to do when the war's finally done?"

McSweeney hadn't thought about that, not since the day the United States had joined their allies in the fight against the Confederate States and the rest of the Quadruple Entente. He didn't like thinking about it now. "I work on my old man's farm," he answered reluctantly. "Maybe I'll go back—don't know much else. Or maybe I'll try and stay in the Army. That might be pretty good."

"Well, I'll tell you, sir, you can have my place when they turn me loose," Carlton said. "I've done enough fighting to last me all my days. Don't rightly know what I'll do afterwards—I was sort of odd-jobbing around before I got conscripted—but I'll come up with something, I figure."

"Not cook," McSweeney said. "Anything but cook. When you're good, you're not very good, and when you're bad, even the rats won't touch it."

"Love you, too . . . sir," Carlton said with a sour stare. He looked thoughtful; he might have been a lousy cook, but he knew all the angles. McSweeney cared nothing for angles. He always went straight ahead. After a few seconds' contemplation, Carlton went on, "You want to stay in the Army, I figure they'll let you do it. You've picked up so many medals, you'd fall forward on your kisser if you tried to pin the whole bunch on at once. If the Army tried to cut you loose and you didn't want to go, you could raise a big stink in the papers."

Raising a stink in the papers had never crossed Gordon McSweeney's mind. He'd seen a newspaper but seldom before he had to do his service; when he read, he read the Good Book. So now it was with genuine curiosity that he asked, "Do you think it might help?"

"Hell, yes," Carlton answered, ignoring McSweeney's fearsome frown. "Can't you see the headlines? 'Hero Forced from Uniform!'—in big black letters, no less. Think the Army wants that kind of headline? Like hell they do. They want everybody proud of 'em, especially now that we've finally gone and licked the Rebs."

It sounded logical. It sounded persuasive. McSweeney knew little of logic. What he knew of persuasion he actively distrusted: it struck him as a tool of Satan. With a sigh, he said, "The Army won't be the same after the war is over."

"That's right," Carlton said. "Most of the time, you'd sleep in a barracks. You'd get your meals regular, from a better cook than me. Nobody would be trying to shoot you or gas you or blow you up."

McSweeney never worried about what the enemy was trying to do to him. His only concern was how he could kick the other fellow in the teeth. How to put that into words? "After the war," he said slowly, "how can anything I do seem better than lukewarm?"

"You're stationed in a nice, cozy barracks, you can go into town and find yourself a pretty girl." Carlton had an answer for everything.

Most of the time, though, it was the wrong answer by Gordon McSweeney's reckoning. "Lewdness and fornication lead to the pangs of hell no less surely than blasphemy," he said, his voice stiff with disapproval.

Carlton rolled his eyes. "All right, Captain," he said, using the rank in a way that reminded McSweeney he'd known him when he had none, "go into town, find yourself a pretty girl, and marry her, then, if that's how you feel about it."

It is better to marry than to burn. So Paul had said in First Corinthians. To hear the same advice from Ben Carlton was jolting; few people struck McSweeney as being less like Paul than did the longtime and stubbornly inept company cook. "Do I tell you how to arrange your life, Carlton?" he demanded.

"Only when you open your mouth," Ben answered. "Sir."

McSweeney gave him a dirty look. "You are godless," he said. "You have made my life a trial since the moment we began serving together. Why God has not called you to Him to judge you for your many sins, I cannot imagine. By failing to call you, He proves Himself a God of mercy."

"Reckon you're right about that, Captain McSweeney, sir," Carlton said, but the gleam in his eyes warned that he did not expect to be taken altogether seriously. "Maybe He figures that, with you riding herd on me, He doesn't have to do any nagging of His own."

"Get out of my sight," McSweeney snarled. Then he held up a hand. "No. Wait. Get down." Carlton was already throwing himself flat. No more slowly than McSweeney, he heard the screech of cloven air and, intermixed with it, the roar of a river monitor's big gun.

The roar of the shell was like the end of the world. Face down in the black, sweet-smelling mud—McSweeney could tell by his nose how rich the soil was—he felt the world shake as the round thudded home. Splinters hissed and squealed past overhead. Dirt pattered down on him and Carlton both. The Rebs hadn't missed them by much. The crash of the shell left his ears stunned, battered.

Dimly, as if from far away, he heard Carlton shouting, "I hate those goddamn fucking monitors—unless they're ours!"

Foul language aside, McSweeney agreed with all his heart. That was why he had sent one of them to its no doubt less than heavenly reward. The U.S. Army still had not brought up guns that could match the monitors' firepower. As a sergeant, he would have guessed about why that was, and only his strong belief would have kept his guesses from being profane. As an officer, he heard official explanations in place of guesses. The only trouble was, the explanations changed from day to day.

Once, he'd been solemnly told that all the really large-caliber cannon were in service east of the Mississippi. A few days later, he heard that the roads down from Missouri were too bad to let the Army move super-heavy cannon down as far as Memphis. The roads *were* bad. He knew that. Whether they were *that* bad, or whether the other half of the explanation was true, he did not know. He did know the U.S. artillery that had made it down opposite Memphis could not match what the Rebels' river monitors carried.

Another shell came whistling down out of the sky. This one struck even closer than had the first. The force of the explosion sent him tumbling along the ground. He felt something wet on his upper lip. When he raised a hand, he discovered his nose was bleeding. If he'd been breathing in rather than out, he might have had his lungs torn to shreds inside his chest, and died without a mark on his body except blood from his nose. He'd seen that happen. After almost three years, he'd seen everything happen.

Ben Carlton was screaming. Because his ears had taken a beating, McSweeney needed longer to realize that than he would have otherwise. He crawled toward Carlton, then stopped and grimaced and shook his head. A shell fragment had gutted the company cook like a trout. His innards spilled into the mud. It put McSweeney in mind of the last time he'd butchered a calf.

"Oh, Mother!" Carlton wailed. "Oh, Jesus! Oh, Jesus fucking Christ!"

That was not the way McSweeney would have called on the Son of God, but he did not criticize, not here, not now. As he took a better look at Carlton's wound, he became certain the cook was beyond his criticism, though not beyond that of a higher Judge. Not only were his guts spilled on the ground, they were also gashed and torn. If he didn't die of blood loss or shock, a wound infection would finish him more slowly but no less surely.

He wasn't in shock now, but too horribly aware of what had happened. "Do something, God damn you!" he shrieked at Gordon McSweeney.

McSweeney looked at his contorted face, looked at the wound, and grimaced again. He knew what needed doing. He'd done it before for wounded comrades. It never came easy, not even for him. He drew the trench knife he wore on his belt and showed it to Carlton. The wounded man was awake and aware and deserved the choice.

"Yes," he groaned. "Oh, God, yes. It hurts so bad."

McSweeney got up on his knees, used one hand to tilt up Ben Carlton's chin, and cut his throat. His comrade's eyes held him for a few seconds, then looked through him toward eternity.

Looking at Carlton, McSweeney hardly noted yet another shell screaming in. Had he noticed, it would have mattered little. The shell burst only a couple of feet away. For an instant, everything was gold-glowing light. Then it was dark, darkness absolute. And then Gordon McSweeney found out whether or not everything in which he had so fervently believed was true.

Richmond shocked Anne Colleton. She hadn't been in the capital since the night of the first big U.S. bombing raid, most of a year before. It had taken a beating then; she'd seen as much as she made her way to the train station. But that had been a house gone here, a shop gone there, and a few piles of rubble in the street.

Now, after months of nighttime visits from U.S. bombing aeroplanes, Richmond was a charred skeleton of its former self. Whole blocks had been burnt out. Hardly a building had escaped getting a chunk bitten out of it. Windows with glass in them were rare enough to draw notice. More were boarded over; still more gaped empty.

"Things have been hard, sure enough," the cab driver told her as he pulled up in front of Ford's Hotel. "Last time they were this hard, I was a little boy, and the Yankees were comin' up the James instead of down from the north." He wore a neat white beard, at which he plucked now. "We druv 'em back then, but I'll be switched if I know how we're going to do it this time."

A colored attendant took charge of her bags. When she registered, she smiled to find her room was on the same floor as it had been during her last visit. The smile held a hint of cat's claws; she'd kept Roger Kimball out of her bed then, much to his annoyance.

After she'd unpacked, she telephoned the president's residence. The aide with whom she talked seemed surprised she'd come into Richmond so nearly on time, but said, "Yes, Miss Colleton, the president looks forward to seeing you. You're booked for tomorrow at ten. I trust that will be acceptable."

"I suppose so," she answered. "Or will we have surrendered by then?" The flunky spluttered. Anne said, "Never mind. That will be fine." She hung up in the middle of an expostulation.

Supper that evening wasn't what it had been the year before, either. "Sorry, ma'am," the Negro waiter said. "Cain't hardly get food like we used to." He lowered his voice. "A couple o' the bes' chefs went an' joined the Army, too."

Anne sighed. "I wish I'd known that before I ordered. I think this so-called beefsteak would neigh if I stuck a fork in it."

"No, ma'am, that really an' truly is beef," the waiter insisted. He dropped his voice to a whisper again: "But if you stick a fork in the rabbit with plum sauce, it'll meow, sure as I'm standin' here. Roof rabbit, nothin' else but." Having thought about ordering the rabbit, Anne let out a sigh of relief.

U.S. bombers pounded Richmond again that night. Anne grabbed a robe and went down to the cellar of the Ford Hotel, where she spent several crowded, uncomfortable, frightened hours. Even in the cellar, she could hear the *crump!* of bursting bombs, the barking roar of the antiaircraft guns, and the seemingly endless buzzing snarl of aeroplanes overhead. She realized how isolated from the war she'd been in South Carolina. It left no one here untouched.

Just after she'd managed to fall asleep in spite of the racket, the all-clear sounded. She went back to her room and lay awake again for a long time before finally dropping off once more.

Ham and eggs the next morning tasted fine. The coffee was muddy and bitter, but strong enough to pry her eyes open, which counted for more. She walked outside, flagged a cab, and went up Shockoe Hill to the presidential residence.

Antiaircraft guns had sprouted on the lawn since her last visit. Holes—actually, they were more like craters—had sprouted in the lawn. Boards took the place of glass here as elsewhere in Richmond. Other than that, the mansion seemed undamaged, for which Anne was glad.

Inside, a flunky of higher grade than the one with whom she'd confirmed her appointment said, "Ma'am, the president will see you as soon as he finishes his meeting with the British minister."

President Semmes stayed closeted with the British minister till nearly noon, too. Had he been with anyone else save perhaps the secretary of war, the delay would have offended her. But the British Empire and the Confederate States were the last of the Quadruple Entente still in the fight against the USA and Germany (Anne didn't count Japan, and didn't think she should— the Japanese were fighting more in their own interest than as allies of anyone else). It was only natural for them to take counsel together.

When the British minister left Semmes' office and came out through the antechamber where she was sitting, she grimaced. His expression would have had to lighten to seem grim. He hurried past without looking at her. Without false modesty, she knew that any man who did that had a lot on his mind.

"The president will see you now," the flunky said, appearing in the waiting room as if by magic.

"Thank you," Anne said, and went into the office from which presidents of the Confederate States had led their nation from one success to another for better than half a century. Gabriel Semmes still led; where the success was to come from, however, Anne could not imagine.

Semmes seemed to have aged a decade since Anne had seen him the previous year. He was grayer and balder than he had been; his skin hung slack on his face, and dark shadows lay under his eyes. When he said, "Come in, Miss Colleton. Do come in," his voice was an old man's voice.

"Thank you, your Excellency," Anne said, and then, as she sat, "Are things really so bad as that?"

"By no means." President Semmes let out a gallows chuckle. "They are a great deal worse. The British Isles *will* starve—save, perhaps, that part of Ireland that has risen in revolution—and we *are* taking blows not even an elephant could hope to withstand for long."

"But the truce in Tennessee is holding," Anne said. "Why would Roosevelt let it hold if the United States weren't also at the end of their tether?"

"So he can hammer harder at other fronts," Semmes said. "So he can threaten us with starting up the war again there, too, if we do not lay down our arms on all fronts. If he does . . ." Semmes shook his head. "We could not hold the Yankees at the line of the Cumberland. I do wonder if we should be able to hold them at the line of the Tennessee."

He shook his head again; Anne got the idea he wished he hadn't said so much. "They've licked us, then," she said. "Colored soldiers and all, they've licked us. We might as well not have bothered with them."

"As it turned out, that is true," Semmes said, "though they did buy us some extra time. Had Russia not collapsed, had France held out, our own circumstances would be very different. And then, when the Empire of Brazil stabbed England in the back . . . our Allies are in a bad way, Miss Colleton, even as we are."

"We had better cut our losses, then, and get out of the fight with the best bargain we can make," Anne said.

"For one thing, that would mean casting aside our allies once and for all," the president answered. "For another, but for the cease-fire in Tennessee, I have seen no sign that the United States want to bargain. All they want is to rub our faces into the dirt. The men I have sent forth to treat with them leave me in no doubt as to how much they want to rub our faces in the dirt."

"We did it to them twice," Anne said, "and they've been burning for revenge since the Second Mexican War."

"We've embarrassed them since, too," Semmes said gloomily. "With Britain and France at our backs, we've been too strong for them to challenge, and so, up till now, we have for the most part had our own way."

"Up till now," Anne echoed. "*Can* we yield? Or do they aim to wipe us off the face of the earth? If they do, I already know how to use a rifle. Teaching the rest of the women in the CSA wouldn't take long."

"I admire your spirit, Miss Colleton," the president said. "But we are not in the state we are in because of any want of spirit. We are in our present state because our allies have failed, and because our Negroes rose up against us, and most of all because the United States outweigh us by about two to one. They outweigh us and Canada combined, and they have been able to take advantage of it. I wish I had something more hopeful I could tell you."

"We must never let this happen again," Anne said.

"In principle, I agree with you," Gabriel Semmes replied. "In practice . . . in practice, I fear, living up to that principle shall not be so easy. The Yankees will grow as a result of whatever peace they force upon us; we shall shrink correspondingly. They will not make it easy for us to gain redress for the grievances they leave us."

"They waited fifty years and more for their revenge," Anne said. "If we have to, we can do the same. But I hope and pray it will come sooner."

"They also spent a lot of time and money preparing that revenge," Semmes pointed out. "Can we do the same, under their watchful eye?" Just when Anne thought his manhood altogether quenched, he added, "Whether we can or not, I don't know, but we shall have to try."

"Yes," Anne said. "I never understood what drove them to want the revenge so badly. Now I do. Nothing like losing to make you want to take back what you've lost and to get even with the fellow who took it from you."

She thought of Jacob, gassed by the Yankees and murdered when the Negroes raised the red banner of revolution. She'd had some measure of revenge—not enough, but some—on the Reds. How could she avenge herself upon the United States of America?

"I do want to thank you for the support you have shown for my policies since I succeeded President Wilson," Semmes said. "I hope that support will continue as we head toward the end of this war."

I hope you still have some money and some influence left, was what he meant. Anne hoped the same thing. She wished she'd sold Marshlands before the Red uprising—that would have given her more capital to invest. Her investments, at the moment, were disasters, but Marshlands was a catastrophe. Not only was it bringing in no money, the taxes she paid on the land were sucking the life's blood from her veins.

She said, "I'll do what I can. We need to get our strength back as quickly as we're able to."

That wasn't a promise that what she would do would involve supporting Gabriel Semmes, although she would not have been brokenhearted to have him take it as one. And so he did, saying, "I knew I could rely on you. And let me say that, even now, I have some hope that the Army of Northern Virginia will yet halt the Yankees' inroads, for which they are paying a dreadful price. If we stop them, if we can drive them back, we may yet get terms more nearly acceptable to the national honor."

"I hope we do," Anne said, and meant it. At the same time, though, she still held to the thought she'd had before: if the war was lost, best to escape it as soon as might be. With this war behind them, the Confederate States could start thinking about the next one.

It was, Lucien Galtier thought, a grand day for a wedding. He felt not the least bit sorry to hold the ceremony in the little tin-roofed church of St.-Antonin rather than the grander structure up in Rivière-du-Loup. Father Pierre, the local priest, got on very well with Father Fitzpatrick. Bishop Pascal would have made a fine show of getting along with Dr. O'Doull's friend, and, while making that fine show, would have done everything in his power to undercut him. Lucien had seen Bishop Pascal in action before.

He fiddled with his wing collar and cravat. Marie had gone on and on about how handsome he looked in his somber black suit. Whether he looked handsome or not, he disliked the way the collar grabbed him around the neck. He sniffed at his sleeve, hoping neither the suit nor the white shirt under it smelled too overpoweringly of mothballs. They spent most of their time in a chest in the closet, coming forth for hardly anything but funerals and weddings.

His sons stood around fiddling with their collars, too. He'd had to tie their neckties for them: it was either that or spend half an hour waiting while they botched the job and then do the tying. Neither of them had had much practice at the art. He hadn't had much himself, and hoped the knot in his own cravat was as straight as those he'd tied for Charles and Georges.

Had Nicole been marrying some young man of the vicinity, he too would have worn a black suit of no particular age (and no particular shape), and like as not a cravat his father had tied for him. Dr. Leonard O'Doull, on the other hand, wore a cutaway, white tie, trousers pressed into creases scalpel-sharp, and a stovepipe hat. When Georges saw him in his splendor, he whistled and said, "I thought I was getting a doctor for a brother-in-law, not a Rockefeller."

"And I thought I was getting a troublemaker for a brother-in-law, and I see I was right," Dr. O'Doull returned. He refused to let Georges get his goat. Lucien reckoned that the best way to handle his younger son, who was indeed a troublemaker.

Father Fitzpatrick came up to them, a little man with a beaky nose and hair the color halfway between rust and a sunset. "We'll do it in just a few minutes, now," he said. He spoke Parisian French with a peculiar lilting accent. When he spoke English with Dr. O'Doull, the lilt remained.

"This is good," Lucien said. "This is very good." He slowed his own speech a little for the priest's benefit. Turning to his daughter's fiancé, he asked, "Are you nervous?"

"Of course I'm nervous," O'Doull answered. Georges looked disappointed; had O'Doull tried to deny it, Lucien's son would have made him pay. The American doctor went on, "Weren't you nervous when you married your wife?"

"Now that I think on it, it could be that I was," Galtier said, and pursed his lips to show he knew he was understating things. He'd been as nervous as a man getting a half-grown lynx out of a tree, and he'd known Marie since they were both children. O'Doull had known Nicole only since they began working together at the hospital. No wonder he was nervous.

Friends and relatives filed into the church. Most of them waved to Lucien; some came over to shake hands with him and O'Doull. A few went inside with rather sour expressions. They were families with young men who might possibly have been matched to Nicole had her father not chosen this outsider. In their shoes, he would have shown a long face, too.

And then it was time to go inside, and for Lucien to lead Nicole down the aisle toward the altar. In her dress all of white, she looked very young and very beautiful. She beamed at him through the veil. He patted the hand she'd set on his arm. If she was happy, he would be happy. And, even if Dr. O'Doull was an American, he struck Galtier as a solidly good fellow.

So did Father Fitzpatrick, though he gave Lucien a start by pronouncing the Latin of his prayers in a most peculiar fashion. Galtier glanced sharply over at Father Pierre. The local priest remained calm. That let Lucien also remain calm. If Father Pierre thought Father Fitzpatrick's pronunciation acceptable, God likely would, too.

After Dr. O'Doull had opened Nicole's veil and kissed her, after he had set a ring on her finger, people headed across the street to the hall Lucien had hired for the reception—the money Major Quigley had paid for back rent for the land on which the hospital stood was proving useful in all sorts of ways. Once there, Lucien got a drink and then found an excuse to get Father Pierre in a corner and ask him about Father Fitzpatrick's Latin.

Father Pierre was also holding a drink. He knocked it back, chuckled, and answered, "You need have no concern over that. English and Irish and American priests are in the habit of pronouncing their Latin as they believe the ancient Romans would have spoken."

"And you, how do you pronounce your Latin?" Lucien asked.

"In the same way as does His Holiness the Pope," Father Pierre said. "I think I have made the better choice, but the other is in no way evil, merely different."

"I also think you have made the better choice," Lucien said. "In your mouth, Latin sounds splendid. In Father Fitzpatrick's mouth, I found it harsh and rather ugly."

"Part of that is because you are not used to it," the priest of St.-Antonin replied. "Their way does have a certain majesty to it—although, as I say, I prefer our own." He rolled his eyes. "Trust English-speakers to pay no attention to what the rest of the world does." Galtier laughed at that.

"Where is the joke, *mon beau-père*?" Leonard O'Doull asked. He could properly call Lucien his father-in-law now.

"Yes, Father, where is the joke?" Nicole echoed. Instead of Galtier's arm, she clung with proud possessiveness to her new husband's.

"It is a matter of Latin," Lucien answered. With any luck at all, that would impress and confuse both the newlyweds.

It worked with his daughter, but not with O'Doull. The doctor thumped his forehead with the heel of his free hand. "But of course! I'm an idiot. Fitz learned his Latin the Ciceronian way, same as I did. But you folks here pronounce it as if the Romans had been Italians, don't you? He must have sounded pretty funny to you."

"If our way is good enough for the Holy Father in Rome, it is good enough for me," Galtier said. Behind him, Father Pierre nodded. "And yes, your friend's Latin did sound odd, though I am given to understand it is also good, of its kind."

He wondered if that would insult the American. Instead, he saw that O'Doull was having a hard time not laughing. "Fitz's Latin is certainly better than mine, these days," his son-in-law said. "Who but a priest has the chance to keep his grasp of the language so fresh?"

"You have reason," Father Pierre said. "I speak no English, I am sorry to say, and many priests who do speak English know not a word of French—unlike your friend Father Fitzpatrick, whose French is very good, if, like his Latin, spoken in an interesting way. But with such folk I speak in Latin, and I am understood. Even with the differences in pronunciation, I am understood."

"It's like the difference between the French of Paris and the French of Quebec," O'Doull said.

"Why, so it is!" The priest of St.-Antonin beamed at him, then turned to Lucien and slapped him on the back. "You are a fortunate man, to have a scholar as part of your family."

"I am a fortunate man," Lucien said. "That is enough. And if I owe some of my good fortune to an American—why then, I do, that is all."

Before either Leonard O'Doull or Father Pierre could say anything to that, shouts from the street distracted both of them and Galtier, too. A couple of people near the doorway called out to learn what was going on. Lucien heard the reply very clearly: "The flag of the Republic of Quebec flies over the city of Quebec!"

Several other people who also heard shouted for joy. A moment later, somebody punched one of them in the nose. Half a dozen men jumped on the puncher and threw him out. To Lucien's dismay, he saw the fellow sprawled in the street with his trousers torn was a cousin he'd always liked pretty well.

Before the reception could turn into a free-for-all, he let out a great bellow: "Enough!" He was loud enough to make everyone turn around and notice him. Still at the top of his lungs, he went on, "This is a wedding, not a political rally. Anyone who wishes to make it a political rally will answer to me." He cocked a fist, leaving no doubt about what he meant.

"And me!" Georges and Charles said in the same breath, standing shoulder to shoulder with their father.

That settled that. People horrified at the victory of the Americans and the Republic of Quebec (very much in that order) over the Canadian and British troops defending the capital of what had been the Canadian province of Quebec kept that horror to themselves. Lucien Galtier felt some, as he watched the world with which he was long familiar crack further. But his manner also persuaded those who were delighted with the success of the Republic to keep their mouths shut. The reception went on.

Marie came up to him and spoke quietly: "You did very well there."

"Did I?" Lucien shrugged. "I do not know. What should I feel? I was torn in two when France lay down her arms to Germany. Now I am torn in two again. What we had is not what we shall have."

"Change." His wife spoke the word as if it were more filthy than *tabernac*. "Why can the world not stay as it has always been?"

Now it was Galtier's turn to whisper: "You ask this at the wedding of your eldest daughter to an American doctor? How many American doctors would have come to the farm a-courting without the war? Not more than six or eight, I am certain."

Marie stuck an elbow in his ribs. "And I am certain you are as much trouble as Georges, which is saying a good deal. I am also certain Dr. O'Doull is a fine young man, even if he is an American."

"I am certain of this as well, else I should never have allowed him to join the family," Galtier said. "And I am certain we have profited since the Americans came, when everything is taken all in all. But in doing so, we have turned our backs on everything that we knew and taken hold of everything that is new. Do you wonder that I worry on account of it?"

"I wonder that you worry so little on account of it," Marie answered.

"This only shows that, wife of mine as you have been these

many years, you do not know every dark place inside my heart,"
Lucien told her. "I worry—how I worry! But I have got by . . .
we have got by. And, old or new, we will go on getting by." Now
he spoke with great determination. After a moment, Marie
nodded.

Lieutenant General George Custer was in a state, and, for
once, his adjutant was damned if he blamed him. "On my front!"
Custer shouted. "Roosevelt accepts a cease-fire on *my* front!
Does he accept a cease-fire on any other front? In a pig's arse he
does! Why my front? Why my front alone?"

"He must have reasons," Major Abner Dowling said, though
he'd been hard pressed to find any that made sense to him.

"Oh, he has reasons, all right," Custer snarled. He had no
trouble finding them, either: "He wants to rob me of my glory,
that's what he wants to do. He always has, damn him. He never
let me go to Canada, to lead our soldiers there. And now this is
the front where we first broke through the Rebels' lines. This
is the front where the U.S. Army learned *how* to break through
the Rebels' lines. And this is the front Teddy Roosevelt chose to
halt. Do I have to draw you a picture, Major?"

"Sir, you can't mean that," Dowling said.

He might as well not have spoken, for Custer ranted right
through him: "That man in the White House has tried to rob me
of the credit I deserve for the past thirty-five years. *I* was the one
in command when we drove Chinese Gordon out of Montana
during the Second Mexican War, but who stole the headlines?
Roosevelt and his Unauthorized Regiment, that's who. Tell me
to my face, Major, that he's not doing the same thing now. Look
at the map and tell me that to my face!"

Dowling obediently looked. The longer he looked, the more
he wondered whether the general commanding First Army
didn't have a point. If Roosevelt hadn't accepted the cease-fire,
how far would U.S. forces have advanced by now?

Custer, inevitably, had his own opinion about that: "Murfreesboro? To hell with Murfreesboro! We'd be pushing on toward
Chattanooga by now, damn me to hell if we wouldn't." Fortunately for him, Dowling couldn't do anything of the sort. Chattanooga was a *long* way away.

"I doubt that, General." The voice came from the doorway.
Dowling turned. His mouth fell open. There, grinning, stood

Theodore Roosevelt. How much of Custer's tirade had he heard? By the look of that grin, altogether too much. Dowling kissed his own career good-bye.

And Custer wasn't finished. Custer wasn't anywhere close to finished. "How dare you inflict this indignity on First Army, Mr. President? How *dare* you?" he demanded. "Whatever you may think of me, the brave soldiers who have given so much to the cause deserve to be in at the kill."

Many of those soldiers would have agreed with him, too, though being in at the kill might have meant their dying. Dowling knew as much; complaints from the front kept flooding into Nashville.

Roosevelt said, "Either the Confederates will yield on all fronts in a week's time, General, or you will be moving forward again. That I promise you. Maybe you will be able to aim toward Chattanooga after all."

"Why the devil did you halt me in the first place?" Custer said, anything but mollified. "Even more to the point, why did you halt me and no one else? You do not serve your country well by bearing a grudge across so many years."

If that wasn't the pot complaining of the kettle's complexion, Dowling had never heard any such. But Roosevelt didn't rise to the bait. Instead, walking over to the map on the wall, he pointed to the ground First Army had seized south of the Cumberland. "I stopped First Army, General, because you have done something no other U.S. force has accomplished."

"You halted us *because* we did better than any other force you have?" Custer howled. "You admit it?"

"That's not what I said, General," Roosevelt answered sharply. "Your unique achievement is easy to describe: in moving south of the Cumberland, yours is the only force to have captured territory I am willing to return to the Confederate States in exchange for concessions elsewhere. We go from the realm of war into the realm of diplomacy here—do you see?"

"Ahh." That wasn't Custer; it was Abner Dowling. He wasn't sure he agreed with what Roosevelt was doing (not that the president would lose any sleep if he didn't), but he was profoundly relieved Roosevelt was doing it for some other reason besides (or at least in addition to) pique against Custer.

Custer himself did not give over sputtering and fuming. "Why on earth should we give any land we've taken back to the Rebs?

When I was a lad, this was all part of the United States, and so it should be again."

"In principle, General, I agree with you," Roosevelt answered. "In practice, the line we occupy—and what we can reasonably hope to take—will not give us a neat, defensible frontier everywhere along it. We'll do some horse trading at the table, and this stretch south of the Cumberland I can trade without a second thought."

"You won't have to do much trading, sir," Dowling said. "We hold the whip."

"That's true, Major, but I can't wipe the Confederate States from the face of the earth, however much I might want to," the president answered. "Kaiser Bill can't make France go away, either. If we weaken them, though, and make them pay, they won't trouble us for a long while."

"Then, by thunder, when we do fight them again, we'll put paid to them once and for all," Custer said. He rubbed his age-gnarled hands together. "Damned if I don't look forward to reuniting the country at last."

He sounded as if he looked forward to commanding U.S. soldiers in the next war against the CSA. If, as Roosevelt hoped, the Confederates would have to lie quiet for a long time, the wait would put him up into his nineties—or beyond. Maybe he didn't think about that. Maybe he thought about it and didn't care: having gone on for so long, he might believe he could go on forever.

Major Dowling asked, "Mr. President, for what land might you want to swap what we've taken south of the Cumberland?"

"What I have in mind getting is the little chunk of southeastern Kentucky the Confederates still hold," Roosevelt answered. "Lord knows it's not worth much as far as land goes, but having the whole state in our hands will make life simpler after the shooting stops. The Confederates won't be able to keep Kentucky in their Congress then, or to go on electing senators and a congressman or two who'll spend all their time speechifying about how the Confederacy needs to take back their home state. I want it gone from their minds, altogether gone, and that will be that."

"That makes a . . . good deal of sense," Dowling said slowly. Because of his bulldog aggressiveness, Roosevelt didn't get the credit he deserved either as a politician or as a statesman. "The

Germans had no end of trouble from France when they took part of Lorraine after the Franco-Prussian War but let the froggies keep some, too. Better they should have grabbed it all, to make the break clean."

Roosevelt beamed at him. "The very example I had in mind, as a matter of fact, Major." Dowling beamed, too; looking smart in front of your boss never hurt. The president went on, "Our allies will correct that omission in the forthcoming peace, I assure you."

Custer coughed, one of those coughs loosed for no other purpose than to draw attention to oneself. "This is all very well, your Excellency, I have no doubt, but why do it at the expense of what First Army has achieved? If you must trade the Confederates land for land, why not give them back some of the vast worthless stretches we've captured west of the Mississippi, in Arkansas and Sequoyah and Texas and Sonora?"

"Not all that land out there is worthless, General," Roosevelt answered. "The stretch of Arkansas we hold puts Memphis under our guns, which emphatically is worth doing. Sequoyah is full of oil and gas, and we can use them: motorized machines grew ever more important as this war moved along. And as for the land that *is* largely worthless—that being so, why would the CSA want it back?"

"It still strikes me as unjust that my forces should be singled out for this halt," Custer said. "We deserve better than that."

I deserve better than that, he meant. Dowling had no trouble understanding as much, and neither did Theodore Roosevelt. He blew air out through his mustache before replying, "General, would you not say that, in your long and distinguished military career, you have already been treated better than you deserve?"

"I haven't the faintest idea what you are referring to, Mr. President," Custer said, bristling, "and I resent the imputation."

"Resent all you like," Roosevelt growled. Abner Dowling did his best to seem a large, corpulent fly on the wall. He listened avidly as Roosevelt continued, "When we were taking our position north of the Teton, you were the one who wanted to move back the Gatling guns that chopped the British infantry to dogmeat. If we had moved them, the limeys probably would have overrun us. The only reason you ever got to be a hero, you pompous fraud, is that Colonel Welton and I talked you out of it."

"That's a damned lie!" Custer shouted.

"The hell it is!" Roosevelt shouted back. "And if your brother hadn't got himself shot, he would have said the same thing."

"Another lie!" Custer turned a dusky shade of purple that had to, surely had to, portend an apoplexy. "Tom and I were two sides of the same coin."

"Both tails, or maybe blockheads," Roosevelt said.

"Damn you, you know why I always wanted to lead in Canada. You've always known, and you've always ignored my requests for transfer. Is it any wonder I resent that?" Custer said.

Instead of answering, Roosevelt shrugged off his coat. Custer cocked his fist and glared a challenge. The two men, one nearing sixty, the other nearing eighty, looked ready to swing at each other. "Gentlemen, please," Dowling said, reluctantly reminding them of his existence. Even more reluctantly, he stepped between them. "If the two of you quarrel, the only gainers live in Richmond."

Roosevelt recovered his temper as fast as he lost it. He'd always been volcanic, but his eruptions quickly subsided. With a nod—almost a bow—to Dowling, he said, "You're right, of course." He also nodded to Custer. "General, I apologize for my hasty words." As if to prove he meant it, he put the coat back on. "I also assure you that, as I said before, I accepted this cease-fire for reasons of state, ones that have nothing to do with personal animus against you, with the memory of your brother, or with disrespect for the sterling fighting qualities the men of First Army have displayed."

"Slander. Nothing but slander," Custer muttered under his breath. Unlike Roosevelt, he stayed angry a long time. But, when the president affected not to hear him, he muttered something else and then said, "I must accept the assurances of my commander-in-chief." From him, that was an extraordinary concession.

It wasn't what most interested his adjutant, though. For years, Dowling had heard whispers about the combat in Montana Territory that said what Roosevelt had said out loud. It did not strike him as improbable. Where sound military judgment required pushing straight ahead, Custer could be relied upon to exercise such judgment. Where sound military judgment required anything else, Custer could be relied upon to push straight ahead.

"General, we've won the damn war," Roosevelt said. "As your

adjutant so wisely put it, Richmond laughs if we disagree among ourselves. I do recognize what you have done here. To prove it, when I get back to Philadelphia I shall propose to Congress your elevation to the rank of full general, and I am confident Congress will confirm that promotion."

Where minutes before Custer had been ready to punch the president, now he bowed as deeply as his years and his paunch permitted. "You honor me beyond my deserts, your Excellency," he said. By his expression, though, he did not for a moment believe he was being too highly honored. Dowling was inclined to agree with the modest self-appraisal Custer gave to Roosevelt, but then wondered if *he* might not be promoted, too. *A rising tide lifts all boats,* he thought, and the U.S. tide rose higher day by day.

XVIII

Chester Martin was no longer in command of B Company, 91st Regiment, and did his best to feel resigned about it. Out of some replacement depot had come Second Lieutenant Joshua Childress, who might possibly have been nineteen years old, but might well not have, too.

"We hit the Rebels one more good lick tomorrow morning," he declared to the weary veterans in the hastily dug trench north of Stafford, Virginia. "That will take us all the way down to the Rappahannock. Won't it be bully?" His voice broke with excitement at the prospect.

Corporal Bob Reinholdt chuckled softly. "Somebody better oil the lieutenant, Sarge," he whispered to Martin. "He squeaks."

"Yeah," Martin whispered back. "We've got to keep an eye on him. He'll get some good men killed if we don't."

"Ain't that the sad and sorry truth?" Reinholdt said with a nod. If he still resented Chester for taking over his section—and for coldcocking him—he didn't show it. Too much water, to say nothing of blood, had gone under the bridge since.

"We must finish the punishment we have given the Confederate States since 1914," Childress was saying. "We are all heroes in this fight, and we must not fear martyrdom in our country's cause."

Reinholdt and Martin both rolled their eyes. This couldn't be anything but Childress' first combat duty. Firing had been light in the couple of days since he'd come down to the front. People who'd served longer were apt to be less enthusiastic about the prospect of martyrdom when the war was visibly won. People who, like Martin, had won Purple Hearts were apt to be least enthusiastic of all.

"Be bold," Childress said. "Be resolute. Be fearless. Now when the enemy totters is the time to strike the fiercest blows."

"Christ," Reinholdt muttered. "Wish you was still in charge of us, Sarge. That stupid prick is going to have us charging machine-gun nests with our bare hands." He got out a tobacco pouch and began to roll a cigarette. "Well, one thing—he ain't likely to last long. Then it's your turn again."

"Yeah," Martin said. "If he doesn't get me shot, too. Thank God for barrels, is all I can say. Without 'em, most of us'd be dead about five times over."

"God knows that's true." Reinholdt's big head bobbed up and down. "If I stay in the Army after the Rebs quit, I figure I'm going to try and get into barrels myself. That way, I'll have some iron between me and the fuckers we're fighting."

Martin considered. "Only trouble I can see with that is, the other guys go after barrels with everything they've got. You'll get in the way of a lot more cannon shells than you would if you stayed out in the open."

"Well, yeah," Reinholdt allowed. "The thing of it is, though, you get in the way of even one shell when you're out in the open and it ain't what you call your lucky day." He stuck the hand-made cigarette in his mouth and brought it to life with a lighter made from a Springfield cartridge case.

In the background, Lieutenant Childress droned on and on. Some of the men in B Company—replacements, mostly—hung on every word he said. The soldiers who'd been in the trenches for a while either took no notice of him or quietly made fun of him the way Martin and Reinholdt did. They didn't need him to tell them how to fight; had he been willing to listen instead of banging his gums, he might have learned a good deal.

The Army of Northern Virginia had taken a hell of a beating, but it hadn't quit. The Rebs interrupted Childress' disquisition with a mortar barrage. Martin hated mortars; they dropped bombs right down into the trenches, which regular artillery had a lot more trouble doing. He was damned if he could figure out where the valor lay in cowering and hoping a spinning fragment wouldn't turn him from a man into an anatomy lesson.

When the barrage eased, Childress picked up where he'd left off without seeming to miss a word. As Chester Martin got to his feet and tried to brush damp earth from the front of his uniform, he hoped that meant the new company commander had some guts. The other choice was that Childress was so full of himself, he hardly noticed what went on around him. Remembering how he'd been at nineteen or so, Martin knew that was possible.

U.S. artillery didn't let the Confederates mortar the forward trenches without paying them back. The USA had more guns and bigger guns than the CSA did; the bombardment went on long into the night. That puzzled Martin, who'd grown used to sharp, short barrages. In the middle of the din, Lieutenant Childress exulted: "See how we thrash the stubborn foe!"

"He makes more noise'n the guns do," Bob Reinholdt said disgustedly.

That gave Martin the answer, or he thought it did. He snapped his fingers. "Bet they're making a racket to keep the Rebs from hearing the barrels coming forward."

"Huh," Reinholdt said, a noise that could have meant anything. After a bit, he went on, "Maybe I never should have given you no trouble, Sarge. Sure as hell, you're smarter'n I am. That's got to be it."

"Nothing's got to be anything." Martin spoke with the deep conviction of a man who had seen almost everything. "It's a pretty fair bet, though."

"Yeah." It was too dark for Martin to watch Reinholdt nod, but the pause before the corporal spoke again was about right. "Last time, they kept the machine guns banging all night long. You don't want to do the same thing twice in a row, or the Rebs'll get wise to you."

"I hadn't thought of it that way, but you're right." Martin swatted at a mosquito. He didn't think he got it. Scratching, he continued, "Maybe I'm the dummy." If Reinholdt finally was getting used to having him in charge, he wanted to help that along as much as he could. Ignoring occasional shells from overmatched Confederate batteries trying to reply to the U.S. barrage, he rolled himself in his blanket and went to sleep.

To Lieutenant Childress' credit, he went through the trenches an hour before the attack was set to begin, making sure everybody in the company was awake and alert. When he recognized Martin in the predawn gloom, he said, "Remember, Sergeant, we are to form behind the barrels and follow them toward the enemy's position."

"Yes, sir." Martin hid a smile. "I've done this before, sir." The last big attack, he'd done it as a company commander. He let out a silent sigh.

Lieutenant Childress might as well not have heard him. "We have to stay close to the barrels, to take full advantage of what they can do for us." He could have been reciting something he'd learned by rote. He didn't understand what it meant, not really, but at least he had it right.

As he was speaking, U.S. artillery came to life again, making the Confederates stay under cover in the key minutes just before the attack went in. Through the booming of the guns and of their shells, Martin caught the sound he was listening for: the rumble of truck engines and the rattle and clank of iron tracks. Sure enough, the barrels were moving up to their jumping-off places.

Darkness slowly yielded to morning twilight. Martin got a glimpse of a couple of barrels not far away, the big boxy steel shapes putting him in mind of prehistoric monsters looming out of the mist. But these monsters were friendly to him and his. Only the Confederates would find them horrid.

And then the note of the engines grew harsher, louder. The barrels waddled forward at their best speed, somewhere between a fast walk and a slow trot, toward the men of the Army of Northern Virginia. Lieutenant Childress' almost beardless cheeks puffed out like a chipmunk's as he blew and blew the whistle that ordered his company forward. He was first out of the trench himself: he would do what he could by personal example.

"Come on, you lazy bastards!" Chester Martin shouted. "If the Rebs shoot you, your family picks up a nice check from Uncle Sam. So you've got nothing to worry about, right?" He suspected that wouldn't hold up if anybody took a long, logical look at it. But so what? It got the men moving, which was what he'd had in mind.

Machine guns winked balefully from the Confederate positions ahead. No, the Army of Northern Virginia hadn't quit, however much Martin wished it would. U.S. machine gunners did their best to make their C.S. counterparts keep their heads down. The barrels began firing on the Confederate machine-gun nests, too. They also began smashing down the wire in front of the Confederate trenches, though those belts weren't nearly so thick as some Martin had seen.

"Forward!" Lieutenant Childress shouted. "Stay close to the

barrels!" He trotted on, doing his best to make sure he was applying what he'd learned in school.

It did him no good. One thing his training hadn't taught him was how to keep from catching three or four machine-gun bullets with his chest. He let out a brief, bubbling wail and crumpled. Martin was only a few feet behind the company commander. He threw himself flat and crawled up to him. Childress' eyes were wide and staring. Blood poured from his wounds and from his mouth and nose. He was still twitching a little and still trying to breathe, but he was a dead man.

That meant B Company belonged to Martin again. He scrambled to his feet. "Come on!" he shouted again. "We can take 'em! Let 'em try and stop us, hard as they want. We can still take 'em."

Talk like that on the Roanoke front in 1915 would have got him laughed at. Taking such talk seriously back then would have got him—and whoever listened to him—killed. Now . . . Now he was right. The Army of Northern Virginia lacked the men and the guns and, most of all, the barrels to halt the vengeful forces of the United States. Each barrel the CSA did get into the fight had to fight off two or three or four U.S. machines.

Also, at last, even the white Confederate soldiers seemed to have despaired of the fight. Instead of battling in the trenches with bayonet and sharpened spade, more and more of them threw down their rifles and threw up their hands and went into captivity pleased with themselves for having outlasted the war. Here and there, in the trenches and behind them, diehards still fought till they were killed in place, but the tide of war flowed past them and over them and washed them away.

Now, finally, everything was going as the generals and politicians had predicted it would go back in 1914. Martin passed through the little town of Stafford—a few homes and shops clustered around a brick courthouse—hardly noticing it till it was behind him. U.S. artillery had reduced most of the buildings to rubble. The Confederates no longer defended every hamlet as if it were land on which Jesus had walked.

"Come on!" he shouted to the men who advanced with him. "Eight miles to the Rappahannock! If we push these bastards, we'll be there by sundown." And if, on the Roanoke front in 1915, he'd heard himself say anything like that, he'd have known he was either shellshocked or just plain crazy.

But only a few Rebs contested the way south of Stafford. Save for those rear guards, most of the Confederates seemed intent on getting to the southern bank of the river, perhaps to make a stand there, perhaps simply to escape. A couple of miles north of the Rappahannock, shells from the far side of the river began landing uncomfortably close to Martin and his men.

Then the shells stopped falling. The rifle and machine-gun fire from the few men in butternut still north of the Rappahannock died away. A Confederate soldier—an officer—came out from behind a ruined building. He was carrying a white flag. "Hold your fire!" Chester Martin shouted to his men. The hair at the back of his neck and on his arms tried to stand on end.

"It's over," the Confederate officer shouted. "It's done. You sons of bitches licked us." Standing there defeated before the soldiers of the United States, he burst into tears.

Jake Featherston had the surviving guns of his battery in the best position he'd found for them since the war began. Back of Fredericksburg, Virginia, up in Marye's Heights, a stone wall protected a sunken road. If the Yankees swung down along the curve of the Rappahannock and tried to force a crossing at Fredericksburg, he could look down on them and slaughter them for as long as his ammunition held out. They would be able to hit him only by luck—by luck or by aeroplane. He kept a wary eye turned toward the sky.

At the moment, he had the guns turned toward the north rather than the east, though—the U.S. soldiers seemed to be heading straight for Falmouth instead of Fredericksburg. That was what he gathered from the beaten men in butternut streaming past, anyhow. He'd given up shooting at Confederate soldiers fleeing the enemy. He couldn't kill them all. He couldn't even make them stop their retreat. And the more rounds he wasted on them, the fewer he'd be able to shoot at the damnyankees.

He climbed up on top of the stone wall and peered north through field glasses. Sure as hell, here came the U.S. soldiers, trailing the barrels that smashed flat or blasted out of existence any strongpoints in their path. U.S. fighting scouts swooped low over the front, further harrying the men of the Army of Northern Virginia.

"Come on, boys," Jake said. "They're inside seven thousand yards. Let's remind 'em they have to pay for their tickets to get in. God damn me to hell and fry me for bacon if anybody else is going to do the job. Infantrymen? Christ on His cross, all the good infantry we used to have's been dead the last two years."

The four guns that remained of his battery of the First Richmond Howitzers desperately needed new barrels. They'd sent too many rounds through these; the rifling grooves were worn away to next to nothing. Featherston knew the guns weren't going to get what they needed. *Fat cats in Richmond get what they need,* he thought. *All I'm doing is defending my country. Does that count? Not likely. What do fellows like me get? Hind tit, that's what.*

When the guns began to roar, though, he whooped to see the shells falling among the leading damnyankees. He'd spent the whole war doing his best to hurt them. Even if the guns weren't so accurate as they should have been, he could still do that. He could still enjoy it, too.

An improbably young lieutenant in an improbably clean uniform came up to him and demanded, "Who commands this battery, Sergeant?"

Jake drew himself up with touchy pride, and took pleasure in noting that he was a couple of inches taller than this baby officer. "I do," he growled, "sir."

"Oh." The lieutenant looked as if he were tasting milk that had gone sour. "Very well, Sergeant. I am to inform you that, as of five o'clock P.M., which is to say, about an hour from now, an armistice will go into effect along our entire fighting front with the United States."

Jake had been braced for the news, or thought he had, for the past couple of weeks. Getting it was like a boot in the belly just the same. "We've lost, then," he said slowly. "We're giving up."

"We're whipped," the officer said. Featherston looked at the men who served the guns. Perhaps for the first time, he let himself see how worn they were. Their heads bobbed agreement with the shavetail's words—they *were* whipped. The lieutenant went on, "We've done everything we could do. It wasn't enough."

"What the hell did *you* do?" Jake asked. The lieutenant stared at him, disbelieving his ears—how could an enlisted man presume to question *him*? Jake shook his own head. Strangling the pipsqueak would be fun, but what was the use? The CSA grew his sort in carload lots. Ask a question with an answer worth knowing, then: "What are we supposed to do with the guns after five o'clock?"

"Leave them," the young lieutenant said, as if they were unimportant. They were—to him. He went on, "The Yankees will take them as spoils of war, I reckon." That didn't seem important to him, either. Off he went, to give the word to the next battery he found.

"Spoils of war?" Featherston muttered. "Hell they will." He looked at his watch. "We got most of an hour, boys, till the war's over. Let's make those shitheels wish it never got started."

Plainly, his soldiers would just as soon have let the fighting peter out. He didn't shame them into keeping on—he frightened them into it. That he could still frighten them with everything they'd known crashing into ruin around them said a lot about the sort of man he was.

At five o'clock, he himself pulled the lanyard to his field gun one last time. Then he undid the breech block, carried it over to Hazel Run—a couple of hundred yards—and threw it in the water. He did the same with the breech blocks from all the other guns. "Now the damnyankees are welcome to 'em," he said. "Fat lot of good they'll get from 'em, though."

His words seemed to echo and reecho. As the armistice took hold, silence flowed over the countryside. It seemed unnatural, like machine-gun fire on a Sunday afternoon in the middle of Richmond. When the gun crew talked, they talked too loud. For one thing, they were used to shouting over the roar of the three-inchers. For another, they were all a little deaf. Jake suspected he was more than a little deaf. He'd been at the guns longer than any of his men.

Before the sun set, Major Clarence Potter made his way to the battery. Featherston nodded to him as to an old friend; in the Army, Potter was about as close to an old friend as he had. The intelligence officer looked at the field guns, then at Jake. "You're not going to let them have anything they can use, eh?" he said.

Jake spent some little while describing in great detail the uses the damnyankees could make of his guns. Major Potter listened, appreciating his imagination. Finally, Featherston said, "Goddammit, sir, sure as hell we're going to fight those bastards another round one of these days before too long. Why give 'em anything they can take advantage of?"

"Oh, you get no arguments from me, Sergeant," Potter said. "I wish more men were busy wrecking more weapons we'll have to turn over to the USA." He wore a flask on his hip. He took it in hand, yanked the cork, swigged, and passed it to Featherston. "Here's to the two of us. We were right when the people over us were wrong, and much good it did us."

The whiskey burned its way down to Jake's belly. He wanted to gulp the flask dry, but made himself stop after one long pull and hand it back to Major Potter. "Thank you, sir," he said, for once sincere in showing an officer gratitude. Then he asked the question undoubtedly echoing throughout the beaten Army of Northern Virginia, throughout the beaten Confederate States: "What the devil happens next? We never lost a war before."

"What happens next is up to the Yankees." Potter drank again. "Unless I read them wrong—and I don't think I do—they'll take us down just as far as they can without provoking us into starting up the war." He thrust the flask at Featherston once more. "Here. Finish it."

"Yes, sir." Jake was glad to obey that order. Once the reinforcements had landed and spread warmth along his legs and up on his cheeks and nose, he found another question, closely related to the first: "What'll they make us do?"

"I'm not Teddy Roosevelt, thank God, but I can make some guesses," Potter said. "First one is, the United States are going to keep whatever they've grabbed in the war. Kentucky's gone, Sequoyah's gone, that chunk of Texas they're calling Houston is gone, the chunk they bit out of Sonora is gone, too."

"Yeah." Jake pointed out north. "Probably hold on to Virginia down to the Rappahannock, too."

"Probably," the intelligence officer agreed. "When the next war comes, that will keep us from shelling Washington the way we have the last couple of times—keep us from doing it for a little while, anyhow."

"The next war," Jake repeated. He assumed there would be a next one, all right. "How soon do you reckon it'll come?"

"That depends on a lot of things," Major Potter answered. "How much the damnyankees make us cut our Army and Navy, for one: how many men and barrels and aeroplanes and submersibles they let us keep."

"Oh, yeah." Featherston nodded. "And on how many we'll have stashed away without them being any the wiser."

"And on that," Potter agreed. "The other side of the coin is, how soon do the thieves fall out?"

"I don't know what you mean," Jake said with a frown.

"Who won the war?" Major Potter asked patiently. "The USA and Germany, that's who. Oh, Austria-Hungary and the Ottoman Empire, too, but they hardly count. Roosevelt and the Kaiser are pals now, but how long will that last? When they start squabbling among themselves, that may give us the chance to get some of our own back."

"Ah." Featherston thought that over, then raised an admiring eyebrow. "You come up with all kinds of things, don't you, Major?" That was genuine, ungrudging praise, and drew a smile from Potter. Featherston went on, "I'll tell you who lost the war for us, though."

"I've heard this song before, Sergeant," Potter said.

Jake went on as if he hadn't spoken: "The white-bearded fools in the War Department and the niggers, that's who. Anybody wants to know, we ought to take 'em all out and shoot 'em. Whole lot of good they did us during the war."

"Take all who out and shoot them?" Major Potter asked interestedly. "The white-bearded fools in the War Department or the niggers?"

"Hell, yes." Without his quite noticing it, the whiskey had mounted to Jake's head. "Country'd be better off without 'em, you mark my words."

"Duly marked, Sergeant." But Potter sounded amused, not convinced. "Nice to know someone has all the answers. I'll tell you one thing: a lot of people in Richmond will be looking for answers, and heads will roll on account of it."

"Some, maybe." Savage scorn filled Featherston's voice. "But not enough. You mark my words on that, too. The high mucky-mucks'll find ways to cover for their brothers and cousins and in-laws and pals, and nothing much'll come out of this. And as for the niggers—hellfire, Major, some of those damn coons'll be voting now. Voting! After they stabbed us in the back, voting! Can you imagine it?"

"You are an embittered man," the intelligence officer told Jake. He studied him for a long moment, then slowly shook his head. "If you turned to good use the energy you waste in bitterness, who knows what you might be able to do with it?"

"Waste?" Jake shook his head, too. "I'm not wasting it,

Major. I'm going to get even. I'm going to get even with everybody who screwed me and my country."

"Forgive me, Sergeant, but I'll believe it when I see it," Potter said.

"You will," Jake said. "Damned if I know how, but you will."

Major Cherney was laying things out for the fliers in his squadron: "All right, boys, this is the last act. The Confederate States are out of the war. It's us against England and Canada now, and we're going to lick them. That's all there is to it. Toronto is going to fall. With the Rebs quitting, we can bring up another million men and another thousand aeroplanes and squash 'em flat."

Jonathan Moss stuck up his hand. When Cherney pointed to him, he said, "Sir, I don't know about you, but I want to finish licking the Canucks *before* all the reinforcements come up from the south. If they do it for us, it's like saying we couldn't handle the job ourselves."

He looked around the tent at the Orangeville aerodrome. Most of the pilots who nodded with him were men who'd been flying against the Canadians and Englishmen for a long time. Percy Stone agreed with him, for instance. Pete Bradley, like a lot of the newer men, didn't seem to care one way or the other. *As long as Canada goes under,* his shrug might have said, *who cares how?*

But Charley Sprague, among the newest of the new, spoke in support of Moss: "That's right. They'll take all the credit, and what will they leave us? Not a confounded thing, that's what. After the war is over, everybody will try to pretend we didn't do anything, anything at all. Is that how we want to go down in history?"

"I agree with both of you," Cherney said. "We've been through too much to let those other bastards grab our glory. That means we have to grab it ourselves. Let's go out and do it."

After almost three years of war, Moss hadn't thought a speech could fire him up for combat in the air. But he went out to his Wright two-decker with a grim smile on his face and a spring in his step. He felt ready to whip the whole British Empire singlehanded.

Perhaps seeing that, Percy Stone set a hand on his arm as he was about to climb up into his flying scout. "Steady, there," he said. "When you try to do more than you really can, that's when you get into trouble."

Moss paused with his foot in the mounting stirrup on the side of the fuselage. "You're right," he said. "I'll remember. Thanks."

"My pleasure," Stone answered. "You brought me home so they could patch me up again. I want you to get home, too." He paused, then looked west. "Or over toward Arthur, if you'd rather do that when the war is over."

Ears burning under his flying helmet, Moss scrambled into the cockpit. Percy Stone went over to his own bus and took his place inside. Moss shook his head. His friend knew how sweet he'd got on Laura Secord, and if doing that wasn't foolish, he didn't know what was. For one thing, she despised Americans. For another, she had a husband. Except for those minor details, she would have made a perfect match.

But he couldn't get her out of his mind. He knew he should, but he couldn't. A groundcrew man spun the fighting scout's prop. Moss checked his instruments. He had plenty of fuel, plenty of oil, and his oil pressure was good. Flying relieved the symptoms of what ailed him. He didn't have time—well, he didn't have much time—to think about it.

He looked to the other pilots. Stone, Bradley, and Sprague waved in turn: they were ready to go. He nodded to the ground-crew man, who pulled the chocks away from his wheels. The two-decker bumped along over the rutted grass of the landing strip till, after one bump, it didn't come down.

The smoke that marked Toronto's funeral pyre guided him south and east. His flightmates followed. He kept trying to look every which way at once, and wished for eyes on stalks like a snail's to make that easier.

For two or three miles inland from the shore of Lake Ontario, the land that made up the city of Toronto rose smoothly from the water. Then it became steeper, even hilly. British and Canadian artillery used the hills to advantage, posting batteries on them and looking down on the flat country through which U.S. forces were slowly and expensively fighting their way.

Antiaircraft guns protected the pieces that were shelling the Americans. Black puffs of smoke burst around Moss' aeroplane as he dove on an enemy battery. The Wright two-decker bucked in the turbulence from the explosions like a restive horse. A piece of shrapnel tore some fabric from the bus's right upper wing. Moss knew it could as easily have torn through the engine, or through him.

His thumb found the firing button on top of the stick. Below, the gunners swelled from dots to toys to bare-chested men in khaki trousers. Englishmen or Canadians? He didn't know. He didn't see that it made a difference one way or the other. He stabbed at the button with all his strength.

"See how you like that!" he shouted as tracers lanced toward the artillerymen. They scattered. Some of them fell.

Early in the war, when he'd thought the principal function of fliers was observation, he'd felt bad about shooting at the foe. It didn't bother him any more. It hadn't bothered him for a long time. The limeys and Canucks weren't shy about shooting at him. They would have cheered their heads off if he'd crashed in flames. His twin machine guns kept things even.

He zoomed back toward the front at just above treetop height, his flightmates on his tail. Every time he spotted a concentration of men in khaki, he gave them a burst and sent them flying like ninepins. They shot back, too; rifle bullets hissed past him, some uncomfortably close. An infantryman had to be amazingly lucky to shoot down an aeroplane. If enough infantrymen fired enough rounds, though . . . He'd never liked that thought.

He brought up the Wright's nose to gain altitude for another swoop on the enemy's guns. That let him look down on Toronto once more. U.S. forces had crossed the Etobicoke and the Mimico; there was heavy fighting in a park—High Park: he remembered the name from maps he'd studied—just east of the latter stream. Farther east still, what had been the Parliament building in Queen's Park was now a burnt-out ruin, wrecked by bombs and artillery.

As always, he checked the air around him for enemy machines. Spying none, he began his second dive on the enemy's guns. Something was different this time. The altimeter wound off a thousand feet before he realized what it was: the antiaircraft guns weren't firing any more. He wondered if artillery hits had put them out of action. "Hope so," he said. With luck, the slipstream would blow his words to God's ear.

Down on the ground, the enemy artillerymen were milling around their guns. His thumb found the firing button again. The men were looking up at him and waving scraps of cloth . . . scraps of white cloth.

Behind his goggles, his eyes widened. He took his thumb away from the firing button and pulled out of the dive a little higher than he would have if he'd been shooting up the gunners in khaki. Instead of grabbing rifles to take potshots at him, they kept flying those makeshift white flags. Some of them waved their hands, too, as if he were a comrade and not a hated foe. Tears that had nothing to do with the slipstream blurred his vision.

"It's over," he said, almost in disbelief. "Can it really be over?"

It could. It was. As Moss once more led his flight back toward the American lines, none of the British and Canadian soldiers on the ground fired at their machines. Like the artillerymen, they waved whatever bits of white cloth they could find. U.S. soldiers in green-gray were beginning to come out of their trenches and approach the enemy line. No one shot at them, either.

Jonathan Moss wished the racket from his aeroplane's motor didn't drown out everything else. He would cheerfully have given a month's pay to hear the silence on the ground where only minutes before rifles and machine guns and exploding shells had created hell on earth.

He wanted to find a landing strip and put down, just to be able to savor that silence. He needed all the discipline in him to fly away from the front where the fighting had finally ceased and back toward the Orangeville aerodrome. If he'd suffered a sudden case of fortuitous engine trouble, he had no doubt Stone's aeroplane—and Bradley's and Sprague's as well—would have come down with similar miseries.

When he finally did land at the aerodrome, the groundcrew men knew far more about what was going on than he did. "Yeah, we got word of the armistice about half an hour after you took off," a mechanic said. "We could have called you back if you'd had a wireless telegraph in your bus."

"Canucks kept fighting up till the last minute, then," Moss said. "They did their best to blow us out of the sky the first time we strafed their artillery."

Charley Sprague asked, "Has England given up the fight, then?"

The groundcrew man shook his head. "Wish the limeys had, but they haven't. The armistice is for land forces in Canada. The Royal Navy's still fighting us and the Germans both."

"They can't win that fight—not a prayer," Sprague said. Had

his flightmate not beaten him to it, Moss would have said the same thing.

"Well, you know that, sir, and I know that, but the limeys haven't figured it out yet," the mechanic answered. "Been a hell of a long time since they lost a war; I guess they don't hardly know how to go about it."

"We've had practice," Moss said. "How many Remembrance Day parades have you watched?" That was a rhetorical question; everybody in the USA had seen his share and then some. Moss went on, "About time they threw in the sponge. Quebec—the city, I mean—is gone, Winnipeg's gone, Toronto's going, Montreal's blasted to hell, and we've finally broken out of that box between the St. Lawrence and the Ottawa and the Ridea where they'd penned us up since the start of the war. Another few months and they wouldn't have had much left to surrender."

"Now we've conquered them," Percy Stone said. "What the devil are we supposed to do with them?"

"Sit on 'em," Pete Bradley said. "If they give us a hard time, we'll shoot some of 'em. That'll give the rest the idea."

"Oderint dum metuant," Sprague said. Moss, who'd had Latin, nodded. The groundcrew men stared in blank incomprehension. Sprague condescended to translate: "Let them hate, so long as they fear."

Moss thought of Laura Secord. She hated. He didn't think anything could make her fear. He wondered whether her husband had come through the war in one piece. If he had, he had; that was all there was to that. If he hadn't . . . Moss did intend to make a trip back to Arthur, so he could find out one way or the other. He suddenly smiled. With the fighting done, that trip looked a lot easier to arrange than it had when he took off earlier in the day.

Rosenfeld, Manitoba, blazed with light as the U.S. soldiers occupying the town celebrated their victory over the forces of the British Empire in Canada. Every so often, somebody would fire a Springfield into the air. Every shot set off a fresh round of raucous cheers.

Arthur McGregor crouched behind a bush in the darkness just outside of town. If a patrol caught him here, he was in a lot of trouble. He shook his head. If a patrol caught him here, he was a dead man. He didn't usually take chances like this. But he wouldn't get another chance like this, either. If ever he could catch the Yanks with their guard down, now was the time.

He stiffened. Someone was coming his way along the dirt road that led out from Rosenfeld. A moment later, hearing how erratic the footsteps were, McGregor relaxed. The drunken U.S. soldier, a little gamecock of a man, staggered past him and out into the deeper darkness where night still ruled absolutely.

After ten or fifteen minutes, another couple of soldiers meandered by. McGregor stayed concealed. One of the drunks paused not far away to throw up by the side of the road. Then he stumbled after his friend, who hadn't stopped.

Fifteen or twenty minutes more passed. Out of Rosenfeld came another soldier looking for fresh air, or perhaps only for a quiet place to heave. He was a big, broad-shouldered fellow for whose lurching strides the roadway did not seem wide enough.

As the U.S. soldier passed the bush, McGregor got to his feet. He carried an axe handle, a good, solid chunk of wood. Since he'd had not a drop to drink, his movements were swift and sure. The soldier, his face a mask of surprise, was just starting to turn when the axe handle slammed into the side of his head. He dropped as if shot—but a shot would have made noise, and McGregor could not chance that.

He dragged the soldier back to his hiding place. Once there, he finished the job of smashing the fellow's skull: he might have been recognized, after all. Then he stripped the dead man of tunic and trousers, puttees and boots. He took off his own clothes and put on the American's. They weren't a perfect fit: the tunic was loose, the trousers and boots tight. But they would do. For what he had in mind, they would do. He opened a wooden box he'd carried from the farm and set the alarm clock inside to ring in two hours' time. Then, carefully, he replaced the lid and used the axe handle to drive in four brads to keep it closed.

That done, he stepped out into the roadway. The dead soldier's brimless service cap lay there, knocked off his head when McGregor hit him. The farmer picked it up and put it on. A lot of soldiers in town would probably not be wearing theirs, but he wanted to look as much like one of them as he could.

Into Rosenfeld he went. He didn't stand out on account of his age: the Yanks had conscripted men who looked older than he did. Plenty of them were carrying this or that. One was giving a piggyback ride to a laughing woman waving a whiskey bottle.

McGregor knew Rosenfeld's two or three whores by sight. She wasn't any of them; the Americans must have brought her in from some other town.

"Hey, pal, whatcha got in the box there?" a soldier asked.

McGregor had known he might get that question, so he had an answer ready: "Beer for Colonel Alexander." The colonel named for his son was fictitious, but the soldier wouldn't know that.

"Reckon he could spare a bottle or two?" the fellow said.

McGregor shook his head. "He'd skin me alive." The U.S. soldier grimaced, but went off instead of trying any more wheedling. The Americans were more submissive to their officers than McGregor remembered being from his own days in uniform. *Comes of having Germans for teachers,* he thought.

He found a spot opposite the sheriff's station Major Hannebrink was using as his headquarters. Lights were on inside; the Yanks arrested their own men as well as Canadians, and were probably hauling in lots of them tonight.

That thought had hardly crossed his mind before Hannebrink came out to stand on the porch and look around, hands on hips in indignation at the chaos victory was creating. He saw McGregor, but didn't recognize him. After a couple of minutes, he shook his head and went back indoors.

"Now," McGregor muttered to himself. If he couldn't do it now, he'd never do it. He staggered across the street toward the sheriff's station, suddenly acting much drunker than he had before. He got down on hands and knees by the wooden steps leading up to the porch where Hannebrink had stood, as if about to lose whatever he had in his stomach. He knew he wasn't the only man in uniform doing that. When he thought—he hoped—no one was paying him any special notice, he shoved the box under the steps.

He got to his feet. Nobody shouted, *What are you doing?* or, *What's in that box?* or even, *Wait a second, buddy—you forgot something.* After that, he had no trouble walking as if he were drunk. He was drunk, drunk with relief.

He got out of Rosenfeld and made his way back to the bushes where he'd hidden. Once there, he put the dead American's clothes back on him—an awkward job—and got into his own shirt and overalls and shoes. He took the man's billfold and stuck it in his pocket. With luck, the Yanks would think one of their soldiers had robbed and murdered another.

He was tying his shoes when another American wobbled up the road past him. Several of them—he didn't know how many—were farther from Rosenfeld than he was. If any of them saw him, he might be in trouble. Instead of getting up and starting along the road, he crawled away over grass and dirt, then got to his feet and made his way north and west across a field: whatever he did, he was not going to leave a trail that led straight back toward his farm.

When he came to a little rill, he threw the American's wallet into it after taking out the banknotes. He stuck those in his pocket and splashed along in the rill for a couple of hundred yards. If they set dogs on his trail, he wouldn't give the beasts an easy time.

Not long after he came out, he kicked a stone. He lifted it and stuck the dead American's paper money under it. With luck, the money would never be found. If the empty wallet was, it would make robbery look more likely.

"Thank you, sweet Jesus," he whispered when he found a road. The wheeling stars gave him the direction he needed to head home. On the hard-packed dirt, he'd make good time. He wouldn't leave much in the way of tracks, either.

He'd been walking almost an hour and a half when a bang louder than any of the sporadic rifle shots came from the direction of Rosenfeld. He made a fist and thumped it against his thigh. He had no way of knowing whether Major Hannebrink was still at his post when the bomb went off. Sooner or later, he'd find out. Even if the major had gone, he'd still hurt the Americans. He could console himself with that—but he didn't care about consolation. He wanted vengeance.

Going down back roads and sneaking across the well-traveled highway east of his fields after a line of trucks rattled past, he got back to the farmhouse as twilight was beginning to stain the eastern horizon. He still had a full day's chores ahead. By the time he finished them, he'd wish he were dead. Right now, he hoped someone else was.

Maude was making coffee in the kitchen when he came inside. "Well?" she asked. It was as close to a direct question about what he did when he went out at night as she'd ever given him.

He came close to giving a direct answer, too: "It worked. I wasn't there, though, so I don't know how well."

"All right." His wife looked him over. "Go change your

clothes and bring the ones you have on downstairs. I'll wash them. Set your shoes by the stove first."

He bent down and felt of them. They were still damp. "Good idea," he said. He sighed as he pulled off the shoes. "Feet are tired."

"I'll bet they are," Maude said. "Go on, now. I'll have coffee and eggs waiting when you come down again."

By the time he'd changed and splashed water from the pitcher on the chest of drawers onto his face, Mary and Julia were up, too. Julia sliced bread for him, to go with the fried eggs Maude set out. "You look tired, Pa," she said, which was not a question at all but at the same time was.

"Everything's all right," he replied, an answer that said nothing and at the same time quite a lot.

Mary's face glowed. "Does that mean you—?" she began, and then abruptly stopped, as if she did not want to hear what it meant. Arthur McGregor only shrugged. With food and coffee in front of him, he didn't want to think for a while.

He went out to work in the fields. When he looked back toward the farmhouse, he saw the overalls and shirt and socks and drawers he'd worn the night before out flapping on the line. The breeze was strong. They would dry quickly.

In the middle of the afternoon, a green-gray Ford parked between the farmhouse and the barn. McGregor didn't notice it till the soldiers who got out fired a couple of shots in the air. That brought him in at a shambling trot that told him just how worn he was.

Three privates in green-gray surrounded a tall, skinny U.S. captain McGregor had never seen before. Without preamble, the officer snapped, "Where were you last night?"

"Here at home in bed," he answered. He felt drunk with joy now, and had to work hard to make sure it didn't show on his face. If he'd failed, Major Hannebrink would have been the one to bark questions at him. But sending sullen looks toward the occupiers wasn't hard, not even a little. "Why? What are you going to try and blame on me this time?"

"Somebody set off a bomb in Rosenfeld," the captain said. "A lot of good men died. Somebody's set off a lot of bombs in this part of the country since your son received military justice. A fair number of hostages have died on account of them, too."

"You Yanks have murdered a lot of people in this part of the country besides my son—including those hostages," McGregor returned. "I don't love you, but I haven't bombed you. Major Hannebrink turned this place upside down trying to show different, but he couldn't show what wasn't there."

"Major Hannebrink is dead," the U.S. captain told him.

"I'll not shed a tear," McGregor said. Again, he had to remind himself not to exult. "I wish I had settled him, but I didn't." That lie came easy. He'd had lots of practice using it. His conscience, which had once sickened at any untruth, troubled him not at all.

"Shall we search the house and barn again, Captain Fielding?" one of the privates asked.

McGregor waited for the tall officer to say yes. If the Yanks found what he'd hidden under the old wagon wheel, he could die content now. But Fielding shook his head. "No evidence," he said. "Nothing but Hannebrink's suspicions, and I can't see that he had anything more than suspicions to go on. You keep your nose clean, McGregor, and you can help us put this country back together again."

He gestured to his men. They and he got into the Ford and drove away. McGregor stared after them. He'd won his battle, and cherished that: the man who'd ordered his son executed was dead himself. But the Americans had won the war, and still aimed to reshape Canada to suit themselves. If he was going to keep on resisting, he had to get ready for the long haul. Grimly, he resolved to do just that.

Nellie Semphroch came downstairs to start another day at the coffeehouse. She smiled at the plate-glass windows replacing the boards that had fronted on the street. Once word got around that President Roosevelt had given her and Edna medals, people started going out of their way to do them favors, as people had gone out of their way to cut them when they'd thought them collaborators.

Across the street, Hal Jacobs' cobbler's shop still presented boards to the world. Nellie didn't think that was fair. Jacobs had done much more than she had to hurt the Rebels inside Washington. If Roosevelt had given him a medal, Nellie didn't know about it. Maybe he was naturally modest. Maybe being self-effacing went into making a good spy. Whatever the reason, Jacobs had let no one know he'd done anything out of the ordinary during the war.

Nellie unlocked the door and turned the sign in the window so it read OPEN. As she was doing that, Jacobs opened his own door and came out onto the sidewalk. Seeing Nellie through the window, he waved to her.

A little reluctantly, she waved back. She knew how much she owed him. The coffeehouse never would have made a go of it, let alone flourished, without his help. But, very likely, she never would have had to set eyes on Bill Reach again if not for his dealings with Hal Jacobs. As far as she was concerned, that went a long way toward canceling her debt.

Edna came downstairs. "Morning, Ma," she called as she started making the day's first coffee.

"Morning," Nellie answered. Edna had been subdued since Roosevelt put the medal she did not deserve around her neck. Maybe that was because she realized she didn't deserve it, and appreciated the contribution her mother had made toward a U.S. victory. More likely, Nellie judged, Edna missed the handsome young Confederate officers who'd filled the coffeehouse for most of three years. That might not have been charitable, but Nellie reckoned it close to the mark.

A U.S. officer came in. He was neither handsome nor young. When he ordered a fried-egg sandwich and a mug of coffee, though, Nellie looked on him with benevolent eyes. When he left a quarter for a tip on top of his tab, she reckoned him a paragon among men.

Another officer came in a few minutes later. All he wanted was coffee. Nellie served him with the best smile she could muster. Business was better than it had been when people shunned Edna and her, but not what it had been when the Confederates held Washington. She didn't suppose it would ever be that good again, and was glad she'd managed to save some of what she made.

Hal Jacobs walked into the coffeehouse as that second officer was leaving; they did a little dance in the doorway to keep from bumping into each other. Jacobs asked for a cup of coffee, too. When he set a nickel on the table, Nellie shoved it back at him. "Your money's no good here, Hal," she said. "You ought to know that by now."

"This is foolishness," Jacobs said. "You can use this no matter where it comes from."

"Like you can't?" Nellie answered. "I know how many people go in and out of your place every day. It's a wonder you've got any money to spend at all, if you ask me. But even if you had plenty, I wouldn't take it from you."

"You are more generous than I deserve," the shoemaker said. "I was happy to help you and help our country at the same time."

"Well, you did, and now I'm going to help you, too," Nellie said. From behind the counter, Edna gave her a look that meant, *We can use every nickel we get.* She ignored her daughter, as Edna was in the habit of ignoring her.

Jacobs said, "I know how you can help me, Nellie."

"How's that?" Nellie asked cautiously. She thought she knew what kind of thing the shoemaker would say. Sooner or later, every man in the world said that kind of thing. Edna leaned forward so as not to miss a word. By the leer on her face, she thought she knew what kind of thing the shoemaker would say, too. And, by that leer, she wouldn't let her mother forget it after he said it, either.

Then, to Nellie's surprise, Hal Jacobs slipped out of the chair in which he was sitting. To her even greater surprise, he went down on one knee before her and took her hands in his before she could pull away. "Nellie, will you please marry me and make me a happy man for all the rest of my days?" he asked.

Nellie's face heated. She was sure her cheeks had to be red as raw meat. She glanced over at Edna, whose jaw had fallen and whose eyes were wide and staring. Whatever else her daughter might do, Edna wouldn't be able to tease her about getting a lewd proposition.

She'd been ready to deal with—to deal forcefully with—a proposition. A proposal was something else again. A man who wanted her enough to ask to marry her without even trying to sample the merchandise first? She'd never known—indeed, never imagined—such a thing. Her experience had always been that men were a lot longer on sampling than on proposing.

And so, after a silence that stretched longer than it should have, she could only stammer, "Mr. Jacobs, I—I don't know what to say. This is so sudden."

"Not when we have worked side by side for so long," Jacobs said, still on his knees. "I know what I would like. I can only hope and pray you would like it, too."

Before Nellie could find any way to respond to that, Edna hissed, "Say yes, Ma! Where are you going to do better?"

Unlike a good many from her daughter, that was a good question. Nellie looked down at Hal Jacobs. He wasn't too young and he wasn't too handsome, but she knew he had a good heart. She'd never tried living with a man with a good heart. Maybe it would make a difference.

And maybe, on their wedding night, he would show his heart wasn't so good after all. She had seen how men who outwardly were pillars of respectability could turn into animals, brutes, when they found themselves alone with a woman. If she said yes and Jacobs turned out to be that kind of man, what would she do? What could she do then? Maybe one fine morning he would wake up dead, in as inconspicuous a manner as she could arrange.

Even if he wasn't an animal, did she want him in her bed? No man had been to bed with her in a lot of years, and she hadn't felt that to be a lack: on the contrary, if anything. But, when he'd kissed her the year before back in his shop, she'd been glad to have the kiss—and astonished that she was glad. What, exactly, did that mean? Did she want to take a chance and find out?

If she didn't, what would she do? Stay the way she was and try to keep an eye on Edna till her daughter found another young man and moved away? Knowing Edna, that might happen in a matter of weeks, maybe even days. What then? Spend the rest of her life alone and getting more sour by the day? That didn't sound like such a good bargain, either.

She looked down at Hal Jacobs again. She wished he'd never asked her. By asking her, he was making her think about things she would sooner have ignored. No matter what she did now, no matter what she said now, it would irrevocably change her life. She hated having to make choices that big, and hated having to do it on the spur of the moment even more.

Or perhaps it wasn't exactly on the spur of the moment. Edna said, "Come on, Ma—you've got to tell the poor man *something*."

With a sigh, Nellie realized her daughter was right. With another sigh, a longer and deeper one, she said, "I'll marry you, Hal. Thank you for asking me." She wondered how much she would regret that. More or less than saying no? One way or the other, she'd find out.

Edna let out a cheer that sounded almost like the yells with which Confederate soldiers went into battle. An enormous smile spread over Hal Jacobs' face. He squeezed her hands and said, "Oh, Nellie, thank you so much. You have made me the happiest man in the world."

"Don't be silly," Edna said. She came out to the front of the coffeehouse as Jacobs was getting to his feet. Kissing him on the cheek, she went on, "Teddy Roosevelt's got to be the happiest man in the world now that the Rebs have quit. But if you want to say you're running second, that's all right."

Jacobs laughed. Edna laughed. After a moment, Nellie laughed, too. She felt giddy and foolish, as if she'd been drinking whiskey, not coffee. Was that happiness? Or was it just surprise at what she'd gone and done? For the life of her, she couldn't tell.

A customer came in then, distracting her. He wasn't a military man, and he wasn't one of the locals Nellie knew, either. He wore a black suit, a black cravat, and a black homburg, and carried a black leather briefcase. "Ham and eggs and coffee," he said, like a Confederate plantation owner giving orders to his house niggers. "Eggs over medium, not too hard."

"Yes, sir," Nellie said; some of the Rebel officers who'd frequented the coffeehouse had been that peremptory, too. "Would you like your coffee now, or with the ham and eggs? And would you like toast to go with that? Like the menu says, an extra ten cents."

"Coffee now. No toast. Had I wanted it, I should have requested it." The newcomer looked around. "This is one of the few places I've seen since coming here that we won't have to tear down and start over from the ground up."

A light went on in Nellie's head. "You're from—" she began.

"Philadelphia?" the newcomer broke in. "Of course. You wouldn't think I'd live in Washington, would you?"

"*We* manage," Nellie said. The Philadelphia—lawyer?—sniffed. People from the *de facto* capital of the United States were in the habit of sneering at those from the legal capital. Nellie got him his coffee as Edna started the ham and eggs. His money would spend as well as anyone else's.

"I am going back to my work, dear Nellie," Jacobs said. "Thank you again. We will talk more of these arrangements as soon as we can." He blew her a kiss as he went out the door.

Over the pleasant hiss and crackle of frying food, Edna spoke to the man from Philadelphia: "Mr. Jacobs there just asked my ma to marry him, and she said yes."

"How nice," the fellow said. "Given the way the tax laws are, it will likely prove an advantageous move for both of them."

Nellie had worried about a lot of things before saying yes. Taxes weren't one of them. Maybe she didn't need the cold-blooded Philadelphian's money so badly after all. Maybe, on the other hand, he was trying—coldbloodedly—to do her a favor.

Edna gave her the plate of ham and eggs, and she set it in front of the man who was helping decide how to restore, or whether to restore, Washington. She didn't know a whole lot about taxes and how they worked. Maybe she should ask him for more good advice. About one thing she needed no advice whatever. Hal Jacobs, she resolved, would never, ever learn how Bill Reach had died.

Lieutenant Crowder was lecturing the crew of the depth-charge projector, which meant he was also lecturing George Enos, who, standing nearby at the one-pounder, could hardly escape the officer's words. "We must maintain our vigilance," Crowder declared, as if someone had suggested that the whole crew of the USS *Ericsson* should lie down and go to sleep. "The Confederate States may be out of the fight, but the Royal Navy is still in it."

Carl Sturtevant's sigh was visible but not audible. Out of the side of his mouth, he muttered, "Good thing he gives us the news, ain't it, Enos?" George's nod was half amused, half annoyed.

Crowder didn't notice. When he was talking, he didn't notice anything but the sound of his own voice. "And we must remain alert against submersibles from the C.S. Navy even now," he said. "Some of them may have defective wireless gear, and so be ignorant that their government has at last given up its hopeless fight. And others may claim ignorance and seek to strike one last blow against the United States in spite of the armistice now in force."

It was Enos' turn to roll his eyes. Sturtevant's answering snort was almost as quiet as his sigh had been. As far as George was concerned, the lieutenant hadn't a clue about how to keep the men wary. Talking about the Royal Navy was a decent idea, because England was still in the war. Talking about imaginary Confederates who wouldn't surrender, though, made no sense at all. And, if the sailors decided Crowder didn't make sense about one thing, they were apt to decide he didn't make sense about anything, and so not keep an eye peeled for the limeys.

On second thought, George decided it didn't matter so much. Most of the depth-charge projector crew, from everything he could see, had already concluded Lieutenant Crowder didn't make sense about anything. They'd keep an eye on the Atlantic anyhow, for the sake of their own skins.

After a while, the all-clear sounded. Crowder hurried away from the depth-charge projector as if he had a beautiful blonde waiting under the covers back in his cabin. Thinking about a beautiful blonde made George think about Sylvia. "Christ, I want to go home," he said.

Hearing the longing in this voice, Carl Sturtevant burst out laughing. "You want to kick your wife's feet out from under her, is what you want."

"What the devil's wrong with that?" Enos said. "It's been a hell of a long time."

"Some ships, you could cornhole some pretty sailor if you really felt the lack," Sturtevant said. "The *Ericsson*'s pretty good about that, though—pretty careful to make sure it doesn't happen, I mean."

"I should hope so," George said. "I don't want a pretty sailor. Hell, I don't think there is such a thing as a pretty sailor. I want to go to bed with my wife."

"I wouldn't mind—" The petty officer stopped abruptly. He'd probably been about to say something like, *I wouldn't mind going to bed with your wife, either.* He was smart not to have said that. Giving a sailor of higher rank a fat lip would have got George in a lot of trouble, but he would have done it without hesitation. After a couple of seconds, Sturtevant tried again. "I wouldn't mind going to bed with anything female. Like you said, it's been a hell of a long time."

"Yeah. I know what you mean." Enos remembered that day along the Cumberland when he'd been about to go to bed with a colored whore for no better reason than that he was half drunk and more than half bored. As he'd been going from the ramshackle saloon to the even more ramshackle crib next to it, the

Confederates had blown his river monitor out of the water. If he'd been aboard the *Punishment*, odds were he wouldn't be breathing now.

He drew a mop and bucket and started swabbing a stretch of deck. By now, he understood perfectly the pace he had to use to keep passing petty officers happy. Once, when he fell below that pace, one of those worthies barked at him. Even then, he had an answer ready: "Sorry, Chief. I guess I was paying too much attention to the ocean out there."

"Yeah, well, pay attention to what you're supposed to be doing," the veteran sailor growled.

"Aye aye," George said. But he noted that, as the petty officer paraded down the deck, he made a point of peering out into the Atlantic every few paces. What was he doing, if not trying to spot a periscope? The limeys were still struggling to get freighters from Argentina across the ocean, and their submersibles still prowled: Lieutenant Crowder had been dead right about that. They'd have to quit sooner or later, but they hadn't done it yet.

That evening, attacking corned beef and sauerkraut, the sailors hashed over what they'd do when the war ended. They'd done that a good many times before, but the talk had a different feel to it now. In the midst of the grapple with the enemy, they'd just been blue-skying it, and they'd known as much. Now, when the war would end in days—weeks at the most—life after it seemed much more real, and planning for it much more urgent.

George was one of the lucky ones: he had no doubts. "As soon as they let me out of the Navy, I find me a fishing boat and go back to sea," he said. "Only thing I'll have to worry about is hitting a drifting mine. Otherwise, things'll be just like they were before the war for me."

"Before the war," somebody down the table echoed. "Jesus, I can't hardly remember there ever was such a time."

"Christ, what a load of horse manure, Dave," somebody else said. "You were here on the *Ericsson*, same as me."

Dave was unabashed. "Give me a break, Smitty. All we were doing here before the war was getting ready to fight the damn thing. Wasn't hardly different than what we're doing now, except nobody was trying to kill us back then."

"Nobody but the chiefs, anyways," Smitty said, which got a

laugh. He went on, "We stay in the Navy, what the hell you think we'll be doing? Getting ready to fight the next war, that's what."

"Well, what's a Navy for?" Dave returned. "You better be ready to fight if you get into a war. Otherwise, you lose. Our dads and grandpas had their noses rubbed in that one."

"Look at the clever fellow," Smitty said. "He learned about Remembrance Day in school. Give him a hand, boys. Ain't he smart?"

"Ahh, shut up," Dave said. Since he was half again as big as Smitty, the other sailor did.

Changing the subject looked like a good idea. George said, "Wonder how long it'll be till the next war."

"Depends." Dave, it seemed, had opinions about everything. "If we forget what we have an Army and Navy for, probably won't be long at all. That's what we did after the War of Secession, and Jesus, did we pay for it."

"We do that, half of us'll be on the beach," Smitty said, which turned things back toward what the sailors would do after the war.

Then somebody said, "No Democrat would ever be that stupid. We'd have to elect Debs or whoever the Socialists put up three years from now." That touched off a political argument, the Socialist minority loudly insisting they were Americans as good as any others.

"And better than a lot of people I can think of," one of them added. "The first thing some of you want to do after the war ends is put the workers and farmers into another one."

George asked his question again: "All right, Louie, how long do you think we've got till the next one?"

"If we keep electing Democrats, fifteen years—twenty years, tops," the Socialist answered. "We finally get wise and put in some people who understand what the class structure and international solidarity really mean, maybe it won't happen at all. Maybe this'll be the last war there ever was."

"Yeah, and maybe the Pope's gonna run off with my sister, too," Dave said. "I tell you, Louie, I ain't holding my breath on either one." He got a bigger laugh than Smitty had a couple of minutes before, and preened on account of it.

Fifteen years. Twenty years, tops. Nobody said peace could last longer than that. Well, Louie had, but even he didn't sound as if he believed it. No Socialist had ever even come very close to getting elected president. George didn't see any reason for that to change soon. If war came when people thought it would, his son would get dragged into it. He didn't like that for beans. Hell, if war came again in fifteen or twenty years, he might get dragged into it, too. He wouldn't be an old man. He liked that even less. Wasn't once enough?

He didn't have any duty after supper, so he wrote a letter to Sylvia. If the *Ericsson* went into port before a supply ship met her, he was liable to get into Boston before the letter did, but that would have to mean England was quitting right away, which didn't look likely. *I sure will be glad to sleep in a bed that doesn't have one on top of it and another one underneath,* he wrote. *If they packed us in oil we might be sardines.*

Some of that was exaggeration for dramatic effect. Arrangements aboard a fishing boat were just as cramped, and those aboard the river monitor on which he'd served had been even more crowded. However . . . *I sure will be glad to sleep in a bed that has you in it.*

One of the officers would have to censor the letter before it could leave the destroyer. Most times, George didn't worry about that. Now he wondered if the fellow, whoever he was, would start breathing a little faster if he read something like that. After a moment, George laughed at himself. The *Ericsson* had a war complement of better than 130 men. If the censor hadn't seen anything hotter than what he'd just written, he didn't know anything about horny sailors' imaginations.

He finished the letter, then read it over. He didn't know about the censor, but he was breathing faster by the time he finished. To wake up in a soft bed with his wife beside him . . . he couldn't think of anything better than that. He addressed an envelope and put the letter inside, but didn't seal the flap. The censor would take care of that. George carried the letter to a collection box and put it in.

"Hey, Enos, you want to get into a card game?" the Socialist—Louie—called.

George shook his head. "Go suck in some single guy. I got a wife and two kids at home. Gotta save my money."

"You might win," Louie said.

"Yeah, I might," Enos allowed, "but I usually don't, and that's why I don't get into card games much any more."

He went back to the bunkroom. He didn't usually hit the sack till lights-out, but tonight he stripped to his skivvies and lay down. A fan was doing its best to keep the warm, muggy air moving. Its best wasn't very good; George always woke covered in sweat. But the stuffiness helped him fall asleep fast. He yawned a couple of times and dozed off, smiling as he thought of waking up in bed with Sylvia.

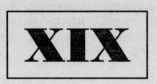

XIX

From the conning tower of the *Bonefish*, Roger Kimball stared gloomily out into the blackness of night on the tropical Atlantic. A million stars hung overhead. The moon's lantern floated low in the east and spilled a long track of pale yellow light across the dark water. It was as beautiful a seascape as God ever made.

He was blind to the beauty. That afternoon, the wireless telegraph had picked up orders directing all Confederate submersibles to return to their home ports, as the Confederate States had been forced to seek an armistice from the United States. Ever so reluctantly, he'd shaped course for Habana.

He'd wondered how the crew would take the news. Most of the sailors had taken it the same way he had: they'd been furious and heartsick at the same time. "God damn it, Skipper, *we* didn't lose the war!" Ben Coulter had cried. "It was those stupid Army bastards who went and lost it. Nobody ever licked us. Why do we have to go and quit?" Several other men had shouted profane agreement.

Since Kimball felt like that, too, he'd had trouble answering. Tom Brearley had done it for him: "If the damnyankees lick us on land, we have to give in. Otherwise, where do we go home?"

"I don't give a fuck," Coulter had answered. "Ain't had a home but for my boat the past twenty years anyways."

Kimball chuckled, remembering the startled expression on his exec's face, as if Coulter had hit him in the side of the head with a sack full of wet sand. The captain of the *Bonefish* agreed with the petty officer. For that matter, he still wasn't sure whether or not the Arkansas farm on which he'd grown up remained in C.S. hands. He hadn't heard from his mother in a long time. And whether it did or not, he didn't want to go back. The Navy was his life these days . . . he hoped.

Brearley joined him atop the conning tower. The exec stayed silent for several minutes, accurately guessing Kimball did not care for conversation. But Brearley, as happened sometimes, didn't keep his mouth shut long enough. "Sir, once we get to port, what are they going to do with us?"

"Don't know," Kimball said shortly, hoping the exec would take the hint.

He didn't. "The damnyankees are liable to make us cut way back on submarines. We've hurt 'em bad; they won't want to give us the chance to do it again."

"Worry about that if it happens." But Kimball had already started worrying about it. He'd been worrying for weeks, even since word of the first Confederate peace feelers came to his ears. He was liable to end up on the beach, not because of what he wanted but because of what the United States decreed. He enjoyed that idea about as much as the idea of a kick in the balls.

A fragment of a curse floated up through the open hatch: "—it, we fought the bastards to a draw out here. Hell, ain't close to fair we have too—"

Brearley broke into it, as he'd broken into Kimball's silence: "The Yankees could cripple our Navy for years. They could even—"

"Shut up." Now Kimball spoke in a flat, harsh tone: the voice of command. Brearley stared, his face a white oval in the moonlight. He opened his mouth—a dark circle in the white oval. "Shut up, damn you," Kimball snapped. He pointed off toward the east, where a ship was suddenly visible against the moon's track.

He raised binoculars to his eyes. The ship leaped closer. How close? Estimating range at night was as tricky a thing as a submersible skipper could do, but he didn't think it was more than a couple of miles. And that silhouette, seen against sky and moonlit ocean, was all too familiar.

"Take it easy, sir," Brearley said as Kimball stared hungrily toward the ship that steamed along unaware he was anyplace close by. "The war's over for us."

"Shut up," Kimball said again, now almost absently. "You know what ship that is, Tom? It's that fucking destroyer that's given us nothing but trouble since she came out here."

"Is it?" Brearley said. "That's too bad, sir. Shame we didn't spy her last night instead of now."

Kimball went on as if the exec hadn't spoken: "And do you know what else? I'm going to sink the son of a bitch."

"My God, sir!" Brearley burst out. "You can't do that! If anybody ever found out, they'd hang you. They'd hang all of us."

"No doubt about it," Kimball agreed. "But England's still in the war. The damnyankees'll blame it on a limey boat—as long as we can keep our mouths shut. To hell with me if I'm going home with my tail between my legs. I'm going to hit 'em one more lick, and I'm going to make it the best one I know how."

"You can't, sir," Brearley repeated.

"Go below, Mr. Brearley," Kimball said. "I can and I goddamn well will. If you don't like it, you don't have to play. You can lay on your bunk and suck your thumb, for all I care." He leaned close to the younger man. "And if you ever breathe one word of this to anybody, I don't know what'll happen to me, but you're a dead man. You won't die pretty, either. Have you got that?"

"Yes, sir," Brearley whispered miserably.

"Then go below." Kimball followed the executive officer down into the stinking steel tube that was the *Bonefish*'s fighting and living quarters. Brearley headed toward the stern: he really didn't want any part in what Kimball was about to do. Kimball didn't care. He was going to do it anyway. In conversational tones, he told the rest of the crew, "Boys, we've got the USS *Ericsson* a couple miles off to starboard. Load fish into tubes number one and two and open the water-tight doors. I aim to put a couple right in the whore's engine room."

Had the sailors hesitated, they might have made Kimball think twice, too. But they didn't. After brief, incredulous silence, they let loose with yells and howls so loud, Kimball half feared the Yankees on the destroyer would be able to hear them. He made frantic shushing noises. Discipline returned quickly, discipline and a fierce eagerness for the kill much like his own.

He took the helm himself, sending a sailor up to the conning tower to watch the destroyer while he made his attack approach. "Give me fifteen knots," he said. "They're just lollygagging along. I want to get out in front of them and double back for the firing run."

"We're in the dark quarter of the sea," Ben Coulter remarked, as much to himself as to Kimball. He grunted in satisfaction. "They'll never spot us."

"They'd damned well better not," Kimball answered, to which the petty officer nodded. Kimball went on, "We'll make the firing run coming in at a steep angle, too, so they won't pick up the reflection of the moon from the paint on the conning tower. And we'll be going in with the wind at our back, pushing the waves along to help hide our wake in the water."

"You don't want to make the angle *too* steep, though, Skipper," Coulter said. "Easy to think it's smaller than it is, and to miss with your fish on account of it. Don't want that, not now we don't."

"Not hardly," Kimball agreed with a dry chuckle. From the bow, a sailor waved to let him know the torpedoes were loaded into the forward tubes. He waved back, wishing he could be two places at the same time: he wanted to be at the helm and up on the conning tower both. He peered through the periscope, which at night was like making love wearing a rubber, for it took away a lot of the intimacy he wanted.

Despite that annoyance, everything went smooth as a training run in the Gulf of Mexico outside Mobile Bay. The destroyer, which could have left him far behind, kept lazing through the sea. He pulled ahead of the U.S. ship and swung the *Bonefish* into the tight turn for the firing run. "Bring her down to five knots," he ordered, not wishing to draw attention to the boat as he closed in.

Like any submarine skipper, he would have made a hell of a pool player, for he was always figuring angles. Here, though, players and balls and even the surface of the table were in constant motion.

He took his eyes away from the periscope every so often to check the compass for the *Bonefish*'s true course. Gauging things by eye didn't work at night—too easy to be wrong on both range and angle. He swung the submersible's course a couple of degrees more toward the southeast. Ben Coulter had been right: if he was going to do this, he couldn't afford to miss.

The lookout on the conning tower called softly down the hatch: "Sir, I reckon we're inside half a mile of that Yankee bastard."

"Thanks, Davis," Kimball called back. He'd just made the same calculation. Having the lookout confirm the range made him feel good. Inside six hundred yards . . . Inside five hundred . . . Inside four hundred . . . "Fire one!" he shouted. If he couldn't hit the *Ericsson* now, he never would.

Clangs and hisses and the rush of water into the emptied tube announced the torpedo was on its way. Even in moonlight, Kimball had no trouble making out the white track of air bubbles the fish left behind it. Maybe somebody on the destroyer's deck also spotted it. If he did, though, he was too slow to do anything about it. Less than half a minute after the *Bonefish* launched it, the torpedo slammed into the U.S. warship just forward of amidships.

"Hit!" Kimball screamed, and the sailors howled out Rebel yells. The *Ericsson* staggered on her course like a poleaxed steer. Water foamed as it poured into the hole better than two hundred pounds of guncotton had blown in her flank. Already she was listing to port and appreciably lower in the water than she had been a moment before.

Up on the conning tower, Davis the lookout whooped for joy. "We-uns is goin' home, but not them Yankees!"

Taking his time now, Kimball lined up the second shot with painstaking precision. "Fire two!" he shouted, and the torpedo leaped away. It broke the destroyer's back and almost tore the stricken ship in two. She went to the bottom hardly more than a minute later. Kimball scanned the sea for boats. Spotting none, he grunted in satisfaction. "Resume our course for Habana," he said, and stepped away from the periscope. "We've done our job here."

Ben Coulter spoke earnestly to the sailors: "Remember, boys, this ain't one where you get drunk and brag on it in a saloon. You do that, they're liable to put a rope around your neck. Hell, they're liable to put a rope around all our necks."

"You do want to bear that in mind," Kimball agreed. He wished he could tell Anne Colleton. If she ever heard he'd gone right on killing Yankees even after the armistice, she'd probably drag him down and rape him on the spot. Warmth flowed to his crotch as he thought about that. But then, slowly, regretfully, he shook his head. He didn't think with his crotch, or hoped he didn't. If she found out what he'd done here, it would give her more of a hold on him than he ever wanted anyone to get. He'd have to keep quiet.

The log would have to keep quiet, too. Kimball went back to an earlier attack and neatly changed a 3 to a 5 on the writeup of the run. That would make the number of torpedoes listed as expended on this cruise match the number he'd actually launched.

He strode toward the stern. Sure enough, Tom Brearley sat on his bunk, looking glum and furious. He glared up at Kimball. "How does it feel to be a war criminal—sir?" He made the title into one of scorn.

Kimball gravely considered. "You know what, Tom? It feels pretty damn fine."

Sylvia Enos threw a nickel in the trolley-care fare box for herself and another one for George, Jr. Next year, she'd have to spend a nickel for Mary Jane, too. She sighed. Even though she was getting her husband's allotment along with her salary at the shoe factory, she wasn't rich, not anywhere close. Nickels mattered.

She sighed again, seeing she and her children had nowhere to sit during the run from Mrs. Dooley's to her own apartment building. She clung to the overhead rail. George, Jr., and Mary Jane clung to her.

As the trolley squealed to a stop at the corner closest to her building, she sighed yet again. Who could say how long she'd keep the job at the shoe factory? With soldiers coming home from the war, they'd start going back to what they'd done before. Women would get crowded out. It hadn't happened yet, but she could see it coming.

She wondered when the Navy would let George loose. He'd have no trouble getting a spot on a fishing boat operating out of T Wharf. As long as he was home with her, she wouldn't have to—she didn't think she'd have to—worry about his chasing after other women. They could try getting back to the way things had been before the war, too. Maybe she'd have another baby.

Mary Jane would be heading to kindergarten next year. If Sylvia didn't get pregnant right away, maybe she could look for part-time work then. Extra cash never hurt anybody.

She paused in the front hall of the apartment building to pick up her mail. It was unexciting: a couple of patent-medicine circulars, a flyer announcing a Fishermen's Benevolent League picnic Sunday after next, and a letter to the woman next door that the postman had put in her box by mistake. She set the last one on top of the bank of mailboxes for her neighbor to spot or for the mailman to put in its proper place and then took the children upstairs.

"What's for supper?" George, Jr., demanded. "I'm starved."

"Pork chops and string beans," Sylvia said. "They'll take a little while to cook, but I don't think you'll starve before they're ready. Why don't you play nicely with your sister till then?" *Why don't you ask for the moon, Sylvia, while you're at it?*

Rebellion came not from George, Jr., but from Mary Jane. "I hate string beans," she said. "I want fried potatoes!"

Sylvia swatted her on the bottom. "You're going to eat string beans tonight, anyhow," she answered. "If you don't feel like eating string beans, you can go to bed right now without any supper."

Mary Jane stuck out her tongue and crossed her eyes. Sylvia swatted her again, harder this time. Sometimes she practically needed to hit her daughter over the head with a brick to get her to behave. Now, though, Mary Jane seemed to get the idea that she'd pushed things too far. She looked so angelic, any real angel who saw her would have been extremely suspicious. Sylvia laughed and shook her head and started cooking.

She'd just set supper on the table and was cutting Mary Jane's pork chops into bite-sized pieces when someone knocked on the door. She muttered something she hoped the children didn't catch, then went to see which neighbor had chosen exactly the wrong moment to want to borrow salt or molasses or a dollar and a half.

But the youth standing there wasn't a neighbor. He wore a green uniform darker than that of the U.S. Army; his brass buttons read WU. "Sylvia Enos?" he asked. When Sylvia nodded, he thrust a pale yellow envelope at her. "Telegram, ma'am." He hurried away before she could say anything.

Scratching her head—delivery boys usually hung around to collect a tip—she opened the envelope. Then she understood. "The Navy Department," she whispered, and ice congealed around her heart.

DEEPLY REGRET TO INFORM YOU, read the characterless letters, THAT YOUR HUSBAND, GEORGE ENOS, WAS AMONG THE CREW ABOARD THE USS ERICSSON, WHICH WAS SUNK LAST NIGHT BY AN ENEMY SUBMERSIBLE. DESPITE DILIGENT SEARCH, NO TRACE OF SURVIVORS HAS BEEN FOUND OR IS EXPECTED. HE MUST BE PRE-

SUMED DEAD. THE UNITED STATES ARE GRATEFUL FOR HIS VALIANT SERVICE IN THE CAUSE OF REMEMBRANCE AND VICTORY. The printed signature was that of Josephus Daniels, Secretary of the Navy.

"Your pork chops are getting cold, Ma," George, Jr., called from the table.

"If you don't eat your green beans, you have to go to bed right now," Mary Jane added gleefully.

Sylvia kept staring at the words of the telegram, hoping, praying, they would twist into some different shape, some different meaning. Twice now, when George had been captured by a Confederate commerce raider and when he'd survived the sinking of the *Punishment*, she'd feared the worst. This wasn't like those times. She didn't fear the worst now. She knew it. She felt it in her bones.

"What am I going to do?" she said, though no one could answer. "What am I going to do without George?"

"I'm right here, Ma," her son said. "I didn't go nowhere. Your pork chops are still getting cold. They're no good if they get cold. You always say that, Ma. You do."

She turned back to the table. She didn't realize tears had started running down her face till Mary Jane asked, "Why are you crying, Ma?"

"Don't cry, Ma," George, Jr., added. "What's wrong? We'll fix it, whatever it is."

They depended on her. She had to be strong, because they couldn't do it for themselves. And she had to tell them the truth. They needed to know. She swiped her sleeve over her eyes. Then she held up the telegram. "This says—" She had to pause and gulp before she could go on. "This says your father . . . it says your father's ship got sunk and he isn't . . . isn't alive any more. He isn't coming home any more, not ever again."

They took it better than she had imagined possible. Mary Jane, she realized, hardly remembered George. She'd been very little when he went into the Navy, and he'd come home but seldom since. How could she miss what she hadn't truly known?

George, Jr., understood better, though he plainly didn't want to. "He's . . . dead, Ma?" he asked, his voice trembling. "Like Harry's father at school, the one the dirty Canucks shot?"

"That's right," Sylvia said. "That's . . . sort of what happened."

A noise in the hallway behind her made her turn. There stood

Brigid Coneval and several of her other neighbors. Somehow, almost as if by magic, everyone knew when a Western Union messenger brought bad news. Had anyone doubted the news was bad, the look on Sylvia's face would have told the tale.

"Oh, you poor darling," said Mrs. Coneval, who, if anyone, knew what Sylvia was feeling at the moment. "You poor darling. What a black shame it is, with the war so near won and all."

People crowded round her, holding her and telling her they would do what they could to help. Someone pressed a coin into her hand. She thought it was a quarter. When she looked at it through tear-blurred eyes, she discovered it was a gold eagle. She stared in astonishment at the ten-dollar goldpiece. "Who did this?" she demanded. "It's too much. Take it back."

No one said a word. No one made any move to claim the coin.

"God bless you, whoever you are," Sylvia said. She started crying again.

Mary Jane said, "You're going to have to go to bed without any supper, because you aren't eating your pork chops." Small things mattered to her; she didn't understand the difference between what was small and what was not.

Sylvia wished she didn't understand that difference, either. Not understanding it would have made life much simpler and much easier . . . for a little while. Life wasn't going to be easy, not ever again. Life probably wouldn't be comfortable, not ever again. If she lost her job at the shoe factory, she'd have to find another one, and right away. If she didn't find another one right away, her children would go hungry, and so would she. Even if she did, money was going to be tight from now on.

What could she do if she lost the factory job? She had no idea. She couldn't think. Her wits felt stunned, strangled. She knew she had to use them, but they didn't want to work.

"Mourning clothes!" she exclaimed suddenly, out of the blue. "I have to fix up some mourning clothes."

Brigid Coneval put an arm around her shoulder and steered her back to the sofa in the front room. When the Irishwoman pushed her down, her legs gave way and she sat. "You wait right here. Don't move, now. Don't even twitch. Back in a flash, I'll be." She hurried out of the apartment.

Sylvia didn't move. She didn't think she could move. George, Jr., and Mary Jane, seeing their mother upset, picked their way through the crowd of neighbors and crawled up into her lap. She did manage to put her arms around them.

"Out of my way, now. Move aside." Brigid Coneval spoke with as much imperious command as General Custer or some other famous war hero might have used. She thrust a tumbler of whiskey at Sylvia. "Drink it off, and be quick about it."

"I don't want it," Sylvia said.

"Drink it," Mrs. Coneval insisted. "He was a good man, your George, sure and he was. Hardly ever a cross word from him did I hear. But he's gone, darling. You may as well drink. What could you do that's better, pray?" She rolled her eyes. "Drink!"

Without much will—without much anything—of her own, Sylvia took the glass and gulped down what it held, choking a little as she did. As far as she could tell, it didn't do anything. Her head was already spinning. "What am I going to do without George?" she asked again, as if one of her neighbors might know.

No one answered. As Mrs. Coneval had, people kept praising her husband. He would have been a happier man had they said all those nice things about him while he was there to hear them.

Then Sylvia started to cry again as another thought struck through the walls of grief and liquor. "He won't even have a funeral," she said. "He would have hated that." Fishermen dreaded being lost at sea. They ate of its creatures, and did not want those creatures turning the tables.

After a while, even in the midst of disaster, routine reasserted itself. Sylvia had to put the children to bed. After she did that, she went to put the pork chops she hadn't been able to eat into the icebox. She discovered a couple of silver dollars and a tiny gold dollar on the kitchen table, along with some smaller coins. When she opened the icebox, she found a dressed chicken in there she had not bought, and also a package wrapped in butcher paper that might have been sausage or fish.

"Thank you," she said. "Thank—" She couldn't go on. Brigid Coneval put her to bed, much as she'd taken care of George, Jr., and Mary Jane. She lay awake and stared and stared at the ceiling. *What will I do?* she thought, endlessly, uselessly. *What will I do?*

When his name was called, Jefferson Pinkard marched up to a pair of officers, his Tredegar on his shoulder. "Pinkard, Jefferson

Davis," he said, and then his pay number. He tossed the rifle down on a growing pile of weapons.

"Pinkard, Jefferson Davis," echoed a Confederate captain from divisional headquarters. He had a list of the soldiers in Jeff's regiment. After lining through his name, he turned to the other officer and spoke in formal tones: "Jefferson Davis Pinkard has turned in his rifle."

"Jefferson Davis Pinkard has turned in his rifle," the other officer agreed. He was also a captain, but wore a uniform of green-gray, not butternut. He lined through Pinkard's name on his copy of the list.

Yankee officers freely crossed the line between their positions and those of the CSA these days. Confederate soldiers had to obey them as they obeyed their own officers. Confederate officers, even those of higher rank, had to obey them, too. The Yanks didn't sneer or gloat, but they didn't take any nonsense, either.

One by one, in alphabetical order, the soldiers of his regiment surrendered their weapons. Hipolito Rodriguez came only a few men after Pinkard. Once he'd thrown his rifle onto the stack, he came over and stood by the big steelworker. *"Finito,"* he said.

That was close enough to *finished* for Jeff to understand it. "Yeah, it's done," he said. "It's done, and we got licked. Who the hell would have reckoned on that when we started out?"

Rodriguez shrugged. *"Así es la vida,"* he said, and then translated that: "Such is life. Now they must send us to our homes once more."

"Bully," Pinkard said in a hollow voice. He hated the west Texas prairie, no doubt about that, but he dreaded going back to Birmingham, too. What had Emily been doing since the leave when he'd walked in at just the wrong moment? Even if she hadn't been doing anything since then (which, knowing her, he found less likely than he would have wanted), could he live with her once he did get home? Or—the other side of the same coin—could he live without her?

And how was he supposed to go on living next door to Bedford Cunningham? That was a smaller question, but not a small one. They'd been best friends and foundry partners for years. But Bedford wouldn't be going back to the Sloss Works, not shy an arm he wouldn't, and how could you be friends with a man when you'd found your wife naked on her knees in front of him?

Hip Rodriguez sighed. "I hope everything goes good for you, *amigo.*"

"Thanks," Jeff said. "Same to you." Here, unlike talk about going home, he could speak freely. "I never knew any Sonorans before you. You're a good fellow. You ever get tired of trying to scratch out a living down where you're at, you bring your family on up to Alabama. Plenty of good farm country there. You'd live high on the hog."

"Thanks, *amigo,* but no thanks." Rodriguez's smile was sweet and sad. "I want to go home. I want to talk *español,* to see my friends and family. And in Sonora, I am a man. In Alabama, I am a damn greaser." He tapped a brown hand with a brown finger to remind Pinkard of what he meant.

In the trenches, Jeff had long since stopped worrying about their being of different colors. Hip was right, though; it would matter in Alabama. Jeff put the best face on it he could: "It's not like you was a nigger."

"Too close," Rodriguez said positively, and odds were he was right. "You go to your home, and I go to my home, and maybe God lets us both be happy."

The last Tredegar thudded onto the pile. The C.S. captain addressed his U.S. counterpart: "All weapons for this unit are now accounted for."

"All *rifles* for this unit are now accounted for," the U.S. officer answered sharply. "This regiment still has two machine guns outstanding."

"Destroyed in combat," the Confederate captain said blandly. "Can't give you what we haven't got."

Pinkard wouldn't have believed that from a beaten foe, and neither did the Yankee. "You're holding out on us," he growled. His sharp, quick accent made him sound suspicious even when he wasn't. When he was . . . "That's a violation of the terms of the armistice, and you'll be sorry for it. Weapons *are* to be turned over."

"I can't give you what we haven't got," the C.S. captain repeated. He waved to Jeff Pinkard and his companions. "This here is an infantry company, not a machine-gun outfit. They've turned in *their* weapons. Why don't you let them go and take the other up with division HQ?"

For a long moment, Jeff thought the U.S. officer would hold them up out of sheer cussedness, if for no other reason. In the end, though, he said, "All right, these bastards can go. But I *am* going to take it up with your superiors, Captain, and heads *will* roll. Yours among 'em, unless I miss my guess." His eyes measured the Confederate for a coffin.

What passed between the two captains afterwards, Pinkard never learned. His company was marched away to the paymaster, who gave each man what he was owed—in banknotes, not specie. He also gave a word of advice: "Don't waste your time before you spend it, on account of it won't be worth as much tomorrow as it is today."

"How come?" Jeff asked.

"Government's gonna have a devil of a time payin' its bills, especially in gold," the paymaster answered. "Yankees'll soak us till our eyes pop—you wait and see if I'm wrong. And everybody's gonna wanna buy things, and there won't be a hell of a lot of things to buy. You put that all in the pot and cook it, and you get prices going straight through the roof. Like I say, wait and see. People'll be wiping their asses with dollar banknotes, 'cause they won't be good for anything else."

With that cheery prediction ringing in his ears, Pinkard marched with the men with whom he'd been through so much toward the nearest railhead. It was, he realized, the last time he would ever march with them. He tried to sort out how he felt about that. He wouldn't miss marching, or the trenches, or the horror that went with war. The men, though, and the comradeship—those he would miss. He wondered if he would ever know their like back in Birmingham.

He kicked at the dirt. He'd thought he had that kind of comradeship with Bedford Cunningham, and what was left there? Dust and ashes, nothing more. After Bedford and Emily had let him down, could he ever trust anybody again? He wasn't going to hold his breath.

He did hold his breath when the company got to the train. Almost all the cars were boxcars stenciled with the words 36 MEN, 8 HORSES. They'd held a lot of horses lately; the stink made that plain. He clambered up into a car and made himself as comfortable as he could on none-too-fresh straw. After all the cars were filled, the train headed east. By the way the engine coughed and wheezed, it, like the boxcars, was what remained after all the better rolling stock had been used in more important places.

Nobody bothered feeding the soldiers or giving them water.

Pinkard emptied his canteen and ate the tortillas and the chunk of sausage he had with him. After that was gone, he got hungrier and hungrier and thirstier and thirstier till, some time in the middle of the night, the train pulled into Fort Worth.

He'd fallen into an uneasy, unpleasant doze by then, and woke with a start. At the station, men shouted through megaphones: "Check the signboards! Find the train heading toward your hometown and get aboard! Men in uniform travel free, this week only!"

Amid handclasps and good-luck wishes and promises to keep in touch, the company broke apart. Jeff found a signboard and discovered, to his surprise, that a train that would stop in Birmingham was leaving early in the morning. He found the right platform after a couple of false starts and settled down to wait.

He hadn't been there more than a couple of minutes before a woman came up to him and snapped, "If you men hadn't been a pack of yellow cowards, you would have whipped those damnyankees." She stomped off before he could answer. It was, he decided, a good thing he'd had to turn in his Tredegar. Otherwise, he might have answered her with a bullet.

Had he had the rifle, he might have shot eight or ten people, mostly women, by the time his train pulled up to the station. Everyone who spoke to him seemed to think he was personally responsible for losing the war. He boarded a second-class passenger car with nothing but relief. It didn't end there, though. About half the people on the car were eastbound soldiers like him. The civilians who filled the other half of the seats showered them with abuse.

And the abuse got worse the farther east the train went. Every time a soldier got off and a civilian took his place, the abuse got worse. The farther from the front the train went, the more convinced people were that the war should have been won, and won in short order, too.

One heckler, a man who had plainly never seen the war at first hand, went too far. A soldier got up, knocked him cold with one punch, and said, "We might not've licked the damnyankees, but I sure as hell licked you." After that, the rude remarks diminished, but even then they did not stop.

The train pulled into the Birmingham station just over a day after it set out from Fort Worth. No one sat close to Pinkard when he got on the trolley that would take him out to the factory housing by the Sloss Works. Maybe that was because he still wore his uniform. Maybe, too, it was because he'd had no chance to bathe since coming out of the line.

He walked from the trolley stop toward his house. He felt as if he were heading toward the doctor's, and likely to be diagnosed with a deadly disease. He tried the front door. It was locked. Emily had gone to work, though how long she'd keep her munitions-plant job was anyone's guess. He had a key in his trouser pocket—about the only thing he did have with him from when he'd gone into the Army. He let himself in. (He wouldn't get that diagnosis till she came home.)

Doing nothing much felt strange and good. He took hot water from the stove's reservoir and bathed and put on a shirt and trousers he found in the closet. They hung loosely on him; he'd lost weight. He got cold chicken out of the icebox, then read an old *Richmond Review*: so old, one of the articles talked about how to drive back the Yankees. Laughing bitterly, he tossed the magazine aside.

At last, the front door opened. Emily stared at him. "Jeff!" she exclaimed, and then, "Darling!"

Was there too much hesitation between the one word and the other? Pinkard didn't get the chance to think much about that. His wife threw herself into his arms. They tightened around her. He'd never stopped wanting her, even though . . .

He didn't get the chance to think about that, either. Her kiss made him dizzy. "Thank God you're home," she breathed in his ear. "Thank God you're safe. Everything's going to be fine now, just fine." Her voice went low and throaty. "I'll show you how fine." She led him back toward the bedroom. He went willingly, even gladly. That would do for now. Later?

"I'll just have to find out about later, that's all," Jeff muttered.

"What did you say, darling?" Emily was already getting out of her clothes.

"Never mind," he said. "It'll keep. It'll keep till later."

Sam Carsten sighed. The exhalation hurt. His lips were even more sunburned than the rest of him. They cracked and bled at any excuse or none. He'd filled out the forms for every kind of cream alleged to help; the pharmacist's mates were all sick of the sight of him. He was sick of the baked-meat sight of himself. As usual, none of the creams did the slightest good against the on-slaughts of the tropic sun.

"God damn Dom Pedro IV to hell and gone," he said. "Stinking son of a bitch should have stayed out of the war."

Vic Crosetti laughed at him. "You're more worried about your hide than you are about licking the limeys."

"Ever since the *Dakota* came up into Brazilian waters, my hide's what's been taking the licking," Carsten said. "And we haven't fought the Royal Navy or even seen more than a couple of British freighters. Waste of time, anybody wants to know what I think of the whole business."

Crosetti laughed harder than ever. "Yeah, I'm sure Admiral Fiske is gonna call you up into officers' country any second now, so he can find out what's on your mind. He couldn't've run the flotilla without you till now, right?"

"Makes sense to me," Sam said. Crosetti grimaced at him. He was about to go on when his ears caught a distant buzzing. He searched the heavens, then pointed. "That's an aeroplane. Now, God damn it, is it one of ours or one of theirs?"

"Escorts ain't shooting at it, so I guess it's one of ours," Crosetti said. "Hope to Jesus it's one of ours, anyways."

"Me too." Carsten kept watching, squinting, his eyes half shut against the bright sky, till he could make out the eagles and crossed swords under the wings of the aeroplane. He breathed easier then. "Aeroplanes," he said. "Who would have thought, when the war started, they'd matter so much?"

"Bunch of damn nuisances, is what they are," Crosetti said as this one splashed into the tropical Atlantic a few hundred yards from the *Dakota* and taxied across the water toward the battleship.

"They're sure as hell nuisances when they spot us or strafe us," Sam said. "But they couldn't do a quarter of what they're doing now back in 1914. I bet they keep right on getting better, too."

"I think everybody on the *Dakota* except maybe Admiral Fiske has listened to you go on like this," Crosetti said with ex-aggerated patience. "You like 'em so goddamn much, go and get yourself a pair of wings after the war's done."

"Don't want wings," Carsten said. "I like being a sailor just fine. But I like aeroplanes, too. Look at that, Vic—isn't that bully?" The *Dakota*'s crane was hauling the flying machine out of the water and up on deck.

Crosetti yawned. "It's boring, is what it is. I think everything about aeroplanes is boring till they start dropping bombs. Then they scare the shit out of me."

"No, that's not boring," Sam agreed. "Tell you something else, though—I'd sooner be bored."

Later that day, the *Dakota* and the flotilla with her, which had been lazing along at ten or twelve knots, suddenly changed course toward the northeast and put on speed. Carsten grunted, waiting for the klaxons to cry out the orders to battle station. One of the other aeroplanes from the flotilla must have spotted a British convoy. He looked forward to knocking it to pieces.

Then rumors started flying: rumors that it wasn't a convoy after all, but a good-sized chunk of the Royal Navy. Sam didn't like hearing that for beans. He'd fought the Royal Navy before, in the tropical Pacific, and had high respect for what the limeys could do. He'd had a lot more of the U.S. Navy sailing along beside him then, too. If they'd run up against a major British fleet, they would regret it as long as they lived, which might not be long.

When the klaxons did begin to hoot, running toward the forward starboard sponson was almost a relief. Once he started slamming shells into the breech of the five-inch gun, he'd be too busy to worry. Whatever happened after that just happened—he couldn't do anything about it.

Hiram Kidde put that same thought into words: "Now we smash 'em—or else it's the other way around."

"Yeah," Sam said. "Well, if they smash us, I hope to God we at least hurt them. We can afford the losses and they can't, not fighting us and Kaiser Bill both."

"I'll die for my country if I have to," Kidde said, "but I'd sooner live for it." He puffed out his chest. "Where the hell else are the United States going to find a better chief gunner's mate?"

"Under any flat rock, I expect," Carsten answered, which won him a glare.

Commander Grady looked into the sponson. "It is the Royal Navy," he announced. "If the flyboy who spotted them had it straight, they've got a force about the same size as ours."

"That's great," Luke Hoskins muttered. "They'll sink all of us, and we'll sink all of them. Last one standing wins."

"Why should this be any different than anything else in the war?" Sam whispered. Hoskins chuckled and shrugged.

Hiram Kidde peered through the sponson's vision slit. "I see smoke," he said, and then, "Jesus, if I see smoke from down here, the fire-control boys up at the top of the mast have been seeing it the past five minutes. And if they can see it, the big guns can hit it. Why the hell aren't they shooting?"

As if to answer his question, the klaxons wailed once more. Sam dug a finger in his ear, wondering if that ear were playing tricks on him. "Was that the all-clear?" he asked, not believing what he'd heard.

"Sure as hell was," Hoskins said.

"Why are they sounding the all-clear, though?" "Cap'n" Kidde demanded. "The enemy's in sight, for Christ's sake." He took off his cap and scratched his head. "And why the hell aren't the limeys shooting at us?"

Somebody ran shouting down the corridor. The shout held no words, only joy. Sam's brother-in-law had shouted like that when his wife, Sam's older sister, was delivered of a boy. "What the hell is going on?" he asked, though he didn't think anyone would have the answer.

But someone did. When Commander Grady came into the sponson, he looked as exalted as the other sailor had sounded. "Boys, we just got it on the wireless telegraph from Philadelphia," he said. "England has asked the Kaiser and Teddy Roosevelt for an armistice."

"It's over," Carsten whispered, hardly believing his own words. To help see if they were, if they could have been, true, he repeated them, louder this time: "It's over." Nobody called him a liar. Nobody said he was crazy. Little by little, almost in spite of himself, he began to believe.

"Maybe not quite over," Commander Grady said. "There's still the Japs, out in the Pacific. But hell, you're right, Carsten: that scrap is liable to peter out by itself. We've shot at each other, but they haven't taken anything of ours and we haven't taken anything of theirs. Shouldn't be too hard to patch up a peace."

Sam nodded. "Yes, sir. And they won't have any big reason to fight us any more, either, now that all their allies have thrown in the sponge."

"That's right." Grady nodded, too. "Matter of fact, if I were England and France, I'd worry about Hong Kong and Indochina and maybe Singapore, too. If the Japs want 'em bad enough, they'll fall into their hands like ripe fruit." He brought his mind back to the here-and-now. "And, since we have an armistice, you men are dismissed from your posts here."

"Sir, since we've won, are we going to head back to the States?" Hiram Kidde asked.

"I don't know the answer to that, not yet," Grady replied. "I hope so, but that's just me talking, not Admiral Fiske or Philadelphia. Go on up topside, boys. Take a look at the limeys we didn't have to fight."

For once, Carsten was glad to go up on deck: the glow of victory, the glow of peace ahead, made him forget about the glow of sunburn. Shading his eyes with a hand, he peered across the Atlantic at the Royal Navy force whose government had finally had to yield. The longer he looked, the gladder he was that the wireless telegraph had brought word when it had. The enemy force looked large and formidable.

In an odd way, he felt sorry for the Englishmen aboard those warships. They'd been top dogs for a hundred years and then some. Coming back to the pack would hurt them a lot. He wondered who the top dog was now: the United States or Germany? He looked east, toward Europe. Wouldn't that be an interesting fight?

He shrugged. However interesting it was, he didn't think it would happen any time soon. Teddy Roosevelt and the Kaiser had just won a war together. They'd take a while to pick up the pieces afterwards. Maybe they'd even stay friends while they were doing it. He hoped so.

One by one, the Royal Navy ships turned away from the U.S.-Chilean-Brazilian flotilla and steamed off toward the northeast, toward Britain. Sam wondered what would happen to them there. Would the limeys get to keep them, or would they have to surrender them to Germany and the USA? That wasn't for him to decide; the boys in striped trousers would have to sort it out.

A U.S. cruiser with the flotilla launched its aeroplane to shadow the British ships. That must have been allowed under the terms of the armistice, because nobody started shooting.

U.S. aeroplanes could have tracked the British ships at the outbreak of the war, too, but neither they nor their wireless sets could have reached as far as they did now. Sam had had that same thought not long before, when he'd spotted the *Dakota*'s aeroplane before it landed by the battleship. Now, reminded of it in a different context, he muttered, "I wish that flying machine could follow those bastards all the way back to London."

He didn't notice Commander Grady standing behind him, also watching the Royal Navy force withdraw. "That would be pretty fine, wouldn't it, Carsten?" the commander of the starboard secondary armament said.

"Huh?" Sam spun around, startled. "Uh, yes, sir." He made himself think straight. "I expect the day is coming when they'll be able to do just that. I expect it's coming sooner than most people think, too."

Grady studied him. "I expect you're right. If we don't do it, some other navy will, and they'll do it to us." He rubbed his chin. "Matter of fact, I happen to know we are doing something along those lines. Would you by any chance be interested in becoming part of that?"

"Would I?" Sam said. "Yes, sir! Hell yes, sir! Where do I sign up?"

"You don't, not yet," Grady answered. "But you're a sharp fellow—sharper than you let on sometimes, I think. When we get into port in the United States, you remind me about this. I think the effort could use you."

"Thank you very much, sir," Carsten said. Part of that was real gratitude—he'd been talking about doing something like this. Part of it, too, was prudent calculation. Even if the Navy did shrink after the war, they wouldn't drop him on the beach if he was part of this new project. Having a job he was sure of wasn't the worst thing in the world—no, not even close.

"Bartlett, Reginald, Confederate States Army, private first class," Reggie Bartlett said to the paymaster in U.S. green-gray. He rattled off his pay number and the date of his capture.

The paymaster found his name, checked both the pay number and the date of capture against his own records, and lined through them. He gave Reggie a sheaf of green banknotes— bills, the Yankees called them—and some pocket change. "Here is the pay owed you under the Geneva Convention, Private First Class Bartlett," he said. "Frankly, between you, me, and the wall, you're damn lucky to get it in greenbacks instead of your own money. These will still be worth something six months from now. God only knows if the Confederate dollar will."

Reggie grunted. From things he'd heard, the paymaster was likely to be right. He put the money into a pocket of the butternut trousers the U.S. authorities had given him—along with a matching tunic—to wear on the train ride back to Richmond, where all released Confederate prisoners were being shipped. Neither color nor cut was quite that of a C.S. uniform, but both were close.

His shoulder ached when he bent his arm to put the money in his pocket, but not too badly. A Yankee doctor had given him chloroform and then gone in there and drained an abscess that refused to clear up on its own. Now the wound really was healing. For a long time, he'd wondered if it ever would.

He could walk with only a bare trace of a limp, too, and his leg hardly bothered him at all. Put everything together and the damnyankees had treated him pretty well. Of course, they were also the ones who'd shot him. Given a choice, he would sooner not have been shot. Then he wouldn't have had to worry about how the damnyankees treated him. But who ever gave a soldier a choice?

Here came Rehoboam, on two sticks and an artificial foot. The Negro prisoner made slow but steady progress toward the paymaster. With nothing better to do, Reggie waited till he too got paid off, then asked, "What are you going to do when you get back to Mississippi?"

"I be goddamned if I know," Rehoboam answered. "Ain't no use in the cotton fields no more. Ain't no good on any kind o' farm no more. Reckon I got to go to town, but I be goddamned if I know what the hell I do there, neither."

"You have your letters," Bartlett said. "I've seen that. It's something."

"It ain't much," Rehoboam said with a scornful toss of his head. "Ain't like I'm gonna put on no necktie and sit behind no desk at the bank and loan the white folks money. Ain't gonna be no doctor. Ain't gonna be no lawyer or preacher. Ain't gonna be no newspaperman, neither. So what the hell good my letters do me?"

"If you didn't have 'em, how could you read all the lies the Reds tell?" Reggie asked innocently.

Rehoboam started to give him a straight answer. Then the black man started to get angry. And then, grudgingly, he started to laugh. "You ain't no stupid white man," he said at last. "Wish to Jesus you was."

"Stupid enough to get shot," Reggie said. "You come right down to it, how can anybody get any stupider than that?"

"You in one piece," Rehoboam said. "I ain't gonna see my foot again till Judgment Day, and I don't believe in Judgment Day no more."

"You *are* a damned Red," Bartlett said. He meant *damned* in a more literal way than he was in the habit of using it. He didn't think of himself as all that pious, but he'd gone to church on Sunday back in Richmond. Hearing Rehoboam casually deny the Last Judgment rocked him.

"Reckon bein' a Red is more dangerous'n the other," the Negro answered. "But if the damn gummint ain't cheatin' me, I'm gonna be a citizen, like you been sayin', so I reckon I can think any kind o' damnfool thing I like, an' say so, too. That's what bein' a citizen's about, ain't it?"

"I suppose so." Reggie hadn't thought that much about it. He hadn't needed to think much about it. Citizenship was natural to him as water to a fish, and so he took it altogether for granted. Whatever else Rehoboam did, he wouldn't do that.

A military policeman in green-gray came up. "You Rebs been paid off?" he asked. When they didn't deny it, he jerked a thumb toward a doorway at the end of the hall. "Shake a leg, then. Trucks to take you to the train station are right through there. You think we'll be sorry to get you off our hands, you're crazy."

As the two men from the CSA made their way toward the door—they could hardly shake a leg—Bartlett spoke in a sly voice: "See? He treats you just like me—far as he's concerned, we're both scum."

"I'm used to white folks what reckon I'm scum," Rehoboam said after a moment. "How about you?"

Outside, Reggie proved he wasn't used to it. Thinking to be helpful, he asked a Yankee guard, "Which one of these trucks is for the coloreds?"

"We ain't bothering with any of that shit here," the U.S. soldier answered. "You and Snowball look like you're pals. You can sit together."

Reggie had to help Rehoboam up into the back of the truck. Conscious of the Negro's eye on him, he said not a word as they sat down side by side. None of the other freed prisoners—all of them white—already in the truck said anything, either.

Most places in the USA, Negroes—a relative handful, not close to a third of the population as they were in the CSA—had to take a back seat to whites, as they did in the Confederacy. Bartlett figured the damnyankees were piling one last humiliation on his comrades and him. He also figured he would survive it—and that he would catch hell if he complained about it. That made keeping quiet look like a smart idea.

The Yankees also made no distinction between white and black C.S. prisoners on the train that set out from Missouri toward Richmond. Reggie and Rehoboam ended up sitting side by side in a crowded, beat-up coach. Bartlett resigned himself to that, too, and told himself it wouldn't be so bad. They knew each other, anyhow; after weeks of lying across the aisle from each other, they couldn't help it.

Until it crossed into Virginia, the train stayed in territory that had belonged to the USA before the war began. Reggie stared out through the dirty window glass at countryside Confederate soldiers hadn't been able to reach or damage. Here and there, in Cincinnati and a couple of other towns, he did see craters and wrecked buildings that had taken bomb hits, but not till the train got into central Pennsylvania, more than a day after it set out, did the landscape take on the lunar quality with which he'd grown so unpleasantly familiar.

"We fought like hell here," he remarked to Rehoboam.

"Reckon we did," the Negro answered, "or you white folks did, anyways. Yankees licked you just the same."

Bartlett sighed; he could hardly argue with that. He did say, "We might have done better if you Red niggers hadn't jumped on our backs while we were fighting the USA."

"Mebbe," Rehoboam said. "You might've did better if you didn't go an' make all the black folks in the country hate you like pizen, too."

Since that held only too much truth, Reggie forbore from replying. He kept looking out the window. Maryland seemed just like Pennsylvania, a hell of wreckage and shell craters and forests smashed to toothpicks. The smell of death was fresher there, and filled the train. And when he rolled through Washington, D.C., he stared and stared. The whole city was a field of rubble, with most of the buildings knocked flat and then pounded to pieces. The stub of the Washington Monument stuck up from the desolation all around like a broken tooth in a mouth otherwise empty.

Rehoboam gaped at what was left of Washington, too. "Didn't see nothin' like this here in Arkansas," he allowed. "This here, this is a hell of a mess."

"Didn't see anything like this in Sequoyah, either," Bartlett said. "But in the Roanoke valley, especially around Big Lick—we saw plenty of it there. Too many men smashed together into too small a space, with no room for anybody to give way, that's what does it. Over across the Mississippi, the fighting didn't get this crowded. The Yankees and us had more room to move."

"When we was fightin' to keep 'em away from Memphis, it got plenty bad, but not like this," Rehoboam said. "No, ain't never seen nothin' like this."

After the train crossed the Potomac on a pontoon bridge and went into Virginia, Reggie expected the devastation to be even worse than it had been in Yankee country. For the most part, it wasn't. It was fresher, but not worse. After a little while, he thought he understood why: by the time the fighting moved down into Virginia, U.S. forces had gained such a preponderance over those of the CSA that the Army of Northern Virginia had to give ground before it and everything around it were pounded completely flat. A war of movement didn't tear up the landscape so badly as one of position.

And then, as soon as the train got south of the reach of U.S. guns, the countryside was the one Reggie had always known, with only an occasional bomb crater to remind him of the war. Coming into Richmond, though, brought it home once more. U.S. aeroplanes had done their worst to the capital of the Confederate States. Richmond was in better shape than Washington, but it wouldn't win prizes any time soon.

"Check the signboards for trains going toward your home towns!" railroad officials—or perhaps they were government functionaries—shouted.

To his own surprise, Reggie reached out to shake Rehoboam's hand. The Negro took the offered hand, looking a little surprised himself. "Good luck to you," Reggie said. "I don't care if you *are* a Red, or not too much. Good luck."

"Same to you," Rehoboam said. "You ain't the worst white man I ever run acrost." He made that sound like high praise.

They got off the train together. Rehoboam slowly headed toward a platform from which a train would leave for Mississippi. He didn't need to hurry; it wasn't scheduled to head out for another six hours, and might well run late. Bartlett left the station. He would have to stay in his parents' home till he found work.

A taxi driver hailed him: "Hey, pal, take you anywhere in town for three beans. Won't find anybody cheaper."

"Three *dollars*?" Reggie stared at him as if he'd started talking Hindustani. The paymaster back at the hospital had known what he was talking about. Bartlett's hand went into his pocket and closed on a coin. "I'll give you a quarter, U.S."

"Deal," the driver said at once.

Reggie wondered if he'd offered too much. By the way the cabbie bounced out of the motorcar—a Birmingham that had seen better days—and held the door open for him, he probably had. He clicked his tongue between his teeth. No help for it now. He gave the driver his parents' address.

"Hope you didn't get hurt too bad," the cab driver said, evidently recognizing the kind of clothes Bartlett had on. Reggie only grunted by way of reply. Not a bit put out, the driver asked, "What'll you do now that you're home?"

"Damned if I know," Reggie said. "Try and find my life again, I reckon." By the way the cabbie nodded, he'd heard that answer plenty of times already.

Colonel Irving Morrell scrambled down into the Confederate works that would have defended Murfreesboro, Tennessee. Without soldiers in them, the trenches seemed unreal, unnatural. Before the armistice, Morrell would have had to pay in blood, and pay high, for the privilege of examining them. Now he had Colonel Harley Landis, CSA, as his personal guide.

Not that Landis was delighted with the job. "If I had my choice, Colonel," he said, "the only excavation of ours I'd show you would be six feet by three feet by six feet deep." He raised an eyebrow. "Nothing personal, of course."

"Of course," Morrell agreed with a dry chuckle. "Believe me, if you were going through our trenches outside Chicago, I'd feel the same way."

"Chicago?" The Confederate officer snorted ruefully. "In my

dreams, maybe. You have the stronger power. We aimed at nothing more than defending ourselves."

Now Morrell was the one to arch his brows. "Aimed at Philadelphia, you mean. Aimed at Kansas, too, for that matter, and Missouri. Talk straight, Colonel, if you don't mind. This poor-little-us business wears thin after the War of Secession and the Second Mexican War."

Colonel Landis stared at him. "But surely you can see . . ." He checked himself, then shook his head. "Maybe not—who knows? But if you can't, the world must seem a very strange place from the Yankee side of the hill."

"Looking at the world from the other fellow's side of the hill is always a useful exercise." Morrell regretted the words as soon as they were out of his mouth. Landis was an enemy—Landis was *the* enemy. If he hadn't figured that out for himself, why hand it to him?

Fortunately, his thoughts seemed to be elsewhere. "All we've tried to do is hold you back a little and keep up with you ourselves. You Yankees have got to be the *pushingest* people in the whole wide world."

"Thank you," Morrell said, which made his Confederate counterpart's mouth twist: Landis hadn't meant that as a compliment. Morrell held his smile inside. Too bad.

He took his own advice, climbing up onto a firing step that was already starting to crumble and peering toward the northwest. If he'd been a C.S. officer defending this position against a whole great swarm of barrels, what would he have done? His first thought was, *turn tail and run like hell.*

Say what you would about the Rebels, he could count on the fingers of one hand the times they'd done anything like that. He turned and looked back over his shoulder, studying the earthworks he hadn't yet explored in person. After perhaps half a minute of contemplation, he grunted softly. "You'd have mounted your guns up there," he said, pointing, "and fired at us over open sights, or as near as makes no difference. I don't know how many barrels you had left at the end, but you'd have put them behind that little swell of ground there"—he pointed again—"to keep us from spotting them for as long as you could."

Harley Landis examined him the same way he'd examined the terrain. The C.S. colonel started to say something, stopped, and started again after a pause: "Has anyone ever told you, sir, that you may be too damn smart for your own good?"

"A whole raft of people, Colonel Landis," Morrell answered cheerfully. "Once or twice, they've even been right." He remembered all too well his own temporary eclipse after the Mormon rebels in Utah had hurt in a way he hadn't anticipated the U.S. troops battling to put them down.

"Only once or twice?" Landis was still eyeing him in speculative fashion. "Well, maybe I'm not too surprised." He took a look at the ground, too, then asked, "How do you think we would have done?"

"You'd have hurt us," Morrell said. "No doubt about that, Colonel, not a bit. You'd have hurt us—but we would have got through. You couldn't have had enough barrels to stop us."

He waited for Landis' irate disagreement. But the Confederate colonel had been the man who brought his commander's request for a cease-fire through the U.S. lines. As well as anyone could, he knew how things stood with his army. He looked as if he'd bitten into something sour. "You're likely right, dammit, but how I wish you weren't."

He got out a pack of Raleighs, scraped a match on the sole of his boot, and lit a cigarette. "Can I steal one of those from you?" Morrell asked eagerly. "You wouldn't believe some of the dried horse manure that passes for tobacco in the United States these days."

"Yes, I would," Landis said. "When we'd capture Yankees, the men'd always let 'em keep their smokes. Here, keep the whole pack."

He tossed it to Morrell. The U.S. officer tapped a cigarette against the palm of his hand, then leaned forward to get a light from Landis. He sucked the fragrant smoke deep into his lungs. At last, reluctantly, he exhaled. "Thank you, Colonel. That is the straight goods. You Rebels make better smokes than we do, and that's the truth."

Landis sighed. "I'd trade that for being somewhere up in Illinois right now, the way you said before."

Morrell nodded as he took another drag. "I haven't tasted tobacco like this in years, though. It's bully stuff." He walked rapidly along the firebay till he came to a communications trench. Then, Colonel Landis in his wake, he zigzagged back until he could inspect the gun position he'd spotted from the front line. He nodded to himself. Field guns there would have done some damage, but not enough to stop a major assault.

He found a question for Landis: "What's your opinion of our barrels as compared to your—you usually call them tanks, don't you?"

"These days, we say *barrels* more often, too," Harley Landis answered. "My opinion? My opinion is that you had too damned many of them, no matter what name you care to use." Past that, he declined to say anything. Morrell hadn't expected him to say much, but had hoped.

To prod the Confederate a little more, Morrell said, "We'll probably confiscate the ones you do have, you know, and do our damnedest to make sure you don't build any more of them."

Colonel Landis muttered something under his breath: "Chicken thieves." Morrell needed a few seconds to understand it. When he did, he thought it wiser to pretend he hadn't.

He did say, "If England and France and Russia had smashed Germany in a hurry and then helped you turn on us, I don't think you'd have given us a big kiss when the war was over."

"No, I reckon not," Landis admitted, which made Morrell like him better, or at least respect him more. He went on, "But that's the way things were supposed to work out, and they didn't." His chuckle had barbs. "I know you're not thinking the same thing I am here."

"No, not quite," Morrell said. They both laughed then, a couple of professionals who understood each other even though they stood on opposite sides of the hill.

"Ask you something?" Landis said.

"You can ask," Morrell said. "I don't promise to answer."

"Here—I'll ply you with liquor first." Colonel Landis took a flask from his belt. To show Morrell it was safe, he drank first. Morrell took a swig. He'd expected moonshine, or at best its more dignified cousin, bourbon. What he got was a mouthful of damn fine cognac.

"You are a man of parts, sir," he said, bowing a little. "First the cigarettes, now this. Ask away. I'm putty in your hands."

Landis' snort had a skeptical ring. He put the question even so: "Suppose the war had gone on, and you did break through here. What would you have done next?"

"I'm not in command of First Army," Morrell said, which was true but also disingenuous, considering the victories he'd helped design. He took another small sip of Landis' brandy and added, "General Custer was talking about an advance to the Tennessee, though, if you must know." He handed the flask back to the Confederate colonel.

Landis almost dropped it. "To the Tennessee?" His splutters had nothing to do with the second swig of cognac he took. "When were you planning on getting there, 1925? The Tennessee! The very idea! We were down, by God, but we weren't out."

"I think he—we—might have done it," Morrell said. "Not a lot of natural barriers in the way, anyhow. And how many divisions of colored troops did you have in the line when the shooting stopped?"

"If you don't know, Colonel, I'll be damned if I'm going to tell you," Harley Landis answered. "I will tell you this, though: they fought about as well as the new white units we were raising toward the end there."

"Of course you'll tell me that and not the other—it makes you look stronger," Morrell said. Landis nodded, unembarrassed. On the whole, though, the U.S. officer thought his C.S. opposite number was right. From what he'd seen and from reports he'd read, Confederate black units *had* fought about as well as rookie Confederate white units. That surprised him, but a man who couldn't see truth when it tried to shoot him wouldn't live long, and didn't deserve to. He asked, "Now that the war is over"— politer than saying, *now that you've lost*—"are you folks going to keep on raising Negro troops?"

"I don't know the answer to that," Colonel Landis answered. "We didn't conscript niggers, the way we did with our own people. What we got were volunteers, and probably a better crop than we would have had if we'd scraped the bottom of the barrel." He sent Morrell a hooded glance. "Other side of that coin is, there are so goddamn *many* of you Yankees."

Morrell's smile was bright and friendly—if you didn't look too close. "Maybe you'll think about that a little harder before you decide whether you'll try picking a fight with us."

"Picking a fight with you?" Landis shook his head. "No, sir. Teddy Roosevelt declared war on us, not the other way around."

"After Wilson declared war on our allies," Morrell said.

"We honored our commitments," Landis said.

"So did we," Morrell returned. They glared at each other.

Then Morrell laughed, a sound more of bemusement than anything else. "And look what honoring our commitments got us. Better—no, worse—than a million dead on our side, likely not far from that for you, and even more wounded, and all the wreckage . . . They shouldn't let civilians start wars, Colonel, because they don't know what the hell they're getting into and getting their countries into."

"You may be a damnyankee, but I'm damned if I think you're wrong," Landis said.

"This must never happen again," Irving Morrell said solemnly. "Never."

"Never," Colonel Landis said. "Never, by God." He took the flask off his belt again. "To peace." He drank and offered it to Morrell.

"Thank you, sir." Morrell drank, too. "To peace."

XX

Jake Featherston slouched down the dirt road toward Richmond at a pace that would have made him scream curses at any soldier using it. No one would scream curses at him, not now. He still wore his uniform, but he wasn't a soldier any more. Along with most of the rest of the Army of Northern Virginia, he'd been mustered out and paid off and sent on his way with a pat on the head.

"Threw me out," he snarled under his breath. "Threw us all out, so the War Department wouldn't have to fret itself about feedin' us or payin' us any more. Payin' us!" He snorted and slapped a pocket. Paper inside crinkled. They'd paid him off in banknotes, not real money. He wondered how far the notes would go when he tried spending them. Not far enough. He was already sure of that.

Dust rose from the pocket when he slapped it. A lot of paid-off soldiers—no, ex-soldiers—were on the road. Every time he took a step, dust kicked up from under his battered boots. Any time any of them took a step, dust kicked up. Thousands of men, millions of steps, a hell of a lot of dust.

"You'd think they'd want to keep a good artilleryman in the Army," he muttered. He'd been plenty good enough to command a battery. But he hadn't been good enough—no, the War Department hadn't thought he was good enough—to get promoted past sergeant, or good enough to keep, either. "Well, to hell with Jeb Stuart, Jr. He can go down there and toast his toes with Jeb Stuart III."

A Negro soldier trudging along the same road turned his head at the sound of Featherston's voice. Jake stared unwinkingly back at him. In the days before things had gone to hell in the CSA, a couple of seconds of that look from a white man would have been plenty to make any black buck lower his eyes. Now the Negro, a big, burly fellow, tried to stare him down.

It didn't work. Featherston might have been on the wiry side, but rage had kept him going during the war, and that rage hadn't got any smaller now that the war was lost. It blazed out of him now, almost tangibly, and the colored soldier flinched away from it. Jake laughed. Instead of trying to start a fight, the Negro flinched again. "Do Jesus!" he said softly, and let Featherston pass.

That night, Featherston slept by the side of the road wrapped in a blanket, as he had slept by a lot of different roads in several blankets during the war. He had turned in his pistol when he was paid off. Again, no: he had turned in *a* pistol when he was paid off. He took *his* pistol out of his pack and set it where he could grab it in a hurry. The precaution proved needless; he slept undisturbed.

When morning woke him, he started walking again. He took the fifty-five miles from Fredericksburg to Richmond in three medium-easy days, not the two harsh ones he would have used if still in the Army. That meant he got into the Confederate capital this side of exhausted but empty as a cave: the men who'd moved faster had got what food there was on the road.

Richmond was full of dirty scarecrows in butternut. The gray-uniformed police seemed to have not a clue about what to do with so many men odds-on to be tougher and shorter-tempered than they were. The best answer they found was, *as little as we possibly can*. That struck Jake as showing better sense than he expected from police.

He went into a saloon to take advantage of its free-lunch spread. The meal—ham and deviled eggs and pickles and salted peanuts and other thirst-inducers—was indeed free, but the mug of beer he had to buy to avail himself of it set him back a dollar, not the prewar five cents. "Christ!" he exclaimed.

"I'll take fifteen cents in silver, if you've got that," the barkeep said. "Hell, I'll take a dime. It's just as well the banknotes are already brown, on account of that's what people will be using them for."

"Don't have enough silver to want to spend it quick," Featherston said. "If a beer is a bean, what do I have to pay for a bed?"

"Paper? Five easy, and the bugs'll carry your mattress in for you, you get anything that cheap," the fat man in the black apron answered. "Why didn't you bastards win the war instead of laying down for the damnyankees? Then they'd have to pay—"

Featherston reached across the bar and grabbed a handful of the white shirt showing above the apron. "You don't ever want to say anything like that again, you hear me?" When the bartender didn't say anything, he shook him, lifting his feet off the floor with no particular effort. "You hear me?"

"I hear you," the fat man wheezed. Jake set him down on the floor. He went on, "Drink your beer and get the hell out of here."

"I will," Featherston said. "You ain't crowded here. And while I'm drinking it, you keep both hands where I can see 'em, hear? You try hauling out whatever kind of persuader you got under the bar there, I promise you won't like what happens after that."

He took his time finishing the beer, then turned and walked toward the door. He hadn't gone three paces before the bartender shouted, "Don't even breathe, soldier boy!"

Featherston looked back over his shoulder and found himself staring down the barrels of a sawed-off shotgun. After gas and machine guns and Yankee traveling forts, that was not so much of a much. If the bastard did pull the triggers, it would be over in a hurry, anyway. "Fuck you," Jake said, and kept walking.

No blast of shot tore into his back. He stood on the street for a few seconds. Five dollars for a flophouse bed? He shook his head and made for Capitol Square. Sleeping in the park was free. Maybe a congressman or a senator would come by and see what the aftermath of war looked like.

He was not the only soldier in Capitol Square—far from it. As evening fell, several campfires started flickering. That was probably against the rules, but no policemen came in to do anything about it. Jake saw them on the sidewalk and clustered around the bomb-scarred Capitol. "Cowardly bastards," he muttered.

"Wish they *would* try and break us up," another ragged veteran said. "Look at 'em there, fat and happy. Nobody who ain't been through what we been through can know what it's like, but we'd give 'em a taste, goddamn if we wouldn't."

"That's right, by Jesus," Featherston said. "Wonder who their pappies were, so they didn't have to put on a real uniform."

"Amen," the other soldier said. "You can sing that in my church any old day." He stuck out a hand. "Name's Ted Weston. I'm in the 22nd North Carolina Infantry—or I was, anyways."

"I'm Jake Featherston, First Richmond Howitzers."

"I've heard of that outfit," Weston said. "Pretty la-de-da, ain't they? You might could have had a pappy of your own, get into a unit like that."

"Hell I did," Jake growled. "I was good at what I did, is all. Good enough to lead a battery for a year and a half, but not good enough to take the stripes off my sleeve and put a bar or two on my collar. La-de-da, my ass—hadn't been for a la-de-da officer with a fancy pa gettin' hisself killed . . . ahh, the hell with it." He spat in disgust.

Weston eyed him in the dim, flickering light; they weren't close to a fire. "Sounds like you got a powerful load of angry rilin' your belly, Jake."

"Oh, a touch," Featherston allowed. "Just a touch. Don't get me started, or I'll sick it all up." He waited to see if Weston would ask him more. He would have brought it all out; he might even have purged himself of some of it. But the infantryman from North Carolina shrugged and moved away.

Nobody gives a damn, Featherston thought. *Nobody.* He went away himself, to the base of the great statue of Albert Sidney Johnston, the Confederacy's chief martyr during the War of Secession. The war now ended had martyrs in plenty, but he didn't think he would see statues to them any time soon. He wrapped himself in his blanket and went to sleep.

When morning came, he found a cheap café, the saloons not yet being open. Ham and eggs and biscuits and coffee cost him two dollars he could not afford. He fumed at the price, as he fumed at everything these days. And then he spotted a couple of neatly turned-out sentries in front of a building at the southwestern corner of Capitol Square. Those sentries drew him as a lodestone draws nails. Sure enough, that was the War Department building, the source, as he saw it, of all his miseries and all his country's miseries as well.

One of the sentries wrinkled his nose as Featherston approached. He turned his head and spoke to his comrade: "Dogs find more rubbish to drag out these days."

Jake didn't think he was meant to hear that, but hear it he did, artilleryman's battered ears or not. "You can kiss my ass, too, pal," he said, and started past the spit-and-polish boys into the War Department.

The one who'd spoken swung his rifle down horizontally to

block his way. "Where do you think you're going, buddy?" he demanded. "State your business."

"Kiss my ass," Jake repeated. "I'm a citizen of this country, and I'm a real soldier, too, goddammit. I'd rather smell the way I do than be a perfumed pansy in a uniform that never once saw dirt. Now get the hell out of my way. I aim to have me a word or two to say to the bonehead generals who cost us this war."

"I don't think so, sonny boy," the sentry said. "They've got better things to do with their time than listen to—and smell—the likes of you."

"Like hell they do," Featherston said. "I want to tell you—" Without a single telltale motion or glance, he kicked the sentry in the crotch, then whirled and coldcocked his chum while the other man was just beginning to raise his rifle. The only difference between them was that the first went down with a groan, the second silently.

Whistling, Jake started to walk by them and into the War Department. Then, reluctantly, he checked himself. He'd get caught in there. He was liable to get caught out here; a couple of men were coming across the street toward him.

He did what they must have expected least—he charged straight at them. Neither of them cared to try tackling him. They were middle-aged and prosperous and no doubt thought anyone who did anything out of line would politely wait around for the police afterwards. He taught them otherwise in a hurry. Then he was back in Capitol Square, one discharged soldier among hundreds. How were they supposed to find him after that?

They couldn't. They didn't. They didn't even try, and the sentries, who'd got a better look at him, were in no condition to help. He stopped running and started sauntering, looking like any of the rest of the men in the square who had more time on their hands than they knew what to do with.

At least one of those soldiers had seen what he'd done. As he strolled past, the fellow said, "Damn shame you couldn't give that bastard Semmes a good shot in the nuts, too."

"You'd best believe it's a damn shame," Jake said. "One of these days, though, if this poor, miserable country ever gets back on its feet again, we'll pay back everybody who ever did us wrong—and I mean everybody."

"Hope that day comes soon," the other veteran said. "Can't come soon enough, if anybody wants to know what I think."

"I don't know when," Featherston said. "We'll have to go some to put our own house in order, I reckon. But we'll walk tall again one of these days, and then—and then everybody better look out, that's all." The other soldier clapped his hands.

Not even a funeral. Sylvia Enos thought that was worst of all. When scarlet fever took her mother, when her brother died in a trainwreck, there had been an end to things, dirt thudding down on the lid of a coffin, and then a wake afterwards. Once that was done, people had been able to pick up the threads of their lives and go on.

But fish and crabs and whatever lived at the bottom of the sea in the middle of the Atlantic were giving George the only burial he would ever get. Fishermen shuddered when they talked of things like that. Along with all his friends, George had hated the idea of going down at sea. Sylvia knew men who wouldn't eat crab or lobster because of what the shellfish might have been eating.

She stirred the dress she'd thrown in the kettle full of black dye. It would be ready pretty soon. She'd used a good deal of coal heating water to dye clothes for mourning; that was cheaper than buying new black dresses and shirtwaists. She hoped the Coal Board wouldn't cut the ration yet again, though.

Mary Jane came into the kitchen and said, "I want to go out and play."

"Go on, then," Sylvia said with a sigh. Mary Jane wasn't really mourning; how could she mourn a man she scarcely remembered? She knew Sylvia was upset, but had trouble understanding why. George, Jr., had known his father well enough to miss him, but he was also far less wounded than he would have been had George come home every night. School seemed far more real and far more urgent to him than a father long at sea.

Sylvia wished she felt the same way. Now that George was gone, she found herself far more forgiving of his flaws than she had been while he was alive. She even—almost—wished he'd gone to bed with that colored strumpet, to give him one more happy memory to hold on to when the torpedo slammed into the *Ericsson*.

"Not fair," she muttered, stirring again. The Confederacy had already dropped out of the war, and England had been on the point of giving up. Why, how, had a British submersible chosen her husband's ship in those waning moments of the war? Where was the sense in that?

George hadn't even mentioned British submersibles to her. All he'd ever written about were Confederate boats. Why had the Royal Navy decided to move one of theirs into that part of the ocean?

She didn't suppose questions like that had any answers. A minister would have called it God's will. As far as she was concerned, that wasn't any answer, either. Why had God decided to take everybody on board the *Ericsson*? Because her husband had wanted to screw a whore? If God started taking every man who'd ever wanted to do that, men would get thin on the ground mighty quick.

Men *had* got thin on the ground. So many women wore mourning these days, or had worn it and were now returning to less somber wear. Sylvia looked at the alarm clock, which she'd brought out of the bedroom. The dress had been in the kettle long enough. Sylvia carried the kettle over to the sink and poured out the water in which she'd dyed the dress. Then she wrung the dress as dry as she could and set it on a hanger to finish drying. That done, she scrubbed at her hands with floor soap to clean the dye from her knuckles and around and under her nails.

She was just drying her hands—and noting that she hadn't got rid of all the dye—when someone knocked on the door. Her mouth twisted bitterly as she went to open it. She'd already had the worst news she could get. Opening the door held no terror for her now.

Brigid Coneval stood in the hallway. The Irishwoman still wore black for her own dead husband. "And how is it today, Sylvia?" she asked. Where nothing else had, their common loss left them on a first-name basis. They understood each other in a way no one who had not shared that loss ever could.

"It's . . . about the same as always," Sylvia said. She stepped aside. "Come in, why don't you?"

"Don't mind if I do," Brigid said. She nodded when she saw the big kettle sticking up out of the kitchen sink, which was not very deep, and smelled the acrid odor of the dye still hanging in the air. "Och, I did enough of that and to spare, so I did."

"As long as I'm doing things, I don't have to worry about what happened," Sylvia said. "And so I keep finding things to do." She waved a hand. "This place has never been so clean."

"My flat'll never be clean, I'm thinking, but then I'm after having three boys," Brigid Coneval said. "But I do know what you're saying, indeed and I do. In bed of nights, I keep thinking *What if he'd stopped to piss?* or *What if he'd fallen down before that damned bullet came by?* or—or I don't know what, but anything to make it different than it was."

"Anything to make it different," Sylvia echoed. "Oh, Christ, yes. What was that stinking English submarine doing where there hadn't been any English submarines? It had no *business* being in that part of the ocean. The Confederates had already given up, and—"

"It does no good—dwelling on it, I mean," Brigid broke in.

"I know that. Sometimes I can't help it, though," Sylvia said. "Sometimes even when I'm working . . . I was thinking about that *damned* submarine"—she brought out the word not casually, as her friend had done, but with savage relish—"even while I was dyeing my dress."

"It does no good," Brigid Coneval repeated. "Well, the truth is, there's not a thing that does any good, but there is a thing, sure and there is, that keeps you from thinking so much about it." She opened her handbag and pulled out a flat pint bottle of whiskey.

Sylvia got up, went over to the cabinet by the kitchen sink, and brought back a couple of glasses. She watched as the coppery liquid gurgled into them. She didn't drink that much or that often, not least because whiskey tasted like medicine to her. But Brigid was right—whiskey *was* medicine here, because it kept her from thinking clearly when clear thought was the last thing she wanted.

"Ahh!" Brigid smacked her lips and poured another shot into her glass. She thrust the pint toward Sylvia, who shook her head. Brigid Coneval shrugged and drank. She wasn't shy about whiskey: on the contrary.

George, Jr., came in. "Hello, Mrs. Coneval," he said.

"And hello to you," she answered with an extravagant gesture that almost sloshed the refill out of her glass. "What a fine, polite boy y'are."

The fine, polite boy had a new bruise on his cheek, very possibly gained by roughhousing with one of Brigid Coneval's sons. He wrinkled his nose and said, "That dye stinks, Ma."

"I know it does," Sylvia answered. "It can't be helped, though." She looked toward the clock. "Go find your sister and tell her to come in. It's later than I thought. I'll feed the two of you and get you ready for bed. I have to go back to work tomorrow, and you're going back to school."

"All right," he said, and hurried away. He liked the idea of going back to school. Sylvia wondered where he came by that. School had always bored her to tears, and George had never been any sort of scholar, either.

"A good boy. A fine boy." The whiskey made Brigid Coneval even more emphatic than she would have been without it. She got to her feet. "You tend to your wee ones, now. I'll have to be laying hold of mine before long, too." Sylvia also rose. The two women hugged each other. Brigid left, heading back to her apartment with great determination.

Mary Jane was mutinous when she came back with her big brother. "Did you really tell him I had to go in?" she demanded of Sylvia, and looked surprised and disappointed when her mother nodded. Not even fried scrod for supper did much to cheer her up; she seemed convinced Sylvia had betrayed her.

Nor was she enthusiastic about going to Mrs. Dooley's the next morning. Once Sylvia warmed her bottom for her, she moved well enough. George, Jr., got off the trolley and bounded toward his school. He'd grown tired of being cooped up at home.

At the shoe factory, everyone greeted Sylvia with a warm show of sympathy. Gustav Krafft, the foreman, was a man of few words. Even he was kind. "From your fellow workers," he said as he handed her an envelope. It not only crinkled, but also clinked.

"Thank you so much," Sylvia said. "Thank you all so much." Money could do only so much, but she was glad to have it. No one could do much without it. Eventually, she would get a payment from the government, but God only knew how long that would take. If the Coal Board was any indication, it might take forever.

"You poor dear," Emma Kilgore said. "Jack's coming home, thank the sweet Lord, but I know how you got to feel, Sylvia, sweetheart. If it was me, I'd be out of my mind."

"I feel like I am, sometimes," Sylvia answered. The redheaded woman at the sewing machine next to her did not know how she felt, regardless of whether she thought she did. She was counting the days till her husband came back to Boston from Tennessee. What did Sylvia have to count? Nothing at all.

The work was steady, and demanded enough concentration that Sylvia couldn't let her mind drift, as she often had back at the mackerel-canning plant. Thinking about anything except the pieces of leather in front of her was asking for a punctured hand. She couldn't dwell on losing George, not unless she also wanted to dwell on what the doctor would have to do to repair her.

Toward the middle of the afternoon, the woman who had hired her came into the factory hall and said, "May I see you for a moment, Mrs. Enos?"

"Of course. Let me finish this first, please." Sylvia joined the pieces of leather together and tossed them into the box by the machine. Then she caught Gustav Krafft's eye. Only after he nodded permission did she rise and accompany the hiring clerk. As she did, she said, "I hope nothing's wrong."

"You've done a very good job with us, as a matter of fact," the woman said as they left the factory floor. If she noticed Sylvia was wearing mourning, she didn't mention it. She waved her to a chair: the very chair in which she'd been sitting, in fact, when she was hired.

"Miss, could you please tell me what's going on?" Sylvia asked.

"Yes, I will tell you," the hiring clerk answered. "Like I said, all the reports on your work have been very good, and Krafft isn't easy to please. But our orders have been cut because of peace, and we have men coming back, and you are one of our most recent employees. And so—"

"You're letting me go," Sylvia said dully.

"I am sorry," the woman said. "I do feel bad about it, because you've worked out very well here." That did Sylvia exactly no good. The woman who'd hired her went on, "I wish we could keep you, but business doesn't allow it. And our brave men in uniform will be returning, looking for the jobs they—"

"*My* brave man in uniform won't be returning," Sylvia broke in, "and my children and I will be going hungry because of this."

"I *am* sorry," the woman repeated. "I'll be happy to give you the very best of good characters, which will surely help you get a position at a firm that is hiring."

"But firms aren't hiring," Sylvia said. "Firms are letting people go. Firms are letting women like me go so they can hire men, like you said." She sighed. "I'll take that good character. It won't do me any good, but I'll take it." *What am I going to do now?* she asked herself. *What can I do now?* The question was far easier to ask than to answer.

Cincinnatus was walking to the trolley stop when someone whistled behind him. He looked back over his shoulder and saw Lucullus, Apicius' son, waving at him. He didn't grimace—not on the outside where Lucullus could see. Instead, he waved. Lucullus came toward him at a heavy trot: he was on his way to putting on his father's massive bulk.

"What you want?" Cincinnatus asked him. "Whatever it is, you better make it snappy, on account of I'm gonna be late for work if I miss this here trolley car."

"Well, ain't you high and mighty?" Lucullus said. He was getting his own man's confidence; he wouldn't have been so sharp with Cincinnatus a year before. "My pa says, he got to figure out whether to fish or cut bait with you pretty damn quick, an' you won't like it if he decide he got to cut bait."

"You tell your pa that if anything happens to me, I got myself a little book," Cincinnatus answered. "First thing that happens *after* somethin' happens to me is, that little book goes straight to Luther Bliss." He'd been bluffing when he said that to Joe Conroy. He wasn't bluffing any more. Anyone who tried to bring him down would go down with him.

Lucullus screwed up his face. He could see that. He was no fool; Cincinnatus would never have thought Apicius'—Apicius Wood's—son could be a fool. He said, "My pa says you ain't got the right attitude, Cincinnatus. You is for yourself 'fore you is for the people."

"I take care of myself and I mind my business," Cincinnatus said. "That's all I want to do. That's all I ever wanted to do. Anybody tries to keep me from doin' that, he can get lost, far as I'm concerned. I don't care who he is."

"You *do* got the wrong attitude," Lucullus said reproachfully. "If the proletariat ain't united against the oppressors, it ain't anything."

"And what about if the party of the proletariat tries oppressin' me?" Cincinnatus returned. Instead of answering, Lucullus made another sour face and strode off. Cincinnatus watched him go, then hurried on to the trolley stop. The Reds wouldn't leave

him alone for no better reason than that he asked them to. He
knew that only too well.

He threw his nickel in the trolley fare box and went to the back
of the car with something approaching relief. While he rode the
trolley, as when he was driving a truck, nobody bothered him.
He sometimes thought those were the only times when no one
bothered him. Oh, every once in a while at home, but that wasn't
the same.

New graffiti marked several buildings along the trolley route.
Some were blue X's, others three horizontal lines of paint, red-
white-red. Only after Cincinnatus had seen several of them did
he realize what they were supposed to suggest: the Confederate
battle flag and the Stars and Bars. The diehards were busy again,
then. Others in Covington were bound to be quicker on the up-
take than he was. No sooner had that thought crossed his mind
than he saw a work crew splashing whitewash over one of those
blue X's. No, the Yankees didn't miss a trick.

Somehow, Cincinnatus was not surprised to find Luther Bliss
waiting at the trolley stop where he got off. The chief of the Kentucky State Police didn't get on the trolley, either. He fell into
step beside Cincinnatus as the Negro headed toward the shed
where Lieutenant Straubing's crew gathered at the start of each
new run.

"Mornin', *Mr.* Driver," he said, irony in his voice at ad-
dressing a Negro by his surname. "Hope I won't take up too
much of your precious time today."

"Mornin' to you, Mr. Bliss," Cincinnatus answered. "I hope
you won't, too, suh. I don't know nothin' more'n I did last time
we talked, and the Army gets powerful riled if I'm late to work—
it don't matter how come."

Bliss gave him a nasty glare. He'd mentioned the Army on
purpose; it was the one institution that had more power in Covington than Bliss' secret police. After a couple of silent strides,
the chief said, "I'll make you a deal—you tell me who punched
that bastard Kennedy's ticket for him and you'll never see my
face again. That's a promise."

Cincinnatus laughed in the aforementioned face. "You don't
know who done it, an' the Reds don't know who done it, an' the
Confederate diehards don't know who done it, an' you all reckon
I know who done it. Only thing I know about Tom Kennedy is
that I used to work for the man."

He knew a great deal more than that. He also knew Luther Bliss did not know how much he knew. Had the secret policeman known that, Cincinnatus would not have been heading in to work. He would have been in jail, or more likely dead.

Bliss did know he wasn't telling everything. "You only knew Kennedy because you worked for him, what was he doing on your doorstep better than two years later?"

"Damned if I know," Cincinnatus answered. "He got shot before he could tell me anything. Maybe he was running from the Kentucky State Police."

"Not right then, I don't reckon," Bliss said. "If he was running from us, he'd have been stupid to run to you, because he must've known we were keeping an eye on you, too. And whatever else you could say about the goddamn son of a bitch, Tom Kennedy wasn't stupid."

Bliss was undoubtedly right—nobody harassing Cincinnatus was stupid. Cincinnatus didn't say anything about that. The less he said, the better the chance the Kentucky State Police chief would give up—give up for the time being, anyhow—and go away. But Bliss, with his odd eyes the color of a hunting dog's, stuck with him like a hunting dog on a scent. Side by side, they approached the shed where Lieutenant Straubing's drivers gathered.

Straubing was waiting outside. "Good morning, Cincinnatus," he said. "You'll have to tell your friend good-bye here."

"Good-bye, friend," Cincinnatus said at once, smiling in Luther Bliss' direction.

Now Bliss laughed at him. "You don't get rid of me that easy. I have some more questions that need answering."

"Ask them some other time," Lieutenant Straubing said. "Nothing interferes with my men when they're supposed to be working. Nothing. Have you got that?"

"Listen, Junior, I'm Luther Bliss, and I'm looking into a killing," Bliss said. Maybe the Army didn't faze him after all. Maybe nothing fazed him. That wouldn't have surprised Cincinnatus one bit. "Far as I'm concerned, that's a hell of a lot more important than if one nigger hops in a truck on time. Have you got that?"

Straubing wasn't any older than Cincinnatus. He was skinny and on the pale side. And, as far as Cincinnatus could tell, he never backed down from anybody or anything. "Sounds like you're trying to sell me the Brooklyn Bridge," he answered. "Cincinnatus didn't kill anybody. If he had killed somebody, you wouldn't be grilling him here. He'd be in prison. If it's about somebody else doing some killing, I think it can keep—doesn't sound like fresh news, anyhow. Now just who's supposed to be dead, and why do you think Cincinnatus knows the first thing about it?" That was Lieutenant Straubing to the core: methodical, precise, unyielding.

"Why do I reckon he knows something about it?" Bliss asked with a chuckle. "Because the fellow who's dead got his head blown off right on your little darling's front stoop, that's why. Bastard was a Rebel diehard name of Tom Kennedy."

"Oh. Him." Straubing waved a hand in a careless gesture of dismissal. "You may as well leave Cincinnatus alone, if that's what you're exercised over. He doesn't know anything about it."

"And you do?" Luther Bliss asked. Calm as ever, Straubing nodded. Bliss spoke in an exasperated growl: "And how come you know so goddamn much, Lieutenant, *if* you don't mind my asking, of course?"

"It's not very hard, Chief," Straubing answered, still calm. "I shot that Kennedy bastard myself."

"*You* shot Tom Kennedy?" For once in their lives, Cincinnatus and Luther Bliss said the same thing at the same time with the same intonation: one of astonished disbelief.

But Lieutenant Straubing only nodded. "I certainly did. He needed shooting. Cincinnatus is one of my better men, and Kennedy was distracting him from his work. He might even have managed to get Cincinnatus involved in something subversive if he'd kept pestering him long enough."

Kennedy had got Cincinnatus into several subversive things, but Straubing didn't know that. Neither did Luther Bliss, who proved it by saying, "We've never pinned anything on Cincinnatus here. But *you* shot Kennedy, Lieutenant? Why in hell didn't you say something about it to somebody?"

"I don't know." Straubing shrugged. "It never seemed that important. I was only doing my job and making sure one of my men could do his. It's not like Kennedy was anything but a Rebel diehard. I didn't think anything more about it than I would have thought about stepping on a cockroach."

Cincinnatus believed that; he'd had a long time to watch Straubing's mind work. After some small pause for thought,

Luther Bliss evidently decided he believed it, too. "Lieutenant, you'd have made a lot of people's lives simpler if you didn't play your cards so goddamn close to your chest," he said at last. His eyes flicked to Cincinnatus. "Reckon this fellow'd tell you the same thing."

"That's a fact," Cincinnatus said. "Everybody reckoned I had somethin' to do with it. Folks kept tryin' to cipher out who I done it for. Made my life livelier than I really cared for, believe you me it did."

"How unfortunate." Lieutenant Straubing looked as distressed as he ever did, which wasn't very. "I just thought of him as rubbish who wouldn't be missed. But if that ends Chief Bliss' business with you . . ."

"Ends this business, anyway." Bliss touched a finger to the brim of his straw hat. "Obliged to you, Lieutenant. Would have been more obliged if you'd spoken up sooner, but obliged all the same." Off he went, brisk and competent himself. *Ends* this *business*, Cincinnatus thought. That would have to do, though it was far less than he wanted.

Once inside the shed, Lieutenant Straubing wasted no time and no words: "Let's get moving, men. We've got food and munitions heading down to First Army. One more thing you need to know: with the armistice holding, we'll be laying off our civilian drivers after this run. We're hauling less now, and we'll be doing it with Army personnel only from now on. You civilians have done a good job, and the United States are grateful to you."

"What are we supposed to do now?" one of those drivers, a white man, demanded before Cincinnatus could get the words out of his mouth.

"Find other work, of course," Straubing answered. "I wish you the best of luck, but I'm not your nursemaid."

"Some of us got killed haulin' for you," Cincinnatus said. "Is that all you got to say, Lieutenant—'I ain't your nursemaid'?"

"Their families are taken care of," Straubing said. "If you'd been killed, your family would have been taken care of, too. Since you weren't, you can't expect the government to hold your hand for you now that your labor is no longer required."

He cared about the job. When the job was done, he didn't care any more. When the job was done, nobody cared any more. Cincinnatus wondered where he'd find work now. He whistled softly under his breath. "God damn," he said. "Welcome to the United States."

Secretary of State Robert Lansing had come before the Transportation Committee to discuss the integration of the railroads in lands conquered from Canada and the Confederate States into the rail network of the USA. Chairman Taft plainly feared some members' questions might go further afield, but fearing that and being able to do much about it were two different things. "I recognize the distinguished Representative from New York," he said with a strange sort of polite reluctance.

"Thank you, Mr. Chairman," Flora Hamburger said. She knew she had to follow her course with care, lest she be ruled out of order. "Now, Mr. Secretary, will these railroads be brought into our network to make trade easier with the CSA and whatever is left of Canada after peace is finally established?"

"Yes, ma'am." Lansing paused to draw on a cigarette and to run a hand through his fine head of gray hair. "That is one of the principal purposes of the integration. The other, of course, is to provide for the defense of the United States, railroads being so important to the transport of men and matériel." He spoke with the precision of the longtime lawyer he had been.

"I see." Flora nodded. "And against which parts of Canada does the administration see a need for future defense?"

"Those parts not annexed to the United States or to our ally, the Republic of Quebec," Lansing answered.

"I understand as much, yes," Flora said. "Which parts will those be?"

"We anticipate that the Republic of Quebec will have borders substantially similar to those of the former province of Quebec," the secretary of state said.

When he said no more, Flora asked, "And the rest of Canada?"

"Areas under military occupation, we anticipate annexing," Lansing said. "Areas not presently occupied are being negotiated with British and Canadian representatives. Whatever we do not annex will naturally fall within our economic sphere of influence, as Holland and Belgium will fall within Germany's and Serbia and Albania within Austria-Hungary's."

He made fewer bones about exploitation than Flora had thought he would. She asked, "And what of the Confederate States?"

"Again, we shall annex such land as we now hold, pending adjustments to create frontiers appropriate to our needs and acceptable to the Confederate States, which may be required to exchange territory for any we yield back to them," Lansing said. "I remind you that this land is different from that of Canada, as it was formerly part of the territory of the United States."

"Did we not abandon our claim of sovereignty over it when we recognized the CSA?" Flora asked sharply.

"So the Confederates now say," Lansing returned—he might look dry and dusty, but he was dangerous, tarring her with the brush of the beaten enemy. "The view of the president is that recognition of the CSA was granted under duress and maintained by coercion on the part of the Confederates and their allies."

"The peace, then, will be as harsh as you can make it," Flora said.

Congressman Taft looked unhappy, but the question followed logically from others Lansing had answered without hesitation. He answered this one without hesitation, too: "Yes, ma'am. The stronger the peace from our point of view, the better off we shall be and the longer our foes will need to recover from it and menace us again."

"Wouldn't we be better off making them our friends?" Flora asked.

"Perhaps we might be, if they showed any interest in friendship," Lansing said. "The next such interest they do show, however, will be the first."

Democrats up and down the committee table laughed. Some of them even snickered. The chairman rapped loudly for order. Flora felt her face flush. The question, while heartfelt, had sounded naive. "If we do annex Canada, I expect a large influx of Socialist voters," she remarked.

"No one, as yet, is speaking of making U.S. states from Canadian provinces, so the question of voter affiliation in them is moot," Lansing replied. "Again, this differs from our approach to territory formerly under Confederate administration."

"Of course it does," Flora said. "Ex-Confederates are likely to make good Democrats, since they're reactionary to the core."

Taft's gavel came down again. "That is out of order, Miss Hamburger."

"Is it out of order to suggest that the administration will make whatever peace is to its advantage, and will worry about its advantage before it worries about the people's advantage?" Flora asked. "Perhaps the administration is out of order, and I am not."

Bang! Bang! Bang! Taft plied the gavel with such vigor, his beefy face turned red. "We shall have no more such outbursts," he declared.

Flora inclined her head to the committee chairman. "Never ask any questions that might be difficult or inconvenient, is what you mean, isn't it, Mr. Chairman?" she said. "Never ask any questions where the American people really need to know the answers. Never mind the First Amendment. Is that what you mean? If it is, Teddy Roosevelt is a lot more like Kaiser Bill than he thinks, or than he wants us to think."

A couple of other Socialist congressmen on the Transportation Committee loudly clapped their hands, and the lone Republican with them. William Howard Taft, however, turned redder still: almost the color of a ripe beet. "It is intolerable that you should impugn the administration and the president in this way," he boomed.

"Is it tolerable that the administration and the president should impugn the truth?" Flora returned.

She got no answer. What she got was an early adjournment of the committee. Robert Lansing stuffed papers into his briefcase and scurried away, looking back over his shoulder as if he expected dogs to come after him with teeth bared. His alarmed expression gave Flora some satisfaction, but not enough.

She went back to her office and stared in dismay at the mountain of paperwork awaiting her there. She'd wanted to go visit David at the Pennsylvania Hospital, but she wouldn't have the chance, not today, not if she was going to do the job she'd been elected to do. Duty ran strong in her.

If she couldn't take the time to visit, she could telephone. When the hospital operator answered, she said, "This is Congresswoman Hamburger. I'd like to speak to one of the doctors seeing my brother." In this matter, she did not hesitate to use her influence. She could learn from the doctor, but she couldn't make him do anything he wouldn't have otherwise except talk to her.

"Please wait, ma'am," the operator said, as Flora had known she would. Flora impatiently drummed her fingers on the broad oak surface of the desk.

"This is Dr. Hanrahan, Congresswoman," a man's voice said at last. Flora brightened; of all David's doctors, Hanrahan seemed the most open. "We tried fitting a prosthesis on your brother this morning. The stump isn't ready yet, I'm afraid, but he tolerated the padded end of the artificial leg better than he has. Things *are* healing in there, no doubt about it. And it was very good to see David upright, if only for a little while."

Tears stung her eyes. "I wish I could have been there to see that," she said. "How soon will he be walking? How well will he walk?"

"No way to tell how soon," Hanrahan said. "I wish we had some better way to fight infection than we do, but his body will have to win that battle. How well . . . He's always going to have a rolling motion to his stride, ma'am; that's the way the knee joint on the prosthesis works. But I hope he'll be able to get by without even a cane."

"Alevai," Flora said, which surely meant nothing to an Irishman. She returned to English: "I hope you're right. That would help a lot." She wondered if it would help enough for her brother ever to find a wife.

Maybe Hanrahan was thinking along with her, for he said, "A lot of good men got wounded in this war, Miss Hamburger. People won't hold injuries against them, not nearly so much as they did before the fighting started. You don't mind my saying so, there ought to be a law against people who do dumb things like that, anyhow."

"I am going to write that down, Dr. Hanrahan," Flora said, and she did. The Democrats, no doubt, would scream that such laws were not the federal government's job. The only federal laws they liked readied the country for war. Maybe she could make them think about the aftermath of war, too.

After she got off the telephone with the doctor, she attacked the papers on her desk, only to be interrupted by Bertha, her secretary, who said, "Congressman Blackford would like to see you, Miss Hamburger."

Flora blinked but nodded. Into the inner office came Hosea Blackford, a wide smile on his handsome face. "From everything I hear, Flora, you sent Mr. Lansing home with a tin can tied to his tail. That's not easy; he's a clever fellow."

"Yes, I saw that," Flora said. "But if he insists on treating everyone else like an idiot, he's not as smart as he thinks he is."

"A song one could sing about a great many people, from TR on down," Blackford said. "But what one could do and what one does are often different. One thing you've become since you got here, Flora, is the conscience of the Congress."

Nobody had ever called her anything like that before. She felt herself flush, and hoped Blackford couldn't see her blushing. "Thank you very much," she said at last. "I'm just doing the best I can." Her smile was wry. "There have been times when you've said I was trying to do too much."

"Not here, not now," the congressman from Dakota answered. "Maybe I was wrong before, too. But certainly not now. You'll have given Lansing and Roosevelt both something to think about." He hesitated, then changed the subject: "Will you let me take you out to supper to celebrate a splendid day of witness grilling?"

Flora hesitated, too. The memory of Herman Bruck's pestering still grated on her. But Blackford was as smooth as Bruck, back in New York City, wished he were. An invitation to supper was not necessarily an invitation to anything else (though it wasn't necessarily *not* such an invitation, either). Well, she always had a hatpin. "All right," she said.

Blackford ate shad at the Bellevue-Stratford Hotel, not far from city hall. "I never got seafood in Dakota, but I make up for it here," he said. "If only oysters were in season." Flora would never have thought of eating an oyster, no matter how secular she became. She contented herself with a beefsteak that did indeed provoke contentment.

Over supper, she told Blackford of the idea she'd got from Dr. Hanrahan. His eyes glowed. "I think we can pass that," he said. "The Democrats won't want people—people like us, for instance—to say they don't care about cripples."

"No, especially when their war made so many cripples." Flora scowled. "And speaking against it is useless. Everyone says, 'But we won!' You warned me it would be that way. I didn't believe it, but you were right."

"I wish I'd been wrong, but that's the way the world works." Blackford beckoned to the waiter. "Let me have the bill, please."

He drove them back to the apartment building where they both lived. It was natural for them to go upstairs together when their flats were across the hall from each other. "Thank you for a very nice evening," Flora said in the hallway.

"Thank *you* for your excellent ideas—and for your excellent company." Hosea Blackford tipped his hat, then leaned forward and kissed Flora on the mouth. He drew back before she even thought of yanking out a hatpin. Instead of trying to get into her apartment, he went into his own. "Good night," he said, and shut the door.

"Good night," Flora said, slower than she should have. She went into her own apartment, locking the door behind her. Then she sat down on the front-room sofa. Her thoughts whirled. She'd been glad of the kiss. Blackford was twice her age, and a gentile to boot. But she'd been glad of the kiss. She was too honest with herself to deny it. And she was far too surprised and confused to have any idea what it meant. She wished her family's apartment had a telephone, but it didn't. All she could do was go to bed and think and think and think.

After rumbling through Tennessee inside a barrel, Colonel Irving Morrell found Philadelphia mild and dry by comparison. To anyone coming from anywhere else, the *de facto* capital of the United States would have been its usual hot, muggy summer self. For once, Morrell was not sorry to return to the General Staff. With the shooting over, the action, such as it was, would be here.

He sat in a little room with a littler window and an overhead fan doing a desultory job of stirring the air. "Good to see you again, Colonel," General Leonard Wood said. "You being one of our leading experts on barrels, we want your ideas on how thoroughly to restrict the CSA in building and deploying them."

"Sir, my view on that is very simple," Morrell said. "I think we ought to forbid them to have anything to do with barrels, on pain of war. The more of them they have, the more they do with them, the more trouble they'll cause us. Those machines knock everything we thought we knew about defense in war into a cocked hat."

The chief of the U.S. General Staff frowned. "That won't be easy. They have a sizable motorcar industry. A plant that manufactures motorcars won't have any great trouble turning out barrels, too."

"Yes, sir, I understand that," Morrell said. "If I had my way, though, I'd put that in the treaty: no barrels. I expect they'll cheat, or try to cheat. As soon as we catch them at it, I'd take a new bite out of Arkansas or Texas or Tennessee—and make them cough up the barrels, too. Do that once and they aren't so likely to take a chance on our doing it twice."

Brigadier General Mason Patrick, who wore a pilot's wings on his left breast pocket, said, "I told you the same thing in regard to aeroplanes, didn't I, General Wood?" He nodded to Morrell. "Good to see there's someone else with his head on his shoulders. We just licked these bastards. I want to kick 'em while they're down. If they build up to where they can take another whack at us in ten or fifteen years, we've wasted a lot of lives since 1914."

Leonard Wood sighed. "The other side of the coin is, if they sit tight for ten or fifteen years and then start building barrels and aeroplanes and submersibles and all the other tools of war we don't want them to have, will we have the will to go in and set a foot on their necks, or will we say, 'Look how much trouble we had beating them the last time. They've only got a few of these little toys, so why should we worry about them?' That's what makes me wake up sweating of nights."

"Philadelphia is what makes me wake up sweating of nights," said General Patrick, who had just come down from Canada.

Morrell stared at Wood in a kind of horror he'd never known on the battlefield. "Sir, as long as Teddy Roosevelt is president—"

"That gives us till March 4, 1921," Wood broke in. "March 4, 1925, if he decides he wants a third term, and if the people remember to be grateful. After TR isn't president any more . . . what then? We spent a generation twiddling our thumbs after the War of Secession. We could do it again."

"All the more reason to punish the Rebels now, sir," Morrell said. "The farther they have to climb, the harder it'll be for them."

"Bully!" Brigadier General Patrick clapped his hands together. "General Wood, this pup said it better than I could."

"He's a bright lad," Wood said, and Morrell felt as if he'd been given the accolade. But the chief of the General Staff went on, "The harder we hold the Confederates down, the more we make them hate us and want to get their own back."

"I honestly don't see the problem, sir," Morrell said. "They already hate us, the same way we hated them before the war. Somebody licks you, of course you hate him. What we have to do is make sure they can't hurt us no matter how much they hate us."

General Wood sighed again. "I've been in touch with General Ludendorff in Berlin. If it makes you gentlemen feel any better, our friends the Germans are having these same sorts of arguments about how rough they should be on France."

"The CSA will have an easier time cheating than France will, though," Morrell said.

"How's that?" Wood said. "I don't follow."

"France isn't even as big as Texas," Morrell said.

"It is now," General Patrick said. "We carved a good chunk off Texas when we made the state of Houston."

"How much will Germany carve off France?" Morrell gave the man he thought was his ally an annoyed look: this was not the time for nitpicking precision. Having got the glare out of his system, he resumed: "Be that as it may, the Confederate States are a lot larger than France even after they've lost Houston and Sequoyah and Kentucky. They have more room to hide armaments than the frogs do."

"And they could go down into the Empire of Mexico, too," Mason Patrick said. "The only way we'd hear about anything down there is by luck. Hell, half the time the damn greasers don't know what's going on inside their own country, so how are we supposed to?"

"We have more ways than you'd think, as a matter of fact," General Wood said. "But never mind that; I take the point. So you gentlemen agree we should squeeze the Rebels till their eyes pop, do you?"

"Yes, sir," Morrell and Brigadier General Patrick said in the same breath.

"Well, I'm hearing that from the Navy Department, too, I will admit," Wood said. "They want to go and bombard Charleston and Habana and New Orleans if the Rebels ever even think of building submersibles again."

"That sounds good to me," Morrell said.

Wood looked grim. "As a matter of fact, it sounds good to me, too. We had a destroyer, the *Ericsson*, torpedoed the night after the CSA quit the war. The Royal Navy swears up and down that they had no boats anywhere near her. If I had to guess, I'd say a Rebel skipper thought he could get away with one—but I can't prove it, mind, and the Confederates deny everything."

"I hadn't heard that before, sir," Morrell said slowly.

"We're keeping it under wraps," the chief of the General Staff said. "Don't see what else to do. Can't prove it, as I say."

"Filthy piece of business." Morrell realized his right hand had folded into a fist. He made it open. "They ever catch that Reb—if it was a Reb—they ought to hang him."

"You get no arguments from me," Wood said. "But back to the matter at hand. In your view, we allow the Rebs enough in the way of guns to keep order inside their borders and put up a halfway decent fight in case Mexico decides to invade them?"

Morrell let out a wry snort. "If Mexico invades them, sir, they can shout for help, as far as I'm concerned."

As he spoke, he worried at the thought General Wood had put in his mind. How long could any country, especially a republic like the USA, keep watch on a neighbor? Sooner or later, the voters would tire of the effort vigilance took. When they did, or maybe even before they did, the one-time enemy would begin to rebuild and become an enemy once more.

"We have to do the best we can," he said at last. "We have to do the best we can for as long as we can. If we drop the ball later on, or if our kids do, that's one thing. But if we drop the ball now, we don't deserve to have won the war."

"That's the way it looks to me, too," Mason Patrick said. "The day the Confederate States start building aeroplanes with machine guns in them again, you'll be able to see the next war from there."

"Very well. Thank you for your thoughts, General, Colonel. They will go into our recommendations to President Roosevelt, I assure you," Wood said. Morrell and Patrick stood up to go. Casually, Wood went on, "Colonel, could you give me another minute or so of your time?"

"Of course," Morrell answered. He waited till the aviation officer had gone, then asked, "What's up, sir?"

"Colonel, President Roosevelt has asked me to give you a choice of assignments, in recognition of your outstanding service to your country," Wood said. "You may, if you like, remain in the field; the president is keenly aware of how much you enjoy the strenuous life, as he does himself."

"Yes, sir, I do," Morrell said. "I can't imagine a choice that would be preferable to staying in the field."

"Let me see if I can give you one," Wood said with a smile.

"How would you like to have charge of what we might as well call the Barrel Works? It's plain the machines aren't everything they ought to be. It's just as plain nobody has a sounder notion of doctrine for them or more experience with them in the field than you do. What do you say to a free hand at making them better?"

"What do I say?" Morrell asked the question as much of himself as of Leonard Wood. He glared at the chief of the General Staff. "Sir, with all due respect, I say *damn*. That's a job that needs doing. It's a job I can do. It's a job I should do, because, as you say, I can do it well." He hesitated, grasping at a straw. "Unless you'd rather have Colonel Sherrard?"

"He recommended you," Wood said. "His opinion was that you had a better feel for all the issues involved than he did. He said he never could have conceived, much less brought off, the crossing of the Cumberland. You did, and that makes you the man for the slot."

"He's extraordinarily generous." Morrell scowled; he'd never known this mix of elation and disappointment. When would he ever get away to the woods and the mountains again? "Sir, you're right. It's such an important position that, if you believe I'm the best man to fill it, I don't see how I can possibly decline."

"I was hoping you would say that, Colonel," General Wood replied. "The more work we do on barrels while we're holding the Confederate States down—holding them down as best we can, I should say—the further ahead of them we'll be, and the harder the time they'll have catching up with us."

"Yes, sir," Morrell said enthusiastically. "I've got some ideas I want to try. And if we get far enough ahead of them, maybe they'll never be able to catch up again."

"You're reading my mind," Leonard Wood said. "That's just what I'm hoping for." Solemnly, the two men shook hands.

Every train that pulled into St. Matthews, South Carolina, brought a few more soldiers home, some from Virginia, some from Tennessee, some from the distant battlefields west of the Mississippi. The men in beat-up butternut tunics and trousers got off the trains and looked around the station, looked around the slowly rebuilding town, in worn wonder, as if amazed even so much peace as St. Matthews provided was left in the world.

Anne Colleton saw a lot of the returning soldiers, for she spent much of her time at the station waiting for her brother to get off one of those trains: she didn't trust Tom to wire ahead, letting her know he was coming. And, sure enough, one morning he stopped down from a passenger car looking about as battered, about as bewildered, as any other soldier Anne had seen.

He looked even more bewildered when she threw herself into his arms. "What the devil are you doing here?" he demanded. "I wanted to surprise you."

"Didn't work this time," Anne said. "I wanted to surprise you, and I got what I wanted." She kissed him on the cheek. Some of the whiskers in the scar that seamed it were coming in white.

"You generally do," Tom said after a moment, with more of an edge to his voice than would have been there before the war. Then he sighed and shrugged. "We—the CSA, I mean—generally got what we wanted, too. Not this time."

"Come back to my rooms with me," Anne said. "There's one more thing I want, and you can help me get it."

"Can I?" Her brother shrugged again. "I'll come with you, though. Why not? With Marshlands burned, I haven't got anywhere else to stay."

He walked through the streets of St. Matthews with his shoulders slumped but his eyes darting now here, now there, ever alert, waiting and watching for shooting to start. "It's not that bad," Anne said quietly. "We hit the niggers a good lick not so long ago. One more good lick and they're done, I think."

"Wasn't worrying about Reds," Tom Colleton answered with an embarrassed chuckle. "I was worrying about damnyankees." When they got back to her apartment, Anne poured him some whiskey, hoping to ease him. He drank it down, but still seemed nervous as a cat. Pointing at her, he asked, "What's this other thing you want, Sis?"

"Another good lick against the Reds," Anne said at once. "When we hit them from this side, they go deeper into the swamp, over by Gadsden. The militia on the other side of the Congaree are worthless. The Reds—Cassius and his pals, mind—whip them every time they bump together."

"Get me another drink, will you?" Tom said, and Anne rose. While she was pouring, her brother went on, "How do I help you get it? I figure I do, or you wouldn't have mentioned it to me."

"Why, Lieutenant Colonel Colleton, of course you do," she said, handing him the drink. "And it's because you're Lieutenant

Colonel Colleton that you do. I want you to recruit as many veterans as you can, arm them, and take most of them across to the north side of the Congaree. Don't you think they'd be able to clean out the nest of Reds that's been in the swamp the past year and a half?"

"If they can't, the Confederate States are in even more trouble than I reckoned they were." Whiskey hadn't fuzzed Tom's wits; he asked, "What happens to the soldiers I don't take over to Gadsden?"

"They stay on this side of the swamp," Anne answered. "You drive the niggers into them, and they finish off any you don't get."

Tom considered, then slowly nodded. "And who commands the stay-at-homes?"

"I do," his sister told him.

She waited for him to pitch a fit. He didn't. "Odds are you'd be better at the job than any man I can think of," he said slowly. "Are you sure you wouldn't rather have the post you just assigned me?—driving, I mean, instead of catching."

Anne shook her head. "You have much more real combat experience than I do," she answered, "and you'll be leading men who won't know so much about what I've done since the uprising, because they haven't been here to see it. I'll keep a lot of militiamen, too. They're used to doing what I tell them, and it should rub off on the soldiers."

"You've got it all figured out, don't you?" Tom raised his glass. "Have one yourself, Sis. Seems to me you've earned it."

Anne got a glass of whiskey, too, but stared moodily at it instead of drinking right away. "The one thing I don't have figured out is how to be sure we kill Cassius. He killed Jacob and he almost killed me—and he wrecked Marshlands. He's kept the Reds a going concern since we drove them back into the swamp, and he knows the place better than anybody. If we don't get him, we'll only have to go back again later on."

"Kill the head and the body dies," Tom said. Anne nodded. She knocked back the whiskey. It snarled its way down her throat. Tom spoke with a certain grim anticipation: "Kill enough of the body and the head won't live, either."

He went about recruiting with both skill and persistence he wouldn't have shown before he'd joined the Army. Nor did he have any trouble gathering followers. The ex-soldiers hardly seemed to think of themselves as ex-; they obeyed his orders as readily as they would have done if still serving under the Stars and Bars. Anne couldn't help noting that with a touch of resentment when she thought of the cajolery she'd had to use to get the militiamen to go along with her ideas even though they'd had none of their own.

A few Negro soldiers came back to St. Matthews, too. Tom Colleton did not recruit them—who could guess which of them had fought for the Congaree Socialist Republic? No one quite knew what to make of them or how to behave toward them. Anne vowed to worry about that later. For now, she hoped none of St. Matthews' blacks was bringing the rebels in the swamp word of the move against them.

She and the militia and some of Tom's recruits headed in the direction of Marshlands (and the swamps beyond) as ostentatiously as they could, hoping to draw as much attention to themselves as they could. Once at the edge of the ruined cotton fields, the veterans automatically began to entrench. She didn't argue; in such matters, she was willing to assume they knew what they were doing.

Some of them laughed at the beat-up old aeroplane buzzing above the swamp. "Jesus, I wish the damnyankees had been flying crates like that," a sergeant said.

"If the other side hasn't got any aeroplanes, ours doesn't have to be up to date," Anne answered coolly. No one, she noted, laughed at the pair of three-inch guns that deployed behind the infantry. One veteran, in fact, respectfully tipped his tin hat to them, as to a couple of old friends.

Veterans and militiamen were still deploying when a brisk crackle of small-arms fire broke out to the north. Although Anne knew she'd chambered a round in her own Tredegar, she checked again to make sure the weapon was ready. The aeroplane flew in the direction of the shooting. A couple of minutes later, the militiamen at the field guns began banging away, presumably at instruction they got from the wireless telegraph the flying machine carried.

Perhaps fifteen minutes after that, a couple of ragged Negroes, a man and a woman, emerged from the swamp a few hundred yards from Anne. Both carried rifles; both looked around to find the best road for escape. They did not look long. They found no escape. A volley from the men in the new trenches knocked them over. The man never moved after he fell. The woman twitched for a little while, then lay still.

Before long, another pair of Negroes, both men this time, came trotting south as if they had not a care in the world. The veterans and militiamen let them approach to near point-blank range before shooting them down. A savage smile stretched across Anne Colleton's face. The Reds had never met a trap with jaws on both north and south before.

"Come on, Cassius," she crooned quietly. "Come on." Some of the Negro rebels in the swamp, seeing the last bastion of the Congaree Socialist Republic crumbling, would fight to the death defending it. Having known Cassius all her life (not so well as she'd thought she did, but even so), she did not believe he would be one of them. His eye was always on the main chance. As long as he lived, he would figure, the revolution lived, too. That held an unpleasant amount of truth. He would try to escape.

A few more Reds blundered out of the undergrowth and died before the rest realized the sort of trap they were in. That was too late. By then, from the sounds of the gunfire, Tom's men had drawn a good semicircle around them. The only way out lay to the south—and that was no way out, either.

Anne felt like Alexander the Great or Julius Caesar or Robert E. Lee. The whole design was hers, and it was working. Paint a picture? Write a book? She shook her head. Using men, not paint or words, to create . . . that beat everything.

But the men of the Congaree Socialist Republic had tried to create using men's lives as their canvas, too. Now, realizing what sort of obstruction barred them from breaking free of their pursuers, they tried once more.

In their own way, they were also veterans, and veteran bushwhackers to boot. That made them too wily to charge headlong at their foes' position. But they had to get through it, or they would never go anywhere again. At a shouted word of command—was that Cassius' voice?—they attacked the trench line.

"Damnyankees couldn't have done it better," a veteran said admiringly, once the shooting was over. The Negroes advanced by rushes, one group firing from cover to let another leapfrog past them, then moving forward in turn.

A man next to Anne staggered back with a gurgling croak, clutching at his throat. She spared him not a glance—she was drawing a bead on a Red. The Tredegar slammed against her shoulder. The back of the black man's head blew out. She worked the bolt and fired again.

For a few minutes, the fighting was very hot. The Red rebels battled for escape with desperate courage. Anne's men had skill, anger, and position on their side. The Negroes got into the trenches even so. That was a worse business than she'd ever imagined, screams and shouts and bullets whipping—several right past her head—and the iron smell of blood and the outhouse stink of guts spilled in the mud.

The Negroes got into the trenches. They did not get past them, not anywhere. The veterans and militiamen outnumbered and outgunned them. A handful of Reds tried to flee back toward the swamp. Anne didn't think any of them made it.

Cautiously, her men began showing themselves. They drew no fire. She went up and down the trenches, inspecting Negro corpses. She did not find Cassius' body. Cursing, she blew out the brains of a black who wasn't quite dead. Had the revolutionary leader slipped through her net again?

Halfway through the afternoon, the veterans who'd slogged down from Gadsden began coming out of the swamp. They had no prisoners with them. When Tom emerged, so filthy she hardly knew who he was, she cried, "Cassius got away again!"

"Oh, no, he didn't." Her brother grinned at her. "I shot him myself."

All she felt was envy bitter and poisonous as prussic acid. "God damn you!" she shouted. "I should have done it."

"Jacob was my brother, too, Anne," Tom said quietly, and that brought her back to herself. "Anyhow, you got Cherry," he went on. "Cassius, now, Cassius was sneaky to the last. Instead of coming south, he tried to wait for my men to go on past him. Then he could have headed north and been home free. He'd done it, in fact, or he thought he had. But I kept a few backstops, and I was one because I had to drag myself out of some quicksand. I was behind a cypress when along he came, a big smile on his face 'cause he'd outfoxed us. But not this time. I put two in his chest from inside thirty yards before he knew I was there. He was still smiling when he fell in the water. He won't come out again, Sis."

Anne Colleton heaved a long, long sigh. "It's over, then—the Congaree Socialist Republic, and Cassius, too. I wonder if

Scipio's dead in the swamp with him. But I don't care so much about Scipio."

"Cassius was the big fish," Tom agreed. "He's feeding the fish now."

"It's over," Anne repeated. "This whole stretch of South Carolina can start picking up the pieces now. The Confederate States will have to start picking up the pieces now." She looked north, not into the swamp but far beyond. "We've got the damnyankees to catch up with, after all."

Read on for a preview of

AMERICAN EMPIRE: BLOOD AND IRON

The first book in a new series by
Harry Turtledove

Available in hardcover August 2001

When the Great War ended, Jake Featherston had thought the silence falling over the battlefield as strange and unnatural as machine-gun fire in Richmond on a Sunday afternoon. Now, sitting at the bar of a saloon in the Confederate capital a few weeks later, he listened to the distant rattle of a machine gun, nodded to himself, and took another pull at his beer.

"Wonder who they're shooting at this time," the barkeep remarked before turning away to pour a fresh whiskey for another customer.

"Hope it's the niggers." Jake set a hand on the grip of the artilleryman's pistol he wore on his belt. "Wouldn't mind shooting a few myself, by Jesus."

"They shoot back these days," the bartender said.

Featherston shrugged. People had called him a lot of different things during the war, but nobody had ever called him yellow. The battery of the First Richmond Howitzers he'd commanded had held longer and retreated less than any other guns in the Army of Northern Virginia. "Much good it did me," he muttered. "Much good it did anything." He'd still been fighting the damnyankees from a good position back of Fredericksburg, Virginia, when the Confederate States finally threw in the sponge.

He went over to the free-lunch counter and slapped ham and cheese and pickles on a slice of none-too-fresh bread. The bartender gave him a pained look; it wasn't the first time he'd raided the counter, nor the second, either. He normally didn't give two whoops in hell what other people thought, but this place was right around the corner from the miserable little room he'd found. He wanted to be able to keep coming here.

Reluctantly, he said, "Give me another beer, too." He pulled a couple of brown dollar banknotes out of his pocket and slid them across the bar. Beer had only been a dollar a glass when he got into town (or a quarter in specie). Before the war, even through most of the war, it had only been five cents.

As long as he was having another glass, he snagged a couple of hard-boiled eggs from the free-lunch spread to go with his sandwich. He'd eaten a lot of saloon free lunches since coming home to Richmond. They weren't free, but they were the cheapest way he knew to keep himself fed.

A couple of rifle shots rang out, closer than the machine gun had been. "Any luck at all, that's the War Department," Jake said, sipping at the new beer. "Lot of damn fools down there nobody'd miss."

"Amen," said the fellow down the bar who was drinking whiskey. Like Featherston, he wore butternut uniform trousers with a shirt that had seen better days (though his, unlike Jake's, did boast a collar). "Plenty of bastards in there who don't deserve anything better than a blindfold and a cigarette, letting us lose the war like that."

"Waste of cigarettes, you ask me, but what the hell." Jake took another pull at his beer. It left him feeling generous. In tones of great concession, he said, "All right, give 'em a smoke. *Then* shoot 'em."

"Plenty of bastards in Congress, too," the bartender put in. He was plump and bald and had a white mustache, so he probably hadn't been in the trenches or just behind them. Even so, he went on in tones of real regret: "If they hadn't fired on the marchers in Capitol Square last week, reckon we might have seen some proper housecleaning."

Featherston shook his head. "Wouldn't matter for beans, I say."

"What do you mean, it wouldn't matter?" the whiskey-drinking veteran demanded. "Stringing a couple dozen Congressmen to lampposts wouldn't matter? Go a long way toward making things better, *I* think."

"Wouldn't," Jake said stubbornly. "Could hang 'em all, and it wouldn't matter. They'd go and pick new Congressmen after you did, and who would they be? More rich sons of bitches who never worked a day in their lives or got their hands dirty. Men of good family." He loaded that with scorn. "Same kind of jackasses they got in the War Department, if you want to hear God's truth."

He was not anyone's notion of a classical orator, with graceful, carefully balanced sentences and smooth, elegant gestures: he was skinny and rawboned and awkward, with a sharp nose, a sharper chin, and a harsh voice. But when he got rolling, he spoke with an intensity that made anyone who heard him pay attention.

"What do you reckon ought to happen, then?" the barkeep asked.

"Tear it all down," Jake said in tones that brooked no argument. "Tear it down and start over. Can't see what in God's name else to do, not when the *men of good family*"—he sneered harder than ever—"let the niggers rise up and then let 'em into the Army to run away from the damnyankees and then gave 'em the vote to say thank-you. Christ!" He tossed down the last of the beer and stalked out.

He'd fired canister at retreating Negro troops—and, as the rot spread through the Army of Northern Virginia, at retreating white troops, too. It hadn't helped. Nothing had helped. *We should have licked the damnyankees fast,* he thought. *A long war let them pound on us till we broke.* He glared in the direction of the War Department. *Your fault. Not the soldiers' fault. Yours.*

He tripped on a brick and almost fell. Cursing, he kicked it toward the pile of rubble from which it had come. Richmond was full of rubble, rubble and ruins. U.S. bombing aeroplanes had paid repeated nighttime visits over the last year of the war. Even windows with glass in them were exceptions, not the rule.

Negro laborers with shovels cleared bricks and timbers out of the street, where one faction or another that had sprung up since the war effort collapsed had built a barricade. A soldier with a bayoneted Tredegar kept them working. Theoretically, Richmond was under martial law. In practice, it was under very little law of any sort. Discharged veterans far outnumbered men still under government command, and paid them no more heed than they had to.

Three other Negroes strode up the street toward Jake. They

were not laborers. Like him, they wore a motley mix of uniforms and civilian clothing. Also like him, they were armed. Two carried Tredegars they hadn't turned in at the armistice; the third wore a holstered pistol. They did not look like men who had run from the Yankees. They did not look like men who would run from anything.

Their eyes swept over Jake. He was not a man who ran from anything, either. He walked through them instead of going around. "Crazy white man," one of them said as they walked on. He didn't keep his voice down, but he didn't say anything directly to Jake, either. With his own business on his mind, Jake kept walking.

He passed by Capitol Square. He'd slept under the huge statue of Albert Sidney Johnston the night he got into Richmond. He couldn't do that now: troops in sandbagged machine-gun nests protected the Confederate Capitol from the Confederate people. Neatly printed NO LOITERING signs had sprouted like mushrooms after a rain. Several bore handwritten addenda: THIS MEANS YOU. Bloodstains on the sidewalk underscored the point.

Posters covered every wall. The most common showed the Stars and Bars and the phrase, PEACE, ORDER, PROSPERITY. That one, Featherston knew, came from the government's printing presses. President Semmes and his flunkies remained convinced that, if they said everything was all right, it would be all right.

Black severed chains on red was another often-repeated theme. The Negroes' Red uprisings of late 1915 had been crushed, but Reds remained. JOIN US! some of the posters shouted—an appeal from black to white.

"Not likely," Jake said, and spat at one of those posters. No more than a handful of Confederate whites had joined the revolutionaries during the uprisings. No more than a handful would ever join them. Of so much Featherston was morally certain.

Yet another poster showed George Washington and the slogan, WE NEED A NEW REVOLUTION. Jake spotted only a couple of copies of that one, which was put out by the Freedom Party. Till that moment, Jake had never heard of the Freedom Party. He wondered if it had existed before the war ended.

He studied the poster. Slowly, he nodded. "Sure as hell do need a new revolution," he said. He had no great use for Washington, though. Washington had been president of the United States. That made him suspect in Jake's eyes.

But in spite of the crude illustration, in spite of the cheap printing, the message struck home, and struck hard. The Freedom Party sounded honest, at any rate. The ruling Whigs were trying to heal an amputation with a sticking plaster. The Radical Liberals, as far as he was concerned, played the same song in a different key. As for the Socialists—he spat at another red poster. Niggers and nigger-lovers, every one of them. The bomb-throwing maniacs wanted a revolution, too, but not the kind the country needed.

He peered more closely at the Freedom Party poster. It didn't say where the party headquarters were or how to go about joining. His lip curled. "Goddamn amateurs," he said. One thing spending his whole adult life in the Army had taught him: the virtue of organization.

With a shrug, he headed back toward his mean little room. If the Freedom Party didn't know how to attract any members, odds were it wasn't worth joining. No matter how good its ideas, they didn't matter if nobody could find out about them. Even the damned Socialists knew that much.

"Too bad," he muttered. "Too stinking bad." Congressional elections were coming this fall. A shame the voters couldn't send the cheaters and thieves in the Capitol the right kind of message.

Back in the room—he'd had plenty of more comfortable bivouacs on campaign—he wrote for a while in a Gray Eagle scratchpad. He'd picked up the habit toward the end of the war. *Over Open Sights,* he called the work in progress. It let him set down some of his anger on paper. Once the words were out, they didn't fester quite so much in his mind. He might have killed somebody if he hadn't had a release like this.

When day came, he went out looking for work. Colored laborers weren't the only ones clearing rubble in Richmond, not by a long chalk. He hauled bricks and dirt and chunks of broken stone from not long after sunrise to just before sunset. The strawboss, of course, paid off in paper money, though his own pockets jingled.

Knowing the banknotes would be worth less tomorrow than they were today, Jake made a beeline for the local saloon and the free-lunch counter. He'd drawn better rations in the Army, too, but he was too hungry to care. As before, the barkeep gave him a reproachful look for making a pig of himself. As before, he bought a second beer to keep the fellow happy, or not too unhappy.

He was stuffing a pickled tomato into his mouth when the fellow with whom he'd talked politics the day before came in and ordered himself a shot. Then he made a run at the free lunch, too. They got to talking again; Featherston learned his name was Hubert Slattery. After a while, Jake mentioned the Freedom Party posters he'd seen.

To his surprise, Slattery burst out laughing. "Oh, them!" he said. "My brother took a look at those fellows, but he didn't want any part of 'em. By what Horace told me, there's only four or five of 'em, and they run the whole party out of a shoebox."

"But they've got posters and everything," Jake protested, startled to find how disappointed he was. "Not *good* posters, mind you, but posters."

"Only reason they do is that one of 'em's a printer," the other veteran told him. "They meet in this little dive on Seventh near Canal, most of the way toward the Tredegar Steel Works. You want to waste your time, pal, go see 'em for yourself."

"Maybe I will," Featherston said. Hubert Slattery laughed again, but that just made him more determined. "By God, maybe I will."

Congresswoman Flora Hamburger clapped her hands together in delight. Dr. Hanrahan's smile was broader than a lot of those seen at the Pennsylvania Hospital. And David Hamburger, intense concentration on his face, brought his cane forward and then took another step on his artificial leg.

"How does it feel?" Flora asked her younger brother.

"Stump's not too sore," he answered, panting a little. "But it's harder work than I thought it would be."

"You haven't been upright since you lost your leg," Dr. Hanrahan reminded him. "Come on. Give me another step. You can do it." David did, and nearly fell. Hanrahan steadied him before Flora could. "You've got to swing the prosthesis out, so the knee joint locks and takes your weight when you straighten up on it," the doctor said. "You don't learn that, the leg won't work. That's why everybody with an amputation above the knee walks like a sailor who hasn't touched land in a couple of years."

"But you *are* walking, David," Flora said. She dropped from English into Yiddish: *"Danken Gott dafahr. Omayn."*

Seeing her brother on his feet—or on one foot of his and one of wood and metal and leather—did a little to ease the guilt that had gnawed at her ever since he was wounded. Nothing would ever do more than a little. After her New York City district sent her to Congress, she'd had the chance to slide David from the trenches to a quiet post behind the lines. He wouldn't have wanted her to do that, but she could have. She'd put Socialist egalitarianism above family ties . . . and this was the result.

Her brother shrugged awkwardly. "I only need one foot to operate a sewing-machine treadle. I won't starve when I go home—and I won't have to sponge off your Congresswoman's salary, either." He gave her a wry grin.

As a U.S. Representative, Flora made $7,500 a year, far more than the rest of her family put together. She didn't begrudge sharing the money with her parents and brothers and sisters, and she knew David knew she didn't. He took a brotherly privilege in teasing her.

He also took a brotherly privilege in picking her brains: "What's the latest on the peace with the Rebs?"

She grimaced for a couple of reasons. For one, he hadn't called the Confederates by that scornful nickname before he went into the Army. For another . . . "President Roosevelt is still being very hard and very stubborn. I can understand keeping some of the territory we won from the CSA, but all he's willing to restore is the stretch of Tennessee south of the Cumberland we took as fighting wound down, and he won't *give* that back: he wants to trade it for the little piece of Kentucky the Confederates still hold."

"Bully for him!" David exclaimed. He had been a good Socialist before he went off to war. Now, a lot of the time, he sounded like a hidebound Democrat of the Roosevelt stripe. That distressed Flora, too.

She went on, "And he's not going to let them keep any battleships or submersibles or military aeroplanes or barrels, and he's demanded that they limit their Army to a hundred machine guns."

"Bully!" This time, her brother and Dr. Hanrahan said it together.

Flora looked from one of them to the other in exasperation. "*And* he won't come a dime below two billion dollars in reparations, all of it to be paid in specie or in steel or oil at 1914 prices. That's a crushing burden to lay on the proletariat of the Confederate States."

"I hope it crushes them," David said savagely. "Knock on wood, they'll never be able to lift a finger against us again." Instead of knocking on the door or on a window sill, he used his own artificial leg, which drove home the point.

Flora had given up trying to argue with him. He had his full share of the Hamburger family's stubbornness. Instead, she turned to Dr. Hanrahan and asked, "How much longer will he have to stay here now that he's started to get back on his feet?"

"He should be able to leave in about a month, provided he makes good progress and provided the infection in the stump doesn't decide to flare up again," Hanrahan said. Flora nodded; she'd seen he gave her straight answers. He finished with a brisk nod: "We'll shoot for November first, then."

After giving her brother a careful hug and an enthusiastic kiss, Flora left the Pennsylvania Hospital. Fall was in the air, sure enough; some of the leaves in the trees on the hospital grounds were beginning to turn. She flagged a cab. "The Congressional office building," she told the driver.

"Yes, ma'am." He touched the shiny leather brim of his cap, put the Oldsmobile in gear, and went out to do battle with Philadelphia traffic. The traffic won, as it often did. Philadelphia had been the *de facto* capital of the USA since the Confederates bombarded Washington during the Second Mexican War, more than thirty-five years before. Starting even before then, a great warren of Federal buildings had gone up in the center of town. Getting to them was not always for the faint of heart.

"I have a message for you," said Flora's secretary, a plump, middle-aged woman named Bertha. She waved a piece of paper. "Congressman Blackford wants you to call him back."

"Does he?" Flora said, as neutrally as she could. "All right, I'll do that. Thank you." She went into her inner office and closed the door after her. She didn't turn around to see whether

Bertha was smiling behind her back. She hoped not, but she didn't really want to know.

Dakota, a solidly Socialist state, had been returning Hosea Blackford to the House since Flora was a girl. He was about twice her age now, a senior figure in the Party, even if on the soft side ideologically as far as she was concerned. And he was a widower whose Philadelphia apartment lay right across the hall from hers. He had left no doubt he was interested in her, though he'd never done anything to tempt her into defending herself with a hatpin. To her own surprise, she found herself interested in return, even if he was both a moderate and a gentile.

"Now," she muttered as she picked up the telephone and waited for the operator to come on the line, "is he calling about Party business or . . . something else?"

"Hello, Flora," Blackford said when the call went through. "I just wanted to know if you had seen the newspaper stories about strikes in Ohio and Indiana and Illinois."

Party business, then. "I'm afraid I haven't," Flora said. "I just got back from visiting David."

"How is he?" Blackford asked.

"They've fitted the artificial leg, and he was up on it." Flora shook her head, though Blackford couldn't see that. "Even with one leg gone, he talks like a Democrat." She inked a pen and slid a piece of paper in front of her so she could take notes. "Now tell me about these strikes."

"From what I've read, factory owners are trying to hold down wages by pitting workers against each other," he said. "With soldiers starting to come home from the war, they have more people wanting jobs than there are jobs to give, so they're seeing who will work for the lowest pay."

"That sounds like capitalists," Flora said with a frown. A moment later, she brightened. "It also sounds like a political opportunity for us. If the factory owners keep doing things like that—and they probably will—they'll radicalize the workers, and they'll do a better job of it than we ever could."

"I happen to know we've urged the strikers to stay as peaceful as they can, unless the bosses turn goons loose on them or their state governments or the U.S. government move troops against them," Blackford said.

"Good." Flora nodded. Blackford couldn't see that, either,

but she didn't care. Something he'd said touched off another thought. "Has Roosevelt made any statement about this yet?"

"One of the wire reports quotes him as calling the factory owners a pack of greedy fools," the Congressman from Dakota said, "but it doesn't say he'll do anything to make them stop playing games with people's lives."

"That sounds like him," Flora said. "He talks about a square deal for the workers, but he doesn't deliver. He delivered a war."

"He delivered a victory," Hosea Blackford corrected. "The country was starved for one. The country's been starved for one for more than fifty years. You may not like that, but you can't stick your head in the sand and pretend it isn't so."

"I don't intend to do any such thing," Flora said sharply. "The people *were* starved for a victory. I've seen as much, even with my own brother. But after a while they'll discover they have the victory and they're still starved and still maimed and still orphaned. And they'll remember Teddy Roosevelt delivered that, too."

Blackford's silence was thoughtful. After a few seconds, he said, "You may very well be right." He did his best to hold down the excitement in his voice, but she heard it. "If you are right, that would give us a fighting chance in the elections of 1918, and maybe even in 1920. A lot of people now are afraid we'll be so badly swamped, the Democrats will have everything their own way everywhere."

"A lot of things can happen between now and the Congressional elections," she said. "Even more things can happen between now and 1920."

"That's true, too," Blackford said. "But you've seen how many Socialists are wearing long faces these days. Even Senator Debs is looking gloomy. Maybe they should cheer up."

"Maybe. The real trouble"—Flora took a deep breath—"is that we've never won a presidential election. We've never had a majority in either house of Congress. Too many people, I think, don't really believe we ever can."

"I've had doubts myself," Blackford admitted. "Being permanently in the minority is hard to stomach sometimes, if you know what I mean."

"Oh, yes," Flora said quietly. "I'm Jewish, if you'll remember." On the Lower East Side in New York City, Jews were a majority. Everywhere else in the country, everywhere else in the world . . . *permanently in the minority* was as polite a way to put it as she'd ever heard.

She wondered if reminding Blackford she was Jewish would make him decide he wasn't interested in her after all. She wondered if she wanted him to decide that. In many ways, her life would be simpler if he did. With a large family, though, she'd rarely known a simple life. Would she want it or know what to do with it if she had it?

The only thing Blackford said was, "Of course I remember. It means I have to eat crab cakes and pork chops by myself." His voice held nothing but a smile. "Would you care to have dinner with me tonight? If you like, I won't eat anything that offends you."

"I'm not offended if you eat things I can't," Flora said, "any more than an Irishman or an Italian would be offended if I ate corned beef on Friday. I'd be offended if you tried to get *me* to eat pork, but you'd never do anything like that."

"I should hope not!" Blackford exclaimed. "You still haven't said whether you'll have dinner with me, though."

"I'd like to," Flora said. "Can we wait till after six, though? I've got a shirtwaist manufacturer coming in to see me at five, and I aim to give him a piece of my mind."

"Six-thirty, say, would be fine. Shall I come to your office?"

"All right." Flora smiled. "I'm looking forward to it." She hung up the telephone and went to work feeling better about the world than she had in some time.

Reginald Bartlett was discovering that he did not fit into the Richmond of late 1917 nearly so well as he had in 1914. Fighting on the Roanoke Valley front and in Sequoyah, getting captured twice and shot once (shot twice, too, actually: in the leg and the shoulder from the same machine-gun burst) by the Yankees, had left him a different man from the jaunty young fellow who'd gaily gone off to war.

Richmond was different, too. Then it had been bursting with July exuberance and confidence; now the chilly winds of October sliding into November fit the city's mood only too well. Defeat and autumn went together.

"Going to rain tomorrow, I reckon," Reggie said to Bill Foster as the two druggist's assistants walked along Seventh Street together. He reached up with his right hand to touch his left shoulder. "Says so right here."

Foster nodded, which set his jowls wobbling. He was short and round and dark, where Bartlett was above average height, on the skinny side (and skinnier after his wound), and blond. He said, "I heard enough people say that in the trenches, and they were right a lot of the time." He'd spent his war in Kentucky and Tennessee, and come home without a scratch.

After touching his shoulder again, Reggie said, "This isn't so much of a much." He'd had a different opinion while the wound stayed hot and full of pus, but he'd been a long way from objective. "Fellow I worked for before the war, man name of Milo Axelrod, he stopped a bullet with his face up in Maryland. He wasn't a bad boss—better than this McNally I'm working for now, anyhow."

"From what you've said about McNally, that wouldn't be hard." Foster might have gone on, but a small crowd had gathered at the corner of Seventh and Cary. He pointed. "I wonder what's going on there."

"Shall we find out?" Without waiting for an answer from his friend, Reggie hurried over toward the crowd. Shrugging, Foster followed. "Oh, I see," Bartlett said a moment later. "It's a political rally. That figures, with the Congressional election next Tuesday. But what the devil is the Freedom Party? I've never heard of 'em before."

"I've seen a couple of their posters," Bill Foster said. "Don't rightly know what they stand for, though."

"Let's get an earful. Maybe it'll be something good." Reggie scowled as his wounded leg gave a twinge, which it hadn't done in a while. "Couldn't be worse than the pap the Radical Liberals and the Whigs are handing out."

"That's about right." Foster nodded. "Everybody who's in is making noise about how he never much cared for the war, and everybody who's out is saying that if he'd been in he never would've voted one thin dime for it."

"And it's all a pack of lies, too," Bartlett said with deep contempt. "Why don't they admit they were all screaming their heads off for the war when it started? Do they think we've forgotten? And when Arango ran against Semmes for president two years ago, he said he'd do a better job of fighting the Yankees than the Whigs were. He didn't say anything about getting out of the war, not one word."

The Freedom Party spokesman didn't have a fancy platform or a fancy suit, which proved he belonged to neither of the CSA's major parties. He stood in his shirtsleeves on a box or a barrel of some kind and harangued the couple of dozen people who were listening to him: "—traitors to their country," he was shouting as Reggie and Bill Foster came up. "Traitors and fools, that's what they are!"

"A crackpot," Bartlett whispered. He folded his arms across his chest and got ready to listen. "Let's hang around for a while. He may be funny."

Somebody in the crowd already thought he was funny, calling, "By what you're saying there, the whole government is nothing but traitors and fools. You've got to be a fool yourself, to believe that."

"I do not!" the speaker said. He was an overweight, balding fellow of about fifty-five, whose fringe of gray hair blew wildly in the fall breeze. His name was Anthony Dresser—so said a little sign Reggie needed a while to notice. "I do not. I tell you the plain, unvarnished truth, and nothing else but!" His eyes, enormous behind thick spectacles, stared out at his small audience. "And you, my friends, you hug the viper to your bosom and think it is your friend. Congress is full of traitors, the War Department is full of traitors, the administration—"

Reggie stopped paying much attention to him about then. "And the moon is full of green cheese!" the heckler shouted, drawing a roar of laughter from the crowd.

Dresser sputtered and fumed, the thread of his speech, had it ever had one, now thoroughly lost. Reggie and Foster grinned at each other, enjoying his discomfiture. The speech surely would have been boring. This was anything but. "Not as easy to get up on the stump as the old boy thought, is it?" Foster said with a chuckle.

"You are all traitors to your country, for not listening to the plain and simple truth!" Dresser shouted furiously.

"And you're a maniac, and they ought to lock you up in the asylum and lose the key!" It wasn't the first heckler, but another man.

Dresser looked to be on the point of having a fit. Somebody reached up and tugged at his trousers. He leaned over, cupping a hand behind his ear. Then, with a fine scornful snort, he jumped down from his perch. "All right," he said. "All right! You show them then, if you think you know so much. I can tell you what you will show them—you will show them you do not have any notion of what to say or how to say it."

Up onto the platform scrambled a lean man somewhere in his thirties, in a day laborer's collarless cotton shirt and a pair of uniform pants. He looked around for a moment, then said, "Tony's right. A blind man should be able to see it, too. The government *is* full of traitors and fools."

Dresser had been argumentative, querulous. The newcomer spoke with absolute conviction, so much so that before he caught himself Reginald Bartlett looked north toward Capitol Square, as if to spy the traitors in the act.

"Yeah? You can't prove it, either, any more than the other jerk could," a heckler yelled.

"You want proof? I'll give you proof, by Jesus," the lean man said. He didn't talk as if he had any great education, but he didn't seem to feel the lack, as did so many self-made men. "Look what happened when the Red niggers rose up, back at the end of '15. They damn near overran the whole country. Now, why is that, do you reckon? It's on account of nobody in the whole stinking government had the least notion they were plotting behind our backs. If that doesn't make everybody from the president on down a damn fool, you tell me what in the hell it does do."

"He's got something, by God," Foster said, staring at the new speaker.

"He's got a lot of nerve, anyhow," Reggie said.

"That's why you ought to vote for Tony Dresser for Congress," the lean man continued: "on account of he can see the plain truth and you can't. Now the next thing you're going to say is, well, they're a pack of fools up there, all right, with their fancy motorcars and their whores, but they can't be traitors because they fought as long as they could and the Yankees are pretty damn tough.

"Well, this here is what I've got to say about that." The lean man let loose with a rich, ripe raspberry. "I know for a fact that people tried to warn the government the niggers were going to rise, on account of I was one of those people. Did anybody listen? Hell, no!" Contempt dripped from his voice like water from a leaky roof. "Some of those niggers were servants to rich men's sons, important men's sons. And the rich men in the Capitol and the important men in the War Department shoveled everything under the rug. If that doesn't make 'em traitors, what the devil does?"

"He *has* got something," Bill Foster said in an awed voice.

"He's got a big mouth," Bartlett said. "You throw charges like that around, you'd better be able to name names."

Instead of naming names, the newcomer on the stump charged ahead: "And after that—after that, mind you, after the niggers rose up—what did the government go and do? Come on. You remember. You're white men. You're smart men. What did they go and do?" The lean man's voice sank to a dramatic whisper: *"They went and put rifles in those same niggers' hands, that's what they did."* He whispered no more, but shouted furiously: "If *that* doesn't make 'em traitors, what the devil does?"

Reggie remembered Rehoboam, the Negro prisoner of war who'd shared his U.S. hospital ward after losing a foot in Arkansas—and after being a Red rebel in Mississippi. Things weren't so straightforward as this new Freedom Party speaker made them out to be. The older Reggie got, the more complicated the world looked. The lean man was older than he, but still saw things in harsh shades of black and white.

And he contrived to make his audience see them the same way. "You want to put Tony Dresser into Congress to give the real people of the Confederate States a voice," he shouted, "the working men, the men who get their hands dirty, the men who went out and fought the war the fools and the traitors and the nigger-lovers got us into. Oh, you can throw your vote away for somebody with a diamond on his pinky"—with alarming effectiveness, he mimed a capitalist—"but who's the fool if you do?"

"Why the hell ain't *you* runnin' for Congress instead of that long-winded son of a bitch?" somebody shouted.

"Tony's the chairman of the Freedom Party," the lean man answered easily. "You promote the commander of the unit, not a new recruit." He took out his billfold and displayed something Bartlett could not make out. "Here's my membership card—number seven, from back in September."

"Where do we sign up?" Two men asked the question at the same time. One of them added, "You ain't gonna stay a new recruit long, pal, not the way you talk. Who the hell are you, anyway?"

"My name's Featherston—Jake Featherston," the lean man answered. "Sergeant, Confederate States Artillery, retired." He scowled. "The fools in the War Department retired damn near the whole Army." With what looked like a deliberate effort of will, he made himself smile. "Party office is a couple blocks down Seventh, toward the Tredegar works. Come on by. Hope you do, anyways."

"Damned if I'm not tempted to," Bill Foster said as the little rally began to break up. "Damned if I'm not. That fellow Featherston, he's got a good way of looking at things."

"He's got a good line, that's for certain," Reggie Bartlett said. "If he were selling can openers door to door, there wouldn't be a closed can in Richmond this time tomorrow. But just because something sounds good doesn't make it so. Come on, Bill. Do you think a stage magician really pulls a Stonewall out of your nose?"

"Wish somebody'd pull one out of somewhere," Foster answered.

Reggie's laugh was rueful, five-dollar goldpieces being in notably short supply in his pockets, too. He said, "The world's not as simple as he makes it out to be."

"Well, what if it isn't?" his friend returned. "I wish it was that simple. Don't reckon I'm the only one who does, either."

"Reckon you're not," Bartlett agreed. "But most folks are the same as you and me: they know the difference between what they wish and what's really out there."

"Yeah?" Foster raised an eyebrow. "How come we just fought this damn war, then?" Reggie thought about that for a while, but found no good answer.

Guided by a pilot intimately familiar with the local mine-fields, the USS *Dakota* made a slow, cautious entrance into New York harbor. Sailors on tugs and freighters waved their caps at the battleship. Steam whistles bellowed and hooted. Fireboats shot streams of water high into the air.

Sam Carsten stood by the port rail, enjoying the show. The late-November day was bleak and gloomy and cold, but that didn't bother the petty officer at all. Anything more clement than clouds and gloom bothered him: he was so blond and pink, he sunburned in less time than he needed to blink. After Brazil entered the war on the side of the USA and Germany and their allies, the *Dakota* had gone up into the tropical Atlantic after convoys bound for Britain from Argentina. He was only now recovering from what the cruel sun had done to him.

Off to the west, on Bedloe Island, stood the great statue of Remembrance, the sword of vengeance gleaming in her hand. Carsten turned to his bunkmate and said, "Seeing her gives you a whole different feeling now that we've gone and won the war."

"Sure as hell does." Vic Crosetti nodded vigorously. He was as small and swarthy as Carsten was tall and fair. "Every time I seen that statue before, it was like she was saying, 'What the hell you gapin' at me for? Get out there and kick the damn Rebs in the belly.' Now we gone and done it. Can't you see the smile on that bronze broad's kisser?"

Remembrance looked as cold and stern and forbidding as she had since she'd gone up not long after the Second Mexican War. Even so, Carsten said, "Yeah." He and Crosetti grinned at each other. Victory tasted sweet.

"Carsten!" somebody said behind him.

He turned and stiffened to attention. "Sir!"

"As you were," Commander Grady said, and Sam eased out of his brace. The commander of the *Dakota*'s starboard secondary armament was a pretty good fellow; Sam cranked shells into the forwardmost five-inch gun under his charge. Grady said, "Do you recall that matter we were discussing the day the limeys gave up the fight?"

For a moment, Carsten didn't. Then he nodded. "About aeroplanes, you mean, sir?"

"That's right." Grady nodded, too. "Were you serious about what you meant about getting in on the ground floor there?"

"Yes, sir. I sure was, sir," Sam answered. Aeroplanes were the coming thing. Anyone with an eye in his head could see that. Anyone with an eye in his head could also see the Navy wouldn't stay as big as it had been during the war. Since Sam wanted to make sure he didn't end up on the beach, getting involved with aeroplanes looked like a good insurance policy.

Commander Grady said, "All right, then. I have some orders cut for you. If you'd said no, you'd have stayed here. There wouldn't have been any trouble about that. As things are, though, we both catch the train for Boston tomorrow morning. You'll see why when we get there." His smile made him look years younger.

"You're leaving the *Dakota*?" Vic Crosetti demanded. When Sam nodded, Crosetti clapped a hand to his forehead. "Jesus Christ, who'm I gonna rag on now?"

"I figure you'll find somebody," Carsten said, his voice dry. Crosetti gave him a dirty look that melted into a chuckle, then slapped him on the back. Sam had a gift for getting in digs without making people angry at him.

"Only problem with this is the train ride," Commander Grady said. "This Spanish influenza that's going around is supposed to be pretty nasty. We might be better staying aboard the *Dakota*."

"Sir, if the limeys couldn't sink us and the Japs couldn't sink us and whoever was flying that damn bombing aeroplane out from Argentina couldn't sink us, I don't figure we need to be afraid of any germs," Sam said.

Grady laughed. "That's the spirit! All right, Carsten. Pick up your new orders, get your paperwork taken care of, and we'll go ashore tomorrow morning—if you can stand an officer for company, that is."

"I'm a tough guy, sir," Carsten answered. "I expect I'll put up with it." Grady laughed and mimed throwing a punch at him, then went on his way.

"What's this about aeroplanes?" Crosetti asked.

"Don't even know, exactly," Sam said. "I joined the Navy five years before the war started, and here I am, buying a pig in a poke. Maybe I need my head examined, but maybe I'm smart, too. Smart, I mean, besides getting away from you. I hope I am, anyway."

"Good luck. I think you're crazy, but good luck." Crosetti shook Sam's hand, then walked off shaking his own head.

Getting orders was the easy part of getting off the *Dakota*. Carsten filled out endless separation forms. Only after the last of them was signed would the paymaster grudgingly give him greenbacks. With money in his billfold and a duffel bag on his shoulder, he walked down the gangplank from the *Dakota* to the pier with Commander Grady.

Even at the edge of the harbor, New York boiled with life. When Grady flagged a cab for the ride to the New York Central

Railroad Depot, three different automobiles almost ran him and Sam down in the zeal for a fare. The drivers hopped out and screamed abuse at one another in both English and a language that seemed entirely compounded of gutturals.

Grady knew his way through the crowded old depot, which was fortunate, because Sam didn't. He had to step smartly to keep from being separated from the officer; the only place where he'd felt more crowded was the triple-decked bunkroom of the *Dakota*. Everyone here was moving, intent on his own business. About every third man, woman, and child was sneezing or sniffling or coughing. Some of them were likely to have influenza. Carsten tried not to inhale. That didn't work very well.

He and Grady got a couple of seats in a second-class car; the Navy saved money on train fares that way. They were the only Navy men there, though soldiers in green-gray occupied a fair number of seats. The civilians ranged from drummers in cheap, flashy suits to little old ladies who might still have been in Russia.

Once Grady and Carsten pulled into Boston, the officer paid for another cab ride, this one over the Charlestown Bridge to the Navy Yard on the north side of the Charles River. Seeing the battleships and cruisers and submersibles and tenders tied up there made Sam's heart swell with pride. A few ships from the Western Squadron of Germany's High Seas Fleet stood out from their American allies because of their less familiar lines and light gray paint jobs.

Sam followed Commander Grady, each of them with duffel bag bouncing on his back. Then, all at once, Sam stopped in his tracks and stared and stared. Grady walked on for a couple of steps before he noticed he didn't have company any more. He turned and looked back, a grin on his rabbity features. "What's the matter, Carsten?" he asked, sounding like a man trying hard not to laugh out loud.

"Sir," Sam said plaintively, "I've seen every type of ship in the U.S. Navy, and I reckon damn near every type of ship in the High Seas Fleet, too." He pointed ahead. "In all my born days, though, I've never seen anything that looked like *that*, and I hope to God I never do again. What the hell is it supposed to be?"

Now Grady did laugh out loud. "That's the *Remembrance*, Carsten. That's what you signed up for."

"Jesus," Sam said. "I must have been out of my goddamn mind."

The *Remembrance* looked as if somebody had decided to build a battleship and then, about a third of the way through the job, got sick of it and decided to flatten out most of the deck to hurry things along. An aeroplane sat on the deck aft of the bridge: not a seaplane that would land in the water and be picked up by the ship's crane but a Wright two-decker fighting scout—a U.S. copy of a German Albatros—with utterly ordinary landing gear and not a trace of a float anywhere. Sam shook his head in disbelief.

Laughing still, Commander Grady clapped him on the back. "Cheer up. It won't be so bad. You'll still mess forward and bunk aft. And a five-inch gun is a five-inch gun." He pointed to the sponson under that unbelievably long, unbelievably level deck. "You'll do your job, and the flyboys will do theirs, and everybody will be happy except the poor enemy bastards who bump into us."

"Yes, sir," Sam said dubiously. "What the devil did she start out to be, anyway? And why didn't she turn out to be whatever that was?"

"They started to build her as a fast, light-armored battle cruiser, to slide in close to the Confederate coast, blast hell out of it, and then scoot before the Rebs could do anything about it—a monitor with legs, you might say," Grady answered. "But that idea never went anywhere. Some bright boy got to thinking how handy it would be to take aeroplanes along wherever you needed them, and . . . there's the *Remembrance*."

"I thought of that myself, after the *Dakota* got bombed off Argentina," Carsten said, "but I never imagined—this." He wondered if he'd get into fights because sailors on ordinary, respectable vessels would call the *Remembrance* the ugliest ship in the Navy. Dammit, she *was* the ugliest ship in the Navy.

"Come on, let's go aboard," Grady said. "She won't look anywhere near so strange from the inside."

Even that didn't turn out to be true. The hangars that held nearly three dozen fighting scouts and the supply and maintenance areas that went with them took up an ungodly amount of space, leaving the bunkrooms cramped and feeling like afterthoughts. As a petty officer, Carsten did get a bottom bunk, but the middle one in the three-tier metal structure was only a few inches above him. He could stand it, but he didn't love it.

The only place in which he did feel at home was the sponson. The five-inch gun was the same model he'd served on the *Dakota*, and the sponson itself might have been transferred bodily from the battleship. The chief gunner's mate in charge of the crew, a burly veteran named Willie Moore, wore a splendid gray Kaiser Bill mustache. He wasn't half brother to his counterpart from the *Dakota*, Hiram Kidde, but Sam couldn't have proved it by the way he acted.

He turned out to know Kidde, which surprised Sam not at all. "If you served with the 'Cap'n,' reckon you'll do for me," he rumbled when Carsten mentioned the name of his former gun commander a couple of days after coming aboard.

"Thanks, Chief. Hope so," Sam said, and punctuated that with a sneeze. "Damn. I'm coming down with a cold."

He was off his feed at supper that evening, which surprised him: the *Remembrance*, however ugly she was, boasted a first-class galley. Everything was fresh, too—an advantage of sitting in port. But Sam didn't realize how sick he was till the next morning, when he almost fell out of his bunk. He stood, swaying, in front of it.

"You all right?" asked George Moerlein, who slept just above him. Sam didn't answer; he had trouble figuring out what the words meant. Moerlein peered at him, touched his forehead, and then jerked back his hand as if he'd tried picking up a live coal. "We better get this guy to sick bay," he said. "I think he's got the influenza." Sam didn't argue, either. He couldn't. He let them lead him away.

Arthur McGregor took a certain somber satisfaction in listening to the wind howl around his farmhouse. That was just as well; the wind in Manitoba was going to howl through the winter whether he took any satisfaction in it or not.

"One thing," he said to his wife. "In weather like this, the Yanks stay indoors."

"I wish to heaven they'd stayed in their own country," Maude answered. She was short and redheaded, a contrast to his rangy inches and dark hair that was beginning to show frost as he edged into his forties.

Her eyes went to the photograph of their son, Alexander, that hung on the wall of the front room. The photograph was all they had of him; the U.S. troops who occupied Manitoba had executed him for plotting sabotage a year and a half before.

McGregor's eyes went there, too. He was still paying the Americans back for what they'd done to Alexander. He would never be done paying them back, as long as he lived. If they ever found out he made bombs, he wouldn't live long. He couldn't drive the Yanks out of Canada singlehanded. If they were going to try to rule his country, though, he could make their lives miserable.

Julia came in from the kitchen. She also looked toward Alexander; these days, the family almost made a ritual of it. McGregor looked at his daughter in what was as close to wonderment as his solid, stolid nature could produce. Some time while he wasn't looking, Julia had turned into a woman. She'd been eleven when the Americans invaded, and hardly even coltish. She was fourteen now, and not coltish any more. She looked like her mother, but taller and leaner, as McGregor himself was.

"What are you going to do about that school order, Pa?" she asked.

The wind gusted louder. McGregor could have pretended not to hear her. His own sigh was gusty, too. "I'm going to pretend I don't know the first thing about it for as long as I can," he answered.

He'd pulled Julia and her younger sister, Mary, out of school a couple of years before. The Americans were using it to teach Canadian children their lies about the way the world worked. Since then, McGregor and Maude had taught reading and ciphering at home.

Now, though, the occupying authorities had sent out an edict requiring all children between the ages of six and sixteen to attend school at least six months out of the year. They didn't intend to miss any chances to tell their stories to people they wanted to grow up to be Americans, not Canadians.

"It'll be all right, Pa," Julia said. "I really think it will. You can send Mary and me, and we won't end up Yanks, truly we won't." She looked toward Alexander's photograph again.

"I know you won't, chick," he said. "But I don't know that Mary would be able to keep from telling the teacher what she really thinks."

At nine, Mary wore her heart on her sleeve, even more than Alexander had. She also hated Americans with a pure, clear hatred that made even her father's pale beside it. Letting the Yanks know how she felt struck McGregor as most unwise.

Julia had washed the supper dishes; Mary was drying them. After the last one clattered into the cupboard, she came out to join the rest of the family. She was sprouting up, too, like wheat after planting. She would, McGregor judged, make a tall woman. But she still kept some of the feline grace she'd had since she was very small, and also some of a cat's self-containment. McGregor hadn't needed to teach her much about conspiracy. She understood it as if by instinct.

Now he said, "Mary, if you have to, do you suppose you can put up with listening to the Yanks' lies in school without telling them off?"

"Why would I have to do that, Pa?" she answered. "Maybe they can make me go to school, but—" She caught herself. Her gray eyes, so like those of her father and her dead brother, widened. "Oh. You mean put up with them so I wouldn't get in trouble—so *we* wouldn't get in trouble."

"That's right." Arthur McGregor nodded. No, no one needed to teach Mary about conspiracy.

She thought it over. "If I have to, I suppose I could," she said at last. "But telling lies is a sin on their heads, isn't it?"

"So it is." McGregor smiled to hear that, but not too much: he'd passed his own stern Presbyterian ethic down to the new generation. "The Yanks have so many other sins on the book against them, though, that lying doesn't look like so much to them."

"Well, it should," Mary said. "It should all count against them, every bit of it. And it will. God counts *everything*." She spoke with great assurance.

McGregor wished he felt so sure himself. He believed, yes, but he'd lost that simple certainty. If he'd had any left, Alexander's death would have burned it out of him, leaving ashes behind. He said, "You will go to school, then, and be a good little parrot, so we can show the Americans we're obeying their law?"

His younger daughter sighed. "If I have to," she said again.

"Good," McGregor said. "The more we look like we're doing what they want us to, the more we can do what we want to when they aren't looking."

Julia said, "That's good, Pa. That's very good. That's just what we'll do."

"That's what we'll have to do," Maude said. "That's what everyone will have to do, for however long it takes till we're free again."

"Or till we turn into Americans," Arthur McGregor said bleakly. He held up a work-roughened hand. "No, I don't mean us. Some of our neighbors will turn into Americans, but not us."

"Some of our neighbors have already turned into Americans," Julia said. "They don't care about what they were, so they don't care what they are. We know better. We're Canadians. We'll always be Canadians. Always."

McGregor wondered if, with the strongest will in the world, his grandchildren and great-grandchildren would remember they were Canadians. And then, perhaps wondering the same thing, Maude spoke as if to reassure herself: "Germany took Alsace and Lorraine away from France almost fifty years ago, but the people there still remember they're Frenchmen."

Canadians had heard a great deal about their ally's grievances against the Kaiser and his henchmen (till the Americans overran them, after which they'd had to endure lies about Germany's grievances against France). Now France had more reasons to grieve, for the Germans were biting off more of her land. And McGregor, still in his bleak mood, said, "The Germans settled a lot of their own people in Alsace and Lorraine to help hold them down. If the Americans did that . . ."

His wife and daughters stared at him in horror. Mary spoke first: "I wouldn't live next to Americans, Pa! I wouldn't. If they came here, I'd . . . I don't know what I'd do, but it'd be pretty bad."

"We won't have to worry about that till next spring at the earliest," McGregor said. "Won't be any Yanks settling down to farm in the middle of winter, not here in Manitoba there won't." His chuckle was grim. "And the ones who come in the spring, if any do, they're liable to turn up their toes when they find out what winters are like. We've seen that the Americans don't fancy our weather."

"Too bad for them," Julia said.

After the children had gone to sleep, McGregor lay awake beside his wife in the bed the two of them shared. "What am I going to do, Maude?" he whispered, his voice barely audible through the whistling wind. "By myself, I can hurt the Americans, but that's all I can do. They won't leave on account of me."

"You've made them pay," Maude said. He'd never admitted making bombs, not in so many words. She'd never asked, not in so many words. She knew. He knew she knew. But they formally kept the secret, even from each other.

"Not enough," he said now. "Nothing could ever be enough except driving them out of Canada. But no one man can do that."

"No one man can," Maude said in a musing tone of voice.

He understood where she was going, and shook his head. "One man can keep a secret. Maybe two can. And maybe three can, but only if two of them are dead." That came from the pen of Benjamin Franklin, an American, but McGregor had forgotten where he'd first run across it.

"I suppose you're right," Maude said. "It seems a pity, though."

"If Alexander hadn't hung around with a pack of damnfool kids who didn't have anything better to do than run their mouths and make foolish plots, he'd still be alive today," McGregor said harshly.

Maude caught her breath. "I see what you're saying," she answered after a long pause.

"And the strange thing is, if he was still alive, we wouldn't hate the Yanks the way we do," McGregor said. "They caused themselves more harm shooting him than he ever would have given them if they'd let him go."

"They're fools," Maude said. That McGregor agreed with wholeheartedly. But the American fools ruled Canada today. God must have loved them, for He'd made so very many.

The notion of God loving Americans was so unlikely, McGregor snorted and fell asleep bemused by it. When he woke up, it was still dark; December nights fifty miles south of Winnipeg were long. He groped for a match, scraped it alight, and lit the kerosene lamp on the nightstand.

He didn't want to get out from under the thick wool blankets: he could see his own breath inside the bedroom. He threw a shirt and overalls over his long johns and was still shivering. Maude got out of bed, too. She carried the lamp downstairs as soon as she was dressed. He followed her.

She built up the fire in the stove and started a pot of coffee. It wasn't good coffee; if the Americans had any good coffee, they kept it for themselves. But it was hot. He stood by the stove, too, soaking in the warmth radiating from the black iron. Maude melted butter in a frying pan and put in three eggs. McGregor ate them along with bread and butter. Then he shrugged on a long, heavy coat and donned mittens. Reluctantly, he opened the door and went outside.

It had been cold in the bedroom. As he slogged his way to the barn, he wondered if he would turn into an icicle before he got there. A wry chuckle made a fogbank swirl around his face for a moment, till the fierce wind blew it away. People said there wasn't so much work on a farm in winter. In a way, they were right, for he didn't have to go out to the fields.

In spring and summer, though, he didn't have to work in weather like this. The body heat of the livestock kept the barn warmer than the weather outside, but warmer wasn't warm. He fed the horse and cow and pigs and chickens and cleaned up their filth. By the time he was done with that, he was warmer, too.

His eye fell on an old wagon wheel, the sort of junk any barn accumulated. Under it, hidden in a hole beneath a board beneath dirt, lay dynamite and fuses and blasting caps and crimpers and other tools of the bomb-maker's art. McGregor nodded to them. They would come out again.

Rain, some of it freezing, poured down out of a bleak gray sky. A barrel rumbled across the muddy Kansas prairie toward Colonel Irving Morrell. The cannon projecting from its slightly pointed prow was aimed straight at him. Two machine guns stuck out from each side of the riveted steel hull; two more covered the rear. A pair of White truck engines powered the traveling fortress. Stinking, steaming exhaust belched from the twin pipes.

The charge would have been more impressive had it been at something brisker than a walking pace. It would have been much more impressive had the barrel not bogged down in a mud puddle that aspired to be a pond when it grew up. The machine's tracks were not very wide, and it weighed almost thirty-three tons. It could have bogged on ground better than that it was traveling.

Morrell snapped his fingers in annoyance at himself for not having brought out a slate and a grease pencil with which he could have taken notes here in the field. He was a lean man, nearing thirty, with a long face, weathered features that bespoke a lot of time out in the sun and wind, and close-cropped sandy hair at the moment hidden under a wool cap and the hood of a rain slicker.

His boots made squelching noises as he slogged through the ooze toward the barrel. The commander of the machine stuck his head out of the central cupola that gave him and his driver a place to perch and a better view than the machine gunners and artillerymen enjoyed (the engineers who tended the two motors had no view, being stuck in the bowels of the barrel).

"Sorry, sir," he said. "Couldn't spot that one till too late."

"One of the hazards of the game, Jenkins," Morrell answered. "You can't go forward; that's as plain as the nose on my face. See if you can back out."

"Yes, sir." Lieutenant Jenkins ducked down into the cupola, clanging the hatch shut after himself. The engines changed note as the driver put the barrel into reverse. The barrel moved back a few inches, then bogged down again. Jenkins had spunk. Having shifted position, he tried to charge forward once more and escape the grip of the mud. All he succeeded in doing was getting deeper into it.

Morrell waved for him to stop and called, "You keep going that way, you'll need a periscope to see out, just like a submersible."

He doubted Jenkins heard him; with the engines hammering away, nobody inside a barrel could hear the man next to him screaming in his ear. Even so, the engines fell silent a few seconds later. The traveling fortress' commander could see for himself that he wasn't going anywhere.

When the young lieutenant popped out through the hatch again, he was grinning. "Well, sir, you said you wanted to test the machine under extreme conditions. I'd say you've got your wish."

"I'd say you're right," Morrell answered. "I'd also say these critters need wider tracks, to carry their weight better."

Lieutenant Jenkins nodded emphatically. "Yes, sir! They could use stronger engines, too, to help us get out of this kind of trouble if we do get into it."

"That's a point." Morrell also nodded. "We used what we had when we designed them: it would have taken forever to make a new engine and work all the teething pains out of it, and we had a war to fight. With the new model, though, we've got the chance to do things right, not just fast."

That was his job: to figure out what *right* would be. He would have a lot to say about what the next generation of barrels looked like. It was a great opportunity. It was also a great responsibility. More than anything else, barrels had broken two years of stalemated struggle in the trenches and made possible the U.S. victory over the CSA. Having the best machines and knowing what to do with them would be vital if—*no, when,* he thought—the United States and Confederate States squared off again.

For the moment, his concerns were more immediate. "You and your men may as well come out," he told Jenkins. "We've got a couple of miles of muck to go before we get back to Fort Leavenworth."

"Leave the barrel here for now, sir?" the young officer asked.

"It's not going anywhere by itself, that's for sure," Morrell answered, with which Jenkins could hardly disagree. "Rebs aren't about to steal it, either. We'll need a recovery vehicle to pull it loose, but we can't bring one out now because it would bog too." Recovery vehicles mounted no machine guns or cannon, but were equipped with stout towing chains, and sometimes with bulldozer blades.

More hatches opened up as the engineers and machine gunners and artillerymen emerged from their steel shell. Even in a Kansas December, it was warm in there. It had been hotter than hell in summertime Tennessee, as Morrell vividly remembered. It had been hot outside there, too. It wasn't hot here. All eighteen men in the barrel crew, Jenkins included, started shivering and complaining. They hadn't brought rain gear—what point, in the belly of the machine?

Morrell sympathized, but he couldn't do anything about it. "Come on," he said. "You won't melt."

"Listen to him," one of the machine gunners said to his pal. "He's got a raincoat, so what the devil has he got to worry about?"

"Here," Morrell said sharply. The machine gunner looked alarmed; he hadn't intended to be overheard. Morrell stripped off the slicker and threw it at him. "Now you've got the raincoat. Feel better?"

"No, sir." The machine gunner let the coat fall in the mud.

"Not fair for me to have it either, sir. Now nobody does." That was a better answer than Morrell had expected from him.

Lieutenant Jenkins said, "Let's get moving, so we stay as warm as we can. We're all asking for the Spanish influenza."

"That's true," Morrell said. "First thing we do when we get in is soak in hot water, to get the mud off and to warm us up inside. And if thinking about that isn't enough to start you moving, I'll give two dollars to any man who gets back to the fort ahead of me."

That set the crew of the barrel into motion, sure enough. Morrell was the oldest man among them by three or four years. They were all veterans. They were all convinced they were in top shape. Every one of them hustled east, in the direction of the fort. They all thought they would have a little extra money jingling in their pockets before the day was through.

Morrell wondered how much his big mouth was going to cost him. As he picked up his own pace, his right leg started to ache. It lacked the chunk of flesh a Confederate bullet had blown from it in the opening weeks of the war. Morrell had almost lost the leg when the wound festered. He still limped a little, but never let the limp slow him down.

And he got to Fort Leavenworth ahead of any of the barrel men. As soon as he reached the perimeter of the fort, he realized how worn he was: *ridden hard and put away wet* was the phrase that came to mind. He'd ridden himself hard, all right, and he was sure as hell wet, but he hadn't been put away yet. He wanted to fall into the mud to save himself the trouble.

Soaking in a steaming tub afterwards did help. So, even more, did the admiring looks he got from his competitors as they came onto the grounds of the fort in his wake. He savored those. Command was more than a matter of superior rank. If the men saw he deserved that rank, they would obey eagerly, not just out of duty.

That evening, he pored over German accounts of meetings with British and French barrels. The Germans had used only a few of the traveling fortresses, fewer than their foes. They'd won anyhow, with England distracted from the Continent because of the fighting in Canada, and with mutinies spreading through the French Army after Russia collapsed. Morrell was familiar with British barrels; the CSA had copied them. He knew less about the machines the French had built.

When he looked at photographs of some of the French barrels—their equivalent of the rhomboids England and the CSA used—he snickered. Their tracks were very short compared to the length of their chassis, which meant they easily got stuck trying to traverse trenches.

Another French machine, though, made him thoughtful. The Germans had only one example of that model: the text said it was a prototype hastily armed and thrown into the fight in a desperate effort to stem the decay of the French Army. It was a little barrel (*hardly more than a keg,* Morrell thought with a grin) with only a two-man crew, and mounted a single machine gun in a rotating turret like the ones armored cars used.

"Not enough firepower there to do you as much good as you'd like," Morrell said into the quiet of his barracks room. Still, the design was interesting. It had room for improvement.

He grabbed a piece of paper and a pencil and started sketching. Whoever designed the first U.S. barrels had thought of nothing past stuffing as many guns as possible inside a steel box and making sure at least one of them could shoot every which way. The price of success was jamming a couple of squads' worth of soldiers into that hellish steel box along with the guns.

If you put the two-inch cannon into that turret instead of a machine gun, you got a gun firing every which way all by itself. You'd still want a machine gun in front. If the cannon were in the turret, the driver would have to go down into the lower front of the machine. Could he handle a machine gun and drive, too?

"Not likely," Morrell muttered. All right: that meant another gunner or two down there with him.

You wouldn't always want to use the turret cannon, though. Sometimes that would be like swatting a fly with an anvil. Morrell sketched another machine gun alongside the cannon. It would rotate, too, of course, and the gunners who tended the large gun could also serve it.

That cut the crew from eighteen men down to five or six— you'd likely need an engineer, too, but the machine had better have only one engine, and one strong enough to move at a decent clip. Morrell shook his head. "No, six or seven," he said. "Somebody's got to tell everybody else what to do." A boat without a commander would be like a boat—no, a ship; Navy men would laugh at him—without a captain.

He was forgetting something. He stared at the paper, then at the plain whitewashed plaster of the wall. Forcing it wouldn't work; he had to try to think around it. That was as hard as *not* thinking about a steak dinner. He'd had practice, though. Soon it would come to him. Soon . . .

"Wireless telegraph!" he exclaimed, and added an aerial to his sketch. Maybe that would require another crewman, or maybe the engineer could handle it. If it did, it did. He'd wanted one of those gadgets in his barrel during the war just finished. Controlling the mechanical behemoths was too hard without them.

He studied the sketch. He liked it better than the machines in which he'd thundered to victory against the CSA. He wondered what the War Department would think. It was different, and a lot of senior officers prided themselves on not having had a new thought in years. He shrugged. He'd send it in and find out.